Also by Anjana Appachana

*Incantations and Other Stories*

# LISTENING NOW

# LISTENING NOW

## ANJANA APPACHANA

RANDOM HOUSE
NEW YORK

Library of Congress Cataloging-in-Publication data is available

ISBN 0-679-45215-X

Random House website address: www.randomhouse.com

Printed in the United States of America on acid-free paper
24689753
First Edition

For my daughter, Malavika, who at two and a half, tearfully urged me not to write this book, for my writing, she sobbed, made her feel very, very sad. For my Kunji, who then begged me to cook and to clean, for then, she assured me, she would be very, very happy.

# CONTENTS

# THE FIRST STORY

In that deep and distant time, there lived in my house my permanently stricken mother, my mother's vivacious, laughing sister, and my absent father, whose presence in our house was shaped by my grieving mother's awful silence. Our house was like a well, holding his absence and her silence, and within those waters, my story began.

Once, long ago, my mother had enveloped those she loved with radiance and with joy. But I, so consumed by her love, knew neither its radiance nor its joy. My mother kept her story from me. And in doing so, she also kept mine.

In that distant and dreamlike time a magic man came into my life. He gave me what my mother could not—his tender, sunlit story. Was he, my magic man, like that elusive, wondrous creature, the unicorn, born of my own longing, my own belief? My friend Prabha also longed, she too believed. And we held our knowledge till the time after we turned twelve, the year that my childhood ended, the year when secrets began to heave and moan.

Once when I was five, my mother said to me, after we returned from a circus, that clowns were not happy people. Behind their painted smiles, she said, often lay very sad men. I did not believe my mother. Her sister, my Shantamama, who was also with us, was most upset with my mother's remark. How can you say such a thing to a child, she scolded. But the words stayed with me. The words formed the way I now think of my magic man. For now I know how a story that smiles can be rooted in a heart stunned and stunted with grief.

Magic and grief. I knew both long before his time. In my mother's womb, floating, unfurling, I fed off their waters. My mother bore them when she bore me, stories swirling with their enchantment, suffused with their mysteries. Later I knew them in the stories I read, and in the stories I imagined.

Then, the disgorging. Beneath the unrelenting heat of one revelation and then another, and yet another, coming up one after the other, the magic dried up, leaving behind only its tortured remains.

Once, in that dreamlike and echoing time, enclosed deep within those waters they lived, that magic, this grief.

# MALLIKA

Even at the age of five, I knew from all the mythological stories and films that God was a capricious, temperamental being, given to loud and unrestrained displays of passion, yet bafflingly silent in the face of His seeker's most impassioned questions, quick to anger and as swiftly mollified, not always susceptible to flattery and obeisance, yet demanding both, quirky in His ability to grant or not grant one's prayers, often spiteful and jealous, always ready to weep and recriminate, perennially busy and preoccupied with the burdens of the world, usually fed up with looking after just about everyone, which was why half the time He didn't listen to their prayers, but if He really wanted to, He could do anything, for He had this bottomless pit of love. Of course, whether He chose to do what you wished Him to, for the sake of love, was quite another matter.

And perverse Being that He was, it was in this very mould that He had cast my two mothers.

In a fit of generosity, or perhaps, simply guilt (for my father was dead), God had given me two mothers. Ma was the mother who had borne me; her sister, Shantamama, who came to stay with us twice or thrice a year, was the mother who had done all but given birth to me.

"Ma, tell me a sad story." I pulled Ma's book out of her hand.

Outside the night expanded, under the sheet Ma's softness enveloped.

"You never let me read, oh you never let me read. Mallika, Mallika, I can't *live* without books," said Ma despairingly.

"But, Ma," I exclaimed indignantly, "yesterday you said you couldn't live without *me!*"

I could read Ma's expression. She wanted to tell me a quick story from her head, get it over with.

"No, Ma, not a happy story." Dead and dull, Ma's happy stories—no twists, no tears, no sighs, no fears. "Tell me a sad story which becomes happy in the end."

Ma's whole body heaved.

"Don't cry, Ma, don't cry, Ma," I wept.

"Amma, Amma, Amma," Ma sobbed, calling out to her own mother.

My body shuddered with terror.

"Amma I want to die, Amma, I want to *die*," Ma cried out.

We cried loudly, both of us. I kissed Ma's arm in a frenzy, put my wet cheeks against hers. Ma's arms went around me, "I'm sorry, I'm sorry," smothering me with kisses. "I'm sorry, I'm sorry," stroking my hair, my back, my arms, my face in her neck breathing in her lovely smell. Nothing so full-blooded and fierce as the love Ma gave me after she was angry with me, nothing so satisfying.

Ma quietly stroked my head.

I knew my mother's silence, even at three I knew it. Worse than her weeping, this silence. No love to be had from her when she was silent. No fierce aftermath. I knew this silence better than any other. This was the silence which crippled my mother, this was the silence that held my father, this was the silence which excluded me completely. There was more terror in this than in all of Ma's tears.

"Don't die, Ma. Say promise."

"I won't die, my love. Promise."

First stories bloomed in the books that Ma and Shantamama read to me. The story that Ma didn't tell me was shrouded in silence.

"Once upon a time there lived a mother goat and her seven kids. One day—"

"Where was Dada goat?"

"He'd gone out to work. So, one day, Mama goat said to her kids—"

"Did Dada goat come back in the evening?"

Shantamama came in as Ma lay down, exhausted. "My darling," Shantamama took me in her arms, put her cheek against mine, "I will tell you the story."

Shantamama read, "Once upon a time there lived a mother goat and her seven kids. One day—"

"Where was Dada goat?"

"He. Oh he . . . one day when their Dada went to the forest to get food for his seven children, the bad wolf caught him and ate him up. And not satisfied with that, the bad wolf wants to eat up his seven children too."

She reached the end when mother goat cut open the wolf's tummy and took out her kids.

I burst into tears.

Ma removed her arm from her eyes, and said, tenderly, "Suddenly mama goat hears a voice that says, What about me, my dear?"

I stopped crying.

Shantamama continued, "Dada goat! Mama goat gives a bleat of joy and out he leaps and all the kids prance around him, overjoyed. And mama goat puts another stone inside the wolf's tummy and stitches him up and they all live happily ever after."

So potent the women, so powerful! What an absence of fathers, what a profusion of good and evil mothers! Where were all the fathers while the mothers battled, protected, rescued, nurtured? While all the stepmothers plotted and schemed?

Where, indeed *were* they? Sita gave birth to Luva and Kusha in the absence of Rama (no unwitting absence, this), brought them up fatherless. Kunti's son, Karan, also fatherless, son of the Sun God, who impregnated Kunti, then, in the bewildering manner of men and Gods, disappeared. Shakuntala left with a child, forgotten by Dushyanta. Ma, telling me these stories, her voice unsteady, the women bearing Ma's face, Ma, my black braided Rapunzel, my father, the elusive Indian Prince.

Indeed, so deeply stricken was God at my fatherless state, that in addition to giving me two mothers, he bestowed upon both of them this awful gift by which means they could telepathically communicate with Him and find out not only what I was doing when I was no longer within their vision, but worse, what I was thinking.

"Don't say you're feeling vomity," Shantamama warned me as I looked at the karelas which I would have to eat for lunch.

"And don't say I should feed you," Ma said, the circles under her eyes looking darker than ever. "I'm tired."

Sobs racked my body. I picked up the fruit knife from the table. "*Don't* feed me. *Don't* feed me. Let me *starve* and *die,* and *then* you can be happy. *Then* you'll never be tired. Here," I thrust the knife at my mother, "*take* it. Take it and poke it into my heart and *be* happy."

"Chee," said Shantamama slowly, taking the knife from my hand.

Ma's body heaved.

"You're *laughing* at me. I'll die and you won't even *cry,* you'll *laugh.*"

Ma held out her arms. No sign of laughter in her eyes. I fell into them, sobbing, oh the sweetness of her neck, the softness of her cheek, what would I do if she died.

The love that my Shantamama bore me was like Infinity, she had told me once. This Infinity Love meant I always came first, it was that simple. But there was nothing simple about the way that Ma loved me. Huge, suffocating and passionate, it was still lesser than her other love—the one she never spoke of. Ah, Finity Love was what my grieving mother bore for me.

Yet, how fiercely burnt both Infinity and Finity. What power they held. Relentlessly, my mothers combed out my secrets with a fine comb; and out my secrets came, held mercilessly between the teeth. In the womblike world created by Infinity and Finity, my every movement and mood reverberated through my mothers, tore them apart. If I sniffed, Ma became pale, if I coughed, Shantamama's eyes widened with fear. You can't go here, you can't go there, no talking to strangers, no going to the terrace in Mahima's house, no, no, no. Once, having got up early in the morning to go to the bathroom, I heard Ma's voice cry out, "Mallikaaaaa." I entered my room, to find Ma frozen, staring at my empty bed. Then she saw me and, moaning, held me tight.

"Ma and Shantamama know *everything,*" I told my best friend, Prabha.

"Mumma also knows everything."

"Ma and Shantamama know what I'm *thinking.*"

"Only *God* knows that."

"They know *Him.*"

"Don't tell lies."

"I'm *telling* you. *He* tells them."

"How?"

"Through ex-re-ice."

Ex-re-ice was this invisible tube, I explained to Prabha, through which a gleeful God communicated with my quivering mothers. I told her how, as I sat in the bathroom, carefully removing the scabs from a wound on my knee, Ma's voice spilled in from under the door, "Don't do that, don't do that." How, as I reached out to touch the kajal container on Ma's dressing table, Shantamama's voice floated towards me, from the next room, "No, no, no."

"But then," asked Prabha, "why didn't God tell them about that papaya man?"

The man had beckoned to us when I was playing in the street behind our houses with my three friends, Prabha, Mahima and Gauri. We went over to him and he looked down, and we looked down and saw what he was showing us. In terror, we ran back to Mahima's house.

"It was as big as a papaya," Mahima said.

"He was not a normal man," Prabha said, "that's why it was so big."

I asked, "Why did he show it to us?"

Gauri exclaimed, "Because he was a madman, Mallika, that's why."

An abashed God had conveniently forgotten to tell my two mothers about this encounter. "Because," I told Prabha, "He was too scared to tell them."

Shantamama's relations with God were intimate, and in the manner of those who are intimate, there was in it an almost casual dependence. Not so, Ma. God was not her friend. He was someone whom she forgot about till He reminded her, quite pointedly, of His existence. I would fall sick after school, and my Ayaji, who had looked after me since I was a baby, would tuck me into bed. Up in heaven, God would snigger. Down in her college, Ma would hear. Ma, who was to come home at four, would rush home at one and sit by my side, small whimpering sounds coming out of her throat, her trembling hand on my burning forehead, and looking up, whisper all His names—Rama, Krishna, Anjaneya, Shiva, Ganapathy . . . again and again and again.

And summoned up by the power of her raised eyes, God floated sulkily on the bedroom ceiling. I knew a bargain was being struck. I knew Ma was tearfully throwing accusations at Him, watching the guilt on His face as He drew out my illness and threw it truculently back at her. Such was Ma's power, that she took my illness upon herself. I recovered, and Ma lay in bed with fever instead.

Shantamama too bent God to her will, but her way in this was quite different. God was her best friend. She talked to Him constantly. She had asked Him for a daughter and He gave me to her through her sister Padma. (In fact, the first few months Shantamama, who also had a small baby, had fed me at her breast as often as Ma.) Shantamama's method of dealing with God was by putting her idol of Lord Ganapathy in a bucket of water, saying, "You stay there till you make my Mallika all right." Of course, I got all right, and Lord Ganapathy was taken out of his miserable surroundings and tenderly mopped dry.

And if God couldn't do His job, then she'd do it for Him. My Shanta-mama bent over me, her clenched fist circling my face, round and round, in utter silence, round and round. "Shantamama," I said, and Shanta-mama rolled her eyes and put a finger to her mouth . . . silence, silence, she gestured. In her fist lay a dry red chilli, salt, mustard seeds, skin of gar-lic and onion, tamarind, mud and a small twig from the broom. She com-pleted the circles around my face, spat into her fist, bent down, beat her fist on the floor, then went out of the room and into the kitchen, where she threw all this into the fire. I got better.

Anu Aunty, Prabha's mother, did exactly the same for Prabha and cured her. In fact often Prabha's stories and mine about our omniscient mothers merged so closely that after some time we could never be sure which story belonged to whom. It was the same way with our dreams and the stories we told one another; with each telling, they became richer and more lux-urious; a time always came when they belonged equally to both of us. Prabha was certain that the dream of the wolf entering the house through the window, mouth open, eyes red, was her dream, I equally certain it was mine, for wasn't I standing there, petrified, the scream struck in my throat, waiting to be eaten up? No, Prabha said, no, it was her dream, for she re-membered how he had in fact eaten her up, it was like being swallowed by darkness, she remembered that, so how could it be my dream? But it was, I said, for I too remembered it was black inside the wolf's stomach, I couldn't breathe, I called out to my mother, my voice a whisper, and she murmured, my pet, my love, her hand stroking my forehead, my hair, my arms, her lips in my ear, there in bed beside me, holding me close against her body, stroking, crooning. No, said Prabha firmly, the dream was hers, because there in the wolf's belly which was red, not black, she called out to her father, and he whispered, Meri bitiya, meri pyari bitiya, and he was there, sitting at her bedside, stroking her forehead, her hair, her cheek.

In Mahima's dreams God descended from the heavens in every poss-ible shape—Rama, Krishna, Shiva, Ganesh, Lakshmi, Saraswati, Jesus, Mary—and blessed her for being so good. Boring dreams, as Prabha said dismissively. I agreed loudly. But I was seized by jealousy. God, Mahima told us meaningfully, never gave bad dreams to the sinless.

Gauri's dreams, like her stories, varied, depending on what she felt we wanted to hear. When Prabha and I related our terrifying dreams of wolves and witches, Gauri would do better with dreams of blood-sucking vampires and malignant ghosts. When Mahima spoke of how Lord Krishna had played his flute for her the previous night, Gauri would relate her dream of how she had chanted "Ram, Ram, Ram," a thousand times and how Hanuman had flown into her dreams and how, when she woke up, she saw him flying out of the window. "If you say Ram, Ram a thousand times," Gauri told me humbly, "then all your wishes will come true." She whispered in my ear, "If you say Rama, Rama a hundred times every night, then even your father can come back to you."

*"Shut up."*

In a way Gauri operated the way my mothers did, except that Gauri didn't have the right.

"Rama, Rama, Rama," I chanted every night. Oh, I knew this man, my father, as well as the lines on my palm, the whorls on my fingertips. For, not long ago, when Ma was in her college, I had discovered his photograph at the bottom of Ma's saree trunk, within the folds of a never-worn yellow saree. A noble face with aristocratic angles and planes, gentle eyes, a musing smile. They stood next to each other, he and my mother, shoulders barely touching, Ma looking at the camera with all that she felt for him in her eyes. She was radiant. It was a radiance born not only of what she felt for him, but one born of itself, that which had been almost extinguished in the life after.

My parent's love belonged to the distilled world of my books, without the ever-after; it was painfully evident in their youth and in their beauty, in her misty eyes, in his tender smile. Behind the photograph was written in faded blue ink, "10th March, 1953." Three years before she got married, four years before I was born.

It is a terrible thing to know one's mother the way I knew mine. It was a terrible thing to know the unspeakable nature of Ma's mourning, which denied me all knowledge of my dead father. I knew how, at nights, she wept for him, silently, bitterly. The night harboured secrets like fireflies. Secrets withheld during the day poured out at night into the darkness of Ma's room, creeping out like smoke from under her door. In the night I heard her beloved, clear voice turning viscous and unfamiliar, as she twisted in the embrace of a familiar, dreaded nightmare. In this, Ma's grief, I could taste what I sought. But that which should have been tender and sweet, tasted rancid and decaying.

The weight of all that Ma didn't tell me about my father had left its permanent imprint in our lives. The nature of his absence shaped his presence in our house, a shape that had inhabited our lives from the very beginning, one that enveloped and consumed Ma. If Ma had once been a woman of natural radiance, I had never seen it. But I knew it must have been there because of the photograph, and because of the diffused, muted nature of what now remained.

In my letters to Ajji, my mother's mother, I did not ask the questions I wanted to ask, but in her letters Ajji gave me their answers. Your mother, said Ajji, used to envelope us in her sunshine. **Do you know, child, wrote Ajji in her first letter to me, that when you want something very badly, it can really happen?**

The doorbell ringing. It would happen now, it would happen.

*Ma opening the door. Dada standing there, eyes bruised, face gaunt with sorrow, voice hoarse with suffering. "Padma, I have come back to you." Swiftly catching her before she falls in a faint, looking down at the beloved, unforgotten face. A sound—looking up, there before him, his child, his free arm opening wide, I within it, his face wet against my cheek.*

Alas, when the doorbell rang it would be either Anu Aunty—Prabha's mother—or Madhu Aunty—Mahima's mother—who lived on either side of our house and who were Ma's best friends. Their familiar stories and their clicks of sympathy and understanding beat a regular rhythm in the house. Madhu Aunty, fat, fair and full of energy, inhaled and exhaled gossip ferociously. Tantalizing gusts would reach me as Madhu Aunty spoke of the goings-on in the neighbourhood. Dark, slim Anu Aunty's talk was not so interesting, but Ma listened as hungrily. "Bas, I talk to you, then I go back and listen," Anu Aunty would laugh, referring to her mother-in-law, who lived with her.

Anu Aunty, who sang like an angel, couldn't even sing because of her mother-in-law. On one occasion, as she sang for Prabha and me, her mother-in-law opened the door. "If you have to make a noise, have the kindness to do it when I'm not sleeping," she said. Prabha exclaimed, "Dadima, you never sleep at this time," and her grandmother sighed and said to Anu Aunty, "Very nicely you've coached your daughter, Bahurani, very nicely."

"You talk too much," Anu Aunty said to Prabha later.

"Mumma, I told the truth, I told the truth."

"Sometimes it is better to keep quiet than to tell the truth."

"Daddy never tells me to keep quiet. Daddy always says, Speak the truth."

"Yes, yes," Anu Aunty laughed. "Your father is a Harishchandra."

Ma never laughed. She was always tired, always sick. She taught in her college all day, came back and went over my lessons, then took tuition in English for ten neighbourhood children, then, late at night, studied for her doctorate. Every time she was sick Madhu Aunty drove her to her college and back so that she didn't have to take the bus. Madhu Aunty and Anu Aunty came home with vegetable soup and porridge for her, sat opposite her and watched her eat it. Madhu Aunty made the soup herself every day, not even letting her servant chop the vegetables or onions for it. "Same thing I do for my children also," she said to Anu Aunty.

No Ma to greet me or feed me when I came back from school. Comfort only in my Ayaji, waiting for me at the bus stop, umbrella in hand to protect me from the summer sun. I'd walk back home with her, soothed by her scoldings, her hands, hard and comforting, massaging me later with mustard oil, the water cool against my skin as she soaped me. Ayaji fussing over me as I ate lunch, then later, the comforting clatter of dishes being washed as I sat at my desk doing my homework, waiting for Ma to come back, waiting, waiting. And at dinnertime, Ma sitting me on her lap, her arm around my waist, her cheek against mine, her breath sweet against my face, feeding me, her fingers soft and tender in my mouth.

Shantamama's husband, Narayana Uncle, was in the railways, so they always travelled free. Sometimes she came with him to Delhi, but usually without. Her sons, Vikram and Varun, after spending an obligatory week with us would rush off to their uncle and cousins in old Delhi for the rest of the weeks. My Shantamama spent hours in the kitchen, chopping, kneading, stirring, frying, grinding. No comfort as deep as the sight of my Shantamama rearranging my cupboard, changing my sheets, stitching my buttons, knitting my sweaters, altering my frocks. No sight as reassuring as Shantamama swabbing and dusting and sweeping and attacking cobwebs. No movements as brisk and fluid and graceful, as I followed Shantamama all around the house while she arranged and rearranged, moving swiftly from room to room, calling me her love, her pet, her darling. When I urged her to dance, for she had ten years' training in Bharatnatyam, she wrapped her saree accordingly, put her ghungrus around her ankles and obliged. And how beautifully she moved, hips swinging, eyes large and expressive, fingers long and mobile, the bells on her ghungrus filling the house with joyous sounds. There was grace in her movements, passion in her body's rhythms.

Ma's passions ran a different course. My mother, so lovely and graceful, so kind and good, so tender and true, was strangely inept in the things that mothers do. Her love was bountiful but it did not get translated into a mother's natural rhythms. I longed to see her beautiful profile bent over a needle and thread. I longed to see her face frowning with concentration as she briskly stirred the chicken curry, kneaded the dough, checked on the oven where the cake was rising, cleared the dishes around her, wiped the counters, her movements quick and assured. Alas, my mother's love blossomed in unfamiliar ways; the path she tread cut through an unknown territory.

Only Dada's love allowed me to articulate my pain. For unlike my two mothers, he had the fortitude to withstand it. I could tell him how I longed to be all that Ma wanted me to be, and how short I fell of it. She wanted me to be strong, fearless, sure of myself. I was wavering, scared and diffident. But, Ma could not speak of this any more than she could speak about her silent grieving. And to my father I could say, Dada, I cannot bear Ma's suffering, it smothers me. Her grief has, since the beginning, been my own, I wear it in the same manner that she does, then tell me, what comfort can we give one another? Not that I had any words for all these things, but then, such articulation lay beyond words.

**Yes, child, wrote my grandmother, Ajji, the power of the mind is such that it can make anything happen.**

The doorbell ringing. It would happen now. I knew it would.

*Ma opening the door. Dada's face, distraught. "I have come back to you, Padma. It was my memory that went. For years I wandered, a prisoner in my own mind. Then my memory returned. I have come back to you, my sweet." (His eyes widen in disbelief. His arms open.) "And this, this beauty is my child?"*

Even my own imagination balked at this last bit. For I defined the word *ordinary.* Mahima would have been perfect in the role—petite, fair, pink-cheeked—Mahima, who was not only beautiful but brainier than anyone we knew. Even long-legged, dishevelled Prabha would have done, for she was not only brainy but redeemingly fair, and when she smiled, her whole body lit up. No, Gauri wouldn't have done at all, dark, thin Gauri, with her straggly hair, ill-fitting frocks and rubber slippers. Gauri, if possible, had even less of a claim on Dreams-Come-True than did I.

Yet, I, unlikely heroine, was no stranger to the extraordinary.

The heroes and heroines of my books, who had adventures and solved mysteries, all lived in foreign lands. Adventures and mysteries could not happen to brown-skinned, black-eyed children who lived in a land where neem and mango trees grew, where there was no containing the heat or the sweat, where there were no rainy days but instead, a monsoon, a time when the skies opened in such an immoderate fashion and trees heavy with fruit dropped jamuns, which stained tongues and teeth purple. Where there were no light pinks, pale yellows and mellow blues, but instead, fiery reds, golden yellows and deep purples like the sarees our mothers wore. Adventures and mysteries could not happen to children whose mothers smacked them and yelled at them and smothered them with kisses, and whose fathers wore crumpled pyjama kurtas, children who lived in neighbourhoods where snarling dogs, possessed with a passion to bite, sprang triumphantly out of houses.

No. Adventures and mysteries could only happen to golden-haired, blue-eyed children who lived in lands where daffodils and daisies grew, where dinner was called supper, when you ate things like mince pies and puddings using forks and knives, where mothers sighed Yes dear, and No dear, where fathers in tweed coats smoked pipes and sat in large armchairs, reading newspapers, and where beautiful, intelligent dogs behaved with pedigreed decorum. Magic could work its wonders only in the lives of Pats and Peters, as they climbed up trees which opened up into different lands—lands full of unfamiliarly delicious sweets with foreign names like liquorice.

And there was so much more magic within the covers of Mahima's hardbound, glossy books which her aunt had got her from England than in my Indian editions.

Ah, but now we had *our* own story, Prabha and I. With adventure *and* mystery *and* magic. And *we* were its heroines.

"Prabha and I were playing behind her house," I said.

"And then," said Prabha, "those badmashes Bunny and Pawan saw us there. The way they were laughing, so quietly, and coming near us . . ."

Prabha pulled up her sleeve, put up her arm, flexed her muscles. "I said to them, Ullu ke patthe, I'll finish you both in one minute."

"They began hitting us," I whispered. "I fell down, and then I prayed to God, and then he came."

"Who came, who came, who came?" asked Gauri.

"You knew to ask God for *him*?" Prabha asked.

"I didn't say any *words*," I said. "I just . . . you know . . . *thought* it. Like in *King Arthur and the Knights of the Round Table*?"

"Lancelot." Prabha understood immediately.

A brave and kindly knight to rout Bunny and Pawan well and proper. "And then—"

And we told Mahima and Gauri of how our tall and kindly knight materialized, raised Bunny and Pawan up in the air, threw them into the ditch.

"Just like a story!" sighed Gauri.

But this time the story was ours.

We told them how he didn't even look at the fleeing boys. Gently, he just said, Are you hurt? Ah, what sad eyes he had. He helped us get up, looked at our elbows and knees to see if we were hurt, then he said, Thank God.

"As though he was . . . he was . . . *breathing* the words."

"As though he would *die* if we were hurt. Oh, the *way* he said it!"

*"Thank God,"* Prabha and I moaned together.

"Lying is a sin," declared Mahima.

"Tell, tell, tell no!" moaned Gauri.

We described how Prabha patted my arm and said, Mallika? I said, I'm all right, Prabha. And his face lit up, his eyes filled with warmth. He took out three coins from his pocket and laid them on his palm. He closed his hand, then opened it. No coins. He said, Oh, oh, and took one out from behind my left ear, and then two more from behind Prabha's right ear. How we laughed. Do you like to read? he asked me. And I said, Ma and Dada and I all love books.

"Liar," pounced Mahima.

"It *isn't* a lie. Shantamama told me Dada loved books."

"Then you should have said, Dada *loved* books, not *loves* books."

"No one's forcing you to listen to the story," Prabha said to Mahima.

How to explain to Mahima and Gauri the nature of our conversation? The way he asked me, What kind of books do you like? I said, Adventures. Mysteries said Prabha. With magic, I said. With scary things happening, said Prabha. But in the end it gets all right, I said. He said, I have a book about two friends called Kiran and Abhimanyu. With adventure and mystery and magic and scary things happening, but in the end it gets all right. Kiran and Abhimanyu? I exclaimed, How can Kiran and Abhimanyu have adventures! He looked surprised. Then he said, You don't like their names? I said, They should have proper names. Like Beth, Claire, Irene, said Prabha. Like Frederick, Harry, Frank, Douglas, I said. I asked, Who wrote the book about Kiran and Abhimanyu? He said, Close your eyes and slowly count to fifty. So we began to count. When we reached forty-five he said, Open your eyes. He was breathing a little heavily. He gave us a notebook and said, Don't show it to anyone. We opened the notebook and inside was written, "Kiran and Abhimanyu in the Land of Talking Trees." He bent down, smiling a little, and said, I wrote it.

"So *lucky*," Gauri sighed gustily. "You're so *lucky*."

Ah, the sprouting of our very own story, the very stuff of fantasy!

Mahima tossed her head, "Show me the notebook."

"The magic man's story," said Prabha, "is about a girl called Kiran, who, like her name, is a ray of light . . ."

"And a boy named Abhimanyu, who like Abhimanyu in the *Mahabharata*, is very young and very brave."

Best friends. In a land drenched with colour, where trees and birds and animals talk. Where the sun rains down like the monsoons. Happy, fearless Kiran is the leader. Quiet, circumspect Abhimanyu doesn't always want to do what she expects him to. The story is written in blue ink, the handwriting is impeccable. The drawings which fill the notebook are in ink as well as in colour pencil. Some scenes of the magic land are drawn on the whole page, and other drawings of the birds and animals are right in the middle of the writing, small and clear, so instead of calling a bird or animal by its name, it's drawn. The flora and fauna of this magic land bear no resemblance to those in our world.

"And each," we chorused, "has a special magic that Kiran and Abhimanyu discover during their adventures!"

Kiran and Abhimanyu don't exclaim gosh and golly. They say hai and oho. They don't eat pies and scones but gulabjamuns and pedas, and they pluck not apples, but mangoes and jamuns. They never say that they can't do without each other, but it is evident, even as they fight, often in the middle of their magical adventures. It is Kiran who takes the initiative, and

Abhimanyu who follows her. Not that Abhimanyu is a coward—far from it. He is merely cautious and not given to impulses of any kind, whereas Kiran does not know what caution means. But she is brave, generous and full of laughter and far more willing to forgive Abhimanyu after their squabbles than he is ready to forgive her. None of this is said in so many words. But knowing them, Prabha and I know it is so.

Ah, what a story, so tender, so intense. If magical things happen to them it is because Kiran makes them happen with her impulsiveness, her fearlessness, and her wholehearted love of life. Because Abhimanyu, beneath his quiet exterior, eventually wants all that Kiran wants.

"Show me the notebook with the story," said Mahima.

"It's *magic*," I said.

Later, Mahima asked Prabha's grandmother. "Does magic happen in real life, Dadima?"

"Why not, why not?"

"But why does magic happen?"

"Ask Him." She pointed upwards.

"But He won't tell us, Dadima."

"One day, Beti, He will. If not in this life, then in the next."

*"In the next life!"*

"Learn patience. Pray to God. Learn to love everyone. Learn humility. Learn compassion. Then all your questions will be answered. Arre, Bahurani, lunch still is not ready?" Dadima called out to Anu Aunty. "By the time she makes lunch the sun would have set. Churail," she muttered.

Outside the world of our magic man, nothing but the old, familiar tunes. Words shifted and slid around us as Prabha, Mahima, Gauri and I played hopscotch in the courtyard.

"But look, how this Mallika's mother dresses, like a married woman, bindi also, mangalsutra also, and such bright sarees! Are all Madrasi widows like this?" Dadima asked Madhu Aunty.

"Padma does it to protect herself, Mataji. This way no one will approach her."

It was about the fifth or sixth time the conversation was repeating itself. It meant that Dadima was feeling content and expansive.

"Ram Ram. Such a sad life she has. That too, after a love-marriage." She turned to Anu Aunty. "And tell me, where is my tea?"

Anu Aunty smiled and went into the kitchen.

Madhu Aunty said, "I do not believe in all this love-shuv. Look at these Western people, so much love, so much love, and next minute, divorce."

Anu Aunty emerged with a glass of tea.

"Arre, so quickly?" her mother-in-law said. "You think you can reheat old tea and give me?"

"It is fresh tea, Mataji, I had kept the water earlier."

"Hai Bhabi, even I want some tea," said Kamala Bua, Prabha's father's sister. She too lived with them.

"My child, take mine, take mine." Anu Aunty's mother-in-law turned to Anu Aunty. "Bahurani, what would have gone of yours if you had made a little more tea?"

"I did make extra tea, Mataji, I will get it."

"Accha, Bahurani, before you get, a little bit if you can oil my hair . . . my back also, for so many days there is this pain, one has to bear it, old age is a curse . . . oof, Bahurani, open my hair a little gently, what need is there to pull like that? Lecturer of History . . . Padma is from a good family, well educated, why didn't she marry a man with a proper job?"

Anu Aunty said, "I told you before, Mataji, Padma's husband qualified for the civil services while he was a lecturer."

"Enough oil, Bahurani, now massage the left side. Ah, yes, yes, ah yes. Hai Ram, what a heavy burden on Her slender shoulders."

Madhu Aunty shook her head. "Oof, I cannot work like Padma. It is His fault; He spoils me so much that I forget what hard work is." ("He" was Nanda Uncle, her husband.)

"Ah, ah, very nice, very nice, for such a thin person, Bahurani, you have strength in your hands, hai, hai, yes, yes. Bahurani, tell me, Padma's husband's side, as well as her own parents, still they are not talking to her, still they are not visiting their grandchild?"

"They are still angry. Both parents were against the marriage."

"Ram, Ram. Such anger, it is unnatural. Especially after a child is born. Nothing he left behind for her? Money . . . property?"

"I don't know, Mataji."

"Very nice, Bahurani, very nice, ah, ah. A little higher, on the shoulder, yes, very nice. Ahhh. Have you seen Padma's petticoats? All of them have lace at the hem, sometimes when she walks I can see it, if it is a white petticoat, then white lace, if pink, then pink lace."

"Mataji, Padma's sister, Shanta, makes all her petticoats," said Madhu Aunty. "Also all Mallika's frocks."

"So talented this Shanta is. A little bit learn from her, Bahurani. More to the right, more to the right, bas, ah, ah. Such pretty frocks. But nothing suits the child. Higher, Bahurani, higher, ah, that is better, very nice. The girl hasn't even got her mother's sweet nature, all she has got is her mother's dark skin."

"She is a bright child, Mataji. And good and kindhearted," said Anu Aunty.

"What of that. Why should a man want a beautiful heart when he can get a beautiful face?"

Familiar these rhythms, familiar their tune. No proper stories here, no dark, delicious tales of woe. No quivering ecstasy or twisting pain, no deep deprivation or desperate desire, no terrible anger or unbearable sorrow, no all-consuming love or burning hate. What could they possibly know of it? What could Shantamama, who was married to the kindest man in the world? And my grandmother, Ajji, who in her letters spoke of so much that I didn't understand, said that she was more content than any of her children could ever be. **You are too young to understand, child, wrote Ajji—but life is full of the strangest coincidences. I believe there is a reason for them. The reason lies within us.**

The doorbell ringing. I believed in strange coincidences. Now, it would happen.

*I open the door. He stands there, his eyes full of pain, his heart full of longing. He cries out, "My child." Behind me I hear Ma take in her breath. "Padma," he whispers, "oh, Padma."*

"Padma, oho, I disturbed you." Madhu Aunty came in.

Whisper, whisper, went Madhu Aunty. Poor Mrs. Moitra, Ma sighed.

Beautiful, wicked Mrs. Moitra lived all alone and drank and smoked and painted strange pictures in her veranda. Late one night I heard Mrs. Moitra's voice floating across the road to my house. I crept to my window, saw her sitting on her lawn with someone else, her voice filling the street like moonlight, "Tiger, tiger, burning bright," she was reciting, and my skin prickled to its beauty in the same way as when Anu Aunty sang Raga Malhar.

"Tiger, tiger, burning bright," repeated Madhu Aunty the next day, as she sat with Ma finishing her third cup of tea, "I tell you, Padma, in class five my boys are learning 'Tiger, tiger burning bright'; if Mrs. Moitra is that much cultured Bengali then why she is reciting children's poem?" She lowered her voice and whispered something to Ma about a nervous breakdown.

Gauri who knew everything, explained. Nervous breakdown meant going mad. In the afternoons after school Gauri, Mahima, Prabha and I all took turns to be Mad Mrs. Moitra, having a nervous breakdown. We laughed and cried, tore our hair and screamed. "Mad she is," Madhu Aunty whispered to Ma, "all the time painting, painting, painting. And what she is painting, Padma, I do not understand, no scenery no people, all round things and square things."

If Mrs. Moitra was mad it had to be because she did whatever she wanted to do. Surely it would be lunacy for any of our mothers to do whatever they wanted to do? The sonorous strains of Raga Malhar filling Anu Aunty's house as Dadima fetched water for herself from the fridge, Ma reading all day and night, Madhu Aunty doing her B.A., leaving Mahima and her brothers alone in the house, Shantamama becoming a professional Bharatnatyam dancer . . . Alas, no stories in the lives of our mothers. So much more juice in the stories we invented. Like beautiful, orphaned, long-suffering Grace, who lived with her ugly, wicked stepmother and stepsister. Each of us took turns playing hapless Grace. Prabha, as Grace wept loudly, banged her head against the wall and threw herself on the ground. Mahima's Grace, songlike, wailed, "Oh what a life, oh what a life." I, as Grace, wept silently, endlessly. And Gauri's Grace was the best, weeping hysterically, and trying to slash her wrists with a kitchen knife. Salvation lay only in Prince Charmings; till then suffer, Grace, suffer.

Gauri had a stepmother and two stepsisters. When we first met Gauri's family, all our expectations were bitterly dashed—her stepmother was fair and pretty, the two stepsisters, plump, fair and red-cheeked. It was poor, bereft Gauri who was so unfairly unattractive.

"Does your stepmother beat you?" Prabha would ask Gauri.

Mostly Gauri said no, but sometimes, when pressed she said yes.

"How many times?"

"How hard?"

"I'll tell you a secret," Gauri whispered. "Married people take off their knickers at night."

Oh what a haven of unlawfully acquired information and seething stories was Gossipy Gauri. Always smiling eagerly, always quivering with terrible tales to tell! Bunny and Pawan call ghosts, Nehru died today, Bunny's servant Kailash dresses up in women's clothes and dances. Gauri told us all that she saw and heard, and if she wasn't true to the text it was not an act of deception, but one of faith: Gauri believed everything.

The nuns in our convent had no keener ear in their moral science classes than Gauri's, who, as they spoke of the ills of scandalmongering and deceit, nodded her head vigourously and exclaimed, "Hai re, hai re!" Yet Gauri failed in moral science and all the other exams except Hindi and English. For Gauri, unlike any of us, had a flair for languages, and could even read and write Kannada fluently.

Gauri loved Ma, for Ma would ask her questions, listen wide-eyed to her terrible tales. Something in my mother was deeply moved by Gauri, somewhere inside Gauri Ma found a pain similar to her own, and this she was determined to soothe. And with Ma, Gauri's eyes would lose their quick, birdlike movements, her smile its uncertainty, her thin arms their sharp, awkward gestures. For a time, however briefly, Gauri's face would be serene.

"When you fail, does your stepmother beat you?" Mahima asked.

Gauri's eyes grew large. "Moitra Aunty's husband used to beat her."

"Liar."

"By God it's true," Gauri said, her hand on her heart.

Impossible. Such things happened only to servants. In fact, Mahima had overheard her mother say that women of the servant class even had babies without marriage, and such babies were called Bastards.

"And," continued Gauri triumphantly, "nowadays Mrs. Moitra commits adultry."

"Adultry?" Prabha asked.

"Adultry," Gauri whispered, "is what adults try."

"What do adults try?"

"A Man comes to her house at night. Yesterday his car was parked outside her house."

"Liar."

"I promise on my real mother's name. By God."

"Mrs. Moitra's house is opposite ours. I've never seen him," I said.

"You sleep at eight. I saw him at twelve."

That night, which was Saturday, Prabha spent the night with me, as she did every other week. "I've asked Gauri to wake us up if he comes," Prabha said as we lay in bed. "I've unbolted your bedroom door."

Much later. Prabha's voice in my ear, "Mallika, Mallika. Get up."

"He's come." Triumph in Gauri's voice.

We crept to the window. A car was parked opposite our house next to Mrs. Moitra's. Someone was sitting inside.

"Mrs. Moitra will flash a torch, and then he'll go inside."

"Till then he's sitting there thinking of her."

"Why should he think of her? She's right there."

"When you fall in love then you think like that."

"But how can he fall in love with her? She's got a husband."

"Her husband used to beat her. He was a Bad Man."

"So the adultrer wants to marry her, but her Bad Husband is alive."

"The Good Adultrer knew her before she got married to the Bad Husband."

"But her parents forced her to get married to the Bad Husband."

"He knows he can never forget her."

"So every year the Good Adultrer comes once or twice, just to look at her. He parks his car next to her house and thinks, Inside this house is the woman I love."

"Look, look."

The man was slumped across the wheel.

"He's dead."

"He's fainted."

Prabha and Gauri ran out of the door. After a moment's hesitation, I followed them. It was a cool summer night. The street and houses were dark and silent. We ran across the street soundlessly, to the side of the car where he lay, his arm on the wheel, his head on his arm, and stood at his window, staring at him. Then Prabha put her hand through the window, and experimentally prodded his back.

He moved so suddenly that we all shrieked. The next second Gauri was running away towards her house.

"As the man in the car turned towards us," I said softly to Gauri the next day.

"He became—" said Prabha, her voice rising.

"The magic man," we whispered together.

A sound emerged from Gauri's throat. Her face was suddenly radiant.

And we told Gauri how he looked at us, incredulously. Hi, I said. After some time he said, What on earth are you doing here at this time? I said, We were watching you from my window. We thought you were dead. He said, Go home. Quickly. I said, I loved your book. He smiled. Then he took out two notebooks from a briefcase lying next to him, and gave them to us. Now run back home, both of you, he said.

"But why was he carrying those notebooks in the middle of the night in his car?"

"Because he's a *magic* man, Gauri."

He asked me, Did you like Kiran? I said, I like Abhimanyu also. He said, You did? Then, after some time he asked, Which school do you go to? We told him. Then I said, Where do you come from, magic man? And he answered, From the land where stories grow, my magic girl.

There was a long, luxurious silence. Then together, the three of us whispered, *"Where do you come from, magic man? From the land where stories grow, my magic girl."*

"Suddenly—"

"We saw Padma Aunty's bedroom light was on."

"We didn't even say bye. We *ran* home and got into bed."

"Where are the stories?"

In the silence that followed Prabha tapped her head and said, "Here, silly, here."

And we tell Gauri our two new stories. I take the part of Abhimanyu, my counterpart, the dreamer, the quiet one, the one who is never quite sure of what he wants. I understand his cautious and circumspect nature, I share his unformulated dreams. Prabha takes the part of the laughing, generous, fearless Kiran who is always so oblivious of danger. She never cries, not even when she once hurts herself very badly. In fact, she never tells Abhimanyu about it. Always, their adventures get them into dangerou situations, always, Kiran ignores the signs. She knows less than Abhimanyu about the birds and animals, but she's the one who understands them better, reads their expressions, anticipates their desires.

Kiran and Abhimanyu go everywhere. And Everywhere is where I too want to travel. I want Everywhere to envelop me, to feel its texture the way Shantamama feels silk between thumb and forefinger, to taste it, bite by delicious bite, the way Prabha's grandmother eats besan ka laddoos. Abhimanyu too dreams as I do, he wants to see every animal and bird and tree that belongs to other lands. No wonder he's often so impatient with Kiran—because he thinks she comes in his way. Yet, I cannot imagine Abhimanyu ever travelling without Kiran.

We feel bereft every time we finish reliving the stories. It is not only because the stories are over, but because of the feeling of danger outside the magic land, quite different from the tangible dangers within it. For there is a hint of impending doom that surrounds the magic land like an invisible barrier. It is that which catches and holds all of us. It is that which gives us the awful feeling that any minute now it will all be over, that the flowers will fade, the animals lose their voices, the birds stop singing. We relive the stories again and again, not only for the vicarious pleasure of adventuring with Kiran and Abhimanyu, but to try and envision that fog of grief within which the magic land lies. Yet, nothing in the stories mentions, or even hints at either grief or pain.

"All right, then, show me the notebooks," said Mahima. She looked at us and made a scornful sound.

That night I wept bitterly. Ma's footsteps coming towards my room, Ma climbing into my bed, her warmth as she held me. "Mallika," she whispered, "Mallika?"

Writhe, Ma. Scream out his name. Hit your head against the wall. Show me the whites of your eyes.

"Where did you get all your books from, Ma?" I asked her the next morning.

In the kitchen, Ma stopped stirring her coffee.

Utter the unuttered. "My father gave them to you, no?"

"Mallika. Stop playing with the knife."

"He didn't write anything in the books he gave you?"

Her face was white. "He . . . would pick them up at . . . a secondhand bookshop . . . and . . . give them to . . . me. *Mallika!*"

Scream louder Ma, louder. Louder, louder. Louder.

Ma's hands on my wrists, the knife falling on the floor, nothing soft about Ma's fingers now, the whites of her eyes showing, my bloody finger under the running tap, hideous sounds coming out of Ma's stomach.

My mother could not know how instinctively and how wordlessly I comprehended the world of Kiran and Abhimanyu to which such blinding utterance had been given. If I hadn't understood her as instinctively, I would have been kinder to her, gentler with her.

That night, my finger bandaged, my arm still hurting after the tetanus injection, I slept with Ma. That night she broke her silence.

Alas, her story, instead of throbbing with passion, pain and despair, was a muted and steady rendering which did not tell me what I wanted to know.

I asked her again and again, night after night, month after month, year after year.

"Ma, didn't he fall in love with you the first time he saw you in the bookshop?"

*Never had he thought he would succumb so instantly to Cupid's arrow. Lost, he was lost.*

"No."

*Drowning in her beauty, drowning. But it was not just this—for she was also intelligent and well read! They were, he knew at last, kindred souls.*

"Tell me *properly*, Ma, *please* tell me properly."

A courtship conducted in bookshops. Ma, her brother Madhav and my father going to bookshops, for walks, for dosas. But he came from a U.P. family and his parents didn't want him to marry a South Indian girl. A Madrasi. Ma's parents refusing to accept the marriage without his parents' consent. Getting married against both parents' wishes. He getting into the civil services at the time. Before he could join—the accident. His parents and Ma's father, still unforgiving.

"But Ajji, Ma?"

"As long as my father doesn't forgive me, my mother can't come to me."

**I will keep all the books in my house for you, wrote my grandmother, Ajji. Once I used to think that people who love books have a hunger that is never satisfied. I saw it in my children. And life cannot satisfy this hunger. Then what can? you will ask. And I will say to you—I have it too, this hunger, and such hunger eats you up, child, it eats you up.**

The doorbell ringing. I know Ajji, I know this hunger too.

*She opens the door. He stands there, his heart in his eyes. Silently, her mouth utters his name. "Padma," he says, "it has been death without you." He sees me. "My child, oh, my child!"*

"Aunty, can Mallika come home for breakfast, we're having aloo parathas?" asked Prabha as Ma opened the door.

And I continued to gather the same old stories, stories grown blunt and rusted with repetition.

"Hai, Bhabi, your parathas are too good," Kamala Bua said to Anu Aunty.

"Eat another, Kamala." Anu Aunty put the paratha from her plate onto her sister-in-law's.

"Mumma, where is your paratha?" Prabha asked.

"Bahurani, one more you make for Kamala," Anu Aunty's mother-in-law said. "So unassuming my Kamala is, never wants anything for herself, never asks, always thinks of other people first."

Anu Aunty got up. Prabha and I picked up our plates and followed her.

"Kamala Bua," Prabha called out from the kitchen, "for your one paratha Mumma has to knead flour again."

"Keep quiet," Anu Aunty hissed to Prabha.

"Teach her more, Bahurani, teach her more," Dadima said, entering the kitchen. She looked at the vessel on the gas. "Bahurani, what is this?"

"Khir, Mataji."

"I see, I see. Khir you are making and not so much as a word out of you."

"Dadima," Prabha said, "the khir is for those friends of Daddy who are coming for dinner today."

Dadima filled two large bowls full of khir. "My bitiya, Kamala, look what I have got for you." She shuffled out of the kitchen.

"Keep quiet. Not one word," Anu Aunty said to Prabha.

"Wonderful, wonderful," Kamala Bua said five minutes later, entering the kitchen. "Bas, one more bowl I will have, that is all."

Dadima entered behind her. "Here, fill mine also, Bahurani, and one bowl get for Anirudh also, the poor boy has not had at all."

"I also haven't, Dadima," Prabha said quietly.

Prabha and I began drying the dishes. I loved to watch Anu Aunty at her work, the way she lingered, considered, tasted, mulled, her movements swift and fluid. So unlike Ma. It was never passion for cooking which quickened Ma's movements, but impatience. No desire to clean, swab, dust, arrange, rearrange. Things fell out of her cupboard. Her books lay all over the house. On weekends, looking despairingly at the house, she would say to me, "Mallika?" Inevitably, we would start laughing, get dressed, take the bus to the library or to one of the secondhand bookshops in Shankar Market, and spend the whole day there.

"Ma, when Dada's parents refused to accept you, he must have been so angry with them."

*Enough. Do not speak of the woman I love in this manner. It no longer mat-*
*ters to me what you want, or do not want. She will be my wife.*

"He . . . didn't discuss that . . . with me."

"Did Dada write poetry for you, Ma?"

She shook her head.

"Letters?"

She nodded.

"And in them he said . . . ?"

*Without you, Padma, the days pass like years. Every second without you is*
*an eternity.*

"He . . . talked to me about the things he observed around him."

"*Ma!* How *boring!*"

"No . . . no. He could paint a picture in a sentence. He could . . . draw
a story in a morning walk."

When Ma was in college, and Ayaji asleep in the sitting room, I carefully and systematically went through her saree box. Then, her cupboard.
In a plastic bag containing her underclothes, I found a box of matches and
a packet of cigarettes. I climbed up on a chair and looked through the top
shelf of her cupboard. At the very back, I found a very sharp knife wrapped
up in an old petticoat. No letters.


And I continued listening to the old familiar refrains.

"Bahurani," Dadima said, "half a glass of tea for me also. And do not be
miserly with the sugar. There is no shortage of sugar in this house."

Anu Aunty went back into the kitchen and came out with a glass of tea.

"Arre, so fast you have made it?"

"I made two glasses, Mataji, when I made for Kamala."

"And then you grumble about household expenses. One glass Kamala
asked for, and you made two glasses. It is a good thing I wanted some, otherwise that also would have been wasted. Learn not to waste, Bahurani.
Even now it is not too late to learn."

Anu Aunty began combing Dadima's hair.

"This Padma, sometimes the poor girl looks so tired. I hope you know
how lucky you are to have a husband who does all the work and gives you
all his money."

Anu Aunty laughed. "And who does the work in the house, Mataji?"

"When I was your age I ran the house on one tenth the money that you do. My mother-in-law, God bless her soul, everything she used to leave in my hands." Dadima wiped her eye with the corner of her saree. "Everything I learnt, I learnt from her. May God keep her soul in peace."

"Amma," Kamala Bua said tearfully to Dadima, "as big a heart as yours no one has. I know how badly my grandmother treated you. Like a servant. Yet you have only kind words for her."

Dadima sighed, closed her eyes, folded her hands.

Anu Aunty began massaging her legs. "These days, Mataji, things cost ten times what they did when you ran a house."

"How she answers back. I know how much water you put in Kamala's milk, don't think I can't make out."

"Mataji, I don't put water in the milk. Everyone has the same milk."

"Yes, yes, that is why the bloom has already gone from Kamala's face, my poor Kamala. No need to say anything. I cannot bear it."

"Mataji, I don't drink milk."

"So what can I do if you don't drink milk? Am I stopping you from drinking milk? The way she talks. Bahurani, do not massage my legs as if your hands are made of rubber. Use some strength. Ah yes, ah yes. Not so hard, Bahurani, hai Ram. A little on the left side, Bahurani, yes, yes, ah, ah."

The same dreadfully dull stories.

And Ma's story? Every time she told me I extracted a new detail—my father buying her gulabjamuns to eat, a shelf of books falling on my mother and he laughing, the books he would give her from time to time. And yet it felt that her story, as if dug out of a coffin, was all bones.

And Kiran and Abhimanyu's story? That its soft breath, that the pure peal of its laughter.

But how could bones or breath suffice when I hungered for what neither could give me—flesh and blood?

I needed to hear its sound. And I had heard its sound, briefly, the day I had cut myself. That sound, in its entirety was Ma. Not my mother this woman so shrouded in silence. That in its entirety my mother, that hideous sound, those rolling, white eyes, that in its entirety, my father.


Prabha was in bed, down with the flu, looking miserable. I said to her, "When I was eating my sandwich in school, guess who came?"

Prabha looked at my face and said, almost pleadingly, "The magic man?"

"And in his hands," I said.

"Were the notebooks," sighed Prabha.

I told her how I said to my magic man, They're the best books I've read in my whole life. And how he smiled. I asked him, Why doesn't Abhimanyu say nice things to Kiran? He looked wondering, and said, Abhimanyu thinks nice things about her. I said, Then why doesn't he tell her? He didn't answer. Then I said, You know everything that will happen to them? And he said, No, nothing. I exclaimed, But you're the author! Then he said, When I begin their story, I don't know what will happen to them. As I write, I find out. I said, You don't have it all in your head? He said, No. I said, Why do you write these stories? He said, For you. I said, But when you wrote the first book you didn't know me. Then he thought for some time and said, I wrote it because I had a story to tell. I gave that to you. After that, all the stories were for you. I said, But you said you didn't know what would happen to Kiran and Abhimanyu. He said, I didn't. I said, Then why are you saying you wrote the first book because you had a story to tell? You didn't know what the story was. He said, I didn't. That was why I had to write it.

"Real people don't talk like that," Prabha said.

"*He's* not like *real* people."

Prabha nodded slowly. "When we tell Gauri and Mahima, remember, I'll also be in the story. O.K.?"

"O.K."


Why do I talk to you like this, child, wrote my grandmother, Ajji, when I do not do so with my own children? You, whom I have never seen! If your father were here to know you, I know what all his heart would hold. And of that, child, I think and I think, day and night, and day and night.

The doorbell ringing. Yes, I too know what his heart will hold.

*Ma opens the door. Dada stands there, unmoving.*

"Hi." Gauri came into my room where I sat with Prabha and Mahima.

Our eyes brightened. For Gauri had promised to tell us the story of the latest Hindi film, the one where the heroine has a baby before her marriage.

"See, the Hero and Heroine sing a song in the rain, and then both of them get wet and take shelter in an old house in the forest."

"Haaw," giggled Mahima, putting her hand to her mouth.

Prabha and I looked blankly at her.

"That's how she has the baby," Mahima explained.

"They sit in front of the fire inside the hut and he sings another song to her and she feels very shy because he is looking at her," Gauri said.

Mahima put her hand to her flat chest. "Her pom-poms show in the wet saree."

"In the morning they show two birds flying up in the sky," Gauri said.

"It means they are like married people now," Mahima said.

"Why?"

"When a man and a woman take off their clothes in the same room, then they have babies. It is a sin."

"Sin?"

"When you sin," Gauri said, "you have to suffer. Like Eve. That's why you have to have babies after you sin. It's a punishment. That's why babies come out of the same place that you do number two." She watched our stupefied expressions with satisfaction. "I saw Pawan's dog having puppies."

"Mothers shit out babies?" I gasped.

Gauri nodded vigourously.

"Haiii!" moaned Prabha.

"I saw a film with a cabaret," Mahima said. "She had such big pom-poms and she kept shaking them."

"Why?"

"Men like big pom-poms that go up and down."

And Mahima tells us the story. Not only does the cabaret dancer have big pom-poms, but she fancies the Hero. And the heroine? As Mahima describes her, she swims before my eyes, a beautiful orphan, her saree palla drawn around her shoulder, her hair drawn back into a bun, exposing her vulnerable neck and soft features, her eyes large with suffering, standing quietly next to a tree in the moonlight, singing, as behind her, unseen, the smitten Hero watches.


"Bahurani. This tea, it is like ice. Bahurani, have you gone deaf?"

Anu Aunty came out of the kitchen. "I will just get, Mataji."

"Just get, just get. A little systematic you have to be, that is all."

Anu Aunty went back to the kitchen. Dadima wiped her eyes and turned to my mother. "Padma, Beti, now that my child Kamala's marriage has been fixed, I have just one prayer, and that is that my Kamala's in-laws realize that they have got a jewel. May they give her the love that she has got from her mother and her father and her brothers and her sisters."

"Yes, Mataji."

"Padma, Beti, my Kamala has such tender hands. We have nurtured her with so much love. How will she look after such a large family? My heart, it breaks to think of it. And—arre, Bahurani, what colour is this tea?"

"The milk is finished Mataji," Anu Aunty said.

"Accha. So the milk is finished. You think you can get the same amount of milk these days when the house is full of guests?"

"Mataji, I got more, but I did not expect five more people to come today. They were supposed to come the day after tomorrow."

"Yes, yes, for everything you have got an answer. Take this tea. I do not want to be poisoned. Accha, Bahurani, my hair it needs to be oiled."

Anu Aunty looked at Ma and broke into laughter.

"All over the world people are suffering and all she can do is laugh."

"Mataji, if I stop laughing will they stop suffering?"

"Laugh more, laugh more. Arre, Bahurani, that mango pickle I made—I kept one bottle for Padma, and still you have not given her?"

"I gave it to her yesterday, Mataji."

"Gave it to her yesterday she says. Did not even ask me, churail."

The same old stories, the same repetitive lines. Where, oh where was Passion in the world I inhabited? It was not Passion that had joined the lives of all the mothers and fathers I knew, that was not why their lives were lived. Would we find it, Prabha, Mahima, Gauri and I? Mahima certainly would, her very loveliness would persuade Passion to draw her into its mysterious folds, whereas I would have to wait a little, grow a little, try not to get tanned, rub basen, haldi and malai on my face, mustard oil on my body, coconut oil in my hair. "Wait and see," Shantamama said, massaging my scalp, "at thirty you'll look ten years younger and prettier than Mahima."

"Imagine," I told Prabha, "imagine, *thirty.*"

Thirty. All end to romance, yearning. All end to turbulence, passion. All end to dreaming, longing, sighing. A time to express quiet pleasure at photographs in the *National Geographic,* never despair for not being in them. Whining children, flabby arms, hair smelling of food, voices drowning under the sound of the pressure cooker.

I, thirty? Impossible. All passion directed to chopping and cleaning? No reading, no dreaming, no lazying in bed? Making the bed first thing in the morning, eating karelas with enjoyment, bargaining heatedly with the sab-jiwalla for vegetables and the phalwalli for fruits, saying two rupees if they said three, settling for two-fifty? Trying to get three rupees more out of the kabadiwalla, if not, refusing to part with the old newspapers? Denying my-self what gave me the greatest pleasure? Like Anu Aunty, in the middle of listening to classical music on the radio, looking guiltily at her sister-in-law and changing it to filmi music? Like rich Madhu Aunty, travelling by bus to Connaught Place rather than in her car, then grumbling about hav-ing to wait forever for the bus in the terrible heat? Like slim, tall, Shanta-mama who loved chocolates but never ate them? Always cooking what my family liked and not what I did, always eating the worst pieces of chicken and fruits, and helping myself to the watery part of the dahi?

Did one grow into thirty the way one grew into green vegetables? When the knowledge of dirt in the corner behind the fridge swept you away like the final pages of a book?

The time hadn't come. The time would never come, never, never. For one day Adventure and True Love would sweep me to unexplored shores and I would have it long before pallid domesticity wet my ankles and rose unbidden, to my neck.

"Ma, tell me, did he keep your hanky close to his heart?"

*It smelt of her, and it was as if she was once again, next to him.*

Ma smiling, her face full of something remembered.

Gauri came running to Mahima's house, breathless. "I saw Mrs. Moitra's boyfriend again last night."

"Haaw!" Mahima exclaimed.

"He's her lost love."

"Loyal to her till the end."

"Living in the hope of just seeing her face at the window of her house."

"That hope keeps him alive."

"Unseen, undemanding."

"Undeterred, unswerving."

"Beneath his handsome, but unsmiling exterior beats a tender heart."

"Does he go inside when no one is looking?"

"Mummy says men like that," Mahima declared.

"My father isn't like that," Prabha said.

"Not fathers, silly. Men."

The summer holidays had begun. Ayaji washed the dishes. Shanta-mama washed them again. Ayaji cleaned the kitchen. Shantamama cleaned it again. Ayaji fuming. Ma's voice, soothing. Shantamama's voice in the kitchen, rising and falling. "How our brother Madhav doesn't see through that wife of his I can't understand, Padma. I heard her say to Amma, What pretty bangles you're wearing. Can you imagine, Padma, Amma so nice and healthy and already Ratna is eyeing her gold bangles? Later I said, very casually, Amma is keeping those for Mallika. Anyway, I'm giving my emeralds to Mallika—why should I give my emeralds to my sons' wives? They'll have my sons under their thumbs, so why should I? Oh, Padma, do you know what our dear brother said . . ." the English words blooming mysteriously into Kannada, the whispering waving and winding its way from kitchen to dining room to sitting room to bedroom, and finally to the bathroom, as Ma rushed in and Shantamama, standing at the door, indignantly hissed the unimaginable conclusion.

I buried myself in my books.

White and blond, the long-suffering heroines of my dreams, blond and blue-eyed the young Lochinvars. And I, black-haired, brown-eyed, squirming as my admonishing mother massaged my scalp with coconut oil, brown skin resistant to the lime that Shantamama rubbed to make me fair. Would roses ever bloom in my cheeks, would my feet ever stop grow-ing? Would the frocks that Shantamama made so painstakingly for me from patterns in *Woman and Home* ever bring about the breathtaking transformation? Would my two mothers never, even temporarily, with-hold their love and cause me suffering? I would suffer silently, I would ac-cept, I would endure, suffering would change my features, lighten my skin, lay bare my innocence, my beauty. Would my mothers never with-draw their love and thus allow my story to begin? For wasn't it only in such absence that He appeared: Her reward, Her salvation, Her promise for a life to be lived blissfully ever after?

"In Kamala's horoscope," Dadima said to Ma and Shantamama, "it is writ-ten that she will stay by her husband's side and serve him all her life. Bas, what need is there for more."

Anu Aunty looked troubled. "In Prabha's horoscope it says that because she will be like a man, she will have a troubled life."

"So much brains my Prabha has," Dadima said, "she will grow up and use it. She is not one to burn it up in the kitchen like some people I know."

Prabha's father, Prasad Uncle smiled. "My mother, she was born much ahead of her time. In the West, now they are talking of equality for women. My mother has believed in it from the beginning. Mataji refused to fix my elder sister's marriage till she finished her M.A. Now my sister is a lecturer and she always tells our mother, it is only because of you."

After Prasad Uncle left, Dadima turned to Anu Aunty. "Bahurani, you must have meditated for several births to get a husband like my son—a man so good, so pure, so kind. Do not think I have forgotten what happened that time when my son's friends came for dinner. They could not even have a second helping of khir—so little you had made. Other sons would have said many harsh things. But my son, only one thing he said to you—a little more khir you should have made—that is all he said."

"But, Dadima," Prabha said, "that day during breakfast itself you and Kamala Bua finished most of the khir, and you didn't listen when I said it was for the dinner party, and Mumma couldn't get milk from anywhere else so—"

"Quiet," Anu Aunty hissed.

"Very nicely you have coached your daughter, Bahurani, very nicely."

"I'm going to play cricket," Prabha, burst out, moving towards the door.

"Bahurani, in this heat the girl is going out—can't you exercise some control on her—"

The door banged shut. After some time I quietly followed Prabha towards the cricket field.


And we told Gauri and Mahima how the streets were quiet and shimmering with heat. We told them how we saw a tall figure batting in the cricket field and how the ball flew outside the maidan. The boys threw up their hands and cheered. Prabha ran towards him, faster, faster. Behind her I ran, panting. He gave the bat to one of the boys and began walking towards us. We met under the shade of that big tree in the maidan. He saw our faces and he knew. He bent down and said, very softly, I'll get them.

"Ohhh," breathed Gauri.

"All lies," said Mahima.

Three thick notebooks. Before we could open them he said, Later. Now tell me about the books you're reading. For five minutes we talked to him.

He listened to every word. I said to him, My father reads even more than Ma. He buys me tons of books. When I was a child he read to me every night.

"*Liar*," said Mahima.

"Then go, no. No one's forcing you to listen."

He didn't look happy. He said, as though he was forcing himself to talk, Do you like cricket? I said, Ma too gives Dada books—And then he smiled, but his eyes weren't smiling, and he went away.

"That's not a proper story!" accused Mahima.

"The stories, the stories about Kiran and Abhimanyu?" Gauri begged.

Prabha and I exchanged glances.

Kiran is now a doctor of sorts, a mender of broken bones and broken hearts, abrasions and sorrows. She tends to the animals and birds who come to her, listening to their tales of sorrow, making them smile, laugh. In her presence, every living, suffering thing heals.

It takes us two afternoons to tell Mahima and Gauri the first two stories. They are not prepared, the next afternoon, for the third.

Abhimanyu enters the magic land without Kiran.

"Why?"

"Don't know."

And when he enters the land, the trees lose their colour, the animals their magic, the flowers their smell, the birds their voices. It appears before us, this magic land and its animals and birds and flowers, in strokes of stark grey and white. In this grey-and-white colourless world Abhimanyu loses his bearings completely. Finally, after a long and painful journey, he finds his way out of it. And Kiran is waiting for him. He confesses to Kiran that he had gone without her. He tries to tell her what the experience has been like. Like dying. He cannot say it. Kiran says, I know. Stupefied, Abhimanyu asks her, You've been there without me? Scornfully, she answers, I'm not like you. I don't have to go there to know. Abhimanyu says, apologetically, We'll go back tomorrow. Together. Kiran replies, We can't. Abhimanyu looks at her incomprehendingly. Kiran says, It was all grey and white and grey, wasn't it, the magic land, as if it was fading away? Abhimanyu nods. Kiran says, Now it's faded away completely. And sadly, she begins walking away from him.

Gauri stared at us. "Then?"

"Then nothing." Prabha shrugged cruelly.

"The End," I taunted.

Gauri's face crumpled. "*Prove* it," Mahima said unsteadily, dashing her hand across her eyes.

Prabha and I watched them with proprietary satisfaction. We knew, oh we *knew* how they felt. Thus must a true story strike its unsuspecting listener. Or else, of what use is it?

My punishment, for all the lies I lived, came that evening. It had withheld itself from me all these years so that when it came, it could do so in all its horror. I would die of it, die dreadfully of it, I *deserved* to die.

Shantamama held me as I wept, saying, tenderly, "There's nothing to be scared of, my darling."

"Oh, my baby," said Ma, also holding me tight, "never hide anything from us again."

"It happens to every girl," said Shantamama, "and it means that now she is old enough to have babies. And eleven isn't all that young. I know girls who have had it at even ten."

"Come to the bathroom. I'll tell you what to do." Ma kissed one cheek.

"No need to tell your friends about it." Shantamama kissed the other.

And so we kept our secrets, every one of us, till that long-ago summer when I was twelve. Ma. Shantamama. Ajji. Anu Aunty. Madhu Aunty. They all kept their secrets. And I kept mine.

Almost as well as my father kept his.

We could not know how, that summer, the secrets would begin to splinter. How could I imagine, that as they splintered, my long-dreamt dreams would come monstrously true?

Oh, a time of such hunger, before that splintering. Before that splintering, such fierce longings. Yearning, in my thirteenth year, to know the absolute nature of passion as I had experienced in my books, in all the mythological stories, and on four luminous, dreamlike times, in my own ordinary life.

But where was passion in the world that I inhabited? The passion of a mother's love was one I knew only too well, but it was not this that I sought; it was passion as a very condition of being; that compulsive and obsessive thing which twisted hearts and tortured souls, from which stories could not help but burst achingly open. It was that chafing against the ordinary, that frustration with the daily groove, that yearning for something more than what one had, that surge of fury against what everyone else expected you to be content with. But alas, outside my books such passion was miserably absent.

Worse, our mothers didn't seem to miss not having it. And most depressing of all, its potential was completely absent in their happy, predictable lives. How, without it, could they bear to live? Yet, they were all, except Ma, living their repetitive lives quite happily, without a cry or even a sigh of longing.

And what of my mother, so different from all the other mothers? Her deafening silence about her own long-ago love spoke of great possibilities. Yet when I urged her to speak of it, hers was such a bland rendering. Her disinterest in the house and all the things the other mothers did was also full of possibilities. Yet even this lacked the accompanying turbulence. As for her work outside the house, she hardly ever spoke of it.

No proper stories in the lives of the mothers I knew; lives lived in kitchens. Talk of the nastiness of mothers-in-law, the indifference of married brothers, the vagaries of the vegetable seller and washerman and sweeperess, the cost of food, gossip about the neighbours. Inside kitchens sharing their familiar lives, telling and retelling the same old stories, stories rendered hot and smouldering with repetition. Within these walls creating their food, living their lives. Here, like Macbeth's witches, stirring and examining, hissing and chanting, prophesying and sighing. Eyes widening, hands going to mouths, heads shaking in consternation and dismay and delight, as they comforted and cried and sighed, all the while chopping, peeling, grating, cleaning, washing, drying, stirring, tasting. The same old stories smouldering and smoking within stainless-steel vessels and copper pots, each outburst mixing irretrievably with every spice (so much more golden was the turmeric for it, so much more fiery the red chilli powder). And then finally, the exquisite relief of having said it not once but again and again, invading every nook and corner like the smell of tadka.

But this was not passion, not this, not that, not this.

"You can Do It ten times a day?"

"Oh *yes*. When you are in the Throes of Passion, everything else fades."

"How long does It take?"

We looked at Gauri.

"Twenty minutes."

*"Only twenty minutes!"*

Well, perhaps I couldn't have access to passion in real life. But it would have been enough to know it was *there*. Enough to overhear someone I knew shout—*I hate you, may you rot in hell*—or burst out—*Life is a prison, I its prisoner*—or speak through gritted teeth—*I will never forgive you till my dying day*—or moan—*I cannot bear this happiness, I could die of it.* Just one of these protestations would have been enough. I would even settle for the knowledge of a certain wistful sighing, a curious yearning.

No such luck. Whenever Shantamama viewed the prospect of widow-hood (which she did every time she ran out of household money), she would tell Ma, "Nothing Narayana has provided for me, Padma, no house, no life insurance, nothing—if he dies tomorrow how does he think I'll feed and educate my boys?" Oh, if only Shantamama had said, *Padma, I cannot even think of life without Him. For though he has given me two chil-dren, I will be alone without him. Padma, my dearest sister, my body might live, but my soul will be with Him.*

Well, perhaps Shantamama couldn't say that aloud. But even had she had thought it, there would have been some hope. And I knew that my Shantamama didn't think it at all.

Never had my life seemed so dull than in this, my thirteenth year, never had I read more. I no longer let Ma or Shantamama oil my hair every day. Prabha and I read like gluttons: Victorian fiction, Mills and Boon ro-mances, throbbing best-sellers. The British Council Library hadn't yet pruned its fiction section, membership to the USIS library was free and now there was a secondhand bookshop-cum-lending library in the market from where we could borrow four books at a time, so among us, Prabha, Gauri, Mahima and I had sixteen. The English films that our mothers al-lowed us to see once a month, augmented my dreams of tall men with slow smiles. The boys of my age and older had concave chests and thin voices, the hair on their faces was straggly, their eyes never glinted with amuse-ment, their smiles would never be sardonic, and when they walked, it wasn't with the grace and strength of panthers. And Prabha, Mahima, Gouri and I approaching our teens and the horizon so stark—what possi-bility then for tempestuous encounters with men whose eyes smouldered? And I knew how incomplete my life was, how attenuated, and I feared it would always be so.

"An inflexible will," Prabha said, gazing at my father's photograph.

"A romantic heart," I said.

"He has a sensitive face. Men should be strong and sensitive."

"They should have a sense of humour."

"They should have a sense of adventure, they should take risks, they should feel passionately about everything."

"Deep voices."

"Piercing eyes."

"They should read a lot and like music."

"Have the courage of their convictions."

"Walk with long, easy strides."

"Faintly smelling of cigarettes."

"Long, sensitive fingers."

"Under his calm, sensitive exterior beat a passionate heart."

"Beneath his warm smile lay a turbulent soul."

"Mallika, hide the photo, your mother's coming."

At various precariously confidential moments, Shantamama had communicated strange, unpalatable messages to me. Once, when I had been asking her about her childhood and Ma's, and then about Ma's marriage to my father, this man who so loved books and music, I sighed, "Shantamama, my father and Ma would have been so . . . so . . . intellectually compatible."

Shantamama laughed till she began to cough. When the fit subsided she said, "No man wants intellect in a wife, my love. Your mother would have had to look after your father's nasty sisters and his witch of a mother. These U.P. and Bihari mothers-in-law are all the same. The minute they get a daughter-in-law they come to live with their son, and lie prostrate in bed, and groan of aches and pains. Your mother would never have been able to get her doctorate. Or for that matter, have this job."

"Why?"

"Darling, you need *time* for all that, *time*. Look at Anu Aunty. Understand? They'd even have expected your mother to pray and fast!"

"But my father—"

"You think he'd have known?" She kissed me tenderly. "Men are—" She stopped.

Now, in our thirteenth year, Prabha and I were writing love stories. In Prabha's fifty-page novel, her fiery red-haired twenty-four-year-old Heroine went "all the way." Worse, it wasn't with the Hero. I don't believe in double standards, the Heroine tells the Hero, eyes flashing, as he confronts her, his grey eyes icy cold.

"How *could* you, Prabha!" I exclaimed, equally thwarted.

The Hero tears his hair, his grey eyes grow fierce, then dark with desire, and He flings her on his bed. Prabha devoted two pages to His wonder at what He sees as He removes each layer of Her clothes, the kiss that each new expanse of Bare Flesh receives from His Expert Lips. After the Final Moment (for which Prabha used a flurry of euphemisms), the Hero rises from the bed, hairy-chested, and gazing at her Alabaster Body, groans, You lied. She smiles. The Hero, fingering Her mass of red hair whispers, had I known, beloved, I would have been gentler. And She, raising Her smooth white arms, replies huskily, Now you can.

"And they're not even married," I said to Prabha, only partially relieved.

He was Jake. She, Maria.

In my own sixty-page novel the nineteen-year-old Heroine was an Orphan, blond, blue-eyed, gentle-but-willful, with a sixteen-inch waist and thirty-six-inch bust. My Hero had a scar on His right cheek and looked Saturnine. He laughed Mockingly, stood Loose-Limbed and Arrogant, and periodically kissed Her against Her will while Her Legs Turned to Jelly. In the end it was Her innocence and refusal to succumb to His Ardour that won Him. You may not be the first woman in my life, He groans, His fingers exploring Her long virginal neck, but now I am done with all that. As Her lips part beneath His, He pushes Her away, groaning, you're enough to tempt a saint—no, not till we marry, not with you.

"Oh, Mallika, what a bore!" Prabha burst out.

She was Jane, and He, David.

My invasion of Ma's bookshelf had begun; Victorian fiction had me by the throat. I read, weeping steadily. It could only be borne if I read on, only in reading on was there hope. And as I did, love bloomed, love was requited, the men and women were united. If I ended the books dry-eyed, if at all I could forget the dead mothers, it was because of this.

"Ma, when did he first kiss you?"

*His eyes, after the kiss, gleaming with laughter, her own averted. He, bending down again, she whispering, What are you doing, he laughing softly, enchanted by her sweet reluctance.*

Ma finished plaiting her hair, then went to the bathroom.

Oh quieter, quieter, this daytime weeping, than the weeping in the nights.

"You think your Ma would have been suited to the life of an I.A.S. officer's wife?"

"What life, Shantamama?"

"Entertaining his colleagues, going for official functions, having parties . . . all she wanted even as a child was to read and have conversations of an intellectual nature—huh—fat lot of good such conversations are."

*Dada's face gaunt with suffering. Padma, my love, forgive me. I did not know what my mother was doing to you. Now I see how your blouse hangs on you, how red with weeping your eyes are. Yet you work so uncomplainingly, not grumbling, not uttering a word of protest. My sweetest wife, no more.*

(Better still.) *Doctor? She is dying?* Padma! (Later, after he has given her his blood.) *She lives, blessed be God. I have been blind. Blind to Padma's goodness, blind to my mother's villainy. Forgive me, my heart, forgive me.* (Then, to Ajji.) *I will never forgive myself, never.*

True Love. Prabha had no patience with the delicacies of Romance, only the turbulence of Passion held its sway over her—her favourite book was *Wuthering Heights,* and in our own mythology, it was the story of the Mahabharata that she wanted Dadima to tell her again and again, never the Ramayana; it was Karan whose story moved her, not the Pandavas; she preferred Draupadi to Sita and defended Ravana's abduction of Sita. "Lakshmana had no right to cut off Surpanaka's nose," she told her horrified grandmother.

True Love. Mahima's imaginings took its roots from Hindi movies, of which she had an unadulterated diet. Her favourite scene was in the film where the Heroine saw that the Hero's shirt was torn. "They show a closeup of her eyes full of tears, so we know that she wants to marry him and mend his shirts. So symbolic."

"Symbolic?" Prabha.

"See, his whole life is full of holes and she wants to mend it with her love."

"Tell, tell, tell, no."

"See, they get married and the Heroine looks after the Hero's mother who is dying, she tutors his younger sister, makes barfis for her brother-in-law, and when she burns her hand in the kitchen, she doesn't tell anyone."

"Then? Then?"

"She rubs aata on her hand and hides it under her saree palla. For two days. The pain is terrible, then her hand gets septic. Still she does all the cooking, she massages her mother-in-law's feet every afternoon and night, see, her mother-in-law can't see her hand because she's half blind."

"Then?"

"Then it's the third day and the pain is so bad, so bad, that as she works in the kitchen she is crying. Then her husband enters and says, Kalpana. Her back is turned to him so he can't see she's crying. He comes next to her, turns her around and lifts her chin, then he says, You are crying? Mallika, even then she smiles, and she says, No, no, this is what happens when you cut onions. So he's very relieved, he smiles."

Stupid man. Stupid man.

"Then the milk begins to boil."

Ahh.

"And when she rushes to lift it from the gas, he sees her hand, and he shouts, *Kalpana!*"

Ohh.

"His voice, Mallika, the way he says, *Kalpana!* He says, if you are in pain, my pain is that magnified a hundred times. The doctor says her hand has to be amputated. And you know what she says, she says, what I did with my right hand I can learn to do with my left, she is so brave, Mallika. Her husband, he cries and cries, but she doesn't cry, she tells him, crying will achieve nothing, keep yourself strong. So he goes to the temple and prays and prays with such concentration, such concentration that the sky becomes dark. Then you know something is going to happen. He says to God, Give her back her hand and take mine. Suddenly there's a flash of lightning and the eyes of Kali—it's a Kali temple—flash. She gets all right, the doctors say, We just can't understand it, and you know, Mallika, one week later he has an accident and his hand is cut off."

"How stupid," said Prabha, "if she almost lost her hand it was her fault."

"Prabha," Mahima said earnestly, "these are sentimental things, you have to understand that."

No such events in the plain and mundane lives lived around us. What knowledge did Shantamama or Anu Aunty or Madhu Aunty have of love and hate, of deprivation and desire, of longing, or dreaming—the stuff of stories? What knowledge of it did my grandmother Ajji have, of whom Shantamama said, "Appa treats her like a queen—he has given her a house, money, jewels, every possible comfort—she lacks for nothing." No hidden passions in their lives, no tales of terror, no husbands or lovers crying out for their pain. Instead, plotting and scheming, saying one thing, doing another, sounding exasperated with our constant questions, always preoccupied with money, extracting nuances from every statement, drawing conclusions from things unspoken, in voices high-pitched and shrill, speaking to us of the virtues of patience.

Our magic man's Kiran, when grown-up, would never be like that. As a woman, married to Abhimanyu, she would be full of radiance and laughter, always young at heart and joyous, her spirit as free as it had been when she was a girl, and her innocence, untarnished.

And it seemed to me as Prabha and I lived and relived the stories, that the sense of impending doom which enshrouded the magic land grew out of what would happen to Kiran if this innocence were to be destroyed. And that the instrument of its destruction, coiled and waiting to strike, lay cradled in Abhimanyu's unknowing hands.

Oh my secret life, so teeming with stories. Oh, the reality, so ludicrously devoid of the fantastic!

"But, darling, you should never wear these nylon ready-made panties," Shantamama exclaimed. "It's unhealthy, specially in the summer. Don't blindly follow Mahima."

"She wears *panties*, Shantamama, not chaddis."

For Shantamama stitched my underwear of thick white cloth, ran long strings through them, then wrote my name behind each in indelible ink in case the dhobi was tempted to steal them.

But lucky Mahima got her underwear from Abroad—all so lacy, so pretty—and it was a ritual for us to examine them every weekend, touching, sighing, longing. Madhu Aunty was also collecting perfume, lipsticks, tea sets, dinner sets, linen and synthetic sarees from England, for the day when Mahima would get married. One day lucky Mahima would go to this land of perfume and lacy underwear, of deodorants and hand lotions, and till she did, these would come to her.

"Darling, strings in your underwear are *good*—you can *adjust* them."

Whatever you want badly enough, wrote Ajji, you can get. Better not to ask for it, better not to think of it. Oh, my child, may God protect you, may He keep you safe.

The doorbell ringing. I would ask for it, I would. If I wanted it badly enough, I would get it.

*She opens the door. "Padma," he says, his voice breaking. "You," she says, her voice trembling.*

"*Telegram!*" shouted the postman as Ma opened the door.

My grandfather. His first, fatal heart attack.

Madhu Aunty drove to the station and bought two tickets for Bangalore. It wasn't the right time for me to go with them, Ma said, pale, but not weeping, holding Shantamama who was making the most terrible sounds. Ayaji had gone to her village for a month and Anu Aunty, her arm around me, said that I would stay with them. She and Madhu Aunty packed food for the journey, and filled a surhai with water. My mothers hugged and kissed me, then Madhu Aunty drove them to the station.

Now I knew with chilling certainty that the end was coming. And my mothers, for the first time, were no longer there to protect me.

That evening, going for a walk with Prabha, Mahima and Gauri. Out of the blue, two men on scooters, their arms reaching out, hitting my chest, grabbing Mahima's thigh, grabbing Prabha's breasts. Their laughter as they roared off, loud and triumphant.

*My darling. I'll kill them.*

*My pet. Don't cry.*

*These things happen, my love.*

*It isn't your fault, my baby.*

*Dada's eyes blazing with anger. Picking up the men by the scruff of their necks, shaking them till they begged for mercy. Contemptuously, throwing them into the ditch. Saying through gritted teeth, Next time I won't be so merciful.*

The chill sinking deeper, deeper. The end coming closer, closer. Shantamama had told me that when people were dying it was only their earliest childhood that they remembered, and those who were part of that time, nothing else. Now, so it was with me. Every thought in the present returned to me a memory of something else in a deep and distant past. Thinking of Ma and Shantamama in the train. Memory returning to me the picture of a young man sitting cross-legged in front of me in the park, his hands cupping his mouth, making wonderful train sounds. Ayaji laughing, he tickling my chin, I chuckling. Thinking of Ma back in her parents' house after thirteen years. Memory returning to me the picture of

Ma lying still on the bed, like a dead woman with open eyes. Like a still life, memories of that time.

The end drawing closer, closer. At night, in Prabha's house, old memories, playing, replaying. Early childhood memories flashing. Like snapshots. Just that moment. Nothing before or after. But that moment in its entirety. Examining a watch in my hand, a grave young man lying on his stomach opposite me. Shantamama feeding me, the spoon poised in the air, her eyes bright with tears. Laughing, laughing in the park, both I and the young man who is holding me up in his arms, a feeling of absolute joy.

The end arriving at the door, breathing, waiting.

**Never trust fate, child, wrote Ajji, or for that matter, tempt it. Remember that whatever happens, you must keep your belief in yourself intact. With that belief, you can survive anything. For, in life, anything can happen. Anything.**

Anything. The doorbell ringing.

*He stands at the door. I have come to meet Padma, he says to Anu Aunty. She asks him to come in. Mallika, Prasad Uncle calls.*

Madhu Aunty burst into Prabha's room where we all sat and said, breathlessly, "Today we will have lunch in my house, hurry up, we are going now." Then she looked at us, blinked, said, "No, no, keep sitting," and sat down next to us, breathing very fast. We looked at her, astonished.

Prasad Uncle's voice, "Mallika."

Madhu Aunty's eyes widening in terror.

Getting up. Going to the sitting room. Stopping.

My father. Right out of the photograph.

Sitting next to Prasad Uncle.

Looking at me without recognition.

A polite smile on his face.

Prasad Uncle saying something. Anu Aunty saying something.

My father smiling politely.

The sound in my ears not stopping.

Someone's arms around me.

# THE SECOND STORY

 That, then, is my first story. That was how I saw it as a child.

Woman now, I hear another story. And that must be my second.

Yes, we are women now, Prabha, Mahima, Gauri and I, long past that unimaginable and impossible age—thirty—strangers no more, in one way or another, to the passions we dreamt of, or to the other passions of which we had no knowledge. And yes, now we know how secrets can grow like fungus, how guilt ripens and rots, how anger burns and smoulders. We know how all of this is directed away from the source and how the source is cocooned in silence. Almost as if anger must accumulate and swirl around the periphery and be expressed accordingly. No words for the dark core within. Women now, we understand our mothers.

We have all learnt our mothers' guilt, even motherless Gauri. Guilt stains our thoughts like sweat under the arms. So like our mothers, seeing and hearing what our fathers and brothers and husbands and lovers do not, grasping the hidden nature of things, shackled by what we must not expect, or do.

And if this rankles? The knowledge that it must be our fault.

Now we speak to each other of all this, as we continue living with each other's secrets, and tending to one another's wounds. With one another, we complain and compare, weigh and balance, measure and count. Only with each another, not needing to explain, to justify, for we have all felt it, these formless, wordless things lying in those subterranean depths. Oh what a ritual of sharing and commiserating, comparing and comforting. Words, sharklike, glide to the surface.

We who always thought we were so different from our mothers, now express the fundamental nature of our feelings for one another with the same ritual that our mothers did. We feed each other. Cooking and talking, eating and talking, year after year after year. For one another, we make khir, rajma, kadhi, parathas, dosas. Have more, have more, we urge, filling each others' plates. What is this, so little you're eating, we scold. Oh God, I've eaten so much, we groan. And then we get tearful. Voices rise, fall. No one else does this for me except Ma and Shantamama. Except Mumma. Except Mummy. No one does this for me except Amma. Except you, Shantacca. Except Mummy. Except *my* Mataji.

Such resonance. Their voices everywhere. Speaking of our mothers, telling each other their stories, telling each other our own, living our stories through our mothers', our mothers' lives through ours. And as we talk, I hear my mother's voice in our stories. Shantamama's voice. Ajji's. Anu Aunty's. Madhu Aunty's. I hear their voices in my own.

So now I sift their voices like flour, looking for threads where there is only grain. Add water then. With hard knuckles, knead. I sift their voices, the rhythm my own, sifting, sifting, a rhythm my own, kneading hard, knuckles moving, between my palms, quietly rolling, bringing into it the woman I am, my fingers, slowly, turning. Voices in the present rising, calling, and from the past, all their voices echoing, answering.

*None of us to whom this story belongs is yet free of it, Mallika, or free from its secrets. It will never be over, my child, it can never end.*

I know that now. Help me. Help me find the story.

**Stories.** *Two stories, Mallika, two.*

I know. The way I saw it as a child, that was the first story.

*And the way that you hear it as a woman, that is the second.*

But its cry deafens me. For each time you tell me this second story, I also hear your own.

*Child, each one of us brought something different into your story, and each of us took something different out of it.*

But with the years your stories keep growing, keep changing.

*As do we, Mallika. As does the way you listen to us.*

But then there is no separating my story from yours. Or yours from mine.

*There isn't. And* **that,** *is your true story.*

That . . .

*Does the knowledge that you have of your story come only from what happened to you and to your mother and to your father?*

The knowledge that I have of my story comes from . . . what I now understand of . . . all your stories.

*Then?*

But then the story is no longer mine.

*But it is. For the knowledge you have of it has less to do with what happened, and more to do with what you are.*

*So, once more, child, and once more—listen.*

# MADHU

The very next day Madhu had told Anu. But Anu as usual was stirring and chopping and grinding in the kitchen, listening to her with one ear and to her mother-in-law's grumblings with the other, and when she finished, Anu vaguely said, "Accha?" No sign of excitement in the accha, no curiosity; she, Madhu, might as well have been telling her the story of the latest Hindi picture she had seen, actually even that usually elicited a more enthusiastic response since Anu hardly ever saw pictures.

"You don't believe me," Madhu said accusingly.

"No, no," Anu protested, lowering the gas and covering the vessel, then wiping her neck and forehead with her saree palla. "It's so hot, difficult even to think in this kitchen." Then, "What you are saying I understand, only, there are many people who look like each other, that is all I am saying."

Madhu clicked her tongue in exasperation. "Listen, Anu. What I saw I saw, my eyes they are never wrong. It is not a question of resemblance, it is a question of being ditto—height, features, smile, everything, ditto. Think a little bit, Anu, if you understand what I have told you, then you will understand everything about Padma."

Anu pulled out the saree palla from her waist and wiped her face and neck again.

"All right, Mataji," Madhu said loudly to Anu's mother-in-law as she stepped out of the kitchen to the dining room, "Namaste, I am going."

"All right, beti," Mataji said pinching her chin to take out a hair, "drink something before you go, Bahurani, give her something."

"No, no, Mataji, in your house there is no such formality," Madhu said automatically. Double-faced creature, Madhu thought, Telling me, Drink something, as if she cares, to Padma she gives bottles of pickle every month, even once has she asked me if I want?

Anu came with her to the front door. "Accha, you didn't tell Padma, no?"

"Tell her what?" asked Madhu.

"That only," Anu said, "what you told me just now."

Madhu felt a thrill run through her body. So that was it—it had sunk in all right, but Anu didn't want to show her. Deliberately she hesitated.

"Vaise," Anu said, "there is no need for her to know."

"Arre, Anu," Madhu said, just the right note of indignation in her voice, "what do you think I am, I also have some sense you know."

"Yes, yes," Anu said, smiling and shaking her head, "I know you won't . . . I just thought . . ."

Madhu smiled too and went home, her blood coursing with delayed satisfaction.

It never ceased to irritate her, Anu's protective attitude towards Padma. As though she, Madhu, didn't care, when Anu knew very well how much she cared. Acting just now as though what she had told her made no difference, as though it was just another piece of gossip. Madhu had almost been deceived. She shouldn't have told Anu the whole thing at one go. She should have stretched it out, got Anu to ask questions, hesitated at appropriate intervals. But she had been so bursting with the news that she had had no thought of prevarication. She had assumed that Anu would ask the very questions that she, Madhu, was dying to ask, especially the last big question, Why? She had taken for granted that after she finished telling Anu they could spend the next hour going over it bit by bit, lingering over Padma's silence and Shanta's explanations, delicately lifting each layer, weighing this possibility, then that. Or at least, she, Madhu, could—after all, she had already reached her own conclusions about it which she would have told Anu in every detail had Anu showed even a little curiosity.

If what she now knew was about anyone other than Padma she would have told Padma first. There was no listener more avid than Padma, there was nothing more rewarding than telling Padma the latest gossip or speculating in her presence about something she had heard, overheard or observed. Wide-eyed Padma would be, her face reflecting amusement or indignation or shock, as the case was, her hand would go to her mouth, she would heave deep sighs, she would draw in her breath, her response would provide Madhu just the fuel she needed to paint her story in its most intricate detail and then go on to the next one. "So, Madhu, what news?" Padma would ask every time Madhu dropped in to Padma's house. "What news, no news," Madhu would reply, settling down in the veranda chair or in the sitting room sofa. She had never thought that there was so much about her life to discuss, but even the ordinariness of her life and family seemed to appeal to Padma. Padma knew Madhu's childhood, was familiar with her mother and her father and her brothers, her aunts and her uncles and her sisters-in-law and her nieces and nephews. Padma knew as much about Madhu's family as she did, and when Madhu found herself musing about some family misunderstanding or the other, then Padma would point to another facet of the whole complex issue, through the eyes of another member of Madhu's family and Madhu would find herself nodding vigourously and saying, Yes, yes, that is true, it could be that way too.

She told Padma about her school and college days and how she got married in the middle of her B.A., how difficult things had been initially, especially when her husband retired from the air force and began his business, how she sold most of her jewellery to build this house they now had and He didn't even know, she had supervised the building and everything, gone to the bank, taken the loan, talked to the contractor. And sometimes her thoughts would take an unexpected turn and a strange melancholy would fill her and she would say to Padma, "I don't know, Padma, life is so strange," and Padma would nod and say, "It is." God knows what they began talking about and what they ended up talking about. The problem with Padma was that she had a way of drawing you out till you found yourself going inwards and saying things that you afterwards regretted, not because you had said it to Padma but because once uttered, it gave form to what had once been only bits and pieces floating inside you, and worse, because it contradicted things that you had always maintained about yourself.

How unexpectedly matter-of-fact Padma was about some things and how naive about others. She had not been married long enough, that was the reason. Padma did not get embarrassed about some things like Anu did, but on the other hand there seemed to be a whole world which she knew nothing about. Like the time Madhu told Anu, "Too much He is wanting me, Anu, what to do," referring to her countless pregnancies, and Anu had gone red and continued with the chopping and frying. But when she told Padma, "Too much He is wanting me, Padma, all the time I am getting pregnant, what to do," Padma looked not embarrassed but startled. What, indeed, to do; He wanted it every day almost and wouldn't use anything. Nothing will happen, He would say at night with such assurance that she really believed that nothing would, in spite of her past experiences.

"Pregnancies?" Padma had asked.

Madhu nodded. "Again I have to go and have abortion."

"Oh *Madhu,*" Padma had said with her heart in her voice.

"Arre, it is all right," Madhu had said shrugging, she was not asking for Padma's sympathy, why was Padma giving it, "in half an hour it will be over, then I will drive back home."

"Isn't Mr. Nanda taking you?"

"Why should he, I also can drive," Madhu said shortly.

"I'll come with you."

"Don't be silly. I can manage perfectly, it is like having a tooth out. At least this time I have found doctor who will do it, previous times I only had to do it." With pleasure she noted the look of astonishment on Padma's face. She nodded benignly. "Two times it happened on its own. But two times I only made it come out." She laughed at Padma's expression and patted her hand indulgently. "Padma, twenty times a day, every day for one week I used to do skipping. Then I used to boil cardamom, cinnamon, cloves . . . all that with water till it became very strong, and I used to drink that. Every day."

Padma, predictably wide-eyed asked, "Why?"

"It is heaty, no, so it induces abortion, that and skipping will do it, with me always it works." She noted that Padma was bereft of speech and smiled fondly. "But it used to take so long, and always I used to think, Hai re, if it does not happen then what am I going to do with another one?"

"I'll come with you, Madhu."

Madhu smiled and pinched Padma's cheeks. "No, no. I will be all right." She giggled and put her hand to her mouth, shaking her head, "Even when I go to see my brothers, then also He wants me to come back to him in a week, that much He wants me. Frankly, Padma, I do not understand how Mr. Prasad is letting Anu go to Lucknow for two, three months. No?"

In one such conversation Madhu suddenly found herself talking of how she never finished her B.A. because she got married in her third year because her father had cancer and wanted her settled before he died. She had found herself saying, "At that time I said, after marriage I will finish it, just final year papers I have to give." She laughed wryly and shook her head.

"You can do it now."

"What are you saying, Padma! Now if I do B.A. I will have to do all three years."

"Oh," said Padma frowning. There had been a short silence, then Padma said, "I can find out what your requirements are, we can go together to the university and find out the details."

"Padma," Madhu said angrily, "when *I* do not want to do it why do *you* want me to?"

"I thought you wanted to."

Madhu made a dismissive sound, "Wanting to, not wanting to, nothing comes from that." She hadn't meant to say that. She looked sharply at Padma's face but could read no skepticism in it. She smiled and said, "Yesterday only I told Him, I think I will complete my B.A., after all, I have only one year left, and he laughed and said, B.A., She-A, Ph.D., T-hd, what will you do with it? You are a wife, you are a mother, that is a full-time job. Even if I die, with my business, investments, insurance and all, you can marry off the children, and still there will be enough to live on for the rest of your life. I don't know, Padma, why he loves me so much, he treats me like doll, thinking, a little bit of work I will do and I will break." She sighed and sipped her tea reflectively. "What will I get out of B.A. now."

It wasn't a question, she didn't expect an answer, but Padma said, tentatively, "Satisfaction?"

Madhu shook her head gently and said, "Padma, satisfaction I have already. Too much satisfaction. He gives me everything. My children give me everything. Where is there bigger satisfaction than this? *I* don't need degrees to get satisfaction." Madhu's anger was mollified only slightly by the sudden stillness that descended on Padma's face.

Sometimes, resentful and a little angry, Madhu would widen her eyes reproachfully and say to Padma, "What do you mean, give me news, give me the news, *you* give me news for a change."

Then Padma would say, "Madhu, what news can I give you, whom else do I know except for you and Anu."

Which was true, Padma didn't mix with anyone else, she didn't go out, she never went to her parents' for a holiday, she had no social life at all. All she did was go to her college, teach, come back, tutor Mallika, take tuitions in the late afternoons, send off Mallika to play, correct papers, prepare for her lectures, spend about an hour or so chatting with Madhu and Anu, then it was Mallika again, and after Mallika slept she would work on her doctorate. On weekends she and Mallika went to the library, and Padma read and slept. How she slept, till nine in the mornings on weekends, Madhu noted disapprovingly. Sometimes Madhu would ask Padma about her college and the girls she taught and her colleagues, and Padma would tell her an anecdote or two about her teaching experiences and the conversations she had with the other lecturers, but since she never met any of them after she left her college and never spent any time with them unless it was between classes, there wasn't very much to talk about. And what there *was* to talk about, about that Padma wouldn't say anything.

Padma's brother-in-law had told them nothing either, yet he had elicited their support all those years ago. He had come to their house, a man with a strong face and clear brown eyes. He was considering buying the house that lay between theirs and the Prasad's for his wife's sister, he told them. But, and here Padma's brother-in-law paused, then said, "My sister-in-law is a widow with a baby and I want to be sure that she has two families with children as neighbours."

In other words, thought Madhu watching him carefully, good neighbours, no bachelors, no widowers. She said, "I have three children, youngest she is a girl, she is one year old and on other side, Prasads, they have one baby girl."

He had nodded and said, "Yes, I have met them, they are also very good people."

Madhu found herself softening against her will. How lucky this man's wife was to have a husband who felt so responsible for her sister. The suspicions arose. "Your sister-in-law, her parents, they—?" she asked.

His reply was spontaneous, "They are in Bangalore, but you see, my father-in-law, he isn't in good health so he could not come to Delhi. My sister-in-law, she has got a job as a lecturer in Delhi University."

Madhu nodded, her suspicions not assuaged.

Madhu's husband said, "There is nothing to worry about, she will be safe, I will be like her brother, my wife, she will be like her sister."

Padma's brother-in-law had smiled, and suddenly Madhu was conscious of his charm. She was full of questions, but somehow couldn't ask them. He said, "I have asked Mrs. Prasad to let me know if there is an ayah she could look out for."

Madhu said, "I have ayah whom I do not need, she is very honest, very trustworthy, if you want her then she can work for your sister-in-law." From the corner of her eye she saw that her husband was looking at her with amusement.

Padma's brother-in-law's face lit up. "Can I meet her?" Madhu nodded and went to the children's room to get her.

And so, Ayaji, who had been taking care of her children, had been transferred without any ado to Padma. For Madhu's mother-in-law and Ayaji clashed terribly. The last time Madhu's mother-in-law had come to stay and criticized Ayaji's work, Ayaji had turned around and said, No need to talk to me like that, I am not your daughter-in-law. Madhu, who had been in a bad temper all day, had overheard, and rushed to the bathroom to laugh. When she came out, she felt she could now go on quite equably with her day.

"But where will she go?" Madhu had asked her husband when he told her Ayaji had to go. "Ayaji does not have any family." Her husband had said impatiently, "What do I know, it is your decision."

But it wasn't her decision. The decision had already been made. Her job, as in all such matters, was to carry it out. Madhu, who had wrestled with larger problems in her life, suddenly found that she didn't have the energy to deal with this one.

And now here, like a godsend, was someone who wanted a dependable ayah. They couldn't have been more suitable, Ayaji and Padma, Madhu thought later. Padma, who was incapable of managing the house, left everything to Ayaji; Ayaji, who hated any kind of interference, did exactly as she pleased. As for Mallika, Ayaji's love for her had a fierceness that had never been there for Madhu's own children. That first day when Madhu had taken Ayaji to Padma's house in the evening, Padma had been holding a wailing Mallika, shaking her in her arms, up-down, up-down. Ayaji put out her arms towards the baby and Padma handed the baby to her. Ayaji put the crying baby over her shoulder and began thumping her hard, muttering something loving and unintelligible. Within less than a minute the baby stopped crying and within less than two she was asleep against Ayaji's shoulder.

Before she came, Anu and Madhu had wondered about Padma. Madhu had imagined someone black and thin like the Madrasis she had seen, someone smelling of sandalwood and coconut oil, with curly hair tied into a tight plait, her bathroom slippers showing underneath her silk saree, who spoke English with a strong Madrasi accent, if, that is, she spoke English at all.

"But she is lecturer in English, Madhu," Anu reminded her.

"Vaise, Anu, these Madrasis are not very friendly, they are keeping to themselves."

"No, no," Anu replied comfortingly, "they are nice people, very honest, very noninterfering."

Then Padma, Shanta and her husband had arrived. From the boys' bedroom window, Madhu watched the two sisters and the brother-in-law getting down from the taxi. The first thing she noticed was that one sister, the older one, was fair and the other, dark. The fair one was the one who struck you at first, beautiful, tall and statuesque, her hair in one long plait, she moved like a dancer, holding the baby as if it were her own. Next to her, the younger, dark sister, shorter and very slim, with smaller, more delicate features and hair of the same length. Such a pity her skin was so dark. Even so, she wasn't bad-looking. Madhu went to Anu's house and into her kitchen. "Bilkul they don't look like Madrasis," she assured Anu.

Within an hour she and Anu were next door with two large tiffin carriers full of food. Madhu had not known what to expect. And when the fair sister, Shanta, said in a trembling voice, "I prayed, please God, let my sister have good neighbours, and my prayers have come true," Madhu was aware of a thrill of gratification.

The dark sister, Padma, came out of the bedroom, the baby in her arms, and when Madhu saw her eyes, she closed her own for an instant and thought, for all that you have blessed me with, I give you my thanks, God.

Then Madhu turned to Shanta and said, "Furniture-shurniture, carpets, gas, curtains, everything I will help you get, I have a car, if you want, I will take you tomorrow."

"Oh, Mrs. Nanda, God bless you!" Shanta exclaimed, so much gratitude on her face that Madhu felt her whole body glowing.

"In the evening I will show you the market, everything you get there—fruits, vegetables, rations, everything," Anu said.

"Also," Madhu said, "the phalwalli and sabjiwalla come every morning before ten to our side houses, buy fruits and vegetables from them, not from the market, they are cheaper."

"I will send the jamadarni to your house tomorrow," Anu said.

Padma, who had been sitting quietly all this time, said, "Thank you for all your help."

"What help, this is nothing, with us please do not do formality," Madhu said.

"When I first came here," Anu said, "Madhu did everything for me. When my Prabha was born, she gave her all Mahima's baby clothes, Mahima's cot, bottles, everything." Anu had smiled at Madhu, and Madhu saw that Padma was smiling at her too in exactly the same way. As though she really likes me, Madhu thought, astonished.

The baby began to cry and Padma took her inside.

They sat quietly for a while, Madhu could hear the baby still crying in the next room. "Colic, the baby must be having," she told Shanta, "dissolve some heeng in hot water, then dip a cloth in that and put it on baby's tummy—all gas will go."

Shanta nodded as though she wasn't listening. She said, "Mrs. Nanda, Mrs. Prasad, something I have to tell you." Her expression was troubled and Madhu felt excitement run through her body. "It is about my sister." Then she told them Padma's story, her marriage to the man outside her community against the wishes of both his parents and theirs, of how his parents had refused to give him permission to marry her, and so they had got married when she was still in her final year M.A., at which time he was a lecturer in Delhi University. "My parents would have accepted her husband if his parents had accepted Padma," Shanta said, her voice shaking, "but when his parents refused, then my father said to her, I do not want you marrying into a family where you are not wanted. How could we have imagined that she would still marry him? That is what my sister is like— she will always stand by what she believes in, whatever the consequences." But shortly after he got into the civil services, he had died in a car accident, leaving Padma alone, penniless and pregnant. Their father had still not forgiven her. "I want you both to know the truth," Shanta said finally, fat tears running down her cheeks, "better you hear it from me than from anyone else, I don't want you to think badly of my sister, she is a good girl."

Madhu who had been shocked that the gentle, soft Padma had done something so scandalous as marrying against her parents wishes, found herself crying too, and so did Anu. Later Madhu would always recall with a thrill how Shanta's nostrils had flared as, wiping her face, she declared in angry, ringing tones, "As for Padma's in-laws, for them their daughter-in-law and granddaughter do not exist. I will never forgive them, never. They will suffer for what they have done to my sister, they will suffer." Madhu had got goose pimples at the tone of Shanta's voice. Shanta had said, "Of course, I don't need to tell you, but still, people will ask you questions, do not tell them the whole story, she is widowed, that is all they need to know."

Anu's eyes had widened, "Never, never," she had said, "your sister, she will be like our sister."

"Arre," Madhu exclaimed, "whatever you have told us, it is going nowhere. But . . ." she paused, "how did . . . he die?"

Briefly, Shanta closed her eyes as if to see better this terrible event of the recent past. She opened them, said, "A car accident. That too, not his car—how could he as a lecturer afford a car? Fate, that was what it was, fate. His friend was going out of Delhi, he left his car with my sister's husband, told him to use it, keep it running. Usually my sister's husband would either cycle to the university or walk. That day he decided to run the car. It was a black car. Padma said she said goodbye to him, and watched him leave from the window, he was wearing a pin-striped blue shirt and dark blue pants. For some reason, Padma said later, she kept standing there, and then she heard it as it moved down the road—the sound of the brakes and then the sound of the crash—then the sound of a woman screaming. It was a big truck. Travelling very fast from a side street. Hit his side of the car."

Then? Then what happened, Madhu wanted to ask but did not, the tears were pouring out of her eyes and out of Anu's, neither could speak. "To be a woman," Shanta said finally, to Madhu and Anuradha, blowing her nose, "is to suffer." Right out of her heart Shanta had taken the words, right out of her heart. After some time Shanta said, "Another thing, my sister, she will not speak of all this. It causes her great pain, she will never talk about it." In other words, Madhu thought, don't ask her.

Madhu would have had some measure of satisfaction if Padma had volunteered a glimpse of that pain. But no, Padma never spoke of it, even if it was there for all to see in the bleakness of her eyes. "How much she can keep inside herself, *some* time at least it has to come out," Madhu told

Anu. Come out it did—in her health. Madhu recalled the time after Shanta left. Padma had fallen ill with an attack of flu, the cough lingered, the weakness refused to go, when she came back from the university she literally collapsed in her bed. The child cried all the time, Padma didn't have the energy to look after her, Ayaji did that, and cooked and cleaned. "This is too much," Madhu told Padma finally, and ignoring her protests, drove her to and from the university for her classes for a month till she had recovered her health. "I'm sorry, Madhu, I'm sorry," Padma would keep saying like a cracked record, as though her illness were her fault. "Enough of this sorry-vorry, I do not want to hear it," Madhu would tell Padma, and Padma would stop for a few days and then before long, look at Madhu again with that familiar, miserable look and start apologizing again.

For two months Madhu and Anu had fed Padma with daliya and saag parathas and soup, and slowly watched the colour returning to Padma's thin face. And Padma, instead of accepting all this as the kind of thing any good neighbour or friend would do, would start thanking them, then apologizing to them, till Madhu said in exasperation, "Arre, Padma, if you say sorry one more time, then you will be truly sorry." Then, for some time, Padma was quiet.

What had hurt Madhu more than anything was to see that the emptiness in Padma's eyes didn't go away even when she saw Mallika. She had found Padma's readiness to hand Mallika to Ayaji almost impossible to bear. "I don't have any energy for her," Padma had told her despairingly once. "Oh Madhu, what kind of a mother am I?" Madhu had been asking herself the same question, but now that Padma acknowledged it, she replied, "What you can do, Padma, that you are doing." Too tired she was, Padma, those first few years, hardly able to cope with her new job, her child, her tuitions, her ill health, her sleepless nights. Too tired even to take Mallika to the park. Ayaji would take the baby instead, every evening at the same time. Once, she had accompanied Ayaji, wheeling Mahima in her pram. A young man in the park had come up to Mallika and Mahima and joined her, saying, "Such lovely children," and she had watched him indulgently as he played with them. He had lifted Mallika in his arms and held her up high, then lowered her, put his cheek against her and put her down. "Do you have children?" Madhu had asked, and then she saw his eyes, bleaker than any eyes she had ever seen, and he said, without looking at her, "I lost mine," and after some time he left. But not before she had seen the hunger in his eyes as he looked at Mallika, and as she walked home she thought, Mallika will get nazar the way he was looking at her, as if she were the child he had lost, poor man, such a tragedy, so young, God has his ways. And sure enough that very evening Mallika fell very sick with fever and there was Padma, frantic as usual, and then Anu came and took the nazar out of Mallika, and Mallika got better.

She had never forgotten how tenderly the boy held the child, for boy he was, not a day over twenty-five, just a few years younger than she was, though she could never think of herself as a girl, or for that matter, think of Anu and Padma as girls. Did that man touch his wife with equal tenderness? Was such a thing possible? She had never known it. When He had finished with her at night He would move away and back to his own bed. Once she had said to Him, "Stay with me for some time," hoping He would understand what she wanted, and He said, "You smell." But when He had been on top of her, there had been no smell. After He had finished with her, her breasts were always sore—He kneaded them the way Anu kneaded flour. Gently, gently, she would say, wincing, but by then He would have finished and got off her bed, tying up His pyjamas and pulling down His kurta, and she would pull down her nightgown and sleep too. She had never known the touch of His skin.

Why ask for something that could only be given if it was there? He needed his release, bas. If that was what it was, then who was she to want more? Who was she to feel bereft every time it happened?

Only for one's children could it be there, only for them. Even now, years later, she still got up every night to check if her children were covered properly, if they were breathing. If they were there. It seemed that Death was just around the corner, waiting to grip its tentacles around her children; every illness they survived was because she wrestled so fiercely with It. When she prayed, she prayed only for her children. Something inside her whispered that the minute she began asking favours for herself or even for Him, God would give it at the expense of her children. Unless of course, she was dying, then to ask to live would be for her children, not for herself, so then she could ask for that.

She had been very ill once, only once. She had been so ill that she had actually wanted to die. It was after one of her abortions; something had gone wrong, she didn't stop bleeding, it went on and on till she just collapsed one day. She had had to be hospitalized. Padma and Anu had come to see her, full of concern, bringing food and fruits. They had taken turns spending the first four nights with her, while the one at home looked after the children. On the fourth day, when her depression had become unbearable, Mahima had come to the hospital and seeing her, had burst into tears and said, "Don't die, Mummy, don't die." Hai Ram, she had been so badly jolted that she had begun to recover almost immediately.

Mahima. Her Mahima. She had always been self-possessed, poised and polite to her elders, she had always had impeccable manners. She didn't have to be told she had better not fail in her subjects—she always did well. And the wonder was, Madhu marvelled, that she didn't let anyone walk over her either. If anyone could have a perfect daughter, that daughter was Mahima. The thing about children was that their love for you made up for everything else. With them you didn't measure, weigh, balance, as you did with everyone else. You could anticipate their needs as you could anticipate no other's. Who else would do it for your daughter . . . 'specially after marriage? After marriage your daughter would have to learn to live without it.

She had spoken these thoughts aloud to Padma. Till she did she hadn't known she had them. Padma's face had become small, she had said, "Madhu, don't talk about these things." Madhu had sighed deeply. "Best thing, Padma," she said, "is you get Mallika married to someone in Delhi, then she will be near you, also in her case it is better that she is not in some joint-family shoint-family." Padma's face had become even smaller. "When Anu and I are looking for boys for Prabha and Mahima then we will also look for Mallika," Madhu said reassuringly. "We will find an intellectual boy who likes books just like you." She looked sharply at Padma. "Caste-shaste, community-shammunity, it does not matter for Mallika's marriage, no?" Padma shook her head slowly.

Over the years, from time to time, questions nagged Madhu. Why was Padma's father still not talking to her? It had been many years now, the child was growing up, why was he holding on to his anger even now? She had known of other women who had married against their parents' wishes, but in every single case the parents came around after a child was born.

"I also don't know why," Shanta had sadly agreed with Madhu when Madhu asked her during one of her trips to Delhi, "in fact when I go to Bangalore to see them, my father doesn't even mention Padma."

"And your mother?" Madhu asked knowing a mother's heart, and knowing Shanta's answer before it came.

"What can my mother do."

"And," Madhu paused delicately, "His parents?" She knew the answer to that but she wanted to hear it again from Shanta, wanted to see the anger in her face and see her nostrils flare.

"*They!*" said Shanta with magnificent scorn, and Madhu had to be satisfied with that.

But the next year when Shanta came, Madhu asked her, "Only son He was, three sisters He has, so Shanta, when they die then *something* at least they should leave for Mallika, property, jewels, *something*, no?"

Shanta's reaction had been all that she had anticipated, it had given her enough excitement to last days. "Never!" Shanta had said, her eyes flashing, "Never, never, never! In their life if they are acting as though their granddaughter doesn't exist, then they can have no claim on her when they die."

Madhu waited, her expression full of sympathy, but Shanta didn't say anything else. Later, Madhu said to Anu, "That Shanta, she should have been an actress."

Anu looked upset, "It is all real, Madhu, she isn't putting on anything."

"That even I know," Madhu said, irritated. "What I mean is that inside her she has so much fire."

Then what about her brother, who never came to Delhi, who had never even seen Mallika? "He wanted to adopt Mallika," Shanta told Madhu, "he said the child needed both parents. Padma said, Nothing doing. Big fight they had. He hasn't spoken to her since."

"But why don't they make up?" Madhu asked, her body tingling.

"They're both headstrong and obstinate," Shanta said dryly, "you know Padma, does she ever do anything she doesn't want to do?"

Madhu, who hadn't given this much thought, reflected now, and nodded. Padma didn't cook, didn't clean, didn't pray, didn't dress like a widow.

"She hasn't forgiven him for losing his temper with her at a time when she needed love and sympathy," Shanta said.

This wasn't what Madhu expected. She looked suspiciously at Shanta. "After all these years?"

"Would you give away Mahima to your brother under those circumstances."

"Never, but—"

"And my brother's wife, Ratna, awful woman. Shows you one face and behind your back it becomes another."

Triumphantly, Madhu said, "See, see, that is why. That is why your brother hasn't made up with Padma, it must be this Ratna's doing."

"Oh," said Shanta, looking at her in wonder, "yes, yes, I didn't think of it."

Later Madhu told Anu, "Imagine, so unforgiving Padma is." Anu didn't say anything. "Vaise," said Madhu ominously, "that sister-in-law of Padma's sounds very bad."

"After marriage brothers are no longer brothers."

Madhu nodded, suddenly sad. "Their wives, they twist our brothers around their fingers." She watched Anu peeling almonds for Mataji. "Anu, sometimes I feel that Padma is hiding something."

Anu finished peeling the almonds, put them in a bowl and said, "What is there in that? I hide things, you hide things. It does not mean that what we hide is big or shocking, mostly we women hide small things." She smiled. "Then these small things, they become big in our minds."

Madhu smiled too and shook her head with indulgence. She was used to Anu's little homilies.

Often she had wanted to ask Padma directly about her runaway marriage, about Him, about her in-laws, about how she felt now, but somehow, she couldn't ask directly. She had tried. It wasn't as if she hadn't tried. She had given Padma chance after chance by casually bringing up the subject of women who had married out of the community or wanted to, of parents who disowned their children for doing so, of nasty mothers-in-law and recalcitrant daughters-in-law, and she had done so as though for her these things were not shocking at all, as though, unlike other people, she took such matters in her stride. She had given Padma innumerable opportunities to say, That's true, Madhu, see, in my case . . . Instead Padma would nod as if it had no bearing on her past, and not a choo would come out of her. Once when Madhu was telling Padma about a particularly nasty remark Mataji had made to Anu, she concluded on a note of amusement, saying, "Oof, Padma, so lucky you will never have to look after *your* mother-in-law." Padma had laughed and nodded. Madhu persisted, "Vaise," she said, "who can say, maybe she is very nice woman, after all, my mother-in-law is very good."

Padma had looked at her, still smiling, and said, "If she was good then she would have acknowledged Mallika and me, no?"

"Oh," Madhu said, wanting to bite off her tongue. "Of course, of course." Another time, talking about someone she knew who had married a Christian, Madhu had seized the opportunity and said, "I am very broad-minded, Padma, it is true I am not for interreligious marriage, but I fully believe in intercommunity marriages, it is a very good thing in our country. Only that way our country will become united." Saying it she was suddenly struck by the truth of this sentiment.

"You don't mind if Mahima doesn't marry a Punjabi?" Padma asked.

Madhu's eyebrows suddenly came together. She shrugged. "Who knows," she said. "For that, there is plenty of time, accha, tell me, I know your husband was U.P., but his caste, it was?"

"Kayasth."

"Accha, accha," Madhu said, though she already knew this. "These U.P. Kayasths, they think too much of themselves." Madhu waited. Padma nodded. "Now," Madhu continued, "if my brother he wanted to marry a person of your type, I would say, So what if she is a Madrasi, so what if she is a little dark—she is still beautiful, and she is also educated, comes from good family, such a *good* girl, that also, Brahmin—marry her." She smiled at Padma. Padma smiled back. "Padma," Madhu said, thwarted, "it is a good thing that even when his parents they said no, even then he married you, he sounds like a man with strength." Padma nodded.

But she, Madhu, saw what Anu didn't see. She was observant, she drew parallels, she drew conclusions. If Padma's silence told her that the past was too painful a subject to discuss, then Padma's reactions to Madhu's stories told her other things. It told her, for one, that objectivity wasn't Padma's strong point, either with regard to herself or her friends. Bechari, how could it be? Having lost her husband, her parents, her brother, all in one go, she was starved for love and when she got love from them—Madhu and Anu—her own response blinded her to their faults. Which was why Madhu sometimes couldn't give credence to Padma's belief in her, couldn't accept Padma's rare but genuine declarations of faith in her character. Oh, no doubt Padma was true and sincere in what she said, but her belief was misguided. Madhu also knew that Padma, who lived such an exemplary life, who had such a strong moral code, did not hold other women to this code, that nothing really shocked her the way it shocked Anu, even though everything that happened around her interested her vastly, no doubt, because, poor thing, she had no life of her own.

When Madhu told a piece of gossip to Anu she could be sure that Anu would be as shocked and disapproving as she was. When she had told Anu about how Mrs. Moitra had left her husband and run off to England with her son and Another Man, Anu's eyes had widened gratifyingly. "She was married, she has a *child*?" she whispered. Madhu nodded. "With Another Man she ran off?" Anu asked, breathless. Madhu nodded ominously. "Why didn't she marry him?" Anu asked.

"Her husband, he said, I will never give her a divorce."

"Accha," Anu had said faintly.

"For two years she was living in England, then her mother in India was dying and wanted to see her and grandson." She paused, watching Anu's rapt face. "Bas, she came here with her son, her mother died, her husband took her to court, got divorce, got custody of the son—finished."

"Ahh," Anu said, stunned.

But when Madhu told Padma, Padma's first reaction was, "Why didn't she get custody of the child?"

"How could she get custody when her moral character is so bad?"

"Ohh," Padma said in a tone very different from Anu's "ahh." "She should never have come back to India."

"What are you saying, Padma!"

"Madhu, she would not have lost her child then."

Madhu opened her mouth to speak, then closed it again. What could she say. Everything Padma saw, everything Padma observed, every conclusion Padma came to revolved around Mallika. Naturally Padma couldn't be objective.

"Why did she leave her husband?"

Madhu shrugged. "Who knows, people say that he was having many affairs or something." Padma looked at her, her head turned to one side and Madhu found herself slightly confused. "Oof, Padma," she said, "that is no reason to run away from your husband, men they are like that, if every woman does that then there will be no marriage left."

"Why did *he* get custody?"

Madhu sighed. Sometimes Padma talked so foolishly. "Padma, one thing you observe from now on," she said, "when a father is having affairs, the children are not affected. But when the mother is having affairs, then the children are affected, the husband is affected, everything is affected. A mother is everything in the house."

Padma's nostrils had flared, just like Shanta's. "How come none of us have seen her son?"

"Because," Madhu said, suddenly, unexpectedly sad, "the court ruling said that she could not visit her son, he proved that she was of a very loose character—having an affair, smoking, drinking . . . all that."

Padma swallowed. "She hasn't seen her child for . . . what . . . years?"

Madhu nodded slowly, "I think so. The husband is not even in Delhi, he is somewhere else."

"In her place I would have done the same thing," Padma said.

Madhu felt her whole world rock. "What are you saying, Padma—*you!*"

"I would have also run away with my child—I would never have let him take my child from me."

"Oh that," Madhu said, overwhelming relief flooding her. Quietly she said, "A child needs both parents, Padma."

Padma didn't reply.

She and her stupid mouth. Why did she have to say that? She had intended one thing, it came out like another. Who was she to tell Padma that a child needs both parents? It was like putting salt on a wound. Padma could hardly be unconscious of the fact, but worse, Padma would be so hurt that she, Madhu, had made an insinuation. What kind of friend was she—the worst, the worst.

Madhu spent a sleepless night and the next afternoon went to Padma's house and into her bedroom and without any preliminaries burst out, "Padma, I feel very bad for what I said to you yesterday, I didn't mean it that way."

Padma, who had begun to remove her saree, looked up in surprise. "Mean what?"

Madhu said tearfully, "That only, Padma, when we were talking about Mrs. Moitra . . ."

Padma looked even more surprised. She removed her saree, put on a dressing gown and began to fold the saree. "Why should you feel sorry just because you . . . I . . . we think differently?"

"No, Padma," Madhu said, "not that, I said to you that a child needs both parents, I didn't mean it that way, I have never thought that way about you, you are a better mother than Anu and me, you are a father you are a mother, everything you have sacrificed for Mallika, you—"

"But Madhu—" Padma said, comprehension lighting her features.

"No, no, listen," Madhu continued, "I meant in Mrs. Moitra's case, not for you, I—"

"I *know*, Madhu, I *know.*"

Madhu felt her heartbeat slowing down. "You mustn't misunderstand me."

"How can I ever misunderstand you, Madhu?" Padma said, the familiar wounded expression coming back to her face. "All that you've done for me, year after year after year—"

Mallika entered the room. "Ma, help me with my maths homework," she said.

Madhu rose. "Accha, Padma," she said and Padma accompanied her to the door.

"Tell me, Madhu," Padma said at the door, "what happened to the other man?"

"Who?" asked Madhu, frowning.

"The man she ran away with, the man Mrs. Moitra ran away with?"

"Accha. He." She paused. "What to say, Padma, even you will be shocked."

Padma waited, her eyes fixed gratifyingly on Madhu's face. Madhu sighed and said, "If one time we do wrong act, then afterwards doing wrong acts becomes easy. Then one does not have any shame left."

"What *happened,* Madhu?"

"It is still going on, what else."

"What do you mean?"

"Oofho, they are still carrying on. One or two times I have seen a car outside her house in the middle of the night."

"But I thought he was working in England."

"He *went* with her to England and he was staying with her for some time, but job he has here."

"Then," said Padma looking puzzled, "why don't they get married?"

Scornfully, Madhu said, "Why should he marry her when everything he gets from her without marriage?"

"Accha," Padma said unhappily.

Madhu softened. "He is already married but he does not live with his wife. She will not give him a divorce." To Madhu's amusement and exasperation, Padma's face lit up. Madhu shook her head, "Padma, Padma. Now you are thinking, if his wife gives divorce then he will marry her. Who knows? And no need to feel sad for her, if she cares so much for her son then why is she getting involved with This Man?"

From behind them Mallika's voice called, *"Ma!"*

Madhu sighed, "Chalo, I will go now."

So jealous, so possessive that daughter of Padma's. No grace, no smile, no looks, no charm. Only brains, but what was brains without the rest, nothing. Probably took after her father. Already she was taller than Mahima and Prabha, but she was neither small-boned and self-possessed like Mahima nor loose-limbed and confident like Prabha. Gawky, that was what she was, gawky.

She had often asked Anu how much Padma had told her, but Anu said that Padma had never spoken to her of Him either. "If she still has so much pain in her heart then how much she must have loved him," Madhu had said to Anu.

"He also," Anu had replied, kneading the dough, "how much he also loved her."

Madhu stared at her. "She told you?" she asked accusingly.

Anu shook her head. "Shanta, she told me."

Madhu frowned, "But she has never met him."

"Oho, so what, Padma must have told her." She began to make balls out of the dough.

Madhu shrugged, "What is there to show for all that love. Bechari, everything she is now doing on her own, money also He didn't leave her, nothing."

"At least she knew what it was to be loved like that."

Madhu's heart twisted. "*I* know, my husband, he—"

"When he lived and after he died this much at least Padma knew that he took her side, and not his parents' side." She slapped the chappati on the tawa and began rolling the next one. "The rest of us have to live without it and die without it."

Wordlessly, Madhu turned the chappati over.

In the beginning people had asked her about Padma. Neighbours were curious. As Mataji said, "Widow she might be, but see how much saj-dhaj she does—lipstick, mangalsutra, bindi . . . and see her sarees—red, yellow, green."

"Arre, Mataji," Madhu told her, "she wants to look like a suhagini."

"Accha?" Mataji had said disbelievingly.

"Yes, Mataji," Anu said, "in her college she hasn't told people she is a widow."

Mataji snorted, "Like a woman without brains you are talking."

"Oho, Mataji," said Madhu, "it is true, she told us herself. This way . . . people will not approach her."

"Accha, accha," Mataji exclaimed, "*now* I understand." She shook her head in admiration, "Very sensible girl she is."

Anu said, "Mataji, this way no one will take liberties."

Mataji raised her hand, "Bahurani, I do not need your explanations. I have lived longer in this world than you have."

Once when Madhu was at Anu's house, a neighbour, Mrs. Sahani, who happened to have dropped in, asked Mataji about Padma. "What is there to tell," Mataji had replied.

"What kind of person is she," Mrs. Sahani persisted, "she keeps so much to herself."

"How you are talking," Mataji said, "is this something to ask, why a widow who is supporting a daughter is keeping to herself?"

Mrs. Sahani had looked flustered and changed the subject.

Later, when Mrs. Sahani dropped in at Madhu's house to borrow sugar she said, casually, "She is your good friend, no, you must be knowing everything about her."

"Bilkul. She is my close friend, what she is suffering all alone, that I only know." Mrs. Sahani's expression showed a deep and profound sympathy, she shook her head and clicked her tongue. "He died in a car accident," Madhu whispered, "so much sorrow Padma has that she does not even talk about it."

"Hai Ram," Mrs. Sahani said avidly, "not even to you?"

Madhu tossed her head and looked reproachfully at Mrs. Sahani, "Whatever she tells me about her sorrows, that is between her and me."

"Of course, of course," Mrs. Sahani exclaimed with a disclaiming gesture, "Bas, only general idea I wanted to have, that is all." She made a move to leave, then she said, "Her sister and brother-in-law, such nice people they are, they don't even look like Madrasis."

Madhu nodded vigourously.

Mrs. Sahani looked troubled, "But her parents don't come to see her?"

Madhu struggled. Her loyalty to Padma won. "They are in very bad health," she said.

"For so many years!" Mrs. Sahani exclaimed.

Madhu nodded, and improvised, "Her father, he had a heart attack, then her mother fell ill, then her father had another heart attack, now her mother is unwell again."

"Accha, accha," Mrs. Sahani said without conviction, "then why is she not going there?"

"Oh, that," Madhu replied, thinking fast, "where does she have the money, she has a lecturer's job, a small child, her life is too difficult." She gave a gusty sigh.

"But *they* can send her money to go, no?" Mrs. Sahani said, "that much they can do."

Anger began to spurt inside Madhu. She said, "That much they can do, much more they can do, plenty they have done, who do you think has bought this house for Padma?"

"Her parents?" Mrs. Sahani said, startled.

"What else," Madhu laughed scornfully, "why, do you think Padma rents this house on a lecturer's salary, you think she can pay rent for a two-bedroomed house?" Mrs. Sahani was still looking at her in astonishment. Madhu said, "You tell me, how many parents are there who will build a house for a daughter; me, I cannot think of one even, for sons they will build one, they will build two, but for daughters?" She saw Mrs. Sahani's expression and noted with satisfaction that her dart had gone home, everyone knew that Mrs. Sahani had taken her own brother to court because he had got both their parents' houses after their death; it showed what kind of woman she was to take her own flesh and blood to court, now let her burn to know about Padma.

"Her in-laws, why don't they come to see her?"

Shameless woman, Madhu thought. She schooled her expression and shook her head. "*They*—coming to see her!" she laughed mirthlessly.

"Accha, accha," said Mrs. Sahani comprehendingly. "Oho, oho," she added commiseratingly.

Madhu said, contemptuously, "They were Kayasths, thought she wasn't good enough for their family."

"Arre," said Mrs. Sahani looking offended, "*she* is a Brahmin."

"What happens from that. Some people have no sense at all, they think all Madrasis are the same."

Mrs. Sahani shook her head indignantly. Then she frowned. "But Rao, it is South Indian name?"

"She did not want to take her husband's family's name. She said, How I can do that when they have nothing to do with me or Mallika?"

"Rao, it is her parents' name, no?"

Madhu nodded. "I told her, Absolutely you are doing the right thing, your Mallika she is Rao, one hundred percent she is Rao."

"Hai Ram, and I grumble about *my* in-laws, bechari, from *her* fate at least God has saved me."

Madhu folded her hands. "Me, I always thank Him that he has given me in-laws who treat me just like a daughter, a bigger blessing than that what can there be after marriage?" Mrs. Sahani looked sceptical. "I am telling you," Madhu said.

"Chalo, I have to go," Mrs. Sahani said.

Madhu watched her walking back to her house on the opposite side of the street. Much she thinks of herself, she thought, and shut her door with a bang.

Now no one asked. Everyone knew that Padma's lifestyle was irreproachable, that she was strong and brave. Even Mrs. Sahani said to Madhu with approval, "To men she is not talking at all, not even to our husbands, Madhu."

Madhu said briefly, "What are you saying, that I know from the beginning itself." Who did Mrs. Sahani think she was?

Madhu regularly told Anu about all her conversations with Mrs. Sahani. Once she had said accusingly to Anu, "No one talks to *you* about Padma."

"You they meet more often than me, that is why," Anu assured her swiftly. Was that why? It was true that Anu had no time to interact at leisure with the other women in the neighbourhood. Cook, clean, chop, grind—Anu should have been born with ten hands instead of two. And ten ears too, everyone asking her to do this and do that, Mataji's endless demands and constant criticism, all those relatives descending on her . . . When Madhu saw Anu on her bad days she would say silently, Thank God I am not Anu; God, you have blessed me. Why He had she didn't know, she didn't deserve it.

She often told Padma so. "In my previous life itself I must have done something good, otherwise why am I getting so much in this life?" It was a hypothetical question. "I am so lucky, Padma, He loves me so much, see how He takes care of me, two houses he has built for me, so many sarees and jewellery he has given me."

Oh it was such a joy to talk to Padma. It wasn't as if she didn't talk to the others, she did, frequently, but every time she did she regretted it because their nazar invariably fell on her and her family. Once when she had told Mrs. Darruwalla about the kundan set she had bought for Mahima, Mahima had promptly fallen ill. Another time when she had told Mrs. Maheshwari about how He pampered her, He had had an accident and broken His arm. But Padma shared Madhu's joys, even though she herself had so few. Anu too was never jealous, but one's conversation never *went* anywhere when talking to Anu. Sometimes she even felt that Anu wasn't really listening, that instead of thinking, How lucky Madhu is, she would be thinking, oho, the potatoes are finished, I'll have to go to the market today, can't wait till tomorrow, then I might as well get some palak and some dhanya . . .

Sometimes, though, Madhu felt that even Padma, who listened so completely, wasn't making the conclusions that Madhu wanted her to make, the only affirmation she got from Padma was in her nods. Then a small knot of anger inside Madhu would begin to grow harder. Then she would find herself giving oblique hints, saying, "Oh, you know, Padma, that day I was asking Anu, What did He give you for your birthday, and Anu just began laughing and said, He never remembers. So sorry I felt for her."

"Oh, Madhu," Padma said, "men forget these things all the time."

"*He* doesn't," Madhu said triumphantly. She waited, but Padma only nodded. She put her hands in front of Padma and said, "See, Padma, touch. Soft, no?"

"Yes," Padma said with a smile, "you have lovely hands, what cream do you use?"

Madhu tossed her head, "Cream I hardly use, Padma. When we got married, then only He said, Madhu, such beautiful hands must never become hard and wrinkled. He said, Now that you are my wife, your soft hands will always be protected from work meant only for servants. Tell me, Padma, how many other husbands treat their wives with so much consideration?" Padma nodded. "Big heart he has," Madhu said.

"*You* have a big heart."

Madhu looked at her, nonplussed. "Me?"

Padma nodded.

The sudden desire to weep was so sharp that Madhu had to look down fixedly at her cup of tea. If she cried Padma would understand, Padma would comfort. She didn't want Padma's understanding, she didn't want Padma's comfort. At such times she felt she didn't even want Padma's love, which she had as surely as Padma had hers. She hated weeping in front of anyone. Yet she had done so when Shanta had said that first day, "My sister is completely alone," as if Shanta thought this needed to be explained. Madhu had wanted to shout, We all are, we all are. It was the same feeling that she had sometimes when she wanted to stamp her feet and cry, as she had as a child, "I want to go home, I want to go home." But she couldn't go home, her father and mother were dead. If home meant a refuge, then she didn't have one. Even Anu had it, Anu who went home to her parents in Lucknow for two whole months every year, coming back pink and glowing as if she had shed her skin.

*You* have a big heart, Padma had said. Once, in the lifetime before her marriage, when Madhu had been another person, people had thought that about her too. She had been twelve when her mother died, her brothers had been older. With her mother's death she had quite naturally taken over all the cooking and housework, doing what she could before going to school early in the morning and the rest after she returned from school, then doing her homework and preparing for all her subjects. One day she had gone to her father's room to find him sitting at the corner of his bed weeping, and he had taken her in his arms and said, "You are God's gift to me."

She had closed her mind to That Life till Padma had opened it again. Not intentionally, she knew Padma didn't do these things intentionally, but Padma loved to listen and so Madhu talked. Then when she went back home the thoughts would whirl round and round and she would find herself distracted and ill-tempered. The problem in thinking about the Life Before was that it was like recalling someone you had known intimately who had died without warning. Her father's death had been expected, but not this one. In fact she had barely known she thought this way till she began talking to Padma about her childhood.

It seemed that the life before had no bearing at all on the life after. In the life after she hadn't recognized herself anymore. All the old bearings were gone—the people, how they felt about her, what they thought about her. The new bearings had to be learnt like learning a new language. But in this new life it was not only what people expected of you that was different—that she had been prepared for—but what they thought about you. Now she knew why her father and brother and aunt were all wrong. Now she knew that what they had thought about her—and as a result, what she had unconsciously accepted about herself—was all a lie. It had taken her years to discover the solution which was actually so simple: her family's love for her had blinded them to the very flaws in her character that were so obvious to others.

"Padma," Madhu said, feeling that sharp pain again, "you think like that because you are like my sister. Actually, Padma, my heart is very small."

Padma shook her head, kept shaking it.

"Padma, it is because you love me that you think I am good and generous. Now Anu, she is the one who is truly unselfish, see how she smiles all the time, how she never counts what she is doing. Padma, I sometimes have bad thoughts inside me even when I am doing good things. I count and say, I did this for my mother-in-law, I did that for my sister-in-law. And they are good people, Padma. Then whose fault it is? My fault, no?"

"Madhu, you're underestimating yourself."

"Oofho, Padma," Madhu exclaimed, exasperated. That was the problem with Padma—once she had made up her mind about something, telling her it was not so was like water off a duck's back.

You only think of others, now think of yourself, Madhu's aunt had told her once. If you want to get along in this world, try and be a little selfish, her brothers had said. How much care you show me, her father had said. And then without any warning, in the life after, it had become the opposite. Try and be a little less selfish. Think of others instead of yourself. Show some consideration. It had been said to her that very first year when her in-laws had come to stay with her, and she had once given Him breakfast a little later than usual. It had been said to her when she cried in front of Him and said his mother had called her selfish, that a few months ago his sisters had implied the same thing. He said, "Think then, think sensibly, if four people think something is wrong and one person thinks it is not wrong, then where does the truth lie?" She saw the truth of it, she saw His calm face and thought, gratefully, He could have been angry but He is not. Then He said, "Sometimes think of others instead of yourself." He had spoken so calmly that she saw how true it was; suddenly it struck her that unlike so many other husbands she had seen, He hadn't once complained about His meals being late and she was full of remorse and guilt.

It was true what her mother had told her when at the age of eleven Madhu had begged her for days to see a popular film: "Beti, listen, you have to learn to do without. One day your marriage will require you do it without thinking; remember, marriage is not song and dance like the films you want to see, marriage means sublimating your desires, so learn to do that now." Her mother had done it; Anu did it; Padma, who had no husband, did it. Only she, Madhu, was the selfish one and at no time did it strike her as harshly as when she found herself unaccountably bursting into tears for no apparent reason. In the middle of her meals, when she was lying in bed . . . at the oddest of times she would find herself suddenly crying, the sobs tearing her throat apart. She had no business crying like this, she who had everything.

Then of course, there was the question of money. About that nobody knew how calculating and selfish she was better than herself. Even now, even after all these years she found herself calculating how much extra she spent every time her mother-in-law came to stay, thinking of how this woman wanted to eat mutton, pistas and almonds daily, of how when her daughters accompanied her she wanted Madhu to provide everything that they liked for every meal. In the early days of her marriage the housekeeping money He gave her had never been enough for such times. "You have to learn to stretch it out, that's what my mother did," he used to say. She had had to ask him for more money. He had said she didn't know how to run the household. She then showed him the accounts for everything—fruits, vegetables, rations. He had looked at it and shrugged. "Something you must be doing wrong," he said. "My mother also managed a house and my father also had a limited income." Madhu had a little money that her brothers had given her from time to time. She used it. It wasn't that she couldn't ask him for more, but she wanted to show him that she too could do what his mother had done, that she too could stretch out what he gave her. The money had finished in a week. Then she had to ask him for more. He had given it to her, impatiently, and said, "With this you have to manage."

But what was managing? Managing was doing without. She who now had everything that money could buy, knew well what it had been to do without. Her mother had managed, her mother had done without, all her life. In her mother's house so had Madhu in little ways, automatically, like breathing; she had learnt not to take the last chappati and the last spoonfuls of dahi, she had learnt not to look longingly at the last sweet, she had learnt to wait so that her brothers first took what they wished, she had learnt to serve them so that she gave them the best, the biggest, the hottest. The one who managed was the one who did without, and Madhu, who had done without in lesser ways in her mother's house, automatically did without in larger ways in her own. In the life before it hadn't angered her, in fact she had given no thought to it at all. Yet, now, when everyone had had two helpings of rasgullas and she hadn't had any and He affection- atelly said to her, "Have one more, Madhu," she wanted to throw the empty plate at Him.

She had never been an angry person. Her father and her brothers had said that if there was laughter in the house it was because of her. When things irritated her she spoke her mind exactly in the manner her brothers did and then she forgot about it. Nothing lingered, nothing accumulated, she was not given to brooding. But in the life after even that had changed. She found herself lingering over little details, she found herself going back obsessively to past incidents, sometimes she felt her insides becoming so knotted that she wanted to scream. She hated herself then. Look at Anu, she would tell herself, how calm she is, how she laughs, how she lets Mataji's nastiness just slide off her like water, look how she works from morning to night. Look at Padma, all alone, so alone, and look how much she has to work to secure a future for herself and her daughter. Neither of them complain. They have more to be angry about, they have the real problems, not you, think of them and be satisfied. But her unruly mind would not listen.

If her mother-in-law and sisters-in-law disliked her she deserved it. She tried to make up. In those days when they didn't have money she had saved desperately from the housekeeping money, she gave up milk and fruits for herself, she didn't buy herself any new sarees. She used the money she saved to buy sarees for her mother-in-law and sisters-in-law. Once— through Shanta, to whom Madhu had given the money—she even bought them Hyderabadi pearl chains. But her sisters-in-law said that the colours of the sarees were all wrong and her mother-in-law said that she already had pearls, pearls strung in gold. It served her right for not knowing their tastes better. The worst was that even when their money problems got over, nothing changed. Her gifts were more expensive, the silks heavier, the jewellery all gold, but no one seemed enthusiastic even though they ac- cepted everything she gave as though it were their due.

For years now, whenever she felt the familiar anger or pain gnaw at her

insides she would open her Godrej and open The Book and look at the figures that were hers alone and think, This I have. Then she would put it in
the compartment inside her Godrej, lock the cupboard and sail outside to
face whatever had to be faced. She had her youngest brother to thank for
it. Once, when she was leaving his house after a short holiday with him,
he had given her a cheque for an astonishingly large amount of money. "I
couldn't give you anything for your wedding," he had said. "I didn't even
have a job at that time." He pressed an envelope into her hand. "Do not
spend this on housekeeping. Open an account in your name." "How?"
Madhu asked, astonished. He told her. She had done that, she had done
better than that, she had put it in a fixed deposit in a bank in Connaught
Place, and she had never told Him. And after that, whenever her brothers
gave her money, or when relatives gave her money for the children she
would wait till she had enough and put it in another fixed deposit. During those difficult days before he began the business, when they were always short of money, when she had to struggle for every paisa, she had
been overwhelmed at the enormity of her action. When they ran out of
money before the end of the month, when they had staying guests and he
had to borrow money to keep going, she had been stricken by guilt. When
he had to help his father get his two sisters married and taken a loan
against his provident fund, she had despised herself. She would get up at
night sweating, dreaming that he had found out about her money. Her
nightmares had got so bad that she finally told Anu, who had just arrived
as a bride. Anu had laughed and laughed. "What is there to feel so bad
about, Madhu? You hide hundreds of rupees in your bank every month, I
hide two, three rupees in my trunk every week!" Madhu had laughed in
sheer relief, of course. The principle was the same, her mother too had
done it, and her grandmother. Now she had quite a tidy sum all in her
name, she didn't even need it, they had so much money, but she still put
away money in it every month.

She tried to explain to Padma in other ways. "One day He said to me,
What you do you must do with an open heart, if you think and then do,
it is not a big thing. See, Padma, how wise he is, how foolish I am."

"Madhu," Padma said, "whatever you do for me and Anu you do from
the heart."

That was the problem with Padma. She interrupted. It was love that
prompted her, Madhu didn't doubt it, but she interrupted. Padma made

her measured stream of thought come to a halt and then it could never continue in the same direction. "I have done nothing for you," she said, "nothing."

"Even that day, after the mela, you didn't think of yourself, you only thought of us," Padma said, her face twisting. "Madhu, if it hadn't been for you I . . . ," she trailed off. Suddenly bereft of speech herself, Madhu finished her tea in quick gulps.

They had not mentioned that day till now. What was there to speak of. It had happened. Worse had happened to other women. She had worried most for Padma, but Padma, after that day, had been surprisingly composed. And now Padma was attributing a selfless and generous role in it to Madhu, when in actuality it was she, Madhu, who had set the evil wheels in motion.

It had begun so harmlessly. There was a fair on in a nearby neighbourhood, and Anu had said, wistfully, "From the time I was a child I loved melas."

Madhu had watched her as she put the lid on the pressure cooker and began washing the dishes. She said, "Anu, tomorrow let us go, you and I and Padma, no children, no one to look after. Hmm?"

Anu had stared at her.

"Oofho, don't look like that, I have the car, Prabha and Mallika can stay in my house, Ayaji can look after them, bas."

Anu's eyes began to shine, then suddenly the brightness faded. "No, Madhu, I can't leave Mataji alone."

"Alone, what do you mean alone, Kamala is there, your husband will be back from office," Madhu said exasperated.

"What will I tell them?"

Thank God, thought Madhu, thank God I have a husband who gives me freedom. She said, "I will tell them, I will say we are all going to Chandni Chowk to . . . that I need your help to buy . . ." She thought a moment. "Some . . . some . . . jewellery for Mahima. Just now I will tell Mataji." Before Anu could protest Madhu went to the courtyard where Mataji was sitting on the charpai with a glass of tea and the newspaper.

"Come, beti, come," Mataji said, "tell me all the news."

She also—Madhu thought indignantly—as bad as Padma.

"I have to go home now, Mataji," she said briskly, "but I wanted your advice, something in gold I have to buy for Mahima, her grandmother gave her money, what do you think?"

Mataji shook her head approvingly, "Bilkul, gold only it is the best, where you are thinking of buying it?"

"Chandni Chowk," Madhu said promptly. "Just now I asked Anu to come with me and excuses and excuses she made—this I have to do, that I have to do—Mataji will be alone, so I told her, we will come back by dinnertime. I have no faith in my choice, Mataji, but Anu she is very wise about these things, so I said, Bas, you *have* to come, still she is saying no, no." Madhu sighed loudly. "So I have come to you, you tell me."

Mataji sighed, "Beti, what can I say, it is not my house, she does what she wants to do."

Madhu nodded, "Accha, Mataji, then tomorrow evening we will go as soon as He comes back from office, we will come back around eight in the evening." Mataji took a sip of her tea. "All right, Mataji?" Madhu said a little louder.

Mataji said, "Eight she comes back, then she has to make dinner, before nine-thirty it will not be ready, beti. He comes back tired from office, that much time he cannot wait for dinner."

"Oh that," Madhu said airily. "She can make dinner before she goes, what is there in that."

Mataji took another sip of her tea. "Why are you asking me, why doesn't she ask me herself. Bahurani," she called. Anu came, wiping her hands on her saree palla. "Has your friend become your tongue now?"

"Arre, Mataji," Madhu exclaimed, "she didn't ask me. That is why I am asking you."

"Let it be, Mataji, I will not go," Anu said.

"Who is stopping you," Mataji said not looking at her, "behaving as if someone has tied you up with a rope." She put the glass below the bed. "Like ice your tea was."

Padma was no problem. Her eyes shining, she said, "Oh, Madhu!"

It was when she went home that it came to Madhu that this was probably the first outing that Padma was having when her sister, Shanta, wasn't there. I'm selfish and thoughtless, Madhu thought fiercely, I should have thought of this before.

It was the first time they had all three sat in the car with no one else. Madhu was feeling heady with delight, Padma kept giggling. Only Anu's smile was somewhat forced. "Don't think, Anu," Madhu ordered, parking the car a short distance away from the mela grounds, "just enjoy."

Anu nodded, her face strained. "Bas, I hope no one I know will see me."

"Anu," Madhu said admonishingly, "no one will see you and so what if they see you, will they go to your house and tell your Mataji? Hmm?"

Later Madhu remembered not Padma's joy or her laughter, but how much she ate, plates and plates of chat and gulabjamuns, as if she had never had them before. She remembered Anu's uncharacteristic diffidence, how Anu had followed her and Padma wherever they went, expressing no preference. One minute, as Madhu recalled, there was bright sunshine and the next minute it seemed the night had fallen, and looking at her watch she saw it was a quarter past seven.

She heard Anu's voice in her ear.

"Speak louder, Anu," she said. The music from the loudspeakers was deafening her.

"Mrs. Sahani, I saw Mrs. Sahani with her husband and children, I think she's seen me," Anu said despairingly.

Her face was so tense that Madhu said with more gentleness than she intended, "She isn't going to tell Mataji, no need to panic."

"Oh, look," Padma said, "gajaras." In front of them a woman sat with a basket full of flowers. Padma almost ran towards her, her palla flying behind her, her plait moving at her waist. She picked up three strings of jasmine, smelt them and, turning to Madhu and Anu, smiled. They joined her as she paid. Then, holding the three gajaras in her hand, she turned to them. Carefully, she tied one gajara around Anu's hair. Gently, Anu touched the flowers behind her, then smelt her fingers, smiling softly, her face suddenly alight. Padma looked at Madhu, her head turned to one side, took out a rubberband from her bag, turned Madhu around, gathered her short hair and tied it into a small ponytail, and wound the gajaras around it. Then she turned Madhu towards her and smiled with pleasure and triumph. The string of her own, Padma pulled through the top of her plait and it hung down over it like a Bharatnatyam dancer's. Madhu was aware of a sudden jolt of shock. Immediately she told herself it didn't matter, after all Padma wore a bindi and a mangalsutra too, she was sure Padma would remove the flowers before she reached home, and anyway who would see her here. A sudden gust of anger against herself shook Madhu—everything Padma had given up, everything, who was she,

Madhu, to feel shocked? And how happy Padma had made her at this moment, she almost felt like a girl again. As they walked towards the gate a large mirror in one of the stalls caught her attention; briefly, she saw the three of them reflected in it like three Apsaras, a swift, lovely vision. She had last worn gajaras in her hair when she was a bride. Once, in college, she had declared to a friend that she would never buy gajaras, she would only wear them if they were given to her. She had forgotten that declaration till then; remembering it, she thought, it has come true, what I said, but this is not what I had meant.

Padma began to scream. Then Anu began to scream. As if in slow motion Madhu saw that like boxers in a ring they were in the middle of a crowd of men with avid eyes, yes, it was the eyes that she always remembered, that Padma was bent over, her hands covering her breasts, that Anu lay crouched on the ground in a foetal position, her legs curled, her hands tight around her body. As Padma screamed Madhu saw the thick ring of men around them move back smoothly like a receding wave, then smoothly, in perfect accord, the wave flowed back towards them and they were engulfed. The hands at Madhu's breasts squeezed and pinched, between her thighs the fingers probed and prodded, they slid down her bra and below her waist under her petticoat, she heard a groan as a hand rubbed her bare bottom up-down, up-down, as if it were sandpaper, she struck out with her bag and hit someone and her long nails scratched someone else's hands, she bent down, her elbows out and hit someone's stomach and as she did she felt a body moving hard against her back, both his hands holding her thighs, she heard her own scream as she fell on the ground, her head hitting the ground. There was silence. The loudspeaker began its next song from the latest Hindi film. She opened her eyes. It was as if nothing had happened, no one was around them, a few yards away four policemen with lathis stood grinning, and beyond them everyone stared. She covered her torn blouse with her palla. Padma was stumbling to her feet. Anu was still lying in the foetal position. Madhu put her hand to Anu's cheek. Then she put her hand under Anu's arm and with Padma's help pulled her up into a sitting position. Padma adjusted Anu's palla around her shoulders and picking up Anu's slippers from the ground put them on for her. Anu's hair had descended from its bun and hung wildly over her back and shoulders, the gajaras hanging askew. Padma gathered Anu's hair in her hand, twisted it and tucked it under Anu's blouse. "Your pleats," Madhu said. Padma looked down to her saree, which was hanging out of the petticoat, she looked around, her eyes wide with fear, and gathering it, thrust it down the front of her saree without pleating it, then lowered her palla so that it fell down low and put the rest over her shoulder and chest. Anu stood up slowly. Madhu rapidly wiped the smudged bindi off Anu's forehead. She held on to Padma with one hand and to Anu with the other and led them towards the gate. From the corners of her eyes she could see that everyone was watching them, she didn't look up till they reached the gate and then she guided them to the car. With hands that were surprisingly steady she opened the doors. "Wait," Padma said thickly and began to vomit into the drain in front of the car. Madhu held her around the stomach, her hand over Padma's forehead as Padma retched. It all came out—the papris, the dahivadas, the golgappas, the gulabjamuns, the rasmalais. She wiped Padma's mouth with her handkerchief and took out a bottle of water from the car which she always carried with her. Padma washed her mouth, gargled and drank some. Madhu gave the bottle to Anu. "Wash your face here, your hands also, they're full of mud." She watched Anu obey her instructions, then Madhu took out a towel from the car and mopped her dry. She did the same for herself. Then she rapidly dusted Padma's saree and Anu's. Then, standing between her car and the next, Padma rapidly pleated her saree. Five twists, one tuck, two pulls, she was almost as good as new. Anu looked at her and did the same. It had hardly taken a minute. They got inside the car, locked it from the inside. The smell of jasmine was overpowering. Padma removed her gajaras and put it on the dashboard. Slowly, she began unplaiting her hair, then she sat as though she didn't know what to do next. Anu ran her hand over her own hair, took out the gajara and put it next to Padma's. She took out her comb from the bag and gave it to Padma. Padma took it unseeingly, then looked again and gave it back to Anu. "I have," she said, opening her bag. They began combing their hair. Madhu took out some cream from her bag, wiped out her smudged bindi, then taking out the bindi box from her bag, made a perfect O on her forehead. She did the same for Padma and Anu. "Nothing is showing, no one will know," she said. She started the car and began the drive home.

Nothing showed, no one knew. The children, who were playing in Mahima's room, greeted them joyfully as if they had been gone for days. Then Padma, Mallika and Ayaji went home and Anu and Prabha began to move to the door. It was eight-thirty. Anu would be in for it.

"I'll come with you," Madhu said, putting Mahima down.

Anu shook her head, "It is all right, Madhu."

"Come," said Madhu and walked back with her.

"Very quickly you have come back, Bahurani," Mataji's voice greeted them as they walked in. Then she saw Madhu behind Anu and sighed, "Sometimes think of us old people, beti, we get worried when it becomes dark."

"Arre, Mataji," Madhu said loudly, "it is my fault, first I saw one thing, then I saw another, nothing I liked. Anu said to me, It is becoming late, Madhu. Then I said five minutes more, those five minutes they became fifteen minutes . . ."

"Accha," said Mataji, "What did you buy finally?"

"I will show you when I come tomorrow," Madhu said, thinking rapidly of what she had in her Godrej, "it is a very pretty gold necklace, like beads strung together, very thin and delicate." She saw Mr. Prasad sitting reading the newspaper and said a swift namaste, he smiled and got up to do the same. What a nice man he was, but he didn't hear anything.

"I am going to sleep," Mataji said. "Now it is too late for me to eat." She groaned as she got up, holding her back.

Kamala came out of the room and smiled at Madhu, "Namaste, didi, Bhabi enjoyed yourself?"

"What else," said Mataji going slowly towards her room.

"Mataji, it will take five minutes to heat the food, don't go to sleep now," Anu said going to the kitchen.

"Five minutes, I know what her five minutes are," Mataji muttered dragging the chair next to the dining table and sitting down. Kamala put on the radio and sat next to her. "If it is old food then I will not eat," Mataji said loudly.

"I made it just before going, Mataji," Anu said from the kitchen.

"Thinks she can give the same thing she made for lunch and I won't know," Mataji muttered into the air.

Kamala, her eyes dreamy, raised the volume of the radio. It was the same song that had been on at the mela as they lay on the ground. "My favourite," Kamala sighed, "hai, I can smell rajma, I love Bhabi's rajma."

Madhu said her namastes and left.

The children had already been fed by the ayah. He still hadn't come back from work. Madhu had a long bath, she used a pumice and scrubbed and scrubbed. Then she dried herself, wore the salwar kamiz in which she slept and walked over to Padma's house. Ayaji opened the door. Padma was lying in bed, the bedside lamp next to her on, and on the other side Mallika was sleeping soundly and Padma was stroking her forehead. "Madhu," Padma said in the same tone that Mahima did, and Madhu sat next to her and hugged her. She looked at Mallika curled up underneath the sheet. Padma didn't usually sleep with Mallika. When she was hardly two years old Padma had put her in the other bedroom. "So soon?" Madhu had asked her, shocked. But what she had meant was, For you what is the need to do this? Padma had said, "I need some time to myself, Madhu." "For what?" Madhu had asked, shocked. Padma had looked guilty, and said, rather weakly, "Just to read, or, you know, just to think." Think, Madhu had thought, everyone in the world buried themselves in work in order not to think and here was Padma trying to find time for it. What had she to think about anyway?

"Madhu, is Anu all right?"

Madhu sighed. "From what I think, no." She told Padma about Mataji's reaction when she dropped Anu home.

That night when Madhu was almost asleep he came home. She heard his sounds in the room, and some time after he got into his bed, she climbed out of hers and got in next to him. He was asleep. She put her arm around him, her cheek against his back, felt a kind of comfort fill her body. She was almost asleep when he turned towards her in the familiar way. "No, not that. Now now," she murmured. He turned his back to her, pushing her away with his body, "Then what are you doing here?" She got up and went back to her bed.

It was as she had predicted. When they dropped in to see Anu the next day she was as normal as ever, cooking and chopping effortlessly, attending to Mataji, laughing. Madhu had taken out the gold chain from her Godrej and she showed it to Mataji in the courtyard.

"Is this Bahurani's choice?" Mataji asked.

"Yes, for that purpose only I took Anu yesterday."

Mataji fingered the chain critically. "It is all right," she said finally, "but it looks a little weak, see, here and here, to me it seems that it will break with the first wear."

Talking was a reaffirmation of your own feelings, an acknowledgement that you weren't alone in what you felt, but some things remained unspoken, unanswered, and what had happened at the mela was one of them.

Her mother had once said to her, Men are different from women, they have different needs. The question was, why did they need *this*? What pleasure did they get from doing it? You have to learn to sublimate your desires, her mother had said, and she understood that it needed to be done for the sake of one's marriage, one's children. But she had never had to sublimate desires like *that*. She had never felt like lifting up her saree to show her private parts to people on the road the way that, on two separate occasions, men had shown her theirs on the road as she walked—educated, middle-class men, one old enough to be her father, one a mere boy, hardly twenty. She had never wanted to grab an unknown man's thighs or worse his . . . it couldn't even be thought of.

But perhaps there was no answer to the why.

She, Madhu, had always wanted to be a boy. With three brothers what else could one want? What was the *fun* in being a girl? No excitement, no adventure. Her childhood memories were vivid with the sounds of her brothers' laughter, the stomping of their feet in the house, their shouts as they played outside. Her sons laughed and played like that now. Unbridled their sounds, unbridled their movements. Naturally, how else could it be when from birth they inhabited a world that allowed such sounds, such movements. Oh it was a joy to hear her sons, to watch them.

Did men ever wonder about women, the world that they inhabited? Why should they? It did not interest them. Why should it? It could not be a world they longed to be part of. That kind of longing only a woman could have.

Once, when she and Padma were chatting, she told Padma about how she had once, when fifteen, unknowingly eavesdropped on this incomprehensible world of men. She had meant it to be amusing, she had meant Padma to laugh . . . somewhere deep inside her she knew that if Padma laughed, she could too. They had been talking about the children and how they were doing in school and Madhu had complained, "My husband, He keeps saying to the boys, if you don't do well in school, I will leave everything for Mahima, business, money, two houses. What to do, Padma. Akhil is only interested in cricket and football, and Randhir he is like your Mallika, reading storybooks, storybooks all the time. Instead of doing homework, he writes stories."

"But Madhu, that's wonderful, to be writing stories at this age."

"Nothing wonderful-shunderful about writing stories, Padma, it is a waste of time, completely useless, if he was a girl I would say, all right, very good, write your stories, but he is a *boy*, Padma, what is the use if he is getting highest marks in English and failing in all the other subjects?"

Padma had said, "Don't worry. He'll be all right. And Mahima is such a bright, responsible child."

Madhu shrugged, "My boys also are bright, but they do not study, that is all." She saw Padma nodding in that polite, noncommittal way. Her irritation rose. "House, each of my boys has, they will inherit the business, there is no need for them to study so hard." She let out a deep, angry breath, looking accusingly at Padma.

"My brother too wasn't interested in studies. My sister, Shanta, would tutor him every day, she would have to force him to study. Boys are different."

There was a long silence, then Madhu said, a break in her voice, "With daughters . . . only thing is . . . so much care we have to take . . ." She saw Padma's stricken face and cursed herself.

She hadn't meant to say that, it had just come out. She searched for something related but different to talk about. She said, "Servant girl, imagine, Padma." Padma looked at her, bemused. "it was happening for so long, in my brothers' room only, and nothing I knew for so long." Now Padma was all ears. Encouraged, Madhu went on. "Young thing she was, Padma, fifteen, sixteen, fair also she was, that must have got inside her head, how she used to walk, mattakte, mattakte, and her payals going *chang-chang-chang.* My brothers used to laugh a lot when she used to come to the house, and big-big eyes she used to make at them. Then only she had started. In the afternoon and night she used to wash the dishes, then go. Such a fool I was, I didn't even notice that she used to stay longer and longer every night, she used to say, Baby, you go to sleep, I will clean up everything and Bhaiyya will lock the door after me. What did I know that Bhaiyya used to lock the door after her in his room!" She laughed, but Padma's eyes were only getting larger and larger.

"Innocent you are, Padma," Madhu said indulgently. "You do not know the ways of this world."

"You said your brother, or your brothers?"

"Two brothers. The youngest he was too young, but the other two—both of them. One was inside the room, the other used to wait outside, after that one would come out, then the other would go in."

She remembered lying in her bed, awake, thinking of her mother, which she did every night. There had been comfort in believing that her mother was still alive, in imagining that any minute now her mother would come into her room and sit next to her and begin chatting about this and that, all the daily observations about food and neighbours and relatives which she hadn't even known was part of her life till her mother had gone. It was as she lay in bed thinking of her mother that she sometimes heard the sound of anklets, but she didn't give it much thought till one day she heard her brothers' stifled laughter in the corridor outside. So she peeped from within the darkness of her room, her door open merely a crack, but it was enough for her to see. Of course, she had known then. She had felt slightly sick, yet, each night after that she had got out of bed, and stood at her door, listening.

From a distance she heard Padma's voice saying, "How do you know she was inside?"

"Arre, Padma, I know!" Madhu snapped, infuriated. "I was peeping from my bedroom one day when I heard them laughing, I saw her go inside with my eldest brother, then a few minutes later with my second brother. Then I saw her coming out looking down at the ground with her chunni covering her head. It did not happen only one time, every day it happened for four months, every day I heard my brothers laughing and the sound of her payals. Padma, women of that class, they can do it any number of times with any number of men." In the morning she would search her brothers' faces but their expressions were as normal as ever and their behaviour with her as indifferent and matter-of-fact as their father's, and the woman's behaviour was no different either. This was what she found hardest to comprehend. Once, in fact more than once, she saw her oldest brother give her money when she asked for it, this was in addition to the money her father already gave her every month. Her mother was ill, she would say, or her brother had to go to the hospital, something like that, and Madhu's brother would peel out a note from his wallet and give it to her without looking at her. Then one day, without notice, she left.

Padma was looking down at her with such an agonized expression that she said, "Arre, what is the matter with *you*, what are you thinking of?"

"About her."

"About *her*? What is there to think about that haraam zaadi woman?"

"How long was she with you?"

"What do I know. Three months, four months . . . just left suddenly, warning also she didn't give . . . arre, why are you looking like *that*?" Padma shook her head as though she couldn't speak. "Too much you are, Padma," Madhu said, and now the rage was building up in her. "Like a bitch she behaved, my brothers didn't force her, they are not like that, money also they gave her whenever she wanted. Ha!" she snorted.

"Stop it Madhu." Her words were almost incoherent. *"Stop it."*

Madhu's body jerked.

"*Think* about what you're saying, just *think* about what you're saying."

"Padma," Madhu whispered, for some reason her voice wouldn't come out louder, "she wasn't like us, she was a servant, those people they can keep doing it."

"She left because she was *pregnant*," Padma panted.

How dare she. How *dare* she. Madhu had to clench her hands in her lap to stop them from trembling. She said, "You are talking about my brothers." Padma looked at her, her eyes still. Finished, Madhu thought despairingly, Our friendship is finished. For a long time neither spoke. Then Madhu muttered something, got up and left.

She wasn't able to sleep that night. How dare Padma, how dare she. Why *now*, why so judgmental *now*? Other things she, Madhu, had also told her, *then* Padma had been wide-eyed and listened without comment. "Imagine, this army officer's daughter, she got pregnant by the orderly. Then she killed herself. Not only that, Padma, my other sister-in-law she knows two cases of orderlies doing it to girl children." Padma had shuddered most satisfyingly. *Then* Padma had had no comments to make.

Madhu tossed in bed this way and that. It was past midnight when He came to the room after some business meeting, and then *He* wanted it and she had to push him away. "Oho, what is the matter," He muttered, trying to climb over her again and she pushed him off again. He made a sound of irritation and went back to his bed. Nothing made a difference to Them. Good mood, bad mood, good day, bad day, fight with wife, no fight with wife, nothing made a difference; they were ready to do it whenever. For her, if even something small was bothering her, then she wasn't in the mood. "For this if you wait for mood then nothing will ever happen," he had told her once.

She had been trying to comfort Padma, trying to make her laugh, and Padma had turned upon her. She felt as though her world was tearing apart. No more talks with Padma, no more confidences, no more laughter. The pain was so deep that she couldn't even cry. The thing was that Padma's own experiences had made her vulnerable. She transferred her pain to every other woman. She had done it with Mrs. Moitra. She had done it now with this haraam zaadi woman. Because her husband had died leaving her almost destitute, because her in-laws had nothing to do with her, because her father and brother had abandoned her, she blamed men for everything.

What would she tell Anu? How could the three of them continue as before? The children would notice. They wouldn't stop playing with each other. Every day she would be seeing her. Then He would ask questions. What could she tell Him? What could she make up that would fit His perception of Padma? To Anu, of course, she would tell the truth. Anu would say, Your brothers did *that*? She would say, *All three*? She would say, *Every day*? After that how could she explain to Anu that Padma shouldn't have said that terrible thing about her brothers. How could she say that these things happened all the time especially amongst the servant classes, haraam zaadi kuthi—the girl knew what she was doing, why should her brothers refuse what was so readily available? Maybe Anu would say, You are right, Madhu, whatever Padma might have felt, she should not have said it. Then Anu would say, Remember what you told me that day about Padma's husband? Madhu, think of that and forget this misunderstanding.

The anger was gone. She was filled with such remorse that if she could, she would have got out of bed and gone running to Padma's house. It was too late for that, almost two at night, or rather, in the morning. First thing tomorrow. Thank God all her bad feelings were gone, thank God. She had Mahima to thank for this, her doll. If Mahima hadn't shown her the photo that day, then she wouldn't have known and if she hadn't known she would still have been angry.

That day in the afternoon Mahima had come running home from Mallika's house and panting, had taken out a photo from underneath her frock, thrust it before her and said, "Quickly, Mummy, quickly look at it, then I will take it back, Mallika doesn't know, she and Prabha are reading in her room." Madhu had taken the photo from her hand and then she had felt her head reeling. Impossible. *Impossible*. No wonder. *No wonder.* She gazed at it, at this young, lovely girl and the young, handsome man with such chiseled features. She wasn't looking at him but at the camera, the look that should have been directed at him was directed outwards. She swallowed. "Mummy, Mummy," Mahima was tugging at her saree, "I have to take it back, hurry." Madhu gave it one more look and returned it to Mahima. She said automatically, "Never take anything from Mallika's house again, all right?" "All right, Mummy," Mahima said. She tucked the photo back under her frock and flew back to Mallika's house.

What a small world it was. That day it had fallen into place. Bechari. What a secret to carry, what a secret to hide from her own child. No wonder she didn't ever talk about Him. She would tell Anu. Together they would take all the separate pieces and put them together.

First she would tell Anu, Something I have found out about Padma's past, Anu. I am so shocked, I just do not believe it.

Accha? Anu would say, wide-eyed, what is it?

What to say, Madhu would reply, how to say. She would pause, reflect, shake her head, then say, Life is very strange, Anu—this is such a small world.

Why do you say that? Anu would ask.

There is a reason for everything to happen, Madhu would say, but the question is, what is this reason?

Anu would exclaim, Tell, Madhu, tell.

Madhu would look at her unflinchingly, she would say what she had to say without preliminaries, in one breath she would say, *Anu, Padma's husband is alive.*

How shocked Anu would be. Stunned. Speechless. They would look at each other for a long time. Then Madhu would say, Mahima showed me a photograph which Mallika has. They were both in it. Oh, Anu, seeing it I almost fainted, I said to myself, Is it Him? It cannot be, it cannot be.

Whom, whom? Anu would ask, agitated.

This man in the photo, Madhu would say to Anu, I have met him. I have talked to him.

No, Anu would say.

Yes, she would say. Ditto same man, older yes, but same, same features, same way of looking, still slim, still thick hair, features like a prince, ditto, Anu, ditto.

Where? Anu would ask, where?

In Cottage Industries Emporium, Madhu would reply. Next to him only I was standing, he was looking at ties, I was looking at ties for Him.

I couldn't decide which to buy so I said to him, I am choosing a tie for my husband's birthday, if you do not mind, please tell me, is this better or is this better? Anu, normally I do not talk like this to strange men, you only know. But on this man's face it was written—honest man, good heart. He said, How about this, and he took out another tie and showed it to me. All right, I said to him, thank you very much. He smiled, so sweetly, Anu, and he said, My pleasure. As I was going out I thought, how nicely this man spoke to me, such a gentleman, such nice English, just like an Englishman.

Hai Ram, Anu would say, looking agitated, Are you sure?

One hundred and one percent I am sure, Madhu would reply, two hundred percent I am sure.

Then the best part would begin. Always I have asked myself, Madhu would say, why she never speaks about Him? Now I have the answer—because he is not dead but alive. Remember, once I was telling you her reaction to Mrs. Moitra's story? Now I understand, Anu. Naturally Padma sympathizes with her, Padma is almost in the same situation. For some reason, who knows, they must have had a divorce, and Padma she must have thought, I will make a clean break, I will go away where he can never find me. She gets custody of Mallika and she comes to Delhi.

But Madhu, Anu would say, why doesn't he visit his own child?

Anu, Anu, Madhu would exclaim, maybe she is divorced, or maybe she is not. But what is certain is that she was pregnant when she left him and he did not know. And she doesn't tell him, because she thinks, I will not let him take away my child. So then she goes to Shanta and has her baby there, and then gets a job here in Delhi.

Anu would nod slowly. Anu would say, So she told everyone the story about her husband being dead, and she keeps the name of her father and not of her husband so that no one will know her husband's name either, so even if her husband looks for her he cannot find her.

Madhu would nod and say, That is why she never ever lets Mallika open the door of the house, even in the morning, even in afternoon when she knows it is either Mahima or Prabha, it is because she is frightened that maybe, just maybe, he has found out about Mallika and wants to take her away.

Madhu and Anu would stare at each other in horror. Never. Never, never, never. They would protect Padma from this, they would not allow it to happen.

After some time Anu would say, But Madhu, he could not be a nice man, this man, otherwise why are he and Padma separated?

That is the thing, Madhu would reply, her brows furrowed, that is the only thing I do not understand. She would shake her head and say, So nicely he said, My pleasure. Just like that. My pleasure.

Anu would toss her head and say pungently, Men are very different with wives and very different with other people.

That also is true, Madhu would reply. She would pause, then say, Difficult to think, Anu. He does not look as if he drinks. Nor [shuddering] like a man who beats his wife.

Anu would exclaim, Do not say such things.

Madhu would sigh and say, And anyway, for this reason no sensible woman will leave her husband.

He does not know that Padma is in Delhi, Anu would say ominously.

And she also does not know he is in Delhi, Madhu would reply more ominously.

Maybe he does not live in Delhi, maybe he was just in Delhi for work, Anu would say. Anu would then think deeply.

If she left him, Anu would say firmly, then He must be a very Bad Man.

Madhu would look at Anu in amusement and say, You always think Padma has no faults at all.

Anu would laugh, toss her head and say, If she left him, then it has to be for a very good reason.

Then after some time Anu would ask, Why are her parents and brother still not talking to her?

Hmm, Madhu would say thinking. Some of the story Shanta told us must be true, no? Probably it was a love-marriage, both parents were against it, then they ran away and got married, then she leaves him, and she thinks, how can I go back to my parents now? Then she finds out she is expecting a baby . . . then her brother who knows whole story says I will adopt the baby and Padma says no, then they fight, and after that . . . after that we know the story.

They would look at each other and the same thought would pass through both their minds—that they would guard this secret with their lives.

Haii! Madhu would exclaim suddenly. If Mallika meets him by mistake, then?

Anu would shake her hands and her head in revulsion—No, no, never.

Sadly Madhu would declare, Poor Mallika. She loves him.

Madhu would want to tell Anu something else. She would want to tell her, Accha, Anu, remember once you told me, At least Padma knows what it is to be loved?

Of course, Madhu's actual talk with Anu hadn't turned out anything like her fantasy. Anu's response to her revelation had been neither one of astonishment nor scepticism. It had been indifferent. Vague acchas. Vaguer it-could-have-been-someone-else. Anu had been unusually harried about the cooking and housework, Mataji's remarks seemed to have been making their mark that day. She had been too preoccupied with all that to pay attention to what Madhu was saying. But somewhere, something must have sunk in, otherwise why had she asked Madhu not to mention it to Padma. As if she would! Who did Anu think she was?

Madhu had thought, later when Anu is less busy then I will talk about it again. But somehow, the occasion had never come up. Once when she had mentioned it Anu had said vaguely, "Who knows, people look alike."

Now, falling asleep, Madhu's last thoughts were, tomorrow I will go to Padma's house and make up. Padma will never hold anything against me. Little bit of awkwardness there will be at first, then everything will be all right.

It didn't sound that simple in the morning. She had thought of going early in the morning before Padma left for her college. But she found herself taking longer to get the children ready for school and the children were fussier than usual about breakfast. The day dragged. She couldn't concentrate on anything. After all, Padma too could have come. Maybe Padma didn't want to make up. She still hadn't forgiven her brother, maybe she would never forgive Madhu. And if she didn't then why should she, Madhu, humble herself by cringing and crawling when actually it wasn't her fault at all?

The doorbell rang. When she opened it her classmate Gayatri was standing there, beaming. "Didi," Gayatri said, entering, laughing, hugging her till it hurt. "First division, didi, you've got a first division, you've come third in the university."

Madhu blinked a few times. Gayatri was still there. "You are sure?"

"See, this is your roll number, no?"

Madhu looked at it. It was. "I do not believe it," Madhu said weakly. "Are you sure?"

"Didi," Gayatri said, "as sure as I am that your name is Madhu Nanda.

I told my mummy, I also have a first division and that is only because Madhu didi explained everything to me so patiently, every day in the library she helped me. Arre, didi, why are you crying, don't cry, don't cry."

This then was happiness, this odd, tremulous feeling. After Gayatri left she had continued to sit on the sofa, unable to think—strange sensations rising and falling inside her—unable to stop smiling. How happy Padma would be. How happy Anu would be.

Why didn't you tell us, Madhu, Padma would ask, her face glowing, For one whole year you didn't tell us?

Chupa rustam you are, Anu would say, Why did you hide it from us?

How ashamed she had felt when she began her B.A. Children her classmates were, sixteen, seventeen . . . sometimes they called her Aunty. If only she hadn't put on so much weight. That was what she thought every single day when she went for her classes. It had happened so gradually, she hadn't even noticed it. How awful she looked next to the other girls, all of them so slim and graceful. She had been like that once. And it wasn't even as if she loved to eat, she didn't. But she ate all the time. She had been so thin at the time she got married that her mother-in-law had said she looked like a shrivelled up old woman. Now her mother-in-law said she looked like a buffalo.

Padma, she would say, I thought, let everyone think I am wandering around as usual. But, Padma, always, on the days I did not have classes in the afternoon I used to come back to give my children their lunch. Padma would look guilty and Madhu would say, My B.A., She-A, everything it is secondary, my children they come first. She would add, meaningfully, I did not read at all, no magazines, no Mills and Boons, nothing.

What was His reaction? Padma would ask.

She would say, Padma, he is so proud of me, so much he encourages me, he has always wanted me to finish my degree, now he says, you must do your M.A.

Madhu was feeding the children lunch when Padma came. Straight from the bus stop she came, Madhu could see her folding her umbrella at the veranda, then entering the open door. "It's so hot outside, Madhu," Padma said, wiping her upper lip with the back of her hand.

"Arre, come and sit, come and have lunch with us," Madhu said, her heart beating very fast. She called for the servant to lay another place. "Here," she said, filling a glass with cold water and giving it to Padma who was now sitting opposite them.

Padma drank thirstily, then put the glass down on the table, looked at Madhu, her eyes full of misery and burst out, "Madhu, I'm sorry, forgive me."

Madhu got up and came across to where she sat, Padma rose from her chair, they hugged each other wordlessly. Padma said indistinctly, "Don't think badly of me, Madhu, please don't think badly of me."

Madhu released her, knowing what she would find on Padma's face and it was there, the expression that she now knew as well as her children's, and she said, "No more talking about it, it is over, finished."

Padma said, almost pleadingly, "You're not angry with me, Madhu?"

"No, no, never, never. Do not say sorry-vorry again, Padma, do not say it."

And Padma, who had opened her mouth to say just that, closed it. Then she said, "Madhu, Mallika is waiting for me, don't bother about lunch."

"What are you saying," Madhu scolded, "wait." She went outside, walked briskly to Padma's house and rang the bell. Ayaji peeped out of the window and scowled. "Memsahib and Mallika are eating with us today," she told Ayaji, "call Mallika." She heard Ayaji's footsteps shuffling towards the door. Then the door opened, Mallika ran out, smiling, Ayaji scowled even more fiercely and said, "And what will happen to the lunch I have made?"

"That you will have for dinner," Madhu said, "come, Mallika."

They walked together to her house.

First they would eat lunch. After they ate, she would take out the box of kaju ki barfi, hold it unopened in front of Padma and say to Padma, Here.

Padma would take the box, put it on the table, then open it. She would gaze at all the barfis, take the largest, then close the box.

Then as Padma took the first bite of the barfi, Madhu would say, Arre, not one, this whole box is for you.

Padma's eyes would widen, she would say, What is the occasion, Madhu?

Then, she would tell Padma.

# ANURADHA

 It was the early mornings she liked best, especially in the winters when it would still be dark at five, and the bird sounds would waft in through the windows. No one got up before six-thirty, so that was an hour and a half to herself, the time not only to get things done as she always told them, but the time for indulgence. Half an hour for indulgence, then one hour to get things done, and that also was an indulgence in a house so quiet and dark. She was bathed and ready in fifteen minutes, and then she would go to the front lawn with a thali and there they were, waiting for her, white and fragrant in the early morning darkness. She would pick the jasmine one by one till they filled her steel plate, and as the darkness slowly dissipated, her thoughts unfurled and expanded. Now, it didn't matter if her head was uncovered; now, if her hurriedly combed hair descended from the confines of its bun, no one saw. Sometimes in the winter when the darkness kept its secrets, she would pull the two pins out of her hair and feel it descend heavy and warm against her neck and waist, merging into the blackness of her shawl. She would put the two pins in the plate among the flowers and walk slowly around the lawn, feeling her hair move softly against her ears. Then, as the sky lightened, she would walk to the veranda and pick up the needle and thread which lay on the table, and make herself her gajara. It didn't take long, just a few minutes, then she twisted her hair back to its usual bun, thrust the pins in and wound the flowers around it. The morning sounds were beginning now, the thud thud of the newspaper boy throwing the paper, the milkman making his rounds on his cycle, dogs barking as they were taken for their walks. She would take the milk from the milkman and go in to the kitchen, pour it into the large vessel and place it on the gas.

Then she would take the small vessel, pour a glass of water in it, a little milk, and cover it. The tea would be ready in two minutes flat, she would spoon in one and a half spoons of sugar, her morning extravagance, and go to the dining room and sit near the window, open the newspaper, and sipping her hot tea, hot as it never would be later, with relish as she never could later, she would open the English newspaper and slowly begin to read.

They bought two newspapers, English and Hindi, an extravagance no one else indulged in. But Mataji had insisted, she couldn't read English and the radio didn't give enough news. In the beginning Anu too read the Hindi paper. But that had changed a few years after Padma had come to the colony. Padma could speak and write Hindi, but her grammar was worse than terrible. One day when Padma was talking to her in the kitchen she mentioned how difficult it would be for her to tutor Mallika in Hindi as she grew older, because of her grammar. "Arre, I can teach you," Anu had replied, surprised that Padma hadn't asked her. And Padma had looked at her as if Anu had saved her from drowning.

So Anu had taught Padma her Hindi grammar so that Padma could then tutor Mallika. She was terrible at languages, Padma had told Anu. "I wish I had taken after Amma—she can speak Kannada, Hindi and English fluently." Anu marvelled, "All that your mother learnt in school?" Padma shook her head, "No, on her own. During Appa's postings in the North she picked up Hindi faster than my sister or brother or I, and imagine, this when she never learnt Hindi in school."

Anu hadn't known then that she would end up learning English. She was terrified of speaking English, her grammar too was all wrong, she could hardly put a coherent sentence together. Already Prabha was speaking it better than her. And when she read English she had to read each word first, one word after another, come to the end of the sentence and then try to understand what the sentence meant, unlike Hindi, where the sentence sprang out at her almost without her reading it. One day when she was teaching Padma her Hindi grammar she had sighed and said that when Prabha and Mahima and Mallika spoke to each other in English she felt ashamed that she couldn't speak even half as well as they did, and they were only five years old. Then Padma said, "Oh Anu, I'll help you with that, please let me," as though she, Anu, would be doing Padma a favour by learning English from her. So after that, during their morning sessions, Padma also taught her. It was Anu's idea, a short time later, that she should speak to Padma only in English and Padma should speak to her only in Hindi, that way they would both learn faster. It worked wonderfully. "Don't tell anyone you're teaching me English," Anu had said. "All right," Padma had replied without asking why. So she told Padma, "Mataji will think I am giving myself too much importance."

They had spent so many hours laughing at each other that it was a wonder that they had learnt anything at all. Every other morning from five-thirty to six-thirty, which was when they taught each other, they discovered each other. As they talked, Anu in her broken English and Padma in her awful Hindi, they found themselves talking about each other. There was so much to talk about with Padma. Not just the big things but the smaller ones, which in talking became suddenly bigger. Strange, how so much could be communicated in alien languages—she telling Padma all about her early married days and Mataji, about her parents, brothers and sisters, all this in faltering English; Padma telling her all about her own family and how she had lost them too, and a few times, even about Mallika's father, but in an oblique way, mentioning that he too liked to read, that he was brilliant in his studies and loved music. Once she said that Mallika had taken after her father in temperament, not her, but she said it in a matter-of-fact way. Anu waited for her to say what Mallika's father was like in temperament but Padma didn't.

The strangest discovery was how unlike Padma was from what Anu had imagined. "When I first began to teach," Padma told her, "I was so scared that I couldn't sleep at night for months."

*"You?"* Anu exclaimed. "Scared of what, Padma?"

"I had no confidence. Even now, there are so many people who know so much more."

"More?"

"More about my subject than I do. More about the literature of other countries."

She could hardly believe what she was hearing, hardly believe the expression she saw on Padma's face, so full of diffidence. Anu began to laugh. "Padma, this job you got without any problem, position you got in the university, so much you read, and then you say these things?"

Padma said, "My brother and . . . Mallika's father . . . neither of them had degrees in literature, and they both knew so much more than me."

And everyone in the neighbourhood—she, Anu, included—thinking, so self-possessed and confident this Padma is.

"Where do *you* have the time to teach her?" Mataji had asked Anu scornfully, "so much time you spend doing God knows what in the kitchen, what you do in four hours I could do in two, and you want to teach her Hindi."

So Anu told Him in Mataji's presence what she was going to do hence-forth in the early mornings—tutor Padma in Hindi, and of course, as expected He said, "Accha, very good," and went back to playing with Prabha. So after that Mataji couldn't say anything directly to her though there were plenty of indirect comments when he wasn't around and had Mataji known Anu was learning *English,* there would have been plenty more.

It had been so easy, so natural, so unexpected. Earlier, while she had always liked and trusted Padma, she had always been conscious of a sense of her own inadequacy. Padma seemed so certain of herself, so well dressed, a working woman with no one to account to, she spoke so well and seemed so self-possessed. Not at all, as Mataji said, like a widow. But, Anu discovered to her astonishment, she was not like that at all. It was all . . . not an act, no not an act, Padma was no actress. It was just what everyone assumed from what they saw of Padma. And they envied Madhu, these people who only saw her rich husband and two sons and two houses and her fair, lovely daughter, her expensive sarees and jewellery, all the things that Madhu herself flaunted. And when they saw her, Anu, they all assumed that she was such a cheerful, happy person.

The truth was, you showed that much of yourself which it was easy to show, and what you showed wasn't the whole thing. The rest, like an ice-berg, lay underneath, and the tip, which was what you saw, made the rest a lie.

The tip she, Anu, showed was a smiling tip, as much part of her as that grim, unseen portion. It was no act, her laughter, there was so much that was amusing in life, one just had to focus on that. Life was comical, more comical than films; when she focused on a particular scene and blanked out the rest, then she could see the scene in a way no one else saw it. She, Anu, was the camerawoman whose focus was different; it gave life quite another twist and her laughter was real.

Once, during their days of teaching each other, she and Padma had talked about Mrs. Moitra. "Mrs. Sahani was laughing about her," Anu said, "so angry I felt, I wanted to tell her, If your child is taken away from you forever then I would like to see you laugh."

"Anu, whenever I think of her I say to myself, God has blessed me."

Hai Ram, Anu thought guiltily, this is what I say to myself when I think about you.

"Were you very shocked when you came to know?"

"What else." Anu suddenly went into peals of laughter. "Padma, about That Thing itself I knew nothing, I used to think the marriage ceremony produced babies!" She couldn't stop laughing.

"Anu, I admire you, you're so . . . you laugh all the time."

"If I don't laugh then I'll cry. Better to laugh, no?" Then, seeing Padma's face she had said, "One has to live, no? Better to do it one day at a time."

"You're talking as if someone has died."

Anu tossed her head, "What else!"

At least when you died and were reborn you thankfully never remembered your past life. But in this life there was no forgetting the Life Before. Now she understood why mothers wept so much when their daughters got married; it had less to do with sentiment and more to do with knowledge. The sentiment belonged to their fathers. When Mataji talked about this birth and the previous birth and the next birth and karmas and having to bear it, it made her want to laugh again. "Previous life, this life, next life," she told Padma. "What difference does it make? What do I care about what happened in my last birth, for what I am suffering in this birth, what will happen in my next birth? Living I have to do in this life. Bas, I want to live happily."

Like anything else, laughter too had to be learnt. The other laughter, the kind that had always been so much part of her nature, that wasn't enough. Once there had been joy in the smallest things, laughter had risen and bubbled out of her as naturally as a mountain spring. Then later she had realized it had to be sought. This is your life now, she told herself. As much happiness as you can get out of it, get, there is no other place to get it from. Bas, it worked. And what joy there was in not letting Mataji get the better of her the way she had the first year of her marriage. It had worked so well that a year after her marriage Mataji had snapped at her one morning, "At least early in the morning show a little bit of restraint when you smile—all her teeth she shows as if she is advertising for toothpaste." She can't bear it, Anu thought joyfully, she can't bear it!

Once, when Anirudh was five, they had been summoned to Anirudh's school. There they were shown Anirudh's report card. At the bottom, in the line for parents' signatures, Anirudh had signed, in a handwriting quite unlike his own, *Mummy.*

Later, after all the commotion died down, Anirudh asked her what her name was.

"Anuradha," she said, laughing.

Mataji snorted. "Your mother's name is Sumati."

"No," Anirudh said triumphantly, "Mumma's name is Bahurani."

Anu explained to Anirudh, "My parents, they named me Anuradha. After I got married your grandmother named me Sumati."

"Then what is your real name, Mumma?"

"Anirudh beta, I don't have a real name." Struck, she began to laugh.

"Madhu Aunty and Padma Aunty call you Anu, Mumma."

"Then, beta, for them that is my real name." She couldn't stop laughing.

"But Dadima calls you Bahurani," Anirudh said, "and Kamala Bua calls you Bhabi."

"For them my real name is Bahurani and Bhabi."

"And Daddy, he doesn't call you anything."

"What he does not call me, that is my real name too." Now she was laughing so hard that her stomach hurt.

"Sumati your mother's name is, Sumati it will always be. Saying it is something else, will not make it something else," Mataji snapped.

"Bilkul Mataji, bilkul," she replied, wiping her eyes, "what you are saying, it is true, saying it is something else, will not make it something else."

And that belief had kept her, Anuradha, intact.

Now she didn't even hear what Mataji said, she had learnt to shut off her mother-in-law's sounds with the same ability as He shut off everything when He read the newspaper. She had learnt to sing in the kitchen as she cooked. That gave her happiness. Her children gave her plenty of it, especially Anirudh. "Such a loveable, loving child I have never in my life seen," Mataji was fond of saying, "*just* like my older daughter he is." Madhu would nudge Anu every time she heard this, her eyes dancing. "And Prabha," Mataji would say, "*just* like my son, so sidha-sadha, so bhola-bhala, such a strong mind." Then Madhu would give Anu another nudge. Madhu, who had so little laughter in her, was an expert in making other people laugh, just watching her expression and hearing her asides were enough to make Anu giggle helplessly.

It was peculiar how thin the line was between laughter and tears. A woman's lot . . . her mother had always spoken philosophically about a woman's lot—that was the strangest thing of all. There was no understanding it. Sometimes when she was arguing with Him, He would say, "Arre, Bhai, two and two do not make five, do not imagine things," and she would get so infuriated that she could never explain what she meant. He never lost his temper, that was the problem, and with him she was always losing hers, not about the things she should have got angry and shouted about, but about other things, little things, things that she needn't have brought up, while the bigger things remained unspoken to all but Padma and Madhu. In her imaginary conversations with him, she could tell him what was in her mind. In her imaginary conversations with him she understood herself, was able to find the words for all that agitated, amorphous mass inside her. She could say, See, this is two, this is two, and two and two equals four. She could say it calmly, logically. And He, on hearing her in their imaginary conversations, would understand and be filled with consternation and remorse. She talked to him as she worked in the kitchen, and in these talks there was satisfaction because he lost his habitual calm. True, there were times when He had lost his habitual calm in real life, but this was because he was incredulous, whereas in her imagination, it was because he believed her. But in the real world that she inhabited she would find herself exclaiming in frustration, "You just don't understand me." Once, he asked her, patient as ever, "Do you understand yourself?"

Who did. Did he? No she didn't understand herself, but at least she understood others, at least she understood Him. When she was pregnant with Prabha she had told him, "I want to change my doctor, I want a woman gynecologist," he had sighed and replied, "This is only a doctor, what is there to be shy about?" How to explain to him what she could hardly bring herself to say aloud even to herself? How could she wail, How was I to know what an examination is, I thought he would check my heartbeat and feel my pulse. She wanted to say, Nothing I knew when I got married, how can you ever understand what that means? They were also part of marriage, These Things, but you could never talk about them, not to your mother, not to your daughter, not to your friend, never to your husband. For a long time you didn't even think about it, in so many words, even though it was there in your mind, loose, amorphous, damaged.

The gynecologist was the second man before whom she had lain with her saree hitched above her waist, that white piece of cloth protecting her from what he could see so clearly, her legs apart, and he wasn't even her husband, he didn't even have the right. When she protested to the nurse, the nurse laughed, not very nicely and said, "*Now* feeling shy won't help," and then the gynecologist had come in. A little reassurance, that's all she had wanted, a little understanding, a little comfort. He had tried to examine her, and she had felt the tears heavy behind her eyes. "Open your mouth," she heard him say in Hindi, and obediently, she opened her mouth. There was a silence, the nurse began to giggle. He said, "Here, not there."

She had never gone back. The new doctor was a woman, Dr. Bhattacharya. It meant going a longer distance for her monthly checkups, but she was a woman. She was reassuring, understanding, comforting. She chatted about this and that while examining her, asked about her husband, her parents, her mother-in-law. "Go and have your baby in your mother's house," she told her, "you need to rest and be looked after for a change, I'll recommend a gynecologist for you at Lucknow." She had told Dr. Bhattacharya it was impossible, that the first child—and Mataji was sure it would be a boy—had to be born in His house. The doctor had sighed and said, "Accha."

When it was time to go, Dr. Bhattacharya had accompanied Anu to the reception, where He was waiting, and said to him, "Look after her, see to it that she has plenty of rest, otherwise she may miscarry the child." Anu's eyes had widened in disbelief and the doctor gave her a warning look. "She has to stay in bed for a couple of months," she said sternly to Him, "no cooking or housework, and special, nutritious food has to be cooked for her."

Pale, He had nodded and said, "My mother will take care of her."

The doctor had said, "My suggestion is that you take her to Lucknow and leave her with her mother till the baby is born. No woman can rest properly in her own house." He had nodded wordlessly.

Back home he had told her to go to bed and told Mataji what the doctor had said. Mataji shook her head. "Poor, poor, Bahurani," she sighed, "beti, you rest now, just now you get into bed."

He sat next to her after she lay down, looking troubled and said, "Now don't work, try and sleep, Mataji will take care of you like a daughter."

Briefly, his hand stroked her forehead, and there was so much tenderness in his touch that for many years afterwards, she had held on to this gesture, which he had never made again. Stay, she wanted to say, stay with me for just ten minutes before you go to office. He looked at his watch and got up. "I have to go now, you try and sleep." She had closed her eyes and when she next got up it was four in the evening, she had slept for four hours. She turned in her bed and looked out of the window, she felt the unaccustomed languor in her limbs, the softness of the old bedsheet around her body. There were no thoughts in her head, there was no past, no future, just the present, just the sun bright on the tree outside her window and the sound of the crows, just the shouts of the children playing pithoo in the houses nearby, and the feel of the pillow next to her cheek and the knowledge of being able to lie like this.

She heard the rustle of curtains and Mataji entered. "Arre, Bahurani," she said, "He will come home in two hours, and I was thinking, there is nothing for dinner?"

Mataji didn't know where the spices were kept. Or the dals and rice. And where were the onions and garlic? Anu showed her. Slowly Mataji took out the tins of dal and rice and bottles of spices, then she stopped and groaned and said, "I don't know why, my hands they hurt so much, never mind, I can bear it, it doesn't matter."

"I'll help you, Mataji."

A little later, as Mataji sighed and muttered, lifting one vessel, then another, Anu said, "Let it be, Mataji, I will do it."

"Can you do it, beti?" Mataji asked sadly.

"Yes, yes, you don't strain yourself," Anu said.

Every day after that she had waited for him to ask but he didn't. He assumed that Mataji had cooked all the meals and cleaned all the dishes and it didn't occur to her to tell him otherwise. Because she now slept every afternoon, he thought she spent the whole day in bed. Every day when he came back from work, Mataji would make tea for all of them, and as they had it she would ask, "Bahurani, did you sleep well?" And Anu would nod and Mataji would smile tenderly. And Mataji would serve the food that Anu had already cooked for dinner and clear the dishes, and Anu would wash the dishes while he sat in the sitting room, reading the paper. What did he think she did in the kitchen, she wondered. But of course, he didn't think of kitchens and what happened within them or where she could be, since she had never sat with him there after dinner, these were not thoughts that came to him. He didn't think.

Then one day Anu went to her corner on the mantelpiece where the idols of the Gods were placed, and she prayed. "Let me have a miscarriage, God," she prayed, "let it all come out. Then he'll know." It had been a terrible thing to ask for but she had wanted it so fiercely that there was no other thought in her head. That night she had begun to bleed, He had rushed her to the hospital. She remembered his face, white and pinched, remembered her own satisfaction at seeing it. After a week her other wish had come true, He had taken her to Lucknow to her mother. The baby survived; Prabha was born five months later in her mother's house and when she came back to Delhi Madhu had got everything ready for her and the baby—Mahima's cradle, sheets, clothes, bottles and new, soft nappies, almond oil, plus an entire new set of frocks that she had made and embroidered herself, and new sweaters and booties that she had knitted herself. Also two large tins of pinne ka laddoos that she had made, "*Only* for you," Madhu said. "*Not* for Mataji or Kamala." She had looked at Anu's tired face and picked up the tins of laddoos. "I know you," she said, "by tomorrow that Mataji of yours will have finished one tin. I will take it home and get you every day." And every day for the next two months, Madhu had come over in the afternoons when everyone was resting, two laddoos folded in her handkerchief, and fed them to Anu in her bed, watching her with vicarious pleasure.

And the purpose behind what Anu had asked God, the whole drama hadn't even achieved that—his knowledge of his mother's perfidy. "You have no one to blame but yourself," he had said after she came back from the hospital, "why did you work when I told you not to? Was work more important than the baby?" She told him then about Mataji and he said, "You are mistaken, in your state of mind, as usual you are imagining all sorts of things, she would never expect you to strain yourself in this condition, she too is a woman, she too has been through all this." Later, she heard Him asking his mother, "Mataji, why did she do all that work?" Anu heard her reply, her voice heavy, "What do I know, beta? I *told* Bahurani, so many times I told her, beti, rest, please rest, but no, she wouldn't listen. Mataji sighed loudly. "Her house it is, beta, she likes to do things her way. Who am I to say anything?"

For the first time she had seen him angry, but like the rest of him, even his anger was controlled. "What has happened has happened," he said to Anu, "it cannot be undone. But you have hurt my mother's feelings, you have made her feel that she isn't part of this house. She is a woman of great sensitivity. If she feels her help isn't wanted she will be the last person to force you to accept help. How can she help you if she doesn't feel part of this house?"

"You don't understand," Anu said helplessly.

"*You* don't understand," he said. "If you want to go to your mother, then I'll take you. But think about it a little, my mother loves you like a daughter, and if you don't give her the love that you give your own mother, you cannot expect her to do for you what your mother does for you." He had gone to the railway station and bought two tickets for the train that would take them to Lucknow the next day.

"First class tickets, that also," Mataji marvelled, "so much he spoils you, Bahurani."

Anu had wept so bitterly that night that at last he had turned to her and said, "What will crying get you, don't cry." She waited for him to put his arms around her and when he did she began crying again in relief. "Don't be angry with me," she cried, and he whispered, "I'm not angry with you, enough, enough, don't cry." Tentatively, she put her wet cheek against his and he rubbed his cheek against her, his hand going under her arm and around her waist. She clung to him as he wiped the tears from her cheek, wanting more but not asking, she never asked, this wanting had to be contained just like all the other things. This he had to want before it could happen, this there was no initiating. What was wrong with her, she had almost lost the baby, she had just returned from the hospital, she was more than four months pregnant, and this was all she could think of? She waited, her head on his shoulder, willing him to come closer, suddenly she knew he wanted it too. Gently he removed his hands, moving away from her slightly, and closed his eyes.

When she got married she had not known that such a thing existed. Was she the only one? Had others—her sisters, Padma, Madhu—been as ignorant about what happened between men and women? That babies came into this world she had thought was the natural consequence of the marriage ceremony, the blessings of the pandit. And he, so ignorant of everything else, had instinctively comprehended her terrible innocence, had smiled at her that first night and told her, as if she were a child, to go to sleep. She had done so, her whole body flushed with embarrassment to be sleeping so close to a man she had only met once before in her parents' sitting room. And so they had slept chastely side by side for three months. They had come straight to Delhi after the wedding, he had to get back to his job. His parents continued living in their house in Lucknow with Kamala, who was still in school. Marriage was a joy. The money wasn't much but enough, cooking took an hour, cleaning even less since she had always been tidy, a bai came in to wash the dishes and do the sweeping and swabbing. Anu planted flowers in the garden and embroidered hankies for her younger sister, dabbled in a little painting, put flowers in every room, even, to his amusement, in the bathroom. In the mornings she would practice her singing for two hours, playing the harmonium that her parents had given her. "Such a beautiful voice you have," Madhu used to say every time. Madhu was pregnant with Mahima those days, and she would drop in at Anu's house or Anu would drop in at hers. Sometimes they would have lunch together, and often, after the boys went to sleep in the afternoon, Madhu would come to her house and they would lie down in the bedroom, side by side, chatting and giggling. Madhu told her about Mrs. Moitra, who got drunk in her own house and once or twice was seen staggering on the lawn, spouting some English poetry. "There are all kinds of people in this world," Madhu said to her, watching her dazed expression with satisfaction. Once, when she was on the point of falling asleep, Madhu said, "What husbands and wives do, that some girls do without marriage." All Anu's sleep vanished, her eyes opened wide, and Madhu told her about a woman she knew in the town where her brother lived who lived on her own and A Man came and spent the night with her every once in a while. "It cannot be," Anu said. "You are a fool," Madhu said. They would fall asleep finally, and when they got up Anu would make them tea and after drinking it Madhu would leave.

Then she would wait for him to come home. She remembered those evenings, how the hours seemed to drag, and his smile for her when she opened the door. Sometimes they would go for a film in the evenings, often they would go for walks and she would chatter happily with him, telling him all about her parents, her sisters, her brothers, her cousins, her friends. He had always been quiet, but she knew he liked to listen to her even when he wasn't always listening to what she was saying, that he liked the sound of her voice and the rhythm of her talk. She liked best the nights when they lay together, side by side, he lying down on his back, she on her side facing him, sometimes quiet, sometimes talking. She would ask him about his family and his college days and his childhood and he would laugh and tell her, all too briefly. Sometimes he fell asleep even as she talked and she watched his sleeping face, wanting to touch it.

It had not been his intent to woo her. But instinctively, everything he had done or not done had been right, and she unknowing, had begun to feel for him a tenderness that was the beginning of love. His own unspoken tenderness nurtured it. Her need to touch him was there long before he touched her, a need so entwined in her growing love for him that one day when she found herself sleeping curled around his back, her arm around him, it seemed perfectly natural. "Such a nice sleep I had," she told him as she pleated her saree in the bedroom, and he said, suddenly laughing, "I did not." "Why?" she asked, full of concern, watching him as he sat on the bed putting on his shoes and he smiled and shook his head.

What followed in a few days was inevitable. He turned to her, she found there was more to this business of hugging than she had imagined, she discovered a strange longing and hunger, but even that didn't prepare her for the shock of what followed. She had cried so much that first time that for days afterwards he hadn't touched her. She wanted to tell him that his touch wasn't what she was averse to, quite the opposite, it was the unimaginable nature of what happened next that had so shocked her, she wanted to tell him that if this is what did happen between men and women, then all she needed was some preparation and she would have accepted it, for hadn't she accepted what preceded it—no, not accepted, but enjoyed?

Then, that too had changed. Her own hunger had shocked her almost as much as that first shock, at times it seemed that she wanted it even more than he did, even when he didn't, and then waiting for him was the difficult part. There were times after it was over when she lay conscious of wanting it to go on, she didn't understand it, what it was that brought her that accidental, sharp satisfaction and why it didn't always come, leaving her impatient for the next time, and she never knew when the next time would be.

It was at this time that his father suddenly died. They rushed to Lucknow, and after the ceremonies were over, the house was wound up, rented out to tenants, and Mataji and Kamala came to live with them permanently. "You won't be so lonely now," he told her.

She had been prepared for changes. What she hadn't been prepared for was for feeling that she was a stranger in her own house. She hadn't been prepared for the loneliness that swept her so completely. She, who came from a large family of several brothers and sisters and knew what it was to give and receive love, hadn't been prepared for an absence of love at a time when she was so willing to give it. As for his oblivion to it all, she supposed she must have been prepared for it in ways she hadn't realized, because it hadn't come as a surprise.

And the things she wanted to ask Mataji, there just didn't seem to be an appropriate time for it. How to ask a newly widowed mother-in-law, Mataji, the jewels that my mother gave me at the time of my marriage, which you said you would keep in the locker, do you have them with you here? How to say to her, Mataji, those five Benarasi sarees that my mother gave to me when I got married, which you put away for safekeeping, can I have them? Fool that she was, fool. She should have known. And even that day when she and He had to go to a wedding, when she asked Mataji, "Mataji, if you have my jewels here I would like to wear them for the wedding," and Mataji had said, without looking up, "What jewels"—even then, she had denied it to herself. Impossible to tell Him, impossible, not when His father had just died.

Some years later when they got Kamala married, she had known. She had known when Kamala's future in-laws had come to the house after the negotiations were finalized, and when in the sitting room, Mataji had taken out several small, lovely boxes and opened them and said, "All these I am giving my daughter, see." And of course, there they were, all the jewelry Anu's mother had collected for her all those years. And yes, the five Benarasi sarees too. Kamala's future mother-in-law felt the silk of each saree with her fingers and examined the silver and gold work.

"See, Padma, how strange life is," Anu told Padma. "All that my mother gave to me, Mataji gave to Kamala, now Kamala's mother-in-law has taken it away from Kamala and kept it to give to *her* daughter when *her* daughter gets married. Which woman, I often wonder, will wear the jewellery my mother made for me?" She shook her head. "When I got married, my parents gave so much to His family. So much cash. Silk sarees to all the women in his family. All of it His family took as if it was their right, said they were not good enough. The day after the wedding I had to sit and watch as they looked at all the sarees and jewellery that my mother had given me, I had to listen to them discuss its quality—the silk was too thin, the zari wasn't real, the gold was less than twenty karat . . . on and on they went for hours, loudly in my presence. Mataji's older sister held my hand and examined every gold bangle I was wearing, then she said to Mataji that the work on them was very poor. My parents gave Mataji a gold set. Mataji was showing it to everyone in my presence the day after the wedding, saying what a horrible set it was. I thought I was dreaming, Padma. My mother never spoke of such things happening to her when she got married. But then my mother did not have a mother-in-law, perhaps that is why.

"I have never wished bechari Kamala any harm, that you know, Padma. Yet see how God also has His ways. Kamala, when she came here after her marriage, she came and cried and cried and said, Bhabi, I miss you, Bhabi, there is no one I can talk to. I said to her, Beti, you come here as often as you can, and she said, That is not possible, Bhabi, my mother-in-law doesn't like it. Then, Padma, she cried again and told me about her mother-in-law taking away her sarees and jewellery. In one part of my mind I thought, see, God has his ways. In another part I thought, Kamala has done me no harm, why should she suffer. I told her, Do not tell Mataji, Kamala, she will suffer if you tell her. Kamala said to me, Bhabi, I told her, it just came out when I saw her, Bhabi—oh, Bhabi, she cried and cried." Anu looked at Padma thoughtfully. "See how Mataji cries and cries for her daughter, but the same things she has done to me, and that she doesn't see."

Kamala's wedding had almost killed them. He had had to take a loan against his provident fund, and it wasn't enough for the two new sets of jewellery they bought, all the sarees, kitchen utensils, furniture. His two younger brothers helped out, but still, the major burden was theirs to bear. By the time it was over there was nothing left—less than nothing. He had told her, "Hereafter we will have to have fewer expenses," and told her how much of his salary was going to be cut to pay back his loans for the next five years. But where to cut from? She hadn't bought herself any new sarees after her marriage, and he hadn't bought himself any clothes either. The children were rapidly outgrowing their clothes, and she bought them the minimum. The school fees and uniforms and bus fees were enormous. Then gas, house rent, electricity, food. Food. She gave up her nightly glass of milk and stopped taking ghee in her food, stopped eating fruits and set less dahi because now she didn't eat dahi. She stopped having sugar in her tea except in the morning—that she still had, that she looked forward to the way she used to once look forward to His return from the office. She dispensed with Saraswati, who came to wash the dishes, and did them herself. She dispensed with the dhobi except for things like bedsheets and towels, the rest she did herself, that meant washing clothes for four people every morning, and when His sisters came to visit it meant washing all their clothes and their family's clothes too. How much could she cut down when they had so many guests so often? "Try and stretch out the money," he said, as if it were the same to feed four people as it was to feed eight. "Like water, you spend the money He gives you," Mataji would say.

It was Madhu who made the dent. At least twice a week, while Anu was having her morning tea, Madhu would come to Anu's house with vegetables that she had grown herself in her vegetable garden, and she would deposit the basket on the dining table. When Anu had visitors Madhu's basket overflowed. Madhu did it for Padma too. There were times, Padma told Anu, when she didn't have to buy vegetables for weeks. Neither of them dared to thank Madhu, they had to take it as if it were their right, as if Madhu's blooming vegetable garden were their own. Greener fingers than Madhu's Anu had never in her life seen—flowers and vegetables grew from her fingers like spring shoots. Anu praised the vegetables, their size, their colour, their taste. That was enough for Madhu, she didn't want thanks.

Praise, that's what Madhu wanted, that was all, so Anu gave it to her in abundance. Not praise for herself but praise for all that she tended and nurtured—her husband, her children, her vegetables, her house, her cooking. That praise she accepted. Padma hadn't learnt, she did it the other way round, praised Madhu but kept silent about Madhu's children and Madhu's house and Madhu's husband. Still, after all these years, Padma hadn't learnt. When Padma spoke highly of Mahima, it made no difference to Madhu, who knew it already; Madhu wanted appreciation of things and people she was uncertain about. These were what Madhu spoke most glowingly about. Padma could not see that all she needed to do was reiterate what Madhu said, and then Madhu would be happy. But Padma would again and again make the mistake of reiterating not what Madhu said, but what she, Padma, believed about Madhu.

Yet, Padma's belief was what bound her to them. In those early days when Padma had first come to their colony, it was her complete acceptance of Anu and Madhu that had drawn them to her. Like Madhu, Anu too had been apprehensive about their new neighbour, almost, like Madhu, suspicious. When Shanta had told them about Padma's past Anu had wept sincerely, right from her heart. Yet, later, she had wondered. What kind of abnormal in-laws were Padma's, who didn't come to see her and their grandchild even after they lost their son? Even Mataji wouldn't do that to her, Anu, under such circumstances, Mataji's first thought would have been for her grandchild. After Padma's sister left, Padma turned to Anu and Madhu as naturally as if they were her own family. So they had become that. And Prabha and Mallika—their attachment to each other was fierce and unconditional.

Long before her, Anu's, fears for Prabha began to grow, she had had Prabha's horoscope cast twice, each time by a different pandit, and both had said the same thing—she should have been a boy. One pandit had said it gloomily, the other had said it delightedly. The one had asked, "Are you sure this is your daughter's horoscope and not your son's?" And when she had seen the foreboding on his face and nodded mutely, he had said, Very difficult life, too difficult, look at her personality—headstrong, obstinate, ambitious, she will do whatever she wants to do, nothing will stop her, nobody will stop her. She will get many degrees, she will travel overseas, perhaps she will work there, she will rise to the top of her profession, get great recognition." He had shaken his head and pursed his lips. "Naturally, she will have problems in her marriage. She might," and he paused and examined Anu's face, "she might even do better in her profession than her husband."

The other pandit had said the same things, but his prediction was different. "Arre, this kind of janampatri, it is remarkable—your daughter, she will be like a son, better than this what can you want? Everything a good son does, all that she will do, but she will do it better. To the highest post she will rise, like a star. So much she will do for her parents, more than any son. Bas, a little problem she will have in marriage, it is all right, that is to be expected."

Looking at her one-month-old baby, Anu had been stricken. She would grow up to be all that? She had told Mataji about the horoscope.

"She is Lakshmi," Mataji said, "she will bring great luck to this house."

"I feel afraid, Mataji."

"You," Mataji replied contemptuously. "Like you my granddaughter will not be, that is for sure. Like my son she will be—fearless, principled, strong."

Anu's husband entered the room at this point and Mataji smiled expansively. "Beta," she said to him, "if the pandit said our bitiya will be like a boy, then what is better than that?" He smiled and said, "Did he say that?"

"Bilkul," Mataji said. "Beta, see, if a boy is born without the qualities that my granddaughter is born with, he will still have a good future because he is a boy. Strong or weak, honest or dishonest, ambitious or without ambition, a man has the right to walk on a certain path. But a woman, if she wants to walk on that path, then she cannot be weak, she cannot be silent, she cannot lack ambition. Not only has she to be strong—she has to be stronger than any man. The pandit is saying that our Prabha will be like a man. It is my prayer that I will live to see this." She folded her hands and closed her eyes.

He had just laughed. Later that day Anu had repeated her fears to him. He had responded in exasperation, "One month old she is and you are talking of her marriage! Why do you believe in all that astrology nonsense?"

All that nonsense, she wanted to tell Him, was the reason why we got married, all that nonsense was what your mother insisted on. Why do you think your mother chose me? Not for my beauty or for my family, though I am not bad-looking and my family is the best, and not for my dowry, which wasn't much, but because according to your astrological chart you are a Manglik and according to mine, I am a Manglik.

He said, "Sometimes maybe you should listen to my mother more willingly. You do not know, but my mother is a very enlightened woman, she is born far ahead of her time."

Yes, yes, she wanted to tell him, I know how enlightened your mother is, I know what she says to me when you're not there and I know what she says to me when you are there. Of course, she didn't say any of these things to him aloud, but only in her imaginary conversations with him, which she had daily in the kitchen. "Don't think I cannot see your mouth moving," Mataji had told her once, "talks to herself like a madwoman and doesn't hear when I call her."

And Prabha, true to prediction, showed no interest in the things she should have been interested in and no inclination to attempt doing them to please her mother either. And all the time Prabha asked, Why?

The problem was that Anu did understand, she *knew* that Prabha merely wanted an answer that she could comprehend. But it seemed that mere understanding didn't make one patient. Then Prabha would go to her father and He would say to Anu, "What need is there for the child to spend her time with a needle and thread when she wants to do other things?"

Anu would say, "She has to learn *sometime*."

And He would reply, "There is plenty of time for that."

Talking like a bewakoof, she wanted to tell him but didn't, interest has to be fostered early, even interest is not important, the fact of doing it well, interest or no interest, that is what is important. But what would He know of that.

Mataji was worse. "If she wants to climb trees, then let her climb trees," she would tell Anu, "now she is a child with a child's desires, do you want her to climb trees when she is in sarees with her maang full of sindoor?"

Arre, Mataji, she wanted to tell her but didn't, the way she is going no one will want to marry her. The child had no sense of when to keep quiet, of what to say when. Bas, what was in her head, that she would say, what was in her mind, that she would do. It wasn't fair, Mumma. That was wrong, Mumma. What else could I do, Mumma? Her bewilderment was genuine, her belief in the rightness of what she did, absolute. At the age of five she had bashed up two boys who had threatened Mallika. She had come home gleefully and told her mother all about it. Laughter had threatened to overcome Anu, but she had managed to keep a straight face.

"Mumma," Prabha said as Anu tucked her into bed that night and smoothed her forehead, "be like this always."

"Like what?" Anu asked, getting up and drawing the curtains. Prabha turned to her and watched her, her eyes bright.

"Without getting angry, Mumma. Like you are with Anirudh."

"With Anirudh also I get angry, beti," Anu said, switching off the light and sitting next to her. She glanced at the next bed where Anirudh had been fast asleep for the past hour and her love for him filled her anew.

"When he's sleeping, then you sit next to him and look at him," Prabha said, "you never sit next to me and look at me when I'm sleeping."

The familiar anger began to spurt inside Anu again. "Everything becomes an argument, everything. I'm tired of it. Next to you also I sit," she lied, "but you're sleeping, what do you know?"

Prabha smiled and held Anu's arm. "When, Mumma?"

"When what?" Anu said tiredly.

"After I go to bed you wash the dishes and clean the dining room, then you give milk to Dadima, then you go to your room. When do you come and sit next to me?"

"After I go to my room, then I come to your room. Go to sleep now." She got up.

"Mumma."

"*Now* what?" Anu snapped.

"You get angry with Anirudh but when you get angry with me it is different."

"From where all you bring up things," Anu said, exasperated.

"When you are angry with Anirudh, you stay angry for only two minutes, Mumma."

"I'm *tired* of you," Anu almost shouted and left the room.

Later that night, after she had washed the dishes and cleaned the dining room and given milk to Mataji and Kamala, she lay in bed full of remorse. This is what always happened, this is how it always ended. She hated herself after she shouted at Prabha. She who had borne all that she had borne with a smiling face, who never lost her temper with anyone, who had learnt to find joy in the smallest of things, she was unable to summon up any patience for Prabha. At times she felt she could slap her and slap her and slap her till she would never again in her life ask why.

"Why are you so impatient with her?" He had asked her on more than one occasion. "She is a child—what is the difficulty in showing some patience?"

She had tossed her head. "I know *your* patience. Getting the children chocolates and sweets and never saying no to them."

"For important things one has to say no. You say no even for small things. You never explain things to her."

"No explanation satisfies your daughter."

"I have heard you with her, you do not even attempt to explain."

"One thing you hear and you judge me," she exclaimed, infuriated, "the other one hundred times what you do not hear, what of that?"

"If a little time you spent, explaining properly to Prabha, then next time she would not ask why."

"If you have the time, you explain, I do not have the time."

"That is what I do," he said quietly, "that is why she listens to me."

Why were children born to the same parents so different? Anirudh. With what ease she had carried him, with what ease he had been born. Madhu had predicted that she would have a boy, but Mataji had had her qualms. "All my daughters-in-law have had sons," she said to Anu, "but with you, who knows." But Anu too had obliged and Mataji's joy had been boundless. When Anu went back to Delhi with Him and Prabha and the baby, her parents sent silk sarees for all the women in His family—his sisters, and his brothers' wives—and many boxes of sweets. There had been a huge hawan for the baby a few weeks later, three times as big as the one they had for Prabha. And from the time he was born Anirudh was a happy, bubbly baby.

And Prabha? At the age of three she had asked Mataji at the dining table, "Dadima, why are you eating?"

Mataji had pinched her cheek and said, "Because it is time to eat food now."

"But, Dadima," Prabha had asked, puzzled, "you were saying Mumma's food is very bad?"

"That it is," Mataji had said, her smile disappearing.

"But everything you have eaten three times," Prabha said.

Later when Anu had told Madhu about this, Madhu had laughed heartily and said, "Very sharp your Prabha is, that I must say."

"No, Madhu," Anu had said, disturbed, "there is an innocence in her, a great simplicity."

Madhu had looked amused. "What you cannot say to Mataji, that Prabha says, what is so innocent about that?"

"She is very young, Madhu."

Madhu smiled meaningfully. "She is learning early, what else."

The conversation had disturbed Anu more than she could understand. But when she told Padma, Padma went into peals of laughter. "Anu," Padma said, "she is an innocent child, she is only saying what she's observing. Tell me, how many children are there like her?"

None, Anu thought later, but it would do her no good. Even now Prabha was so unequivocal about her feelings, about her convictions of what was right and what was wrong. Like Him she was, but He was a man.

It was very well feeling that way, nothing was wrong with that. What was wrong was acting on it, and Prabha acted on what she felt. What was wrong was telling people what you thought, and Prabha told people what she thought. What was wrong was questioning the way things were and Prabha questioned the way things were. How would Prabha survive her nature in a world where women just shouldn't act on their beliefs, where to do so was certain disaster? A sense of fairness was no quality to bring into a marriage. That was a quality that stood you in good stead only in the relationships outside marriage and in the Other World, the world outside the domestic one, and how many women knew that world anyway? To stand by one's beliefs and speak one's mind was necessary in the professional world, good men did that, He did that, it was not the most practical thing as she had seen, after all He didn't get his promotions as fast as his colleagues did, but she understood, she respected him for it.

But His beliefs and his principles were no good at home because they did not apply there. He didn't know the world she inhabited, where words like *fairness* and *justice* rang hollow. He could keep his principles and his integrity for all they were worth. On the homefront it had as much worth as the onion skins which she couldn't even feed to the cows who came mooing to the back of the kitchen door every afternoon. She gave the cows potato skins and mango skins, she gave them the bananas that were too black and overripe even for her to eat. They loved her for it, they nuzzled in the palm of her hand and when they saw her standing at the kitchen door which opened into the back lawn they came to her, mooing joyfully. That was the way to be, like a cow, grateful for the leftovers, that was the way to be, placid, unruffled, peaceful.

Once Mataji had tried to feed the onions skins to her cows. "The less that is wasted, the better it is," Mataji had intoned. But the cows had refused to touch them, turned away and ambled back to the road. "Much they think of themselves," Mataji had said, affronted, "you have spoiled them too much." Then she had looked at Anu and snapped, "What is there to laugh about, Bahurani?"

Arre, Mataji, Anu had wanted to tell her, you think that I too have been spoilt with a diet of leftovers; if you could feed me onion skins you would. She had laughed so much that Mataji had been meaner to her than ever that day. Honesty, Principles, Integrity. How high-sounding, how nice. At home it only applied to His mother and His sisters and brothers, to His nieces and nephews and to His own children. It was she who had to bear the brunt of His principles and His integrity and His honesty.

She, Anu, did have faith in Prabha, but what was the use. She had had faith in Him too and in principle, she still had it. The reality was what mattered, and Prabha was too young to know the consequences of fighting for truth and justice. Acceptance, that was the truth. Justice, there was none. Truth meant violence, assault. On the surface it was what had happened to her and Madhu and Padma that day at the mela, but that was just its outward manifestation. The everyday violations did as much damage. Prabha would have to learn to accept both.

Like the fool that she was she had told Him about the mela incident the same night. Why? Her need for comfort, for understanding? Once, long ago, he had given her both. Then too he had never spoken of his feelings for her, but she had known how he felt and the knowledge had sufficed. Perhaps it was this then that made her speak—her need to know if he too would suffer for her as he had suffered when she began to bleed when she was pregnant with Prabha, perhaps she hoped that the old, never-forgotten tenderness would surface again, would allow her tears to come. She began to tell him and warning bells began to ring; she ignored them. He didn't say anything as she told him, there was nothing in his expression, no anger, no shock, nothing. After she finished He said, "I thought you were going to the jewellers at Chandni Chowk."

She looked at him blankly. She saw the beginnings of something like distaste on his face. "What was the need to lie to Mataji?" he asked.

She had forgotten. Completely forgotten. She continued looking at his face, her own full of panic. He closed his eyes. She said, "Mataji doesn't like me to go anywhere."

He didn't open his eyes as he replied, "I can't force you to like my mother. But what foolish things you imagine, do not attribute those things to her."

After some time Anu said, "Your mother says I put water in the milk that I give her." He turned his back to her and didn't reply. "Did you hear me?" she asked.

"What has that to do with what all this?" he asked. She tried to speak but couldn't. There was too much to say so she said nothing. "You take two and two and you make five," he said. "Mataji must have said the milkman put water in the milk. You hear it as her saying you have done it."

"Mataji used to say I denied Kamala milk at night. She used to say I drank up the milk secretly in the kitchen and didn't give Kamala her milk."

She heard him sigh. "I don't know from where you drag up things."

"Nothing makes a difference to you," she said. She turned her back to him, the tears coming. It was as though those hands were on her again, she could smell those men, she could feel her hair being pulled and the fingers under her saree blouse. The bath hadn't helped, even though her body was red after scrubbing with the pumice stone. She found that she was making a noise as she cried, a horrible noise, trying to stifle it made the sound even worse.

"If Mataji doesn't want you to go anywhere it is because she knows what can happen to you," he said. "You may not believe it, but it is of great concern to her, your safety, your well-being. If you want to lie to her and go out on your own, then you must be prepared to take the consequences." She moved away from him till she was lying at the edge of the bed. "Why do these things happen only to you?" he said, sounding tired.

She should never have told him. Not just this, but the other things which she had told him over the years, about the man who followed her all the way to the vegetable shop and back, about the man who had felt her thigh in the D.T.C. bus. She hadn't been able to help herself—out it came.

"You *told* your husband all these things?" Madhu had asked her, shocked, when she once mentioned it to Madhu.

"Why not, what fault was it of mine?" Anu retorted.

"So what did He say?"

"I don't remember," Anu said vaguely.

"*I* can't tell my husband about these things." Madhu shuddered. "*He* would get so angry that he would kill those men—he is so protective about me, see."

If only He would get angry about these things. But if he got angry at all it was at her, not at the fact that it had happened to her. "These things can always be avoided," he said, "do not travel by bus, take a scooter."

"Where is the money for a scooter?"

"If you want money for a scooter, ask me for it, when you want something for yourself have I ever refused?"

"Have I ever asked for any money to buy something for myself?"

"Keep to the issue we are talking about."

"You always tell me to cut down, cut down, where is the money for scooters?"

"About things like this if money has to be spent, it has to be spent," he said, "use the housekeeping money and I will give you more."

"I am not eating fruits, I am not drinking milk, and you ask me to take scooters."

"If you are not eating fruits and not drinking milk do not blame me, did I ask you not to?"

"No, but you asked me to cut down."

"So cut down on other things."

"What things?"

"The problem with you is that you can never keep to the issue at hand."

"No scooter will go to the vegetable shop—what can I do if some man decides to follow me?"

"Don't walk alone, take one of your friends—Mrs. Nanda, Mrs. Rao."

"Every day I should ask them to come with me vegetable shopping because I am scared that some man will follow me? They have better things to do, I have better things to ask them."

"If that is the case then don't complain."

Silence.

"You just don't understand."

"I understand very well. The problem with you is that all your problems are self-inflicted."

"Much you know about my problems."

"All right, all right."

"When I came back from Lucknow, you had given Mataji money for the house and asked her to give it to me."

"You have started again."

"She never gave me the money. She said to me that she had no money."

"Why must you bring my mother into everything?"

"One day before I came back from Lucknow you gave her all the household money. You said, Take it from her. She said, I don't have any money. What was I to spend for the house?"

"She must have forgotten. Ask her again."

"Where do you think I spent from? I spent the money my father gave me to buy a silk saree for myself."

"For your faults you are always blaming others. Remember this. I did not ask you to spend your father's money. Nor did my mother."

"You ask her for the money. She will never give me."

"I do not ask you to do my office work for me. You do not ask me to do your work. If you have a quarrel with her, sort it out with her. Do not drag me into it."

Anu turned over in her bed, her eyes dry. Outside she could hear the crickets chirping, and the light of the full moon streamed in from the window. In the distance she heard a dog barking. He was fast asleep as usual. No difference it had made. No difference that his wife had been violated. When their children were hurt or upset he acted as if the world were collapsing. When Prabha fell and bruised her knee he coddled her as if she had broken her leg. When Prabha bashed up the boys who threatened her and Mallika he said, It is all right, never let anyone do an injustice to you. From the darkness Anu heard his voice saying, "The people in the outside world will not change. Accept that and try and behave accordingly."

Once she had gone to the dentist to have a cavity attended to. She had sat on the chair, her mouth open, wincing slightly as he began the drilling. Half an hour it had taken, she looked up at the ceiling and the spots over there, she let her mind drift, let the tiredness fill her body, felt the tension ooze away, felt her body relax. Her eyes grew heavy.

She awoke to see the dentist peering worriedly at her. "Are you all right?"

She nodded, shook her head, smiled. "I'm sorry, I fell asleep," she said.

He looked at her as if she were some creature from another planet. "I saw," he said. "You did not feel any pain?"

She shook her head again, stepping down from the chair. "It was a deep sleep," she said and began to laugh.

"Do you drink milk, take vitamins?" he asked.

She shook her head.

"You start, then. This is sign of weakness."

Holding her lips tight to suppress her laughter, she nodded.

But now there was no waking up, most of the time she didn't even feel any pain. Better this way. She tried not to think about the early days, it made her feel ashamed, embarrassed, as though she were a voyeur peeping into the lives of two other people. Now, the nearest He came to her was when He wanted sex, and she never felt so distant from Him as she did then. Two minutes it took, as quick as her single early morning cup of tea, and the tea was infinitely more satisfying. No, not more satisfying. *More* implied that the other was also satisfying in a lesser way, and the word *sat-*

*isfying* didn't apply to something in which she didn't participate. There was a great deal she didn't participate in; how could this need be alive, dependent as it was on the others?

Some things could never be uttered; there was shame in uttering them. And humiliation. Once, when things had begun to change she had wanted to say to him, Will you hold me at times other than when you are on top of me? After all, she had known it once. Once she had known her love for him to be fiercest at such moments. Now, in a process unknown even to her, the quality of her love had changed. It could not be asked for, what he had once given her. But the sadness of it was, he did not even know it had stopped. Did he remember it had once been there? The sadness of it was, she did.

It was strange, how in marriage one had to find time to do everything, most of it not related at all to the man one had married. And for talk and for love there was no time at all, no attempt, no thought. The leftovers—that was what lovemaking and conversations with one's husband were, like the sides of bread that Anirudh left on his plate, like the yellow, sticky remains of dal and rice on the plate.

It was true, what her mother always said: "A woman's fulfillment is her children. Without children what is there?" For your children, and only for them were you Everything. Once on a rare occasion when she had burnt the potatoes a little, Mataji had grumbled loudly at the lunch table. "It *isn't* burnt, it *isn't* burnt," Prabha had said equally loudly and scraped the bowl of potatoes and eaten every one. Then she took the burnt potatoes from Anirudh's plate which he hadn't eaten, and ate those too. "Tomorrow also you make the same, Mumma," Prabha said, looking at her with love.

"Yes, yes, make," Mataji had said, pushing her thali away in disgust, "*I* cannot eat such food."

"Dadima," Prabha said indignantly, "Cinderella's stepmother talks like you."

"Who, who?" Mataji asked.

Anu put her fingers around Prabha's arm so tightly that Prabha cried out. Anu dragged her to her room and smacked her hard. Prabha burst into tears. "Stay there till you learn to keep your mouth shut," she said.

"Teach her to say more, Bahurani, teach her more," Mataji said as Anu came out of Prabha's room, "everything I understand, everything."

It was impossible to remain tender with Prabha, impossible. The day after the mela incident was Anu's fast—nothing to eat all day until after the puja in the late evening, Mataji kept the same fast. His sister, her husband and children were expected for two weeks the next day, so she had to prepare for that too. In the evening, finally, after she and Mataji bathed and did their puja, she made the puris and heated the rest of the food and fed everyone. She wanted to sit by herself and eat, let everyone finish, then she would sit in peace without having to get up a hundred times to get this and get that. Kamala was also with them for a week, which was all the time her mother-in-law was willing to spare.

"What is your fast and puja for, Mumma?" Prabha asked, eating her third puri with enjoyment.

"This is a fast for sons," she replied, serving Anirudh another hot puri. "Why, Mumma?" Prabha looked puzzled.

"For their long life and for them to live in good health and happily," she said going into the kitchen to turn the puris.

"Mumma," Prabha said when she came back and served Him and Mataji, "this fast is for Anirudh?"

"Yes." She nodded and went back to the kitchen to fry the rest of the puris.

When she came back, Prabha said, "Mumma, when do you keep a fast for me?"

Anu paused in the act of spooning some dahi into Mataji's bowl. She served Mataji, then served Him and Anirudh some aloo. She put another puri onto Prabha's plate.

"Mumma."

She went back to the kitchen and finished frying the puris. After they had all finished eating, she cleared the thalis and other dishes, put them in the sink and came back and began serving the khir.

"Mumma, tell me."

She went back to the kitchen. An hour later, after washing the dishes and cleaning the kitchen, she went back to the dining room and began to serve herself. She felt the tiredness seep into her body.

She looked up. Prabha was sitting opposite her, and her eyes were full of unshed tears. "Arre, what happened?" she asked, startled.

"Mumma, when do you keep a fast for me?" One tear rolled slowly down Prabha's cheek. She wiped her nose with the back of her hand, then burst into tears, trying to hold back the sounds that racked her body, but unable to.

"Prabha, beti." Her father put down his paper and came to her. He dragged a chair and, sitting next to her, put one arm around her and with his other hand wiped the tears from her cheek. "What need is there to cry, my child?" he said over and over again. He smoothed her forehead, took out a handkerchief from his pocket, wiped her cheek again. He put his hand on her cheek and drew her head into his neck, murmuring comfortingly. Anu finished her puri, forced herself to finish the rest on her plate. Her appetite had gone.

She got up and cleared the dishes, washed them, cleaned the table again. Tomorrow she would have to get the vegetables and rations first thing after breakfast, His sister and family were coming in the evening. She changed into her old saree and went to the children's room. He was sitting next to Prabha, stroking her forehead. Her eyes were closed, her hand, limp in sleep, was lying in his. Anu went to Anirudh and brushed her finger against his cheek. His cheeks were red, his hair rumpled, his plump hands against the pillow. He was smiling even in his sleep, she found herself smiling too, she wanted to pick him up and hold him the way she used to when he was a baby.

She was fast asleep when He spoke to her, she opened her eyes and looked dazedly at him. "Already you are asleep?" he asked.

She saw his face and suddenly she was wide awake. "What is the matter?"

"Prabha wasn't answering my question as to why she was crying. After a long time she told me. Is it true?"

"Is what true?" she asked wearily.

"That you keep a fast for Anirudh and not for her?"

She took a deep breath and said, "What do you think."

"What can I think. I told her, That is not true at all, if your mother keeps a fast it is for both of you, not for one of you. She just would not believe me, she kept crying." He paused, then said, "When I'm talking to you try and look in my direction," he said.

"When I talk to you, you don't."

She heard him expel a noisy breath.

She said, "Yes it is true, I keep a fast for Anirudh, I have been keeping it all these years ever since he was born, what do you know of it."

He said, disbelievingly, "For one child you keep and not for the other?"

"What your mother told me to do, that I do."

"She told you to exclude Prabha?"

"No. When Anirudh was born, she said, Now you have a son, now you must keep a fast for him once a year. So I kept a fast once a year. That's all." He didn't answer. She said, "Your mother also, she also keeps a fast for you and your brothers. She doesn't keep it for your sisters." She stretched her legs and closed her eyes.

"Do not bring my mother into this. She is of another generation. You, you need not do things blindly."

"That is the only way to do it."

"In answering back you are very quick. Perhaps you should be as quick in thinking."

"Tell your mother that."

There was a silence, then he said, "From now onwards your fast will include Prabha. Tomorrow you tell Prabha that you fast for both of them."

"I won't tell her that. I don't want to lie to Prabha. She knows what the truth is."

"You won't lie to Prabha, but you will lie to Mataji when you want to go wandering about with your friends. Suddenly truth has become very meaningful to you."

"You understand nothing."

"I understand everything. I understand how twisted your mind has become. Your simplicity, your innocence, your softness, everything that I first knew you for, nothing remains." He turned his back to her. "I know how your mind works," and now it was he who sounded tired, the anger all gone, "I know the thoughts you have about me these days. Because I say nothing do not think I don't know. If I am no longer what I was, then remember, you also are not the person I married."

No, she was not. Oh no, she was not. Once, just before one of Kamala's visits, Padma had bought her two tickets for a recital by a famous classical singer. "*You* should be on stage, singing," Padma had said to Anu.

Anu laughed, joy flooding her. "That's what my guru used to say to me," she said before she knew what she was saying.

Padma gazed at her face for a long time, then said, "You had singing lessons."

Anu nodded. "Twelve years," she said, then shrugged.

"I should have known," Padma said. "You have the voice and the training . . . you didn't even tell me."

"What is there to tell."

"We can go, no?" Anu had asked Him, showing Him the tickets and He had given her one of his old, sweet smiles and said, "Yes." There were two weeks more before the performance, and she lived in anticipation of it every day and every night. "We should go for these more often," she had told Him, "the tickets are so cheap," and he had said, "Yes, why not." Why hadn't she thought of it herself? Her longing filled her body like a fever, her eyes were bright with it. She would wear the tusser saree that Madhu had given her, the off-white one with the green border, which had been lying in her trunk for so long. "I know what happens to all your sarees," Madhu had warned her, "my saree you better not give to your sisters-in-law or anyone."

Then Kamala and her husband came.

"Hai, Bhabi," Kamala exclaimed when Anu told her about the performance, "I also want to go, I *love* music."

"Then come with us, both of you," He said, smiling indulgently.

"But the tickets . . . they are sold out," Anu stammered.

"Haii," Kamala wailed.

"Arre, what is there in that, you take our tickets," He said.

"Classical music, I will get bored," Kamala's husband protested.

"No you won't." Kamala pouted. "You will enjoy it."

"Go, beta, go," Mataji said. "Such things, they feed the soul."

"*Come. Please.* I will never talk to you again," Kamala said sounding like Anirudh. Baby talk. Men liked that. She, Anu, should have learnt to pout.

"Accha, accha," Kamala's husband said, resignedly.

Padma had come to the house the day after the performance, as Anu was chopping onions. "Tell me, Anu, tell me," she said, her voice full of anticipation.

Anu smiled, it came out like a grimace. "We didn't go, Padma." She put aside the onion she had chopped and began peeling the next one.

"Kamala and her husband went," Padma said. It wasn't a question.

"They said it was boring. They came back early." She finished chopping the onion and picked up another one, began to peel it. From the corner of her eyes she saw the maroon blur that was Padma.

"Don't cry, Anu."

When you cried it was never for one thing. It began with one thing and then everything else got mixed up with it. There had been compassion in Padma's voice. *Padma* full of compassion for *her*. She, Anu, had no generosity, no kindness. She only thought of herself. She was despicable.

Long after this she had mentioned it to him. For some reason, she couldn't remember what, all those old feelings had surged up like milk boiling over. Finally, when she stopped he said, very calmly, "A small sacrifice like that, and such a big tirade. You have to learn to be less selfish. Perhaps you have forgotten, I also did not go. But I have not spent the last one year brooding about it."

No, she was no longer the person he had married.

She got up and went to the bathroom. She had forgotten to wash the strips of cloth kept aside from her periods. There would be no time the next day with everyone coming. She opened the bathroom cupboard and taking out a bottle of Vaseline, smeared it on the insides of her thighs. They were red and raw, she had barely been able to walk all day, the cloth around her sanitary towel had dug into her and rubbed against the insides of her thighs with every movement. She began washing the strips of cloth on the floor, rubbing them hard with the soap, the tap running. If there was one extravagance, just one that she longed for, it was the use of sanitary pads without cloth, pads that she could use and throw away as everyone else did, instead of using the same one for a whole day and washing five or six layers of cloth every night. Kamala used to have that luxury when she lived with them, for Kamala she used to buy the softest, most expensive sanitary towels. But she shouldn't complain to herself, it was foolish to complain, self-pity was a destructive thing, think of her mother, her mother hadn't even had that, her mother had had to use only cloth, and now her mother bled every day with some strange, horrible disease, she lay in bed and bled and bled, she was thin and wasted, she would go to her mother next month when the children had their summer holidays, but a month was a long time, then her mother would get out of bed and make parathas for her and say, My child, eat, my child, eat, and her mother would spread ghee on her chappatis, but not for long, and that too she, Anu, would have to accept. She too wanted to die, and she couldn't even do that because of the children.

The next day, after she had got her rations and vegetables and fruits and was busy getting things ready for her sister-in-law and family, Madhu came with her news. Perhaps at any other time she would not have felt its effects so severely, any other time she could have withstood it. She listened to Madhu and continued chopping and peeling and cooking and giving vague replies. After Madhu left, Anu went back to the kitchen. For some time she stood there. What to think, what to think, her mind was blank.

It hadn't been blank when Madhu was talking to her, then it had been razor sharp, though her vague response to Madhu's revelation had hidden that. It had come instinctively, that vagueness, that indifference, she hadn't had to think to know it was the best response.

She quickly made tea. "Take, Mataji," she said going with tea to the sitting room, where Mataji sat reading the Hindi newspaper. Mataji took it, "See, Bahurani, like such a befakoof this Chief Minister is talking, he is saying—"

"One minute, Mataji, I have to go to the bathroom."

"Go, go, bathroom, kitchen, kitchen, bathroom, always in one or the other, no interest in what is happening in the world—go."

In the bathroom, Anu sat on the pot and closed her eyes.

She shouldn't be so frightened. Madhu wouldn't tell Padma. That much sense even she had. She shouldn't have told Madhu not to; she had seen the gleam in Madhu's eyes. Now Madhu would know she wasn't indifferent and that would give Madhu a lever in subsequent conversations. Best to act as though she hadn't given any thought to it. Thank God Madhu didn't know anything else, thank God. Madhu would never understand, she would believe that she was full of compassion, she would feel certain that her comprehension of the situation was deep and generous, but inside, unknown even to herself, she would be gloating. What to do, what to do. Should she go to Padma and say, Padma, listen, everything I know, what Madhu doesn't know, even that I know. Padma trusted her. So should she tell Padma? Then at least Padma would be prepared. But prepared for what? Telling Padma would mean that Padma would have to spend every day, every week, every month and year anticipating the worst. Every hour, every minute. She would go mad, she would become even more obsessive about Mallika. After all, if it had to happen what could Padma do to stop it? Nothing.

What a small world it was. Destiny had its own ways, nothing that one did or didn't do could halt its intricate, inexorable workings. Why she had been chosen she didn't know, perhaps that knowledge too would come in time, as this knowledge had that day one year ago in the cramped, dirty, third-class compartment of the train taking her and Him and her children to Lucknow for their summer holidays with her parents. Mataji was with another of her sons for a week. Anu had been having her periods, perhaps that began it all, perhaps that gave birth to the nature of the conversation, a conversation rising from the surreptitious, intimate nature of the help that she as one woman could so naturally give to another. There was one other person in the compartment, a young, pretty woman, with an infinitely sad expression on her face. Prabha was sitting opposite her mother, next to her father at the other window seat, her nose in a book as usual, Anirudh was asleep on the upper berth above Anu. Anu was content to do neither, she liked the sound of the train chugging along, it always brought her a strange comfort, even the peculiar train smell and taste that entered her nostrils and mouth didn't annoy her, reminiscent as they were of her yearly journeys to her mother's house. Already her body was relaxing, moving gently to the rhythm, her eyes soothed by the green fields outside and the distant figures of peasants with their bullocks ploughing the fields. When the voice said something, she didn't hear it at first, then her eyes focussed and she found the girl with sad eyes leaning towards her, whispering, "Something I have to ask you."

"Yes, yes, certainly," Anu replied.

The girl hesitated, looked embarrassed, said in a whisper, "My, that thing, it has started, nothing I have, do you—?"

Anu nodded reassuringly. "It is up there," she said, "I will take it out." The girl nodded gratefully. Anu stood up on the berth, opened the air bag, and fumbling, found what she was looking for. Wrapping a towel around the pads, she climbed down and gave it to the girl. The girl thanked her softly and went out of the compartment.

"She didn't even have her own towel, she had to take your towel?" He asked with distaste.

"Sometimes it can happen," she replied briefly.

All these years he had been married, what was the use. Looking disapproving like that. Didn't see anything, these men. Asking stupid questions. What did he think she, his own wife, did, locked in the bathroom with the tap running every month in the middle of the night when she should be sleeping? Why did he think she took three pills every day for two days every month right in front of him after every meal? Aches and pains, women always have aches and pains, Mr. Nanda had once said, with great good humour. Her husband saying, Your friend, Mrs. Nanda, why are you always telling her to rest, it doesn't seem to me that she has any health problem. Shanta's husband explaining patiently, It is all in the mind, if the mind is sick, then the body is sick. Sickness of the mind, of the body, what did they know of either. How could they conceive that it could have anything to do with them. Like aborted children, their vision, unfinished, incomplete, scarred like Madhu's womb.

The girl came back, holding the towel in her hand, and gave it to Anu. "Thank you," she said softly sitting next to her.

"There is no need to thank," Anu said, smiling. They began to talk. The girl was going to Lucknow too, her parents also lived there. It turned out that it was just a few miles from where Anu's own parents lived. She too was married, but her husband hadn't been able to accompany her. "Do you have any children?" Anu asked. The girl did not reply. Then she shook her head. "You have not been married long, no?" Anu smiled.

There was a silence. "I have been married . . . a few . . . years," the girl said.

Poor thing, Anu thought, full of compassion, bechari.

The girl turned to Prabha, "What is your name?"

"Prabha. And my brother's name is Anirudh."

"Such nice names," the girl said.

"What is your name?"

"Sita."

"Such a good name."

"It is not a lucky name."

"Arre, no, no," Anu said, knowing the truth of what the girl said. Her own mother had said it too. It was a name to which suffering was attached.

"When I got married, my in-laws wanted to change my name, but I told them, all my life I have answered to the name Sita, now I cannot answer to another."

"Accha?" Anu said admiringly.

"But now I think, perhaps I should have listened to them and let them change my name, then my life would have been happier."

Anu opened her mouth to speak, closed it, opened it again and said, "Beti, I have known of women having children after eight, ten years. Bas, you think of God and everything will be all right."

To Anu's shock the girl made a sound, almost of contempt. "God. Everyone says, Think of God. For what?" Briefly, her face contorted. Anu looked up quickly but Prabha and He were still reading.

"So much she reads," Sita said.

"Too much," Anu said, "when she is married with children she can't keep reading."

"That is a long way off. No one can tell about the future."

Anu nodded and told her about Prabha's horoscope. "Both pandits said the same thing," Anu said thoughtfully, "but sometimes I think, maybe it isn't true."

"About these things nothing one can say. I had a . . . my friend's horoscope . . . and I took it to two pandits and they both said different things. One said, She is very strong. The other said, She is very weak. One said, Her marriage house denotes great sorrow. The other said, Her house for children denotes great happiness. One said, She will never get married. The other said, She will. One said, She is an evil woman. The other said, She is a woman of integrity. Better not to believe in all this."

Poor thing. Anu thought, bechari.

"Sometimes, what you know, even that you doubt."

"Accha?"

"Didi, sometimes I feel I am going mad."

Anu patted her hand, looked at her face, patted her face, "Do not think this way, child, do not think this way, everything will be all right."

"I hear voices from the past. I hate going to my mother's house."

Perhaps Sita was really mad.

"My mother-in-law doesn't understand. Didi, the place where your heart and mind feel rested and nurtured, that is your true home. That I feel with the family into which I married. They do not treat me like a daughter-in-law, didi, they treat me like a daughter. Before serving anyone else, before even serving my father-in-law, my mother-in-law serves me. She gives me the best pieces of everything, she buys me my favourite sweets. When I am not well she sits by my bedside and feeds me in bed with her own hands, she even combs my hair."

"Your mother didn't pamper you?" Anu asked.

The soft expression on Sita's face disappeared. "She did. After my brother I was her favourite child. I was the last to leave home, so they pampered me more than anyone else. Especially my brother. He indulged me like a child." She shook her head as though pushing away the memory.

"Mumma, can we have lunch now?"

He looked at his watch. "It is time," he said.

She took out the boxes of parathas and sabji and the steel plates and glasses. "You also eat," Anu told Sita.

Sita shook her head, "I am not hungry at all."

Anu climbed up her berth and woke up Anirudh. They all ate.

After she had cleared everything, Anu put her legs underneath her, facing Sita. As though there had been no interruption, Sita said, "I . . . how should I say it, when I think of my mother's house, then I am filled with dread, it is as if something dark and horrible will swallow me. I can see the shock on your face. It is merely the truth that I am telling you, nothing else. After I got married and began to live with my husband and in-laws, then I knew peace." Sita looked out of the window. The train had stopped at a small station.

"Mumma, can I have some aloo bonda?" Anirudh asked.

"No."

"I have something for you," He said, and took out a chocolate from his pocket. The children cried out in delight. He broke it and gave each half.

"I used to think I imagined it," Sita said, "I can still hear the voices, didi, every day, every night I hear the voices. Whenever I think of her I think of a vulture sitting on a tree, waiting."

"Beti," Anu said.

Sita's eyes moved from the window of the train to Anu's face. "In my house they act as if it never happened. Sometimes I think I have imagined everything."

"Beti—"

"That time they made me swear on the Gita not to speak of it to anyone. But I don't believe in that promise now. If God wants to punish me, let him. What more can He do? He can take away my husband, my in-laws, my mother, father, sisters. Let Him."

"Do not talk in such a manner about death. It is—"

"I was still in school at that time, in Lucknow only. That day I was in the room next to the sitting room which is my father's study, I liked to sit there and embroider, it was always very quiet and no one ever came in. My father had died a few years before. I used to sit in his study, do my embroidery and think about him. I was his favourite child. That day I heard the doorbell ring and after some time some voices but they were muffled . . . I wasn't concentrating anyway.

"Then suddenly I heard a woman's voice talking very loudly in English, but I couldn't hear all the words. I heard the word *son,* then *marriage.* But it wasn't the words that attracted my attention, but the tone of the woman's voice. She was talking as if she was attacking my mother and sisters.

"I put my embroidery down and tried to listen. I heard the woman saying something like, *I will shout it in front of the servants.* I thought, what is happening, have some mad people come to our house? I heard her say, *your brother.* Then I heard my mother's voice and I heard her say something and the word that came to my ears was *randi.* Something horrible is happening, I thought, or else I am dreaming. Never, never in my life had I heard my mother utter any bad word. And that word from her lips?

"Very softly, I opened the door. The door opened inwards into the room, and there were curtains outside that were drawn, so no one could see me. Then the same woman began to speak again and now I could hear her very clearly. She was talking in English and I heard her saying, *I curse you all. You and you, and you. May your son's wife be forever barren. May your two daughters be forever barren. May your house be forever empty of the laughter of grandchildren. May the marriages of your son and your two daughters be as barren as their wombs. May all my sister's suffering come back to you through your children.*

"Everything was quiet. Then I heard another voice, very soft, very gentle. It sounded like someone reciting shlokas. I thought, why is she praying? But they were not shlokas. She was talking in another language. It was a South Indian language—I could make out by the sounds. But I did not understand her words. But this I understood, that what she was saying was something terrible. Softly she was talking, as though she was reciting a poem. Three sentences she said. In those three sentences lay a curse more terrible than anything ever uttered by anyone.

"I parted the curtains and saw them. I couldn't stop myself from going out, it was as if a hand was pushing me there. Ma, I cried. She said, more harshly than she has ever said anything to me in my life—Go inside. The women, they were now looking at me. I stood rooted to the ground. A mother and a daughter, I could see the resemblance. The daughter was in her late twenties, the mother must have been less than fifty, a few years older than my mother. She had jet black hair, the mother, and everything about her was soft, her face, her body, and it wasn't because she was plump. It was a serene face, very calm and quiet, very dignified. The other woman, her daughter, resembled her, she had her sharp features and big eyes, very beautiful, like a dancer. But otherwise she didn't resemble her mother at all, her expression was completely different, the way she held her body was different. I remember when she saw me she looked frightened. Later I used to wonder, why should *I*, a child, have frightened her?

"The mother saw me and she looked at me, she smiled. Before this I had been frightened. Now terror filled me. I wanted to run but could not move. She began to speak and I recognized her voice, it was the second voice that had cursed, the soft voice, the voice that I thought had been praying. She pointed to me and again spoke in her language. Two sentences she said in her soft, evil voice. My legs began to move, I ran to my older sister and put my arms around her. Again the mother spoke, still looking at me. This time she was not saying anything at me. She was speaking to me in her language. Just two sentences, very clearly, very deliberately. Gently. As if she were explaining my lessons to me." She paused, her brows furrowed. "Evil. That was what filled our house that day. It came from her, not from her daughter. It was as though I lay in a snake pit and the words crawled over my body like snakes. I looked at her daughter. All I was feeling, it was reflected on her daughter's face. Her daughter was looking at her mother almost in terror, as though she was saying, Ma, no, no, no, take it back, take it back. My sisters and my mother, who also had not understood what the mother was saying, were also looking at the daughter. The horror on her face was not something to see. No daughter should look like that at her mother. Now when I think of that day, it is the daughter's face that I recall. I think of the daughter's face and I know I am not imagining what I now know about her mother's curse."

For a long time neither Anu nor Sita said anything. Anirudh was fast asleep again in the berth above his father, who was asleep too on the lower berth and Prabha had shifted to the other side and was sitting next to Sita, reading another book. Outside the wheat fields gleamed yellow against an unclouded blue sky. They said the monsoon would come early this year. Now, every time it rained it was Shanta's voice that she heard, describing the day Mallika was born, the thunder and lightning outside, the quietness inside as the baby suckled.

"I never saw them again," Sita said. "The mother said, Shanta. Then they left."

It was true, He was right, she had an overactive imagination. It was true, what He said, her mind was always running amuck. Try and control your mind, He had said. He was right. Two and two do not make five.

"As soon as they left I said to them, What happened, what happened? My mother said, These two women are mad. I asked, What did they say, why did they come? My sister said, It has nothing to do with you, stop asking questions. Why were they cursing, didi, I cried. My older sister, she grasped my shoulders and hissed, What did you hear, tell me, what did you hear? I told her. My older sister took me to Ma's bedroom, put my hand on the Gita which lay on her bedside table, and said, Now swear on the Gita that what happened today, you will not repeat to anyone. But, didi— I said. Swear, my sister shouted, right now swear—*What I heard today, I will never speak of this to anyone.* I repeated what she said. Then she seemed satisfied. I said, Didi, tell me. Be quiet, she said, don't ask any more questions. My other sister said, more gently, Now forget all that, they were mad women, frustrated women. There is nothing to fear. My elder sister said, If you break your promise God will punish you so badly that your whole life will be blighted; remember, you swore on the Gita."

"They were from the South?" Anu asked. She hadn't intended asking. The words came out by themselves.

Sita nodded. "What is the matter, didi, is your head aching?"

Anu, who had been rubbing her eyebrows with her thumb, stopped. "A little bit, it is all right, it happens."

"My mother also she gets headaches," Sita said, "very bad headaches. Do you want an aspirin?"

Anu shook her head.

"After that no one spoke about it. Once, about two years after it happened, I mentioned it to my mother and she looked puzzled and said, What women are you talking about, and when I reminded her she said, dismissively, Oh, those two, God knows what all you keep in your mind, even I had forgotten about those two women."

"What your mother said is right. There is no point thinking about such things."

"Didi," Sita said, "my brother and his wife and my two sisters, none of them have children. That is all right, even that is all right. But my sisters, they—" she stopped abruptly.

"Beti," Anu said, "do not dwell on what cannot be changed. You are going to your mother's house. You go there and rest and become strong."

"There is no rest in my mother's house. My mother's house is like a snake pit."

"Beti—"

"My mother she lives in this snake pit and prays. All day, all night, she prays. All the time, puja-path, puja-path, this havan, that havan. In every room photos of her guru, photos of the Gods. The Gods, they are powerless." Then, for a long time she did not say anything. Anu looked out the window. Sita said, "Now I know the mother's curse. Now I know what the mother said."

"Mumma, I'm hungry."

"Wait. Not now."

"But now my question is why? No one utters curses without a reason, no?" Sita's voice was sharp, persistent. "To put a curse on someone, the person who is cursing must have been greatly wronged. She said, *May my sister's suffering come back to you through your children.*"

"So—"

"The words still ring in my ears. Every day I think, How did my family cause her sister to suffer? My mother and sisters have never harmed anyone. Perhaps every daughter feels this about her family. But I know they cannot deliberately harm anyone, they cannot. Then what? Didi, must a person truly be wronged for a curse to come true?"

Ahalya. Anu shook her head. "Perhaps not. The person who is cursing must really believe that a wrong has been done to him or her. That belief is enough to give the curse its power."

"Then all this suffering, it could be not because any of us did anything wrong, but because someone believes that we have done wrong?"

"Yes, that could be."

"Then what justice is there, didi, what is the meaning of anything?"

"There is no justice in suffering."

"My mother and sisters do not even talk about it amongst themselves. I know. After that day I would try and eavesdrop on their talk. I had sharp ears, soft steps. Not once. Never."

"I have to go to the bathroom, beti, one minute."

In the bathroom she stood silently for five minutes, swaying with the motion of the train. Enough, enough. She washed her face, then remembered she had no towel. She wiped her face with her saree palla and went out slowly. Sita was waiting for her, her eyes fixed unwaveringly on the door. She sat next to Sita, holding her palla out from over her shoulder, and spreading it, began to shake it to dry.

"Sita," she said, "let it go now."

"How can I let it go?" Sita asked. "Never."

Anu said nothing. Her headache was much worse.

"Didi, there was a man with them. I heard his voice when I was in the other room. But when I went out he wasn't there." She opened her bag and took out a packet. She tore it and gave a pill to Anu. "Here, have this aspirin. You will feel better." She poured a glass of water from the surhai and gave it to Anu.

Anu drank. Then she asked, "Where was your brother that day?" Why was she asking?

"He was in Delhi, he was training for the civil services."

"What is it, Sita?"

"They didn't want my brother to know."

"Sita—"

"My brother. The younger woman's sister."

Anu looked out of the window. The blind was down. She could see nothing. She turned back to Sita, who was cracking her knuckles automatically. "But what to ask my brother?"

"All these years you have not spoken of it to anyone. What will be achieved by asking your brother now?"

"I will know."

"Know what, beti. What is there to know?"

"I cannot tell you, didi, I cannot tell you."

They were all still sleeping, He, Anirudh. Prabha also, curled up next to Sita, her book next to her. Sleep, keep sleeping.

"But how can I ask him. I have never in my life asked him anything of a personal nature. He is so much older than me. I can never speak to him about what I feel about our mother. He is devoted to her. He does not know my mother used to read all our letters, my sisters, mine, every letter we got from our friends our mother read as if it was her right. My sisters they used to give her all their letters after they read them. When I used to say, No, you can't read my letter, then they would all laugh, my sisters, my mother. Then my mother used to say, If there is nothing to hide then why not? Once when I came home from my friend's house she was sitting in my room reading all my letters. I shouted, You can't read my letters without my permission. She gave me one hard slap. She said, Mothers have to protect their children, who knows what rubbish your friends write to you, one day God knows you will get letters from some boy and keep it from your mother."

"Are your brother and his wife happy?"

"I told you, no, they don't have children. It has affected his wife very badly."

"It must have affected your brother too."

"I don't know."

"You said he's changed?"

"In the beginning I did not understand. But now I think I see. That spark inside him. That is gone. It's dead. I was too young to see when it happened. And now I cannot reach out to him. He is like a shell, dark and hollow inside."

"Those women who came to your house, what did they—"

"I want to ask my brother about those women. But I am frightened of asking. I want to ask him, and I want to say to the Gods, If you curse me for breaking the promise I made on the Gita, then let your curses rain on me. Rain harder, rain harder."

A long silence. "He . . . has great affection for his wife?"

"In a marriage one cannot say about these things." Sita paused and said, "You look happy."

"I *am* happy," Anu said quietly. "I have good children and a good husband."

"Do not take offence. I meant what I said—you look happy. Before we started talking I was looking at you—you were gazing out of the window and smiling. A lot he loves you."

"Who?" Anu asked, startled.

"He, who else."

Anu smiled.

"You cannot fool me with your smile. When you were feeding your children I saw how he was looking at you."

"Accha."

"He looks at you as if there is no one in this world for him except you and your children."

Padma had said so once. After Padma and Shanta and Shanta's family had had dinner with them, Padma had whispered to Anu in the kitchen,

"Anu, you know what He said?" Anu looked up from the dishes to Padma's glowing face. Padma said, "I told your husband, Anu is looking beautiful today. He smiled and replied, She always looks beautiful. Padma peered into Anu's face. Anu went red. "To me he does not say it," she murmured. "Oh, Anu," Padma said, laughing, "he can't live without you," and began drying the dishes. He could not live without her? Like in the books, in the films? Padma saying He couldn't live without her made it true. At least for that brief moment it was true.

"I didn't tell you something, didi. I know her name."

Anu looked up at Sita's face, bemused.

"It was written on the horoscope."

Anu didn't reply.

"The sister of the woman who cursed us the first time. The daughter of the woman who cursed us the second time. She."

"After all these years it does not matter. All that—"

"But I forgot to tell you that part—after my mother and sisters made me swear on the Gita, they went to my mother's bedroom and locked the door. When I went back to the sitting room I found a piece of paper lying on the side table.

"Destroy it. Do not hold on to the past."

"Remember, earlier when we were talking about horoscopes I told you about showing my friend's horoscope to the pandits? It wasn't my friend's horoscope—it was this girl's."

"What has happened has happened. It is of no use—"

"Didi, what happened in the past is affecting us to this day." Sita had unzipped her bag and was fumbling inside it.

"Everyone has built a life for themselves. You do not know what you are doing."

"What life, didi, our lives have no meaning." She stopped digging in her bag and looked at Anu with a faraway expression. Her eyes focussed on Anu's face. "I know now that something must have happened between my brother and this girl, you also must have concluded that."

"Yes."

"Nothing I understand. My brother, he was not that kind of person. He was . . . is . . . an intellectual. Everything he has read, everything he can talk about—he wasn't interested in girls."

"Maybe, then, he . . . in his college he knew . . . this girl and began to care for her?"

"Didi, if he cared for her he would have married her. My brother, he does not care for people easily."

"Maybe, it was casual from his side . . . men, they . . ."

"No." Sita shook her head firmly. "He is not like that."

"Some men, they—"

"My brother is a man of integrity. Whatever his faults. He used to be moody, completely spoilt by our mother—he is her moon and her sun—all that I know. But he was, is, honest. Maybe the girl fell in love with him and imagined he reciprocated, some girls, they throw themselves at men, they—"

"Never."

Sita's eyes widened. Anu looked away, she felt that she was suffocating. She hadn't intended it to come out so harshly.

Sita gave a small shrug and began looking in her bag again. "I can never find anything in my bag, everything I throw into it. My mother-in-law said if I could pack my sarees in my handbag then I would do that." She pulled out a folded piece of paper. "Here it is. See." She gave it to Anu.

The window next to Anu was closed. She couldn't open it now, couldn't let the wind snatch the paper from her hands. Fool. She was a fool. She and her mad imagination. Two and two do not make five. She opened the paper and saw the astrological chart made with bright blue ink, the incomprehensible squiggles in each house. "Let me see, Mumma," Prabha was awake now, kneeling next to Sita, peering into the chart. "Stop it," Anu said automatically, transferring the paper to her other hand and pushing Prabha back. Two and two do not make five. It was written there, clearly, at the top left-hand corner—*Horoscope of Miss Padma Rao, 1935.*

Nothing had happened after that. A coincidence, that is what it was. Both names. Sita's description of the sister, that also. Their being from the South, that also. There must be hundreds of Shantas and Padmas who were Raos and who were sisters. Her thinking of just them just before Sita uttered their names, that too was a coincidence. To come to the conclusions she had, based on such flimsy evidence, was a sure sign of her overactive imagination, of her ability to take two and two and make seven. If nothing had happened it was because it had nothing to do with this Padma.

But at night as she lay awake, other stories clouded the landscape.

Padma never talking about her husband. Padma living in Delhi so far away from her family. Neither her family nor his having anything to do with her. Now Anu understood. If there was any justice it was in the force of the curses uttered by Padma's sister and her mother. But was he suffering for it? No. His wife was, his sisters were. What did he know of it? So charming, Madhu had said. Such a gentleman. So handsome. Madhu had been charmed off her feet, even while imparting the awful news, she had giggled and simpered. My pleasure, he had said. Bilkul, bilkul. The pleasure was all his. The consequences were all Padma's. Padma. He had charmed her too.

What did Sita know. Women never knew their brothers. With them their brothers were different men. Honesty, integrity—hah. Tenderness, understanding—hoh. All for their sisters. Her own husband, she had caught him brushing the tears from his eyes after Kamala's wedding, when Kamala left for her husband's house. Had he ever wept for her, Anuradha? Whenever Kamala came to Delhi, He treated her with the same tenderness that he treated Prabha. He knew what sweets and fruits to buy for her. He remembered that she liked karelas, even knew that she preferred stuffed karelas to the chopped ones.

Compassion. She could not show hers to Padma. She could not say, Padma, in our mythology, it happens all the time. Look at Kunti. She bore Karan out of wedlock, and what a great man he was, greater than the Pandavas. And Shakuntala. Even Hanuman—he was born of Anjani and the Wind God—they were not married, and don't we all worship Hanuman? And look at Sita, they say she was born of the earth, and the earth took her back. Our Shastras do not condemn.

At night as she lay awake, stories like tornadoes gathered momentum inside her head, whirling into motion and out into the darkness, one after the other, one after the other. Shanta and her mother. They had gone to Lucknow with the proposal. That's why the horoscope. They knew of Padma's pregnancy. In the Lucknow house Shanta and her mother had got to know about his marriage, and then they had cursed them.

Would Sita finally ask her brother? She tried to imagine the scene. Sita would tell her brother what she had overheard all those years ago. He then would ask his mother and his sisters what had happened. Or maybe he would not. Why should he? All right. First scene, he would not ask. Why should he? He had had no intention of marrying Padma. Second scene, he would ask. They would eventually tell him—a proposal came to you from the family of Miss Padma Rao. They would say, This Padma, her family is mad—they cursed us because we told them you were married. They would say, We did not tell you because there was no point, you were already married. He would not ask any more. He had had no intention of marrying Padma.

No, wait. Wait. Randi. Sita's mother had uttered that unmentionable word. It was not addressed to Shanta and her mother. It was the response to Shanta and her mother's revelation about Padma. My sister is pregnant, your son is the father, Shanta must have said. My daughter is going to have a baby, your son's baby, Padma's mother could have said. Sita's mother's response—Your daughter is a whore. Whore. Randi.

Next scene. His mother and sisters telling him about Padma's pregnancy. Then? One: it would make no difference to him at all. Two: he would not believe it. Three: he would believe it but deny it. Four: he would be stunned by the revelation, struck by remorse, he would want his child, he would seek Padma out like a man demented, like a Hindi film Hero, beg her forgiveness, marry her, be a husband, a father . . . fool, fool . . . he was already married. All right then. He would want only Mallika. Then? How would he find her? No difficulty in finding out where Padma's parents lived in Bangalore. Perhaps he already knew where. All right, so he would go there and ask for Padma's address. He would not say who he was. They would give it to him. No, Padma's parents would not give him Padma's address. They would never give her address to a strange man, never. They would scent who he was in a moment. Five . . . ah yes, yes, *this* was the answer: he would deny it to his mother and his sisters, but the truth would be that he already knew. The truth would be that he already knew because Padma had told him about it. And with full knowledge, he had cast her aside.

He was in Delhi. Or was he just visiting Delhi? Fool that she was, fool. She should have asked Sita where her brother lived. It had not even occurred to her to ask. Her mind had been burning with other thoughts, other conclusions. All right, so he was posted in Delhi when Madhu met him. But then, so what? He could be posted out by now. Or, maybe he had never been posted to Delhi but had been there for some other reason—work, holiday . . . ?

What would He say if He ever came to know about Padma? Madhu had told her once, "Such a kind man he is, Anu, your husband." She had said it in a rare moment of weakness, that time when she had come crying to Anu's house in the middle of the night when everyone was asleep and Anu was washing up the last of the dishes in the kitchen. Anu had heard the tap at her kitchen window and seen Madhu's face against it. Anu had unlocked the back door of the kitchen and Madhu, weeping, had entered. That was before Padma came to live with them, Madhu had been pregnant with Mahima. "Where can I go, Anu, tell me, where can I go?"

"What do you mean?" Anu had asked, her body becoming cold.

"This much only I told Him," Madhu said, "that always when I have been pregnant, there has been no one to look after me. I said to him, This time I want to go to my eldest brother's house—his wife she loves me very much, she will take care of me. You remember her, no?" Anu nodded mutely. It was rare to have a sister-in-law who loved you as a sister, but Madhu's eldest brother's wife did. Which was what Madhu, starved for the love of a mother, wanted.

Now Madhu continued, "He said, If you think I am not a good husband, go and do not come back, I am not stopping you. I said to him, I am not saying that, all I am saying is that my mother is dead and at such a time I want that kind of love which only one woman can give to another—my sister-in-law she will look after me like an older sister. He said, All right then, I heard you, why are you repeating it again and again, you pack your suitcases and take the children and go, and there is no need for you to come back, you stay with your brother and his wife only, I am not stopping you." Madhu paused and wiped her eyes. "So I packed and I sat in the veranda and then I came here."

"Are you mad?" Anu said, her voice shaking with fear. "Tell him you're sorry. Everyone has fights. Tomorrow it will be all right."

Madhu had wiped her tears. "What else can I do," she murmured. She looked at Anu and said, "I have some money of my own in the bank, I can—"

Anu raised both her hands, "Bas. Don't talk like that. Money will not solve anything. Go to him before it is too late."

Madhu got up, wiping her eyes with a beautifully embroidered hanky. Madhu always had beautiful things, right down to the lace at the edge of her petticoats. "Such a kind man he is, Anu, your husband," she said before she left.

A kind man. Once, Anu, brooding about Padma, had said to Him, "Padma and Shanta, all the time they worry that they will die and there will be no one for Mallika."

He had considered briefly, then said, "Nothing will happen to them. It only happens to those who do not think about it."

She had been mulling over this when he added, "What is there to worry about. We are there to take care of Mallika."

Perspective. That was what happiness was. That sharp, quivering feeling which she had known in the early days of her marriage, that wasn't happiness, it was something else. Happiness was the absence of unhappiness, not its opposite. If unhappiness meant being plunged into the depths, then happiness had its reign not in the heights, but in the plains. Its nature was not blissful but calm, it did not heighten one's senses but dulled them. It was that middle ground one had to seek in order to live. The problem was, everyone sought the other. And when you really thought about it, whether you sought it or not, it was the middle ground that you inhabited finally, even while your thoughts crouched in those subterranean depths. As Padma often said, It was so much easier to think of those than of the other. The other, this happiness or whatever, just because one did not speak of it, it did not mean that it wasn't there. It just felt that way when you retreated into those depths; that panting sensation, that rhythm which went, this is all, this is all, this is all. Then you crawled out and began to breathe, the air was fresh and clean and the sun against your body warm, and it was there, the knowledge, clear as water, that that wasn't all.

# SHANTA

 It was always the worst after she came back from Delhi. Every year, the wounds went deeper. She couldn't even read in the bathroom after her return, not because of the inevitable external intrusions but because of the internal turmoil; it felt as though her body, like the vessels she cooked in, contained boiling oil to which a little water had been added, her thoughts were hundreds of scalding drops springing up and sputtering, and beneath, the fire burnt on.

The external intrusions were easier to pin down though, even though they never ended, from early morning to late at night they never ended. No time to think, even in the bathroom early in the mornings no peace. All of them helpless, standing outside the bathroom, shouting, Shanta, where are my socks; Mum, where is my maths textbook; Shanta, where did I keep my spectacles. Even in the lavatory she had to feel guilty. There also, work, the drum and buckets to be filled with water, water didn't come again till five in the evening and if she didn't fill the buckets no one else remembered, and just when the drum was filling up, and she finally sat back on the pot, then *they* got the urge and started banging on the door.

And to add to all this, even now she could hear the quiet disgust in her mother's voice as she said, Again reading in the toilet, Shanta—chee. When I get married, Shanta had thought, when I have a house of my own, no one will tell me I can't read in the toilet, no one can tell me anything. She opened the novel to page forty-two and tried to read, but it was hard, after returning from Delhi it was always hard, but she would get into it, she always eventually got into it, even felt a faint flutter as the Hero's mocking eyes turned unexpectedly soft. Narayana too read in the bathroom, but for him it was the morning paper with a cigarette. But no one interrupted *his* cigarette.

Sometimes when she pictured the hero it was Sumit's face that rose before her, so English and handsome, so fair. His sister, Sumi, had been in college with Padma, and she had bumped into him in Bangalore that time when she had gone to see Amma and Appa. He had begun chatting about the lunch Amma had given him and Sumi when they came home as though he had dined with them a few days ago instead of all those years ago. Unable to speak she had smiled and nodded like a schoolgirl with a crush. "How is Padma?" he asked. "Padma's all right," she replied. He will ask for her address, she had thought, her heart beating like a drum, then what will I say, what will I say, I will say I have it in my address book but I do not know it by heart, that is what I'll say, then he'll say, Can you send it to me, and I will nod but I won't send it to him. All this passed in her mind at that moment, but he just nodded and asked her about her children and Narayana and other things, all of which she must have responded to, none of which she remembered later. After they said goodbye she remembered that she had not asked about Sumi at all. Oh God what must he have thought, after all those times that Sumi stayed in our house and after all those years that she and Padma shared a room in college—and she had not asked about Sumi. Too late. It could not be helped, her brain had not functioned. His face stayed with her long after he left, that wonderfully handsome face . . .

"What are you *doing*, Mummy, hurry up." There. There. She should have known. "Go to the other bathroom, Vikram," she answered, knowing his response, and there it was, "Daddy's in the other one, *hurry*, Mummy." Of course, the question of saying, Hurry, Daddy, didn't even arise. And Varun, twelve now, as old as Mallika, and no better than his brother. She pulled the flush (the guilt for this surreptitious reading would never leave her, nothing would ever leave her), and went out. "Where are you, Vikram?" she called and from the bedroom he yelled, "It's O.K., Mummy, I don't want to go now." She should have guessed, a three-year-old or a teenager, it was the same.

"Don't read, Mummy, don't read," Vikram would say to her as a child of three. Like a cracked record he would say it as she sat trying to read after finishing the endless household chores, "*Don't read, Mummy, don't read.*" "*Stop it,*" she would scream, "*stop it will you.*" He would look at her thoughtfully. "Don't read, Mummy, don't read," and he tugged at her saree and she slapped him hard and he burst out crying, clawing at her saree with one hand and hitting her with the other and so she slapped him again and he screamed louder and of course, after that she couldn't read anyway. That's how it always ended, it was as though he was egging her on to hit him every time, and after she did it he cried till she had to comfort him, and he would only be comforted when her anger dissipated and her anger never did. And by the end of it all he had accomplished his purpose and she had to go back to the kitchen to supervise and instruct the bungalow peon about lunch and dinner and keep an eye on him as he cleaned the house and see to it that he shook the sheets and bedcovers while making the beds, and instruct him to keep an eye on the jamadar when he came, because on his own the jamadar never cleaned behind the pot or put Phenyle inside it and more often than not the gardener was sleeping under the neem tree instead of watering the garden, so she had to get after him too. No one wanted to work and getting them to work was another trial, and Narayana refused to reprimand any of them.

"Your husband is in the railways, oh so lucky," Padma's friend Madhu would always say to Shanta and it always infuriated her, this assumption that you had servants and didn't have to do any work. And Madhu had pots of money, two houses and one car and even the only T.V. in the neighborhood. "Oh, money—money isn't important," Madhu would say shrugging her shoulders, "what is money after all, you don't take it with you when you die." Shanta had noticed that it was always people who had money who claimed that it wasn't important. "When are we going to build our house, Narayana," Shanta would ask him and he would turn the page of his newspaper and say, "When we have the money," and that of course, they didn't and never would, and he never thought about it, he never considered what would happen after he retired and where they would live or how she would live if he died.

Sometimes she thought these thoughts in the bathroom, where she soaked in the blessed silence, her thoughts uncoiling and rising. She learnt to hide her book under her saree, put Vikram with his toys in the bedroom and shut herself inside. She began doing it every day. She who had never craved solitude in all her life discovered its pleasures among the toothbrushes, the mugs, the taps and the buckets; solitude smelt of Phenyle and soap, solitude was the sound of the dripping tap and the rustle of pages between her fingers. For a long time Vikram didn't know, and perfunctorily he would call, "Come out, Mummy, come out," and she would reply, "Coming, coming, I'll finish and come," and he would murmur with great comprehension, "You finish and then you will come," and so it went on for some weeks, quite amicably. There was quite a thrill in it actually, this whole business of hiding the book and shutting yourself in the bathroom; when the time came for it every day she would feel her pulse beating faster, her tummy feeling queasy with anticipation . . . rather like having a quick, no-strings-attached affair or eating chocolates on the sly, it kept you alive and it kept your shoulders above this daily business of living, and what was this daily business anyway that like an eclipse consumed so much of your life so swiftly, so that you hardly noticed the day slowly darkening or the evening approaching when it should be morning, and when the unnatural night quietly fell you didn't notice that either, till one day you heard the silence. You knew then, knew too why not to look up to view this other sun; it would damage your eyes.

Vikram caught her one day, slipping the paperback into her saree and as she sat inside he pounded at the door, wailing, "*Don't* read, Mummy, *don't* read." Anger welled up inside her like lava, she fixed her eyes on the page but she couldn't read. Outside, the wailing and pounding continued. Then there was a silence. "*Bad* lady," Vikram shouted. "Bad, bad-bad, not *good, bad.*" She put down her book and waited. There was a longer silence. "Dog," Vikram said, "not *good* dog, *bad* dog." He was getting into form. "*Rascal,*" he bawled, "dog, cat, bear, lion, tiger, hippopotamus, camel." He had stopped sobbing. "Table, chair, spoon, plate, paper, pen, pencil, sky, tree." She came out then, laughing, and tried to take him in her arms, love for him surging up the way it used to when she suckled him, but he would have none of it. "Don't kiss me," he said, irritated, "I don't like it."

It would be different with her next child, she had thought, her hand on her still flat stomach. She was sure that it was a girl growing within her. It was not just the fact of kissing and cuddling which you could do so much more of with a daughter. It was more than that. Her daughter, like her dream-lover, would want to know her mother. Through her daughter, as through her dream-lover, she would discover herself, give words to all that lay within. Her dream-lover, whom she had sustained all her life, and who had sustained her till she got married, was now long dead, but he had known her well, he had asked her the questions her husband never did,

and not a night had passed before her marriage when they hadn't con-
versed at length. He knew that she had something "up there," unlike her
husband who once said, "If you have something up there how can you read
such rubbish." She had tried explaining to Narayana that reading romances had nothing to do with the way one thought, but she couldn't find
the words. Years later the words came to her and she said to him as they
ate dinner, "Reading romances doesn't have anything to do with the way
you think." He had looked blankly at her. She reminded him of the past
conversation and he said, tiredly, "Why must you always bring up the past,
Shanta, I don't remember what we talked about five days ago and you
bring up incidents from five years ago. If you want to talk, talk about *now*."
She wanted to say, "But Narayana, between us nothing happens in isolation, there are patterns, Narayana, can't you see—the same things happen
again and again." But these words too took several years to form, and when
they did, she thought, triumphantly, now I can say it calmly, logically, now
I can say it without shouting. She told Narayana, and he looked blankly at
her and said, "What are you talking about?" She reminded him. He looked
at her as if she were mad. To her shock his voice was shaking as he said, "I
don't know what you're talking about, I've had enough of this, Shanta."
She began to cry then, saying, "I've read all the classics, I've read more than
you have, I read the newspaper too when the children and the servants
aren't sitting on my head." But he wasn't listening, he wasn't there, he had
gone to the bedroom. And though she knew she shouldn't, though she
knew it was the worst thing she could do, she marched into the bedroom
and, sobbing, said some more. He continued reading.

Once, a year after her marriage Amma had asked her, "Have you ever
cried in front of Him?" She had nodded and her mother had sighed and
said, "Then you're finished." "Why, Amma?" she had asked, already knowing the answer in some deep recess of her mind, but she wanted it put into
words. Her mother said, "Once you cry, always you cry, it doesn't even affect them." Shanta said, "It isn't for effect that I cry, Amma," and her
mother replied, "That I know. But that is what happens. Then you hate
them and you hate yourself more. No need for that, Shanta, so much of
our lives we spend hating ourselves." "Amma," Shanta said, shaken as she
saw her mother's veil lifting for the first time, "Amma, you—" And then
their neighbours had rung the bell and dropped in and the moment was
lost. Sometimes Shanta had felt she didn't fully understand her mother,

this woman who never raised her voice and whom she had never seen crying or angry, whom she had never heard arguing with her father, of whom everyone said, So gentle, so soft-spoken. When people said that Shanta had hated herself for the violence that she so often felt against Amma. But now she knew. After that morning in Lucknow she knew. Amma had revealed herself, finally and awfully. Gentle. Kind. Forgiving. Lies. Lies. Wrapped up deep inside that gentleness and softness lay the truth, like the jagged, gaping mouth of a broken bottle.

Shanta's dream-lover was over and done with, burnt to the bones. But she had spoken of all this to her unborn daughter, who in her mind was already old enough to listen—in fact, she was listening now, absorbing her mother's voice, her soul soaking in her mother's dreams. Her daughter would ask her the kind of questions her dream-lover used to ask her once. What were you like when you were five? her daughter would ask. Then she would answer, Full of life, full of confidence, always ready with an answer. My father, unlike my mother, always admired my spirit.

"Too much anger inside you, my child," her mother said once at the dining table.

"But, Amma," twelve-year-old Shanta had said, enraged, "you gave me two pieces of chicken and you gave Madhav *three*. Why are you *always* doing that?"

Her mother put another piece of chicken on Shanta's plate. Shanta dragged the steel vessel of chicken curry towards her, took out the last piece, and put it on her plate.

"Now you have four and I have three," Madhav said in an injured tone.

Shanta ate without talking, her throat full; she couldn't swallow the food.

"See," her mother said gently as the servant cleared the table later, "you left the fourth piece."

After four days of silence her mother took her on her lap, and said, "Control yourself, Shanta, anger must be contained, all right?" Shanta nodded. That evening when her mother poured Madhav a full glass of milk and her three fourths of a glass, Shanta threw both glasses on the floor. The glass shattered, the milk spread slowly, and Shanta waited for her mother to scream. Her mother's lips tightened and she withdrew from Shanta for another three days.

What did Padma know of all this. Whom else did Appa and Amma have to cosset and indulge but Padma while she and Madhav were away at college. There was nothing Padma had to fight for or argue about the way she, Shanta, did, it was as if Shanta had paved the way for her younger sister with her own arguing and fighting. For most of the year it was Padma alone who sat for lunch with Amma and Appa, and they filled her plate with the best pieces of chicken and her favourite, liver. How Padma had adored Shanta. As a child she had listened to her stories, had sighed with pleasure at the frocks her older sister made for her, had sat on her lap with her arms around Shanta's neck in much the same way that Mallika now did. But now only Mallika loved Shanta the way she wanted to be loved, only her love was pure, complete, demanding in the way children were demanding, knowing you were there for them anywhere and any time, which she was, and Shanta thanked Krishna that Narayana was in the railways or else how would she and the boys go to Delhi with this kind of regularity, not once but often twice a year?

Now, it was Mallika who asked, "What did you read when you were young?"

"So much I read," Shanta would answer, her eyes dreamy, "not all these stupid romances—no, no—I read all the classics, the Brontës, George Elliot, Jane Austen, Dickens, all those books—oh, yes—and also Marie Corelli—oh, the romance, the scenery, I had stars in my eyes—and Thomas Hardy—oh, Tess, how I wept and wept for her. When you both went away to Delhi your mother took most of my books, she said, Acca, can I keep them till I can afford to buy some, they'll keep me sane, Acca. How could I refuse, not that I considered refusing, but I felt a wrench, I felt I was giving away part of myself, I said, Padma, Why do you ask, take them all."

When Mallika is older, Shanta thought, I will tell her the rest. Of how I thought to myself, now Padma will never have time to read.

She would tell Mallika how, once in those early days in Delhi Padma had cried, I feel consumed by everything, Shantacca, consumed.

I told your mother, Padma, Padma, do you think you are the only one?

Despairingly, she said, Acca, in one day how much do we do of what we truly love. And then she replied, For me, nothing, Acca, nothing, I can't read, you've given up your Bharatnatyam.

I said, Padma, no point talking this way, no point at all. After marriage and motherhood, you get fulfillment in other things. You only tell me,

Does anyone love you more than Mallika? And tell me, who will be there for you in your old age except your husband and your children?

Oh Acca, she cried, wouldn't you rather read or dance for two hours than cook and clean for two hours?

Padma, I told her, one does not think of what one cannot do.

Tears streaming down her cheeks, wiping her nose with my hanky (even now she uses my hankies, never has her own), she said, I too love Mallika, she's my life, I can't live without her, but Acca, she too is consuming me.

Listen, Padma, I said, stop talking about Mallika as if she were a python.

Padma said, I ask myself, why can't I be a good mother to Mallika and do other things, too?

I sighed, Padma, you might as well ask yourself, Why can't I go to the moon.

We looked at each other and I felt as if we were standing on opposite sides of a broken mirror, each of us reflecting the other.

Mallika, my love, you might have been born of your mother's womb, but as you grew inside her it was my voice you heard, my food you ate. Amma used to say, A woman who is carrying a child should have good, pure thoughts, she should avoid things which make her angry or unhappy, it will affect the child. Amma said, The foetus hears everything outside, voices, music, everything. But your poor mother couldn't help thinking her thoughts any more than you could help growing inside her. Like a prisoner in a dark cell she was with her thoughts, and you, a tumor growing inside her. As you lay inside your mother's womb, it was your Shanta-mama's endearments that you heard, not your mother's, it was your Shan-tamama's hand that caressed you when you moved in your mother's womb. So wasn't it only natural that you suckled me before you suckled her, that it was your Shantamama who could make you go to sleep in two minutes when your mother couldn't even after rocking you for one hour? Isn't it only natural that I know, that I understand all your secret thoughts and dreams? Oh may your secrets never reveal themselves to you.

It was a small world, that was the thing, a very small world. However carefully you guarded your secrets, things from the outside world had a way of moving inexorably towards them. Like Madhu, whose cousin's husband's sister was married to "a very nice Madrasi" and the "nice Madrasi" had turned out to be Narayana's classmate in college years and years ago and Narayana had said to Shanta, almost bashfully, "His sister was the college beauty." Shanta, prodding relentlessly, had found out that Narayana had been quite smitten with the College Beauty for his entire two years in college, her Narayana whom she had thought incapable of entertaining any romantic sentiments; he had even written poetry for this girl, which he never had for his wife. Sometimes Shanta wished she had been this girl so that she would remain frozen in Narayana's dreams as this girl still must, a memory sweet and chaste and tender, and yes, wistful . . . sentiments never associated with a wife. Shanta didn't doubt Narayana's love for her, she knew that if she died before him he would be bereft. But there would be nothing wistful in his memories of her.

She fantasized about dying or being close to death. Sometimes the former seemed preferable, they would know her worth then, all of them, its finality would bring about the realizations long overdue, they would grieve bitterly. But then what of Vikram and Varun and Mallika, how would they survive her death? How would Padma? She wept at the thought, her body heaving as Narayana snored gently beside her. Perhaps it was better then, to be close to death, it would achieve the same purpose and the children would survive, and she would see the others in their agony and their fear, know, at last, how much she mattered to them. But after that? Would a mighty change be wrought, would her life change its course the way some rivers did, leaving in their wake only devastation? Naturally not; once she recovered, life would go on, unchanged. That was the problem with this fantasy of Almost Dying But Not Quite. It was only in books that the Heroine almost died, and the Hero realized in that infinitely satisfying moment of revelation how much She meant to Him. Actually He realized it even if She cut her hand or twisted Her ankle, for Her pain was His.

Shanta's body began to heave. Next to her in bed Narayana opened his eyes. "Are you crying again," he sighed. "No," she said, turning her back to him, her body shaking with laughter. So much for books! How could Her pain ever be His! Her pain was constant. It was the way she lived. She was deformed from the beginning by all that had to be contained. It was a way of life to contain the relentless pain of her monthly periods, it was a way of life to have contained the pain of that torn, unmentionable body part after each childbirth, which refused to heal for so long. It was a way of life to have contained the pain of her two miscarriages and the subsequent scraping and cleaning of her uterus. Everyone believed that she was as strong as a horse, and most often she believed it herself, for none of her physical problems incapacitated her, and her other ailments—the headaches, the skin rashes, the low fever—they came and they went. It was Padma's frequent illness which totally swamped her. Padma didn't complain either but she had the ability to make people rally around her. Madhu and Anu looked after Padma like mother hens, they would do anything for her. Her college friend Sumi would have done anything for her. Why didn't anyone feel this way about her, Shanta? When Padma had been with them and had a bout of flu, Narayana had said to her, "Rest properly, Padma." Shanta had said to Narayana that day, "You would never have said, Rest, Shanta, if I was sick, would you?" Narayana had replied, "There's no point asking you to rest, you never will."

It was when he made such remarks that the rage filled her ears till she felt she could walk out of the house leaving everything behind her including her children. She fantasized about it sometimes, fantasized about Narayana looking desperately for his socks and vests every morning and coming back from the office and tutoring the boys and managing the servants and not knowing what rations to order every month. Oh God, Oh God, Shanta would think, almost laughing at the irony of it. So even in her imagination this was all Narayana would miss, the absence of clothes and appropriate food and a well-organized house . . . this then was the tragedy, her knowledge of what she meant to him now, just a footprint that would in time disappear, nothing deeper, or sharper, or sweeter.

As for the other unfathomable pain—she could never find words for it, the words came out all wrong, when she tried to explain she found herself accusing; instead of sounding measured and logical, she sounded emotional and high pitched. She could never know how or why this pain had taken root, it had been conceived when she had been conceived, she had been born with its seed, as had her mother and her mother's mother. But this pain her mother and her mother's mother had contained with greater ease than she could, they had not allowed it to show its hideous face, whereas she, Shanta, felt that its face had now become hers. What understanding could he have of this pain when she herself had none?

Get married, then you'll settle down, Amma used to say to her, to Madhav, to Padma. Settle down. What was so settling about marriage? The only thing settling was the surface, only the surface was calm and content, one even took on the expression of other married women, their mannerisms, their conversation, one stopped being a girl and became a woman, and this was no gentle blossoming, but instead, an unseen withering. One stopped asking questions about life and love and relationships as in one's college days; instead, one lived it in ways never imagined before. In her college days everything had been so black and white, especially her conception of marriage—something so intimate could only be wonderful or terrible. In truth it was neither. Marriage was grey, perhaps brown, an indeterminate colour, it gave her no excuse for such violent feelings.

Control yourself, Shanta, control yourself. Even now, after all these years, she continued to hear her mother's voice, the refrain of her childhood. Now the incantation made sense. It was a preparation for the permanency of marriage and motherhood; her mother could not help saying it any more than she could help being born a woman. Shanta had raged against her mother, but now there was no one to rage against. Now no one said it to her, now she couldn't blame anyone. Blame anyone for what? She didn't know. Control yourself, Shanta, control yourself. Now she knew her mother's words, now they were ground into her bones. She saw how they sat so easily on every other woman, she saw that this was the only thing to be done. Yet this knowledge changed nothing. Her anger and guilt burned on. Narayana once had said to her, "Other women don't complain, why do you complain?" Other wives looked calm and happy, no doubt, as Narayana implied, because they were nicer, more generous, more exalted beings. She, Shanta, was the exception to this rule, something her mother had always believed anyway.

Was it a question of getting used to it the way one got used to sex? Often she wanted to ask Padma, did you enjoy it, you must have. But one didn't discuss these things with one's sister. Once when Narayana was huffing and puffing above her, she had thought about the whispered conversations she and her friends would have on the subject in college and had begun laughing. Narayana became still and then stopped. But she couldn't stop laughing and he never asked her why, just moved away. You look funny, she had thought, but what she wanted to say, as she had wanted to say after the very first time, was, *This* is it? That first time there had been a little pain and no pleasure; it had been unlike anything she had imagined. And after it was over she had felt a great emptiness; and an ache, which she had never understood, had taken root deep inside her. Easier to pin down was the guilt, for Narayana had not been rough, and he had been patient. But how could she have known that *this*, after the initial fumbling, would become as mechanical as ironing one's clothes or chopping cabbage, one's movements as automatic and unwavering, one's thoughts elsewhere. For a period there was some pleasure before and after as she lay close to Narayana, his arms around her, but after some time there was no before or after either.

The tragedy, thought Shanta, was that if she died Narayana's memory of her would be of someone high-strung and neurotic (his favourite word), and a nag, someone who was selfish and jealous and without intelligence, someone whom he depended on, and incidentally, loved, because she was his wife and took good care of him and the children and who unerringly knew where his socks and his vests were and what temperature he wanted to eat his sambar and drink his coffee, but not someone to admire or cherish or emulate in any way. Often she wondered if this was really true, and if so, then where was the girl to whom her father had said, "You better sit for the I.A.S.," to whom Padma had said, "Acca, you always give, you never take," to whom Madhav had come for years and years to be tutored, and said, "Shantacca, you are better than any of my teachers," to whom her mother, who rarely praised anyone, said, after she topped the university and got her gold medal, "You should have been a boy." Now she played bridge with the other railway officers and their wives, she kept a beautiful house, she tutored her sons relentlessly so that both got glowing reports from their teachers. Once when she had gone home her father had asked, "Have you hung up your gold medal in the kitchen?"

Appa had never got over his disappointment when she had declared that she wanted to get married, that she had no intention of working. "Work. Don't fry your brains in the kitchen," he would say to both her and Padma, and this in the forties and fifties when hardly any women worked. She hadn't taken his words seriously. Other things he said penetrated deeper, formed the shape of her girlhood and early womanhood, "Don't be afraid of the truth, always stand up for what you believe in." Amma uttered platitudes, Appa uttered truths. "Don't ever hide anything from us again," he had said to Madhav when they had found out about that girl with whom Madhav had had a brief but messy entanglement. "We are your parents, if you tell us the truth we will always stand by you." But Madhav, who had a weakness for fair, easy women, had done it again and again, only the subsequent entanglements were quieter, he got out of them with the same ease that he got into them. She, Shanta, knew; he couldn't hide anything from her—she smelt the perfume on his shirt, she knew that look on his face.

It was she, Shanta, Appa's firstborn for whom he had had the highest hopes, it was she whom he had talked to the most about the things he believed in, Amma never listened to him the way she did, Amma was too busy cooking special things for Madhav to listen to anyone. It was Appa who spoke to her of the need for independence and integrity, it was he who guided her as she went through school and college. With what ease she had let him down. After all these years she remembered the incomprehension in his voice as he asked her, "Why? Why don't you want to take up that lectureship?" For she had been offered one as soon as she finished her M.A., it had been offered to her on a platter. Amma had said to Appa, "If she wants to work she can also do it after she gets married, she can get any job, but she might not get such an offer again." Appa hadn't even looked at Amma. "Why, my child?" he had repeated.

But Appa hadn't asked Padma why.

There were some experiences that Shanta relived from time to time, experiences so deeply etched in her consciousness that she could remember them like a film in slow motion. The moments could not be categorized as simply happy or unhappy, they were—in a way—outside the bounds of understanding, beyond words or thoughts. Perhaps that was why she relived them, because even now all she could say to herself was, It was a strange feeling, such a strange feeling. She relived the time that she had gone into labour with Vikram, the long, excruciating hours, then the baby. There had been neither joy nor relief as she held him in her arms, this wrinkled, red new being that she had pushed out of her body. What did she feel for him? Not love, how could she love someone she didn't know? Yet she recognized a fierceness inside her that would kill anyone who might harm him. When she held him to her breast the same fierceness made her dizzy. There was wonder too, but that wasn't all, and she didn't know the rest. Today she could say, I know my son, I love him. But then, when it should have been so much simpler, she had had no words.

The day Padma came to her was another one of those moments that she often relived, trying to grasp the emotions that had risen and ebbed so rapidly. That day she had opened the door thinking it was the dhobi, and she was ready with her speech about cutting his pay for not putting enough starch in her sarees and in Narayana's shirts. But it was Padma who stood there with a suitcase beside her, her eyes red and swollen, Padma who said, "Shantacca, why didn't you come to the station?"

"I didn't know you were coming, darling," Shanta exclaimed, "come inside, come, come."

Padma had stepped backwards.

And Shanta forgot that Narayana was sitting in the armchair at the corner of the room where Padma couldn't see him, she forgot for the first and last time in her life that the milk would boil in two minutes, because already her hands were getting colder and her mouth drier and for a brief horrible moment everything before her swam and became dark as though Padma had already spoken the unspeakable. Then the darkness lifted and turning her head, she saw her neighbour, that nasty, gossipy woman, in the veranda of the next house, looking curiously at them, and Shanta hugged Padma and pulled her in, suitcase and all, and as she closed the door, Padma moaned, "I'm pregnant."

Shanta held her for a long time, felt her sister's soft hair against her neck, felt the sweat at her waist and the saree damp with it, and she thought, Now I won't be able to hide it from Narayana, what will I do. If he tells her to go then I'll go with her but how will I take the boys? Will I get custody? But even if I do then how will we manage? I can sell the jewels till I get a job.

Then she smelt milk burning as it boiled over the gas, and she ran to the kitchen, but not before she saw Padma's eyes dilate as she saw her brother-in-law looking at her from the corner where he sat, and not before Shanta heard him say, very gently, "There's nothing to cry about, Padma, we will look after you." And as Shanta turned off the gas and began cleaning the kitchen counter, her body heaving and heaving, she closed her eyes and whispered, "Krishna, Krishna, thank you, forgive me, I'll never complain about him again." A promise that she broke easily and repeatedly.

How could she help her oft-broken promise, how could she help it. She knew she had betrayed Lord Krishna, and this knowledge ate into her insides. She felt that if she had a soul it would resemble the moth-eaten sweaters that she was always salvaging from Padma's trunk—Padma, who always forgot to put in mothballs or neem leaves, who hated anything that required an extra effort. Everything ate into her insides and there was no escape, not from one's children, not from one's husband, not from one's parents and siblings, not from oneself.

Krishna, Krishna, forgive me, she begged when she prayed every morning, try and understand why I keep breaking my promise. Just today at six in the morning he shouts from the bedroom, Why do you make so much noise cleaning on holidays, can't a man sleep in peace. Only men sleep in peace, I shouted back at him. I don't want philosophy before sunrise, he yelled, and will you stop that khatat khatak noise. That khatat khatak noise, I said, are your shoes, which I'm putting in their proper place, is it my fault if you leave them all over the house, is it my fault if you leave the newspaper in the bathroom, is it—. And he groans, Oh God, stop it, will you. If he and the boys keep the house tidy, then I won't have to spend time cleaning, but no, they don't, then when I tidy up he gets irritated, so whose fault is that? Don't clean on holidays, he says, but on other days I have to get the children ready for school, iron their clothes, get their tiffin prepared, both the boys say, We don't like what the servant makes, we like your food, Mummy, then I get his tiffin ready, he wants something different every morning, he also likes my cooking better than the servants'. Then, half the time the dhobi irons so badly that I have to iron Narayana's shirts and pants again, imagine going to work with a crease on his shirt, they won't blame him, they'll blame his wife, say, Oho, so this is how she looks after her husband, poor man. Then after Narayana and the boys go, what a mess in the house . . . and who tidies that, who? Hardly any time for my bath and breakfast, then the children come back from school, then their lunch, their homework . . . does it ever end? Then on holidays he says, Don't clean so early in the mornings, because he wants to get up late, then he wants a big breakfast and after that no noise because he wants to read his paper in peace and listen to classical music, then lunch and in the afternoon don't do khatat khatak because he wants to read and sleep and in the evening he wants to visit friends or friends drop in and at night I'm too tired anyway. When do *I* read or listen to music or sleep late, tell me, when do *I*? He says, For one day if the house is untidy, then how does it matter. I told him, Because the next day I have two days' work to do, that's why, when people drop in then are you going to run around picking up the newspaper and shoes and toys and books, are you going to run to the kitchen to make a quick meal for our friends who arrive close to dinner-time? So casually he says it, Krishna, so casually, Oh, you must stay for dinner. Then who has to send the servant for vegetables and who begins to chop and grind, who has to wash and clean the china and wipe them while Narayana and our friends have intellectual conversations about politics and history? I tell you, Krishna, my brain has been chopped and ground and cooked, there's nothing left of it, he's right, absolutely right, I have nothing up there, nothing.

Once, after an evening spent with Madhav and his wife, Ratna, Narayana had mused, "What an intelligent woman Ratna is, how well-read."

Shanta said, "Narayana, even I have read a lot, I have read more than her."

He had looked at her mildly and replied, "Did I say you haven't?"

"But you never say that I'm well-read, Narayana, you think I'm empty up there, no?"

"*You* said that, not I."

"But I know what you're thinking."

Narayana had given her one of his tired looks. "So now even my thoughts are not my own."

"I know how she's managed that career of hers in the hotel, she's done it because she employs an ayah to look after the three children, she's done it because the ayah is the mother, not she."

Then Narayana said, very quietly, "Shanta sit down." She sat down, and felt the tiredness take over her body till it settled around her eyes. "There's an advertisement in the paper," Narayana said, "for a lecturer in this college, see, read this," and he opened the newspaper and put it on her lap. Then he groaned, "Shanta, why are you crying, what did I say now?"

Her throat was so full that for a few minutes she couldn't reply. Finally she said, "You and your suggestions. What do I qualify for? Nothing. I've forgotten my history, Narayana. I did my M.A. years and years ago."

"I'm only trying to help. There's no need for you to work like this in the house, Shanta, we have a bungalow peon, we have a dhobi, a mali, a jamadar, if you want we can employ a woman to do what you're doing now, try and relax a little."

She heard her voice grow high as she said, "Relax, what a joke, relax. I don't have money to buy a saree, we don't have money to put aside for a house and you talk about maidservants. And you think these days servants want to work? And where do you think I have the time to train her to work the way I want her to work? Why do you think Padma's Ayaji has lasted so long? She's lasted because Padma lets her do everything the way she wants to. If you really want to make me happy then start planning for our retirement. If you want to lighten my load then you and the boys try and keep the house tidy. So generous you are, so considerate, wanting to pay money that you don't have to someone to do what you and the boys should be doing."

She wanted to say more but didn't. She wanted to say, At whose expense does this generosity come, tell me? When we have meat every day for dinner, who has one piece of mutton and who has five or six pieces? Who has never bought herself even a small box of Mysore paak all these years and no one will buy it for her because no one knows how much she loves it? Who is the one who buys fruits and vegetables for the house that she has no love for because no one likes the fruits and vegetables she likes, and therefore no one will eat them, but of course, she will eat what she doesn't like? Who eats all the leftovers and who eats the fresh food? Who is the one who buys expensive sarees for your mother and your sisters every time we visit them, sarees that she would never buy for herself?

Once for her birthday Narayana had got her a shockingly expensive grey silk saree and watched as she opened it out. I won't say anything, she told herself, but her hands had trembled with the effort. The quality was superb, she could feel its thickness and one look told her that the gold at the border was real, not artificial like in all those North Indian silks that she despised. She opened her mouth to thank him but what came out instead was, "How much did this cost?"

"That isn't important."

She put her hands under the saree to hide their trembling and said, gently, "Narayana, why do you buy me things we can't afford?"

He looked pleased and sat down in the chair and said, "Now you put on your fall or whatever and wear it this evening."

"For what, are we going out anywhere?"

"If you want to we can go out for dinner." He opened the newspaper and began to read.

"Where is the money for that coming from?" she asked, knowing she would have to take out money for her birthday dinner from the household money, knowing that the household money would then fall short and she would have to ask him for more before the month ended and then he would say, So fast it has finished and then she would say, You spent it on my birthday dinner, remember, and he would blink and murmur, Did I, and she would say, Now can I have some money for the household expenses and he would say, You'll have to manage for another week till my salary comes, there's no money right now and she would say, Then when you give me money at the end of this month for next month you have to give me more, and he would look surprised and say, Why, and she would say, To replace what I am short of now because you spent it on my birthday and he would look exasperated and say, All right, all right, whatever you want, just stop nagging me.

He was absorbed in the paper. "Narayana," she said, then louder, "Narayana."

"Hmm?"

"Why did you spend so much money? Where will I have the opportunity to wear this saree, so much work there is in the house, when do I have time to go out?"

He continued reading as he said, automatically, "I told you, we can get another servant."

"Tell me, what colour sarees do I wear?"

"For heaven's sake. How on earth am I supposed to know?"

"But Narayana, I know you like blue shirts, I know you like your sambar thin, I know that you like your omelette without tomatoes, I know your shirts shouldn't be heavily starched, I know you like only white sheets on the bed, I know exactly how much rice to serve you at meal times, I know all these things about your mother and your father and your brothers and your sisters and their children."

He had stopped reading now, but he wasn't looking at her.

"Narayana, all these years that we've been married, you don't know that I never wear grey?" He didn't reply. She said, "Narayana this is a colour for an old woman. I remember the saree you got for your sister. Golden yellow. For her you knew what to get. Because she's your sister. Because she's your blood. I'm not your blood. I'm just your bloody wife." She had broken into a storm of weeping.

He was silent. Like Amma, that's how he held her down, he was like Amma. "Narayana," she said, "what colour are my eyes?"

He looked up and to her despair she saw in his eyes not anger but indifference and he said, "Black."

She went to the bathroom and washed her face and mopped it, she stood inside for a short while, telling herself, Stop it, stop it, calm down. Then she went back and told him, "Brown."

He shrugged and said, "It's the same thing."

Blind, blind. He could not see what stared him in the face. And what he did see he believed was the whole truth. What he knew of subterfuge and dishonesty was what happened in politics or in the workplace, he knew nothing of the subtler, deeper subterfuges. Narayana had seen the worst side of Madhav and so he was full of disdain for Madhav, and full of admiration for Madhav's wife, Ratna, who called Narayana the best brother-in-law in the world, listening wide-eyed to his conversation and nodding as if she supported every opinion he held. Because Ratna called Shanta darling and dearest, Narayana believed she loved Shanta; because she always enquired about Padma, whom she had never seen—her face grave, concerned—Narayana believed that her heart was overflowing with compassion for her.

Ratna was the one who had mastered the art. Perhaps she had been born knowing the art, born knowing that confrontation never worked with men, that telling them what lay in your heart never worked, that complaining to them about their families never worked. The knowledge which was so slow to come to most women, if it came at all, was second nature to Ratna. Shanta told Padma once, "I do my duty and maintain good relations with my in-laws, then I take it out on Narayana, but not Ratna. She'll never argue or disagree with Madhav, but in the end she'll achieve her ends, and Madhav will never know at what expense."

When Madhav and Ratna had come to Shanta's house for dinner, a short while after their marriage, Shanta had given her a silk saree. It was one that she had bought for herself just a month before but never worn, one that she had fallen in love with, so exquisite was it, that for once all practical constraints had flown away and she had taken out the money she had saved for three years from the household money that Narayana gave her. There had been no occasion to wear it, she hadn't even had the time to put on a fall, it was still folded the way it had been when she bought it at the time that Ratna and Madhav came. Of course, she had nothing to give Ratna then, she knew Narayana had no money at all, having just married off another sister a few months before. And so, her heart breaking, she had given the saree to Ratna, who had exclaimed with joy, hugged Shanta, said to her, "How beautiful, how beautiful, oh, thank you, thank you so much."

About a year later she and Narayana had lunch with Madhav and Ratna when passing through the city where they lived. There she saw that the servant woman who was getting food to the table was wearing the same saree that she had given Ratna. Shanta had eaten her lunch in a state of incredulity, smiling, talking, nodding automatically. Then before leaving she went to the kitchen to tip the servant woman, who simpered and said, "Thank you for this saree, so beautiful it is, Memsahib told me, Wear it today, it will make Shanta memsahib happy to see you in it." Back at home, Shanta had found herself shivering with shock. "Why," Padma had asked when Shanta told her, and now Shanta asked herself the same question.

She had told Amma about it. Amma had said, "She. I know her very well. When we were leaving their house after staying with them, Appa gave me money to give to the hands of the children, and when I gave, Ratna said, All this money, what can the children do with it, you keep the money and when you go to Bangalore you buy something in gold for the children with it. Your Appa nodded very vigourously. Ratna knew and I also knew that even the smallest gold earrings cost much more than the money I was giving. So when we were settled down at home I told your Appa, I need more money and he looked shocked when I told him how much. I told him, Yes, now that you've told her it has to be given."

"How much?" Shanta asked. Amma told her.

*"Amma!"*

Amma smiled her soft, gentle smile. "Oho, Shanta, you think I am a fool? For the girls I got the gold earrings, very pretty, like little flowers, and a small gold ring for the boy. With the rest I got ruby earrings for Mallika and also a thin, beautiful ruby necklace set in gold and a lovely little ring. It is all in my locker now. When Mallika gets married I will give it to her."

That day Amma took Shanta to her locker in the bank, took out all her jewels and took them home. After lunch she locked the bedroom and laid the jewels on the bed and divided them into three lots. "For you, for Mallika, for Ratna. All right?" Shanta scrutinized the jewellery, then said, "Amma, give that diamond ring to Mallika, not Ratna. Ratna has plenty of diamonds. Give that plain gold one to her instead." "All right," Amma said, putting the jewellery back in their boxes. Then she touched the earrings that she was wearing. "These are for you when I'm gone." She smiled softly. "Yes. I know. You loved them even as a child." Shanta smiled too. From the time she was a three-year-old Shanta remembered looking at them and touching them, moved not merely by their beauty but by the feeling that they were part of her mother.

Amma opened her trunk and from the bottom took out six sarees. Shanta gasped. "They are new," Amma said. "Every year Appa buys me one or two Cancheevaram sarees. Every year he laughs and he says, You are growing older and your sarees are getting brighter. Then he forgets and he doesn't see that I never wear them. These you take now and keep safely for Mallika." She closed her trunk, locked it and hung the keys at her waist.

"Amma," Shanta said, "the jewellery you have kept for Mallika, give that to me also, I will give it to Padma."

"You think I will give Ratna Mallika's share?"

"What she wants she will get by hook or by crook."

Amma touched Shanta's cheek. "What I want to give I will give by hook or by crook."

By hook or by crook. Amma telling Appa he was not giving her enough money for the household expenses. Appa giving her more. Every year Amma asking for more, Appa giving it without questions, as he had done all his life. Amma putting away money in her trunk every month. Surprisingly large sums of money. She, Shanta, coming home every year and Amma handing over the money to her. Shanta going back and hiding the money in her own trunk. Shanta going to Delhi and giving Padma the money. Padma using it for Mallika's expensive convent school and uniform. Padma telling her every year, "I hate myself for taking it." Shanta replying patiently, every year, "Amma gives money to all her grandchildren when they visit her, this is Mallika's share." Padma taking the money, looking miserable. Shanta saying, "You accepted the house, why so much fuss about this?" Padma replying, "The house is my share, it is from Amma's money, not Appa's, it is what Amma spent on your marriage and Madhav's." Shanta, exasperated, snapping, "Her share, His share, there is no need to quibble over these things, forget your principles, principles won't get Mallika an education." Year after year the money lying in her black trunk between the folds of her wedding saree like hot, burning coal. It lay there when Narayana had to borrow money to buy something in gold for his sister when she got married.

"You don't have any money tucked away?" he had asked her half teasingly, half seriously. She shook her head, meeting his eyes squarely. "I will replace it," he said.

Of course, he had forgotten about the last, the one and only, time. How easily they forgot. And when you reminded them they said you were a nag. When you tried to explain to them they said there was no need to scream, why were you so hysterical. She said, "Only Mallika's money."

He frowned. "Are you a fool to think I will take Mallika's money?"

"You did take it once."

Anger spread slowly over his countenance and she watched it in trepidation. Narayana was slow to anger. "You gave it to me," he said. "You did not tell me it was money given by your mother for Mallika."

She should have kept quiet then. Amma would have. Amma never wanted to make a point, she just wanted to get her way, as she said, by hook or by crook, and she almost always did. It was she, Shanta, who always wanted to make a point and of course, she never got her way, because after she made her point she gave in anyway. All that noise for nothing, being labelled a shrew for nothing. But Amma, she was like Ratna, she got what she wanted, all the while seeming docile and accommodating and gentle and loving. They did it, Amma and Ratna, and their husbands worshipped them. "How Ratna clings to me," Madhav had said once, his voice tender, his eyes soft.

She, Shanta, should have kept quiet when she saw Narayana's expression. But instead, her voice weak with tears, she replied, "You asked me if I had money when your other sister was getting married. Where do I get money from? I only have the money you give me for household expenses. Even my petticoats are on their last legs, I—"

"Quiet."

He said it quietly too, the way one says it to a dog who is whining. Like a dog she responded, with a whimper, then silence. He said, "When I asked you if you had money I was not asking for the money your mother had given you for Mallika. When you gave that money to me you did so of your own will. I don't want to hear any more about it."

Like a dog she went to her room. There she cried. Of her own will, he said. She had no will, her will bent to everybody else's, when had she ever done anything because only she, Shanta, wanted it? When? That time there was Narayana, miserable because he had no money to contribute for his first sister's wedding, ready to go to the bank to take a loan, then, before going, asking her with no hope, "Do you by any chance happen to have any?" As though she could have any, even if she had saved from the household money, which she did, every month, how much could that be, certainly not the sum he needed. She was not like Amma, quietly and confidently taking huge amounts from Appa, and Narayana was not like Appa, giving those huge amounts without question. No, Narayana was not like Appa, who gave Amma two or three sarees every year, cash gifts and jewellery for every birthday and anniversary, who indulged his daughter Shanta and anticipated her every need, there was no one to indulge her now, no one.

"Yes," she had said to Narayana, "I have some money," and taken it all out of the trunk and given it to him. Shouldn't he have asked her then, *So much money, where did it come from?*

Six months later, she said to him, "Narayana, that money you took from me, when are you going to replace it?"

"Money?"

"That money you took for your sister's wedding."

"Oh, that," he went back to eating his breakfast. She waited for some time but he kept eating.

"When will you give it back to me?"

"Don't shout." He finished his egg and toast, drank his coffee, got up.

"Answer me."

He looked startled, as if they had had no conversation at all. "Answer what?" She repeated her question. He shrugged. "I don't know." He went to the bathroom and she could hear him gargling. Then he came back to the room, went to his favourite chair and sat down with the newspaper. She repeated her question. He grunted and continued reading. She went to him and snatched the paper from his hands, walked to the balcony and threw it over. "Now tell me," she said.

Narayana was looking at her now. At last he was looking at her. Never mind his expression, at least he was looking at her. Never mind that he said, "Are you going mad or something?" At least he was responding to her. She repeated her question. He said, "Not only are you going mad, you're going deaf. I told you, I don't know."

"You took a lot of money from me."

"It was money you had put aside for an emergency; well, there was an emergency and we used it. It can't be replaced."

Fury made her speechless. That was the problem. Either she couldn't find the words or when she did they were all wrong. Or she shouted them and then he did not want to hear anyway. She knew it, she knew it, yet she could not change it. Somewhere she had once read that recognizing a problem was the first step to solving the problem. She recognized the futility of her shrill responses and emotional arguments. But she could not change either, she just could not. If there was an in-between step between recognizing things and effecting the change, she did not know it. "Where to put aside money from? Every month one week before your salary comes I run out of money for the household expenses. You say, Stretch what I give you. How to stretch? We have to eat. I don't eat fruits, I don't eat meat in that week—"

"Shanta, I have never told you not to eat fruits or meat. Stop talking in this nonsensical manner."

She began to weep. "It was Mallika's money." The sobs were tearing her body apart. "Amma gave it to me for her education. Padma—"

"Mallika's money? Why did you give me Mallika's money?"

"Yes, yes, nicely gone and spent Mallika's money for your sister's wedding, at that time you never asked me how I had so much money, now you ask—"

"You'll get the money before you go to Delhi."

"Ah. So now you have the money. Now you're singing a different tune. Now—"

He was gone. Picked up his briefcase, opened the door and out he was.

She got the money. Not before she went to Delhi but that very week. "Now where did it come from?" she asked, not wanting to ask. He did not reply.

She knew by the end of the month when he gave her less money for the household expenses, saying, "I can't give you more, more is being deducted from my salary now." Of course. She should have guessed. He had taken a loan from the bank.

"Why?" she asked him, "why? I am not going to Delhi now, I am going only after five months, why could you have not taken the loan then?"

"Because till you have the money I'll never hear the end of it."

Ratna would not have done what she had done. Ratna would not have said what she had said. In her place Ratna would have told Madhav the source of the money and said it did not matter that she was giving the money, she would have said that such sacrifices were necessary. And Madhav, touched and remorseful, would have either refused the money and never forgotten her offer, or having taken it, returned it at once, and never forgotten that it was his wife who had come to his rescue.

Once when she had tried to give Narayana some idea about the kind of person Ratna really was, he merely looked long-suffering and said, "Shanta, please, you're so critical about your sister-in-law, but have you tried looking at your brother first?"

"Don't say anything about my brother. I don't talk about your family."

He shrugged, "There's nothing the matter with my family, *I* don't complain about my family." She had struggled with the tumult inside her, fighting silently for the right words, which as usual she couldn't find. Narayana said, "I'm only saying what you've always said all these years about your brother, though with more brevity than you're capable of."

"You think your family is perfect, don't you," she said, helplessly.

"Not at all. But they're not petty or mean."

Rage overpowered her. Really, Narayana, she wanted to say, really? Do you know your mother and your sister think my family isn't good enough? When Amma and Appa came to visit your mother two years after our marriage, your precious sisters didn't even come out of their rooms to greet my parents. Your mother tells me, Why are your sarees so bright, they hurt the eyes. Do you notice that when your precious mother cuts mangoes after lunch she always gives me the middle part? When they talk to each other when we are all eating at the dining table, they don't include me. Once, five years after our marriage, your sister said to me, Oh, you also have done your M.A.? Five years it took her to find out. Shanta wanted to say all this and more but she didn't, somewhere inside her something held her down, something intuitive that said, He might talk about your family, but you better keep quiet about his. Or else. She wasn't sure what the Or Else was, but it was there.

She had tried to indicate to Narayana the extent of her unhappiness with his mother, who snubbed her so casually, who showed her so wordlessly that she, Shanta, meant nothing to her. Shanta tried to explain to Narayana, "She never talks to me." Narayana said, "My mother is a quiet woman, Shanta, you should learn to adjust to that, adjustments are necessary in relationships." As though that wasn't what she had been doing all her married life.

She could never talk to Padma about all this. Padma had given her trust to Narayana in her typical, total way, her loyalty to him was complete. In Delhi Shanta felt infinitely tender towards Narayana, their few days together were strangely calm and humourous. It was Padma's doing, Padma's belief in his solidity and goodness that rubbed off on her, Shanta. But when Shanta returned home she could not partake of that conviction, inside her the rage began again.

The only time Shanta could remember when she had any respite from her anger against Narayana was that period when Padma was with them. In Narayana's protective shade Padma had rested, and she, Shanta, too. It had been a time when questions grew inside Shanta like weeds, questions she could not ask, questions she slept with and which intruded into her dreams. Every night she thought, Tomorrow I'll ask Padma. But in the morning the words lay heavy on her tongue. The time for asking was ripe the first week that Padma had come to them but she had thought then that it was too early, and afterwards it had been too late.

The second day she asked not why, but what.

"It isn't what you think," Padma said, "we love each other." So, Shanta had thought grimly, the same old story. "He does," Padma said, her voice shaking, "he does, Shantacca." All the cliches were true, Shanta thought, love was indeed blind. She, Shanta, too had fallen in love with Narayana during their brief engagement, falling in love was the easiest part. It was true, the saying that you saw the best of each other before marriage. It was true not because you were hiding anything but because there was no context for the other things to come out. During the months of their engagement Narayana had once said to Shanta, "You're very vibrant." Vibrant. The word stayed with her, adjectives like *beautiful* and *attractive* were shadows next to its radiance, a radiance that she felt was, for this once, hers alone. Later, as the years passed, there were many times when she wanted to ask Narayana, Narayana, do you still think so? But she did not. If she asked him, and he told her, then that too would be gone, the tenderness with which she cherished that old, untainted moment.

"Shantacca, he does want to marry me."

Oh, Shanta thought, of course, of course. "Sumi knows."

Padma looked away from her. Yes, Shanta thought bitterly. Sumi had known, but not Padma's own sister. And where was Padma's Sumi now? Why had Padma not gone to her precious Sumi now?

"Sumi doesn't know about . . . this. Only, about him."

Shanta did not say anything.

"After his M.A. he taught as a lecturer of history in the college. Then he qualified for the civil services. When the college closed for the holidays he went home to his parents in Lucknow to tell them about us, Shantacca."

"In Lucknow?"

"They're from U.P."

At the back of her head a faint voice said, Ask Padma why, ask Padma how. She couldn't. The voice said, insistently, you must know, Shanta, you must understand. But she didn't want this understanding, she couldn't bear it.

"How long have you known him?"

"Four and a half years."

And she had told her sister nothing. Nothing. Padma's eyes were dark with the knowledge of her betrayal. In Shanta's heart the pain was deep.

"Shantacca, I wanted to tell you all after he had spoken to his parents, before that it was too early."

"What happened after he went home?"

"I didn't hear from him. When I found out, I wrote to him."

"How many letters did you write to him?" The same story. The films didn't lie.

"I wrote four times. I didn't get his reply."

Shanta noted her words: "I didn't get his reply," not "He didn't reply." She asked sharply, "You told him you were . . . ?"

"No, Shantacca. I could not. I told him it was urgent, that was all. I could not tell him in a letter." Seeing Shanta's expression she shook her head vehemently. "No, Shantacca, no, he's not like that—I think his mother isn't giving her consent."

"Then why doesn't he write and tell you so?"

"Because he's trying to persuade her, Shantacca. He thinks I'll get hurt if I know she's against the marriage. You see, he was so sure that she would agree."

"I see."

"After he persuades her, he'll write so that he won't have to tell me that she was against it initially."

She waited for Shanta to answer but Shanta was silent.

"Shantacca, the English department had offered me a job, the interview was in a few days. I told Appa I didn't want the job, Acca. He said, Padma, why have you changed your mind, is there someone you want to marry? Then Amma said, If there is, then tell us. She said, Jobs like this don't come when you want them, a teaching job is something you can do if you are married, it is something you can do while you're waiting to get married."

"Amma didn't want me to work," Shanta said.

"Shantacca, *you* wanted to get married."

"Every woman wants to get married, all I needed was some encouragement."

"Shantacca, Appa and Amma used to set you up as an example every time to Madhav and me. In fact when Madhav got into the bank, Appa told him, Shanta could have got into the civil services."

"What did Madhav say to that?"

"He said, Then why didn't she."

It was at such moments that Shanta felt that it was all dust, all that she had, even her children. Appa had had faith in her and as long as she lived in her parents' house, his faith was rewarded. In school she was always first in her class, in college not only did she top the university every year but participated in debates and was on the college badminton team. It was this kind of faith that one internalized, it was this kind of faith that made one fulfill the dreams others had for you.

I could have done it, Shanta thought, I could have done it. But Amma favoured Madhav. Even when he just about made a first class he got more praise from Amma than she did, she who had topped her university. It was as if Madhav now represented what she could have been. All the praise her mother bestowed on him and his job and his promotions should have been hers. If only someone had that kind of faith in her again. Her husband and her children did have faith in their wife and mother, but its texture had everything to do with them and nothing to do with her, unlike the other.

Padma said, "Appa told me, You must go for the interview. I told him, I'm going to Shantacca tomorrow. Then Amma took me to her bedroom and made me sit on the bed and said, You have never lied to us all these years about anything, not even as a child. But sometimes when a man comes into the picture I know that even the most truthful of women can lie because she feels ashamed or embarrassed. There is nothing to feel ashamed about. Any man you like will be a man worthy of you, he will be intelligent, he will come from a good family, he will have a good job, so if you like someone, tell us, and we will go with the proposal to his family."

Clever, clever, Amma, Shanta thought. Amma would win either way. If the man was intelligent, well-placed in his job and from a good family then Amma knew Padma would tell her and she would win Padma's eternal gratitude. If he wasn't, then Amma knew Padma would think twice before pursuing the affair. As things stood, Padma couldn't tell her anyway.

"After that," Padma said, "I came to you."

Not to Sumi, not to Amma, not to Madhav. Padma had come to her, Shanta. She had come almost blindly, instinctively, in the same way that she used to come to her as a child when she fell and hurt herself, in the same way that she would come to her after reading a sad book, her eyes red, asking, "Shantacca, why did it happen like this?" Then Shanta would comfort her. Years later, as Shanta awaited the birth of her first child in her mother's house, sewing and embroidering tiny clothes, she also mended Padma's blouses and put falls on her sarees. A month after Vikram was born, Shanta sat putting hooks on Padma's blouse and suddenly Padma hugged her and said in relief and in love, "Acca, I thought you'd stop indulging me after you had the baby," and Shanta had gathered her words and her hug to her heart and lived on them for days. Padma had needed her once in that way, that irreplaceable way. Even Madhav Padma hadn't needed this way. And what did Madhav do for her anyway that wasn't easy to do, nothing he did for her or for anyone entailed any sacrifice. He bought her books because Amma and Appa gave him more pocket money at college than they gave Shanta, so even here, he had the edge, for if Shanta loved books, then Padma lived in them and breathed them. "What do you need more pocket money for," Amma told Shanta implacably when Shanta accused her of being unfair. It was Appa who overheard the argument and said to Amma, astonished, "You mean the extra money we give Madhav is for his pocket money and not for his fees?" Amma shrugged then, as if she didn't know what he was talking about. Appa dropped a kiss on Shanta's head and said, "Tell me how much more you want and I will give it to you."

What did Appa know of Amma. He did not know how Amma manipulated him in her quiet, unassuming fashion. Amma let him believe that he made the rules and the decisions. She let him make his speeches, but when it came to the crunch, she had her way so easily that he did not even know that it was her way.

Madhav. Always Madhav. He got the appreciation; she, Shanta, the criticism. When he came back from college Amma welcomed him with two meat dishes, chicken and mutton, and khir filled with almonds and raisins. When she came home after her marriage there was one meat dish and no almonds in the khir. "So costly almonds are," Amma said. "You had them for Madhav last year when he came from college," Shanta said. Her mother shook her head, "Silly girl, at that time there must have been almonds in the house, so I must have used them, why are you so childish, Shanta." Shanta got up and went to the pantry, she climbed up the chair and rummaged on the highest shelf, but there were only bottles of raisins, walnuts and apricots. Ashamed, she was about to climb down when she noticed the one bottle behind the row, at the far-end corner. She moved the bottles in the front and there it was, a large jar of almonds. She stood there, weak with more emotions than she could understand, and thought, if I were twelve I could have smashed this. Her mother's gentle voice rose up from below, "Oh, child, it is there. I wondered. I thought it was finished, give, give, I'll soak them today and make fresh khir for you tomorrow." Shanta shut the cupboard and climbed down. "It's empty, Amma," she said, "just as you told me," and for the first time saw an expression pass on her mother's face that told her that she, Shanta, had for this brief moment, triumphed. But with Amma such triumphs were empty.

Control yourself, Shanta. Control yourself, my child. There was more to Amma's refrain than Amma herself consciously realized. Amma's words did not hold anger. Control yourself. That held a note of caution. Then, Control yourself, my child. That was almost a plead. She, Shanta, had a black tongue. And Amma knew. "Shanta, my child," Amma used to say, "be careful of what you say, don't think badly of anyone." Once a girl in her class had stolen Shanta's favourite pencil. "I know you've taken it, give it back," Shanta had said, standing before her. The girl had shrugged her shoulders. "All right," Shanta had said, "by tomorrow if you don't return my pencil the hand with which you stole it will be full of boils." The girl snorted contemptuously. The next day the girl didn't come to school but her mother sent a note for the teacher. When she returned, two days later, her right hand was bandaged and the yellow pus stains showed. The pencil found its way back to Shanta's desk.

The strange thing was that she never said these things with any foregone knowledge of their coming true. It was anger that drove her, nothing else. Once, when Padma was at home during her college summer holidays, Shanta had scolded her for not paying enough attention to the housework and not helping her mother, and Padma had replied, predictably, "What are the servants there for, Acca?" Shanta had tried to explain to her, "No servant will do anything if you don't keep an eye on them, have you instructed them to dust the table's legs. And what about the mantelpiece, just because no one can see it doesn't mean you can let the dust gather, one day you'll have to run your own house you know, and look at your room, such a mess, at least put your books back in the cupboard and—" She hadn't been allowed to finish because Padma put her hands to her ears, and walked out of the room. Shanta followed her to her room and Padma shouted, "I'll have better things to do than running a house, Shantacca, I'll have better things to do than changing nappies every hour." At which point Vikram, who was a few months old, began to wail in the next room and Shanta said, "You will do just that, Padma, just you wait and see, you'll do it and do it and do it. And more."

It was Padma's penchant for categoric statements that infuriated her more than anything else. I'll never do this, I'll never do that, this is wrong, this is right, how could you say such a thing, how could she do such a thing . . . Once, years ago, when Padma had heard Shanta lying about her age, Padma had shaken her head and said, "Really, Shantacca." Another time when Shanta had told a friend in Padma's presence that her emerald set cost one thousand rupees Padma had said when they reached home, "Acca, it cost only eight hundred. Why should it matter what people think, why should the way they think affect our lives?"

Shanta remembered these words. She remembered them all. I'll have better things to do than running a house, Shantacca, I'll have better things to do than changing nappies every hour. You will do just that, Padma, just you wait and see, you'll do it and do it and do it. And more.

It had happened exactly as Shanta said. Padma had done it and done it and done it. And more. Now Shanta understood those people who whipped themselves and cut their flesh with knives and burnt their bodies with cigarettes; it was what she wanted to do to herself to expiate the guilt. She didn't want Padma's forgiveness, she wanted Padma's curse thrown back at her in equal measure. But Padma never cursed her, Padma never referred to it, perhaps she had forgotten it. After all, what was it but one of many fights between sisters. Shanta remembered, and she knew that no amount of guilt or anguish could take back what her words had set in motion. It wasn't as if her words were calculated, or that she said what she did with any knowledge of how prophetic it would be. In fact, when she wanted something very badly, asking for it or willing it didn't make it happen. But it was when her sense of justice and her need for understanding were wounded that the anger twisted and writhed inside her, and words she had never prepared poured out of her, and inevitably she forgot about them till they came true. She had a black tongue, she had a black tongue, or else why was she always confronted with the knowledge of her words coming true, why didn't this knowledge ever keep its distance?

That long ago time, Narayana sat with Padma and Shanta and said, "There is no need for panic." He had sounded so calm and unperturbed that the surging in Shanta's breast had subsided, and looking at Padma she saw the wildness in her sister's eyes subside too. Narayana told them what they would do and it sounded so simple, so practical, that Shanta marvelled why she hadn't thought of it. They would go to Lucknow, Narayana said, he had already got accommodations for them at the railway guest house. Today he would write a letter to the parents, telling them of the proposal from Padma's family, fixing a date when they would visit with the formal proposal. Padma would write another letter to him telling him the same thing—there was no doubt that either he hadn't received her earlier letters or that he hadn't been at home at the time, perhaps he was away for a week or a month. If he was still away when they reached Lucknow, they would send him a telegram wherever he was and ask him to return. There was no need for his family to know about the pregnancy, but they could insist on an early marriage, it need not be a big affair. If he was certain of wanting to marry Padma, and Padma seemed certain that he was, then he could prevail on his parents. Of course, there might be tensions, but these could be ironed out if Padma had his support, and she had that, didn't she? His parents might object because Padma was from a different community, but again, if their son prevailed, no objection could be sustained, and they certainly couldn't have any objections about Padma's family, even as far as the caste went. Padma and her family were Brahmins and they were not. Narayana would go to Bangalore the next day, talk to Padma's parents, tell them everything, and ask them also to come to Lucknow.

Shanta said, "Amma and Appa?" Padma's face had become white.

Narayana said, "They have to be told."

Shanta opened her mouth to argue, then saw an expression on her husband's face that she read instantly and at that moment she began to feel weak and tearful again, and she said, her voice calm, "Yes, you're right."

"Shantacca."

Shanta held Padma's cold hand between her warm ones. She wanted to say, They have to be told Padma, because if this doesn't come through, then how long can you hide it from them, then they must know. That was what Narayana's expression had said, and the knowledge that underneath his practical demeanor, he was as unsure as her, shook her anew.

Appa hadn't come. He hadn't said a word when Narayana told him, Amma told Shanta, he had just gone to his room and not emerged, not even for lunch or dinner. Amma had returned with Narayana. Padma was in the bedroom and Amma went in. From the kitchen Shanta heard Padma begin to weep, but she couldn't hear Amma. When she went in ten minutes later Padma was still weeping, the sounds in her throat long and harsh, and next to her Amma sat quietly.

The next day they all left for Lucknow. "What did Amma say," Shanta asked Padma in the train. Padma said something so softly that Shanta had to bend down to listen. "What did you say?" Shanta asked. Padma said, "Nothing, she didn't say anything."

Many months later, Shanta asked Narayana, "What did Amma say?"

"What could she say."

"For heaven's sake, Narayana. I didn't ask you what she could have said or not said, what did she say?"

"Nothing."

Shanta wanted to ask Narayana, What was her expression like, what was Appa's, did she seem angry or despairing or both, did she know what to do or did she wait for you to tell her. Tell me, Narayana, tell me. He saw her expression and said, as though in answer to her unspoken questions, "Shanta, I'm not a woman, I don't notice all these things."

One hour in That House in Lucknow, Shanta thought. But if she were to add up the number of hours she had spent reliving that one hour it would add up to months. Amma had insisted on taking Padma's horoscope with her. "Amma, there is no need for all this at a time like this," Shanta had said, exasperated. "There is every need," Amma had said implacably. "They will want it. And it is a good horoscope, a very good horoscope. They must know Padma will have success in everything she undertakes, her studies, her job, her child." "You never told me all that before," Shanta said suspiciously. "What was there to say," Amma replied.

They went to the house—she, Amma and Narayana. After the servant had opened the door for them and asked them to come in, they had waited, standing, for ten minutes. Shanta had known then that something was terribly wrong. "Sit, Amma," she had said. "No," Amma had replied, holding the horoscope firmly in her hand. Thank God Padma hadn't been there, thank God Narayana had sensibly said that there was no need for her to come and that she and Vikram must stay behind.

Of course, They had been expecting them. They had pretended they hadn't. She had come first—the mother, short, dark, unsmiling. Her eyes behind her spectacles were cold. The two daughters had come behind her, they must have been around nineteen and twenty, both tall and fair, equally cold. No one asked them to sit. The mother had inclined her head briefly as if in a question, her daughters on either side of her like sentinels.

"Did you get my letter?" Narayana asked in Hindi. Having been educated in the North for some years he knew the language adequately.

"Letter?" the mother repeated, unsmiling. "What letter?"

Shanta had known then, and for a brief moment Padma's future stretched before her in all its stark certainty. Then she heard Narayana's voice saying, in his strongly accented Hindi, "I would like to meet your son."

Shanta knew the answer before it came. The mother said, "He isn't here." Then the mother took her eyes away from Narayana and looked at Amma and then at her, Shanta, then her eyes went back to Narayana. There was no expression in the look.

Narayana asked, "When will he be back?" No one answered. Narayana took out two cards from his wallet, his and Appa's, and wrote on the back of one of them. "This is where we are," he said, handing it to the mother, "please ask him to see us when he returns." The mother didn't take it. Narayana placed the cards on the table.

The mother said, "My son is not here. He got married last month."

It was then that Shanta became conscious of a humming sound inside her ears, her head felt as though bands of wire were being stretched and tied around it, and her heart was pumping so hard and so rapidly that her chest hurt. She saw Narayana turn to her and Amma but she couldn't hear what he said. He said it again, a little louder, but it seemed that Amma too was rooted to the ground. The humming reached a crescendo, then began to subside and when she turned towards Narayana she saw him going out of the house.

He had never asked her what happened those ten minutes while he waited outside. For years she waited for him to ask her, but he never did. She was on the brink of telling him once, but he said, "Shanta, it's over and done with, please," and he raised his hand and she saw the bleakness in his eyes and stopped. It was, she realized with a sudden surge of tenderness, as though he couldn't bear to think of it, for him it could only be dealt with by burying it, whereas for her it could only be borne by the ritual of reliving it, a ritual whose nature was as imperative as it was unknown.

They had stared at each other—the mother, the two daughters, Amma and she. Now with Narayana out of the house the atmosphere had changed from one of cold hostility to something else, they stood like two armies poised for battle. The mother turned to the daughters and said something in Hindi, and the older daughter said, "My mother has to go out now."

Shanta found her mouth stretching in what must have been a smile. She saw the mother's expression change and a smell of fear began to pervade the room. "Tell your mother," said Shanta, her voice loud, "that if she goes I will say what I have to say so loudly that the servants will know and your neighbours will know." The three women, who had turned away, now slowly turned towards her. "Listen to what I have to say," Shanta said, "I will say it in English and you will tell your mother in Hindi, and you will say to her all that I say to you without changing any word or any meaning, do you hear, because I understand every word of Hindi. Tell your mother her son promised marriage to my sister whom he has known for four years in the same college." The sister, her face pale, said nothing. Shanta's voice rose, "Tell or . . . or I will go to your kitchen and shout it in front of your servants." The sister made a convulsive sound, and moved closer to her mother. "Tell her," said Shanta, "that under this pretext your brother made my sister pregnant and then abandoned her."

The mother raised her hand and said in Hindi, "Whatever you are saying, I understand." She looked at Shanta and then at Amma, her eyes were no longer cold but seething with contempt. "So," she said to Shanta, "you want to give our family's name to the bastard of your whoring sister?"

Shanta heard a sound from Amma, Amma who understood and spoke Hindi fluently, having picked it up during Appa's postings in the North. Shanta closed her eyes and when she opened them it was as if she no longer had control over her body or her words, as though each diabolic gesture and word that now emerged had been practiced, so easily did they possess her, and as she hurled them they seemed to speed into a future where retribution curled and waited. It was as though she had no control over her hand, which clenched itself into a fist and then moved to her head, no control over her mouth, which said in ringing tones, "I curse you. I curse you all," and her fist moved from her head towards the three women and opened before each one in a gesture of something being thrown at them. "You, and you, and you," she said. Her eyes closed, then opened, she looked at the mother and said, "May your son's wife be forever barren.

May your two daughters be forever barren. May your house be forever empty of the laughter of grandchildren. May the marriages of your son and your two daughters be as barren as their wombs. May all my sister's suffering come back to you through your children." She folded her hands above her head, her eyes closed. She opened her eyes and there was terror on the faces of the two girls, and the mother now sat on the chair, her hands gripping its arms, her face turned away.

Then, as though in a dream, Shanta heard Amma's voice. Soft it was, almost musical, speaking in Kannada. As though she were chanting her morning prayers—Shree Rama, Jaya Rama, Jaya Jaya Rama—the same rhythm as those words, the same absorption. As though in a dream the words twisted and writhed into the room. As though she, Shanta, lay insulated in a glass bottle which had been thrown into a pit of snakes, nothing would touch her, but she saw everything, everything, and there was no insulation against that.

Later, whenever Shanta relived That Day in Lucknow, she would find herself shuddering. She did not want to know any more about that family, she did not want to know what Amma's curse had set in motion, nothing she wanted to know, nothing. She did not want to remember the contrast of her mother's soft musical voice with the venom of her words. She did not want to remember the gentleness of Amma's demeanor in her off-white saree with the maroon border, her lovely, glowing complexion, the quiet eyes, her unchanged expression; the way she looked when she prayed every morning, serene, absorbed. When she, Shanta had spoken, Those three had been frightened, yes, but unlike Amma, Shanta's eyes had partaken of what she said, she was aware of how her nostrils had flared and how her eyes glittered, of the ringing tone of her voice. And the mother, who understood the language that Shanta spoke and did not understand the language that Amma did, stared not at Amma, but at Shanta; the horror in Shanta's eyes told the mother what Amma's words could not. The mother, the sisters knew its malignancy, they knew it from her, Shanta's, face. They stared at Shanta, all three, and the whites of the Mother's eyes showed through her spectacles.

They had heard a sound then, from the room next to the sitting room, and the mother and daughters turned in that direction, and then, as if in one accord, turned away. The curtain moved and a frightened face looked out. A lovely face, Shanta thought later, just thirteen or fourteen years old, her lips were trembling and she looked at her mother and sisters and said, her voice quivering, "Ma." Her mother didn't look at her, her voice was harsh as she said, "Go inside." Shanta knew what was coming now, she wanted to tell Amma, Don't Amma, don't, she's innocent, but it was useless, the words stuck in her throat. Amma turned towards the girl, who still stood there, and pointing to the mother, spoke again in Kannada. Two sentences. The girl ran to her older sister and wordlessly put her arms around her sister's waist, but the girl's head was turned, and she watched Amma, her eyes brimming with fear. Again Amma spoke, very softly, this time directly to the girl. Then Amma turned to Shanta and said, "Shanta." Shanta looked at her mother and across her shoulder saw the mantelpiece full of photographs of the family. She walked across and picked up the one her eye had fallen on, then, like a lamb, followed her mother outside the house and to the road, where Narayana was waiting for them in the car.

They drove back in complete silence. Confirmed. After all these years they were confirmed, her darkest feelings about Amma. Feelings for which she had not, Shanta realized blindingly, wanted any confirmation. Later as she relived that brief period in that house Shanta knew that it had been easier to wrestle with her doubts, even with her self-hatred and guilt. Once the doubts were gone the knowledge she carried about Amma was far more horrible to carry and she could share it with no one, not even Padma. Especially Padma.

Padma was standing at the window, waiting. She must have watched how they walked back to the room, seen their faces as they approached the guest house. Because when they entered her room she was sitting on the bed as though her legs would not support her. It was Amma who sat next to her and said, "He got married and is now in Delhi."

No, this she had not expected.

Now, Padma merely looked blank, shook her head and said, "No, no. That is not true."

Narayana spoke then. Everything he told her that had happened when he was there, every word. He did not spare her, he did not try to buffer any angle or curve of the encounter.

Padma listened carefully. Then she shook her head again and said, "He is not married." The silence seemed to go on for a very long time. She looked very earnestly at Narayana and said, "They are lying because they do not want us to marry. When you meet him you will know the truth."

Amma said, "It is the truth, Padma."

She, Shanta, was not able to utter a word, it was as though her tongue had been cut out.

Padma got up, picked up her handbag from the side table. "I will go and meet his family."

Narayana raised his arm and his voice. "Padma." Her eyes widened. She stopped. "You are not stepping out of this place." Padma's body jerked, a strange sound emerged from her throat. Gently, Narayana said, "Padma, my child, your mother is right."

Shanta took the photograph out of her purse and gave it to Padma.

What else could she have done. Padma would never have believed them. That was the kind of faith that Padma had in those she loved. That was the kind of faith this man had exploited. The same old story. And Padma must have given in to him, persuaded that if one loved then it was all right. He must have persuaded her of it, having already seduced her before that with all his talk of books.

What else could she have done. It was cruel, it was terribly cruel, but her darling would never have accepted it otherwise. He was a handsome man in an unconventional way, so much taller than the bride, his face so young and his eyes so blank, the garlands sitting almost incongruously around his neck. Krishna, Krishna, Shanta cried out silently, help us. Give my sister strength. Protect her child.

After some time Padma put the photograph on the bed. Her face was contorted as though she had eaten something very bitter. Her body heaved, her arms went around her stomach. She opened her eyes, they were dazed, a strange sound came out of her stomach, "Aa . . . aaa . . kaa . . . a . . ." Later, much later, Shanta realized that Padma had uttered the only word that she could possibly utter. "Shantaccca."

The lies had to be carefully constructed. Shanta and Amma constructed them. Shanta couldn't say to Padma, Do you remember your categoric statements? She couldn't say, Now, I will lie again, I do it well, don't I, I do it easily, don't I? I will invent the lies for you, and you will live them.

It was a small world, people found out things. This was Shanta's secret terror. That they had to prevent, that. They had to make up a story. They did. They had to make people believe it. They, the tellers, had to believe it. And in the telling she and Amma did believe it and so, the people they told believed it too. It was as if all the anguish she and Amma had to contain in front of Padma had to be vented somewhere, and so it came out in their relating of Padma's story to those who had to be told and those who asked, the truth emerging in ways they hadn't anticipated.

"Yes, she fell in love with him," Shanta told Narayana's youngest sister, "you know how Padma is, there was never anyone before, there will never be anyone after. Same university, he was teaching, yes, yes, he got into the civil services, all ready to marry her, he was. No, they wouldn't have anything to do with her—to be fair on him, he didn't expect it either." Shanta's eyes filled with ready tears.

Amma told Appa's sisters and their two neighbours whom they had known for twenty years. They will tell the others, Amma wrote to Shanta. Shanta almost smiled when she read the letter, she could imagine it in vivid detail. She could imagine Amma's face, heavy with grief, saying to her sister-in-law, I told her, we cannot accept it if his family doesn't accept it. She could hear Amma's soft voice saying to Appa's older brother, I told Padma, Think about it with your head, not your heart, this is not the West, this is India, here the family's support is more important than anything else, if you don't have their support your marriage is doomed from the beginning. She could see Amma's fingers clasped in her lap as she told her neighbour, But they got married, sent us a telegram, sent his parents a telegram. Amma's ravaged face must have told the rest, no one would have asked her questions, no one asked Amma questions. Amma had the ability to let people draw the very conclusions she wanted from the things she left unsaid.

Sumi's letter to Padma was waiting for her at home, Amma enclosed the letter to Padma in her own, and said to Padma, I would suggest you do not write to her at all—she knows too much, and who knows if her husband will want to read her letters, so do not write to her.

Padma read Amma's letter in the same manner that she turned the pages of magazines, as though she did not know what she was reading. Then she read Sumi's letter in the same way. "What does Sumi say?" Shanta asked. Padma handed her the letter. Surprise, surprise. Sumi, Padma's best friend, had got married. It happened too fast, dearest Padma, Sumi had written, there was no time to send invitations or anything, we got married within two weeks of meeting each other and I am still dazed. Dazed, but oh so happy. And then it was full of nonsense about how much she loved him and he her and how their hearts beat like one and how her mind was an open book for him and there was nothing that she kept from him because that was what marriage had to be, no secrets, not the smallest subterfuge, they shared everything with each other, she and her husband, their deepest secrets and all their past, he loved her so much that he said he would kill any man who looked at her and no one had felt this way for her before, no one, she felt protected and secure and thanked God that she had found a soulmate.

Things like that, Sumi had written. One never could tell with people. She, Shanta, had always thought Sumi was very sensible. But this was worse than the books Shanta read in the bathroom—at least the books had some semblance of credibility. "What on earth has happened to your friend, Padma?" she asked and Padma shrugged her shoulders as if she had not heard. No, it had not registered. Nothing was registering in Padma. It was frightening how mechanically she went about doing what had to be done. Sumi had ended her letter saying, As soon as you know about your wedding dates let us know, we will definitely come.

Three more letters Sumi wrote, but Padma did not reply.

Like Narayana, there were things that Shanta wanted to bury and sometimes she felt that she had almost succeeded, till a chance remark or an unexpected encounter brought it heaving to the surface again. Many years later she and Amma were shopping when she materialized in front of them—Sumi, hardly a few yards ahead, matching the tassels of a green saree with a row of green falls in a box. "Amma," Shanta whispered, nudging her, and Amma looked up, then took Shanta's arm and turned her around and into the next shop. When they came out, Sumi had gone.

The lies were very carefully constructed. Two weeks after Amma's return to Bangalore she showed a still more ravaged face to everyone she knew. She said nothing, of course, and of course, they asked. Her daughter was a widow, Amma said finally to Appa's sisters. He had died in an accident. The news spread as such news does. Appa's brother said to Appa, "Now is the time to forgive." Appa stared into space as though he hadn't heard. "Go and get her from Shanta's house," Appa's sister said to him, "open your doors to the poor, bereft child." Appa said nothing. Amma too said nothing. All this Amma wrote to Shanta.

Two weeks after their return from Lucknow Shanta and Narayana were posted to another town. Easier to lie to the new neighbours here, tell them her sister was widowed. Everyone believed it. How could they not, seeing the wreck who was her sister, her eyes swollen, her lips dry and chapped, her face devoid of colour. She hardly ate, and Shanta, who had little appetite herself, forced herself to eat. She needed every bit of strength, that she knew, Padma had none at all. That was what having a child taught you. Eat properly, keep healthy. No other way to cope. Sleep properly.

Sometimes when friends or neighbours dropped in to call on them Padma would still be sitting on the chair in which she had sat two hours earlier, oblivious of anyone around her. "It was terrible," Shanta said, "just terrible. He had just said goodbye to Padma, she remembers he was wearing a blue pin-striped shirt and dark blue pants . . . he got into the car, that too a borrowed car, and my sister stood at the window watching him, just kept standing there and then she heard the sound of the crash, it was as if she was waiting for it."

Shanta's neighbour began sewing clothes for Padma's baby, her tears dampening the soft yellows and blues. "Your sister is not alone, Shanta," she said, "all my children's old clothes I will give to her, and I am making more, don't cry Shanta, don't cry."

But there was a second reason why her fear of people finding out the truth hadn't been realized, Shanta thought, and that was because of what everyone believed Padma to be. If they believed in Appa's integrity, they also believed in Padma's, and even as the news spread in the way such news always did, and even as their mouths opened and eyes gleamed, they knew that she wasn't That Kind of Woman. They couldn't say, We expected it of her. "So forthright, so good-natured, so loyal," Amma's friend said to Shanta. Yes, Shanta thought, people believed the story because it was Padma's story, if she fell in love with a man whose parents didn't want her, they thought, what fault of it was hers? "The thing is," Amma's friend said to Shanta, "is that your sister, Padma, she does what her heart tells her to, I have known her all my life, I know how true her love for her husband must have been." And, marvelled Shanta, implicit in that statement was Amma's friend's belief that Padma had done no wrong in eloping, she had merely followed the dictates of her heart, she had done it with the one man she loved, she had loved no other, and her parents should never have disowned her for it.

How would people have reacted if it had happened to her, Shanta? They

would have said, Oh, Shanta, she had such a temper, always fighting with
everyone, thinking no end of herself just because she topped the university, *she*! They would have said of her parents, It's all their fault for giving
her such liberties, serves them right. It seemed that Amma's strictures were
only for her, Shanta—Amma's remarks about loose women who fell in love
were warnings only for Shanta; Amma's quiet disapproval about women
who dressed or behaved in a certain way were only for Shanta. She, Shanta,
who longed for the freedom of travelling in a cycle was never given one,
but when Padma's turn came—when she was in college—not only did
Amma and Appa give her a cycle but did it without her asking for it.
Shanta remembered Amma's face when she, Shanta, wore her first sleeveless blouse, and how one day it just disappeared from her cupboard. "How
should I know where it is," her mother said vaguely when confronted. "I'm
going to have two more made," Shanta said in a fury, and her mother
shrugged and said, "Do what you wish, if you want to look cheap, look
cheap." The sense of having cheapened herself stuck, till the day, years
later, when Padma wore sleeveless blouses, and when Shanta said to her
mother, "Oh, I see, so she can wear them and I couldn't." Her mother
looked surprised and said, "Why couldn't you?"

Now Shanta wanted to tell Amma all this, show her the unfairness of
her treatment, but how could she use Padma in her fight? In life, Shanta
thought, the reasons one kept silent had little to do with being weak or
lacking courage, it more often than not had to do with protecting people
one knew or their confidences, one could never use one's knowledge of the
situation in an argument or a fight, for the knowledge one had was sacro-
sanct. In her fights with Narayana this was what made her rage virtually
sing in her ears, his complacency when he knew nothing, his dismissal of
her words as rantings. She was reduced to ranting because she couldn't tell
him the truth. Once Narayana told her, "Your father's brother seems to
have no sense of shame," referring to his frequent and well-known extramarital affairs. Then she wanted to shout, What about your own mother,
Narayana, what about her? But of course, he didn't know, and even had he
known she couldn't have said it. Narayana had dared to be contemptuous
of her uncle for his extramarital affairs. The fool, the stupid, ignorant fool.
Shanta recalled that day when Lakshmi, Narayana's youngest sister, had
talked to her about the time after their father's death when the family had
moved to their father's married brother's house. Barely a year after that it

had begun. Their uncle would come to their mother's room after midnight, when all the children were asleep. "I used to sleep with my mother—in the bed, next to her, because I was the youngest and because I used to have nightmares after our father's death," Lakshmi told Shanta. "They thought I was asleep, that I couldn't hear." Lakshmi had paused, then said slowly, "I used to think I was imagining the whole thing, because there was no indication in the morning of what was happening at night, my mother continued to treat him with the same formality as before, he was as matter-of-fact in her presence. God knows if my aunt knew, she acted as if she didn't. And then, seeing everyone behaving so normally, I would think, I'm imagining the whole thing, I'm a dirty girl, and then at night it would happen again."

Shanta and her sister-in-law had sat together in the bedroom in silence, and then Lakshmi had said, "Something else happened when we were staying with our uncle. My cousins' friends used to come home often. My oldest cousin's brother's friend once passed me in the corridor and touched my breast and then continued walking away from me as if nothing had happened. Later too, he behaved as if nothing had happened. Is something wrong with my head, am I mad?" Shanta could say nothing, just shake her head in mute response to Lakshmi's question.

Then Shanta said, "Lakshmi, something happened to me also. At the time that I was in college, Amma and Appa called Appa's boss for dinner. He was Appa's age, married with teenage children, very well known, respected. We were having coffee after dinner in the sitting room. I was serving it to him when suddenly the electricity went off. In that instant I felt his hand squeezing both my breasts. As if he was blowing two horns with his two hands, Lakshmi," Shanta demonstrated, "just like that, twice, squeeze, squeeze."

They both began to laugh helplessly. "It isn't funny," Shanta said, unable to stop laughing.

"No, no, it isn't funny," Lakshmi gasped.

"I had the cup of coffee in my hands. I dropped the whole thing on his lap. It was scalding hot. He screamed. At that instant the light came on. I said, So sorry, so sorry. Amma rushed around getting towels and ice and Appa took him to the bathroom. I used to think, This is why Amma tells me not to wear sleeveless blouses."

It seemed as if these unexpected revelations had opened up things in both of them that each had thought long buried, they must have carried the guilt for years and years, for why else was there such a storm of relief? After all these years, talking to Lakshmi had given legitimacy to her own experience.

She hadn't told Narayana's sister the rest. She hadn't meant to tell Narayana. But he had been tender that day, had booked her and the boys to go to Delhi soon after his attack of flu, when she herself was reluctant to leave him. "Padma needs you more than I do," he had said, "you go." She had coddled him more than ever then, made him chicken soup, got him his newspaper in bed. Reading the newspaper, he had commented on a news item about a young woman who had battered her boss with her umbrella after years of putting up with his advances. "She should have done that the first time," Narayana had said.

"Narayana, to me also it happened."

He didn't lift his eyes from the paper.

She took the newspaper from his hands and told him what had happened with Appa's boss. What had she expected at the end? Anger? Shock? Comprehension? It was none of these. He said, "Oh, Shanta," and he shook his head. "I know your father's boss, I also have met him."

"What do you mean?" Shanta said, understanding now.

"Shanta, he was probably just putting out his hands to take the coffee from your hands."

"Narayana, if he touched my breasts by mistake instead of touching the coffee cups, then why did he squeeze them?"

Narayana began to laugh. "You have such a wild imagination, Shanta," he said. He studied her expression and said in a gentler voice, "Shanta, I know you better than you know yourself. You think I don't know why you cry in bed and why you have all those dreams when you get up screaming. Sometimes the world in which you live in your imagination is more real to you than the real world."

When the time came to leave she didn't remind him to write or take care of himself, and when she was with Padma, for the first time in her life she didn't write to him at all, till finally he sent a telegram. After that the ice broke. But the anger never left her. Like all the other things, it merely got swallowed deep inside; the daily ebb and flow washed to the surface—shell-like—the littler things, which was what she could speak of, these little things daily becoming more unmanageable and more unwieldy, and beneath, the heavier things, unuttered, unseen, sunk deep.

In some undefinable way something had changed after her talk with Lakshmi. Perhaps it was her dim realization that just because she wasn't logical in the way Narayana wanted her to be, it needn't mean that she was wrong, as she was often told and believed. Perhaps it was one thing less to carry untold, one thing less to feel responsible for. Yet while it freed her from a remnant of the past it didn't seem to embrace other related things—her guilt when her neighbour's husband looked at her in a way that she couldn't define, her continued inability after all these years to wear sleeveless blouses, her inability to say to Narayana, Narayana, don't call that man for dinner, he stands too close to me. But after this conversation with Lakshmi a deep and enduring friendship was forged, almost making up for the love denied to her by Narayana's other sisters and the mother. The last time they had met, which was on Shanta's birthday, Lakshmi had taken Shanta to a Bharatnatyam dance performance. It was one of the happiest days of her life, Shanta recalled later, this gesture of love and of indulgence. Had she all these years been waiting for Narayana to surprise her with just such a lovely, longed-for gesture?

Once it was Madhav who had indulged her with these precious gestures of indulgence, and Padma, of course, still continued to do it. Even before he got his job, Madhav would spend his pocket money on books for Padma and once he bought two books on embroidery and knitting for her, Shanta, books that she still used. It seemed that Madhav unerringly knew what they loved, and there was a sweetness in his gestures that moved Shanta more deeply than she would acknowledge. When she was with Amma and Appa during the months of May and June, waiting for Vikram to be born, Madhav would cycle to the sweet shop three miles from their house to get Shanta the gulabjamuns that she so craved. He would ration them out to her—one, or at the most two, a day. It was bad for the baby to have more, he would tell her sternly, and then, when there was only one sweet left, he would leave on his cycle to get some more. "Why don't you just get one big box of gulabjamuns," Amma said to him once, "instead of having to cycle twice a week in this heat?" Madhav's brows almost came together as he looked at her and said, "Amma, Shantacca needs *fresh* sweets." It was an unspoken understanding that Shanta would ask Madhav to get the sweets from the fridge after dinner every night. He would do so, open the box and hold it before her, savouring her choice of the largest piece with the same silent joy, refusing to offer it to anyone else or take any for himself. She remembered once when she absentmindedly asked Padma to get her the box, and later as Padma held the box before her, she had seen the look on Madhav's face, a look of such betrayal that in spite of the laughter that threatened to rise, she understood it—it was the way she often felt. Those days, Madhav and Padma would vie for her attention, for their beloved older sister's gestures of love. It was as if everything they did for her during her pregnancy was too little. As Shanta and Amma sewed and embroidered and knitted, Padma would wail, "I can't make anything for the baby." But in the afternoons and at night it was Padma who massaged her swollen feet, and in the mornings, Padma who made her her tea and gave it to her in bed with a biscuit.

Amma would spend hours in the kitchen cooking everything for her that she wanted, and every few days she would oil Shanta's hair with coconut oil, her hard fingers and palms in Shanta's hair moving to the remembered childhood rhythm, then Amma would comb it and say, as if Shanta had not already heard it a hundred times before, "You have to look after your hair now, after childbirth many women lose hair." Appa, who had never done any work in the house, would squeeze out juice for her and make her drink it every morning and evening, and when he went for his evening walks would make her accompany him saying, "Shanta, exercise is essential," and after her protests, she would end up enjoying the walks as much as Appa did. Appa, who had never in his life interfered in Amma's domain, the kitchen, began doing so now, looking critically at the food, commenting that there was too much oil, too much salt, too much sugar. Amma, who was adept at ignoring what she wanted to, nodded and continued to do things in exactly the same way. Every evening Appa would go out and compulsively buy something—almond oil for the baby, fruits for Shanta, once a book on pregnancy and childbirth which Amma glanced at and said, "I did it three times without such books."

It was worth it being pregnant just for this. At night Padma would bring a glass of milk to her in the large bed in which they both slept, then after Shanta had drunk it, would slip in beside her, and they would talk. Then Madhav would come to the room, looking irritated. "How much you two talk," he would say. "Padma, be a bit more considerate, let Shantacca go to sleep." Then Shanta would say, "Madhav, tell us about college," and Madhav would make a sound of exasperation and promptly sit at the foot of the bed and ask in a long-suffering tone, "What do you want to know?" Shanta would fall asleep to the sound of Madhav and Padma talking and arguing. They always argued, each was determined to take the opposite point of view regardless of what the argument was, for the sheer pleasure of thrashing out whatever it was that they wanted to thrash out.

It had been an idyllic time, that summer; there had been nothing like it before or after. Before she went to college and while she was in college, both Madhav and Padma had been too young to be her companions. This was the first time they had been able to enjoy one another's company so fully and with so much laughter. Padma would have what she believed was an intellectual conversation with both Shanta and Madhav, holding forth on life and morality and philosophy with such gravity that both Shanta and Madhav had to hold their laughter back with difficulty. "The problem," Padma told them once, full of indignation, "is that I'll always be the youngest—you'll never take me seriously." Madhav had tweaked her plait and said teasingly, "When you have your baby we'll take you seriously." Prophetic words.

This landscape of Shanta's past was an unfamiliar one to Narayana. In the beginning she had wanted to tell him about it, as her expression of a time both tender and innocent. But Narayana's attention was elsewhere and when she said, tearfully, "Narayana, listen properly," he sighed and said, "I'm listening," and she couldn't go on. Once she told him about an incident when she and Madhav had a race which she had won, and after she finished Narayana looked at her blankly and said, "Then what happened?" "Nothing *happened*," she replied, "for heaven's sake." The disappointment had been acute.

Mallika listened. Mallika asked her questions. She found herself telling Mallika things that she had thought forgotten. For Mallika, every picture Shanta drew and every conversation she recalled told a story, and every story held another which held another which held another. Once Mallika had asked her, "Shantamama, Madhav Uncle doesn't want to see me ever in his whole life?"

Shanta had replied, very carefully, "I think he does, but you see, he hasn't forgotten what happened before you were born, and he is very unforgiving."

"He must have felt so hurt and so . . . you know, so . . . rejected, Shantamama."

It frightened Shanta sometimes how Mallika put her finger so unerringly on situations about which she knew nothing.

And how could Mallika ever know.

It was the day the bungalow peon was down with the flu, so she and Padma had spent the morning cooking. The jamadarni lost her temper with Shanta, saying that Shanta expected too much work out of her. When Shanta went out to the garden the mali was fast asleep under the tree. Then Padma told her, "Shantacca, no need to get so worked up." Normally she would have given Padma a piece of her mind, but there was nothing that was normal now, so she tightened her lips and began to clean the bathroom, which the jamadarni had left half done. Then when she was cooking, Padma, who was chopping the vegetables said, "Shantacca, try and relax, why are you cooking so many things, one dal and one vegetable is enough." Again, she said nothing. Then Padma gave a sigh and in that sigh Shanta saw red. "You work yourself to the bone, Shantacca," Padma said, "then you get angry because you have no time for anything else."

Shanta laid down her knife and raised her finger. "Don't talk like Narayana, all right? Don't you dare talk like him." Padma's eyes flared very briefly, then she shrugged her shoulders. Then, as Shanta stirred the vegetables, Vikram decided he wanted attention and tugged at her saree. She smacked him the second time he did it and he began to cry and persisted in the tugging. Finally she had to take him to the bedroom and tell him a story and when she came back she found that the vegetable had got burnt because she had forgotten to lower the gas, and Padma, who was now chopping the tomatoes had also forgotten. "How could you forget, you're right here, couldn't you smell it burning?" Shanta asked her but all Padma did was shake her head and say, "No, Shantacca, I didn't notice, I'm sorry." Then Padma said, "Shantacca, you go and lie down and rest, I'll make another vegetable." Tight-lipped, Shanta threw the burnt vegetable into the bucket below the sink and began shelling peas. Then she peeled the potatoes, cut them, threw them into the vessel, sprinkled spices and stirred them. Then she took out onions, garlic, ginger.

"What is this for, haven't you finished?" Padma asked her.

"What do you think we're going to have for dinner?"

"Shantacca, leave all that for the evening." Shanta began to chop the onions. Padma said, "All right, give me the other things," and she put out her hands to take the ginger, garlic and onions.

Shanta put her hands over them. "No need," she said, "you go and rest."

"I don't want to rest. You're pregnant too, you also need to rest. Give."

"You want me to leave all that for the evening. You want me to cook in the morning, cook in the evening. Don't you think I need some respite too, don't you think I want to sit and read and sit and knit and relax?"

"Of course you do, Shantacca. That's why I'm telling you to relax, we can have the same thing for lunch and for dinner, it'll be easier on you."

"Padma, don't give me advice about things that you know nothing about."

"Shantacca."

"Padma, just let me do things my way. You go and read or something, two people can't work together in the kitchen."

"Shantacca," Padma said and then burst into loud tears.

She couldn't stop. She cried loudly, the sobs tearing her throat, fat tears rolling down her cheeks. Shanta lowered the gas, stirred the potatoes, covered them and took her to the bedroom, where Padma continued crying. It went on for about fifteen minutes, till Vikram, who was only four then, sat on the bed beside Padma and said, "It's all right, it's all right," patting her back, in exactly the same manner that Padma comforted him. Padma smiled a little, her sobs slowly subsiding and Shanta went back to the kitchen. She had felt nothing for Padma, nothing at all. Her back was hurting, her head was hurting, her varicose veins were killing her and the circles around her eyes felt like lead. Working in the blessed silence, she cooked the dinner and put it aside to cool, laid the lunch, the thalis and glasses on the table, cleaned the kitchen, mopped the kitchen floor. Then she picked up Vikram's toys from the sitting room and the dining room, picked up the newspaper from the carpet and put it on the table, picked up Narayana's vest, underwear and pyjamas and put them in the dirty-linen basket, made a list of the vegetables and fruits to be got that evening, dusted all the rooms, cleaned the fridge and rearranged all the items in the pantry shelves. Then they had lunch. Padma's nose was still red but she was calm now and Vikram sat next to her and sang to her. After they cleared the table Padma went swiftly to the kitchen and began to wash the dishes but Shanta pushed her away. "Padma," she said, "I can do them better and faster." Shanta washed the dishes and Padma dried them and put them away. Then Shanta took out all the dishes from where Padma had put them and put them in their proper places. The sheets hadn't been changed for a week now. The dhobi was coming in the evening. She went to the bedrooms to do that but found that Padma had already taken out the old sheets and put on the fresh ones. She smoothed the sheets, which had wrinkles at the sides, tucked the edges in more tidily, noticed that the flowers were dying in the vase, threw them out, put in fresh water, went to the garden and plucked some more flowers and arranged them in all the rooms. Then she put Vikram to sleep. He wanted her to sing three songs to him and tell him two stories, she sang the songs and Padma told the stories. It was already two-thirty by then. Padma got into bed and was asleep in seconds. Shanta was going to get into bed too when she noticed that Padma's nightie, which was lying at the foot of Padma's bed, had a tear under the arm. She got her needlework box and darned the hole. She noticed that the hooks at the front were missing and that Padma had two pins where the hooks were supposed to be. She shook her head in exasperation and stitched in the hooks. Then she put everything away and lay down on the bed. As her head touched the pillow, everything inside her head began to go round. She felt a little cold, but in order to cover herself with a sheet she would have to summon the strength to get up, so she tucked her feet under her saree and wrapped the palla around her shoulders and chest, curled herself and closed her eyes. From the other room she heard Vikram cry out in his sleep. She tensed up, but there was no sound after that. She was almost asleep when she heard it, a ringing sound from far far away. In her dreamlike state it seemed to go on and on. She opened her eyes. The doorbell was ringing. The dhobi. How dare he. How many times had she told him never to come in the afternoon. She wouldn't get up. Let him go. She closed her eyes. The doorbell rang three times in succession. Suddenly she sat up in bed as if someone had pulled her up. Oh God, she thought, don't let it be a telegram. Appa, Appa, something had happened to Appa. She stumbled to the door, her body heavy with her child, and opened it.

Madhav stood there, looking hot and flushed, and before she could say anything, before she could tell him to come inside, he burst out, "Shantacca, why didn't you tell me?" Then he brushed past her and came inside, flung himself on the chair, took off his shoes and removed his socks, tossing them right in the middle of the carpet as he used to do at home, with Amma hovering around him, waiting to pick them up and put them away. Madhav looked up at her from his chair and said, "You always want to take charge, Shantacca, you always want to exclude me."

It had begun right then, the wrong note had been struck right from the beginning. Perhaps if she had paid more attention to the misery on his face rather than to the accusation in his words, perhaps if she were less tired, the outcome would have been different. But she was tired, and the misery on his face was less evident than the accusation in his words—as if it were all her fault, the same way Padma had sounded in the afternoon, the way Amma had always sounded, the way Narayana sounded, the way even Vikram sounded when she couldn't pay him attention twenty-four hours a day, as if she were in a conspiracy against them that was all her doing. And there was no part of her body that wasn't aching, the ache reaching inwards, her very chest was hurting with things unformed, unsaid. Perhaps things would have been different if he had come another day. Perhaps not. Perhaps this is what fate was, the fact that some people happened to be at a particular place at a particular time and not at another time, perhaps this was what people meant by destiny.

"Madhav," she said, "if you've come all this way to start accusing me, then there's no need for you to have come."

He stared at her and she saw his body tense with growing anger. "I'm not accusing you of anything," he said, "I just asked you a simple question, no need to get hysterical, Shantacca."

"Simple question—ask me what you wish but ask properly. Don't you dare call me hysterical again, keep those words for your wife. Have you had lunch?"

Madhav burst out laughing. He stopped as abruptly as he had begun and shook his head, saying, "You'll never change."

She shook her head too, her ears singing in that horrible, familiar way, and said, "If you've come here to laugh at me, then go." She went to the front door and opened it, ignoring the voice in her head that panted, Don't, Shanta, don't, don't-don't.

Madhav looked at her as if he had been punched in his stomach. "Shantacca?" he whispered.

"Shantacca!" Padma's voice cried from the other end of the room. Shanta shut the door and for some time stood there, her back turned to them, feeling as though her whole body was disintegrating.

When she turned finally, Madhav was standing looking at Padma. Shanta saw that his eyes were very bright, that next to his legs his hands were clenched, he was trying to say something but nothing came out. "Madhav," Padma said, her voice faint, and at the same time Madhav said, "Padma," and they both stopped. It was showing, Shanta realized with a shock, Padma's stomach was showing. She hadn't noticed it before. "Madhav," Padma said again. Madhav raised his hand, brushed his eye impatiently and said, "I just came to tell you . . ." he paused and burst out, "I'll kill him."

Then Shanta began to giggle. She put her hand to her mouth but laughter came out of her like a fountain, she couldn't stop, it was like when Lakshmi and she had begun giggling about the time Appa's boss had squeezed Shanta's breasts—there was nothing funny in it, in fact, quite the opposite, but the laughter wouldn't stop, and this time it filled her with terror because she knew that the irrevocable turn she had feared was coming. She found herself saying, "Madhav, please don't act like a film Hero, this is real life." Inside her the voice whispered, Shanta, why are you saying this, what is wrong with you? Madhav turned towards her slowly, Padma turned away from her, all in slow motion. It really was like a Hindi film, Shanta thought as her laughter spilled out without control. She saw the incredulous look on Madhav's face, the humiliation and anger, and as Padma turned to look at her, she saw the despair on Padma's. Abruptly, her laughter stopped. She sat on the sofa and closed her eyes.

"Madhav," Shanta heard Padma say, "Amma said you were coming to Bangalore soon and then she would tell you. She . . . we . . . didn't want to write. So . . ."

Shanta opened her eyes. Padma was sitting next to her, Madhav was sitting opposite them on the sofa, looking into space as if he hadn't heard. After some time he said, "It is him, isn't it?" Shanta stared at her brother. Padma nodded. "Why didn't you tell me, Padma?" he said.

"When you met him . . . nothing . . . there was nothing."

Madhav too, Shanta thought bitterly, he and Sumi had both known. "What are you going to do?" he asked. So, Shanta thought, he was asking the question she, Shanta, hadn't asked, the question Padma herself hadn't asked. She heard Padma's voice saying, "I've applied for the post of lecturer in Delhi University . . ."

"Padma," Shanta said, "you never told me." Padma didn't reply. Shanta got up. "Have you had lunch, Madhav?" Madhav shook his head. She went to the kitchen and put the rice on to cook. By the time she finished heating the food and laying the table the rice was ready. "Come, Madhav," she said, "eat while it's hot." Madhav didn't get up. He was still looking into space. "Madhav," Shanta said sharply. He really was the limit. This is how he always behaved at home, Amma calling him for lunch or dinner, Madhav not coming on time, Amma reheating the food, Madhav in the bathroom, Madhav finally at the table complaining that the food wasn't hot enough, Amma reheating the food again—if he thought she, Shanta, was going to begin that ritual he was mistaken.

"Padma," Madhav said, "you don't have to worry about anything. Ratna and I will adopt your baby."

Shanta almost dropped the jug of water she was placing on the table. Padma's head had jerked up as if she were a puppet. Shanta put the jug on the table and said, "No, you're not, Narayana and I are adopting the baby."

Then both Madhav and Padma were looking at her—Madhav's face impatient, Padma's face with an expression she couldn't understand. "Narayana and I have talked about it," Shanta said.

Padma said, "You didn't tell me, Shantacca."

Shanta felt the colour rushing to her face as she replied, "I was going to." It was true. It was just that the right moment had never come. Padma wasn't talking about anything, she didn't seem responsive to anything, she didn't mention the baby at all, not once. Shanta had thought, she has to talk about it some time, then I'll tell her, What's the hurry. It wasn't as if the idea had suddenly come to her, it was as if it had been there from the moment Padma arrived at her house that first day. She had told Narayana one night, knowing what his answer would be, and he had said, "If Padma doesn't want the child, then of course." Shanta had made a sound of exasperation. "What do you mean, Narayana, if she doesn't want the child, how can she look after the child alone, what means does she have and no support either, she can't manage." Narayana had turned towards her and said, "Shanta, don't make Padma's decisions for her. Wanting the baby has nothing to do with practical constraints like money or even, as in her case, the circumstances. When she's ready to talk about it she'll talk about it. Then you tell her. As for asking me, why should you feel you have to ask me. One more child in our house, and our house will be a richer one." He put his hands under his head, looking up at the ceiling. "My childhood," he said, "was rich, even after my father died. My mother had six of us, and my uncle with whom we lived had eight. The older ones looked after the younger ones—no dearth of company, no dearth of affection, quite idyllic. Look at Vikram now, the demands he makes on you—he's lonely." He said, a faint laugh in his voice, "Our parents didn't plan to have so many children, only we people plan these things and that's our loss." He yawned and closed his eyes. "I hope at least one of them, ours or Padma's will be a girl." Shanta had gazed at his face, wanting him to go on, love for him flooding her, but he had closed his eyes and fallen asleep. And the next time they lay in bed and she brought up the subject of Padma's baby, just for the joy of hearing Narayana speak of it and of his childhood, he said, "Shanta, I told you what I felt, now go to sleep."

Madhav got up from his chair and went to the window. He turned his back to it, his eyes on Shanta, and said, "I have more right than you, Shantacca, I'm the brother, the child will have my name, not your husband's."

"Don't talk rubbish," Shanta said, enraged, "Narayana and I are keeping the baby."

Madhav's face turned dark, he folded his arms across his chest and said, sarcastically, "Taking charge as usual, no, Shantacca? Wanting to do everything for everyone so that later you can say, No one does anything for me."

Shanta stared at him, stunned. The beginnings of a new grief began to stir inside her. "Madhav," she said, "how can you talk to me like this?"

Madhav shrugged his shoulders, and his voice was hard as he said, "This is no time for sentiment, Shantacca, for once try and be practical. Why should the child be foisted on my brother-in-law? Why should he spend his money on bringing it up, on its education, marriage, whatever? Don't shake your head, don't say he won't mind, I also know him, I also know he won't mind. But I have the right, not he, Appa agrees with me."

"And Amma?"

Madhav made an impatient gesture, "She was dithering as usual."

"I see," Shanta said, "so what does Ratna think of all this?"

There was a silence. Madhav walked back to the chair and sat. He shrugged. "What Ratna thinks or doesn't think isn't important. She knows what her responsibilities are."

They're the same, Shanta would think later as she recalled that day, they're all the same. Later she was able to find the words that hadn't emerged the day Madhav came. In her fantasy the words that came out of her were different, and so the outcome was different. In her fantasy she contained her rage, and said, gently, Oh, Madhav, I understand how you feel. But it isn't fair on Ratna, she is expecting her first child—how can she look after another who is as young? Be practical, Madhav, the poor girl will fall ill with exhaustion. And then she also wants to get back to her job. See,

Madhav, I'm not working. It will be so much easier for me, the child will get so much more undivided attention. In this scenario the hardness would leave Madhav's face, he would continue sitting on the chair in silence, then after some time he would say, with his wry smile, Right as usual, Shantacca. Then Shanta would turn to Padma, hold her hand and say, Padma? And Padma would squeeze her hand in silent assent. Then Madhav would sit down to have his lunch and say, Shantacca, it's cold, and she would give a sigh of exasperation and heat it again and he would eat.

All that Shanta said in her fantasy was true, but it was not her truth. Her truth, uttered neither in the fantasy nor in actuality, was, This child belongs to Padma and me, and you will not have it.

What she finally uttered, also her truth, was "You think Ratna will have any love for Padma's child when she isn't capable of loving anyone except herself?"

Madhav was putting on his socks, then his shoes, tying the laces. Shanta closed her eyes again, feeling the familiar bands tighten around her forehead. It was as if she couldn't open her eyes now, the darkness inside her head bloomed red and purple, her ears hummed. Inside her the baby moved restlessly; she put her hand on her stomach. The baby, a voice said. Not you, Madhav, not Shantacca, the voice said. Shanta opened her eyes with great effort. "I don't want it, I don't want to ever see it," Padma was saying, "it's going to an orphanage," and it was the hysteria in Padma's voice that hit Shanta before the words did.

The silence after that went on for so long that Shanta felt she would begin screaming. Then Madhav said, his voice full of disbelief and contempt, "Have you no sense of responsibility, have you no compassion?"

The look on Padma's face shocked Shanta. "Oh, shut up, Madhav," Padma said, "just shut up."

"An orphanage, do you know what an orphanage—"

Padma put her hands to her ears, closed her eyes and said, "Keep quiet, keep quiet. I don't want to hear anything, just keep quiet."

"Listen to me first. Listen to me. Children need both parents, they need a happy environment, they need security, they need respectability."

"Respectability, respectability," Padma panted, "so you think marriage gives you respectability?"

She knows, Shanta thought, her body thrilling with the realization, she's always known about Madhav's women, and then her body stopped tingling, and she watched them staring at each other like enemies and she thought, You stupid fool, Padma, why did you have to *say* it.

"You better take responsibility for what you did, you lying, deceiving bitch," Madhav whispered.

"Out," Shanta said, taking him by the shoulders, "get out."

He flung her hands off him and went across the room to where Padma was sitting, staring at him. He bent down before her and said, "I didn't mean that, Padma, I—" He put his hands over hers. Padma flung her elbow over her eyes and hit out blindly with her other hand, hitting Madhav on the side of his head.

He got up. He walked to the door where his suitcase was still lying, picked it up and fumbled for the bolt on the door. He unbolted it, and as he went out Shanta saw that his face was streaming with tears. "Madhav," she said, following him, her hand outstretched, but he strode down the steps of the veranda, down the driveway and out of the gate.

She went back to the house. She could hear Vikram prattling in his room, and then Padma's voice asking him if he wanted his milk. Her mind blank, she watched Padma going to the kitchen to warm the milk. She picked up the plate and glass from the dining table, but her hands were trembling so much that she had to put them back. She touched the dal and meat and vegetables, all cold now. She wouldn't have to reheat anything.

During one of her holidays in Delhi Madhu had asked Shanta, "What did you want to do in life?" She hadn't been able to reply, strangely confused, both by the question and by the fact that Madhu had asked it. After some time she had said, "I wanted to go to college, then get married to a nice man with a good job, have a large house and garden and have two children." Even as she spoke she was swept by a wave of such blinding realization that it was as if someone's hand was squeezing her throat. Madhu smiled and said, "Very lucky, Shanta, very lucky you are, in life it is so difficult to get what you are wanting."

Life, more often than not, Shanta thought, gave you what you wanted, but it did so in a nasty, perverse way, so that when you got it (and you usually got it in full measure), it was never the way you had wanted it. Padma had wanted passion, romance, she had wanted to be swept off her feet. All of it she got, temporarily, and all of its residue, permanently. It was the residue which, like accumulated dust in a locked house, you had to sweep away, it was like one of those dreams where you swept and swept and swept to no avail, till the dust was in your nostrils and in your throat and inside your lungs, and you learnt to breathe that way for the rest of your life.

Yes, God gave you what you wished for in ways you never would have asked for. When she went into labour the second time she told herself, This time I'm going to be brave, this time I won't scream and moan the way I did when Vikram was born. And she neither screamed nor moaned, but pushed almost silently, awaiting her reward, and finally she felt the child slither out of her, and it was the nurse who gave a little scream and exclaimed, "*So* lucky, another boy, another boy!" And Shanta's mouth opened, as if of its own accord, and a sound emerged that was so despairing that it filled the room and poured out of the door in one continuous stream, and outside in the corridor another nurse clicked her tongue and said to Padma, "Oho, poor thing, it must be a girl."

The irony, the irony. It was Padma to whom a daughter had been born three months later, Padma who didn't ask to hold the child or look at it, who lay silently in the labour room, her face turned away. And after the child was washed and cleaned, and Shanta held her in Padma's room, waiting for Padma to be wheeled back, it was towards Shanta's breast that the baby turned, and Shanta opened her damp blouse, and the baby nuzzled and began to suckle. So effortlessly, Shanta thought wonderingly; it had taken both her sons two days to learn. She looked out of the window.

It was so dark outside, she would tell Anuradha and Madhu a year later, concluding My Sister Padma's Story, which she now knew by heart—better, much better than the true story, which she didn't know at all. How it was raining outside, she would say, how it was raining, for two days it had been raining like that. And the trees—they were bent by the wind and the whole sky was covered with black clouds, and up on the roof I could hear it drumming and drumming. Shanta didn't tell Anu and Madhu of the sudden peace inside her when the baby suckled so fiercely, of her own silent declaration, She fed at my breast first. She didn't tell them of how she thought, Padma will not prevail; the child is mine, this is how it is meant to be. She didn't tell them of the baby's indignant cry as she had moved it from one breast to the other, and of how she smiled and thought, Krishna, Krishna, is this how you give her to me.

It had been a brief, perfect moment, that time with the baby at her breast, a moment existing only for itself. She had known peace then, and happiness in its purest, most sublime form.

Then Padma was wheeled in. The nurse looked at Shanta in shock. "I have milk," Shanta found herself explaining, "I have a baby." The nurse tucked Padma into the bed and left.

Padma looked at Shanta and said, "Shantacca." Shanta gently removed the baby from her breast, put the infant on her lap and buttoned her blouse. Still holding the baby she dragged the chair to the bed and sat next to Padma, the baby in her lap, and held Padma's cold hand in her warm one. The baby began to cry. Padma looked at her and there were dark circles under her eyes. With her finger she touched the baby's cheek. "So soft," Padma said. Shanta nodded. The knowledge of her loss began to spread over her body like a creeping chill. "How to hold it?" Padma asked. Shanta picked up the baby and put her into Padma's arms, watched as Padma unbuttoned her nightie and put the baby to her breast. The baby began to suck. Padma looked up at Shanta. "Shantacca, is it a girl or a boy?"

"A girl."

"Shantacca, all the sarees and jewels that Amma has kept for my marriage, what happens to that now?"

"It's your share, it should go to you."

Padma nodded, her eyes still on her baby. Shanta could see Padma's mind working as though the words were appearing in print in front of her. "We'll talk about all that later," Shanta said. She watched the baby that should have been hers and found to her surprise that her eyes were dry.

Madhav's daughter was born a month before Mallika. "One thing I must tell you now," Amma wrote to Shanta, "he has not said anything to Ratna about Padma. The story Ratna knows is the story everyone else knows. This you must know." Shanta didn't miss the note of adulation in Amma's letter, how she was thinking, no doubt, My darling, precious son, who is so protective of his sister.

The tears that hadn't come broke when she told My Sister Padma's Story to Anuradha and Madhu. Somewhere inside her a voice said, Cry, Shanta, cry, it won't do you any harm, it will do Padma only good. Cry, Shanta, make up for all the tears Padma will not shed before them, your tears will have to stand Padma in good stead. Look at these two women, Shanta, see. That one, Madhu, affection she has in plenty, she will bestow it in abundance on your sister. But in return she will want to touch every jagged piece of Padma's pain. See how Madhu sobs, already you have weighed the balance in Padma's favour. And the other one, Anuradha, you think she cries easily? No, no, your tears have unleashed something inside her; the unleashing can only be to Padma's benefit.

"To be a woman," Shanta said finally, to Madhu and Anuradha, blowing her nose, "is to suffer." She had heard this line before in some Hindi film, she recalled the beautiful tear-stained face of the actress who hadn't had to blow her nose. Madhu and Anuradha looked back at her in mute agreement, both their noses pink. "You both have daughters," Shanta said, her voice breaking, "and Mallika is as much my daughter as Padma's." She closed her eyes and folded her hands and said, "May none of our daughters have to go through even one tiny portion of what my sister has gone through."

She couldn't have succeeded better had she known she would say all this. Even as she said it the sheer dramatics of it made her want to laugh hysterically, but almost simultaneously came the realization that every word she had just produced in such filmi style was true, and with that knowledge, her hand went to her breast in an equally filmi but completely unpracticed gesture. It was only many years later that she knew she hadn't been crying only for Padma and Mallika, and nor had Madhu and Anuradha. They had each wept for all the reasons that Narayana and Mr. Prasad and Mr. Nanda and Appa and Madhav would never weep, of which Padma and Mallika were only one part.

Once, before Shanta's marriage, when she and Amma were talking about the price of gold and silk, Padma had laughed at them, and when Shanta had said to her, "No need to laugh like that, when you get married all this will be part of your marriage and of your life," Padma had shaken her head with all the indulgence that was possible for a younger sister to give an older one, and said, "No, it won't."

How children changed you, Shanta thought, you became another person when they entered your life. She, Shanta, who had always been so generous, so ready to find time for others, had turned into this person who hid from her children in the bathroom. She, Shanta, who had always taken every illness, hers and her parents, in stride, now lived in dread that every illness her children had would take them away from her. She couldn't live without them, if she lost them her life would be over, yet she often wished them lost, gone, away. She loved them in a way she had no words for, yet at times she knew she actually disliked them. And Padma, look what had happened to her. "I'll write to Amma, Shantacca, later I don't want her to attribute anything to you," Padma had said to her when they returned from the hospital. So while she, Shanta, sat on the sofa suckling Mallika, Padma composed her letter to Amma, asking her for her share of the jewellery and sarees—a cold, formal letter.

"Show some affection at least, Padma," Shanta had said when Padma gave it to her to read.

"She hasn't even come to see the baby, Shantacca."

*She,* Shanta noted. Padma had said *she,* not *they.* As if reading her thoughts, Padma said, "Appa won't come, but Amma should have."

"You think it's easy for her, do you," Shanta said, transferring Mallika to her other breast.

"For Appa it's over, finished, I don't exist. Not for Amma." For the first time Shanta heard the bitterness in Padma's voice. Added to it, her indifference to all that she had once scorned. It is my share, she had written to Amma, so please sell it and send me the money so that I can buy a house wherever I get a job. But, Shanta thought, what did Padma expect? Surely she didn't think that Appa would forgive a transgression of such magnitude? Surely she didn't imagine that Amma could say to her, even though she felt like it, Come, my child, my house is open to you. Bitterness was often the result of things unexpected, gone sour, the turning of events and people away from one's imagined course, the living of a life against one's grain, the losing of one's illusions. It was Him towards whom the bitterness should have been directed, He who had done all that, not Amma and Appa, whom she had betrayed. This is what it did—having a child; things became misdirected.

It was a small house. The money from the jewellery and sarees had been more than any of them expected, but it had been short of ten thousand rupees, which Amma put in. In her letter, addressed to both Shanta and Padma, she had said without sentiment, This is your share, Padma. The jewellery and sarees kept for your marriage, all of it has been sold. Shanta, the amount we spent for your wedding and for Madhav's wedding, that I am adding to this amount. All this I am putting down in writing; later I do not want anyone to say I gave more or less. In money matters, everything has to be clear. Padma, my child, there was no need for you to ask for this. I was going to do it anyway when your letter came.


The day Shanta had found the photograph she had felt such rage against Padma that her fingers had begun to tremble. Careless, careless, careless, she had thought, her breath going in and out in rhythm with the unspoken words. But even as Shanta's anger surged, the expressions of the two in the photograph turned her anger to grief. And with it came a reluctant admiration for Mallika, who had kept it from them all, hiding it so carefully underneath her desk where the board was loose, first putting it in a white envelope, then covering the envelope with a brown piece of paper, then slipping it inside the board where no one could possibly look. She, Shanta, wouldn't have discovered it if she hadn't decided to clean under the desk too. She had seen the loose board then, had told herself, Trust Padma not to have it fixed, better tell Narayana to hammer a couple of nails in when he comes. Then, as she moved the board experimentally with her hand, the photograph fell out.

God knew for how many years Mallika had kept it hidden away, how many times she had gazed at it. Every day, probably, several times a day possibly. Shanta had looked at his chiselled features, his tender smile, and she had known. And Padma's face, glowing, looking not at him but at the camera. This was the girl she had known once, not the woman she knew now. Oh God, Shanta had thought, Oh God.

Did Padma know how her child talked to her father every day, every afternoon, every night? She, Shanta, had heard Mallika murmuring in her room, had stood outside and heard every word. Mallika talked to her father, sought his advice. Mallika's father talked back to her, gave it. Two voices Mallika used, her own, and his. His was quiet and measured and mature. Dada. She called him Dada. Shanta did not want to listen after that first time. But it was as if she were drawn like a magnet to that door of Mallika's room, where she stood silently while Padma slept, listening.

We suffer most through our children, Shanta thought, the sobs catching at her throat, and in the silence her thoughts seemed to echo back into the past, where she had wished something similar on another woman. She had done it for Padma. If there was justice in this world, her curse would fulfill itself. "Krishna, Krishna, forgive me," she prayed. Her prayer was automatic, she knew there was no truth in it. So what. Praying had nothing to do with truth.

Once, in a sudden frenzy of despair she asked Narayana, "What will happen to Mallika if Padma and I and you die before she gets married?" Narayana had laughed for a long time. "We'll try not to do it together," he said finally. Vikram had been at the table demolishing mangoes and he had grinned. Later as she cleaned the boys' room Vikram came up behind her, his mango in his hand, his mouth full and he said, "I'm there." "You're where?" Shanta asked, picking up his shirt and pants and books. Vikram swallowed, took another mouthful of mango and said, "For Mallika," and wiped his mouth with the back of his hand. "Oh, darling," Shanta said tearfully and put her arms around him but he pushed her away. "For heaven's sake, Mum," he said, leaving mango stains on her arm and on the floor which she then had to swab. But his words had stayed with her. At times like this, love for her firstborn threatened to choke her, suddenly she found herself longing for the time when he was still a baby so that she could hold him as fiercely. But now Vikram didn't want it, now Varun didn't want it. It was over, that total, complete dependence on her, finished. She who had felt like fleeing while it was there, now craved it in a way that was almost physical. Now her sons would never say, Mummy, *hold* me. Mummy, *where* are you going? Now neither would wait outside the bathroom for her, jealous of the space she dared to occupy without them. Now her thoughts lingered over each moment of their babyhood and the way their faces had lit up for her as if she were their sun, how their plump hands had moved towards her. She remembered how Varun always asked for water or milk or biscuits just when she was feeding Mallika. Now she wanted their demands, now she sought their possessiveness. When she left them with her brother-in-law for weeks at a stretch during the months she stayed with Padma and Mallika, she waited for them to miss her. They didn't.

If Narayana hadn't had his operation she would have tried for another baby, she wanted one so fiercely that it was like a physical need—she wanted to feel a baby's bare skin against hers, its tender head in the palm of her hand, she wanted to breathe its milky breath. Now she would have to wait till her children had children of their own. But before that they would have wives. Then she would lose them the way she and Padma had lost Madhav. Who knew what her sons' wives would think of Mallika. What need would their wives have to bear any responsibility for a mere cousin. Daughters-in-law now were not the daughters-in-law of her time. They had strange ideas about independence and identity, they no longer believed in responsibilities, duties, adjustment. Her sons' wives would be like that, she was sure of it.

Mallika, my dearest, your Shantamama will explain when you grow older, your Shantamama won't let anyone hurt you. I will prepare you. We were not prepared. If you're prepared, then you will accept it. You have to accept it, otherwise you'll end up like that Mad Mrs. Moitra. Mallika, my darling, I will tell you all this when you're older. You listen, even now, and in such a way you listen that I get frightened, I begin thinking things that I didn't know I thought, sometimes I even say them to you. Then when I see your questioning face, I have to stop myself.

My love. My darling child, listen. What we have given you, your mother and I, don't expect it from anyone else. Mallika, my dearest, understand this now or else you will spend your life seeking it and it isn't there to be sought.

The words would have to wait, they would have to wait. Mallika was too young now, too tender.

The thought was unbearable; for herself she could bear it, but not for Mallika: somewhere there was a man who would marry her darling and already she hated him for what he wouldn't give her, for what he wouldn't understand about her. Padma and she knew Mallika's core in a manner that was fundamental, intrinsic, their learning of her grew from within this core. But for That Man who would one day marry her, what would he know? Nothing, nothing, nothing. His understanding would have to begin from the outside, and there would be blood in this learning, and even then he wouldn't reach the core. And if at all he understood, it would be an understanding of the mind—the kind of understanding one got from textbooks, not one of the heart. That of the heart, only she and Padma had, only she and Padma would ever have.

How to explain to her, how? How to tell Mallika that it was the nature of indulgence that she, Shanta, had craved, thinking, this is what love is about. That love should express itself in anticipating what the other wanted or needed or expected, as her father had with all three of his children, as her mother had with Madhav and Padma, as she and Padma did with Mallika? How to explain to Mallika in mere words the foolishness of women who expected from their husbands and their husband's families the same gestures of love that they got so naturally from their own? How to tell her that love between men and women was by its very nature a blemished thing? That it was gilded on the outside by all the things it was made out to be in books and films, in mythology; by the very vibrancy of the marriage ceremony; by the lie every married woman lived and the smiles she showed. There was no substance to it, it was only the wistful yearnings of those like her who had dreamed, and those who had had the luck to love at a distance, and those who had lost the ones they loved. It was only out of these emotions that the poetry and fiction that Mallika so loved arose, for it was only in the writing of it that one could vicariously realize one's dreams.

But underneath the gilding its centre seethed like thousands of maggots in a rotten fruit. Other women smiled because they had pushed such knowledge to the very edges, where, like low tide, it ebbed and flowed decorously. Once she had thought that tragedy was what afflicted great lives, tragedy was what one read in Shakespeare, but the small lives were the ones more sorely afflicted, so permanent a part was it of these lives, so much was it the very life they learnt to live.

All her life she had sought it. And she had it now. It was the complete-ness of Mallika's love for her that she had sought all her life. Her boys loved her too—that she had never doubted—but the nature of their love was dif-ferent, already it had in it the seeds of another life, already there was a dis-tancing . . . the distancing that was second nature to men. Her sons would always love her, they would always be there for her, but they would never know her. Unlike Mallika. Already Mallika knew her in that fundamental, essential way, already Mallika was asking questions about her childhood and her dreams and her experiences. Her sons would never ask that, Narayana would never ask that. Even now she continued resenting Narayana's disinterest, even though she knew that such questions didn't in-terest him any more than the working of a car interested her. Only Mallika loved her the way she wanted to be loved, only Mallika adored her. Krishna had given her her daughter, but even here he had given with one hand and taken with the other; he had given Mallika to Padma, and Mallika would always love Padma more.

# PADMA

 I want to die, I want to *die.* She had allowed her three-year-old child to hear her frenzied cry. Allowed? She had cried it out *against* her child, *against* her demands, *against* her love. Not once, but night after night after night, she and Mallika weeping in loud unison, Amma, Amma, Ma, Ma. Not wanting Mallika, without whom she couldn't live; not wanting Mallika's demands, without which she wouldn't have survived; not wanting Mallika's love, without which she would have curled up and died. I can't live without you, Mallika. I can't live without you. He had said it to her just once, but she had thought she heard it the other times when he had murmured it against her bare arm, thinking she slept. Sometimes she had wondered if she had dreamt it, *Padma . . . without you . . . can't live,* perhaps she had dreamt it, all of it. Don't die, Ma, don't die. All her doing, Mallika's anguish. The lies coming out like weeds, I won't die, Mallika, I won't die. At three her child had grasped what no child her age should grasp—the unspeakable nature of her mother's grief. She should have protected Mallika, her child who had so little and understood so much. But instead she had, time and time again, exposed her child to her hemorrhaging.

And her child too had exposed her. That was what having a child did. That was what loving so terribly did. It had happened with him, and it had happened with Mallika. That was the price you had to pay for loving in this way. You got exposed to yourself, your true self. I'm talking to you so *nicely* and you're getting *angry* with me, Mallika had wept at three. I love you *so* much and you're *shouting* at me, Mallika had sobbed at three and a half. I only wanted you to give me some love and you're looking at me like

225

*that,* Mallika had wailed at four. And then, the next day, she had looked at her mother apprehensively and said, Ma, *please* don't look at me like that again. Padma had burst out, I'm sorry, my love, I'm sorry, my pet. And Mallika, her eyes large, asked, Ma, when you were looking at me like that yesterday, were you turning into a big bad witch?

That was what being loved so fiercely did. He or she who loved you saw that misshapen horrible thing inside you, and then you saw it too, this thing which you had never known existed.

Karan had known. Mallika knew. Not Anu, not Madhu, not the neighbours, not her colleagues, not her students. Good, honest, brave Padma. The woman of integrity. Good, honest, brave Mrs. Rao. Anu and Madhu indulging her, protecting her, mothering her, standing by her. They did not know how unworthy she was of what they gave. And she kept receiving it, kept expecting it, yes, demanding it, and one day they would find out how they had deceived themselves. No, no, they would find out how *she* had deceived them, they would find out what she was, and perhaps she could bear that. One can bear anything, Shantacca had said. One can recover from anything, Karan had said. She could bear it for herself, but how could she bear it for Mallika? She, Padma, who had boasted so often about truth now had to live her lie. It was true what Karan had said, it mattered what people said, what they thought. How could she ever have imagined otherwise? And Mallika would lose it all, her friends, her surrogate aunts, her belief in her mother, everything, and she did not have the strength to withstand it, she could not have the fortitude to bear it, and if it happened it would be, like the rest, all her, Padma's, fault. She, Padma, was willing to face the consequences. It could be done. Had she already not done it. It could be done again. But it was her child who would suffer the consequences of what she, her mother, had done.

Don't die, Ma, don't die. I won't die, Mallika, I won't die. Once, she, Padma, had thought she would never die. Later, she had wanted only that, and then she had not been able to die because of the child. Even then she had wanted to, wanted it as passionately as she had wanted Karan—yes, even after her child was born. That was the kind of mother she was. I want to die, I want to *die.* Mallika, her child, who read her mind, knew the magic words that held it at bay, Don't die, Ma, don't die. And then her affirmation of this, as much for Mallika as for herself, helping Mallika ward it off with the mantra, I won't die, Mallika, I won't die, like the prayers Amma and Appa chanted in perfect unison to which Padma had once awakened every morning—Shree Rama, Jaya Rama, Jaya Jaya Rama. Don't die, Ma, don't die, Shree Rama, Jaya Rama, I won't die, Mallika, I won't die, Jaya Jaya Rama. The smell of incense, soft and insidious, had permeated every room, Amma's sarees and her hair smelt of it. Shree Rama, Jaya Rama, Jaya Jaya Rama. Shanta was the only one who joined Amma and Appa for the morning prayers, while she and Madhav continued sleeping till Shanta woke them both up and supervised them and got them ready for school. When she was five Shanta was already mothering her and Madhav, already Shanta was asking Madhav to open his mouth to see if he had brushed his teeth, taking out Padma's underwear and school uniform, her socks and shoes and red ribbons, dressing her, checking their school bags to see if all their books were in and all their pencils sharpened, sending her and Madhav downstairs for breakfast then rushing into the bathroom to get ready herself. "No need to wake them up, Appa," Shanta would say whenever Appa grumbled, "It is high time these two also prayed in the mornings." So she and Madhav escaped the morning prayers and had that extra hour's sleep, while Shanta sprang out of bed, bathed, ran out to gather flowers for the prayers and cleaned the table in Amma and Appa's room which had all the pictures and statues of the Gods, and arranged all the flowers, one for each God but two for Krishna. Appa, Amma, Shanta, standing together before the prayer table, incense drifting up, their voices perfectly in tune, Appa's deep and resonant, Amma's soft but clear, Shanta's loud and ringing, chanting in perfect accord, Shree Rama, Jaya Rama, Jaya Jaya Rama. That was how she would always remember them when she thought about all that she had lost so completely.

As though in an instant it had dissipated—her childhood, her girlhood, her family—swiftly and magically as coins in a conjurer's hand. One minute there, the next, nothing.

That was one punishment. The other two were still waiting. The second punishment, then, for all the lies she told, for the lie that she lived, for the love and the respect that she, the unworthy one, received: for this she would lose Anu and Madhu, and everything else built up over the years, and Mallika would lose it all too. Terrible, yes, unbearable, yes, but by no means the worst. The worst was the third, the final punishment. And this would be for the nine months that she had not wanted Mallika, and for the times after that when she had wanted Mallika out, out, away. This wish was waiting to fulfill itself. One day, it would happen. Mallika would die. She would fall ill, shudder, stop breathing, she would be kidnapped, she would fall from the roof and smash her head, she would go to school and never come back, she would go to play with Mahima and never return, and Madhu would say, But she never came here, Padma, she never came here, Padma would go to Mallika's room in the middle of the night and find her quiet, not breathing, in bed, Padma would go to her child's room and Mallika would not *be* in bed, Mallika would cross the road and be run over, someone would enter the house when Padma was at the college and take Mallika away—in one of these forms or the other it would happen to her child. This then, would be her final, absolute punishment. And this, of course, there was no surviving. She kept the knife very carefully, wrapped up in an old petticoat under the towels at the very top shelf of her cupboard. If she kept it outside then Ayaji would use it and it would lose its sharpness, and if the time came, then she would need one immediately—not a minute to mourn, not half a minute, straight to the cupboard she would go and then to the bathroom. And she had decided how to do it too, so that it would be quick, and Mallika, wherever she was, wouldn't have to be alone for very long, because Mallika would be waiting for her, even in death Mallika would not be able to stay without her mother.

All this was mixed up in the two dreams which descended on her and smothered her night after night. They only stopped when Shantacca came to stay. Every year, two or three months of respite from the dreams. When Shantacca came to stay, Padma slept the sleep she had known in Amma's house, deep and dreamless. She didn't even hear Mallika cry out in her sleep at night. Shantacca did, Shantacca went to Mallika's room to caress her out of her nightmare. When Shantacca came to stay, she, Padma, always fell very sick, at least once. High fever, cough, cold, everything. So there was poor Shantacca, nursing her back to health, unable to go out, unable to do anything. Year after year after year.

"Why do you always fall sick when your sister comes?" Madhu never failed to ask. Madhu often asked questions to which she already knew the answers; the questions seemed necessary more to satisfy some need she had at a particular time than to provide any answer, since anyway, she always provided the answer herself. The first few times when she noted Padma's sickness always coinciding with Shanta's visits she clicked her tongue in genuine sympathy and said, "This way only it happens, Padma. When the mind relaxes, the body also relaxes and then you fall sick." To which Padma would nod in relief and appreciation and Shanta would nod too, and say, "I also, I fall ill only in my mother's house, it is true what you say." But at other times Madhu would raise her eyebrows and say meaningfully, "Arre, again you are falling ill when your sister is coming, Padma. What is meaning of this, hmm?" Then Padma would try to tell Madhu what Madhu herself had said earlier, but under Madhu's piercing gaze the words would come out all wrong, guilt and remorse would strike Padma afresh. Then after she had inadequately and unconvincingly said her piece, Madhu would reply, "Illness of the body is because of illness of the mind, you always are under a strain for something or the other. No, no, do not try and deny it, Padma. I know you only too well. You don't speak of your troubles to anyone so don't think no one understands your troubles." Thus within this final sentence, she both condoned Padma's silent courage and implicated Shantacca.

Not that any of it struck her then. Nothing struck her then, but somewhere along the line Madhu's loaded remarks always lost their weight. "The way that Madhu talks and the things she says," Shanta told her time and time again. How to tell Shanta what Madhu and Anu meant to her. Of course, she knew how Madhu imbued the simplest of things with drama; of course, she knew that there was another, simpler, quieter version somewhere there. But she did not want to hear the simpler, quieter, truer version, she would much rather have the dramatic one for the sheer pleasure of listening to it. It did not matter if she, Padma, did not see the stories as Madhu saw them—which, on reflection, she often did not—but she wanted to hear how Madhu saw them.

How to tell Shantacca? What to tell her? One did not go about proving the worth of one's friends the way one went about proving a theorem. And if she did, then Shantacca would school her expression and say nothing, and when she said nothing it was worse than when she spoke because in this case it would mean, Yes, I know, you don't need me anymore. Or, if she said to Shantacca, One can't prove these things, the proof, if any, lies in your knowledge, then it would be on the tip of Shantacca's tongue to say, Like your knowledge of Karan, is it, and Shantacca would stop herself just in time.

How to tell Shantacca what happened. How to tell her, It had less to do with him and more to do with me. That was why it happened. How to tell Shantacca, If anything happens between my friends and me, it will be the same thing, Shantacca. How to tell Shantacca that she waited every day for

Madhu to drop in for her evening gossip, and Madhu did, almost every evening, and when she didn't, how the old fear would begin nuzzling Padma's ankles, the fear that told her Madhu finally knew, that now Madhu would never come, that now she had lost her as she had lost Karan and Madhav and Appa and Amma. How to tell Shantacca that when she dropped in to Anu's house, and Anu sounded preoccupied, she knew the same fear, the fear that told her that gentle and generous Anu also knew, that now, inevitably, she had lost Anu too.

I want to die, I want to *die*. But Karan, like Mallika, didn't allow her that either. He who had bestowed upon her her desire for death, was the one who did not let it obliterate her. At night, after Mallika slept, as she lay in her bed, he entered her room, slid into bed next to her, turned towards her in the familiar, loved manner. Enclosed in his arms, she would remember. From the beginning. The very beginning. When she was sixteen and a half. And he three years older. That first time when he didn't even notice her. That part she would relive in its entirety. Then, the next night—never the same night, for she had to stretch it out—the next night she would relive the second time, in the same bookshop, but now she and Madhav and Karan. And this day she would break in half: half to be relived this night, the other half the next night. She had to stretch it out. Linger. Go over his expression. The way his fingers held his cigarette, that bored expression when he looked at her. Its opposite as he talked to Madhav. All that. Bit by bit by bit.

She could not relive any of it when Mallika slept with her. Only when she slept alone. When Mallika let her sleep alone. Which in the beginning she never did. On the nights when she had begun reliving it Mallika would never sleep. Wide awake she would be, wanting more stories, wanting more love, wanting proper hugs and proper kisses, nothing halfhearted, nothing hurried. Not letting her read, not letting her think. On the nights she had begun reliving it, Mallika would take half an hour to fall asleep instead of five minutes, Padma's hand thumping her on her back again and again and again, Mallika's eyes wide open, unblinking, looking at her, saying, "How much do you love me, Ma? A million?" And she replying, automatically, "More than million, more than words, more than numbers," and Mallika saying, "As high as the sky?" and she saying, as though reciting her multiplication tables, "Higher than the sky, higher, and deeper than the sea," and Mallika wailing, "No, Ma, no, *I* have to ask about the sea first, and *then* you answer," and frustration and anger ballooning inside her, she saying, "Say it then, hurry," and Mallika bursting into tears, sobbing, "All I want is love and you're talking to me like *that*." Then the petting and kissing and embracing, none of it coming from the heart, and Mallika knowing it wasn't, and weeping louder than ever, and then she weeping too, Amma, Amma, I want to *die,* and Mallika's face full of terror, Don't die, Ma, don't die, I won't die Mallika, I won't die. She would not die. No, she would not die, she would never die as long as her child was alive. Hugging and kissing her child, holding her, murmuring into her ear and throat and cheek, and Mallika finally quiet, knowing the love she was getting was hers alone, all of it, the love it had to be, more than words or numbers or heights or depths, and it was coming from her mother's heart, from her mother's gut, from her mother's blood, this was it, what Mallika wanted, this, this, this.

Then tucking her into her own bed, in her own room, her Mallika, her pet, her love, her life. She, Padma, back in her room, all lights off, all doors bolted, Ayaji in her quarter, at last her cigarette, savouring every drag, blowing it out the window, no houses behind this window, no light inside her room, the fan whirring. Flushing all the evidence away, washing the cup, getting into bed, the beginning, that polite smile, that first day in the bookshop, the beginning.

"From the beginning, Ma."

"Don't you get tired of the same story?"

"It isn't the same. Every time you tell me, it's different."

"When Appa was posted out of Delhi to Bangalore, I had just finished school. Madhav was in college then and Shantacca was married. So Amma stayed on in the house for a short time till I got admission in my college and in the hostel, then she wound up the house and joined Appa in Bangalore. When I was in my B.A. first year, Madhav was in his final year, M.A. Sumi and I were roommates. He would come to my hostel almost every other day to see me, and we spent all our weekends together."

"In bookshops."

"In bookshops, going for long walks at India Gate—I've told you all this, love."

"Ma, I want to know what you were like *before* you met Dada, so that I'll know how he . . . saw you the first time."

"Madhav and I used to spend all our spare time together those days. Madhav used to read everything he could get his hands on—fiction, poetry, philosophy, history, mythology, everything. And he knew so much about the arts, especially music. All three of us love Indian classical music, but Madhav, he was knowledgeable about it in ways Shanta and I never were—he could identify all the Ragas and singers and players. He sang beautifully too, but it was an untrained voice. He—"

"When you first saw Dada, you were sixteen and a half and he was twenty."

"Yes. He was in his B.A. final year."

Another girl, another boy, not yet man or woman, passing before her eyes. "Your father, he had some books that he was going to buy, and as he went to the counter they all fell down. So I helped him pick them up." Seven books, all over the floor. He picked them up swiftly, she picked up two that had fallen at her feet. The two books she picked up were of poetry by people she had never heard of. She stood up and gave them to him and he took them and said, with a polite smile, "Thank you," and went to the counter.

"Ma, you never describe Dada properly."

"Lanky, nice eyes. Thick hair."

"Ma, what were you wearing when you picked up his books?"

"A yellow saree Shantamama had given me, a lovely, bright yellow—"

"Like sunshine."

Like sunshine, he had told her later. Again, Mallika was doing it again, absorbing her mother's thoughts and bringing them forth as her own.

It had been Shantacca's yellow saree. When she had told Shantacca how lovely it was, Shantacca had promptly taken it out of the cupboard and given it to her and had a matching embroidered blouse made for her. She had not chosen the sarees that she took to college that first year, Shantacca had—she had bought a few sarees, falls, blouse pieces and material for petticoats, then taken her to the tailor for measurements, and before college began that first year, everything was ready.

"So easily our Padma has grown up, as if on her own," Padma had once heard Amma telling Appa. She knew what Amma meant, for neither she nor Appa had had to instruct her or advise her or reprimand her. She could hardly recall any argument she had had with them—quite, in fact, the opposite of Shanta and Madhav, who were always at odds with one or the other of the parents: Shanta with Amma, Madhav with Appa. "Padma is a good child," Appa had replied with indulgence, "there is no need to tell her anything, she knows right from wrong, weak from strong." "Such an easy child," Amma had said musingly. But Amma was wrong. She had not grown up on her own. Shantacca had nurtured her, Shantacca had loved and bullied her, Shantacca had taught her how to tie her ribbons and make her plaits, and tutored her in the subjects in which she was weak. She, Padma, had been willing and adoring. And Shantacca had endless patience with her demands, told her as many stories as she asked for, made her whatever sweets she craved, bought her books with the meagre pocket money that she got in college, at the expense of buying things for herself.

And Madhav was Padma's protector, her ready escort, philosophizing endlessly on life and death while she listened—his first, best, audience. She could remember from the time she was a child, sitting on the floor and looking up at Madhav and listening to him talk. He would stand on his chair and make passionate speeches to her about the British, about Gandhi, throwing words like *patriotic, sacrifice,* and *courage* at her, he would shake his fists and roll his eyes and at the end she would clap fervently. When his friends came, then they would take turns standing on the chair and making speeches, and the clapping was louder now, the cheers heartier. Later they stopped climbing on chairs but the speeches and arguments continued, all full of nationalistic fervour.

It was Sumi who had pointed out to her, years later in college, how strange it was that Amma and Appa had never said anything to her about spending so much time with Madhav and his friends. "My parents would never allow me to talk to my brother's friends," she said. Padma was struck by Sumi's observation. "I don't think they ever noticed," she said after thinking about it for some time.

With Shanta and Madhav there she had not had to make any demands on Amma and Appa. Besides, she was the youngest, Shantacca and Madhav had already fought for what they wanted and when her turn came she got the same things without even asking for them. "No cycle for me, no sleeveless blouses for me," Shantacca said to her years later, "but to you Amma never said no. She always treated me differently."

But Padma remembered differently. She remembered Shanta and Amma gossiping endlessly in the kitchen, in the bedroom. There was no one Amma talked to as much as she talked to Shanta, or for that matter, in the *way* she talked to Shanta, her eyes so alight, her nods so vigourous, her exclamations so heartfelt. Padma had always felt excluded from their conversations because anytime she entered a room where they were talking, the talk stopped and they would look at her with mild impatience. It had not mattered, she was not interested. But she knew instinctively that Amma and Shantacca shared secrets that no one else was privy to.

If she was asked to recall her childhood what would she say? She would say, I knew happiness then. I knew the comfort of absolute security. I knew freedom. No, no. That was not the way to say it. No, she would say, I grew up easily, comfortably. I did not know what unhappiness was, or pain. I did not know insecurity. I did not know what it was to feel trapped. That was what my childhood was, the absence of such knowledge. Such knowledge I had only from books. I shed tears only for the characters in my books. It was only their pain that was real. Then it happened to me.

There was no preparation for it. As though going through a prism, it had all emerged, refracted and unrecognizable.

People who did not know your childhood did not know you at all. Did Anu's mother-in-law know Anu's childhood, did Anu's husband? Did they know she had learnt classical singing from the age of five, taught by a well-known singer, that he had said she had the makings of a great artist? Or, that as a child, once when her exams came, Anu put onions under her arms so that she got fever and did not have to take the exams and that her father found out and thrashed her for the first and last time? And Madhu's husband, did he know of her love for her loud, boisterous brothers and of how she longed to be a boy, of what her father's loss at the age of seventeen had meant for her? Did he know that Madhu's father liked ginger in his tea and that her mother applied amla oil to her hair? Did Narayana know that once when Shanta was nine her teacher had raised his cane at her for talking loudly in class and that she had grabbed the cane from his hands and deliberately broken it in two? And that Appa, when he got the teacher's letter laughed loudly and said, "What a girl, what a girl!" It was Madhu's favourite story about Padma's family. Anu's favourite was the one where Madhav and his friend were travelling by train with a friend and began to comment in Kannada about the fair, red-haired foreign man sitting in front of them who was so hairy that he looked like a white gorilla. Madhav and his friend kept saying to each other about the foreign man, Look at that red-and-white gorilla, belongs to the jungle, imagine, a gorilla travelling on a train and they chuckled and guffawed, and in the morning when the red-and-white hairy man was ready to get off the train he folded his hands to Madhav and his friend, and bowing, said solemnly in Kannada, "The red-and-white gorilla bids you farewell."

And once at night, when Padma was fourteen and travelling by train, with both Amma and Appa in the same compartment, all fast asleep, the man in the fourth berth had touched her all over her body, it was to the pressure of his hands that she awoke from a heavy sleep and as her eyes opened he picked up his suitcase and got off at the station . . . had Karan known that? Anu and Madhu knew. To Madhu also it had happened. Madhu's brother's friend. Madhu only eleven. Waking up one afternoon to a weight on her body and he on top of her. Anu somehow, during her girlhood, had escaped unscathed. To her it happened later. Padma thinking she had dreamt it, Madhu thinking her smile had encouraged him.

Padma even knew the stories of Madhu's and Anu's husbands' childhoods, the stories told to her friends by their mothers-in-law and sisters-in-law. She knew Madhu's husband had been a hockey champion in school and was so badly behaved that he got a caning every day at school from which he emerged grinning. She knew that when Anu's husband was eleven, he and his brother had a competition to see who could eat the maximum number of chappatis and Anu's husband had lost at twenty-one. That Mataji who was making the chappatis in the kitchen kept thinking, This cousin of my husband who has come, how much does this man eat? And then, discovering the boys were the culprits, slapping them hard. All these stories Padma knew and more. She had known Karan's stories. Once when he was fifteen, they had a house full of guests and he had demanded of his mother that she make laddoos for him. I do not have the time now, there is too much work in the house, his mother had said. Just make two laddoos for me, Mataji, that's all, just two, he had begged. That night at midnight after cooking for all the guests and washing all the dishes and cleaning the house, she made the laddoos. By the time she finished making them, it was past two in the morning, and then she had to wash the vessel and clean the kitchen again, so she could not sleep before three a.m. and she had to get up again at six to make tea for all the guests. "The next day after lunch," Karan said, "she called me to the pantry and took out a tin from behind all the other tins. From there she took out a laddoo and gave it to me and said, One now, the other after dinner, this will last you two weeks, don't tell anyone else, not even your sisters, I do not have the time to make any more."

"Then, Ma, then—the next time?" Mallika asked.

"The next time Madhav and I went to the bookshop in Connaught Place, your father was there again, absorbed in a book."

This much to be told to Mallika, this much not to be told, this much to be relived on her own, waiting for the nights, waiting. Remembering how he had looked up briefly as they entered, then smiled faintly at Madhav. Madhav walking up to him, both of them talking. From where she stood, a few feet away, she gathered that he was in the same college as Madhav. No social graces Madhav had, none at all, didn't introduce her to him, but kept talking and laughing, so she went to her favourite corner and began to browse. Afterwards, as if by mutual consent, they all walked together to the dosa place, he and Madhav deep in a discussion, she listening, getting more and more irritated that she was not included, wanting to express some opinion but she not knowing what, since she did not know the poets they were discussing, she had never much enjoyed poetry, in the middle she interrupted loudly, saying, "But *I* like Keats," and he looked at her as though noticing her for the first time, and then went back to his discussion with Madhav as though she hadn't spoken. This boy Karan (she heard Madhav calling him that), he might as well have been Madhav for all the interest he showed in her intellect. Listening to them she was beginning to seriously doubt if she had one. She was in a frog's well in college, that's what it was, secure in the knowledge that she was better than any of the others in her class, that she had read more than any of them and understood her texts in a more comprehensive way than they did. But now, here with Madhav and Karan, she felt a fool, she had read no Russian writers, no French writers, just the same old British writers, not even any poetry except what was in her literature course, she had not even read Tagore. She could not even *begin* to join their discussion. She was ignorant, that's why they did not include her in their discussion, she had nothing of any worth to say, and if she was better than any of the others in her class, well, that meant nothing because her brother and Karan, who were both doing their M.A.'s in history, knew a lot more about literature than she ever would.

They didn't stop talking at the dosa place either. History, politics, philosophy—on and on and on. Finished their dosas, smoked, talked, drank coffee and tea, smoked, talked. Madhav expounded and Karan listened, then Karan expounded and Madhav listened, then both expounded and neither listened. She finished her second dosa and ordered gulabjamuns. What was it, she wondered, in a family, that children grew up so differently? If she and Shanta had behaved like Madhav they would have had it from Amma and Appa. But Madhav did it all the time, didn't introduce his friends to Shantacca, didn't come out of his room to meet Amma and Appa's friends, or often, even their relatives, and if he decided he wanted to talk to someone he would do so to the exclusion of everyone else in the room. "Teach your son manners instead of getting after me all the time," Shantacca would tell Amma, and Amma would reply calmly, "He can get by without them."

They were laughing now, Karan was lighting Madhav's cigarette and then his own. Appa would kill Madhav if he knew. Appa would say, Smoke with your money, not mine. She heard Madhav tell Karan about their secondhand bookshop, they began to get up, she sat firmly in her chair and said, "I'm still hungry." Madhav looked at her astounded, "You've had two dosas and two gulabjamuns, Padma." She said, "I'm still hungry." She would eat more even if it killed her. "God," Madhav said. He beckoned to the waiter, and he and Karen sat down again. "One plate of rasmalais," Padma said to the waiter.

The rasmalais came. Slowly she ate. She was feeling a bit sick. "Hurry up," Madhav said. She looked up. They were both watching her, Madhav's expression impatient, Karan's bored. She looked at his long, slim fingers which held the cigarette, the nails cut very short. Lovely long nose, his upper lip a bit thin, fuller lower lip, thin face with interesting planes and hollows. "You don't *have* to finish it," Karan said, then turned to Madhav and began talking where they had left off.

Always when she reached this point, she would stop, try to sleep, keep the rest of the day for the next night. Stretch it out, stretch it out, slowly, slowly. The next night she would continue.

They got their bus almost as soon as they reached the bus stop. Inside their secondhand bookshop, Karan gave an exclamation of delight, his long, thin fingers brushing the books in front of him, coming out coated with dust and he wiped them absentmindedly on his trousers. Madhav stood next to him, murmuring with pleasure. She went to the other side. Madhav would buy her five today, his pocket money had come and he was feeling rich. Hers had too, but it was always less than what Madhav got. She began taking the books out of the shelves, one by one, till her arms could hold no more. She kept the ones she had selected on the floor and climbed up on a stool to look at the ones on the top shelf, there were more there. Her hands were full of dust, she sneezed, wiped her nose with her saree palla, leaving streaks of dust on the saree. She opened one and smelt it, yes, the same old musty, delicious smell, Appa's old books smelt the same. She looked down to see Karan looking at her. "Please, could you hold these," she said, and he came across to the foot of the stool, bent down, placed his books on the ground and held out his arms, brown with dust, for her books. She gave him the whole pile. He was smiling, he looked different when he was smiling. She was looking at his face as she stepped down, her foot landed on the uneven pile of books that he had placed on the ground and she fell, her hands held out in front of her, clutching the air. Her right hand knocked the shelf of books in the middle, the bookshelf began to fall, the books to fall over her.

Karan and Madhav were laughing. They were laughing so hard that they couldn't help her up, they stood over her, holding the bookshelf, which they had managed to get hold of before it fell on her, roaring with laughter. The old bookshop owner was clucking like a hen. "Are you all right?" he asked her and she said yes, and began to pick up the books, mortified. Then Madhav and Karan helped her pick up the books and put them on the shelf.

"Such an ass you are," Madhav said, still chuckling. "Here, take my hanky." She took Madhav's hanky and began wiping herself. Madhav went to the old man.

"I'll pay for half, Madhav, you—"

"Oh, shut up."

The following weekend they ran into Karan again, this time at the secondhand bookshop. After a couple of hours there they went to a nearby place for dosas and coffee, Madhav and Karan talking as usual. After she finished eating, she looked at Madhav's plate. "Here," Madhav said, sliding his plate of gulabjamuns across to her, "Finish it." She protested half-heartedly, then ate them. Madhav took out a packet of cigarettes from his shirt pocket and slid it across to Karan. "Could I see your books," she said to Karan. He passed them to her across the table. "Could I borrow them after you've finished reading them?"

"You can borrow them now."

"Don't be greedy, Padma, you have enough of your own," Madhav said.

"So do I," Karan said. "It's all right. I can wait."

She couldn't relive any of it when Mallika fell sick. Nothing was possible when Mallika fell sick. Then they would come, Anu and Madhu, with fruits and soups, send her off to college. In her absence, they took turns at Mallika's bedside. In the shadows, Yama, the God of death, waited for Mallika. Once, in that first terrifying year in Delhi, she almost didn't go to college, and then Anu literally dragged her from Mallika's bedside, took her to her bedroom, shook her, said, "Padma, listen, nothing will happen to her, this is just fever, Padma, it is the flu season, nothing will happen to her." Then Anu had gone to the kitchen and made her tea and toast, taken out her saree and matching petticoat and blouse from her cupboard, pushed her to the bathroom, said, "Now go and have a bath." After she was ready Madhu had driven her to the university. She had managed to make it for her class just in time, and after she finished teaching, Madhu had driven her back. "You have to change, Padma," Madhu had lectured as they drove back. "In life worse things happen. But it will not happen to Mallika. When I pray for my children, then I pray for your child too. I know you don't pray-shay, but I believe in it, and belief is everything." And Padma, hanging on to Madhu's words like a drowning woman, asked Madhu, "Mallika won't die?" and Madhu honked her horn angrily at a cow that sat in the middle of the road saying, "Are you mad? Never." Madhu saying it the way she did, made it true. A few years later, Anu said, "When I went to Vaishnudevi I made a wish for my children and I made a wish for Mallika. Wish I cannot tell you, Padma, but this much I will tell you—do not worry about her." And Anu saying it the way she did made what she had wished for Mallika true, so her child then would live long, for that was what Anu must have wished.

Then Mallika would recover and it would be Padma's turn to fall sick. Lying in bed, trying to prepare her lectures, the fever rising, the doorbell ringing. Madhu's voice at the door, the sound of Mallika weeping. Madhu almost dragging Mallika into Padma's room, bursting out, "Padma, very difficult Mallika is acting, Padma, very difficult." Mallika weeping loudly. Madhu panting as though she had been running, saying, "After all, it was only a picture, that Bambi picture. She was crying so loudly she was crying in the picture hall, so loudly, Padma, that no one could hear the picture. Crying and crying and saying, Is Bambi's mumma dead, is Bambi's mumma dead? Everyone was saying shh, shh. So I told her, Mallika in the end of the picture Bambi's mother will come back. Then when picture finished, she kept sitting in the chair and saying, When is Bambi's mumma going to come? Wouldn't only get up from the chair. By force I had to drag her from the picture hall, Padma. Everyone was staring at me as if I was kidnapping her."

After Madhu left, trying to console Mallika. Mallika refusing to be consoled. Feeling her fever rising, her head splitting, her body aching, Mallika in her arms sobbing, "I want Bambi's mumma to come back, I want Bambi's mumma to come back." No respite even after an hour, Mallika saying, "*You* make Bambi's mumma come back, now, Ma, now." Telling Mallika, "I can't do that, now eat your dinner and go to sleep," and Mallika staring at her in disbelief, saying accusingly, "But Ma, you can do *everything*." The familiar tears starting in Padma's eyes, exhaustion pulling at her eyes, anger beginning to boil in her body, "I can't, I can't I can't." Mallika bursting into louder tears, Padma trying to push her away, Mallika refusing to be pushed, her arms in a vicelike grip around her mother's neck, Padma beginning to weep, "Amma, Amma," Mallika weeping, "Ma, Ma," Padma flinging all her textbooks on the ground, watching them fall on the ground, crying, "I want to die, I want to die," and it beginning all over again, Don't die, Ma, don't die. Two hours and two aspirins later, sweating out her fever, Mallika in bed, lectures unprepared, waiting for Karan—there, at last, his fingers opening her own, the comfort of his arms around her, her eyes closing, remembering.

Madhav and Karan talking, she listening, the three of them walking, browsing in bookshops endlessly. Her resentment had gone, and strangely, she felt an odd comfort in Karan's company, akin to what she felt with Madhav, and she sensed that Karan liked her. Now, while he didn't expect to hear her opinion, he didn't ignore her completely either, at least he looked at both Madhav and her when he expounded on something, instead of only at Madhav. She waited for Karan to say, How did you enjoy that book, Padma? Or, You're not saying anything, what are you thinking of? But he never did.

Men don't look for brains in women, Amma had always said. And if a woman has brains then men don't see it, she had added.

Once at home she, Padma, had asked Madhav, "Madhav, what kind of woman do you want to marry?"

He had looked up from his newspaper, with the familiar pained expression that he wore when Shantacca nagged him, and replied, "How do I know?"

Shantacca who was sitting next to him, stitching a button onto his shirt, said, "I'll tell you. He wants to marry a good-looking girl from a good family who will take care of all his needs."

Padma shook her head, "No, I mean, what should the *girl* be like—what should her interests be?"

Shanta snorted, "You think that matters to Madhav?" She snapped the thread with her teeth and handed the shirt to Madhav.

"Tell me, Madhav," Padma said.

"Can't a man read the paper in peace?"

"Do you want the woman you marry to read books and know about politics and history and all that?"

Madhav burst out laughing. Shanta was laughing too.

Shanta said, "My dearest Padma, your brother wants to marry a woman like his mother. Every man does."

Madhav threw her an affectionate look. "Or like you, Shantacca," he said half teasingly. He shook a warning finger at Padma, "*Not* like you."

There was another snort of laughter from Shantacca. She said to Padma, "Darling, don't think Madhav is paying a compliment to my noble soul or to my intellect."

That evening as she and Shanta were laying the table for dinner, Shantacca said, "You think a man will marry you for your mind? He'll marry you for your lovely face, my dearest." Padma made a sound of dismissal. Shanta laughed. "You think he'll think, Oh, how intelligent Padma is, she has read all of Dickens and the Brontës and Hardy and Jane Austen? You think when he sees you he'll think, How well-versed she is in current affairs, how well she sustains her arguments? You might have read everything and be able to talk about anything under the sun, but if you have a squint or a face full of pimples, no man will care what's in your head."

In league they were, Amma and Shanta, speaking the same language, chanting the same warnings like the chorus in a Greek tragedy.

Now she could speak of all Shantacca had mentioned and other things as well with her students. She spoke what she knew through the Victorian fiction that she taught. She spoke it unprepared; the thoughts did not occur to her as she prepared her lectures, but as she delivered them, out they came. And they listened, her students, rapt, she saw the wonder in their eyes. They spoke, tentatively at first, then more surely, exploring her ideas, they asked questions and she answered saying things she had not known she thought. Year after year her students came back to her. "You opened my eyes," one told her. "My life changed after I took your class," another said.

And then back in the bus, crowded, being jostled and pushed and prodded, and back to her neighbourhood, and the haze of pain would descend silently over her again, Mallika waiting for her at the door, waiting as if her mother would die if she did not stand there willing her to return. Back to her child, back to the house, back to him who had inhabited the house from the beginning. It had begun the day Mallika was born, his face bent over his daughter, suffused with tenderness. With her in Delhi, in bed next to her, talking. Holding his daughter, rocking her to sleep, his long body swaying to a murmured song. In the house when Mallika took her first steps, standing on the other side, bending down, arms stretched out. Next to Mallika when she was sick, mopping her brow, feeding her soup, his familiar worried frown creasing his forehead. Smiling at her report card, taking her to the library and to bookshops, telling her, One day I will take you to the bookshops your mother and I used to go to, winking at Padma above Mallika's head, saying, There is a wonderful secondhand bookshop there, with a section upstairs which your mother loved. His the third presence at the dining table, his the figure that ran behind Mallika as she rode her first tricycle. At night she felt his arms gripping her, hard and satisfyingly. She knew then that she had imagined it all, that she would now wake up in his arms, in his—their—house, open her eyes and see his desk full of books, their clothes on the floor, hear the clock ticking, the fan whirring. Her eyes would open, the arms wrapped tightly around her body would be her own.

The doorbell ringing. Karan. Not the Karan who inhabited the house, but the other, the one coming back to her. Forgive me, Padma. Padma. Forgive me.

And then the monstrous fear, as monstrous as the pain. Mallika, her child, who knew how to keep secrets, had kept this from her for . . . years? She discovered the photograph—much thumbed, much looked at—by accident when Mallika was six. She looked at it numbly, then, after some time put the photograph facedown on the desk, unable to look at the face she had once known so well.

The doorbell ringing.

Stretch it out, stretch it out. Linger, linger. Mallika in her room, the cigarette smoked, back in bed, under the sheets, enclosed in him.

The girls in the hostel thought she had two brothers. Even the watchman at the gate and the hostel warden thought that. Sometimes Karan came to the hostel with an armful of books for her; often Madhav did. Karan seemed to know exactly what she liked, sometimes he would pick up books that she hadn't seen in their bookshop and buy them for her, then they would argue about the money and eventually he would reluctantly take the money for it. It touched her when he found the books that she had been longing for in their bookshop; she longed for him to say, I knew you wanted it so I looked for it, but instead he always said, "I happened to find it, aren't you lucky?" And it moved her unutterably when he borrowed the ones he could not buy from friends and lent them to her with the warning, "Don't ruin them." She noticed he had begun treating her in much the same manner that Madhav did. Any time she wanted to hold a serious discussion with him, she would see only amusement on his face. "I'm listening," he would say, "I promise I'm listening," and so she would begin to talk and after some time she would see the laughter creep into his eyes and that was the end of that. Besides, they didn't have that much time to talk, Madhav was there too, and Karan seemed to find Madhav infinitely more interesting than he found her.

"What do you talk to him about?" Sumi asked.

"The same things I talk to Madhav about."

"You better take care. Karan shouldn't think you're forward."

"God, Sumi. You sound like Shantacca."

Once—and she could no longer remember how it had begun—she had told Shantacca that she would have better things to do than running a house or changing nappies. What on earth had driven her to such an arrogant, thoughtless remark? She remembered how Shantacca was looking then—tired, dark circles under her eyes, her hair uncombed. The baby was crying in the other room. And Shantacca had shouted that Padma would do all that and more. And she had. Shantacca had probably forgotten what she said, she said things like this all the time, no one was exempt from her fits of rage. But Padma remembered. I'll never do this, I'll never do that, this is right, that is wrong, that was how she used to speak those days. Disapproving of Shanta and Amma's constant talk of gold and sarees, disapproving of Shanta's harmless little lies about her age and the cost of sarees. She, Padma, was the one who had demanded her share of the sarees and jewellery barely minutes after she was suckling her child, demanded them without any thought for all those years when she had professed to despise such things. And now, saving and scrimping day in and day out, not being able to stop herself from thinking, Appa's house will go to Madhav, then what about the money, will Amma manage to keep a little of that aside for Mallika? This was how far she thought now, this horribly.

"Tell me, Ma, then?"

"Then the exams came, we were all busy studying, Madhav and I went home for the holidays, he began working a month later. After the holidays I went back to college. Now I was in my second year."

"And Dada was in his M.A. first year."

She missed Madhav's talk, their walks, his indulgence, his scoldings. And Karan did not come to see her. Now, back in the hostel, she chafed against the confinement. She had known freedom with Madhav, she hadn't thought about where she was going or how or whether it was getting dark. Now on weekends she went out with Sumi or with groups of other girls, sometimes she branched out to the library or a bookshop but it was a quick, unsatisfying affair because someone or other was always in a hurry to return to the hostel, so the whole group had to go back. An unfamiliar desolation began to fill her. It was the first time ever, since she was a child, that there was no Madhav to do with her what they both loved to do. Well then, she would have to do it on her own.

The bangle shop was just a few shops away from the secondhand bookshop. The bangle woman knew her well. Padma had often come this way with Madhav, often picking up a dozen bangles that she fancied. This time she chose two dozen in shades of green and mustard that she didn't have. Simpler to wear them than to carry them. After paying the woman, she entered the shop. Karan was there, absorbed in a book, his back to her.

She must have known he would be. "Karan."

He turned. "Hullo," he said, smiling. Delight suffused her features. She hadn't known she had missed him so much. She couldn't stop smiling. "You're looking very happy," he said.

"Yes."

"You always do."

Did she?

"I've got some books for you."

"You were going to come to see me?"

He nodded. He must have seen the question on her face, she saw him pause, then he said, "I didn't have the books earlier."

She laughed. "I like you *and* your books, Karan." She watched the smile on his face. He didn't smile often but when he did it was a singularly sweet smile.

"After you're through," he said, "would you like to have dosas?"

After a couple of hours, during which he browsed downstairs, and she upstairs, they went for dosas.

As usual she was hungry. He didn't talk much as they ate. After some time she said, "Karan, try and pretend that I'm Madhav." He looked startled. She said, "You can talk to me too. I *do* understand the things you talk about, you know."

He dipped a piece of dosa into the chutney and put it in his mouth. "I know," he said. She waited. He didn't say anything else, finished his dosa, ordered a coffee, a plate of gulabjamuns, lit a cigarette.

"I'd like a plate of gulabjamuns too," she said.

"They're for you," he said, inhaling. "By the way, congratulations."

"For what?"

"For standing third in the university."

She smiled, "Thank you. How do you know?"

"I know," he said vaguely.

"And you?"

"I managed."

"You topped. Congratulations to you too." She saw the question in his eyes and said, "I too know." There was a silence. If Madhav were here he wouldn't have stopped talking. Would Karan have asked her for lunch if she hadn't made it so obvious that she was happy to see him? Perhaps Sumi was right.

"Karan, do you think I'm forward?"

"Yes."

*"Forward?"*

"Yes."

*"Why?"*

"I can see through your excuses."

She looked at him in disbelief.

"You think you want books but you actually want me."

*"You?* I—"

"You can have both."

She saw the laughter in his face and relief flooded her. "You scared me. I thought, Sumi's right. She said I shouldn't say whatever I feel. Shantacca says the same thing."

"And do you?"

"Do I what?"

"Say whatever you feel?"

He was drinking his coffee. She began on her gulabjamuns. Irritated, she said, "I think Amma was right, men don't like to talk intelligently with women. Only with other men."

He didn't reply. She watched him as he lit another cigarette. She said, "Are you close to your sisters?"

"Yes."

"Like Madhav and me?"

He shook his head. "You and Madhav are more like friends. My sisters and I are . . . not."

"Why?"

He shrugged.

"Don't you ever wonder why?"

"I don't think about these things." He was leaning back against his chair, amused.

"You're talking just like Madhav."

"My sisters wouldn't be sitting like this with a strange man, eating lunch and talking."

"You're not a strange man."

"They wouldn't sit alone with any man."

"And you'd disapprove if they did."

"They wouldn't dream of being so . . ."—he blew out a stream of smoke—"forward."

She took out her purse and counted some money, put it on the table. "Now I don't know whether you're joking or not," she said, her voice shaking. "All I wanted to do was talk to you, that's all." She got up and went out, walked swiftly to the bus stop. The bus was right there, she got inside and sat down, breathless, the books on her lap. The bus began to move. The day was dark. Heavy rain clouds had gathered in the sky. She didn't even have an umbrella. She wouldn't make it back to the hostel before the deluge began. Damn, as Madhav would say.

She heard Karan coming towards her seat and felt him sit next to her. "I was teasing." He sounded slightly breathless.

She didn't reply.

"I leapt on to the running bus. Almost fell off."

"I wish you had fallen off," she said. It had begun to pour. Water was coming in through the window, she couldn't get the window closed. He leaned over her and tried to close it. "We'd better move to the other side," he said. He took the books from her lap and they moved to the empty seat across the aisle. "You're stuck with me now," he said, sitting next to her, holding her books. She looked curiously at him. This was a new Karan, defensive, slightly sulky. "Can't you take a joke?"

"You weren't even talking properly to me. Smoking and looking superior. Not answering my questions. Making me feel stupid."

"I don't think you're stupid. I don't think you're forward. I don't think you should be like my sisters. Happy?" She looked at him then. He was sitting close enough for her to see that his eyes were clear. "For God's sake, don't look so suspicious," he exclaimed.

"You're more accessible now than you are when you put on that . . . that older, aloof . . . act."

"Is that how I appear?" he asked. She nodded. He said, quietly, "I don't put it on." They were silent.

He gave her one of his sudden smiles. "I like needling you."

"Why don't you just say what's in your head? Like you did just a little while earlier in the bus?"

He looked away from her, "Believe me, I didn't."

He was back to being the old Karan. He said, "Do you still want the books I got for you?"

"Of course I do."

"I'll get them to the hostel."

For some time they were both quiet, then he smiled at her and said, "Say what's in your head."

She smiled back at him. "Whenever you go to any bookshop will you take me?"

"Yes."

"It's difficult going alone, I—"

He said mournfully, "When you smiled in the bookshop I had no illusions that it was my charming self you were smiling at."

What bearing did this life have on the one she had known in college? Conversations about books and politics? Had she ever had them? Now she didn't care what was happening in the world. Before Shantacca left Delhi after settling Padma in, she had sat with her and given her a long lecture. "Wear your mangalsutra all the time," she told Padma, "let people at your workplace think you are married. If they find out you are a widow, tell them your husband would never have wanted you to remove it. Don't talk to any man more than necessary. For God's sake remember you can't treat every man you meet the way you treated Madhav and his friends. Men will misunderstand. Only a brother is a brother. Don't open the door for any neighbour if it is a man. Don't talk to them unless they talk to you, and if they do, say only the bare minimum. And these two neighbours, Mrs. Prasad and Mrs. Nanda, go to their houses only when their husbands are at office. Before their husbands come back, you come back home. All right?"

Of course it was all right. She didn't want to talk to anyone. She desired nothing except sleep. Everything paled before the enormity of having to survive one day after the other, the days rolling into one another, the weeks, the months, the years. She had learnt to sleep in the bus, that is if she got a place to sit. Her brain had timed it exactly, she would close her eyes the minute she sat, be asleep in about a minute, and then, as the bus slowed down at her college, her eyes would open. The same thing on the way back, if she got a seat. Then back home, back to Mallika, her child's fever rising, up all night, Madhu saying, "This is happening to all children, Padma," and she saying to Madhu, "But Madhu, I have only one child," and watching Madhu's expression change and Madhu saying, "One or ten, it is not mattering, Padma, you think if something happens to my Mahima I will care less because I have two more children?" Stricken, her eyes filling with ready tears, Madhu would say, more kindly, "When you are having more than one child, Padma, you become practical. With three children there is no time to imagine this and imagine that."

Some respite on the nights when Mallika let her sleep alone. Linger, linger. The way he smiled. His arms full of books. Watching his tall figure walk towards her hostel. Their arguments. Rather, hers. He hardly argued. If he disagreed with her he didn't say why—he merely dismissed what she was saying. Nonsense, he would say, and go on to something else. It infuriated her. She longed for him to listen to her, say, But that's an interesting point, or, Oh, I hadn't thought of it like that—the way he would to Madhav. Or even, preferably, I disagree, now look at it this way. But no, nothing of the sort. Then when he saw the look of frustration on her face he would begin needling her and predictably, she would rise to the bait.

She never knew which Karan she would see, the one of whom she was still unsure—a little aloof, a little bored, looking older than his age, whose expression she couldn't always read, with his silences and his remarks which she was always uncertain of. Or the other Karan—the boy, irritable, sulky, laughing. The second was the Karan she felt indulgent towards, almost tender: her irritation with this Karan she could deal with. How much easier for him, she would think—she was always the same, always happy to see him, always predictable. Sometimes she felt the boy Karan surfaced only for her, not for anyone else, that actually, as he had once said, the older, slightly unpredictable Karan was the real one.

"Karan, why don't you ever talk properly about your family?"

He looked surprised.

"You never say what you talk to them about, what your sisters and mother and father are like . . ."

"I haven't talked to my father for five years."

She looked up at his face, stunned, saw the emptiness in his eyes. He said, "Once when I was still in school, I heard my mother crying in their room. I had never heard her cry before. My mother is a very restrained woman. My room was next to theirs. I got up and went to the door. It was slightly ajar and I could look inside. I saw my mother standing next to my father. Both their backs were to me, and her hands were over her head. He hit her. I heard the sound. She kept standing there. He walked away from her, went to the side table, where there was a jug of water, drank a glass of water and then lay down on the bed and closed his eyes. My mother continued standing in the same position with her hands over her head."

Appa had always said that a man who raised his hand against his wife deserved to be whipped. After some time she said, "It had happened before?"

"I don't know."

"And then you stopped talking to him?" He nodded slowly. "What did your father say to that?"

"Nothing."

"For five years you haven't talked to him and he's never asked you why?"

"My father isn't like yours."

"So you never liked him?"

"I worshipped him."

"He must have noticed."

A shrug.

"I wonder what he thinks."

"There are certain things that people should realize for themselves without being told."

"Five years."

"I thought my father had no faults. From the time I was a child I wanted to be like him. That night it died. That instant."

"Your mother, your sisters?"

"I don't know. They haven't asked me."

"Oh."

"My sisters' regard for me is more obvious than their love. They consult me about decisions they have to make about which college to go to, what subjects to take . . . things like that. My mother too. They don't consult my father."

"So your mother and your sisters do whatever you tell them to do?"

"I don't usually tell them what to do. I usually listen."

"Hmmm."

"Hmmm. What a serious *Hmmm*."

"Karan. I'm serious."

"Padma. Don't be."

"That's why you don't talk about your family?"

"Once you asked me if I was close to my sisters. You said how much I was missing by not sharing with them what you share with Madhav. That's probably why I enjoy being with you."

"You—"

"No, I don't share that kind of intimacy with my mother and my sisters. Love and intimacy don't necessarily go together."

"You'll never forgive your father."

"Nothing so dramatic. He's like a stranger living in the same house."

"How can you talk about it so calmly?"

"Must I weep and rave?"

"Whenever I'm serious you laugh."

"And whenever I'm serious you don't hear me."

"Answer my question."

"One recovers."

"Really?"

"One can recover from anything."

"I don't think you've recovered. Stop laughing."

"I'm hungry."

"You were talking so *deeply* about it and now you want to change the subject."

"I'm bored of talking *deeply*."

"Tell me about your youngest sister?"

"She's about eleven now. She chatters all day . . . my mother calls her her ray of sunshine."

"Do you talk more to her?"

"Everyone does. My father too. She's the baby of the family."

"And when she's chattering with your father, where are the rest of you?"

"The questions you ask."

"Tell me, Karan."

"When she's chattering to my father in the evenings, my mother and sisters are in the kitchen getting dinner ready and I'm in my room reading. Now you talk."

"I don't know, Karan. My life is very simple. Not like yours."

"Really?"

"How can I talk seriously to you if you keep laughing? You're just like Madhav."

"I'm not like Madhav."

"You too treat me like that."

"I treat you the way you want to be treated. Are you hungry? Yes, of course you are. Let's eat."

My life is very simple, she had told Karan once. And now? Now she had sunk so low that it seemed that the everyday happiness of her sister and friends gave her grief. Thinking, I have lost forever all that Shantacca and Anu and Madhu have. Hating herself for the feelings that shook her when she saw Mr. Prasad tutoring Prabha, teaching her to ride her cycle, Mr. Nanda holding Mahima on his shoulders, Narayana playing cricket with Vikram and Varun. Hating herself for the ache inside her as she saw the miserable, lost look on Mr. Prasad's face when Anu went home to her parents for two months, as she saw the opposite look when Anu returned, the daily letters that Narayana wrote to Shanta when Shanta came to stay with her, the contentment on Mr. Nanda's face as Madhu fussed around him. Watching Mallika as Mallika looked at Prabha's father caressing his daughter's cheek, unable to stifle the voice inside her which said, If Mallika doesn't have it, whose fault is it?

And then she would tell herself, But look at what cost they have it. And when she thought this way she knew that she must indeed be a wretched creature to actually seek comfort in what they didn't have. A low and wretched creature.

Don't think of all that. In the blessed darkness of the night, think of him. Remember the month of October? No classes, hardly anyone in the hostel, not even Sumi, plenty of books, Karan. Madhav had sent her money again, there was enough for her to buy more books and pay her share for their cheap lunches at idli-dosa places. Hours spent in their secondhand bookshop, sitting upstairs in the little loft that had so many books, both of them squatting on the floor, browsing. The old man now gave her books at half the cost that he sold them to others, and when Karan demanded books at the same cost, the man told Karan his books were the more expensive ones.

"Your charm is like a noose around his neck," Karan said to her as they left for their dosas.

"Karan, let's see some films."

"Oh God, no."

"I can't go alone, and Sumi's gone too."

They entered their familiar dosa place, and the familiar waiter came smiling towards them.

He said, sitting, "I can't say no to you." She looked at him suspiciously. "I don't understand how you stay so slim. You eat more than I do."

"You're the intellectual. I'm the plebeian."

He was watching her with a strange expression. "Would you spend any time with me if there was another girl in the hostel who loved books and walking as much as you do?"

She stopped eating. "You think I'm using you?"

"Stop sulking and finish your dosa."

They went to four films in four days. She enjoyed them hugely, she was sure that Karan did too though he refused to admit it. In the middle of the first film she felt his finger tapping her hand, she tried to see his face in the

darkness and felt his fingers opening hers and putting a large bar of chocolate into her palm, then closing her fingers over the bar. "No," he whispered when she offered him a piece, so she ate the whole bar herself. He
had a bar for her each of the following days, and always, at the most dramatic moment in the film, when she was completely absorbed, he would
tap her hand, open her fingers and place it in her palm, then close her fingers over it and withdraw his own. Years later she couldn't remember anything that had tasted sweeter than those chocolates.

By the end of that week the October holidays were over and it was back
to classes and work. "When are you going home?" he asked her as they sat
cross-legged upstairs in their bookshop. She looked up. "The day after the
exams. Sumi and I are going home together, she'll spend a week with me
and then go to her parents." He nodded. "Karan," she said, "will you write
to me?"

"What did he write in his letters, Ma?" Mallika asked.

Once she had known each one by heart. "He wrote about the books he
read, the music he liked—he liked Indian classical music—about the
walks he went for, he wrote about the things he believed in." She had not
meant to say this. Now Mallika would ask.

"What he believed in?"

"You know, like honesty, strength, things like that. Integrity."

"Oh. Like you."

"Me?"

"Everyone says you're like that."

They were so unlike him, his letters; it was as though she were reading
a book, that was how he wrote, each word perfectly and effortlessly chosen, each sentence following the other with grace and humour. Nothing
aloof about them, nothing childish either, but perfectly assured, beautifully expressed. Not like her letters, where she wrote as if she were talking
to him, with many dashes and exclamations, innumerable *you knows* and
*I means,* and then she would forget to say something and add it at the very
end after she had signed off or squeeze it in on the top of the first page
above his name.

No one asked her about the letters.

He told her in his letters that he was reading up for the civil service
exams. He wanted to read at leisure over the next few years, because after
his M.A. he planned to teach. He had always wanted to teach, and if it

wasn't for the fact that it paid so poorly, he would have preferred to do that rather than be a civil servant. He had never spoken to her of these things during their time together. In fact, in his letters he talked to her the way he never did in person. He painted pictures of the early morning walks he went for, the colour of the sky in the early pre-dawn, the sounds of the birds and the thud of newspapers, the men spitting paan, old couples going for their walks. She knew how he felt as he walked, that fullness of feeling, all the senses awake, absorbing. He told her about sleeping up on the terrace at night and looking up and seeing the different constellations in the sky, and how he wanted one day to go to the Southern Hemisphere so that he could see another skyline, different constellations. Her own dreams? Only one. Just to go with him wherever he went. Simple.

Nothing simple now. Endless the subterfuges. Dragging Amma into it, Shanta into it, its slimy arms around her child, her friends, her neighbours. And not just the big lies. The smaller daily subterfuges which had the potential to become so enormous. Madhu knocking at her door at night when she was in the middle of her cigarette, she rigid with fear, hiding the evidence, blowing powder all over the room, throwing cardamom into her mouth, chewing desperately, now Madhu would know, now she would lose Madhu, and Madhu would tell Anu and she would lose Anu too, all over, the life she had built so far, all because of a cigarette, rushing to the door and opening it, bursting into frightened tears. Madhu taking her into her arms, asking her what the matter was, she sobbing that Mallika wasn't feeling well. Madhu comforting her, saying she would look at Mallika the next day when Padma was at her college, not to worry, nothing to worry about. And the next day, Mallika falling ill. In Padma's stained hands did it lie, would always lie, the instrument of her child's destruction.

The fan whirring, the sheet cool against her body, the darkness comforting, his hands unplaiting her hair.

The day after she returned to her college, in January, he was there, waiting for her outside the hostel. "Your brother is here," one of the girls said, knocking at the door, and she went outside, saw his tall figure outside the door. He turned, saw her, smiled. "I have something for you." He gave her a packet he had been holding. She opened it, it was the complete works of Charlotte Brontë, beautifully bound, with gold lettering. He heard her sigh and said, "I know you've read *Jane Eyre*, but I don't think you've read the others." She shook her head, feeling the cover and the letters. "Don't thank me," he said hastily as she looked up at him. She looked at the book again and opened the first page. In it he had written, *To Padma, my friend. Karan.* He was watching her, his expression soft, he said, "Do you want to go for a walk outside?"

Never before had her senses been so alert. She wanted to hold his hand, feel his long fingers between her own, lay her palm against his cheek. She felt she could watch him forever, the way he walked, long easy strides, her saree rustling beside him, the faint smell of soap and cigarettes wafting across to her. How would he describe the day if he were writing to her? Easily, gracefully, every word chosen with care. He would write like a writer. She could see the day through his eyes. He would describe each sound of each bird, tell her the names of the trees and how they appeared, sketch a rapid, vivid picture of the people on the roads which would make her laugh with its droll humour. He said, "You write lovely letters."

She turned to him, astonished, "I was going to tell you the same thing." He looked disbelieving. She said, "You describe everything so beautifully, Karan. You make me see everything you see."

He smiled then in the way she was beginning to love, and said, "Do you see everything I see?"

"Yes, I was just thinking how you would describe this day if you were writing to me about it."

"If I were writing to you about it then it would be different." She looked questioningly at him. He said, "If I were to describe it now, it would be one thing. If I were to describe it to you in a letter, you wouldn't be here walking with me, so it would be another thing."

"That's true. But tell me, why d'you like my letters?"

He didn't reply.

"Karan."

"Hmm?"

She repeated her question. "Oh," he said, "I enjoyed reading about your family. Your letters have a feeling of immediacy. I feel I can hear you talking. See your expression."

She felt her heart leap up. "I thought my letters were awful, you know, yours are much more sophisticated."

He gave a shout of laughter, "Sophisticated! You mean they're dry and dull."

Delhi was cold but beautiful, she would wrap herself in sweaters and shawls over her silk sarees, wear socks, tuck her fingers under the shawl, and walk. He never seemed to feel the cold, a thick sweater seemed to suffice, and on rare occasions, a coat. He talked easily to her now, about the little everyday happenings, about the other boys in the hostel, the lecturers he had, what he was reading. She would ask him about his days in school when his parents lived in Delhi, incidents of his childhood. He always began by saying, "There's nothing to tell," but as she asked he would begin to talk, slowly, almost indifferently, and then he would focus on something—his mother, his grandmother, their ancestral house, the cousins stealing mangoes from the neighbours' gardens—and the boy Karan would spring up before her eyes. Then he would stop, look at her, say, almost accusingly, "Why on earth do you want to know all this," and then before she could reply, say, "it isn't even interesting." He had never spoken of his father after that one time, and she didn't ask. But it was evident that he adored his mother. "She's left us alone only once," he told her as they walked down a long deserted road lined with trees, "when her mother died. But those days I remember we all felt as if we were falling apart." It was dark now, they had, on an impulse, decided to take the road they were now on because of how beautiful it was. But lonely roads always made her feel uneasy. Karan had often chided her when she expressed her need to get back to the hostel before it got dark. "You're not alone, so why are you uneasy?" he would ask. And when she tried to explain by telling him, "I feel apprehensive," he would answer, almost impatiently, "What about?"

Now, as they walked down the road, the same unease gripped her. In the distance on the same side she could see a man walking towards them. She glanced at Karan, who was saying, "My mother is like a rock. If she disintegrates, all of us will. She never spoke of all that she had to suffer. Like the time she was pregnant with my second sister. There was a wedding in the family—my father's sister. As the oldest daughter-in-law my mother was responsible for running the show. Those days, my father's mother was living with us; she was quite a dragon—my mother lived in absolute fear of her. My mother worked so hard for the wedding that after the ceremony got over she fainted. Later the doctor said that she could have lost the baby. I sat next to her bed the following day, and she wouldn't let go of my hand. Strange, even when I was a child, she sought comfort only from me." The end of the road was coming. She could begin breathing properly soon. The man would pass them in a couple of minutes and then five minutes later they would be at the bus stop and safe in the bus. "She still does?" she asked. Karan stopped to light a cigarette, turning away from her, his back against the breeze. The man passed her and hit her hard on the breasts. She made a stifled sound, almost falling back under the impact. The man continued walking. She stumbled towards Karan, who was throwing the match and turning towards her, inhaling. He said, "Yes, she still does." They walked in silence towards the bus stop.

Once inside the bus she sat down, looking blindly out of the window. "Are you cold?"

She heard Karan's voice next to her ear. She didn't answer.

He leaned over and closed the window. "Better now?" he asked. She nodded. He said, "Sometimes I wonder how many other things there are that my mother never spoke of."

"No one should have let her work like that when she was pregnant."

"She always did it uncomplainingly. She was—is—a very strong woman. She has immense courage and . . . fortitude."

"Whom would she have complained to."

"There are enough women who spend all their time complaining. My mother isn't one of them. What had to be done had to be done."

She turned to him, her eyes bright with tears. "What does keeping quiet have to do with fortitude, Karan?" She saw the anger stirring in his face. She burst out, *"You're blind. Blind."*

Evenly he said, "What do *you* know? She's *my* mother."

Neither said anything after that. From the bus stop, they walked in silence to her college.

He was back the next day, Sunday. She wasn't prepared for him, she had thought he would still be angry. It had frightened her, his anger, his speaking so evenly, his expression belying that calm voice. She preferred it when he showed his irritation. Now he looked quite normal, as though nothing had happened—probably, as far as he was concerned, nothing had. For the first time she found it was an effort to act normal. In their bookshop she went upstairs as he browsed downstairs, but once up there, she couldn't concentrate and looked blankly at the books.

She heard him come upstairs. He planted himself on the ground opposite her and said, "It isn't like you to be upset for so long." She looked at the face that she knew so well. Now he would say, What is the matter, tell me, and she would tell him, and he would understand. "Snap out of it, Padma," he said shaking his head, "Be yourself."

"Karan, I'd like to go back."

He looked up at her, "What did you mean, 'I'm blind'?"

"Nothing." She put on her slippers and plaited her hair, which had come undone.

He stood up. "You were talking about something else, weren't you?" he said. She closed her eyes briefly, nodded. "Will you sit for a minute?" he asked. She hesitated, then sat on the floor opposite him, putting her arms around her knees. "I want to know," he said. His eyes didn't move from her face.

She got up. "I want to go out."

He got up too. "Padma, answer me, please."

She didn't want to answer anymore. He wasn't asking for the answer she wanted to give, she could see it in his eyes. He was asking for something else, and that, she wanted away from her, far away. It was too close now to the other thing; she could barely separate one from the other.

She must have gone downstairs, she didn't remember.

Once, the third year in Delhi, soon after Mallika's sickness and her own, standing at the bus stop outside her college, it had hit her that she had not been to a bookshop ever since she returned to Delhi. She would go to one now. She couldn't afford them, not even secondhand books, but she would go anyway, for the sheer pleasure of looking at them, touching them, for the sheer pleasure of being on her own. A car had stopped beside her, she had recognized one of her student's fathers, she had smiled at him, he had asked her where she was going and then if he could offer her a lift since he too was going that way.

It had not even occurred to her to refuse. She had been conscious of only relief—no bus. And so she had entered the car. They talked as he drove, he asked questions, she found herself telling him about her husband's death, her child, what she was teaching, where she lived. At first when it happened she thought she was imagining it. His hand resting on her thigh, nothing deliberate about it, almost casual, as casual as the conversation he was having with her, talking of his daughter and his son. He lifted his hand, changed gears, his hand rested on her thigh again. Suddenly, all Shantacca's warnings screaming in her ear, Shantacca shouting, Get out, Padma, get out, you fool. Her voice came out in a whisper, "Stop the car." He looked at her and she saw his smile, his eyes raking her body, turning away from her and watching the road, his hand moving up her thigh. Shantacca, she screamed silently, Shantacca. The car slowing down before the traffic lights, she opening the car door and jumping out, the car moving on. She falling, sprawled on her back on the road, the bus inches away from her head, and then over her, the vast monstrous underbelly of the bus over her, its wheels on either side of her, Mallika, Mallika, Shantacca, Shantacca, and then the darkness gone and the blue sky above her, the bus moving ahead, hands lifting her up, taking her to the side of the road, a middle-aged woman feeling her, the woman's voice trembling as she said, "This is God's grace, this is God's grace." The woman's husband saying something about a doctor, about a possible concussion, taking her to a private clinic. A wound on her head that her hair hid, but otherwise, she was, miraculously, unhurt. The two of them dropping her all the way back home. Later, the reaction setting in, she sitting on a chair with Mallika in her arms, her whole body shaking, Mallika looking at her face and bursting into tears. Comforting Mallika, Mallika not being comforted but crying for an hour.

Was it only she who felt that there was nothing natural about motherhood? That motherhood meant the virtual end of all desire? No one spoke of such things. She had never read of such things, not in books, not in articles, nowhere. She was the unnatural mother, the aberration. The others gave up things without a murmur, continued smiling, continued laughing—Anu not complaining about giving up her music, Madhu never complaining about not finishing her degree. She was the aberration. She was the anomaly, the unnatural mother. She had always associated motherhood with all that was gentle and tender and soft: a gurgling child, a toothless smile, the mother's smiling face suffused with tenderness. And she had had that too with the child Mallika, but when it came, she was too tired to enjoy it. She had enjoyed it more in the photographs, in the advertisements, in the babies she saw in their mothers' arms, these had given her the delight that she was too tired to get from her own child. Ayaji said how, when she took Mallika for a stroll in the pram, people would stop and coo to her, exclaim over her, how in the park a young man would lift her up towards the sky and break into laughter as she laughed.

Gentle, tender, soft? It was buried under the rest, the rest that was brutal, harsh, all-consuming. From the beginning, from the time the baby pushed its way out. One forgets the pain after the child is born, everyone said—Amma, Shanta, Anu, Madhu, everyone. Perhaps they had forgotten, but she could never forget it. She was the coward, the one without fortitude. Why didn't you tell me, Shantacca, why didn't you tell me, she wanted to scream as she tried to push the baby out, why didn't you prepare me? You had such a short labour, Shantacca said, and later, Anu and Madhu too, when she told them. Ten hours. It had been more than twenty for Shantacca, and even more for both Anu and Madhu. But ten hours of that kind of pain wasn't a short time. But she had been persuaded that it hadn't been so bad because for the others, it had been so much worse. She had not known how her body would change, staring in shock at the huge watermelons that were her breasts, at her once firm tummy, now loose and ugly. There was nothing natural about breastfeeding either, the baby falling asleep at her breast before finishing her feed, crying to be fed within the hour. No one had told her that her breasts would be dripping milk, she had to prepare herself for that before taking the bus to work. Then going back home in the bus, her saree palla draped over her breasts, her breasts aching, reaching home and grabbing Mallika and attaching her to one breast, and then to the other, the relief as the pain subsided.

No one had prepared her for the absolute exhaustion. Once, after several sleepless nights, she lay in bed feeding Mallika. As the baby suckled she closed her eyes. Then she heard a voice, very distant, her eyes opened and she saw a woman bending over her, saying, Padma, do not sleep, you have to eat your dinner first. She saw she was lying in a strange room in an unfamiliar bed, something heavy was hanging at her breasts, a woman she didn't know was bending over her and talking of food. Padma, Padma, the woman was saying, so she said to the woman, Who are you? and the woman's eyes widened, and she said, I am Anu, and Padma repeated blankly, Anu? She closed her eyes, fell into a deep sleep again, then voices around her, someone's fingers around her arm, a peremptory voice ordering her to wake up, she opening her eyes and seeing Madhu and Anu bending over her. "Madhu, Anu, what is it?" she asked, saw the relief on their faces, one of them taking the sleeping baby away from her, she sliding under the sheet and falling asleep again.

The next day Anu told her how frightened she had been. "When you are tired then give Mallika the bottle, Padma," Anu said. But Shantacca and Amma had both told her never to give Mallika the bottle if she was at home. "Vaise," Anu said, "Mallika is already eight months old, Padma, it is time to wean her, 'specially since you are a working woman. I weaned Prabha when she was four months old." But Shantacca and Amma had categorically told her to breastfeed the child for at least ten months, preferably eleven. That much at least give your child, Amma had written.

Why had no one told her that one made sacrifices partly because they had to be made but largely because one was too tired to do anything else? In her case exhaustion had killed her desire for books, for music, for walks, for her favourite sweets, even for Karan. Reliving those four and a half years night after night was like reliving a love story without the desire, like the romances that Shantacca read. It was comfort that she had sought from those memories, and tenderness, both of which he—after those first two years—had had so much to give. The rest she would relive after the constant sickness began to abate, after she was able to sleep without interruption, after Mallika began to read. And when her memory of him returned, it was fiercer and more overpowering than it had been when she knew him, for there was no assuaging it.

Quiet, quiet, Padma. Quiet, lie still in your bed, move a little to the side, better now, his arm under you, the other caressing your neck, quiet.

He came to see her in the hostel, even though they were both so busy studying for the exams. "Why do you come for such a short time, Karan?" she asked once.

"Too much work, too little time," he said, getting up.

"Then come less often, but for longer," she said.

"After the exams."

"Then it'll be time for us to go home," she said mournfully.

"Will you write to me, Karan?" he said in her voice.

She smiled, how perfectly he had got her tone. He waved and was gone.

The work must have been too much, or he was working too hard, but he looked tired and preoccupied the next few times that they spent out. But whenever it was time to go back he seemed reluctant to do so. When he dropped in to see her at the hostel, he would sit quietly opposite her, smoking, hardly talking, and she would think, He doesn't have anything to say to me anymore. But he would be back in a couple of days, and do the same thing.

"Are you worried about the exams, Karan?" she asked him once.

"No."

"You look very preoccupied these days."

"Just tired."

"Then perhaps you should sleep more and come here less often," she said without meaning it.

He smiled, "I feel refreshed when I'm with you."

It was when he said things like this—and how rarely he said them—that she wondered how much she imagined of what she saw in his eyes that morning in the bookshop, when he had asked her what she meant when she had said he was blind.

His eyes fell on the sheaf of letters that she was holding. "You're always reading letters when I come in the evening. Your parents?"

"And Shantacca and Madhav. I'm re-reading them."

"Did you re-read mine too?"

She nodded. "You write so well—it's like reading a book."

She saw the flash of amusement on his face. Then he said, "I met Sumi's brother when I was coming in, he suggested we all spend next weekend together, have a picnic or something."

March. It was warmer, she and Sumi were back to wearing cotton sarees, she could wear her bangles again, all the way up to her arm now that she wasn't hampered with sweaters. On the days she felt the urge to buy bangles she would leave her arms bare when going with Karan to the bookshop, and after she had had her fill of books, she would go to her bangle woman next door, buy and wear her two dozen bangles, then join Karan. "Buy your bangles before, not after," he told her once, and then, seeing her enquiring look, added, "You always make me wait."

Later, she would go over the day in fine detail, trying to understand. It was relaxed, leisurely. Sumit and Karan had got two hampers full of food—in fact, Karan had bought half a dozen of her favourite pastries. They spent the day sitting under the shade of a large tree, eating and talking. They took photographs with Karan's box camera—Padma and Karan, Padma and Sumi, Padma and Sumi and Karan, Padma and Sumit, Sumit, Sumi and Karan—till they finished the whole reel. The morning went by slowly, they were all replete with food. Karan was quiet, but that was nothing new. After lunch, Sumit lay down on the grass and closed his eyes, Karan did the same thing, Sumi opened her romance novel. Padma watched Sumit and Karan as they lay there, their eyes closed—one so fair, with features so chiselled, he looked like a beautiful statue; the other, dark, not exactly handsome, but so much lovelier, such long eyelashes . . .

Karan's eyes opened and he looked at her. She waited for him to say something and returned his look, a question on her face, but he said nothing. She said, "Are you in a bad mood or something?" He closed his eyes without answering.

Then it was time to get back. Sumit had to catch the train. They dropped Sumi and Padma to the hostel. It was still only two. As Sumi and Sumit said their goodbye's, Padma said to Karan, "Do you feel like going to the bookshop?" She didn't. She only wanted to be with him.

He looked at his watch, "Now?"

"Not if you're busy."

She saw him hesitate, then he said, "Next time?"

She tried to smile, "All right."

She had become too dependant on Karan, that was the problem. If he wasn't free she had to learn to do on her own things that she enjoyed.

"Alone today?" the old man at the bookshop said. She smiled and nodded. She climbed up the stairs. Listlessly she began looking at the books. She didn't even have money for them. But he would let her pay next time. After ten minutes she was absorbed. An hour later, holding five books, she began climbing down. Later she could never remember how it happened, one minute she was stepping down, the other minute she was stumbling down the stairs. She fell hard on the ground, the books falling all around her; something very sharp went into her palm as her hand clutched the bookshelf on the side. She drew in her breath in a moan. It was a nail, her palm was bleeding. She got up, took out her hanky from her bag and held it in her palm. Then, slowly, she got up. The pain was so severe that it seemed to go right up her arm. She closed her hand around the hanky and turned around to see Karan at the entrance.

He came to her and picked up her books. "Are you all right?" he asked. She nodded. She could hardly speak for the pain.

Karan said, "I changed my mind. It seemed too late to come and pick you up." She nodded. He said, "Some tea?"

She shook her head.

He looked at his watch. "There are still a couple of hours for you to get back." She shook her head again. "Don't fuss," he said. Come along." In too much pain to argue, she walked with him.

"Coffee or tea?"

"Coffee."

It came and she spooned in plenty of sugar. Perhaps this would revive her. The pain was making her head hurt. "What papers are you giving this year for the exams?" he asked. She told him. He said, "Eat something."

"I'm not hungry."

"That's the first time then." He called the waiter and ordered two plates of rasmalais. It was the first time she was seeing him order one for himself. He had always said he didn't like sweets except the ones his mother made for him—and the ones at the bazaar couldn't ever compare with hers. The rasmalais came. He began to eat. She pushed her plate away.

"Sulking?"

Dazed with pain, she shook her head.

"How's Madhav?"

"All right."

"Is he happy in his job?"

"Karan, I don't feel like talking."

"Oh? All right."

Why was he eating so slowly, hurry Karan, please hurry. Finally he finished and lit a cigarette. She opened her purse, put some money on the table and began to get up. He looked at her. "Please sit with me till I finish the cigarette, Padma." She sat, her legs weak. He talked. Later she didn't remember what he said. After they left the shop there was another wait at the bus stop. The bus journey back was interminable. They walked in silence back to her hostel.

The nail had dug deep inside; there was actually a small hole in her hand. Sumi took her to the doctor, who medicated and bandaged it, gave her a tetanus injection, some pills and some painkillers. She had to get up in the middle of the night to take more painkillers, but she managed to sleep, and by the morning the nightmarish pain had begun to subside.

No tears then. Especially in front of him. And now? Now she was like a leaking tap. In class three Mallika wrote an essay entitled "My Mother." In it she said, *My mother is very beautiful. She cooks for me and takes care of me. She tells me stories. My mother loves me the most. She teaches me my subjects and gives dictation to me. She makes gulabjamuns for me, cakes, and chicken curry. My mother makes my bed and tidies my desk and she stitches my buttons. When I am sick my mother makes me better. She gives me medicines and sleeps with me. When I am sick my mother cries. When I get better she stops crying. I love my mother and she loves me.*

The tears had been there, waiting, when she read Mallika's essay. She couldn't post it to Shantacca because Shantacca would think, Mallika has not written about me. She dropped into Anu's house the next day after her tuitions were over and showed it to Anu in the kitchen. Anu was washing the dishes.

"Why are you washing them now?" Padma asked her.

"His cousins came unexpectedly at lunchtime from old Delhi, they just left fifteen minutes ago. I had to make food for all of them. What is the matter, Padma?"

She showed Anu the essay. Anu wiped her hands and read it. "Almost the same thing Prabha has written in her essay," Anu said comfortingly, giving the notebook back to her.

"That is the truth about you, Anu. I hardly ever do these things for her."

Anu finished rinsing the last dish and put it aside. Padma picked up the cloth and began wiping them, and Anu began putting the dishes away.

"Padma," Anu said, "you are her father and you are her mother. Both jobs you are doing. Correct values you teach her. You cannot do more."

"Mallika does not write about all that, Anu."

Anu finished putting the dishes away and filled a vessel of water for tea. "She will."

"What, Anu?"

"A child will write like a child. A woman will write like a woman. You expect her to write like a woman now?"

"When she is a woman she will not think all this. When she is a woman she will know what a horrible mother she had."

"Don't cry. No, no, don't cry. See, I'm making your favourite tea, illaichi I have put, ginger also. See, Padma. Look at me. I cook and cook, I clean and clean, I wash and wash. What is so great about it? Tell me? Anyone can do it."

Mataji's voice rose from the sitting room. "Bahurani, it is already five-thirty and still there is no tea?"

"I am getting it, Mataji." She spooned the tea leaves into the vessel, let it boil, switched off the gas and covered it.

"When will you get the tea, next year or the year after next?" Mataji called.

"Just now Mataji, just now." She began to pour the tea into five steel glasses.

Padma said, "Every small thing I have done for Mallika, she has made into something big in her essay."

"And every big thing you are doing for her, she has not mentioned at all. It makes no difference. She knows, Padma."

"She does, Anu?"

"You wait and see. About these things I am never wrong." She spooned out sugar into the glasses, and stirred the tea. "Take." She gave one to Padma. "I am just coming." She placed three others on a tray and took them to the sitting room. She returned, took her glass and sat at the kitchen table opposite Padma, who was sipping her tea.

"Now look at Prabha. You think she will ever learn from me? Never. She is not one bit like me. Sometimes I feel you cannot teach your children. They are born a certain way and then you cannot change them. Mallika is just like you."

The unspoken question lingered in the air. "She is also like her father," Padma said steadily. "He was reserved. He also read a lot and was very bright."

"What is this dirty tea you have made, Bahurani," Mataji called querulously from the sitting room. "It is not fit for even the jamadar."

"In temperament," said Padma, "we were quite different."

"Did you hear me, Bahurani, or have you also gone deaf?"

"Yes, Mataji, I will make some more." She got up from the table and put another vessel of water on the gas. Padma rose and stood next to her, leaning against the counter. Anu said, "Padma, Mallika has the right values. She will be strong and upright." She searched Padma's face and said, "And just. Like *you*."

"Bahurani," Mataji's voice travelled indignantly from the sitting room, "are you making tea or are you cooking a meal?

"It is ready, Mataji," Anu called.

She could not sleep that night. Strong and upright and just! That was how others had always seen her, Karan included. But when the test came, she had failed it. Strong and upright and just! That was Prabha. Her test too would come one day, and then, would she too fail it? Padma recalled a time when Prabha was just six, when Mataji said to Anu, "Bahurani, at least sometimes buy oranges for Anirudh." And Prabha cried, "Dadima, you never tell Mummy, Sometimes buy oranges for Prabha, you always say, Sometimes buy oranges for Anirudh."

"The way she goes on," Mataji said, putting her hands to her ears.

"Dadima, when you give us oranges, you give two pieces to Anirudh and one piece to me," Prabha said.

"What lies."

"Dadima, you give Anirudh one piece, then you give me one piece, then before Anirudh finishes you give him another piece, but you give me another piece only after I finish. When I have eaten two pieces Dadima, he has eaten four."

"Oof!" Mataji threw her hands up in the air. "Eat it all, eat it all."

There was something about this business about cooking and feeding one's family that seemed to carry with it a misshapen and silent weight and Prabha was the only one who gave words to it. "Mumma, you've filled all our bowls with dahi but you haven't taken any?" she would ask at lunchtime. Later, as Anu would spoon the leftover dahi, not into Prabha's bowl, but into Anirudh's, Prabha would complain, "You always give *him*, never *me*." When Mataji cut mangoes and distributed them at the table, she always gave Anu the gutli, the meagre middle part with the stone in it, and Prabha would glare at her. But if there was an extra slice of mango that remained after the distribution, Anu gave it to Anirudh, and not to Prabha, and Prabha's lips would quiver. Sometimes Anu made sooji ka halwa, which everyone loved, and after Anirudh gulped down his, she gave him, and not Prabha, whatever was remaining of it, and Prabha would protest again. Often relatives arrived unexpectedly, just as everyone was eating, and Anu would serve them lunch and not eat herself. Then too, only Prabha would say, "Mumma, you haven't eaten, please eat, Mumma." But no one would hear her, not even Anu.

It reminded her of Amma and Shantacca, and how Madhav was always the recipient of the biggest, the last, the best. She noticed that Madhu did it too, in the same, automatic, unthinking manner that Anu did. When Madhu served food, she always put the hottest chappatis, still full with air, first on the plates of her two sons, Akhil and Randhir. If there was only one piece of chicken remaining after everyone had been served, the piece was always divided between the boys. But Mahima, unlike Prabha, never once asked, Why not me, Mummy?

Now that she, Padma, had a daughter, she understood Shantacca's pain at how Amma, with Madhav, had portioned her preference—that extra piece of mutton, that last marrowbone, those almonds in the khir. Now as she gave Mallika the leg of the chicken, as Shantacca served Mallika the thickest portion of the dahi, as they picked out for their child the most succulent jamuns and tenderly watched her eat, she would think of how Karan had once done the same for her, with jamuns, one monsoon day, in the house she would always remember as theirs. Except that while doing so, he had pretended he was picking the best for himself. But that was later, much later.

At first, when Karan didn't drop in one week, she thought, He's working, that's why, he'll come this Saturday. But he didn't come on Saturday, or on Sunday. Or the rest of the week or the following weekend.

"Sumi, something's happened to him, he's ill, or he's had an accident."

Sumi didn't look at her. "Maybe he's all right and just hasn't come to see you."

"I can't even go to his hostel alone—will you come with me, Sumi?"

"Are you mad, Padma, thinking of going to his hostel? He's perfectly all right—I've seen him twice, once last week and then again, two days ago." Padma looked at her pleadingly. Sumi said, "It's true. I wouldn't lie to you even to protect you."

But she couldn't believe it. What did she do now? Wait and wait till she happened to bump into him? Then ask him what the matter was? He was no casual acquaintance. She had the right to ask.

"Don't you have any pride, Padma?" Sumi said when Padma told this to her.

"Sumi, he's my friend. You think I wouldn't want to ask you if it had happened between us?"

Sumi made a sound of infuriation. It surprised Padma, Sumi's anger. "Don't compare me with him. He's a man. Don't be stupid enough to expect the same kind of friendship from him."

"But I did get it."

"Well, he doesn't have it to give anymore."

She buried herself in her work. The exams were drawing closer. She waited for him. Still he didn't come. Then the exams were upon them. Then they were over.

Some men, Shantacca would say warningly, use women and then drop them like hot potatoes. Shantacca was full of such warnings. But he hadn't used her any more than she had used him, any more than Sumi and she had used each other. Why didn't you come to see me? she would ask him. He would look irritated and say, I had a lot of work, I planned to come as soon as the exams got over. She would say, At least you could have told me, Karan. He would say, What was there to tell—isn't it obvious?

He was on his way out as she entered the bookshop. He saw her and stopped. "Hullo," he said. She looked up at him and all the words she had disappeared. "Hullo."

"How were your exams?"

A sick feeling was beginning in the pit of her stomach. "They were all right. Yours?"

"Fine. They were fine."

"I'm going home the day after tomorrow."

"Well, I hope you have a good time."

The sick feeling surged up to her throat. "I haven't seen you for so long."

"Too much . . . work. Well . . . have a happy holiday."

"You too. Bye."

He waved and was gone.

Shanta never asked her, after that first time, about Karan. Or about Madhav. As the long months in Shanta's house had gone by she had waited for Shanta to say, Padma, have you forgiven Madhav? Then perhaps, she, Padma, could have begun to talk. But Shanta did not ask her. Amma she had been able to talk to, about some things at least, but she had known what lay behind her listening face and her gentle nods—Amma did not believe what she said. Amma believed Padma had been deceived and was now deceiving herself. Amma and Shanta had not spoken of compassion or responsibility. Shanta wanted the child, Padma had not wanted it, Amma had wanted it out.

And so they had gone to get it out. How well Amma had done her homework, finding so quickly just the doctor who would do it, of course he would take a lot of money but Amma had come with the money and with a couple of extra gold bangles just in case. Amma had told Narayana she wanted to come with him to his office because she wanted to buy some material to make maternity blouses for Shanta and Padma, and after he dropped her she had climbed into a taxi with her list of gynecologists and visited each one till she found one who would do it. "He is clean, he is discreet, no one will know," Amma had said.

Once, thinking about that day, Padma had asked Madhu, "I wonder if unmarried girls have it done too . . ."

"Of course, Padma, really, you are too innocent. My gynecologist she told me, So many unmarried girls come to me, every day they come, girls as young as fourteen and sixteen, Padma—imagine."

"I wonder how the girls . . ."

"There is no wonder about it, my gynecologist she told me it happens to girls with their brothers-in-law, with their cousins, sometimes they are forced by members of the family itself, and then who can these girls tell? Other times, Padma, the girls themselves want it. You do not know girls these days, Padma, just like men they have become, all this sex and all, girls also want."

When Madhu had told her about her abortions, the old never-forgotten feeling had risen again in Padma, but Madhu had seemed so matter-of-fact about it. Padma had said she would accompany Madhu, but Madhu had not wanted Padma to go with her, had seemed almost angry. Padma could not understand it any more, probably, than Amma had understood why Padma had reacted as she had in the taxi. Amma had not once questioned her reaction. She must have thought Padma had changed her mind. But that had not been the case. She had not made up her mind to have an abortion any more than she had made up her mind not to have one. It was only that feeling, which had its insidious beginnings when Karan did not reply to her letters, that new, unfamiliar feeling, lapping around and nuzzling her ankles, and then in Lucknow, beginning to swirl around her knees, rising up to her waist, over her shoulders and up to her mouth: she had never known terror such as this—and in the taxi it finally rushed up her nose and above her eyes, closing over her head, and she must have cried out or something, and the taxi turned back.

Shanta had never known. Shanta had taken her into her arms when she came home, scolded Amma for tiring her, wiped Padma's tears, tended her. "Rest, my darling, rest," she had said to Padma, tucking her into bed and covering her with a sheet and kissing her, "your Shantacca will take care of you." That had made Padma cry harder than ever, the sight of her pregnant sister bending so tenderly over her. "*I* am all right," Shanta had said as if reading her thoughts, "this is my second pregnancy, this is nothing new for me."

She had never known days longer than those in Shanta's house. She could not read anymore. She stopped talking. As her stomach grew she felt she was someone else. She never thought of the baby, there was nothing to think about it. When it began to move inside her it felt as if some creature had decided to make its home in her body, a creature that did not intend to harm her but merely wanted a comfortable place in which to sleep and grow. It had nothing to do with her at all or she to do with it. Shantacca would put her palm over Padma's stomach and croon to this creature inside, she would say to Padma, "Touch the baby, Padma, caress it, the baby feels and hears everything," but Padma could not. She moved in a kind of stupor, helping Shantacca in the house and kitchen when she could, and otherwise sitting unmoving in the sitting room. She played with Vikram when he wanted her to, and read him his books and gave him his bath. In the evenings Narayana would come back with fruit for her and Shanta, and every week he would take them to a film. After she left the film theatre she could never recall what she had seen, all those black-and-white pictures moving in front of her made no sense. Narayana took them to the doctor for their check-ups. "I hate it when it is a man," Shanta said to Padma the first time they went. But it had not affected Padma—the check-up, the examination of her insides by this strange man. Narayana went to the library and chose books for her. Shanta stitched new, large blouses and petticoats for her. Narayana insisted they both go for walks in the evening, so she walked with Shanta round and round the park, round and round.

Then, when she had completed her fifth month, her brother Madhav came and the stupor left her. He came and she said things to him and Shanta that she had not thought of till she spoke them. She had not thought of giving the child away any more than she had thought of applying for a job, but here she was saying she did not want the child and had applied for a job. As she said it she knew this was what had to be done. The baby would have to go. And then Madhav had said what he had, and he too had gone out of her life forever.

It had been the end of her stupor. Then it all came back to her, and she felt like the dog she had seen crawling into the drain after being hit with stones by some young boys who were competing to see who had the best aim. It had happened near their house when she and Madhav were children. As the boys guffawed and ran towards the drain with sticks in their hands to get the dog out, Madhav also ran from the other side towards them, leapt into the drain where the dog lay whimpering and lay over it, weeping, "I won't let you touch it, I won't let you touch it," and Padma clambered into the drain too, then looked up and saw above her the boys and their sticks, and began to scream at the top of her lungs. Help came in the form of two sturdy men on cycles, who took in the scene, picked up the boys by the scruff of their necks and scattered them about, then the men lifted the children from the drain and Madhav said, "He also," pointing to the dog, so they lifted the shivering dog and put it into Madhav's outstretched arms, and he and Padma went home slowly, Madhav panting with the weight of the dog but refusing to relinquish his hold. As soon as they reached home, the dog, which should have known better, struggled out of Madhav's grasp and went whimpering straight into Shantacca's arms, and was her shadow till it died five years later.

Mallika in bed, the relief of her cigarette, the light off, even now the pain of that time without Karan returning.

Returning from the summer holidays, Sumi a constant, quiet, comfort. In a fit of misery Padma wrote to Madhav. Come and see me, Madhav, she wrote, I feel so homesick and miserable, I miss you so much. She didn't expect to hear from him for a month, but he replied the day he got her letter. He didn't have any leave, he said, but if something was seriously the matter he would take leave without pay and come to see her. She should write immediately and tell him. Moved to the core, she wrote back and said she was all right, that she had just been feeling homesick, that there was nothing wrong at all, but that she missed him, that was all. He sent a money order with the note, Cheer up, buy some books.

The December holidays were easier. She went home and spent most of the time studying, to Appa's approval. Amma said that she must apply for a lectureship in her final year M.A.

One can get over anything, Shantacca had said to her once, she couldn't remember in what context. She wondered now what Shantacca had meant, she who had everything—Amma and Appa, who had given her everything; a husband who was kindness and generosity personified; a bright and handsome son; a secure life. As for her own self, she had intelligence and good looks and charm . . . what had Shantacca meant? But now Shantacca's words came back to her in the way that Shantacca's words always tended to do.

Back to college in January. She had always had the ability not to brood about things, and it stood her in good stead now. She spent long hours working in the library. She read a lot. Most of them were the books she had bought with Karan and the books that he had bought for her. During that year with him she had not been able to do as much reading as she normally did. She had not realized that till now.

Then Madhav's letter came. He would be coming to Delhi in March, just to see her and to have a good time and to blow up all the money that he now had. He would stay in a hotel. She could stay with him. They would then have the weekend plus the two holidays. Madhav. Madhav was coming. So much they could do together. There were some Indian classical recitals on just the days that he would be there. She had never been able to go to one, not even with Karan, because they ended so late and she had to be back in the hostel long before that. Karan, on the other hand, had been to them all. She remembered how she missed him on such evenings, but then there was the next time to look forward to when he would tell her all about it in such wonderful detail. She could never understand the feelings that ebbed and flowed within her as she listened to him describe such evenings—longing, despair, excitement. Jealousy. Resentment. Frustration. He was doing everything she so desperately wanted to do, everything. Effortlessly. Taking it so much for granted. Not questioning why she couldn't go, taking that for granted too—that she couldn't. Taking for granted her acceptance of it. But what would he have said had she expressed all this? He would have said, What's the point of getting upset—if you can't go you can't go.

The day Madhav came she hugged him so hard that he had to disentangle her arm from around his neck forcibly. "Look what you've done to my tie," he grumbled, adjusting it.

"Oh, Madhav," she said as they got into a taxi, "I miss you so much."

He peered into her face. "Are you going to cry?" he asked so apprehensively that she began to giggle. She shook her head. "Thank God," he said fervently, "you just need food, that's what is the matter with you, those people in the hostel aren't feeding you properly. Let's go to my hotel first and get you a room, then we'll eat."

How long it had been since she had been so indulged. How tender he was in his brusque way. He gave her her choice of every restaurant and every film. It was heaven not to have to worry about getting back to the hostel on time, not to have to worry about getting back to it at all. Walks at India Gate, pastries at Wengers. She hadn't known it was possible to do so much in such a brief period of time. He too was enjoying himself hugely. "How is that chap Karan?" he asked once and she said, "I don't know. I haven't seen him for ages." He seemed satisfied with that. For the most part Madhav talked, and she, with pleasure, listened. Just like the early days. She felt nurtured, loved, comforted. Shanta's comforting would have been of a different kind; it was Madhav's unquestioning, matter-of-fact comfort that she needed.

Four days were not very much, after all. He was to leave the next morning; the evening before, he would drop her back at the hostel. She was determined not to sink into a depression. She wouldn't let the prospect of the end spoil what she had. Shantacca did that, could never enjoy anything without thinking it would be over soon. In the taxi on the way to the auditorium where the morning recital was to be held, he said abruptly, "Write to me again if you're unhappy. Don't keep anything from me." She nodded wordlessly.

The recital was superb. A fitting end to their four days. "Now for a good lunch at a good restaurant," Madhav said as they moved out with the rest of the crowd. "Karan. Hullo there."

They shook hands, Karan smiled at Padma, she was too stunned to smile back. They moved towards the foyer, Madhav and he talking about the performance euphorically. They used words she didn't know, they compared this performance with others they had heard, they compared the singer with others they knew. For ten minutes they stood in the foyer, talking and laughing. The only thing she wanted to do was look away, pretend she was absorbed in something else. The only thing she could do was watch them, try to listen. How easily Karan was talking. No sign of awkwardness, nothing. Something was stirring inside her. The old humiliation. A new anger. Did she have to begin dissembling now? It was a new experience. Shantacca could have done it. In her place Shantacca would have said, How *nice* to see you, Karan, after all this time! *How* are you? The afternoon would have been a triumph for Shantacca even if it meant she would afterwards go back and weep. Shantacca would have chattered with him, charmed him and revealed nothing. Madhav was asking him to join them for lunch. He was accepting. They were walking out together, Madhav was hailing a taxi, it was taking them to a restaurant nearby. The restaurant was almost full, but they managed to get a table. Madhav was telling Karan about the last four days, what he and Padma had been doing, the awful Hindi film they had seen, the boring Bharatnatyam performance Padma had dragged him to, the superb recitals they had seen prior to this one. Karan was telling him about his work, about the lectureship that had been offered to him, about working for the civil service exam but not intending to take it for another couple of years so that he could make the most of this time. Then Madhav was talking about his job and how right Karan was and how he had not had the foresight to think this way earlier, so desperate had he been to begin working and so much was it taken for granted by his parents that he would work immediately after college. She had not heard Madhav talking this way before.

"You're unhappy, Madhav?" she asked during a brief silence.

He didn't look at her. "No," he said and turned to Karan, "That old bookshop. Do you still go there?"

"Often."

Madhav said, "Padma, do you mind checking out of the hotel now— then we can spend a few hours at the bookshop, and have dinner somewhere there? I'll drop you back at the hostel after that?" She nodded and helped herself to some raita. "Join us?" he said to Karan, "we can have dinner at that dosa place. It's still there I hope?" Karan nodded. "I miss those days," Madhav said. She listened to them talk as she ate her rogan josh and naan. Why didn't either of them ever talk like this to her? Gandhi, Nehru, the future of the country, what they foresaw, on and on they went. When she had earlier tried to talk to Karan on these subjects during their long walks together he had responded indifferently, as if these topics didn't interest him.

"How is college?" Karan was addressing her.

"Please don't patronize me," she said.

"Padma." The warning in Madhav's voice was clear.

She glared at him, "I *do* understand the things you both talk about. You don't have to have separate questions for me."

"Padma, don't you have any manners?" She continued eating. "Sorry, old chap, she's got into the habit of treating every chap she meets the way she treats me. She does it with all my friends. Didn't mean to be rude. You mustn't mind her. Padma—"

"Oh keep quiet, Madhav."

"It's all right," Karan said. "I don't mind. At all."

Suspiciously, she looked up at his face. He was eating, his eyes on the plate. She couldn't see his expression.

"You're nineteen, Padma, not nine."

"*You* say what you want to, Madhav. *You* do what you want to."

"That's quite different. And anyway . . . I don't."

She opened her mouth, then closed it. Not in front of Karan. This had the beginnings of more than an argument.

"Here." Madhav was serving her the last piece of rogan josh. Her anger dissipated as quickly as it had come. She could feel the tears fighting to come out. When Shantacca indulged her by filling her plate with her favourite food, she took it for granted. When Madhav did it it moved her immeasurably. He had come all the way to cheer her up and she was angry with him and he would be gone tomorrow at this time. She watched him as he lit a cigarette.

"Appa doesn't say anything about your smoking?"

"I do it in my room." Then he chuckled and said, "I didn't tell you what happened last time—Shantacca came in and saw me and she snatched the cigarette from me and said I was doing a terrible thing. I told her, Shut up and try it, so she sat next to me and did. She was blowing the smoke out of her mouth with a horrible expression when the door opened and Amma came in."

"Then?"

"Amma said, Shanta, have you gone mad? You have a small son, what will he think if he sees you, control yourself, Shanta, control yourself. For once Shantacca was unable to say anything because she was coughing, and tears were running down her face. Finally I told Amma, Stop it, Amma, it's her first, I gave it to her. After she finished coughing Shantacca got into an enormous rage—you know Shantacca and her rages—she made her usual speech about how Amma doesn't say anything to me and always finds fault with her."

They were both laughing now. She took another mouthful of her pudding and met Karan's eyes, his expression so bleak that she found herself saying, "What's the matter?" The expression was gone, he answered, "Nothing."

Then to the hotel in a taxi, all three of them. Outside the hotel, Madhav carrying Padma's bag, another taxi to their old haunt, Madhav and

Karan talking. It was like watching a replay. After they reached the book-shop she left them downstairs and climbed up to the top section. Upstairs she sat on the ground between two shelves of books, and took a few deep breaths. She found herself shaking her head. Control yourself, Padma, control yourself, she said to herself in Amma's voice. She closed her eyes briefly then opened them and began looking at the titles.

An hour later she heard Madhav say from just below the steps, "Padma, get your fill of books. I'm paying for them." She answered, "All right, Mad-hav." She heard him climbing up and said, "Madhav, help me choose." He came in, moving across the floor and towards her, coming to where she was and crouching down next to her. Gently Karan took from her hand the book she was holding and put it down on the floor. He took both her hands in his and said, very softly, "Padma, I'm sorry." For some time they looked at each other. He had such warm hands. She removed her hands from his and held them within her own as she had wanted to do for so long. He examined her face and she looked gravely back at him. "Should we go down now?" he said after some time. She nodded. He picked up her books.

Their dinner of dosas and idlis was a quiet affair. Madhav and Karan's ebullience seemed to have subsided, and she had nothing to contribute. After they had eaten they took leave of Karan, and Madhav dropped her to the hostel.

Madhav said, "Nice chap, Karan."

"Yes."

"Do you know him well?"

"No. I don't know him well."

He looked at her curiously. "The way you spoke to him in the restau-rant, I thought you knew him very well."

"Madhav, when will you come again?"

He sighed, "I don't know." He put an arm around her, gave her a brief hug. "Just learn to guard your tongue, that's all," he said severely.

"All right."

"Here," he said, putting some money into her hand.

"Madhav, I—"

He gave her a wave, and walked towards the gate.

Madhav, her beloved brother. She didn't think of him now, she had shut him out of her mind, the way she had shut out Appa. That was the only way. Shantacca had never forgiven Madhav for that day in her house. For four years they had not spoken to each other, Shanta had timed her holidays to Bangalore so that they would not coincide with Madhav's. Then, one summer Shanta reached Bangalore to find Madhav, his wife and two daughters there. They had suddenly decided to come for ten days. "How to stay in the same house and not talk, Padma," she said. "It was not possible, the strain drove me mad. So I went to Madhav when he was alone in the dining room one day. Amma was feeding him as usual. We had finished breakfast at eight-thirty but our dear brother decided he would sleep late and eat at ten-thirty, so of course, there was Amma making breakfast again, and not toast and eggs mind you—dosas. And Amma, like a cracked record saying, Have more, child, have more, child. I sat opposite him and said, There is no point going on like this, Madhav. He didn't say anything, just kept eating his breakfast. You better look at me when I talk to you, I told him, so then he looked up, but he continued eating. He must have enjoyed the scene, his older sister cringing and crawling before him. I said, all this nonsense about not talking to each other should stop. He said, How can I talk to you when you don't want to talk to me? Even then I held my tongue, I told myself, I will not say anything I'll regret. I said to him, Madhav, don't you want to meet Padma and her child? His expression changed, as if his face was closing. He said, Are you speaking on her behalf? I said, No, I don't carry Padma's messages, I just want you and Padma to start talking again and I want you to know her child. I shouldn't have mentioned Mallika; till I mentioned her I was all right, Padma. I was perfectly in control. Madhav said, If Padma wants to start talking to me again she can. I said, Madhav, you can go to her. I wanted to say, You *should* go to her, it was all your fault—but I didn't. I should have said it, Padma, I should have said it. He said, I don't go where I'm not wanted. By now I was crying, so I got up to go, and then, Padma, you know what he said, he said, She also has not seen my children. I shouted at him, I said, Madhav, that is not the same thing. He just continued eating, very calmly, he said, I don't see why not. So then I left, Padma. Ten minutes after I went to my room Amma came in and sat next to me and told me not to cry and all that rubbish, then she came to the point—she said to me, You and Madhav must start talking to each other again, this kind of rift between brother and sister is very bad. I replied, Why don't you tell *him* that? Of course, she didn't answer my question, she said, Do not broach any controversial subjects with Madhav, just be normal. So in the end that is what I had to do—act 'normal.' "


How tense Karan was when he came to her hostel that Saturday, the week after Madhav left. When she went outside the hostel, where he was waiting, his greeting was strained. "I thought . . . would you like to come for a walk?" he asked diffidently.

Outside they walked slowly. After some time Karan said, lightly, "Well, you haven't told me how I would write about this day if I were writing about it to you."

She stopped in her tracks and burst out, "Oh shut up Karan, stop playing all these idiotic games with me. Talk simply, talk so that I can understand you. Otherwise *don't* talk." He stopped too, looking a little stunned. She said, "I just don't understand you. You think you can be a friend for one year and then drop me like . . . a hot potato the next year, and then you think you can come and say sorry without any explanations—all right, that I accepted. And then you start asking *stupid* questions just because you don't know what else to say—well if you don't know what else to say, don't say *anything*." She was panting a little by the end. If he smiled now she would hit him. He did not. He looked a little grim.

"I owe you an explanation, don't I," he said almost to himself.

"You don't owe me *anything*. The way you're talking, Karan. You don't owe me *anything*. If you *want* to give me an explanation, you can give me one; if you *don't* want to give an explanation, then *don't* give me one. Just don't *pretend*." He looked even grimmer now. Good. Let him. She wanted him to.

"I was . . . going through a . . . rough patch. I can't talk about it. It's over now. I didn't want to meet you during that time. I'm . . . terribly sorry."

"I'm not going to ask you about your . . . rough patch. But I do want to say that . . . that if any other friend I had was having problems she . . . he would not . . . would not have been . . . ." She couldn't find the words. Damn. As Madhav would say.

Karan said, penitently, "I know that. I behaved awfully."

She took a deep breath and asked, "Did you stop talking to your other friends too?" They began to walk again, slowly.

"No."

"At least you're being truthful now."

He gave her a strange look. "I've always been truthful with you. It's because I am that—forget it," he said abruptly.

"What."

"I've always been truthful with you." He was struggling to find the words. "It's just that . . . I can't . . . . discuss it."

"I see." They walked on. She said, "So why was I the only one you avoided when you were going through your . . . rough patch?"

He didn't answer immediately. Then he said, with difficulty, "Because I felt I could not meet you while . . . I was . . . that I couldn't meet you. If I told you about it . . . it would upset you. If I did not tell you . . . and continued . . . meeting you, I would . . . it would . . . upset me. It was simpler to keep away."

"And now the rough patch is over."

"You could say it is."

"Well, either it is or it isn't."

"Not so. If something is over it doesn't mean you have . . . resolved what it . . . ummm . . . your thoughts about it."

"Hmmm."

"Hmmm. I missed your *hmm*'s."

"Karan, were you having an affair?"

His head jerked up.

"It just came out. I didn't mean it to come out." They had both stopped again. She felt a little weak in her legs.

"Yes," he said and began to walk again, leaving her a little behind him.

She followed and he slowed his pace without looking back. Blindly she kept walking. After some time he said, "I meant to tell you. I wasn't ready to tell you . . . so soon." He paused, then said, "You're very young, Padma." Seeing her expression he said softly, "I know. I'm not much older. I didn't mean your age. You see things very . . . simply."

"Can we go back now?"

"Yes."

The walk back seemed endless. When they reached the gates he said, "Can I see you again?" She looked up at his face, which suddenly looked vulnerable. She nodded and began to walk back to the hostel. She heard him coming after her and waited. He came to her and said, "When?"

"I don't know."

She buried herself in her work. It was her final year and it was crucial that she did well. Then the exams were upon them and then they were over, and it was time to go home again. She began her packing, her mind no longer blank. Karan had said she was simple. There was nothing simple in her thoughts. She no longer understood anything. A burning sense of humiliation possessed her. What could he have thought of her? They had never had any claims on each other. Then why did he feel compelled to stay away from her while it was happening? Because he thought she had a crush on him? And she, she had not dispelled that notion either, her shock and misery so clear on her face when he had answered her question in the affirmative. She felt he had betrayed her, but of course, he had not, she had never had that kind of claim on him. He had never given her to feel otherwise. In the bookshop he had said he was sorry. It was not an apology for his silence but for what he knew she would regard as his treachery. He had known how she felt and it had embarrassed him. As for his involvement, whatever it was, it happened to men. Why had she assumed that it would not to him? Probably with him it had meant something. She could not imagine him cold-bloodedly embarking on an affair. It must have been something important to him and he stayed away from her because he knew he was becoming important to her, and in all honesty, he could not let that happen. She had to talk to him.

Try the bookshop again. At the bus stop, waiting for the bus, she saw him in the distance, walking in the other direction.

She began to run towards him, holding her saree above her ankles, then stopped as she came closer. He didn't turn around, he was whistling softly to himself. She came up behind him and said, "Karan." He stopped in his tracks. She said, "I want to talk to you."

"I've been wanting to talk to you too."

They began to walk. She asked, "Will you be teaching here next year?"

He nodded, "And you're going to do your M.A."

She nodded. "Well, I'll be back and you'll be back, but I wanted to talk to you before next term."

She heard him take in a deep breath. "I did too."

"But I want to talk first."

He nodded.

She said, "All right. What I wanted to say was this. I didn't understand it then, but I understand it now. You don't have to feel upset about what you did—I mean, your involvement—because of me. You didn't have to apologize to me about it. I mean, Madhav too does it. He thinks I don't know but we all know. So that's what I wanted to say. And also, I was very shocked and I shouldn't have been. No, wait, don't say anything yet. I *shouldn't* have been. It's none of my business. I understand—"

"You don't understand a thing." He sounded goaded.

"All right. I don't understand. But I'm back to normal now. So let's start talking again, that's all I want."

"That's not all *I* want." He stopped and faced her. "*Stop* treating me like Madhav. *Stop* comparing me with Madhav. I am *not* your brother."

Her legs were trembling. "You want to have an affair with me also?"

"*Padma!*"

"Karan," she said, her voice unsteady, "I'm not that young, you know."

"What?"

"To have an affair with you."

"*What?*"

"That's what you meant, didn't you, about being sorry, that you chose her to have an affair with instead of me, because I was too young?"

"*No.*"

"I don't think in a simple fashion."

"You don't understand a thing."

"Then explain to me."

"I don't know what to explain."

"See, you're going in circles again."

"Can we walk a little more—when do you have to get back to the hostel?"

She looked at her watch. "In another hour."

"All right, let's walk a little more." They turned around and began retracing their steps. After some time he said, quietly. "She didn't live very far from our college. I had a parcel for her from her parents who know mine—they gave it to me when I had gone home. That's how I got to know her."

"How old was she?"

"Five years older than me."

"*Five years older than you? Twenty-seven?*"

He didn't answer.

"She was living on her own?"

"She was a widow. Her husband had died four years ago. It was his house. She . . . taught in a school."

"So . . . you went to give her the parcel."

"We had tea. She asked me to come again for tea. I didn't plan to."

"But you did."

"Yes."

"And she gave you more than tea."

He stopped and glared at her. She bit her lips. Better to laugh than to cry, much better.

He turned away from her and said, "You seem more curious than concerned."

"I'm very concerned."

He glared at her again. She could deal with him when he was like this. He was just like Madhav. This look she could understand. He looked his age now, he felt nearer hers.

"When did it start?"

He hesitated then said, "The day we had that picnic with Sumi and Sumit."

Her laughter had gone completely. "But . . . you . . . were in the bookshop after the picnic."

"After that."

Her throat was hurting. "You went to her house after that."

"Yes."

"And how long . . . did it go on?"

"Till . . . the end of last year."

March. Half of March. April, May, June, July, August, September, October, November. Half of December. Nine months.

"Did you go home for the summer holidays?"

"Yes."

Minus two. Seven months.

"In the Dusshera holidays?"

"No."

"You spent it with her."

"Yes."

And she had thought the time she and Karan spent the October before that had been special.

"You stayed in her house?"

"Padma."

"I want to know."

"No."

"You went to her every day?"

"Please, Padma."

They walked for some time in silence.

"In late December she got married to a widower with a small son, and left for America."

She looked up at him, amazed. "She never told you?"

"She did."

"Then?"

"I knew from the beginning that she would get married if the chance came. She told me."

"I don't understand."

"She was . . . honest."

"You loved her?"

"We . . . cared for each other."

"But she got married to someone else?"

"You won't understand."

"Then make me understand."

"Marriage wasn't an . . . the . . . issue."

"Just sex."

"Padma. Please. Don't make it out to be sordid. It wasn't."

"Then what was it?"

"You won't . . . I can't explain."

"What was her . . . background?"

"Her background. She has a B.A. from Delhi University. Her father is in the army."

"You . . . met her often?"

"Yes."

She didn't want to ask. "How often?"

"Several times a week."

There was not even a remnant of laughter left. Not a shred of dignity in her questions.

Did you talk, she wanted to ask. She wouldn't ask. "What did you . . . talk about?"

"Padma."

"Did she like to read?" She hated herself.

"Yes. Done with the interrogation?" He was looking tired now. He looked at his watch. "We should go back, you'll be late." They began walking back.

"You don't think any less of her . . . now?"

"If I thought any less of her for any reason," he said steadily, "I would also think less of myself for the same reason."

They were quiet for some time. The calm that had washed over her before the meeting was all gone. She had wanted to ask him something else, something to do with herself, but she didn't know what, it wasn't clear anymore.

As though he had been thinking, he said, "I didn't *choose* to have an affair with her or *choose* not to have one with you."

She was silent.

His voice was very low, "I wasn't looking for an affair. With either of you."

They had reached the college gates. They entered, walking towards her hostel. He said, "When are you leaving tomorrow?"

"In the evening." She looked at his face and saw the strain on it. Gently she said, "Karan, do you want to meet tomorrow?"

She saw the relief on his face. It passed. "Yes."

She remembered later that night as she tried to sleep, what she had forgotten to ask him. *That's not what I want,* he had said. He didn't want her to treat him like she treated Madhav. But if so, why had he gone to this other woman just when they were getting to know each other so well, just when she had felt so full with the knowledge of his affection for her? If it had happened before, yes, then she would have understood. But it happened right after that day they had spent with each other, he lying on the grass, looking at her in that unsmiling way, not talking, then saying bye to her, meeting her at the bookshop, then going to *her* house for tea. For *tea.* Some tea it must have been. Week after week, several times a week. How did these things happen? What were the preliminaries the first time? It was not sordid, he had said. They liked each other, they were even fond of each other. They must have talked too. And what had he said earlier, before? That he had not resolved . . . what was it . . . that just because something was over did not mean one had resolved one's thoughts about it . . . something like that. What thoughts? That also she had not asked him. Other images crowded her mind, of the woman and Karan together, and misery washed over her in waves.

They were both quiet the next day as they took the bus to their bookshop. All her questions had retreated into a corner of her mind. He did not look as if he was ready to entertain any more. He seemed to be steering her carefully away from anything personal, talking about his studies, what he would be teaching, the house he planned to rent. "It's not very far from the college," he said. "About a fifteen-minute walk. But it's very private, so I'll be able to work without distractions for the exams once I get back after teaching." So she would hardly see him then. "Though it doesn't take very long cycling," he said, answering her unasked question, "so I'll be able to come and see you in the evenings."

"You can invite me for tea."

He gave her a furious look. She looked back at him. Then, his fury seemed to abate and he said, equably, "Stop baiting me."

The old man at the bookshop smiled when he saw her. "After one year you have come," he said to her reprovingly. Karan threw him a grin and began climbing up the stairs. She stood where she was. "You go ahead, Karan," she said.

He was stepping inside, he looked down, "Don't you want to look at some too?"

She shook her head, "The dust will show on this pink saree."

He looked surprised. "All right." He disappeared inside.

She wanted to lean her forehead against the books. She could not have borne the proximity. What was happening to her. She looked blankly at the titles in front of her.

The old man shuffled out of the shop. "I will be back soon," he said to her. That meant at least an hour. He had done it before on the days she and Karan used to come here. She suspected he did it knowing how long they took, and went back to his house above the shop for a nap or tea or whatever, trusting them to be the shop's custodians. She sat on a stool, her chin on her hand, looking out of the door.

"Padma?" Karan was peering down at her. "Are you all right?"

"Yes."

"First time I've known you not to look at books."

"All right, I'll come up."

She climbed up. "Here," he said, taking her to where she had sat the last time, and picking up the books he had chosen for her. "And these for myself," pointing to the other pile.

She looked at them. "Thank you."

He sat down cross-legged on the ground. "Do you mind waiting?" he asked, looking up, "I want to pick up a few more." She nodded. He took out a hanky from his pocket and put it on the ground next to him, "Here. Your saree won't get dirty." She moved the hanky a little away from him and sat, her arms around her knees. He was absorbed in the books, frowning a little. What on earth did she have to be so tense about. At least they were talking to each other now. She hadn't lost him. Then she had her holidays to look forward to—Shantacca would be at home for at least a month. Madhav had said he would try to come too. He always kept his leave for the time when he knew both she and Shantacca would be at home. She had plenty to look forward to.

She looked up, he was watching her. "Why does the dust bother you now?" he asked.

"Dust?" she asked blankly.

"First time I've known you to be bothered about dust on your saree."

"Oh that. It's the colour of the saree. Pink. Dust shows."

He was leaning back against the bookshelf behind him, looking at her. His eyes were naked with pain.

"Karan," she said softly. She moved towards him and put out her hand, touching his bare wrist. His eyes didn't leave her face. Her fingers curled around his wrist, involuntarily it seemed, her other hand reached up, curving around his cheek and chin. He closed his eyes. Her hand moved up his arm and under it, the other down his neck and around it, she was kneeling, holding him against her, her cheek against his. He was very still. This then, was what it felt like to hold him. Why had she not done it before. Why had he not done it before. This then was his smell, this the feel of his skin, this the warmth of his breath on her face. She closed her eyes and held him closer. Never, never had she known a lovelier feeling. Never, never would she know anything like it. She heard him take a deep, shuddering breath, felt his arms go around her, drawing her onto his lap, his mouth moving from her ear, across her cheek and opening her mouth, kissing her fiercely, kissing her as though he would never stop. This then was the taste of his mouth, his tongue. More, she wanted more. She felt his arms on her shoulder, he held her away from him, she saw how dazed his eyes were, she moved towards him again, felt his hands move up her bare waist, felt them stop, then his hands were holding her by the wrists, elbows down, holding her away from him. She shook her wrists and tried to move towards him again. He lifted her up, then got up, leaning against the bookshelf, breathing as though he had been running. He tried to say something, but could not. He shook his head. She stepped over to him where he stood leaning against the bookshelf, she stood on her toes and put her arms around his neck, she would not let him go anywhere, not backwards, not forwards, she nuzzled her face against his, found his mouth, she wouldn't let him put her away like a sack of potatoes, she wouldn't let him go, he was responding now, kissing her back, oh it was lovely, lovely, lovely the feel of his bare back under his shirt, and his tummy, nice and flat—

"*No.*" He was gripping her arm above the elbow this time, holding her away from him. She stood still, looking up at him. He dropped her arms and moved away from her a little. She was trembling. Suddenly he sat down, leaning against the bookshelf, his face turned away from her. She continued standing where she was, her hands getting colder and colder. It was as though he couldn't bear to look at her.

"My father's dying of cancer."

Slowly she sat beside him.

"He has about a year left."

After some time she asked, "How long have you known?"

"Since . . . last February." From the time before the silence. He hadn't told her. That was why he had seemed so preoccupied those days when she thought he was working too hard for the exams. Hadn't he needed to talk? Hadn't he wanted comfort?

"You . . . you've started talking to him again?"

He nodded, not looking at her. He said, "It makes no difference." She looked at him, uncomprehending. He said, "To him."

She didn't know how to comfort. He didn't want her to touch him. "We'd better go down," he said, getting up. She got up too. She wanted to weep. What do you want of me, Karan, she wanted to cry out. I don't understand you at all. He picked up the books and said with a faint smile, "Don't look so serious. I'm all right. I've learnt to accept it over the . . . last one year."

"You . . . they . . . you didn't want to stay with him?"

"I did. But I could do nothing and they all said it would be of no use. If . . . when he takes a turn for the worse, they'll call me. This summer . . . I'll be there anyway." She nodded. Was that all he was going to say?

She was selfish, she was horrible. His father was dying and all she could think of was how awful she felt because he did not talk about it to her the way she would have talked about such a thing to him. All she could think about was that she still did not understand what he felt for her, or wanted of her. "Brazen hussy," Shantacca had once said about a woman whom she had seen flirting with a married man at a party. That's what she, Padma, was. Of course, he had responded. What man would not. But she had not, at first, wanted what it became. She had just wanted to take away that expression from his eyes.

"Wait," he said as she began to move towards the stairs. He held her arm gently and brushed the dust off the back of her saree, then off the side and front. "You're right," he said. "It does show." He turned her around so that she faced him, holding her hands loosely. "No dust," he said, examining her face.

"Karan, this isn't the right time, but I want to ask you something." He didn't reply. The strained look was returning. She said, "When I said yesterday that all I wanted to do was talk to you, you said that wasn't all that you wanted."

"Was it all *you* wanted just now?"

"Karan, you said you didn't choose to have an affair with her or choose not to have an affair with me." He let go of her hands. She said, "I don't understand what you want of me."

Carefully he said, "I think you have to first ask yourself the same question."

Almost tearfully, she said, "You never answer me directly, you always go round and round."

He looked apprehensive, "Are you going to cry?"

She blinked back her tears and said furiously, *"No."*

"Thank God." He sounded like Madhav. She wanted to hit him. He said, "If I had a direct answer I would give it to you."

"All I want is the truth, that's all, there's nothing complicated about that."

"The truth *is* complicated, and the truth is—I don't know. It's simple for *you. You* think this is the beginning and the end of everything, like in your books. It *isn't.* I . . . when you were . . . we were kissing, I knew how it was for you—it was simple, you did it as if . . . as if there wasn't anything more natural for you than to . . . be with me. I wish *I* were like that. I *wish* I were." He said it almost savagely.

She felt as if she were being steadily battered. The words came out of her mouth slowly, "You said you didn't want me to treat you like Madhav."

"I was sick of your . . . brotherly treatment." He saw her face and said, "You don't understand how different you are from other women. Women don't behave the way you do."

"I see."

"You don't see. You don't see because it doesn't matter to you. That's why you've spent so much time with me. That's why you haven't once thought of what people might say or think. It never occurs to you to think of these things. I used to wonder about it in the beginning. Don't say that you see. You don't see. When I said women don't behave the way you do I wasn't saying it with disapproval. It was merely an observation."

"And it matters to you that people might be talking."

"If they talk about you, yes, then it matters."

"It didn't stop you from seeking me out."

"It didn't."

"You didn't misunderstand me."

"Because I first got to know you with Madhav. I knew it was against your nature to . . . hold back if you . . . liked someone. Once you asked me if I thought you were forward. If I had not met you first with Madhav I might have thought so. How on earth would I have known otherwise?"

"I don't understand what you're trying to tell me, Karan."

"That you're different from others and that's why I—that's what matters most to me . . . about you."

"So?"

"It should have been enough."

"Why?"

"It should have been enough."

"*Why?*"

"It isn't . . . the right time."

"Then why did you say you didn't want me to treat you like Madhav?"

"I couldn't keep it up."

"I don't understand. Which way do you want it?"

"I don't know."

She scanned his face. The look of misery was back.

"Sometimes I feel I don't want either," he said.

With difficulty she said, "You had neither, for a long time."

"That didn't help, did it."

"You had her."

"I don't want to talk about her."

She said, "Let's go down."

It was very bright outside. The sun hurt her eyes.

"Are you hungry?" he asked.

"I suppose we might as well sit somewhere."

At their dosa shop they sat in silence. "I just want coffee," she told Karan.

He ordered a tea and a coffee and lit a cigarette. "You're very naive, Padma."

"Oh keep quiet, Karan. Don't sound so patronizing."

"Calm down."

"Sometimes you talk as if you were thirty-two, not twenty-two. You'll be an old man ten years from now. I can just imagine you in the civil service, you'll fit in perfectly, pontificating ponderously all day."

"That's better."

"You should hear yourself talking. *You're so naive, Padma.* You should hear yourself."

"I hear myself."

"You don't. You complicate things unnecessarily. There's no need for it. I'm sorry about going on like this when you're suffering for your father but I had to say it all today because I can't wait for three months and I can't say it in letters. All this about not knowing this and not knowing that, maybe you should trust your instincts the way simpletons like me do. Instincts. At this moment all my instincts are telling me, Keep away from you."

"I see."

"You said I think love is like what I read in books. Actually it's you, not me, you who talk as if it is. All those books on philosophy and modern poetry, they've addled your brains. No wonder I can't read the stuff. You're not even listening to what I'm saying, you think nothing I say is worth anything, you—"

"Oh, *stop* it."

She stopped, trembling with anger. It was not unfamiliar, the look on his face. She had seen Shantacca's husband wearing it when Shantacca went on and on. Now she knew why Shantacca couldn't stop going on and on. She didn't want to stop either. He looked at his watch. "I think we should go back."

Nastily she said, "Maybe I should invite you to tea. Then you might not be in such a hurry to leave."

"You did invite me for tea. Remember? Up in the bookshop."

Her ears were hurting with her anger. "You declined," she said childishly. He shrugged.

She wouldn't talk, she wouldn't talk, she wouldn't say a word. "What did you mean, it was simple and natural for me, and not for you?"

For some time he was quiet. Finally he said, "It's not the first time I felt . . . the way I did."

The burning, humiliating feeling was coming back. There was dignity only in silence. Like Amma. She couldn't behave like Amma. She couldn't look at his face for fear of what he would see on hers. "I know that."

"You don't know anything. You're too naive."

She wanted to scream. Through clenched teeth she said, "I know you slept with her for seven months."

"Well then."

Keep quiet Padma. Shut your mouth. Don't open yourself to more humiliation. "It's over with her. Then why."

"I told you. Because something is over doesn't mean you've . . . resolved your thoughts about it."

"What thoughts?"

"God. The way you go on."

She burst out, "You're making me feel like a worm for asking you all this, when *you're* the one who can't talk sense—I hate it when you make me keep asking you, I hate it. If you can't be truthful with me . . ." her voice began to tremble, she looked away.

"I don't know the truth myself."

"At least try and answer my questions instead of getting impatient."

"All right."

She took a deep breath. "What is it that you haven't resolved about your involvement with her that's confusing you in your . . . relationship with me?"

"The fact that I got involved with her when I knew you. At a time when I knew my father was dying. That I knew it would hurt you. That I could have helped it. That I did not want to help it."

Well. She had asked for it. She didn't want to hear any more. "All right," she said.

"When you kissed me I wanted you. I had wanted her too. I . . ."

"It's all right. I don't want to hear any more."

"I haven't been able to reconcile this part of myself with the part that I thought I knew."

She had to withdraw. Now. She could not bear it any more. "All right. Let's stop talking about it."

"No, don't get up. Hear me through. The moment you kissed me I knew you'd start digging for the truth and . . . I . . . I didn't . . . wasn't ready to start . . . thinking about it."

She wasn't either. Not now. "Yes," she said, "I'm sorry. It's the wrong time to ask you . . . your father—"

"No. Not my father. You."

She opened her purse to take out money.

Unsteadily he said, "Please, Padma."

She took out the money and put it on the table.

"You. Not my father. You. I thought I'd lose you."

She looked at him.

"Did you hear me?"

"Yes, I heard you. You wanted my friendship. Then you didn't want only my friendship. Then when you knew you had more than my friendship you didn't know if you wanted it. Then you didn't want to talk about it because you weren't ready to start thinking about it. Then you thought that if you talked to me about it you would lose me, which seemed to matter to you even though you weren't sure if you wanted me. As you were at such pains to explain to me, the truth, which I see simply, is in fact, complicated, and you wish you were like me—simple and uncomplicated and naive. Though of course, actually you don't think anything of the sort because you enjoy believing that you're as complicated as the people in *your* books who don't believe in *anything*."

Her brain was clearing. The battered feeling was subsiding. She was feeling in control again. There was no feeling more liberating than this. She had felt it before. The problem was, with Karan it never lasted. But at least she could look at him now without flinching. He hadn't moved his eyes from her face but she couldn't read his expression.

He said, "I believe in *you*."

She said, without meaning to, realizing the truth of it only as she spoke, "But you see, I don't, in you."

"Yes," he said quietly, "I know that. That is what I had . . . feared."

There wasn't anything more to say. They both got up. When they reached her hostel they said a formal goodbye.


After their return from Lucknow Amma had said to her, "If you begin thinking of the long, lonely years ahead you will think they cannot be borne, so take it one day at a time." Amma spoke as if Karan were dead. He is alive, Amma, he is alive, she wanted to say but did not. It is your daughter who is dead, she wanted to say but did not. Amma had had a lifetime of experience condoling bereaved wives. It was Amma whom every relative and friend wanted at such times. She gave them strength, they said, she gave them fortitude. Rukmini is always there when you need her, her friends and relatives said. But she was not there for Padma after that first time.

Padma understood. Amma had no choice. Even so she had come running to Padma that one time. She wanted to tell Amma that she understood, but could not. It was difficult to say such things to Amma.

Now, when Shantacca came to Delhi, Appa and Amma and Madhav materialized in her imagination the way they had been before, strangely disconnected from the life after, she could enjoy them, savour their conversations, the tiny everyday incidents that she had heard so often before, made more vivid, not less, by endless repetition . . . "Three sweets Amma had made for Madhav, the day he came home, Padma. Imagine, three. When I come she makes one, and the way she was running around the house, was this all right in Madhav's room was that all right in Madhav's bathroom, had she got the soap that Madhav liked, new printed sheets, so expensive, she bought them 'specially for her precious son, for me white sheets will do, and then he comes in like a lord and there is Amma, fawning over him, Eat this, Madhav, eat that, Madhav. At lunch she gave him the marrow bone again. I said, I also like marrow bones, Amma, and she said, The poor boy has not had his mother's food for so long, and I said, Nor has the poor girl, then Madhav began to laugh and put the marrow bone on my plate and I put it right back on his." She brooded darkly for a few moments. "Amma never had any dreams for us. Always Madhav. Madhav has done so well in school, Madhav is doing so well in college . . . I did better than Madhav but Amma never praised me, Padma, never."

"She always praised you to me, Shantacca. She always said I should learn from you."

"Learn from me. Cooking, embroidering—all *that* she wanted you to learn from me. Oh, Padma, Appa had dreams for us. Appa treated us like sons."

"If Madhav had had a child before marriage Appa would not have stopped speaking to him forever."

"Keep quiet, Padma, you—"

"Why should I keep quiet, you—"

"Do you know you have broken his heart? Do you know he hasn't eaten your favourite banana chips since you left the house? He—"

"What does all that count for, Shantacca? All those lectures that Appa would give us, what do they count for? Amma never gave us all those lectures, but . . . when I . . . she was there for me."

"Appa loved you like a baby. He would have done anything for you."

"Shantacca, don't cry."

"Appa had dreams for us. We have both let him down. I no less."

"No, Shantacca, no. You're the best mother, the best sister, the best wife."

"Here, take my hanky. Why you don't carry your own I don't understand. Every year I make for you, every year you lose them. You just won't change."

"Amma might believe one thing but she is willing to accept its opposite if it has to be accepted."

"All this high-flown talk, keep it for your students."

"My students, Shantacca, understand me."

"All theory. Your students understand nothing. They know your ideas. They don't know you. All this high-flown talk. Very seductive it is. When it comes to the crunch this high-flown talk won't get anyone anywhere. One long fart, that's what it is."

"But Appa's high-flown talk is all right, is it? Appa will never accept the consequences of his beliefs where his daughters are concerned . . . Shantacca, Shantacca, they've both deserted me, Shantacca. When will I see them again."

Later after she had washed her face and drunk some water, Shanta said, softly, "Like Mallika you are, what you expect from Amma."

"I only want her to come and see Mallika, Shantacca."

"Darling, you should know better. Mallika wants you to do things that are against your inclination and you get so irked because you feel she should know it isn't what you enjoy doing. But Mallika's a child. You're not a child. But even you want Amma to do what she cannot possibly do."

She never meant to say all these things to Shantacca. Especially about Appa. But with Shantacca too, it seemed, she was a child again.

Tiring, thinking of all this. In the quiet of the night, think of the other. That summer she went home, telling herself, I won't think about what happened, I won't. She did not succeed. It came back to her, night after night, everything he had said. Worse, their brief, frenzied lovemaking, she remembered every detail, found herself going over it again and again and again. She found herself imagining scenes where they continued from where they had left off, though it always got a little hazy after a point. And then what he had said to her would come back, that it was not the first time he had felt this way, which meant, didn't it, that it was the same to him whether it was Her or Padma? She had been shameless, throwing herself all over him like that, he had to hold her off once, twice, thrice. He had said he was not able to reconcile what he had done with what he thought he was. She did not find any difficulty in that where she was concerned. It was a part of herself she had not known ever existed, this part which suffered from a complete lack of guilt or shame or any sense of right or wrong. If he had not pushed her away from him and if they had been elsewhere she would not have let him stop. And it would not have been wrong. The burning shame she suffered came only from his determination to keep her away from him, it came from the hurt he had knowingly inflicted on her, it came from his knowledge of what she felt as opposed to his ambivalence about what he felt. As Karan said, It wasn't simple. She was beginning to understand a little now. She had told him she didn't believe in him. It was true. What was belief after all? It was what she felt for Amma and Appa and Madhav and Shanta and Narayana and Sumi. It was something she had never thought about, her belief in them, so integral was it a part of her existence. They would be there for her, her family and her friend, whatever happened. Their feelings for her would never be ambivalent. She would trust them with her life. Could she say all this about Karan? Yet, she felt he was as integral to her existence as they were. Was it possible to feel this way about someone in whom you did not have belief? Books, books, books. They had distorted the truth. Of course, Karan was right. There was nothing simple about the truth. Things were not clear to her either, anymore. But they had been, once.

Several times she began letters to him, then tore them. He didn't write. But he had a reason now. His father was dying. But if he felt anything for her, surely he would want to share his grief with her? Could she share hers with him if she had a similar grief? Should she write to him and ask him about his father? That would only be an excuse, wouldn't it? She had lost it, her direct, simple (as he would have said) way of looking at things. He had made her lose it. Once she would have written without all these considerations. Once she would have said, Let us start talking again. He had to resolve his feelings, his thoughts, he had said. Perhaps he would, and realize that she did not fit into his scheme of things at all. Then what good would a letter do? It would cause him embarrassment, open her up to more humiliation. She would not write to him.

*Dear Karan, I have been thinking of your father and of you. I wanted to tell you that day how terrible I felt to know that he had so little time left. But I didn't know how to say it and other things seemed more important to me then. I'm writing to tell you that I hope you and your family are bearing up, and that your father is not suffering. I could not bear it if it were happening to someone I loved in my family, and I don't know how you are bearing it. I know you don't like to talk about these things so I won't go on. I just wanted to tell you that I am praying that his last few months will be as peaceful as possible, and that all of you in your family will be strong for each other.*
*Padma.*

He did not reply.

Madhav got married. All fixed within two weeks. Amma found a girl whom she liked, Ratna, who came from a well-to-do and cultured family. Madhav met her and liked her. The engagement, and a month later, the marriage. It happened so quickly that Padma could hardly believe it. A terrible sense of loss possessed her. She hadn't expected it of Madhav, not like this. And he seemed happy, full of smiles. Then off they went for their honeymoon, and Shantacca and Vikram and Narayana left too, and she was alone.

The letter arrived four days before she went back to college.

*Padma, your letter arrived the day after my father died. That is why I did not reply earlier. It happened sooner than we expected, but it happened for the best. He had been suffering terribly. He was prepared for it, as were my sisters and I. We have accepted it. My mother has not been able to. She, it seems, does not have the strength. My youngest sister, whom I thought would be the worst hit, is taking care of my mother and comforting her.*

*Thank you for writing. It is difficult to say this but I must, to you, since I cannot say it to anyone else. People have been pouring into the house and condolence letters are arriving every day. I am sick of them all. I don't want them here. I don't want to read their letters. What I actually want to say, I suppose, is that death does not heal. What happened all those years ago, about which I told you, that has not healed even though he is no more. I have not been able to lay to rest what I saw. More so now. I have tried. It isn't that I don't forgive him. Forgiveness is not part of it. He destroyed my belief in him. The memory of what I saw surfaces even more vividly now.*

*I feel better after having written about this to you. Don't look serious and concerned as you read the letter. I am all right. There are enough serious people here. When I tire of them I think of you as I saw you in the shop that first day. You looked like sunshine. Actually you always look like sunshine. Even in pink. Especially in pink.*

*I should be more serious. I began in utter seriousness. But even from this distance I can't sustain that with you. In spite of everything that has happened between us.*

*You gave me my belief in you. Whatever else I doubted, I never doubted that. Or will. But I destroyed your belief in me. I did it knowingly. Now I understand how much more I have destroyed. I have no words for it, or for what I feel now. K.*

So. What had changed? The same mixture of seriousness and levity. The same ambivalence. Did he think he was making himself clearer? He wasn't. She had reread the letter ten times—he wasn't. It was the decent thing to say, what he had said at the end of the letter. It made her feel a little better. If he had no words for it, if he felt that rotten, she was glad. Let him feel rotten for a change. She was *very, very* glad he was feeling rotten. But she still didn't know what she wanted to know. What it boiled down to was that he was repeating what he had already said, except that he was repeating it in a simpler, more coherent fashion. A very nice mixture of seriousness and levity. He knew how to do it. Looked like sunshine in pink. She could imagine his face as he said it. What was she doing having these uncharitable thoughts. She couldn't even think about his father. But why should she. Why should she feel compelled to feel sad. She was tired of feeling sad. She would not be sad.

It was with this determination that she went back to college. She told Sumi about what had happened, everything. After she finished Sumi said, "Here, I meant to give this to you but you started talking and I forgot." It was a note from Karan. *If you feel you can still talk to me will you meet me in the bookshop at 10 on Saturday? K.*

The next day. She looked at Sumi. Sumi shook her head. "You have to decide, Padma."

She was at the bookshop at 10:10. She wore neither pink nor yellow. She wore green, a bright green with a maroon border. He was there, not inside but at the entrance. She went up to him and said, "Karan, I'm sorry about—"

"It's all right. I'm all right." He was smiling, his eyes were clear.

There was a sudden silence. She forced herself to look at him, her legs suddenly trembling. He was looking down at her, still smiling. "You look lovely." She murmured something. Like one of those coy women in her class, she thought furiously. He said, "Should we walk?" She nodded. They began to walk. "Did you get my letter?" he asked.

"Yes." She should not have met him at the bookshop. She did not want to remember that day upstairs.

"How is your family?"

"Fine. Madhav got married."

"Congratulations. What is his wife like?"

"I don't know her. She must be nice if Madhav married her."

"The days must have flown."

"Yes."

"I thought about you a great deal."

She didn't reply. She couldn't.

"Have you forgiven me?"

It was too much. Too soon. "Karan. Don't. Forgiveness isn't . . . part of it." It sounded familiar, she didn't know why.

"All right. Why aren't you looking at me?"

She looked up at him, he wasn't smiling anymore. "Because of last time. I don't know what to say."

"Unfinished business."

She felt her face burn. "Let it be now. It's over."

"Padma, look at me. Please."

She swallowed, schooled her expression and looked up again. His face was very gentle. He said, "Should we finish it then?" He saw the shock on her face and said vehemently, "I meant, what we were talking about."

She shook her head as vehemently and said, "It's all right, Karan. I have been thinking about it too. You're right. It wasn't simple. Don't try and explain now."

He stopped. "I have to talk to you. I've spent three months thinking about what I want to say to you."

She couldn't go through it again. She said, "You don't understand. We always do this, go round and round the same way. Every time."

He said, very quickly, "You can ask me whatever you want and I'll answer. I won't go . . ."—he paused and tried to smile—"round and round."

"When you talk to me I take you seriously. You have to take me seriously too."

"I do."

She ignored the inference.

He said, "My house isn't far from here."

She said curiously, "Where?"

"It's a fifteen-minute walk from here—want to see it?" She nodded.

They changed direction and continued walking. She said, "It must be a nice change from the hostel."

"Much nicer. A woman comes in the morning and cleans for me and then she cooks lunch and dinner and leaves by ten. I just have to heat it up. It's private too, the neighbours aren't too close, it's very quiet. It's a good place to study."

"Are you going to take the exams next year?"

He nodded. "That'll give me about two years more of . . . freedom."

"You seem sure of getting in."

"Yes." He said it quite naturally.

The neighbourhood was quiet. His house, a little apart from the others, was small. He pointed to it from where they stood, then said, "Well, you've seen it now—should we go back?" She nodded. "Or," he said, "would you like to come in for tea?" She looked up swiftly at him, he was grinning. No, nothing had changed. He was not in the least remorseful. Well, *she* had changed.

"Yes," she said, moving towards the house, "I would love some tea."

With satisfaction she heard the uncertainty in his voice as he said, "Padma, I don't think—" but she walked ahead. He followed her.

Inside it was sunny and cheerful. The living area was furnished sparsely. "And inside, on that side is the bedroom where I study, bathroom and kitchen," he said, pointing. She took off her slippers and sat on the diwan, her legs underneath her. She liked the house. It made her feel relaxed. How quickly her tension was dissipating. One minute there, the other minute gone. It was always like that with Karan. She looked at him, smiling, and said, "Tea?" He smiled back and disappeared into the kitchen.

It really was very quiet. So. Here she was.

He came ten minutes later with two cups of tea, placing it on the centre table. "One spoon?" he asked. "One and a half," she said. He spooned the sugar for her and then for himself. One. He stirred the tea and came to where she was. She took it from him, unable to stop the smile that came to her face. He peered into her face and she saw the same amusement on his. Neither said a word. Well. He sat on the carpet opposite her and sipped his tea, his face still alight with amusement. Think of something serious. Something very, very serious. Think of the last time with him. Of what he had said.

"You're looking serious."

"I'm waiting to hear what you wanted to tell me."

"Yes." He got up and put his half-finished tea carefully on the table. Then he took out a crumpled packet of cigarettes from his pocket. She watched him as he lit one, shook the match stick and placed it on the ashtray, inhaling deeply. He said, "I tried to tell you in my letter."

She didn't reply. She wouldn't. She didn't know what it would be this time. She would not be humiliated again. She would not let him make her feel like a fool. He had tried to tell her in his letter, had he. If so she was none the wiser for it.

He said, again, "I tried to tell you in my letter. Did . . . you understand?"

"Yes."

He looked at her a little warily. "What did you understand?"

She said, generously, "Everything."

He looked taken aback. "Everything?"

She nodded.

He nodded, looking a little bemused now. "I see."

She put her cup and saucer on the carpet next to her. He picked it up and put it on the table. He sat opposite her again, smoking.

"Well. You . . . did you want to say anything . . . in response to my letter?"

"I understand."

"Oh."

"Hmm."

"What do you understand?"

"Everything."

*"Padma!"*

She bit her lips. She was feeling very giggly now. He was looking a little angry. Composing her face, she said, "You tell me whatever you want to, Karan."

"I told you. In the letter."

She nodded. "I also told you. I understood. The letter."

He stubbed out his cigarette a little violently. "You know," he said, "you weren't like this before."

"No."

He threw her a furious look. She returned it blandly. For some time they looked at each other. Then she began to laugh. "You should see your expression," she said finally.

"You're not taking me seriously at all."

Ditto.

"If I were to kiss you now you would."

He must have seen the surge of shock on her face. She got up. His hand gripped her wrist. "Don't go."

He expected her to struggle. She said, "Please don't touch me."

His hand dropped from her wrist. She sat down on the far end of the diwan. She said, furiously, "You haven't changed at all. Everything that's happening now is the same. That's why I didn't want to talk about it. If you feel I didn't understand your letter, then say what you want to in another way. Don't expect *me* to give you the answers that are in *your* head. I'm not going to do that anymore. I'm not going to do that anymore." To her horror she found her voice trembling. "Please get me some water."

He was back in an instant. He gave it to her, then sat next to her. She said, "Please don't sit next to me."

"Padma," his voice was soft in her ear, his breath warm against her face. She raised the glass and poured the water over his head.

She watched it drip down his hair, his eyes, his nose, his chin. His shirt was wet and the diwan too. She got up and put the glass carefully on the centre table. She sat on the chair opposite the diwan. She watched him run his hand over his hair, shake his head, wipe his face with his hands, then turn his face, raising his arm to dry it against his shirtsleeve. He said, "I can't live without you." He wiped his face on his other arm. He closed his eyes briefly, then opened them. "It's that simple."

Her hands were very cold. So were her feet. So was the rest of her. Very, very cold. She folded her hands across herself. Her teeth were chattering now. From a great distance she heard him say something. She didn't know what. He was asking her a question. What was it he was asking? With great effort she looked up at his face. He was sitting down now, looking up at her face, holding her hands in his, rubbing her hands, then her feet. The shivering was subsiding. He was still rubbing her hands and her feet. "Do you want some tea?" he asked. At last she could hear his voice. She said, "Coffee." He went away, then came back with a bedcover and put it around her. Then he went in again. In no time at all he was back with the coffee and a couple of biscuits. The coffee was hot and very sweet. She ate the biscuits. She felt better. She looked at her watch and then at him. He was standing, watching her carefully.

He took the cup and plate from her and put them on the table. He had changed his shirt but his hair was still damp. She removed the bedcover from around herself and put it on the ground. Can't even fold anything, Shantacca would have said. She watched him as he folded it very neatly. Then he sat on a chair opposite her.

"Are you feeling better now?"

She nodded.

He lit another cigarette and threw the empty packet across the room towards the wastepaper basket. It missed, touched the edge and fell onto the floor. She looked at the damp patch on the diwan.

"What else do you want to know?"

Let it go, Padma. Let it go. "Tell me about her."

"I can't."

She looked at him, feeling the old pain return. He was watching her, a similar pain in his eyes. He said, "I wouldn't talk about you with anyone. Either."

"I see."

He fumbled in his pocket.

She said, "It's the same thing, then."

"No, it isn't," he said. He went inside and came out with another packet of cigarettes. He shook one out and lit it. He said, "Let it go."

All right. Say it. She couldn't. She tried to hold back her tears. She looked down steadily.

"I'll tell you whatever else you want to know."

She looked up. "You can't separate it from the rest."

"It's over. It won't happen again."

She didn't reply. She would not cry. "Have you . . . resolved your thoughts about it?"

"No."

"Do you miss her?"

"No."

"She used you."

"Stop it, Padma."

"When you went to her, what did you feel for me?"

"I didn't want to think about what I felt for you."

"Is that why you went to her?"

"No."

The same pattern. It would not change.

He said, "It's your turn now."

"I don't know about my . . . faith in you, Karan."

He flinched a little. "I expected that."

"It isn't simple for me anymore."

"Yes. I destroyed it didn't I?"

She said nothing.

"Did I destroy the rest too?"

She shook her head. She watched him stub out his cigarette and get up. He came to her and sat on the table opposite her. "So," he said, trying to smile, "where do we go from here?"

He was too close for comfort. She said, "For lunch."

He looked at his watch. "We can eat here if you wish. I just have to heat the food."

"All right."

He didn't get up. She forced herself to look at him. "You're too close for comfort," she said. He was giving her the old smile now. As if everything was fine again. She looked down at the floor, her face turned away a little from him. Let it go, he had said. Just like that. He wouldn't talk about her either, he had said. As if that woman and she were the same to him. He had said, No, they were not the same. So? What was that supposed to mean? She should have asked him that.

"Tea?"

She shook her head despondently. He got up from the table and bent down towards her, his arms on either side of her chair. She felt his breath soft on her cheek. He kissed her tenderly next to her ear, then looked at her face questioningly. She gripped her fingers together on her lap. He bent and kissed her again on the other side. He smelt of himself, that familiar, longed-for smell. He murmured, "You smell lovely." He kissed her eyes, one after the other. She closed them. Gently, he separated her hands and opened them. He held them and pulled her up and stood looking at her for some time. Then he put his arms around her so that her arms remained enclosed within them, and held her. She felt her body relax, her eyes close. After some time he whispered in her ear. "I'm sorry." His arms released her, briefly his hand smoothed her hair, then he said, "I'll heat some lunch."

She could hear him in the kitchen. After some time she got up and, parting the curtains, entered the corridor. She could see him in the kitchen, his back to her. She walked down and entered the bedroom. A desk, a chair, a side table, a large bookshelf full of books, a bed with a blue bedcover. Next to a pile of books and notes on the desk were some photographs. She picked them up. They were the ones taken that long-ago day with Sumi and Sumit. She had forgotten all about it. How well they had come out. There was one, in particular, of her and Karan which was lovely.

She heard him behind her. "They've come out so well, Karan," she said, turning around.

"Yes, they have. Keep them. I'll get copies made for myself. Lunch is ready." She followed him to the kitchen. She was ravenous now. She helped herself to the chappatis, dal and vegetables and watched him as he served himself. Slowly, like a steady trickle, happiness was flowing into her again. They went to the sitting room. He put the bedcover on the ground and they sat and ate quietly. "Padma," he said as they were finishing. It felt so natural to be here with him like this, as if it were their own house. "Hmm?" He drank some water and said, "You should go back after this." He picked up her empty plate and put it over his. She picked up the glasses. "I don't want people to talk," he said. She followed him to the kitchen. He put the dishes in the sink. "The woman will wash them to-morrow. Leave them. The bathroom is next to the kitchen." She went to the bathroom. People would talk. She didn't care.

When she went back to the sitting room he was sitting on the diwan, smoking, his legs stretched in front of him. She sat next to him and said, "I don't care if people talk."

"I do. You can't keep coming here."

"No one whom we know lives in this neighbourhood. I want to stay."

"If people see you coming here, your name will be mud."

"They won't get to know. Your neighbours aren't near enough. I can come here on my own. I don't have to be seen coming with you. No one from college will know I'm coming to you." He hadn't even kissed her properly. "Very principled all of a sudden," she said sullenly.

"You don't know what you're saying."

"I do know what I'm saying."

"Listen to me. I teach every morning. I'm free only in the afternoons. That's when I study. I *have* to study. I work all afternoon and late into the night. I'll come and meet you every evening. We can spend our weekends together. But not here."

"Then where? Walking round and round sweating in the heat, and necking in the bookshop?"

He choked and she thumped him hard on the back. "You're smoking like a chimney," she said. "I'll let you work, Karan. I'll get my books and work too."

He shook his head, looking down at his cigarette, smiling. "No."

"Yes."

"Be sensible. Otherwise I'll spend all my time making love to you instead of working."

"You can do both."

He looked at her incredulously.

"You don't have to look at me like that. I'm just *saying* it. You *did* it."

"Can't you stop going on about it?"

"Then don't say things like God knows what you'd think of me if you didn't know me better. Hypocrite." She heard him make a sound of infuriation. Didn't even want to kiss her properly. Sitting there smoking and being principled. Waiting for her to fling herself on him so that he could push her away.

"When I first met you I thought what a nice peaceful girl you were. You're not in the least peaceful."

She looked at the displeasure on his face and snapped, "You don't do much for my peace of mind."

"Is this how you fight with Madhav?"

"I don't fight with anyone. Only with you."

"I think I'll take you back."

"You don't need to take me back. I can go on my own."

"All right." He lit another cigarette.

She got up and said nastily, "Don't think you look like a Hero smoking like that."

"The way you're going on we might as well be married."

She put on her slippers. He got up, stubbing out his cigarette. She put up her hands. "No need. I'm going back on my own."

"All right."

"Go and sit on your diwan and smoke another cigarette."

"I will." He went to the door, unbolted it and opened it.

Her purse. She went back, picked up her purse and went to the door, which he was holding open for her. She was stepping out when his arms went around her waist from behind. She felt herself being pulled back against him, watched the door shut, his arm appearing in front of her, bolting the door, the other still around her waist. Then both arms were around her, she felt his mouth on the back of her neck, on her ear, the side of her cheek. She turned around and felt the blessed relief of his mouth on hers. Endless. "Padma." Opening her eyes, his looking smudged. Such lovely languor, his hands on her skin, her fingers in his hair, no wonder it was forbidden, all good things were forbidden. "Padma." Taste like no other, his taste, no breath as sweet, smooth his back, tender his mouth, a slight roughness on cheeks and chin, neck slightly damp, salty its taste . . . "Padma." More to come, that was the best of it, better now, better, much lighter without her yards of material, without his, damp skin against skin, feel of soft sheets under her, all good things are forbidden, the sound of his breathing in her ear. "Karan." His mouth everywhere, nothing so tender, so true. And then the new rhythm, the new pain, his mouth stopping her cry.

The novels she had read had always stopped short of this. If one had to go by the preliminaries that always ended such novels, then what followed would have to be as natural as what began it. That was the impression she had always been left with. The first time, in the bookshop, she had not known much beyond her own instinctive response to him. It had seemed so inevitable, given how natural she felt with him, that the rest would be as instinctive, as enjoyable.

But it was not.

One of the girls in their hostel had got married in her second year and returned to the hostel after that to finish her degree. She had told her four friends all about It, and one of the four friends had told Sumi and Padma. "He had to use cold cream," she told Sumi and Padma.

Sumi nodded sagely.

"Cold cream?" Padma asked.

Sumi pinched Padma.

The girl said, "We asked her, What was it like? She said, I don't know what's so great about it. We asked her, How long does it take? She said, Two to three minutes."

There were other stories too. Vasu in the hostel knew how to tell who was a virgin and who wasn't.

"Show me your arm. Hold it up." Sumi held hers up, Vasu felt the upper arm and nodded, "Yes you are." She said to Padma, "Show me your arm." Padma held out hers. Vasu felt the upper arm and said, reassuringly, "You too are."

Sumi asked, "How do you know?"

"If you're not a virgin, then the flesh on your upper arm is loose."

Sumi nodded comprehendingly.

"Why?" Padma asked Sumi later.

"I don't know."

That first time, both of them awake, above them the fan whirring. His arms around her, her face buried under his arm, not thinking, not knowing what she felt, not wanting to get up, not wanting to talk. Closing her eyes, trying to recapture the beginning for which she had been so hungry, which had so little to do with what followed, even though he could not have been gentler.

"Padma."

"Hmm."

"Time to go back."

But he didn't make any move to get up.

She must have fallen asleep. It was not the sleep of languor, but one of sheer exhaustion. She couldn't think anymore, she didn't want to think anymore. She didn't have to. He couldn't live without her.

Can't live without you, heavy the sleep, heavy the weight on her body. No weight more beloved than this. Can't live without you, he didn't know she was half awake as he whispered into her neck, his body pinning her down, was he whispering it or was it out of her dream, the heavy sleep beginning to lift, his mouth moving against her neck. She stirred, opened her eyes, he lifted his head and looked at her, she touched his face.

Time to go back. When she came back from the bathroom he was dressing. She looked at her clothes lying on the ground, and picked them up. She shook the saree, held it up to see if the wrinkles showed. He sat on the bed and watched her as she pleated the saree and tucked it in, folded the palla and put it over her shoulder. She went to the sitting room and picked up her bag from the ground, opened it, took out her box of kum kum and cream, and went back to his room. She stood on her toes in front of the small mirror that hung on the wall and applied her bindi. She combed her hair and plaited it. He got up. "Ready?"

She looked up at him. He made a sound and put his arms around her very tightly. She closed her eyes.

Less than two years, the time after that.

Mallika's arms around her, her cheek against hers, Mallika murmuring with happiness. Mallika demanding her in a way he had never demanded her, claiming her in a way he had never claimed her. Telling her what he had never said to her, knowing the shape of her thoughts in a way he had never known, at night she weeping and in the other room Mallika moaning, even in her sleep Mallika knowing her mother's anguish. Curling up to her mother, sighing, "Ma, my heart, it is empty, give me love." Holding her and loving her and Mallika sighing and murmuring, "Now my heart, it is becoming full."

And then, after she was six, all of it stopping. Wanting the same things from her mother, but never asking. No declarations. Not once, the word *love*. After Mallika went to school, Padma would go into the bathroom for her bath, and begin to weep for all that she had lost, all that she had taken for granted, all that had made her so impatient. Would her child never say those things to her again? Her child never did. But her child wanted it. So she continued loving her the way she had always done, continued telling her child the things she had always said, and Mallika, silent now, drank it all in, her body warm in her mother's arms.

As the years passed, enjoying her child whom she had once been too tired to enjoy, with the years, beginning to dream for Mallika. She had never known ambition, but with Mallika's growing, it began to grow in her. Now she understood Appa's dreams for her and Shanta, because the same dreams were stirring in her. Once, when Mallika was three, Padma had asked the child, "What do you want to be when you grow up?" Mallika looked at her blankly. Padma said, "Do you want to be a doctor, a schoolteacher, a lecturer like your ma?" Mallika had considered the question carefully, then replied, "No. I want to be a butterfly."

When she said such things she would think of him, of his delighted smile, of his arms sweeping Mallika up into the air. She thought of him when Mallika came first or second in her class, as she read Mallika's English essays, as she watched her read, as they both browsed in bookshops. She wouldn't let what happened to Shantacca happen to Mallika. Shantacca said that Padma drove Mallika, made her work too hard, and perhaps Shantacca was right, but it would bear its fruit one day, Mallika would be all that she and Shantacca were not.

Karan would have been able to give Mallika the security that only a man could give. She had thought of him the day after the mela incident, of his arms around her, comforting her, taking away all that now continued to lie like sewage within her. If his love hadn't died and they had married, she would have had with Karan what none of the others did with their husbands.

Close your eyes, Padma, turn your face. Feel his mouth move across your stomach. No, wait. The time which followed that first day in his house—that first. Those two years together. Like her two dreams. The same sense, in the beginning, of anticipation, of promise, of pleasure and joy. She would start from the beginning, knowing the happiness that was to come in the living of it again.

He would be waiting for her the three afternoons of the week that she went there. In his house by two o'clock, out by five-thirty. And then there were the weekends. She would be in his house by eleven on Saturday, and out the next evening by four. He gave the woman who cooked and cleaned for him the day off on Sundays. So she got her way—sleeping with him once a week. That was the best part of it, this sleeping together, going to bed in his arms and getting up knowing she would still be there. Then the quiet happiness of slowly awakening in the morning, late—she always woke later than he did. He would have been awake for an hour at least by then, waiting quietly for her eyes to open—and when they did she would turn to him, just so she could hold him closer, but now he was the way she had been that first time in the bookshop, so the quietness of her awakening never lasted. If he had once seemed reluctant, that reluctance was gone. As for her, she had never known it. Even that very first time in his house she had not known it, in spite of the awkwardness, in spite of the pain.

Once she had known the boy-man with his moods and his laughter, she had known his confusion and his reluctance to deal with it. She had known the holding back, he had always held back, it was as natural for him, it seemed, as it was unnatural for her. She had seen the rapid change of expressions on his face in the course of a few hours, from amusement to anger to quietness, to that odd, expressionless expression. But now, in this house she saw the other part—the part that knew no reluctance or reserve, the part that longed for her and showed it; there was no need to wrestle with this. Now she did not have to beg him to let her visit him, he would be waiting for her in the afternoons—for tea, as he always laughingly called it. Sometimes she would want to talk first, tell him about her day. But that had to wait. Often there was no time for it at all till the weekend came, and then they talked. But not often in the afternoons. It was like the first day in his house when she stepped in. Now she entered and barely did he close the door behind him before his arms closed about her, his mouth opening hers, walking her backwards to the bedroom and to his narrow bed.

It had to be learned, even this. And not by her alone. He was a willing learner, discovering, slowly, what she enjoyed, as she did. It hadn't occurred to her ever to add the word *fun* to the others that she had always read about—*passion, desire, love*—but it was that too. Who would have thought it. Who would have imagined so much laughter.

The Pleasures of the Flesh, Shantacca would have called it. But that was the thing, it was not that. That sounded sordid, loveless, that was a hollow, meaningless coupling. This was merely an extension and culmination of everything else. It was what went on in smaller, sweeter ways at other times. It was the touch of his hand on her hair as she talked, the way he opened and closed her fingers as they sat silently, it was the way he held her as they slept. He worked at night even on Saturdays and she was usually asleep by the time he finally got into bed with her. When she got up in the morning he would be awake, watching her face. No mornings lovelier than those. Lovely the warmth and smell of his body, lovely the touch of his hands, lovely his expression as he lay back waiting for her, loveliest his laughter. The clock ticking on the table next to them, the curtains drawn against the sun, his books all over the desk, their clothes on the floor, no laughter now, no talk, no silence. Her sounds in his ear, her mouth against his, always awaiting that deeper, sharper pleasure. He, knowing what she was awaiting, knowing what she wanted. Later, drowsy, damp, he blowing into her neck to cool her down, blowing over her face and her breasts, getting up to lift the sheet, covering them, murmuring something, she smiling, both of them burrowing into each other.

"Padma. Read this."

A book about safe times. Avoidance. She read it. "Note it on the calendar," he said, leaning back from his chair, watching her as she read on his bed. "Note the dates."

She made marks on the calendar.

"No. Not now."

"Karan."

Wrestling with her, holding back her arms, laughing, shaking his head, giving in.

"Padma, will your parents accept me?"

"Of course."

"Your brother and sister's marriages were arranged."

"Shanta wanted it. Madhav too."

"How do you know they aren't looking for a boy for you too?"

"Not till I finish my M.A. Then I'll tell them about you."

"Don't you want to tell them now?"

"No. I want this . . . time just with you. Once they know . . . then how can I come here, Karan?"

"It worries me. What if they find out?"

"How can they? Anyway, you haven't told your family either."

"I will. Once I get a job. It's too soon after . . . it's too early now."

"I can't tell mine till you tell yours."

"I suppose not."

"Will they accept me?"

"They will love you. 'Specially my mother. She'll teach you to cook." He was grinning.

"Your mother's not looking for a girl for you?"

"I had fantasies of you making me chicken pulao in this house. You barely make me tea."

"Stop laughing at me. Answer my question—isn't your mother looking for a girl for you?"

"Yes. She'll find one and I'll marry her and forget all about you."

"And I'll do the same the next instant."

"Oh, oh. *Very* serious."

"Don't laugh. I meant it."

"On our wedding night you'll have to keep very quiet. No moaning."

"Mmm."

"You girls discuss everything, don't you, including your wedding nights?"

"Karan, we people only talk about it. You people do it."

"I never talked about it."

"Then how did you get to know about it?"

He groaned, "How would I remember that?"

He had put down his book on the diwan. She looked down at his beloved face. He rolled over on to his front and kissed her stomach. She could feel the lovely languor stealing over her again. How could she read when this was what she wanted. All the time. Never, never was he so tender with her as he was at such times. It was this tenderness, which he had always been so slow to give words to, that she sought every time they loved each other.

She couldn't, wouldn't stop going to him. Whether people found out or not, whether Karan worried about it or not, she wouldn't stop going to his house. It was only in this house, his house, their house, that he knew how to love her. It was only in these rooms that he instinctively responded to what she wanted, even when she wasn't sure what it was that she wanted. It was only in this house that she felt his body and face relax, it was only here that the old, familiar withdrawal didn't occur. It was only in his narrow bed, where they both slept, that she would wake up to hear him murmuring to her, not knowing she was awake. "You always sleep so heavily," he said to her once. It was true, she fell asleep the instant she closed her eyes, and on occasions when he tried to wake her up, the sleep wouldn't let her open her eyes, not till he began kissing her awake, and even then it would be like a dream—the touch of his mouth and tongue, his skin against hers, like a dream her longing for more, her own movements a dream, her eyes opening and already the waves of pleasure upon her. But on the days that she awoke to his voice murmuring against her bare back or neck, on those days she would not move at all, but instead, listened, trying to gather the words tickling her skin . . . "live without you . . . Padma . . . only you . . ."

And for that she would break all the rules in her hostel, for that she would not let him go, ever.

Less than a year, the time after that.

"Ma, when did you tell Ajja and Ajji about Dada?"

"Later. After . . . after he got into the civil services."

No end to the lies. It was true what Appa had so often said, that one's true colours came out in a crisis. What had this crisis shown her of herself? That she was a liar, a hypocrite, a failure as a mother and selfish to the core. All these long years, preoccupied with her grief, thinking only of herself, oblivious to what was happening around her, oblivious to what mattered to her friends. So long before she knew that Anu had learnt classical music for years and years. Not once guessing that Madhu was quietly getting her degree, going for classes every day, thinking that Madhu was off wandering in Connaught Place again. Having no idea that Madhu was capable of doing what she had so quietly done. Content to let her two friends take care of her, indulge her, look after her and her child, allowing them to do everything for her, allowing them to anticipate her needs and never, never being able to do the same for them.

Switch off the light, Padma, calm your mind. Under the sheet, turn to your side. Your head under his chin, his regular breathing, his fingers long and warm around your waist. Remember how irregular the visits to the bookshops became? No time to read when they were together in his house. Not many walks at India Gate either.

She hadn't wanted to listen to him when he said he didn't want people to talk. "I don't know what kind of world you live in," he said.

"Don't talk as if you're not part of that world, Karan."

"I'm a man, no one will talk about me the way they might about you. I only say these things to protect you."

"It hasn't stopped you from doing what you want to do."

He exhaled, exasperated. "I'm not saying we shouldn't do it, I'm saying we should be discreet because if we're not, *you're* the one who'll suffer, not I." He watched her face then added, "Though in retrospect perhaps we shouldn't have."

"So it's all my fault now."

"I did *not* say that."

"Talking as though it means nothing to you."

"I did not say *that* either. Don't twist my words."

"Isn't it rather late in the day for principles?"

"The problem with you is that you can never sustain a logical argument."

"How superior you sound."

"I say one thing and you argue about another thing."

"So you feel we shouldn't have."

"Yes, I do. I'm beginning to think that if it can't be done openly it perhaps shouldn't be done at all. I feel guilty as hell at the thought of meeting your parents. If they find out— Or mine—"

"I thought it meant something to you."

"It means a great deal to me and if you don't know that, you're stupider than I thought."

"Just because you've read more don't think you can call me stupid."

"Use your common sense. It's not what we're doing but the way we're doing it that disturbs me."

"A bit late in the day to get disturbed about it, isn't it."

"Stop it."

"I will stop it."

This time when she went out of the house he did not stop her.

It didn't last more than a week. He was back at her hostel in six days. She was back in his house that afternoon. Afterwards, as they lay under the damp sheet, he said, "How can you think it means nothing to me."

"I don't think that." She put her head on his arm, looking at his troubled face.

"Then?" he asked, his fingers running softly through her hair.

"I just said it."

"Because I was truthful and the truth hurt, you wanted to say what you knew wasn't the truth, just to hurt me in return?"

"It might be the truth, what you said, but what has happened has happened, and there's no point wishing it hadn't, 'specially when it isn't going to stop. I don't see the point of having qualms about something once it happens. You should have had qualms before."

He smiled faintly, "I didn't have much of a choice, did I?"

Fiercely she said, "Everyone has a choice, Karan. You were no exception."

"I had plenty of qualms before."

"Just don't blame me."

"There. You're starting again. I'm not blaming you."

"You make things too complicated, Karan. Try and enjoy the time we have together."

"I do. But we will have plenty of it later."

"I don't want to think about later. I want to enjoy what we have now. That's the only way to be happy. Everything you *can* enjoy, you spoil by thinking about what *could* happen. That way you'll never be happy, ever."

Sumi asked Padma many questions about Karan's family. "How will they manage?"

"There's enough money I believe, their father's provided for all the sisters and there's quite a lot of family money."

"Padma, I don't want any drishti to fall on you. You're both so happy with each other, I feel scared for you."

"I told him the same thing. He said I was talking like an uneducated woman."

"But actually you're not superstitious. It's just about this, isn't it?"

"Just about this. I feel I don't want anything more. I have everything I want."

Sumi touched her head. "Don't ever utter these things, Padma."

Less than eight months, the time after that. It came and then it went, and everything went with it.


The exams were upon him. He did not want her to stop visiting him. She took her books with her and worked in the sitting room while he worked in his bedroom. Sometimes he worked all night, taught in the mornings and would be asleep when she came in the afternoon. He would open the door for her, tell her, "Wake me up before you leave" and stumble back to bed. She would get in beside him and he would put his arm around her and fall asleep again. She would try to read in that position, the book held behind his back, but mostly, she couldn't. Then two hours later she would kiss him awake, make him tea and leave. On the weekends she would leave after breakfast after spending the night with him.

The exams ended; the long, lovely days resumed. The weeks, months, passed. During the October holidays she would spend two, three days at a time with him. He gave his bai three weeks off. Between them they managed to clean sporadically. Once she tried to cook but it was such a disaster that she never tried again and they ate all their meals out. She told him the stories of her childhood, of Shantacca's childhood, of Madhav's. His own were less easy. She had to ask him questions: What do your sisters like to do; Do they have good friends; Did you fight when you were children; Does your mother like to read; Did your father laugh with your youngest sister. No, he would not answer any more questions. Why wouldn't she talk about something more interesting? Her letters? No, he didn't have them with him here. They were at home. Inside a drawer in his cupboard. Certainly not, it was not locked. No one locked anything in their house. Why not? No one snooped in his room or opened his things. She and her feelings. Next subject. No, he would not discuss Her. It was over and behind him. Yes, he had resolved his thoughts about it. No, he would not tell her what they were. Now what? Of course he wanted children. Didn't she? Two. First a girl, then a boy. Not a girl like her. He couldn't handle another one like her. What was there to wonder what kind of a father he would be. Certainly not like his own. His children would know him.


She was at home that December when she received his letter. He had got his call. He would wait for the final results before telling his family about her. Unless she felt otherwise—what did she think? The advantage of telling them now would be that the marriage could be arranged for May before he went for his training in Delhi. But if he didn't make it, then it would be a terrible embarrassment to everybody. However, if he did make it, and he was sure he would, then there wouldn't be time for the families to correspond or for anything to be arranged till much later, probably after the training—and that would mean another year. Or perhaps they could get married during one of the short breaks . . . but that would mean she couldn't join him while he was training. But she could stay with his family and he would try to make it to Lucknow whenever he could for one or two days. Or better still, she could apply for a lectureship in Delhi and live near him. That was probably the best idea. What did she think? She wrote back her congratulations. She thought it would be better to wait for the results of his interview before telling either family. She didn't tell him it was only because she wanted to have him to herself for the rest of their time in Delhi.

Back to Delhi, back together. Now he didn't say anything about people talking. She had told him in the beginning, "Don't worry, they all think you're my brother."

He hadn't found it amusing at all. "A few years from now you'll find yourself introducing me as your husband to someone from your hostel. What then?"

She laughed. "What then? Nothing. We'll be married."

He looked at her, "You really don't care, do you?"

She said, gently, "If I did, would that make it easier for you?"

He didn't answer.

Marriage would change all this. No hurry, no hiding, all the time that they wanted. "We've been so happy in this house, Karan. I don't think I could bear to leave it."

He sat on the diwan and lit a cigarette. "There'll be other places. Better than this one."

It gave her a curiously hurt feeling when he spoke like that. "Doesn't this one mean anything to you?"

He shrugged. She said, "Here's where we . . . we would have spent two years, Karan . . . don't these two years mean anything to you?"

"They do. But there'll be others. Better years."

"You won't later think of this time as . . . special?"

He said, "This time, yes. This house . . ." He began to grin.

"You know what I mean. Try and say nice, sentimental things to me sometimes."

He pulled her to him. "I'll *do* nice things to you."

She returned his kiss and said, "Karan, let's go to Agra."

He began unplaiting her hair. "Agra?"

"I want to go to Fatehpur Sikri and make a wish at the Chishti."

"What wish?" He removed the clips and spread out her hair.

"I can't tell you," she said. "Not till it comes true."

He lay down and pulled her down on top of him. "And how long will it take to come true?"

She looked down at his smiling face. "I don't know that. But it always does come true. You can wish too." She put her palm on his cheek.

He put his hand over hers, then brought it to his mouth and kissed her palm. "What's this mark?"

"An old wound. Karan, will you also make a wish?"

"All right, I'll make a wish. What wound?"

"A nail went in. Can we go this weekend?"

"When?"

"This weekend—later it'll be too near the exams."

"No, I was asking about the mark—when did the nail go in?"

She put her cheek against his. "Long ago." He raised her palm, kissed it again. She said, "So we'll go this weekend?" His eyes were closed. She tickled his neck. "Indulge me, Karan."

His eyes opened. "You don't have to plead. We'll go this weekend. Make as many wishes as you want."

There was such unhappiness on his face that she stared at him. "Karan. What's the matter?"

"Sometimes I hate myself."

"What's—" But he was kissing her so fiercely that she couldn't go on.

They went that weekend and each tied one red thread at the Chishti.

"Have you wished properly?" she asked him after he finished. He nodded. She said, "I know you don't believe in all these things, Karan, but all you need to do is to wish for what you want with faith. Then it'll come true."

"Yes, I think it'll come true. What did you wish for?"

"I can't tell you."

"Of course. You'll tell me when it comes true."

She shook her head again. "I can't ever tell you."

He laughed. "You and your superstitions."

She said, anxiously, "Karan, whatever you wished for, don't tell anyone till it comes true. Not even me. All right?"

"You'll be the first to know."

How could she ever tell him hers? Never. That day when she asked him to go to Agra, it had suddenly come to her that she wanted nothing more, that she had all that she wanted. The last two years had been a time of such happiness that like Sumi, she was beginning to feel superstitious about it. Soon they would be married. She tried to imagine the years ahead with him. She did not want to imagine it; her mind found it difficult to contain the prospect of so much happiness. Shantacca always said that a period of happiness was always followed by a period of bad luck. Shantacca said, When good things happen, they all happen together; when bad things happen, they all also come together. But what could happen to them? It had come to her that only one thing could happen to end it. He could die.

At the Chishti she tied the red thread, closed her eyes and wished. I want him to have a long life. April came, and the exams were upon her. She was in the middle of the exams when the results of the interview were splashed in the newspapers. He was in.

Less than two weeks, the time after that. It came and then it went, and everything went with it. Time passes, Shantacca had said once to her.

"Padma, we can't get married till October at the earliest. There won't be any time between now and the time I begin my training."

"After you get your mother's consent, write to me and I'll tell my parents."

"All right."

"Karan, stay longer in Delhi."

"We have four more days together. After that we have the rest of our lives."

"Stay just a couple of days more."

"I can't. My mother's expecting me. She even sent me a telegram asking me to confirm the date and time I was coming—she knows she can't rely on my letters! How come you're going home so late?"

"I told them I'd come later. They think my exams finish later."

Abruptly he sat up on the diwan. "You told them that?"

"I don't remember what I told them. They're expecting me to leave in four days."

"Why did you have to lie to them, for heaven's sake?"

"I didn't *lie*. I just let them assume that my exams are finishing later than they actually are."

He was sitting away from her now, frowning. "You shouldn't have let them assume that."

"Karan."

"I hate this. Lying to your parents because of me."

"I did *not* lie."

"It amounts to the same thing."

"I just don't understand you, Karan. Suddenly being so holier than thou. Our families still don't know about us—that hasn't bothered you."

"I didn't tell my family because I was in no position to support a wife and family. Now that I am, I will."

"I also couldn't tell my parents for the same reason, and because you have to get your family's consent first. I—"

"That's not true. You didn't tell them, because, as you told me once, you wanted the time just with me. Because if they knew, you could no longer come and spend it with me. Just a minute, don't interrupt. I understand that. I'm just pointing out that your reason was not the same as mine."

"You don't understand a thing. If I'm deceiving my parents, then so are you. It's exactly the same thing."

"It certainly is not. I never tried to give my mother the impression that my holidays begin at a time when they don't."

"I just can't believe this. *They* don't know either that you're spending all this time with me."

"I can't tell them. They won't accept it in a girl I marry."

"Exactly. Exactly. Mine won't accept it in the man I marry."

"You're not getting my point. I know you can't tell your parents what we've been doing. Any more than I can. I'm not a fool. But now you've begun lying to them. There's a difference."

"Your family too is ignorant of what we've been doing. You too have kept it from them, Karan. That's also a lie."

"Not telling them something is not the same thing as deliberately giving them the wrong impression about something."

"I see. What should I have told them?"

"The truth. That your exams are over but that you have decided to come home a few days later. That's all."

"How on earth do you expect me to tell them that without giving them a reason? Your parents won't ask you, but mine will."

"You asked me why I reacted the way I did and I told you. Now forget it. Let's not fight."

"Karan, what do you think I've been doing the last two years?"

"Doing?"

"How do you think I've been managing to come to see you and spending all those nights out of the hostel? Don't look so impatient. Answer my question."

"How would I know."

"Use your common sense, Karan."

"Oh, for heaven's sake."

"We do have rules, you know, unlike in your hostel."

"We had rules too."

"Well, you could go out wherever you wished without breaking the rules."

"You can go out too."

"Only at certain times. If we have to stay out longer or spend the weekend out we need our local guardian's signature."

"You don't have a local guardian."

"I did in my first year—Amma's cousin was my local guardian. After they left Delhi it was just easier for Madhav to . . . sign for them so that I could go out with him. Nobody knew."

"He *forged* their signature?"

"How do you think I spent those four days with Madhav? He used their signature again."

He was looking at her with disbelief.

"So now you know."

"Hold it." He sounded unlike himself. "I don't. What did you do?"

"I used my local guardian's signature permitting me to go out with my brother. What else."

He stubbed out his cigarette and looked at her aghast. She said, "I tried to tell you once. I told you they think you're my brother."

He said, "So now you want me to take the blame for it?"

"I'm trying to tell you that this deception about which you're so upset began two years ago. If you chose not to see it, then—"

"*Chose* not to. What d'you mean, *chose* not to?"

"It was convenient for you not to ask, wasn't it?"

"I didn't in my wildest dreams *imagine* that you were forging anybody's signature."

"Then what, Karan, did you imagine?"

"I didn't think about it."

"How convenient."

"I can't believe this. Not only are you not remorseful, but you want me to take the blame."

"No, I'm *not* remorseful. This was the only way I could be with you, so I did it. I'm not like you, doing something and feeling guilty about it, doing something and not knowing why I did it, having to spend all my time trying to reconcile my thoughts about this or that. If I feel guilty about something, then I *won't do it*. And I don't want you to *take* the blame. I just want you to know that you should have given it some thought too, instead of enjoying your time with me and then turning around and blaming me for breaking the rules to be with you."

She had never seen him look so upset. He said, "I have never felt guilty about being with you. I wanted to protect you from gossip. I had no idea about all this."

"Well you know, now."

"I would not have wanted it if I had known."

"You never wanted to know."

"You had no intention of telling me. You knew how I'd react."

She watched him as he stood opposite her, his hands folded across his chest. Slowly he said, "I didn't know you were capable of deceit on such a huge scale."

Words crowded in her throat. None would come out. His anger she could deal with. Not this. She got up and tentatively put out her hand to touch him. He moved away. Slowly, she went and sat on a chair. She said, "I just wanted to be with you." He didn't answer. He was standing at the window, looking out unseeingly.

Remorseful. Remorseful for what? For the two loveliest years she had ever spent? For the blossoming of her deepest feelings?

He said, "And on top of all this you try and defend yourself."

In the past he had hurt her terribly. Now he was hurting her again. "I'm sorry it had to be this way, Karan. We just have four days together. I don't want to talk about it anymore."

He turned from the window and she saw the amazement on his face. " 'It had to be this way.' After all this, all you can say is, 'It had to be this way'?"

She had lost her will to fight. "All right. It shouldn't have been this way. Let's not fight."

"A maze of lies—that's what I can't believe. An absolute maze of lies. *You*. I thought you were the one person who was incapable of lying."

No, she hadn't lost her will to fight. "Hypocrite. That's what you are—

a hypocrite. You've done everything I've done. And more. Much, much more. But you could do it because you didn't have to break any rules to do it. You didn't have to break any rules in the hostel, you didn't have to break any of the rules in your home—because you're a man, and none of those rules apply to you."

"Should we stop this now."

"No. No. If you want to accuse me, then you have to listen to me too. I broke the rules. You did not. That doesn't make you any more honest than it makes me. You do what you wish, you go where you please—you always have. You've gone for every music recital that's been held here, every one. I can't go. I have to be back in the hostel by a certain time. I can't go alone. I can't go with you because I shouldn't be seen with you in such a public place. Even a simple thing like listening to a live performance of Indian classical music I can't do without breaking the rules. So I deny myself what I love. Have you ever thought of it that way? No, you couldn't have because it's never happened to you and it never will. Had the rules applied to you, you too would have broken them. But the rules will never apply to you. Never."

"Have you finished."

"Yes, I've finished."

"Padma—"

She banged the door shut.

She went to the station, cancelled her ticket and bought one for the next afternoon. Then she sent a telegram home to tell them about her change of plans. She went back and began to pack. "Another fight?" Sumi asked, smiling. Their squabbles always seemed to amuse Sumi. She told Sumi about it. "Here, let me do that," Sumi said, folding Padma's saree and putting it in her trunk, then beginning on the others. "Padma, you're going tomorrow. Don't fight just before you leave. Go and make up. I'll finish your packing. Go."

He was standing at the door, smoking.

"I'm going tomorrow afternoon," she said.

"Good," he said blandly. Making it difficult for her as usual.

"Listen," she said patiently, "stop acting like that. Be pleasant. This is our last evening together."

Silently he opened the door and she followed him in. "Don't get into one of your moods, Karan."

He shut the door. "Tea?"

She sighed in exasperation. "All right." Indulge him.

He stubbed out his cigarette, put an arm around her, kissed her very hard. When he stopped she looked up at him, trying to read his face. This was not how she wanted it. He kissed her again. Was this how it was with the other woman? She wanted none of it.

He went into the kitchen. She quickly wiped her eyes with her palla, surreptitiously blew her nose into it. She would never let him see her cry, never.

He came back with two plates of dosas. "The problem with you," he said, "is that you always behave like this when you're hungry. Have you had your lunch?" Slowly, she shook her head. He spread a bedcover on the ground. "It's cold," he said. "I got it an hour ago. What are you waiting for. Come and eat." She sat opposite him and began to eat. After she finished he said, "Another one?" She nodded. He got up. He returned with another plate of two dosas and a vessel filled with gulabjamuns. She ate her second dosa. Then she had two gulabjamuns. "Coffee?" he asked. She nodded. He came back ten minutes later with two cups of coffee. She sipped hers. He peered into her face. She began to smile. He blew her a kiss. He finished his coffee and they picked up the plates and glasses and took them to the sink.

"Karan."

"Yes, Padma."

"Don't kiss me without affection."

"I was testing the waters."

"Then don't."

"They were very cold."

"Don't kiss me without affection."

"Is that better? Hmm?"

"Hmmm."

"And this?"

"Hmmm. How did you know I'd come back?"

"Your lust for me, my dear, overcomes everything."

"So you went and got the dosas."

"So I went and got the dosas. Dropped chutney all over my shirt."

The bedroom was clean, his books all packed, his suitcases lying at the side. A surge of such misery shook her that she gave a stifled cry. He looked questioningly at her. She shook her head. She said, "I love our house."

"We'll have another. Better."

"I don't want to leave this house, Karan."

He lay down on the bed and she sat next to him. It was being abandoned, their lovely room. They were deserting it, their lovely house. His thumb caressed her wrist. He put out his arms and she went into them.

How quiet he was. She smoothed his forehead, watched his eyes close as she kissed his cheek, feeling the roughness of his skin, the smoothness of his back. He would never know how she had longed for him before she came to this house. She had never known it herself. He would never know how she longed for him still, even though she had him. Twice, when she had gone home for the holidays she had taken his hanky home with her, just so that she could smell him at night. Like the dog that Madhav had rescued which had become Shantacca's dog, who always slept on Shantacca's old nightie . . . that was how she was.

Once when they were bathing, Karan had said to her, curiously, "How is it that you never smell?"

She was sitting on the ground, scrubbing her toes with an old toothbrush; she said, "I must be when I'm hot and sweaty."

He poured water over himself and shook his head. "No, never. You always smell as though you've just had a bath and powdered yourself."

She stood up and began to soap herself. "I don't powder myself."

"I know," he said, reaching out for the towel.

Hopefully she said to him, "Do you want to keep my hanky?"

Astonished, he stopped wiping himself. "For what?"

"To remind you of me when I'm not with you."

He burst out laughing. "I'm not a dog, you know."

She had begun drying herself, still smiling. What would he have said if he knew what she had done?

That last day together, asleep in his arms.

"Padma."

He was murmuring into her arm when she awoke, but this time she couldn't hear the words.

Less than a day, the time after that. It came and then it went, and everything went with it. Time passes, Shantacca had said once to her. Less than a day, the time after that, it was death without him, her own.

She went home the next afternoon. He and Sumi took her to the station and put her on to the train. He was very quiet, hardly said a word. The train began to move, he and Sumi raised their hands, waving goodbye. She watched them from her window, two figures waving, growing smaller, smaller.

This was the end of their story. What happened subsequently, that was another story. The years that they had shared were not tarnished, would never be tarnished. The night that it finally came to the end, Karan and Sumi waving goodbye to her, two figures growing smaller and smaller, those nights when this memory replayed were the worst. For many days after that she would not think about it at all, because she had to recover from it again.

But after some time, a few weeks at the most, the thirst would begin to consume her and she would begin again, all the way from the beginning, from the first day to the last, four and a half years, dipping into it carefully, like a miser, lingering over this, and that, slowly, carefully, stretching it out, and out.

Tell me, Ma, tell me.

And what did she know of this child of hers who had once deliberately cut herself with a kitchen knife in order to tear her mother's silence? As Padma held her daughter's hand under the tap Mallika watched her with a look on her face that Padma could never forget. She had no name for what her child had done to her that day. Was this thing-without-a-name what Mallika was in her entirety? Was what she knew of the other Mallika the lie? She didn't want to think about it—bury it, bury it, bury that look, bury the sight of the finger.

Telling Mallika what could be told, leaving out the rest. It was this—all that she left out—which made everything she told Mallika a lie. And what she left out about other things too, all that she couldn't tell Mallika of what lay so heavy in her heart, and how the tentacles of the past, of one's very childhood, tenaciously grasped every present moment. Such griefs were not meant for children.

Mallika must not find out. Never. If she did she would learn to hate those who had wounded her mother, hate her mother, hate herself. Mallika did not have the strength to withstand it. She did not have the confidence. She was not like Prabha, who was born with the belief in herself. Mallika was the one who had to come by such belief. Perhaps Mallika would learn from Prabha; Prabha, who had got it from her mother—Anu doing all that she had to do so cheerfully, keeping that part separate from that inner bit of her which was inviolable. "Let Mataji say what she wants to say, Padma. I know what I am," she had said once, laughing. Padma had been so struck by Anu's remark. "It doesn't affect you, what Mataji says?" she had asked. Anu said, "If I let it, then what will there be left of myself?"

She, Padma, needed to learn from Anu. She recalled Anu's son Anirudh standing in front of the mirror when he was barely two, singing, "Anirudh is fair, Daddy is fair, Prabha didi is fair, Dadima is fair, Mumma is black, black, black," and Mataji laughing in delight, pinching Anirudh's cheek tenderly and saying, "Like a crow my daughter-in-law is. My grandchildren have got their fair skins from their father, and for that I thank Him." And Anu threw a conspiratory smile at her, Padma, and continued clearing the table, while her husband's family who had come to stay for a month, sat around, neither hearing what had been said, nor helping her. And she recalled how Anu's parents sent Mataji an expensive silk saree every year through Anu, and how Mataji always wore it, saying, "Cheap, raddi quality." Now, after all these years, whenever Mataji wore these sarees, Anu would laugh and declare, "What to do, Padma, poor Mataji is forced to wear cheap, raddi sarees!"

It was Anu's spirit Prabha had inherited. Everyone said the girl was like her father. But she was like Anu; she had her mother's spirit. Prabha was the lucky one who was born with the knowledge and conviction of what was right and wrong, and Mallika, the other who had to come by such knowledge and conviction.

At first when it was late she didn't worry. But when the second week passed and she still did not get Karan's letter, she went to a doctor many miles from home. She told Amma she was going to the library and would not be home for a few hours. Before entering the clinic she put Shantacca's mangalsutra around her neck. Shantacca had left it behind during her last visit. The appointment didn't take very long. Yes, the doctor said, smiling, her first? She nodded. Karan's letter would be waiting for her when she went home. Letters had been delayed before. If they got married within the month, or if it came to that, even within two months, it would be all right. Babies did arrive prematurely. She had written to him once, before suspecting anything, now she would write to him telling him what had happened so that he could persuade his family to have the wedding quickly. Or should she write such a thing in a letter at all? Perhaps not. He never locked his letters. What if the letter got into the wrong hands? What if he left it lying somewhere and someone read it? They would think she was a . . . no, she would write to him and tell him that it must be soon, stress the need for a quick wedding. She went home. There was no letter from him. She wrote to him and posted it.

She waited for the postman. A strange feeling was growing in the pit of her stomach. It could only mean one thing. His mother had said nothing doing. His mother must have said, You must marry a girl from our community. He would try and reason with her. She would not be reasonable. He would think, first I have to see to it that she agrees, then only will I write to Padma. He had been so sure of his mother's compliance. Well, then, he was wrong. If only he had written and told her so. But he would probably be thinking, I do not want Padma to be hurt on that score, let her not know that my mother was initially unwilling. He would be thinking, once my mother comes around—and she will because she loves me— then I will tell Padma. He would be thinking, anyway there isn't a terrible hurry—we can't get married till October at the earliest.

Another week passed without a letter. She wrote again. She told him to hurry with whatever he was doing, that she knew his mother was unwilling and that she accepted it, that these things happened and it was not his fault. She told him to write to her and tell her exactly what was happening so that they could then quickly decide what to do.

Two days later she wrote again. She told him that if his mother did not agree, then they should get married without her blessing, rather than wait indefinitely. She could not wait. She underlined this several times. She said she was willing to marry him without her own parents' consent if need be, but it was imperative that they marry soon. She could not wait. She underlined this again. Then she wrote, You're hurting me more by trying to protect me, Karan. I need to hear from you soon. I can bear anything, don't hide your family's displeasure from me. I understand, these things happen. Nothing matters, nothing, except you.

No reply. She told Amma and Appa she wanted to go to Shantacca's, that she was missing her sister terribly. And then the whole drama about the job. Going to Shantacca.

Then Amma came to Shantacca's. Then they went to Lucknow. Then they came back.

It came and then it went, and everything went with it. Time passes, Shantacca had said once to her. It was death without him, her own. The pain a monster inhabiting her body, imprisoned in her flesh, growing larger than her. Eating her brain, chewing off her tongue, swallowing her eyes, gnawing off her ears. Easier after that to hold it, it was satisfied. Then Madhav coming and going, and the monster awakening again.

Everything came back after Madhav left. She had numbed her mind to it till he came. Then he came and he went and she knew she was alive and that her skin had been peeled off her. Memories crowded, heaved. The question why filled her brains till her head was a constant throb. Why, why why. The rhythm beat its beat all day and all night. How how how. The rhythm beat its beat all day, If this has happened then anything can happen if this has happened then anything can happen if this has happened then anything can happen. She felt she was going mad. Perhaps she had gone mad. Later she couldn't remember anything of the months that followed, nothing except the monstrous pain which she carried along with the other growing thing in her body. The other thing moved and turned and kicked, the monster bit deeper and deeper all the way from her chest to her stomach till her insides felt raw. Shantacca started sleeping with her, Shantacca caressed the thing that was in her stomach at night, talking to it.

The haze had never really left her. That's what no one knew. It was still with her. It cleared when she went to teach, at such times it lifted almost miraculously. Then as the bus began taking her home the haze would begin to descend, because he was in her house. He had inhabited it from the very beginning. She hadn't meant it to happen. She hadn't wanted it to happen. In fact, some time after Madhav left she had destroyed everything, almost, that remained of him. She had been ruthless. That was the only way to cope. Some time after Madhav left she had opened her trunk and taken out all his letters and the photographs. She did not read the letters, she knew each one by heart, but the photographs leapt out at her. She had heard the word *heartache* time and time again but had never imagined that it was literally that—a physical ache in the heart. It was palpable, the pain; it was there, right there inside her heart. It went from her chest down to her stomach, she had to press her palms across her swelling stomach to try and hold it in. She took them all out of her trunk then, the letters and the photographs, went to the sitting room, took Narayana's ashtray and matches and then went to the veranda. She put the first letter, the first in fact which he had written to her that summer, the one where he described his walks, and burnt it in the ashtray. Then she took the second one and burnt it. The one about the constellations. Then she had to go back to the kitchen to get the bucket, she took it to the veranda, threw the ashes in the ashtray over the eggshells, onion peels, coriander stems and bean strings, and began on the third letter. She did it in the order that she knew them. Then she began on the others. The one he had written after his father's death, with that note of seriousness and levity. The "you were like sunshine" one. Then the others. The ones where he talked to her the way he used to talk to Madhav. These too went, one by one.

Shantacca came to the veranda as Padma was burning the last letter. "Padma—" She stopped abruptly as she saw the photographs on the table in the veranda. Almost unwillingly she lifted them from the table, and as Padma watched, she held up one and asked, "Is this him?" Padma nodded. Shantacca looked at all of them, one by one. Then, wordlessly, she put them down on the table and went inside. The photographs took a little longer. They would not burn properly. Some burnt halfway and she had to light the match to them again. Then she came to the last.

She could not burn it. If this starting afresh had meant putting the past behind her, then she was trying to do it. But did it also mean destroying what she did remember of all that she had once been? And it was there, in this photograph, all that she had once been, more than in any of the others. It was there in the radiance of her expression, the way she stood, her head held high, her limbs free and unhampered, it was there in the expectation that her eyes held, the promise.

Was it not for this that she kept the photograph finally? It must have been. Not for him, not for him. If it had been for him she would have kept the rest. It was for herself, for all that she had lost of herself, for that part of herself that was now dead.

Fool that she was. The physical fact of burning these things she had accomplished. But she had not been able to control her mind. The years that they had shared were not tarnished, would never be tarnished. She had severed what happened subsequently from what they had shared before.

It could only be done by putting the rest aside, the rest that she had so painfully constructed over the years. Now she knew why he had been so quiet that last day when he said goodbye to her. He had been in mourning for what was dead in him—his love for her. He could not bear it, that it had gone. He had been very quiet as they went to the station. He did not write to her and tell her why. Just like he did not tell his father. He had expected his father to understand what he himself had done because it was so clear to him what his father had done. And that was not the only reason he had not written. Also because he could not bring himself to write . . . so deep was his disillusionment and pain and loss. Like with his father.

She, Padma, had erred not in what she had done with him, but in what she had not seen of herself, which he had seen. She should have waited. He had wanted to. She should have been willing to continue meeting in the evenings, going out occasionally for lunch, for walks, to their bookshops. But no, she was not content with that, she had wanted him completely. And since that could not be done honestly, she had done it dishonestly. And when he had found out and realized what she had done, she had lost him. No, not merely his realization of what she had *done*. His realization of what she *was*.

And then, so quickly, he had married another. Thinking, probably, that it made no difference now, his mother must have produced someone on his return, he must have shrugged, saying, Whatever you wish. So she knew now, why it had happened. She knew now what she was.

If she had been less impetuous, less impatient, more willing to listen to Karan, then they would have got married and Mallika would have had a father. And she who had denied her child what was every child's right—this child gave her the kind of love that she deserved least of all. She expected her child to be all that she had never been, and her child, her poor child, believed that her mother was all that.

Karan, Karan, you should have written and told me. It has taken me years, years, to slowly, painfully, construct the reasons for your betrayal. Such a brutal silence, Karan, such a brutal silence.

The doorbell ringing.

At last.

Forgive me, Padma. Forgive me.

It came and then it went, and everything went with it. Time passes, Shantacca had said once to her. It was death without him, her own. The pain a monster inhabiting her body, imprisoned in her flesh, growing larger than her. Eating her brain, chewing off her tongue, swallowing her eyes, gnawing off her ears. Easier after that to hold it, it was satisfied. Then

Madhav coming and going and the monster awakening again. Carrying it for longer than she carried Mallika, for months and months and years and years, no simple confinement, this. Never to be aborted, no cutting or scraping or sucking out, no such luck. In her blood now, dissolved into the red stream inside, it would not leave her now, no, never, running through her veins, no parting, no bleeding.

They came back to her, night after night, the same two dreams. In the first dream, which occurred more often, Amma and Appa's house was waiting for her, large and gracious, the sunshine bright in the sky, the roses in full bloom. Always in the dream she was opening the gate and walking in knowing she would find them all inside—Amma, Appa, Shanta, Madhav. All was as before, she was still in school, always in the dream it was the sense of comfort and security that she remembered as she walked towards her house, and her recognition in the dream and outside it that this, this was happiness—this feeling of coming home, of love waiting for her in that house. Walk faster, Padma, walk faster, she'd think, but the house came no nearer, endless the walk to the house, endless. Then she would wake up. Then the relief, the relief that it was this dream and not the other one.

Because in the other dream, the one where she did reach the house, she would silently open the door and walk in. Nothing had changed, all was as before, the sitting room drenched in sunshine, the mantelpiece with photographs of all of them as children, the comfortable sofa and chairs, the glass cupboard full of books, Amma's flowers on the centre table, even the smell of cooking wafting in from the kitchen. There was no one down-stairs, so she climbed upstairs towards the bedrooms. She passed Madhav's bedroom; he was sleeping. Madhav, Madhav, she would say but he could not hear. Madhav, Madhav, she would say, but he still slept, his school bag flung at the corner, his pens and pencils all over the floor. Then she would walk to Amma and Appa's room and there they were—Amma, Appa and Shanta—praying in perfect accord, their eyes closed, the smoke from the incense curling upwards. Appa, she would say, Appa, but they could not hear her above the sound of the chanting, so then she would walk up to Appa and reach out to touch his arm and Amma's eyes would open and she would frown very slightly and make a small gesture which meant wait, but of course, she could not wait, how could she, there was no time to wait.

Shantacca, she would say, but the sound would not come out. Shantacca, she would say again, but again there would be no sound, Shantacca's eyes would flicker open, Shantacca would walk past her without recognition and walk into Padma's room and Padma would follow her and Shantacca would be sitting on Padma's bed, waking Padma up, saying, Get up, get up, you'll get late for school. And there she was, the girl Padma lying in bed in a heavy sleep, and then the woman Padma would say, Shantacca, Shantacca, *I* am Padma, look at me, look at me. That is what she would want to say but the words would not come out, Shantacca not even looking at her, the girl in the bed was Mallika, she was stirring. Take her away, Padma, take her away, Shantacca saying, eyes full of terror. But where will I hide her, Padma saying, wrapping a white sheet around Mallika, round and round Mallika till she was completely covered all the way up to her nose. Quietly, quietly, Shanta saying, don't make any noise. Padma carrying Mallika down the stairs, slowly, carefully, all the way down into the dining room and to the sitting room at last, reaching the front door, putting out her hand to open the door, grasping the handle, but the door not opening, saying, Shantacca, Shantacca, holding on to the door handle with one hand and Mallika with the other, saying, Help me, help me, but no words coming out. No Shantacca, no Amma, no Appa, no Madhav— she all alone in the house from which all sunshine had withdrawn, the curtains drawn, no view from the window, no looking out, dark inside, very dark, her child wrapped up in a white sheet. Was her child breathing, she could not see, she could not hear. The doorbell ringing, someone outside the door, she shaking the door handle, the door opening, not her hand opening the door, someone else's hand outside the door, Karan's hand, Karan risen from the dead, coming to take Mallika's body away.

Waking up soaked in sweat, stumbling out of bed, running to Mallika's room, Mallika lying under a white sheet covered up all the way to her nose, pulling the sheet down, feeling her heart, then to be sure, her pulse, then to be surer, putting her face to Mallika's nose, feeling her soft breath against her cheeks. Then closing her eyes, taking deep breaths, feeling the pounding of her heart slowly subsiding, getting into bed next to Mallika, turning her gently to her side, curling her body around her child's, her arm around her waist, the other arm over her head, the birds outside beginning their chirping, she sleeping.

# RUKMINI

 A couple of years after her daughter Shanta had got married she had asked, "Amma, when we were all children, in those days did you have different thoughts?" She had looked at Shanta, bemused. Shanta explained, "I meant, did you think differently then from the way you think now?"

"Think about what thing?"

"About us—about Padma, Madhav, me, about . . ." Shanta waved her hands vaguely, "about everything." She looked at her mother's enquiring face and said with exasperation, "Amma, you must have had *some* thoughts in your head, what did you *think* about?"

Astounded, Rukmini answered, "Where was the time to *think*?"

What did you *think* about. *Think.* That was the luxury that men had. They could even write books about their thoughts and about more than their thoughts, about where their thoughts led them, about how one thing connected with another and that with another and so on, and there it was, the miraculous conclusion, like a newborn baby, and so much simpler to nurture. But these days women had some of that luxury—and much good it would do them. Her own daughters, Shanta and Padma. That was what thinking did, that was what having the time for it did. It was all right for men to get agitated; they got agitated about ideas and work and things like that. But when women had the luxury to think and get agitated, they got agitated about other things; so much the worse for them. She knew. Now she had all the time in the world to think. And what good was it doing her? What good would it have done her if she had had the time to think when He was alive? No good. Great harm. But with Him gone, and she alone in

Madhav's house, with both Madhav and Ratna out at work and the children at school and no work to do and no one to talk to, what else could she do but think; even when she tried to push the thoughts away from her head they swarmed in like locusts and tore up her brain. Sometimes, when she thought about her daughters and the granddaughter whom she would soon see, then she would talk aloud, sharing her thoughts now with Shanta, now with Padma, now with Mallika. It was very clear in her head, what she could share with whom, she didn't have to think about *that*, that came as naturally to her as breathing, she had done it all her life: this can be told to her, this to her—the possibility of leaks didn't occur to her any more than the possibility that she would one day forget how to breathe. Hide this from one person, hide that from another, tell her this part of the story, tell her that part of the story. Shanta, do not tell Padma this. Padma, do not tell Shanta that. Mallika . . . Mallika . . . would she need such warnings? Or would she know, instinctively, how to gather all that her grandmother told her into herself till it nestled deep within her heart, accommodated comfortably or uncomfortably with everything else, to be examined carefully sooner or later?

Mallika would ask her questions. More questions than Shanta, more questions than even poor Padma. That she knew from the letters Mallika wrote to her. She knew from all that Shanta had told her about Mallika. Mallika asked questions, Mallika lived experiences vicariously. Innocuous questions to begin with, Shanta told her mother, then these leading on to the others, till things began to come out of Shanta one after the other, Shanta said, tumbling out like the things that Padma stuffed willy-nilly into her cupboards. Each time Shanta left Delhi she would think, That I did not mean to tell Mallika. But Shanta had told her that and that and that. And Shanta had felt better for it, her heart soothed, her mind calmed. Curiosity wasn't the reason Mallika asked, Shanta told her mother, it was something more, perhaps she asked because that was the way she lived, by wanting to know about people, not in order to tell other people, but for herself.

When Shanta came to Bangalore every year and told her mother all about this granddaughter whom Rukmini had never seen, then she wanted to say to Shanta, The child is not like you, Shanta, learn from her, learn from her. Because when Shanta asked questions it was to assuage her curiosity, or to set the record straight, or to seek justification—oh yes,

Shanta was a great one for seeking justification. When Padma used to ask it was because she wanted to know why, that was all. Madhav never asked, but his wife did—oh yes, Ratna did—and she, Madhav's mother, knew exactly how to look vague and forgetful, that also she had had practice with. Madhav's wife would not get the better of her, not now, never now. What right did Madhav's wife have? Shanta, only Shanta, had the right, Shanta her firstborn, who was as different from her mother as night was from day. Yet that day in Lucknow when there had been no preparing what happened, they had acted as one, she and Shanta, they had thought as one.

That day the time had been ripe to utter the words that they had uttered. But the problem with Shanta was that she spoke at other times too. Whatever she felt, whenever she felt it—it came out of her mouth. That was all very well with her parental family, but she, foolish girl, also did it with her husband. For someone so intelligent she had no sense about these things. For someone who had topped the university and got a gold medal and had two degrees, she was almost stupid. She, her mother, who had no college degree and had read nothing compared to her children, it was she who was attuned to what a marriage and what a husband required. To separate, that was the thing, separate—one had to know how to keep things separate. What one thought, felt. What one said, what one did. They should have no bearing on one another. In watertight compartments, each one, each with a separate function. The minute you began to connect one with the other—finished.

The problem was that she, Shanta's mother, knew Shanta inside out—better than Padma, better than Madhav, almost better than she had known Him. She knew how Shanta's mind worked, she knew exactly what the expression on her face meant. From the time Shanta was a child, her mother had known. It was a mistake to know anyone else this well, even one's child. It made them vulnerable to you and they hated you for it. It was a bigger mistake letting the person know that you did. She had made that mistake with Shanta. Big mistake. After all, Rukmini had known Him too. Better than He knew Himself. But not once had she let Him know that. She had never blamed Him for anything. She had never attributed this and that to Him. She had never withdrawn into injured silence, never nagged, never flung accusations. If she had needs, He had not known what they were, she had never expressed them to Him. She had protected Him as a wife just as He had protected her as a husband. He had believed that He had been a good husband, as indeed He had. He had believed that she was happy and contented and that her needs had been fulfilled. No, no, He hadn't thought about these things, these were not things to think about, but the knowledge was there for Him like the air he breathed.

The problem these days was that people thought education taught you everything. Actually it taught you nothing at all. It fed your intellect, that was all. It didn't teach you how to live your life. In marriage it was useless. Worse than useless; it gave you ideas, it misled you. She had come into marriage without even finishing school, compared to her children she was illiterate. But she had what her children did not have—the right instinct. No amount of education could give you that. No amount of education could teach you what she had known from the beginning—that if there was a rightful place in marriage for anything, that if there was anything a woman could legitimately bring into marriage besides her children, that thing was her silence. Nothing could thrive without her silence—not her husband, not her children, not her marriage. Mouth closed gently over a captive tongue, that was all, the knowledge as inborn as a baby's instinct to open its mouth and suckle.

It was education that eroded instinct. Shanta opened her mouth. Shanta grumbled. Shanta wept. Shanta accused, attributed. Shanta blamed Narayana for this, for that. Foolish girl. She had no one to blame but herself. Shanta fished out the dregs. To what effect? That was the question: to what effect? Narayana did not hear her. If he did, he disregarded what he heard, dismissed it. Men did not want to hear about their wives' unhappiness. It was not because they had no knowledge of unhappiness. Far from it. It was because their knowledge of unhappiness grew out of contexts external to the contexts their wives knew; their wives' unhappiness sprang out of a territory so near and so foreign that to acknowledge it would destroy the men. The dregs inside that rotting place within you—the dregs belonged right there. It was not meant to be shown to Them. It was like showing Them the bloodstained cloth of your monthly periods, thinking, let me shame Them. You showed it to Them and the shame became yours.

In her own case what would have breaking her silence been worth? Would anything have changed? Nothing. And she would have lost that thing most precious to her—her dignity. She would have lost that most precious thing that He had given her—his reverence. He more than anyone else had revered her. Given her complete freedom in the running of the house and the bringing up of the children. Complete freedom with money, with the hiring and dismissing of servants. His parents had loved her as a daughter, his sisters and brothers had looked upon her as a sister. She as the eldest daughter-in-law and sister-in-law had had a say in everything—the arranging of the marriages of her husband's sisters and brothers, the buying of the sarees and the jewellery, the naming of her nieces and nephews, the conducting of all the religious ceremonies. It was she everyone had come to for advice. She had given it when asked, never otherwise, and they had taken it and been the happier for it. Even now everyone said, "It is She who has kept our family together." When her father-in-law lay dying it was she who tended him till the very end; he had died with his blessings on his lips. Within a week her mother-in-law had died too, true to her word that she did not want to live without her husband. Then too, Rukmini had been with her mother-in-law till the end. When they died she had felt a far deeper grief than she had felt even for her own parents, but she had been forced to be strong for the others, who bore their grief with less fortitude than she did. He had said nothing to her, but she hadn't needed Him to. The knowledge of His complete dependence on her was enough. She was not like Shanta, constantly wanting reassurance, constantly demanding verbal assurances. Words counted for nothing, they were meaningless. What people felt for you, it came out in other ways. If you gave with your heart and were strong for them, then they revered you and this did not need words. Even after Padma, He had revered her. She had almost broken her silence then, almost. He hadn't stopped her from going to Padma that first and only time. She hadn't even asked His permission to go. She had gone, just like that, packed her trunk and gone, done what she had to do and come back. When she came back He had said, "Next time you go, you can stay with her."

Death was a strange thing. In some ways it numbed you completely, in other ways you felt as if your skin had been peeled from your body. It was only now, in Madhav's house, that she was beginning to recognize His permanent absence. She had not felt it in her own home; there it had felt as though He would walk through the door any minute, place His walking stick in its usual corner, sit on the sofa and remove His shoes and socks. It was as though He had gone on one of His tours, one of the longer ones and that it was only a question of waiting for Him to come home.

That time, with her house full of her children, her daughter-in-law and her son-in-law, she was numb to the fact of His death but not to the change in her children. These three who had been born in this house, lived and loved in it, these three who shared the same blood and who had tended to each other did not come together in their shared loss. In this house of death the past was alive and stinging. How they had changed, these children whom she had borne. Grief had snatched Shanta's pungency from her. It should have made her soft and compassionate, but instead she was flaccid and colourless. Temporary, it had to be temporary. She would go back to her normal self in due course, she had to. There was nothing temporary about the change in Madhav. It had happened gradually but like lines on an aging face it now showed clearly. For years now the only animation that showed on his face was when he spoke of money and promotions and who was in what position in the government—the higher, the better. No luxurious conversations now on politics and history and philosophy. Now, in this house of death, her once affectionate, mercurial son was distant and cold. And Padma, no one had changed more than her. Her soft, warm-hearted, sweet-tempered child had gone. She was cold and brittle; it was as if the woman who wept in fits for her father was another woman. Once, just once she saw the old Padma. It was very early in the morning when everyone else was asleep. She was going to the kitchen when she saw Padma moving like a wraith from one room to another, looking around her, touching the walls, the doors, the furniture. She didn't hear her mother following her, and when finally her mother said, "Padma," she turned slowly, then put out her hand and touched her mother's hand, her fingers encircling her mother's wrist, as if to be sure that it wasn't a dream. She, Padma's mother, took Padma in her arms and held her for a long time. There was no comfort to be had from Padma, but she, her mother, could give Padma a little of it. That was all. That one time. Padma and Madhav spoke to each other like strangers. Ratna's attempts at talk with Padma were met with indifference. Shanta, who at any other time could have been the only one to bring Padma and Madhav together, was dazed with grief. There was no comfort at all to be had from her children.

What had happened to her son, who had taken care of his pregnant older sister and cycled miles to get her fresh sweets? Who had spent most of his pocket money on books for his younger sister? What had happened to Shanta, who had mothered Madhav and tutored him, of whom he had said as a young boy, "When I become big, then I want to marry Shan-tacca"? And Padma, her youngest? Whenever she pictured the children of her past, the picture she had of Padma was of her slim figure waiting at the window either for Madhav or for Shanta.

In her mother's house for the first time in thirteen years, Padma hardly looked at Madhav after the initial, constrained greeting. They didn't speak to one another at all. Ratna made overtures—oh yes, she did. Still full of curiosity, that Ratna, still suspicious of the story of Padma's runaway marriage. There too Madhav had been loyal to his sister—he had said nothing to his wife of the true story; the story she knew was the one the neighbours knew. "See, Shanta, see," Rukmini had told Shanta once, "so loyal Mad-hav is to Padma, see." Shanta had snorted. Incapable of acknowledging anything, Shanta, incapable. Rukmini had said, "Shanta, be fair to your brother. After all, Narayana also knows the truth." Shanta had turned on her in such fury that she blanched, and shouted, "Don't you compare that Ratna with my Narayana."

Now in this house of death, Padma met all her aunts and uncles and cousins with composure, she answered their queries about Mallika and no one asked her anything. Her mother had expected ripples at Padma's arrival after all these years; there had been nothing. Rukmini saw her husband's sister take Padma aside and say something to her. Later, her heart pounding, she asked Padma, "What did she say?" Padma replied, "She said, Now try and forgive."

That was all. After thirteen years, that was all. That was why they thought Padma hadn't come home, thank God. That was what they had been thinking all these years. That is, if they thought at all, which, of course, they hadn't, because they had all been getting along with their own lives. While Padma's story and its consequences had become bigger and bigger in her mind till it stretched her head and her heart to tearing point, they had all forgotten. What for Rukmini had become her quietest, heaviest burden, had been for them just another incident. If only she had had the foresight to see that. If only she had had the sense not to equate their curiosity with her guilt, their knowledge with her own. All those slow, heavy years, could not she have been spared at least that—her own monstrous fear?

What did you think when you were young? That's what came of reading novels—you asked stupid questions. All of them—He, Shanta, Madhav, Padma. Now, Mallika. Reading, reading, reading. Thinking, thinking, thinking. Luxuriously speculating about people, about situations, about relationships. For what? Useless, utterly useless. "My children, they love to read," He had said so often, so proudly, "they have got it from me." With His daughters He discussed literature, philosophy, politics, everything. "A great man, Shakespeare," He said to Shanta, "a great man, the greatest. His characters speak to me here," and He tapped His chest and shook His head and sighed. They used to enjoy themselves, He and Shanta, His firstborn, His favourite child, discussing books and arguing about them. He would tease Shanta about her love for Jane Austen, saying, "Oh, *she,* she is the mistress of trivia." Shanta herself wasn't sure, when put this way, that Jane Austen wasn't. All those English books and all those English people. Gave them the wrong ideas. Him, Shanta, Madhav, Padma. Now Mallika. "The problem with women who write," He said to Shanta once, "is that they write only for women. Men, they write for everyone." "Oh, *Appa!*" Shanta had exclaimed, but with amusement. They amused each other, father and daughter, indulgence like water lapped gently around their relationship. Amusement and indulgence, the domain of fathers and daughters. Not for mothers and daughters. Never for husbands and wives. No such simplicity here.

What it boiled down to was that all this thinking, all those high-sounding words, all those lofty ideals, they were bubbles. Looked good, flew high. Then they burst. Nothing left to show they had been there, not even a noise to proclaim their death. Many lofty ideals He had had. Many high-sounding words Padma had had. She knew what the results were of that. What people thought had nothing to do with what they did. And that was how it should be, but they, her husband and her youngest daughter, had not known that. People who thought could not act. Should not act. Ideals rightfully belonged to the head. That was where they were meant to be nurtured and sustained. If they were meant to be translated, well, then, that's what books were meant for. The minute you began to incorporate them into your life—finished. That had been His problem. That had been Padma's. With Him it had been His own ideals. With Padma it had been her admiration of the ideals she saw in others—she saw others as they saw themselves. She had seen her father as He saw himself. She had seen this Man she loved as He saw himself. Because these men believed what they said, Padma too had believed. That had been Padma's downfall.

Oh yes. Intellect. That also. Great ones for admiring the intellect, her family. No, not Shanta. Shanta, the brightest, did not give much thought to such matters, either her own brilliance or that of others. She had no interest in the kind of conversations Madhav and his friends frequently engaged in when Madhav was in college, those so-called intellectual conversations . . . philosophy, politics, history . . . back and forth, back and forth Madhav and his friends would go, endlessly. Padma listening, enthralled. Then after Madhav's friends went, she would try and engage Madhav in the same fashion and he would ruffle her hair and tease her. "You never take me seriously," Padma would exclaim in frustration. Yes, Padma had been the one seduced by intellect. She had been the one who connected intellect with sensitivity, with comprehension. That's what came of reading so much. She had been the one who made the foolish connection that what the head thought, the heart felt. That also had been Padma's downfall.

Books, thinking, intellectualizing . . . where did that get you in life, what did it get you in life? Would He have been as proud of her if she read the way her children did? No, then He would have said, Why is the food cold? Did any of this get you security, wealth, happiness? Ah, yes, respect. Sometimes it got a man that. But not a woman. She knew. Hadn't she arranged marriages all her life? How many men had she known who when asked, said, I want a girl who has brains? Not one. Beauty they wanted, accomplishments in the kitchen and house they wanted, culture they wanted, girl from a good family they wanted. The other things—purity, humility and all—they took for granted. These days even education they wanted. Should have a B.A. at least. But intellect? No. No one she knew had asked for that. Naturally not. Of what use was a woman with brains? Marriage and motherhood demanded common sense and intuition, not brains. A woman should command respect for her resilience, for her fortitude, for her integrity and for how she brought up her children. The complementary qualities in a man were strength, courage, honesty and his ability to provide for his family. For a woman to sustain her intellectual abilities meant neglecting the home and children; to sustain the home and children meant neglecting the life of the mind. The choice was clear. Intellect got you nowhere in the kitchen. Contemplating one's life meant burning the rice. Thinking about relationships meant starving the children.

Shanta had made the right choice, even though He had chafed against it for the rest of his life. I want my daughters to be like sons, He used to say from the very beginning. She never argued with Him. There was no point, it changed nothing. She let Him think what He wished and say what He wanted. My daughters should have the best education, He had said. Well and good. She had kept quiet. But when the time was ripe, then she had her way, and Shanta hadn't protested at all, in fact, Shanta had wanted to get married. It was only natural. I want my daughters to join the civil services, He had said, dreaming no doubt of the day when He could say, My daughter is joint secretary in the such-and-such ministry, my other daughter is the under secretary in such-and-such ministry. Or, at least, My daughter is a professor. Even that He would have accepted for Shanta. But later, even that Shanta had resisted. Naturally. Why shouldn't she.

Saying to His daughters, Stand on your own feet, be independent, be free. Use your education. Your parents will always stand by you. What are parents for if they cannot stand by their children? Do not allow any man to treat you badly. Come to me. I am your father. I will protect you. I will see to it that you will never have to depend on anyone. Saying to Shanta, There is no hurry to get married. Telling her, If you find someone you want to marry, tell me. Very appreciative He had been of those so-called love-marriages. Praising Padma's friend Sumi for having found a man on her own and marrying him. Didn't have anything to say when she got divorced. Too preoccupied then licking the wounds Padma had inflicted on Him. She wanted to say to Him, This is how these love-marriages end up. She would have said it if not for what had happened to her own youngest child. If Shanta had married for love would she have found a man like Narayana? True gold he was, Shanta's husband, twenty-four karat gold. But like all people who had it, Shanta was unappreciative. Love. Outside books it had no reality, that kind of love. Inside marriage it had no place, that kind of love. She snapped her fingers at It.

After Shanta He had tried it with Padma. Apply for this lectureship, apply for that lectureship. And the job had fallen into Padma's hands, and she hadn't been able to take it. She too had let Him down, and in a manner so grotesque. Nothing He could say, nothing, with This Thing like a monster looming and grinning before him. He had taken refuge in silence. Didn't even talk to her, his wife. Wrapped the tentacles of His silence around her like their marriage vows so that she couldn't even say, Tell

Padma to come and stay with us, tell her you forgive her. Nothing she could say, nothing, so formidable was His silence, so terrifying. In retrospect she never understood how she had gone to Shanta and then to Lucknow. It was a single act of monumental courage. After Padma had settled down in Delhi she had wanted to go there with a longing that excluded everything else. Her heart yearned for her child and her child's child. She had written to Shanta. Try and explain to your father, she had written, to you he might listen. My arms are aching to hold Padma's child. Try and make him understand. But Shanta, she had been useless. Nothing Shanta had said to her father, nothing. All those years of her going to Delhi and everything, everything she shared with her mother in detail. Even photographs Shanta got for her. But she allowed her father his silence; her love for Him neither changed nor diminished. Till the day he died she loved Him more than she loved her mother.

Madhav, for all his brains, had not wanted a woman of intellect. He had wanted to marry a woman who would take care of him, so she, his mother, had found him one. And all said and done, Ratna took care of him. She tended to him, she clung to him. She didn't spout theories or argue. Ratna knew as well as his mother did, that Madhav, who had all of Shanta's brilliance and Padma's passion, had two other things—ambition and a fierce desire to be appreciated. The ambition had got him where he was now in his job; Ratna had fostered it. And Ratna had given him the appreciation he had felt so lacking in his family. Madhav, more than Shanta or Padma, had set store by how his love was received. She, his mother, like a bottomless pit, had received it. Ratna successfully gave the impression of doing so.

The appreciation that came from those who sought their strength from his—that was all Madhav wanted. Once, long after his marriage, he had told Shanta, "Ratna, how she clings to me." There had been indulgence in his voice, and affection. Shanta's face had darkened briefly; she had ignored the remark in the manner that she often ignored Madhav's remarks, but her mother could see that it had struck home. Her mother could see how deeply Shanta felt that her own husband would never speak of her with such tenderness. She wanted to tell Shanta, I understand, but it is your fault. Tenderness has to be fostered. Subsume your needs to His. Silence will foster this tenderness, that is all that is needed, that is all. How to tell. Madhav felt it for his wife, a great tenderness, a fierce desire to protect and cherish . . . and what more could a wife want? All Madhav wanted—

strong, proud Madhav—was the acknowledgement that he was there, ready to take care of you, ready to shoulder your burdens. All he wanted was appreciation of that fact, appreciation not for his work, not for his accomplishments, but for himself, purely and simply for himself. That was all. She, his mother, had given it. It had to be demonstrated. She, his mother, had demonstrated, both in action and in words. All her life nobody had needed her the way Madhav had needed her. Till he got married.

Of course, Madhav was mistaken in his belief about his wife. Ratna needed nobody, she was someone unto herself. Ratna knew exactly what cards to play and when and how. She had insinuated herself into his deepest recess by appearing to be that which he most wanted her to be. Clever, clever Ratna. Her insidious games he was blind to. Not that Rukmini blamed her son for it. All men were like that. Shanta could learn a few things from Ratna. But Shanta's problem was her jealousy, all her life she had been jealous. Always weighing and measuring, watching and counting, storing it all up in her mind to use weaponlike in the next round. Yet, Madhav had loved her, more than he loved his own mother and his father, and almost as much as he loved Padma. That was the thing about Madhav—his generosity, his ability to give unstintingly. That was the tragedy about Madhav, that this very thing in him, once so pristine and clear, was now muddy and maimed.

It was a good thing one never knew, in spite of seeing it all around every moment, what went into the raising of one's children. There was nothing automatic about it, even though one seemed to do it automatically. Look at Madhav, maimed for life. Look at Shanta, born maimed, jealousies coursing through her body like blood. And then there was Padma, with her misshapen life, and it was Padma who had finally claimed her mother and maimed her. That claim was rightfully Madhav's, that was his prerogative—Madhav, whom his mother had always loved as unstintingly as he wanted to be loved. Even Shanta, who eroded her mother, acidlike, could have made that claim, for her mother had expected it all her life and it would have been no surprise. But, no, it was Padma, her youngest, least troublesome child, of whom everyone had said, Such a simple, innocent girl.

Now she understood why. But what was the point of this understanding? What did it change? What difference did it make? The calmness and dignity that everyone had always admired about her, Rukmini, now sometimes there were ripples across its surface. That's what thinking did. There was no dignity in it. It made you retrieve the dregs, all dirty and stained. It forced you to examine them. It made you gloat. Now she spent hours gloating; there was great pleasure in it. So much pleasure that sometimes she would spend the whole night awake and gloating. She remembered everything. Every word, every gesture, every tremor. Like Shanta she had become. Even Shanta had been shocked and written to her, "Amma, now stop thinking about it, it is over, it is over, Amma." But she couldn't stop.

There had been no speaking of it while He was alive. No speaking of what had happened in the Lucknow house, no speaking of what had happened years after that, no speaking of what had happened two weeks before He died. He had died—unforgiving, ignorant. He had died keeping His own secret. He had had to die before her youngest daughter could come home for the first time in thirteen years. "My child, you have come home at last," she had whispered to Padma, when Padma came home, putting her arms around her. When she had let Padma go, Padma had clung to Shanta, without once looking at Madhav and Ratna. Shanta, only Shanta. Thirteen years she had not seen her mother but she had sought comfort with her sister. It was all right. It was as it should be. She, Padma's mother, had forfeited that right. And for that, Padma had never forgiven her. She wept for her dead father, who had not spoken or written to her for thirteen years, but she had not forgiven her mother.

All three of them. All three of them unforgiving, unforgetting. Not towards Him. Towards her. Shanta, born unforgiving. For everything Shanta had blamed her, all her life for everything. Nothing she had done was right for Shanta. Always watching, waiting, comparing. Always accusing her mother of favouritism, of hypocrisy. Attributing meanings to each innocent act. Storing it all up in her mind to pull out when she fought. Never forgetting, never. Not to this day. If Shanta could remember the trauma of birth then for that also she would have blamed her mother.

Madhav. Ah, Madhav, he too. Accusing his mother of being unkind to his wife. Accusing her of interfering in his wife's affairs. Accusing her of causing his wife great unhappiness. In some ways it seemed that the loss of one's sons after marriage was more irrevocable than the loss of one's daughters. Daughters took on another name and belonged to another family, but their deepest feelings were rooted in their parental home; for them, as long as their parents lived, that was Home. But they who carried on the family name, your sons, they lost their hearts and their minds to their wives, their home now was where their wives were, they basked like cats in their wives' cancerous love. So be it. Even as Madhav accused her and even while she protested, she accepted the fact that he now felt this way.

But Madhav also blamed her for what had happened to Padma. "You are her mother, how could you have not seen it happening?" he asked after he came back from Shanta's house. But Padma was in Delhi, she in Bangalore, how could she have known? "You should have," he had said, "you should have. You're her mother." Blaming her for not instilling the right values in Padma, in giving her too much freedom. "You never said no to Padma for anything," he had said. "But child, what was there to say no to, Padma never asked for anything that was wrong, she never did anything that was incorrect." He had replied angrily, "Sometimes you should have said no anyway." All this and more he had said to her after coming back from Shanta's house after seeing Padma, but nothing about what had happened there.

About what had happened there, Shanta had told her. And for what had happened between Madhav and Padma, Shanta had blamed her. "You've spoilt Madhav completely, Amma," Shanta had said bitterly. "He thinks he is God." Rukmini had tried to make Shanta see the other side, she had tried to tell Shanta that all he wanted to do was help Padma in much the same way that Shanta herself was helping her sister. But Shanta had dismissed that angrily and said, "Amma, everything your precious son wants to do he wants to do for himself, not for anyone else. He wants everyone to think how noble and good he is." But he is good and noble, Shanta, she wanted to tell her but didn't. "Listen, child," she said, "tell Padma to write to him and say that she appreciates what he wanted to do for her, but that she cannot accept his offer, of course I understand why she cannot, if she says she is sorry, then he—" Shanta had given her a look of such fury then that her words faltered. "*Padma* apologize to *him,* are you *mad*?" No point. No point explaining to anyone. They all blamed her—Padma, Madhav, Shanta.

What did you think about when you were young? When had she ever been young? Married at fourteen, a mother at sixteen, three children, innumerable miscarriages, a womb that never stopped bleeding, a tumor within that grew and grew and grew and poisoned her body because the doctor said she was imagining the pain. Out with the tumor, out with the womb. All before she was thirty. And before she was forty, out the others came tumbling, her grandchildren, one after the other after the other, and Shanta, running to her mother for her confinement, and she, running to Ratna for her three confinements. But no running to Padma except that one time.

She had written to Padma all these years. She enquired about their health, told them to take care. She told Padma that she herself was well, that Appa was. Nothing else about Appa. What to write when so much could not be written? Padma's replies were also brief, she wrote about Mallika, but not about herself. After Rukmini read Padma's letters she would leave them out in case He wanted to read them too. But He never read them.

Please write to Mallika, Amma, Padma had said when Mallika was six. So she wrote. In English. She knew English. She had learnt it in the fourth form in school, she had done better in the English exams than anyone else in her class. Then after she got married there had been no need for it for some years till Shanta began going to school, then Madhav, then Padma. She heard them talk, she understood everything. She read their classroom notes and their homework, she answered their teacher's notes. She had always had a flair for languages. Hindi she could speak more fluently than her children, having picked it up during His postings in the North. When her children went away to college they wrote to her in Kannada, and she to them, but when the grandchildren came they wrote to her in English and she replied in English. Plain, ordinary letters, beginning and ending with love, nothing more, nothing less. Till she began writing to Mallika.

Mallika replied the day she got her letter. Mallika asked, Do you have books in your house, Ajji? She replied to Mallika. *So many books we have, so many. All for you. Children's books, your Ma's and Shantamama's and Madhav uncle's when they were children. Other books also. All the classics. For you only I will keep.* Mallika wrote back the same day. Such joy in Mallika's letter, such joy. The books had done it. She, Mallika's grandmother, had done it. For this spontaneous, heartfelt gesture, she had Mallika's devotion. She had not planned to get it this way, no. She had not planned to get it at all. All she had done was write to her and respond to her letter and speak to her of what lay in her own heart and tell her in all truth that what she so craved for would one day be all hers. She had not expected such an outpouring of gratitude or of love.

Once, long ago, He had seduced their children with books. Getting them from libraries, buying them from bookshops, spent more money on books for Shanta, Madhav and Padma than on clothes. Then His grand-children came. Not interested, any of them. How ironic that reading was a chore for Shanta's boys, not a pleasure. Madhav's two girls and the boy were hardly better. Her husband used to buy his grandchildren books too. They did not read them. So He stopped. She knew how disappointed He was. Shanta only read rubbish now. Madhav hardly had the time to read. Only Padma managed, in spite of everything. Shanta told her that. Once He had caught Shanta reading one of those trashy books. From the cover itself it was clear what the book was about. Not one of those usual ro-mances, it was by some American man, so it was worse. "Is this what you read these days?" He asked Shanta, shaking his head. She took the book from his hands, her face flushed, and said, "It's light reading, Appa." He had not said anything but she had seen the disgust on His face. Later that holiday Rukmini managed to get hold of Shanta's book when both she and He were out, and went through it swiftly. She found what she was looking for, several pages of it scattered all over the book, and read it with aston-ishment. Was this what they did, these Americans? Or was it what they wanted to do? She read on, skipping the superfluous parts. Chee. How could they? And even if they did, why describe it so graphically? She looked at the back of the book, where there was a picture of the author. Wasn't even handsome. Look at his eyes. Couldn't trust a man with eyes like that. That too—pink, plump cheeks.

*I only have one hobby, reading,* Mallika wrote. *What are your hobbies, Ajji?*

She wrote to Mallika, *Many hobbies I have. Cooking I like, gardening also. What else. Stitching, flower arrangements. About books you asked me. Now I have some time to read. Mostly Kannada books. Every day I pray to Saraswati. You know Saraswati, Goddess of Learning. May my Mallika get many degrees and become learned. That I pray for you. For learning and for wisdom. To Lakshmi also I pray, you know, Goddess of wealth and prosperity. Saraswati, what she gives you she does not take away. No, Lakshmi she has not taken away anything from us, I am not saying that. But Saraswati, what she gives, she gives for life. People when they see how Saraswati has blessed you, they will not be jealous, they will not say, Oh why is she so learned, why is she so intelligent. They will not say, I want that wisdom, I want that intelligence. No, they will never say that. For what Saraswati bestows on you, everyone else will give you only respect. Lakshmi, for what she is giving you, for that people will not give you respect. Only envy. That is why I pray to Saraswati for you. My prayers, they always come true. Saraswati, she has also blessed your Ma. May God bless you, my child.*

These were the kind of things she chatted to Mallika about. She could not write such things to her children. To them she wrote about what she did, whom she met, who had got married, had children, things like that. To her children she could not write her thoughts. They were not used to it. After she began writing to Mallika and getting letters in return she began talking to Mallika every night. Sometimes even when she did not get Mallika's letter because of some delay in the post she would write to her with her thoughts. Not only with her thoughts. She described her garden, the house, each room, what the rooms had held at the time Shanta and Padma were children. Mallika wanted to know. All that Mallika wanted to know and more. Not once did Mallika ask, When will you come to see me, Ajji?

He had to die before she could begin to think of seeing her grandchild. The dream that she had been nurturing so tenderly for twelve years began to shrivel as she thought of Mallika waiting for her, then asking, "Ajji, why didn't you come to us all these years?" What could she say? Did she start blaming Him to the granddaughter whom He had never seen and now never would? One did not blame the dead. What would she say? Would this granddaughter whom she had never seen shrink from her as she held her in her arms? Mallika had the right to do so; she, Mallika's grandmother, had forfeited the right to take her in her arms.

She, Rukmini, should have died instead of Him. She should have been the one her children and her husband should have been grieving for. She, Rukmini, should have died; it should have been her body lying in the house waiting to be cremated and He should have been the one alive, standing at the door as Padma came home, He should have been the one alive as Mallika asked him the question.

All these thoughts she had had in that house of death. All these thoughts she had nurtured as they went through the ceremonies. Instead of praying for Him she found herself praying that God would protect her from Mallika's rejection. From Padma's rejection. From Shanta's, from Madhav's. She found herself begging Him silently to give her the strength to bear it when it happened. And then, just in case, she prayed that it might not happen.

Prayers did come true. But what you wished for turned on you when it came true, that was what happened. It never came true the way you wanted it to. Shanta had said exactly that to her once. She now knew that Mallika's rejection would have been a smaller price to pay, that she would have paid it willingly if she had been able to foresee what would happen, that she would have then bargained with God and said to Him, All right, let Mallika reject me, and for that let her never know that part of the truth. All right, let Mallika never love me, let her hate me, but let not the truth confront her in such a grotesque way. Had she been able to foresee what was just waiting around the corner, she would have prayed, For this not to happen, I am willing to forfeit Mallika forever.

Two days before the eleventh-day ceremony Shanta came to her mother's room, where she sat on the chair next to the window. She sat on the bed next to her and said, "Amma, has Appa left you enough money?"

"Enough."

"Madhav is renting out our house." Shanta's throat moved convulsively, she burst out crying.

"My child," Rukmini said getting up from her chair and sitting on the bed next to Shanta, "my child." She caressed Shanta's hair.

Shanta wiped her nose with her saree palla. "Madhav was with some man downstairs talking about how much rent he should give, Madhav was telling him to write out the cheque to him, Amma."

She removed her hand from Shanta's head. "Yes," she said. "Yes."

Shanta looked at her fiercely, her eyes still streaming. "Amma, the cheque should be coming to you, not to Madhav, Appa's eleventh-day ceremony isn't over as yet and Madhav is getting rid of our house."

Rukmini was silent. Then she said, "The sooner these things are done the better. No point delaying."

She looked up. Padma was standing there. She did not know how long she had been listening. "Sit, child," she said. Padma sat on the other side of her.

"Amma," Padma said, "Appa has left the house to Madhav, not to you?"

She looked at her two daughters, sitting on either side of her. She said, "How does it matter to whom Appa has left the house. None of us will be living here now."

Padma said, "Ratna is already packing up all the things in this house. The books and everything, Amma."

She nodded. "Yes."

Padma said in a choking voice, "Amma, you promised Mallika all the books."

She felt a cold hand twist her insides.

Shanta said, "Amma, before Ratna decides she'll have all your jewellery too, you give us our share."

Padma said, "Shanta—"

Shanta made a sound and said, "Keep quiet, Padma, this is no time to mince matters. Amma, open your eyes, look at me." She got up and bolted the room. "Do it now, Amma," Shanta said. Padma went to the door and began unbolting it. In one swift movement Shanta followed her and dragged her back. "Proprieties. Proprieties my foot," Shanta said to Padma through clenched teeth.

"Shanta—" Padma said, a sob bursting out of her.

"Oh, keep quiet, will you. Keep your mouth shut." Shanta said. "*I* will open my mouth. Don't I always. *I* will do the dirty work. It is my job, isn't it. I am not doing it for you. I am doing it for Mallika, all right? When Mallika gets married she will get married with what is her share of jewellery from her grandmother's side. Open your cupboard, Amma. Do it now."

Like that Shanta had spoken, and her father not even ten days dead. Ruthless, completely ruthless. Standing before her mother, her hand outstretched, saying, "If you can't do it then I will do it, give me the keys, Amma." Then Shanta turned scornfully to Padma, saying, "Books, talking about books at a time like this, is something wrong with your head, Padma?"

And Padma looking at her mother, saying, "Amma, in your second letter you promised Mallika, she remembers everything, she—"

And Shanta shouting, "Keep quiet, will you, books, books, you think you're more principled than me because you remember her promise about books and you want to show your contempt for me by walking out of this room because I am talking not about what books have been left to whom but what jewellery, is that it? Listen to me, Padma Rao, don't you dare walk out on me again. Listen. You think the matter lies in the books or the jewellery? Padma Rao, the matter, it lies in the asking. You asked Amma for one thing. I asked Amma for the other. Both things were promised for Mallika. You remember one promise. I remember the other promise. Don't think your asking is more seemly than mine because it is books and not jewellery. Yes, Amma, what is it now? Why are you not answering me? Has Ratna packed away your jewellery and sarees too?"

She was just talking, Shanta. Just getting her anger and her sorrow out. From the time she was a child she had always been the worst at such times. Anger and sorrow always combined to throw the most appalling words out of her mouth. But it always ran its course and then she was all right. She would have been all right this time too if the bedroom door hadn't opened then. The door had been unbolted when Padma tried to walk out of the room and Shanta had dragged her back, Shanta had forgotten to bolt it again, and there Shanta was now, the cupboard keys held like a banner in her hands, saying, as the door opened and Ratna and Madhav walked in, "Has Ratna packed away your jewellery and sarees too?"

Madhav came to where his mother was sitting and put his arm around her shoulder. She closed her eyes. This is what she had wanted since her children came, just this, but none of them had given it to her, not even the demonstrative Shanta, this was what she had craved, the arms of her children around her. They probably thought she did not need it, they probably thought she had no needs. That was how children always thought about their mothers. Feeling Madhav's arms around her she wanted to weep, but did not. He said, "Amma, don't let Shanta wear you down. These things can wait." He looked up at Shanta. "You are ruthless, Shanta. The eleventh-day ceremony is not yet over and already you want to take possession of our widowed mother's jewellery?"

When it came to the crunch Shanta could never fight. The preliminaries were her forte, she was magnificent in the preliminaries. Rukmini did not look at Shanta's face but she knew how it must be, full of anger and speechless with frustration, soon she would begin to stutter and weep. Oh God, do not let Shanta weep, she prayed, let her keep her dignity in front of Ratna, let her.

"You are in no position to talk, Madhav. You've taken possession of the house. You've decided on the tenant and the rent and you're pocketing the money. I saw Ratna putting away Amma's jewellery and sarees in her suitcase without so much as asking Amma what she wants to do with it."

Padma.

No reconciliation, then. No forgiving, no burying the past. It could never be buried, the past, never. They will come together, my children, she had thought when He went away. When death comes it brings with it forgiveness. This house holds too many memories for my children, they will come here and be healed, they will leave the house and bury the past. That is what she had imagined, the fool that she was. For of course, there was no burying the past. From the time Padma and Madhav had met that terrible day in Shanta's house—which Shanta had described to her so graphically—from that time they had all changed, her children. They were no longer the children who had once loved and lived under this roof; this was not a meeting of the same sisters and brother. Too much water had flowed under the bridge.

Even then it need not have become what it did, even then. She could have sorted it out later, she could have explained to Shanta and Padma. All that was needed then was Shanta's silence. She, their mother, could have easily silenced Padma. But no, Shanta who did not know, had never known, when to speak and when not to, she turned to Padma and said harshly, "Enough, Padma, enough."

And Padma, who had already become pale in the wake of her words to Madhav, flushed a bright red and not even looking at Shanta, said to Madhav, "*I* know who is ruthless."

She had never seen Madhav's lips curl in that manner. He was looking at Padma and there was nothing but contempt in his gaze. Madhav said, "Oh, were you waiting for Appa to die so that he would leave you another house?"

Shanta said, "Keep quiet both of you, this is not the time to talk about these things."

Everyone talking very softly, very nastily, no loud voices, no shouting, only Ratna keeping very quiet, just the right expression, neither overdone nor underdone, just the right amount of innocence and bewilderment. Padma ignoring Shanta completely, saying, "My house came out of the money and jewellery kept aside for my wedding, and out of the money Amma got from her house—one third, one third, one third—that is what all of us got, I got nothing more, nothing less." Then adding, "My house equals what was spent for your wedding." And as if that were not enough, saying, "And *Shanta and I* are not taking what has been promised to you."

Ratna looking at Shanta, her eyes full of bewilderment, saying, "Shanta,

I packed away Amma's things because she is coming to live with us now."

Then Madhav saying, "Keep quiet, Ratna. You do not owe an explanation to my sisters." Ratna shaking her head, her eyes full of tears, Shanta saying nothing, just looking at her mother.

Then Padma saying, very clearly, "*You* owe us an explanation, Madhav. Amma told Shanta she was dividing her jewellery into three parts. She will never wear any of it now. How can you and your wife empty out Amma's cupboards without asking her as you did yesterday? That is for Amma to do."

Madhav's expression was venomous. Ratna, tears running down her cheeks, said, "What was there to ask, Padma, everything I was packing, so Amma's things I also packed."

Padma said, "Unpack then. Let Amma divide what has to be divided before she shifts to your house. She promised Shanta that this will be done."

They had changed. Yes, they had changed. It was Shanta who felt this way, not Padma, who was speaking Shanta's thoughts. It was Padma to whom these things had never made a difference, it had always made a difference to Shanta. No, no, it still did not make a difference to Padma. Padma was not fighting for the jewels, she was fighting for other things, the jewels were incidental. Not that it mattered, what did motives count for, what should never have been said had been said, and at a time such as this. There was Padma looking steadily at Ratna, there was Shanta, very quiet, her whole body tense, Ratna gazing innocently at all of them, Madhav looking at his sisters, his eyes narrow.

So in the end it was she, their mother, who had to say it, in the end it was she who had to live with it. That was how it had always been, how could she have ever thought that His death would change it. What you began doing because you knew the Other Person wanted it soon became the pattern of your daily deeds, your daily admonitions, you could never escape it. It was the Other Person, the one who expected it to be done but did not say Do it, who escaped. Always He had said to her, "Shanta must dress more moderately." When He had seen Shanta in her first sleeveless blouse He had said to Shanta's mother, a look of disgust on his face, "What is she wearing?" Not to Shanta, but to her. So she did what had to be done. When it came to Padma's turn He said nothing. He didn't even notice, that much change those few years had wrought in Him. "I don't want Shanta cycling around like those Other Girls," He had told Shanta's mother. And she, who had been quite charmed by the sight of those Other Girls Cycling, had had to tell Shanta that a cycle was quite out of the question.

So in the end it was she, their mother, who had to say it. "Ratna is keeping my things safely for me. Do not misunderstand simple things."

Shanta's body jerked very slightly. Then Padma, looking as though she had been slapped, said, "Amma, you promised—"

Then Madhav's voice, very loud, saying, "My mother has given you both enough." He said, looking at Shanta, "Sarees and jewellery to last you a lifetime," then to Padma, "A house. And you come here asking for more. Amma has promised Shanta. Don't talk to me of promises. Are you going to look after our mother? Are you going to feed her and pay her hospital bills on your pittance of a salary when you don't have enough to marry off your daughter and come demanding jewellery for your daughter from our widowed mother? Or is my brother-in-law going to look after our mother?"

No. No no. Madhav. Madhav. Why did you speak of Padma's child, son? All over now, no forgiveness, no forgetting, never never never. She had been watching Padma. She had known Padma could not keep it up, did not want to keep it up. She could see the expression on Padma's face as she said all those things in that first flush of anger against Madhav in defence of her beloved sister, whom Madhav had wronged. Already that fire was dying when Madhav fanned it. Now it did not surprise her when Padma's eyes became very bright and she said, "You will not be paying for Amma's upkeep or her hospital bills. The rent you get from Amma's house, which should have gone to Amma, but is now being sent to you in your name, that will be paying for Amma's upkeep and her hospital bills."

Yes, she had truly lost Padma. Hard and cruel, her Padma. Was she like this with others too? Would she have said all this if Madhav had not said what he did? Not that it mattered. Not that thinking about any of these things mattered. Thinking changed nothing. Madhav said, "So be it. It is my house now. Every day that you sleep and eat here, you are sleeping and eating in my house."

A long silence. The clock ticking. Downstairs the sound of dishes being washed. The morning sun streaming into the room and over the bed. "As for all this talk about jewellery, what Amma is supposed to have told you is not what she told Ratna." Her daughters both looking at their mother. Ratna wiping her eyes, whispering, "I don't want anything, Madhav, really,

I don't." Madhav saying firmly, "Nonsense, Amma is a woman who keeps her word. If she has promised you her jewellery then she will keep that promise." Shanta and Padma exchanging a swift glance, laden with realization, then looking at their mother. No compassion in their eyes, not one bit. Not even in Shanta's. I did not promise her, she wanted to say but could not. It is them I have to live with. Not you. Till the day I die. Shanta left the room, followed by Madhav and Ratna.

Then Padma slowly said, "Amma, this letter is addressed to me," and picked up the letter on the bedside table. Sumi's letter. Rukmini cursed herself. She had meant to destroy it. She was not one for reading other people's letters. The first time this was and the last. She had to protect Mallika. It had not been gummed properly, she had been able to open it, and after reading the letter, had gummed it again and closed it. Now Padma was looking at the envelope, turning it, saying, softly, "Oh, Sumi," sitting down on the bed, opening the letter and beginning to read it. She continued sitting on the bed, her hand smoothing the warm bedcover on which the sun lay. She, Rukmini, knew what the letter said.

*Padma, I often wondered why you never wrote to me. Then I bumped into Madhav one day (did he tell you?) and he told me what had happened to you. Now I understand why you did not write. When Madhav told me that your husband died so soon after you got married, I was devastated. I never knew, Padma. And you have Karan's child now. I do not know how to write condolence letters. All I can say is that I don't know how you recovered, or what you must have gone through.*

*I meant to write to you again (you must have got my first few letters) but then I was caught up with my own marital problems, the separation, getting a job, etc. etc. Those days I used to think that I wanted someone to love me the way Karan loved you. I wanted to love someone the way you loved him. When my parents found this boy and suggested marriage, I proceeded to fall in love with him. I told him my secrets, I showed him my diaries. I believed that love meant baring your soul so I bared everything. Later, he used it all against me. He laughed about the things I had confided in him. He quoted things I'd written in my diaries and flung them at me. It's a long story—this isn't all. One day I'll tell you the rest. But after two years I left him. It took another four years for the separation to come through. He did not want one and created endless trouble. Of course, no one supported me except my* brother, who helped me financially and helped me get the job. Everyone said how intolerant I was and how selfish and how badly I had treated my husband, a man from such a good family with such a good job, who did not drink or smoke or beat me.

I have been thinking of you very much of late, it has all been coming back to me, our years together—you, Karan, all that we had shared. I remember so vividly saying goodbye to you at the station and how quiet Karan was as we walked back to college. Then he began talking to me about you. I remember how surprised I was, because it was so unlike him to talk like that. I think he was very upset, and you had left and I was there—so it all came out.

He told me about the argument you both had had and how upset he was with himself for reacting as he had with you. He said he felt culpable for allowing you to get into a situation where you had to deceive your parents and break the hostel rules, and for being such a willing party to it himself. He said he always saw the truth of what you said much after you spoke it, and it wasn't ever easy for him to admit it to you because with you both the argument invariably seemed to become more important than what you were arguing about. He said you made it difficult for him to admit anything. He said how young and innocent and unthinking you were and how he should have been the one who held back, and yet how it was your lack of inhibition that drew him to you, the fact that you never held back, either where he was concerned or where anything else was. He kept saying that he should have known better than to get you into such a situation because he felt you were going against your grain by hiding this from others. He was talking as if he was thirty-four, not twenty-four! I told him you knew perfectly well what you were doing and not to brood about it any more, that you would be married soon and done with all the deception—if that indeed was what he wanted to call it. He said he did not want to call it that. He said nothing had meant so much to him as the years that he had shared with you. He said it was difficult telling you all these things because you always imagined that you regretted what you both had started, when in fact it was not what you did that he regretted but the fact that it all had to be so secretive, that you were not meant to live life hiding things, that other women could do it and did do it, but not you. He said that if he had not known you he would never have known the magic of laughter or wonder or faith. (You understand, don't you, why I was so determined to fall in love.) You should have seen his face. It was full of you.

*Then he began to laugh. He said it was foolish of him to continue in this strain when it was just a question of time before you both got married, that thank God he did not have to wait anymore, he was sick of waiting, that now he had to take your advice and be happy instead of complicating everything by anticipating problems, that at this point in his life he wanted nothing else, absolutely nothing, and that he didn't understand why he felt so sad.*

*He must have had some premonition that your time together was very short. Please write. Your mother will probably redirect this letter to you, wherever you are. With my love, Sumi.*

The shock and anguish on Padma's face. Ah, she, Padma's mother, understood. She also knew what Padma did not understand. She could not tell Padma. She and Shanta had decided there was no point telling her. No point at all.

She sat next to Padma and held her. After some time Padma said, "Amma, why didn't you give me the letter?"

"I forgot, my child. It came when Appa took ill." Now what to do. Padma would meet Sumi. Before she did, Padma had to be told. She would have to talk to Shanta first. Shanta knew everything. A thirty-page letter she had written to Shanta two weeks ago. Shanta would tell her what to do now and how to do it. Her brain wasn't functioning. She would talk to Shanta. After breakfast the next morning. She was too tired now, too tired.

No one talked to anyone the next morning. First she, Madhav and Ratna ate breakfast. Then Shanta and Padma. All very silently, no talking at all. Then, loudly, the doorbell ringing. Padma opening the door and there she was, Sumi.

Like a premonition it was when she saw Sumi over Padma's shoulder. As if a gust of wind had suddenly taken root and swept into the room, flattening her into her chair. Then it was gone and there was Sumi, kneeling next to her chair, murmuring condolences. Later she couldn't remember a thing of what had been said. She remembered sitting in her chair while Sumi and Padma hugged each other for a long time. Then when she next looked they were no longer in the room. She sat up, her hands cold, and Shanta from opposite her said, "They have gone inside, Amma." So they sat there, she and Shanta, waiting for Padma and Sumi to come out.

And yet, she recalled later, there had been no need for all that fear,

Sumi's presence with all of them after all these years would not have changed anything. It was just their knowledge, that was all, that so charged the room with fear. How were they to know when Sumi came that she came as a messenger? How were they to know that the grotesque fantasy had already realized itself in exactly the fashion that they had each fantasized? Except that fate had been crueller than they could have imagined, for neither Padma nor Shanta were there when it happened to Mallika. So much for trying to protect one's child, one's children.

Padma and Sumi came out after one hour and fifteen minutes. Rukmini looked at Padma's face first; she had been crying. Swiftly her eyes went to Sumi. She too. So. Padma had told Sumi about Karan. It was all right, Sumi had a right to know. As for the other thing, the only thing to be done was for her to tell Sumi. How foolish of her not to have thought of it before. She and Shanta had let it become a monster. They would explain everything to Sumi, and say to her, You see, this is our fear, so now you know and now you will not let it happen. She would say, Once we saw you at a shop, Sumi, and it was completely irrational, but we actually hid from you. We knew you would ask about Padma, for her address. And how not to give it to you? Sumi would nod and say, I understand, nothing of what you fear will happen, I will see to that. How simple it was now. Only one thing more she would have to say, What I have told you, do not tell Padma, ever.

Sumi was taking leave of all of them, then she was telling Padma, "I'll come tomorrow and take you home in the morning, will eleven o'clock be all right?" and Padma nodding and Sumi saying, "And I'll drop you back after tea," and she, Rukmini, opened her mouth to say, Sumi, something I have to tell you before you leave, and Sumi smiled and said, "I forgot to tell you, my brother is in Delhi these days. He wrote to me last week and said he had got your address from Madhav and that he would look you up."

A moan came out of Shanta's throat and Sumi looked at her. Padma was leaning against the sofa, terror on her face. "Padma?" Sumi said. "Shanta?" Shanta's face had blanched. Across the room Padma's face began to crumple. She knows, her mother thought, she knows, oh my child, my precious child, this too you kept to yourself. "Amma," Padma said and it came out like a wail as her body began to shudder, but in the sound was her own recognition of her mother's knowledge.

Three times the doorbell rang. Madhav was there, opening it, looking over his shoulder at the tableau behind him, then turning to take the telegram and signing for it. Then there was Padma, walking to Madhav as Madhav opened it, and Madhav reading it and not showing it to Padma, putting his arm around her and saying, "Nothing to worry about, I will book you a flight to Delhi, you'll reach today itself, it's all right, it's all right," and then he had his other arm around her, holding her up. And she, their mother, took the telegram from him and read, *Mallika very ill stop come immediately stop Madhu.*

If only Narayana were there. But he had had to go back and the boys were with his parents.

She couldn't remember when Sumi left. She remembered sitting on the bed in Padma's room as Padma packed, saying to her, "Padma, my child, tell her the truth, only the truth." Padma nodding, packing in a frenzied fashion. Then going to Shanta's room, where Madhav was sitting next to her on the bed, watching her drink a glass of tea (he made it himself, she thought tenderly, my son, my child), and saying to her, "You also go with Padma." And Shanta looking up at her, tears streaming down her face, and sobbing, "What do you mean, You also go, I *am* going. She's as much *my* child." Madhav making soothing noises, patting Shanta's shoulders, saying, "It is all right, Shantacca, it is all right, now you pack up, the flight leaves this afternoon." Then patting Shanta again and adding, "If you want me or Amma to come to Delhi, then write and tell us, we will be there."

Her son. Her gem. Not one question had he asked. His sister's child was very ill, nothing else mattered at that point, nothing. Paid the money for two tickets to Delhi for his sisters, arranged for a colleague to pick them up at the Delhi airport and take them home. And Shanta, still unforgiving of what her mother had said so innocently, saying, "Telling me to go to Delhi, I won't forget that, telling me to go to Delhi, did you tell Padma to go to Delhi?"

Now the guillotine had fallen. Now there was no more hiding the whole story. Only Shanta and she knew. But the end of the story, the one that neither she nor Shanta had been able to gloat about, that had made it impossible for them to tell Padma. Let it be, Amma, Shanta had written to her, there is no need for Padma to know. She will not be able to take it. I know Padma, in some part of her there has always been hope.

But they had both thought, fools that they were, that Padma hadn't known about the photograph. And she, Padma, her poor, burdened child, had thought that Shanta hadn't known. They hiding their knowledge from Padma, Padma hiding it from them, Mallika hiding it from everyone, and all of them hiding their knowledge of Mallika's secret from her.

Ah, secrets. What to keep from whom. Protecting, hiding, pretending. Knowledge, what a tenuous thing it was. Stories growing, growing, one here, another there. None of them growing in isolation, each growing out of something the other had touched, each touching something else. Somewhere perhaps, in the larger picture, each had its place, but in this life at least they would never know what that larger picture was or why it had to be there. How blithely the young Madhav would talk with his bright and voluble friends about Life and Death and the randomness of things. How casually he and his friends had spoken about the God who didn't exist, these young men who hardly knew what life was. Everything was an accident, they used to declare, Life was an accident. There was no meaning in life said these young men who had everything. And Padma, listening, bright-eyed, enthralled.

Talk. A luxury. Meant nothing. Life taught you otherwise. Her Madhav was the believer now, her Madhav was the one who prayed every morning and every evening, who made regular pilgrimages to all the religious places. Shanta's daily rituals were nothing compared to his. Shanta's knowledge of the religious texts was like her reading of those film magazines—she knew all the gossip and all the intricacies of all the relationships. When she told Mallika the stories of the Ramayana and the Mahabharata, all they remained were stories. But Madhav, he knew what lay beyond them. He knew the philosophy, he knew the deep moral dilemmas. And Padma, who never prayed, who didn't have a single picture of the Gods in her house? It indicated a dependence on herself for such things, and there was great danger in that. Padma would break.

She hadn't broken yet. But it was there, the crack, deep within her, all the way across her.

An hour before they left for the airport she and Shanta sat down with Padma in her bedroom. She said to Padma, "Child, it is not the right time to tell you. But Mallika must know the truth now. And if I do not tell you what I know, then you will not be able to tell Mallika the truth. Do not tremble like that. There. There. Mallika will be all right. Your friends are taking good care of her. She cannot be in better hands. She will be all right. Remember, children who are loved the way you and Shanta have loved

Mallika, such children have great resilience. There. There. Mallika will be all right. Now listen, my child. Listen."


As a young girl she had once heard with wonder about some desert flowers which bloom just once in a lifetime, then die. She had thought then, There can be no satisfaction greater than this, to wait and see it bloom that one time; for a thing like this I could wait forever.

Like that she had been waiting for Him. She had been patient. She had known it was only a question of time. Full circle. It had to come full circle. Most things in life did not. More the pity. But this, this would. The knowledge was there in her, as certain as her heartbeat.

Thirteen years she had waited. That day, she had been tending the garden after breakfast, breaking off the dead leaves, gazing at the roses. He had gone off, swinging his walking stick, to his brother's house a mile away. "Do not get worried if I am not back for lunch," He had told her. That meant He would not be back for lunch. It had been a particularly beautiful day, the blue of the sky, and the green of her garden all scrubbed and tender, and against this canvas, her roses—yellow, pink, white and red. She heard the gate opening and turned, thinking, the postman is early today. But it was another man in his thirties, tall and dark but with North Indian features. He closed the gate, and turning, folded his hands and asked, "Mrs. Rao?"

She nodded, looking up at his face, his thick, straight hair cut very short, his almost thin upper lip with the fuller lower lip, his unexpectedly gentle eyes, the wide shoulders beneath the blue pin-striped shirt. "Are you," he paused, "Padma's . . . mother?"

She nodded again. She could hear a ringing in her ears, briefly. She closed her eyes. She opened them. He was bending down slightly, saying something, she heard him say his name, " . . . Karan . . ."

He had come. Thirteen years it had taken him.

"Come," she said. "Let us go inside." Thirteen years. A few years ago she had thought the time was ripe for his coming. In fact, she had been sure of it. A miscalculation.

In the room she walked to the mantelpiece and put the picture face-down on it. Then she turned to him, gestured to him to sit, sat opposite him. "Tea, coffee, what will you have?" she asked after they sat.

He shook his head, his eyes beyond her where the photographs of her children were framed, taken when they were children—laughing Shanta, solemn Madhav, radiant Padma. I will say nothing, she thought, let him ask, I will make nothing easy.

"Some water?" she asked.

He looked at her then as though he hadn't heard her, shook his head, then said, "Yes. Thank you."

She called the servant to get some water. No, he wasn't as dark as she had first thought. But it was as if some inner light had been extinguished, giving the impression that he was darker than he was. The servant got the water and he rapidly drank half a glass. He placed the glass on the side table. He looked at her. She waited, her hands folded on her lap. Outside she could hear the gardener talking to the servant, inside the sun streamed in through the windows and from the kitchen came the faint clatter of dishes being washed.

He said something. She blinked. He said again, "Is Padma in . . . is . . . she . . . all right?"

Fury twisted her insides. She asked, "Who are you?" It surprised her how gentle her voice sounded, how soft.

Uncertainly he said, "I thought . . . I'm sorry . . ." She continued looking at him. He said, "Padma and I . . ." he stopped and began again. "We . . . she must have told you that we . . . knew each other in college." His eyes did not leave her face. "About . . . thirteen years ago you had come to my parents' house in Lucknow . . . ?"

She didn't reply. In what a cultured, deep voice he spoke his Hindi. What would he think of her heavily accented Hindi? Not that it mattered. It was an intelligent face, a sensitive face. She hadn't expected it even though Padma had told her mother how much he read, how informed he was. Padma had told her, but what she actually meant to say was, This is not the kind of man who would . . .

Who would what? Who would betray me? Had she meant to say, Amma, a man of such intellect does not have double standards. There is no wrong in what we have done because we love each other. He is not like other men in this. Ah, yes, this is what her foolish daughter had wanted her mother to glean from her talk about this man who was well read and well informed.

Connections, connections, her daughters were forever making connections. Connections between thought and action and speech, connections between intellect and action, connections between marriage and love and the so-called act of love, which had nothing to do with love. This too they attributed significance to. But it was insignificant, irrelevant. The problem was that they associated the act with love. But the act was as far removed from love as it was from the child who was the result of the act. What love did the act express? What love did the act evoke? What did it partake of tenderness? What did she have to do with it? For Him it was a release, as imperative as an itch that must be scratched. She was the means of assuaging that itch.

Once she had overheard Shanta using the phrase *making love* when she was talking to Padma, God knows in what context. It always amused her how Shanta spoke to Padma in English when she didn't want her mother to understand, when Shanta knew fully well that her mother knew English. Like an ostrich she was, Shanta. Especially when Shanta and Padma were talking about film actors and actresses and who was doing it with whom and who had got pregnant and had an abortion and all that . . . she never spoke in Kannada but in hushed English. She, their mother, knew everything. What did her daughters think she was? After all she spoke to her grandchildren only in English, had done so ever since they started going to school. She also read English magazines. She knew very well what young people were up to these days and what young people thought love was. *Making love.* What a meaningless phrase. She had mulled over it for a long time, she had spent many nights thinking about it. She quite enjoyed it actually, all this thinking, though it was quite useless, a complete waste of time. Making love . . . no, no. *Making love* implied a closeness, both emotional and physical, that went before and beyond the act. Now He, He had in all those years never touched her except at such times as when He wanted It. Never had she felt more distant from Him than at such times. Touching, that was the wrong word, there was no touching about it; a brief, hard grip, that was all. Here too, she was the receptacle.

The act had nothing to do with love. It was a thing apart. That man Shakespeare, He had got it all wrong. That was to be expected; He was only a man. She knew the things He said, she had heard her husband and her children and now she was hearing her grandchildren too. Not that they ever talked to her about That Man Shakespeare, but they talked around her. Plenty she had picked up from that, ah, plenty, what would they know. They thought all her ears heard when she cooked and chopped and made pickle was the sound of the knife or the pressure cooker. Her hands were quite independent of her eyes and her ears. Especially her ears. Something That Man, whoever he was, had said about love being a woman's whole existence. If He had meant *love* in a larger sense, then there was some truth in it. But He had meant *love* in its narrow, romantic sense, the foolish man, he had meant *love* in the way it existed in one's imagination. How could He know any better than any of Them that Her existence was something quite different. Something about love being a thing apart for a man. No, no. The thing apart was not the love, it was the other thing. He had loved her. She knew it as surely as she knew the grass was green. Without her He would have been a man adrift. He himself had never known how adrift. If she had died before Him, then He would have known. But he had died without that realization. That realization also He had denied her.

For thirteen years she had dreamt that this man whom Padma loved would sit before her in her house and he was, his gaze was not guilt-stricken but intent, not remorseful but watchful. Time, it was a question of time. Four hours at least for Him to come back from His brother's house, time enough for her to change the expression of this man, change his expression to what it should be, four hours would suffice, time enough to do it slowly, very slowly, twist his features to her dictates.

"Why have you come here?" she asked. She hadn't meant to ask. He was the one who had come to her to ask. But it was out. No more, she would say no more. He had to do the asking, not she. That was why He was here. "It has taken you a long time to come," she said. His eyes on her face were very still. Like Shanta she was behaving, out it came, out, before she could stop it, like Shanta. Quiet, Rukmini, quiet, shut your mouth, Rukmini, thirteen years you have been patient. "Who told you finally?"

No longer still, his eyes. Like a patient He was, now. One who was finally hearing what his mind had shut itself to, His eyes on the doctor, his saviour, His eyes saying, Say what you have to say, but say it with compassion, with kindness, help me bear it. Now she saw it in his eyes and an ecstasy of triumph swept and held her quiet body.

He got up and gave her a piece of paper and went back to his chair. *Horoscope of Miss Padma Rao,* she read, her hands steady. This she had forgotten about completely. Now she remembered. She had left it on the table.

"My sister," he said quietly.

"Your youngest sister," she said.

"She told me that you and your daughter Shanta had come to our house thirteen years ago."

"Yes."

"About . . . about Padma?"

"Yes."

"I— She— I did not know. That you had come."

He was telling her what she already knew. He thought this would satisfy her did he. He would find out. "Is that all she said to you, your youngest sister?"

"She said all kinds of things. Her imagination . . . she . . . one cannot believe all she says, she is disturbed. Something happened to her, it—that is another story." His eyes were still pleading. Let him wait, let him wait. What would his wait be in comparison with hers?

"What did your sister tell you?"

For some time he did not say anything. "She told me she heard raised voices, that there was . . . anger."

"That is all?"

"Something about curses—"

He stopped as he saw her smile. She couldn't stop smiling. "Did she tell you what we said?" she asked gently. He said nothing, sitting still in his chair, looking at her. She said, "First Shanta cursed your family. She said, *May your son's wife be forever barren. May your two daughters be forever barren. May your house be forever empty of the laughter of grandchildren. May the marriages of your son and your two daughters be as barren as their wombs. May all my sister's suffering come back to you through your children.*"

No expression on his face. It would come. If not for this, then for the other. Time enough to bring it back.

"Then it was my turn. I said to your mother, *I add my curse to hers. To her curse I add, you will always have hope, from one year to the next you will have hope. It will always come to nought. From year to year the wombs of your children will carry not life but death.* That is what I said."

Now he was looking at her the way a person looks at a snake curled in the corner of a room. Still. Unblinking. Fascinated and repulsed. She said, "Then your youngest sister came to the room. I told your mother, *Your third daughter, she also. To her also it will happen.* She was looking at me, your youngest sister. What did she know. Nothing. An innocent she was, untainted, ignorant. It is the innocent who must suffer the most. Like my youngest daughter. It is the blood of the innocent, no other, that must be spilled. I told your sister, *Child, one day you will understand.* I told her, *Child, I will wait for that time to come.*"

He said nothing. She had not expected him to say anything. "Now the time has come," she said simply.

His expression had changed now, it was no longer the one that had held her gaze as she sat chanting that old chant. This expression was familiar. Withdrawal. Faint but unmistakable. It was the expression she had seen on many men when women talked of things they did not understand. She had seen it when men were forced to listen to their wives when their wives did not come to the point. Come to the point, Narayana would say to Shanta. Keep to the subject, her brother-in-law would say to her sister-in-law. The stage after the withdrawal was the stage when disgust surfaced. She would not let it come to that. Careful. She would be very careful. Was there this withdrawal on his face when His youngest sister talked to him? No, no, not for her, no withdrawal for his sister. To her, his sister, He would have said, with kindness, You are an educated woman, why are you talking such nonsense about curses?

His eyes had not moved from her face. She sat back in her chair and waited. She could do with him what she wished. What he wanted her to tell him she would not tell him till the end. Then, in the end, he would get to know what he wanted to know and more. Much, much more. There would be no withdrawal on his face for her then. Ah no, ah no.

They must have sat for at least five minutes like that, He looking at her, she at him. Good thing it wasn't Shanta here. Shanta would have raved and ranted. She would have told him everything without getting anything out of him. So hysterically would she have accused him that he would have left the house feeling free of guilt and responsibility. He would have walked out the door sure that all they said, these overwrought women—his mother and his sisters, Padma's mother and her sister—was mere hysteria. Then, instead of tunnelling inwards to find the answers that lay in His own cursed soul, he would have burrowed his way outwards, found no answers, blamed them. That was what Shanta would have done to Him. She had done it with Narayana, with Madhav, she was doing it with her sons. They no longer heard what she said, Vikram and Varun, they were immune to her chantings.

"My mother and sisters did not tell me you had come with a proposal, because when you came I was already married."

This was how men told such stories. The bare essentials, that was all. The bare essentials he was giving her. He thought that she would be satisfied with that, did he? She would give him the flesh, the blood. But later. In the meantime she could imagine what had been said, and how. His mother, her face full of compassion, would have said to him, Beta, how could we tell you? Of what use would it have been—you were already married. Yes, it is true, the mother would have said, they came, this mother and daughter. We told them you were already married. Ram, Ram, you should have heard them. Shouting and cursing. In our house. Behaving like Punjabis, not Madrasis.

She watched his eyes slowly glaze. It wasn't pain, it was something more, something held back for years, surfacing now. She watched it with interest, the slow darkening of those brown eyes, the almost imperceptible flare of those fine nostrils . . . he was still looking at her face but his thoughts were beyond it now. "When Padma and I said goodbye and I went home," he said, "I was going home to tell my family about her."

It was as if there were no house, no sunlight, nothing, all she saw now was Him, sitting before her, and herself. Yes, she saw herself as if she were watching a picture, a close-up, sitting still, her eyes on his face, nothing between them, no table with flowers, no carpet, nothing behind them, no walls, no pictures, and no sound except that of his low voice and her soft breathing. "When I reached home, I found the house full of people, dressed as if for a marriage." Abruptly he stopped. Just before the words came out of his mouth she knew, and they uttered it together like a chant, her words curving softly against his:

"Your marriage."

"My marriage."

This time it was a very long time before he spoke.

"It was to take place in four hours. All my relatives were there. Hers also. The shamyana had been put up next door. They told me to get dressed—"

"Next door?"

His eyes focussed briefly on her face as though he had forgotten he was speaking to her. He said, "They were our neighbours. Family friends for years. They had a son and a daughter, and my mother and sisters sometimes used to tease me saying how nice it would be if she and I were to marry one day. I thought it was all a joke. I had hardly spoken to her. We must have met during family occasions a few times. It seems I was wrong. It seems that there was an understanding that we would get married. I did not know."

He loves his mother dearly, Padma had told her that night before they left for Lucknow. What had Padma meant to convey by that? That he was a man capable of great love? Which man didn't love his mother dearly? What had that to do with the quality of the love they bore their wives or their . . . what was the word . . . lovers? Was that what Padma had been to him, his lover? His whore? His beloved mother had called Padma that. Randi. Whore. Ah yes, the whore's mother had heard, the whore's sister had heard, the whore's mother and sister had invoked retribution. Retribution had come. He told me all about his family, Padma had told her, they're very closeknit, very devoted to each other. His mother, Amma, she has sacrificed her whole life for her children, He told me she lives for them and for nothing else. Foolish girl, foolish Padma. Talking as if what his mother was and what his mother did were any different from what they all were, what they all did. Talking as if the children's devotion to her was any different from the devotion of all children to their parents. His mother has had a very difficult time, Amma, Padma had said, especially when they were children—they didn't have much money or anything, but she was the one who managed and kept the family together . . . such a strong woman, Amma. She had listened to her daughter speak with awe of this mother of the man she loved, her daughter who was expecting this man's child, and she had almost laughed. No money . . . managing . . . keeping the family together . . . foolish Padma, her foolish child, seeing it as a singular, illuminating example.

And what had she meant to convey to her mother by this? That he spoke tenderly of this woman who was his mother, that he was aware of her tribulations and so he was an understanding and sensitive man? That he was a family-oriented man? That he had shared all this with her because he loved her? That it was such a man, who belonged to such a loving family, who wanted her?

But the mother had not wanted Padma. She, Padma's mother, could surmise the rest. "Your mother did not tell you about the marriage."

"She wrote to me. I never got the letter."

Perfect. Diabolic.

"In the letter she wrote and said that now that I had got into the civil services the time was right to get married. She never got my answer, naturally. So she assumed that it was all right. I was never the best of correspondents. She went ahead with all the arrangements. She sent me a telegram a couple of weeks before I went home, asking me to immediately confirm by which train I was coming. I wondered . . . briefly . . . why a telegram? But . . . I didn't give it much thought . . . I sent her a wire with the details of my arrival."

A long silence.

"I told her, I cannot get married. My mother collapsed. She has always had a weak heart. The doctor had to be called. My sisters took me to another room and said that I would not only bring dishonour to my family but to the girl's family. They said everyone had come—all her relatives, all ours, all their friends, all ours. About five hundred people were expected for the ceremony that night." He stopped, she saw his throat move. "I refused. My mother called me to her room. The doctor was there too. He said she had suffered a great shock and that if she suffered another, it would be a serious matter. Then my mother said she would never force me into a marriage I didn't want. But she begged me not to leave Lucknow because she felt she would die, and she wanted me by her side. After saying that she collapsed."

"And so you got married."

She understood now. Not only why he had done what he had done, but the other—the absence of disillusionment with his mother and sisters. That day as she and Shanta stood in the Lucknow house, she had known that this man, whom Padma loved, would never be told of their visit. But she had also known that her words and Shanta's would fulfill themselves, that he would then come to her, that she would then hear in his voice and see in his eyes his knowledge of his mother's and sisters' betrayal, just as she had seen in Padma's, her knowledge, finally, of his betrayal. But it was absent. So this too she now held in her hand, this too she would watch dawning in his eyes. She hadn't expected this. It was a bonus. She would tell him, she would watch realization streak across his face like the early dawn. Like a leaking drain she would spill the truth of his mother's part in it, watch the slow contamination of unsullied waters. It was a bonus. This then had not been left for her to imagine. This then would be there for her to see. And then, there would be more.

They had suffered, his mother and his sisters, as she had meant them to suffer. But there was more of it for them. For, like a hunchback, he would carry his knowledge back to them. Then they would know that they had lost him forever. That would finish his mother. No, she would not die, such women always lived long. But she would be finished, finished. That scenario she, Rukmini, would have to imagine. In imagining it there would be pleasure to last her for years and years. In imagining it there would be pleasure to last her for the rest of her life.

"I went through it. My mother was very ill. She was a little better when it was time for me to go to Delhi for the training. I had no leave during the training period, except for weekends and holidays. I needed at least four days' leave in order to go to Bangalore."

"For what."

"To tell Padma."

"Tell her what."

"To explain. That's why I did not write. Nothing could be said in a letter."

"You would tell her, and after that?"

No answer. The same expression on his face as the one she had seen on Padma's thirteen years ago. Lovingly, her eyes lingered on it.

His turn to suffer now. Ah, yes, he *thought* he suffered, like the Hero of those romantic books and films against whom fate had played a nasty trick. For even now, that was how he perceived himself, as one wronged by fate. The biggest thing he still did not know, as she had always known he would not. Always she had known that this revelation was hers to unfold. She would keep it for the last. That is what Shanta used to do, keep her favourite sweet for the last, so that she could savour it, this best part, right at the end. But in this too Shanta did not succeed, because in the end she was too full to eat it. One would have thought that it would teach her a lesson, but no, every time she would do it again, and there it would lie every time, her favourite Mysore paak, on the plate, uneaten. In such desires too she and Shanta were alike. But she, Shanta's mother, knew what Shanta did not—how to savour not just the best part but the others too, and yet not be too full for that last, most delectable piece. Careful. She had to be careful. She had to make a concentrated effort not to behave like Shanta. She had to make sure that he did not withdraw again. Not for her.

He was saying something. Her eyes focussed on him. He was saying, "Is Padma happy now?"

She looked at him blankly. His face was so full of what she had once seen on Padma's that if he had been anyone else she would have looked away. "Happy?" she repeated.

There was despair on his face. "I'm sorry," he said, "I should not ask. I will not ask." Despair. Already? He asked, "When did she hear about my marriage?"

"The day we came to your house. She had come too."

His face jerked.

"No, she was not with us. She was at the railway guest house." She waited. No, no, she would not ask. Let him do the asking. The answers she wanted would come to her.

He was frowning a little. He said, "You came to our house . . . do you remember the date?"

She told him.

He shook his head as though trying to understand something, sharp lines etched on his forehead. He said, "Are you sure that was the date?"

"I am sure of everything I say."

"Then when did she get married?"

She stared at him.

He repeated, almost sharply, "Then when did Padma get married?" Her mind had become stupid. He said, "Your husband . . . Padma's father, he told me Padma was married."

Did her face show her horror? No, it could not have. He was saying, "I see. I understand." What did he understand?

"When did you meet Padma's father?"

"I did not have any leave during my training period in Delhi. I told them my mother was critically ill, and I took the train to Bangalore."

"When?"

"About a month and a half after the marriage." He read her expression correctly and said, "Yes, it would have been at the same time that all of you went to Lucknow."

With difficulty she said, "And you met my husband and he told you Padma was already married."

"I should not have told him I was married."

"You told him you were married?"

"I did not mean to tell him that. It was Padma I had to tell." He stopped. The colour had gone from his face.

"But you told him."

He did not reply immediately. She watched him as he picked up the glass lying next to him and drained it. He said, "He asked me, Are you the man Padma wanted to marry? I said to him, Yes, but I am already married and— He did not let me finish. He opened the door and said, Leave. Padma is married too."

So he had had his secret too. Thirteen years it had taken for this to come to her knowledge.

His voice low, he said, "I understand. What else could he say." She felt her head beginning to pound. He said, "But actually she must have got married after you returned from Lucknow." She did not reply. Her tongue was so heavy her head felt as if it would burst. Horror blanched his face. He tried to say something, failed, then said, in a voice not his own, "Is Padma alive?"

Anger like ice chilled her blood. She said harshly, "She is alive." She watched him lean back against the chair as though spent, watched his eyes close briefly, then open, an almost terrible relief passing like waves across his face.

"Padma wrote five letters to you."

His eyes were very still. He reached for his pocket and took something out of it, something wrapped in his handkerchief. He opened the handkerchief carefully. He held them out to her, her child Padma's five letters. He saw her expression. He said, "I did not read these till a few days ago." She could feel her nostrils flare, feel the band tight across her heart, she could hardly breathe. "I never saw them. In all the confusion of the wedding—guests, my mother's illness, my leaving for Delhi . . . they must have got misplaced."

"Where were the letters all these years?"

"My sister found them, my youngest sister."

"Where?"

He took in a deep breath, withdrawing his hand and placing the letters carefully on the table. She watched him struggle for words. "My sister . . . my youngest sister is . . . sometimes gets . . . strange ideas. She hardly speaks to our mother. She imagined that my mother read and hid these letters. When my mother was out, my sister searched for the key to her trunk, and after finding it, opened it and found the letters along with some other letters and documents. My mother had put them all away at the time of the wedding, and then forgotten about them."

"Your mother told you that."

"She said that is what must have happened. She does not remember."

What Padma had said was still true then. He adores his mother, Amma, she will do anything for him, he too for her, Amma. So much she has sacrificed for him, Amma, so much. Once, Amma, he told me that everything he was, everything he achieved, it was because of his mother. He said that she was like the air that they breathed, that they took her for granted in every way, yet could not live without her. Imagine, Amma, Padma had said, her eyes soft and tender. Imagine, she had answered silently, thoughts seeping into her like sewage.

"Then you read them and came here."

He nodded, his eyes begging for the answer that she would make him wait to hear. So. What is it that he wanted to hear? Did he want her to say, It is all right. The desperation in Padma's letters—it is not what you think. Yes, she did think so, but in a few days she knew otherwise—when women are tense their body functions can get delayed. That is what happened to her and she imagined the worst. Or, did he want her to say, What you think happened, yes, it did happen, but we went to a doctor, he scraped it out, now go, it is all in the past. Or, did he hope she would say, She was desperate because we had found a match for her and were pressing her to agree, that is why she wrote to you like that. Was that why he had come, to hear Padma's mother say to him, finally, I absolve you—you tried to do what you could, you went to Bangalore, and now you have come here. Most men would not have bothered. Is that what he had come to hear? To hear her say, You are a man of integrity. You could not help what happened to you, I understand, there is nothing else you could have done. Padma has forgiven you, she is happy now, the past is behind all of us, give me the letters and go. For, of course, he thought that Padma was married.

She watched his hands as they lifted the letters, his eyes as he read the address. What was there to see there? Of course. Her handwriting. Shanta would have died of jealousy. Shanta would have thought, Narayana would not savour my handwriting like that. Shanta would have thought, Narayana's face would never contain such anguish for me. Ah, my child, she wanted to tell Shanta, don't you see, don't you see. One only lingers over what one has lost.

"So," she said, "you thought Padma was fickle like you."

He looked up, almost blindly. "No. I thought that she had . . . somehow heard about my marriage . . . and then . . . accepted an offer from . . .

someone else. Once . . . long ago, she had . . . said that if I did . . . she would . . . we were joking . . . I thought." He could hardly speak. She had to lean forward to make out his words.

"So," she said, "what is it about her five letters that compelled you to come here?"

He still did not say anything, but his eyes did not leave her face, his hands still holding the letters like a secret. In the background the grandfather clock ticked loudly. No, not a handsome man, but a striking one. Had his features been as strong when Padma knew him? Probably not. So. He had loved her. In a manner of speaking. Romantically. For the pleasure it gave him, the joy. Believing in it as Padma had, because that is what they, like all the others, had sought all their lives. Unlike many of the others they had found it. Didn't go very far. When it came to the crunch it collapsed like a flat tyre. Fair enough. Either one or the other. Shanta hadn't had it. Still craved it. Didn't appreciate what she did have. Shanta, my child, either way you will be left craving. Mutually exclusive, that's what they are. Padma had one. You have the other. Padma craves what you have. Never talks about it, but I know. Thinks her loneliness will be assuaged. Thinks Mallika's future will be assured. And you, you think that what you don't have will fill that emptiness in you. Both wrong. Love, take that from books and films. Joy, you will get it from your children. Sustenance—emotional and spiritual—only from your parents. From your husband, the greatest thing of all—security. A good man will stand by you.

He said, "I thought . . . you may have been pressing her to get married." One. You hoped it was that. "For that you came here?"

He said, "I was not sure . . . it was that."

She would not help him. Let him find the words for it.

"I thought it . . . might be worse."

Two. You hoped it was not that. "Worse?"

"Forgive me for saying it. I thought she imagined she was with child."

Three. You hoped she imagined it. "And if she was?"

She lingered on the misery etched across his face. He burst out, "Tell me."

For years she had imagined the meeting. For years she had fantasized how it would take place. What he would say. What she would say. How he would look. The sequence of revelations. Sometimes in her fantasies she had been in control. More often than not she had not. More often than not she had found herself shuddering with tears. Lashing out at him. Sometimes even screaming. Had she been able to fantasize the perfect unfolding of events, she would have imagined this.

The flower was beginning to bloom.

"Thirteen years have passed," she said. "The circumstances that drove Padma to write these letters are not your concern anymore."

"They are my concern."

"They were, once. But when you did not come, they became ours and Padma's alone."

He knew she would tell him, eventually. She watched his throat move, his eyes still on her face. She said, "Your wife."

"My wife?"

"She too suffered."

He did not understand.

"To her also you caused suffering."

He thought she was meandering. He thought she was dithering in the way women often did. She saw it in his expression. "Like you," she said, "your wife also came to me."

Ah, his stunned expression. That itself she would relive many times for many years. The last but one fold. Her fingers, opening it, slowly. Completely in control, completely controlled. It was her due. For all the tears she had not been able to shed. For all the tears Padma had shed. In the railway guest house. Padma had wept so bitterly that she had been unable to get up from the ground, where she crouched like a wounded animal, her arms about her stomach. Like the heroine in a Hindi film. Always she had thought that such films exaggerated, but Padma had been the actress then. Only Padma did not say anything, just made those hideous sounds. But now the balance was beginning to tilt.

The flower was beginning to bloom, its petals unfurling.

"Like you," she said, "your wife came to me some years ago." All expression had been sucked out of his face. She was looking at the mask now. This was the face his wife had met every morning for years. "Nothing I could understand," his wife had told her, "nothing. When you see the Ramleela, the people who play Ravana and the Rakshashas wear masks, but at least the masks are fierce and frightening, at least you know what you are looking at, how you should feel. With Him, what He wears has no expression at all." Her own expression had been full of sadness on a face still soft and innocent. A fair face. His mother had seen to that too.

"When the grandchildren did not come," she said to him, "yours and your sisters'—then your mother told your wife that there was a curse on the family and that it could only be lifted by her, your wife. They told her to come to me, to beg me to remove the curse."

Prema had entered the house one afternoon when He was having his afternoon sleep, asked if she was Mrs. Rao, bent down and touched her feet, saying, "Forgive us for whatever we have done, Mataji. I touch your feet and beg you, remove this curse." She had stayed in that position, unmoving, her hands lying like leaves across her feet, her head bent down, covered by her plain cotton saree. That was how Padma would have been if she had married him, that was what his mother would have turned her into. Prema did it naturally, she was born into it. If she had been trained by the mother-in-law, it was not training of any fundamental kind. But Padma would have had to be changed fundamentally. And whether his mother succeeded in that or not, he would have been ignorant of the process and never known what it meant to Padma.

She bent down and lifted Prema, put an arm around her, looked at the soft face on which suffering had laid its permanent scars, found herself stroking her forehead the way she used to stroke her children's, saying in Hindi, "How did you know where to find me, child?"

Prema looked at her face then, and said, "What my mother-in-law said, I do not believe it, Mataji."

She walked Prema to the sofa, sat next to her, her arm still around her, "Believe what, my child?"

"She told me you were an evil woman." And then, after some time, almost irrelevantly, she said, "She gave me this," and she gave her the card with their address that Narayana must have left behind that long-ago day in Lucknow.

She had come by train and taken a taxi to their house. She had not been able to eat or sleep. "I did not know what to think. I did not know what to say," Prema said as Rukmini served her rice and sambar and vegetables. Prema ate slowly. Rukmini found herself watching her the way she used to watch Madhav while he ate, the way she now watched her grandchildren eat. After Prema finished she took her to the spare bedroom. Prema put her small bag in the corner and stood there, her eyes heavy.

"Where did you think you would spend the night?" she asked Prema, folding the bedcover and spreading fresh sheets on the bed.

"I did not think."

"Sleep now. When do you have to go back?"

"Tomorrow evening."

"Here," she said, handing Prema a towel, "the bathroom is across the room. After your bath you come here and sleep. My husband, I will tell him that you are . . . Shanta's friend. He does not ask questions." She turned to go, then said, "We will talk later."

Expressionless, he was waiting for her to go on. She said, "Do you know your mother blamed her for not having children?" Behind the mask something flickered. "Your mother used to say to her, Our family will die if a son is not born to you. All these . . . years, your mother has blamed her for being childless." No, she could not read his expression. Patient. Be patient. Think, all these years you have been patient. Do not be like Shanta. No accusations. Be moderate. Remember, love does not die in an instant. Remember, knowledge does not suffice. Time. That is the killer. Do not be greedy. Love has its own way of dying. Even he within whom it happens cannot know its workings. Let it suffice to know, it will happen. Imagine it. Yes. One more thing to imagine after he goes. And if this does not do it, well, then, the last one will. He will know how she has hidden that also from him. For that there will be no forgiveness. Even ashes will not remain.

"In all these years, Mataji, I have spoken to no one," Prema said to her that evening as they sat outside in the veranda. "Of these things, how to speak?" Ah, yes. How to. "But you will understand. When I talk to you I do not feel shame. When I talk to you I do not feel I am a dirty woman." She looked down then, her hands clasped tightly in her lap. "In all these years he has not touched me once."

So were stories born. Untold, so did stories die. Prema looked up, fear in her eyes for the disgust that she imagined she just might see, and seeing instead its opposite, looked down again and said, "After the first year I thought, this thing that I thought which happens between men and women, it does not happen. That is the lie, born of my wicked mind, not this."

She looked at him. He was staring beyond her at the photos of her children when they were children. Had he heard her? Had he switched off the way Narayana did when Shanta was speaking? She said, "Your mother sent her to me. Your mother told your wife that there was a curse on your family and sent her to me to ask that the curse be removed."

"The women in my house—my mother, sisters, my wife. They are superstitious. Astrologers, curses . . . they believe everything. What you said in anger they took seriously." He shook his head, frowning. "She should not have come to you."

"Your mother told your wife to go to a gynecologist to see what was wrong with her." Ah. Now he was looking at her. "Your wife went."

It had been a woman, the gynecologist. "For small things at least I should thank God, perhaps," Prema told her. "If it had been a man the humiliation would have been worse. Afterwards she said to me, You are a grown-up woman. You come to me not knowing how children are conceived? I said to her, I thought I knew, but after I got married, I distrusted what I knew. She said to me, I will tell you again, and she told me. She said, I do not know what advice to give you. After that, every time I went to Lucknow, my mother-in-law would send me to the same gynecologist and every time I would make an appointment with her and go and then she and I would talk. Divya, her name was. With Divya I used to laugh a lot. Only with her. She was young, under thirty. She liked me. But one year when I phoned to make an appointment with her I found that she had left Lucknow. That day I went out, stayed out for about two hours, then came back and told my mother-in-law that I was barren."

He was waiting.

"Your wife went," she said. "Every year. She told your mother, The doctor is doing tests. Then finally she said to your mother, The doctor said there is no hope of having a child. I am barren." The arrow had gone home. He flinched. She continued, "Your mother said to her, What sin my son must have committed in his last birth I do not know, to be cursed with a barren wife." He was looking at her but they focussed beyond her. Had he heard. Look at me. Look at me. She said, "Your wife's mother knows." His eyes focussed on her.

"This was two years after my marriage, Mataji," Prema had said. "I did not want to ask her, but I was desperate. All the time I was thinking, I must know, it does not matter if He does not come near me, if He does not talk to me, but I must know. This was before I went to Divya. If I had sisters, older sisters, it would have been different. But I only have one brother. My mother said to me, Keep quiet. Shut your mouth. Talking of such things, has a demon entered your mind? I said, Mataji, Just tell me, is it normal, what is happening, just tell me, if he does not touch me can I have a child? I do not know how I asked her, how I had the courage. She said, You dirty girl, stop all this talk. I shut my mouth. But from her face I knew that she understood."

His attention was hers. Yes, he was listening. But what was he thinking? She said, "All your wife wanted to know was, How are children born. That is all. But there was no one whom she could ask. She was desperate. She asked her mother. Her mother called her a dirty woman. Other things also. Year after year your wife went to the gynecologist. Year after year it was with full encouragement from her mother. To your mother your wife's mother would say, Do not worry, the doctor will cure her, she will have a child. Your wife's mother, it was she who found this gynecologist whom your wife visited every year."

Softly, slowly, continuously, Prema had talked, pausing only to drink water. "Everything I accept. I accept my mother's betrayal. I accept His behaviour. If this is what has been written for me, then it is written. Only one thing I have wanted all these years, and that is someone to whom I could talk. Someone who would listen. Understand. For some time I had Divya. Now you. I think of God and then I feel at peace. That is the only truth."

Rukmini's husband had talked to Prema warmly enough, accepted that she was an old friend of Shanta's. He was used to women coming and going in his household, his daughters' friends, his wife's sisters, his own. He was used to them chattering and whispering constantly. He missed not having anyone to buy fruits and chicken for, sweets and tender coconut. But now His child Shanta's friend was there, He went out after breakfast and came back laden with fruits and chicken and sweets for her.

Now the man sitting opposite her said, heavily, "She never mentioned . . . all this."

"Is that her fault?"

He did not reply.

"He is a good man," Prema had said, "an honest man. He knows everything. He reads everything, every book, every magazine, every newspaper. His mother and his sisters, they do not have to ask him for anything, before they ask he does it for them. His sisters, they say, Our brother, he is

like ten brothers put together. That highly they think of him, that strong
he is, like a rock. Do not mistake me, he is not cruel to me. No one could
be more kind. He gives me more money than I need for the house, he
never asks me for any accounts. Does not interfere, does not question.
Never criticizes me, never. When I say to you, he does not talk to me or
touch me, it does not tell the whole story. For Diwali people send him baskets of sweets and fruits. All of it he sends back. That honest he is. Does
not take favours from anyone, will not do favours for anyone. His mother,
she says, Tell me, bahu, in this birth you have been blessed with a husband
like him; do not think you will be so lucky in your next birth." For some
time she was silent.

"All my life I wanted to be first in someone's heart. As a child I used to
think, Why does my mother love my brother so much more than she loves
me? When I was in school, I used to think, When I grow up, then I will
become a teacher. I used to think, this way I will have my own children
and I will also have all those other children. I used to think, when I have
a daughter I will not send her to a school different from my son."

"Different?"

"I should not complain. It is not different from what the others have
done. They sent my brother to the best convent school, they paid a lot in
fees for him, they could ill afford it. If they had the money they would have
sent me too, but they did not. So I was sent to a government school. I did
not do well in school, the standard of education was very poor. So then I
did not get admission in a good college. I could have been a teacher if I
had a chance."

"If you were my daughter," Rukmini said to Prema, "you would have
been a teacher. My husband, he believes in a good education for all his
children more than anything else. Shanta, she topped the university in her
B.A., in her M.A. Gold medals, prizes, everything. My husband is a man
far ahead of his times. Both my girls have done their M.A.'s. My husband,
he always said, In the civil service you will do better than any man."

She had said this many times. She had said it to his sisters and brothers
and to their friends. She had said it before any of them could say, as they
thought, *three* children in convent schools, *three* children doing their
M.A.'s, and *two* of them in the hostel? How would they get their daughters married at this rate? And He had not cared, he had not given one
thought to his daughters' marriages or where the money would come for

it. "I have given my children the best education, the rest will follow," he said to her, as if education would buy gold and Cancheevaram sarees or pay for wedding dinners.

And indeed, who had paid for it eventually? She had, she, their mother, with the money that had come to her when her only unmarried brother died, her brother who had inherited their parents' house and money. She sold the house and she was able to celebrate her children's marriages the way they had to be celebrated, and Padma's share, which she had kept aside for Padma's marriage, that went for Padma's house. Now no one could sneer, No wonder they celebrated their children's marriage so simply—it isn't because they believe in simplicity but because they have nothing; you see they have spent it all on their daughters' *education.*

He believed in simplicity. "We should celebrate our children's marriages very simply," he used to say, "just the immediate family, and no gold, three sarees at the most, that is all." Simplicity was all very well for those who had money, she wanted to tell him, people would know that this is what they had chosen, not that this was what they were compelled to do. But for those who did not have money simplicity had no place.

"Which cadre are they in the I.A.S.?" Prema asked. She saw Rukmini's surprise and added, "Your daughters, which cadre?"

"Oh. No, they—my younger daughter is a . . . lecturer."

"Accha. So the older is in the I.A.S.?"

"Oh, no, two children she has, a large house, her husband is in the railways. There is no shortage of money, free railway passes they have, travel all over India first class several times a year. No, no, she does not need to work."

Prema said thoughtfully, "It is all right. There is no need for me to feel bad about . . . who knows . . . if my parents had money and sent me to a convent school and I had got into a good college and all . . . even then my life might have been the same." Prema looked at her. "Is something the matter, Mataji?"

She shook her head.

"Mataji," Prema said, "I have to know before I leave you. Why did you curse them?"

They looked at each other.

Then Prema said, "I heard you that day when you came to the house."

Rukmini continued looking at her.

"My husband was training in Delhi and he could not take me with him. I should not say, could not, for had he been able to take me, even then he would not have. But I heard voices and could not help coming to the door that opened into the sitting room. It was then that I heard you. But I do not understand Kannada. You were speaking softly. As though you were praying. Was that how you cursed?"

She nodded.

Prema sighed deeply. "Then it has come true, your curse. One does not need a language to understand these things."

A fierce surge of triumph shook her still body, she lowered her eyes. When she raised her eyes Prema said, "My older sister-in-law, she has had three miscarriages. The second one, she had a fallopian tube pregnancy and had to be operated on, after that she has not been able to have any children."

So, this was what fulfillment was. This. This. She almost shuddered with the violence of her pleasure.

"You will think, my mother-in-law says things about my own inability to bear children when her own daughters . . . ? But that is how it is. For them she has only compassion. For them she has only tears." She was quiet for some time.

"I cursed them because your husband promised marriage to my daughter, whom he had known for four years when they were both in college. We came to the house with the proposal and it was there that we learnt he was already married."

For a long time, neither spoke.

Prema opened her eyes. "So. He is a normal man."

"I do not understand, Prema."

"It is your daughter. It is she he has lived with since the day he married me."

"I do not understand why he married you."

"I do not understand either. We were promised to each other from the beginning. I knew, he knew, our families knew."

"Why are you looking like that, Prema?"

"My mother-in-law, she is a shrivelled, twisted thing now, like a dead tree. It is not unhappiness, it is terror. That is why she has sent me to you. Her youngest daughter is expecting her first child."

"Ah."

Now, to the man sitting opposite her, she said, "Your mother sent your wife to me four years ago with these five letters that you now hold in your hand. She asked your wife to beg for my forgiveness and remove the curse that she is convinced we put on your family. Before your wife left I told her, Take these letters back to her. Your wife asked me, What should I tell my mother-in-law? I told her, Nothing."

The time was ripe. Now there would be no holding back. Now there would be no need for it. Now he would listen. See, Shanta, see. This is the way to do it. Otherwise They will not listen. Otherwise They will not hear.

Painfully he said, "My wife did not tell me all this." His face searched hers, retreated from what he saw there. He said, "I did not know."

They did not know. They did not know. The cruelty, the cruelty. They thought it absolved them, this not knowing. They thought it had nothing to do with them, this not knowing. They thought that not knowing, they were not culpable. Like armour this not knowing was, and thus protected, they slowly turned the knife. We did not intend to hurt you, they said. We did not intend to cause you any pain, they protested. Why did you not tell us, they asked. We did not know, so do not blame us. We did not know, so we are absolved.

She said, "You did not know anything, it seems."

He said, as though she were finding an excuse for him, "No, nothing."

Now, Rukmini, now. Remove that armour, Rukmini, expose the skin. Peel off the skin, Rukmini, reveal the flesh. Even as they flail, Rukmini, they will blame you. Even as they thrash, Rukmini, they will scream, What are you doing to me, why. Even as the pain sears their flesh, Rukmini, they will say, You are revengeful, mad. Strike, Rukmini, strike. When *you* hurt *them*, Rukmini, there is nothing unintentional about it. When you plunge the knife in, Rukmini, you know what you are doing. You, Rukmini, will not say, I did not know. You, Rukmini, you will not say, I did not know I was causing you pain. Instead, Rukmini, you will say, It is without such knowledge that you live. You will say, We, it is with such knowledge that we survive. We do not know of any other way to live. Then, Rukmini, will you say to them, What need have *you* for such secrets? Then, Rukmini, will you tell them, What need have *you* for such vengeance?

"So you see, your mother did not misplace the letters. She read them and hid them. You can ask your wife. She also held them in her hands as you now do, with their envelopes torn. Your wife is a good woman. She did not read them. Do you know, some criminals refuse to destroy evidence that will incriminate them? The reason for this I do not understand. Whatever the reason, your mother all these years has refused to destroy the letters, even after your wife took them back with her. Your mother knew about Padma and you. She must have read Padma's letters to you when you went home for the holidays. So she fixed your marriage in your absence. She gambled on the chance that you would not be able to do anything if it happened the day you came home, 'specially if she fell ill at that very time." Spell it out, Rukmini, spell it out. "She knew you better than you knew yourself. Her gamble paid off."

A bonus, this. God was bountiful. He believed her. His eyes were bruised, and the disbelief they held was not for her, Padma's mother.

"Padma never married."

Slowly, like the early dawn, horror was lighting his face. Horror? Already? Then she saw the other thing growing in his face, growing, growing, growing. Nothing new, it had been there when she first saw him, but she had not recognized it for what it was. It was the same monster that she had seen inhabiting Padma thirteen years ago. He could barely hold it now. His face and body were rigid with its force.

Ahhh. If her body could have moved, each limb would have grasped this moment with the hunger that only lovers knew.

Softly she asked, "You still do not know?"

He was unable to speak.

"That day when we came to your house in Lucknow, Shanta told your mother and your two older sisters that Padma was carrying your child."

He closed his eyes.

"Your mother said, *So, you want to give our family's name to the bastard of your whoring sister?*"

Word for word from her fantasy. It was only his expression that she had never been able to visualize in her dreams. Now she saw it. Once before she had seen it from the window of Madhav's first-floor apartment, two men hitting a third, she hearing the thud of each blow, the man just standing there, swaying. That same expression.

The flower was blooming, its petals unfurling. Such beauty she had never seen.

Watch those limp hands, the way his body lies back in the chair. Watch those bruised eyes. It seems he has stopped breathing. No, do not wait for him to say anything. He has nothing to say. Just wait a little. Let him be sure before the rest takes over that this too his mother hid from him. Let him know that this is what she thought of it.

With this knowledge, he will go back to her.

"When we went back, I said to Padma, Get rid of the baby. Even now it is not too late. We will find someone who can do it."

She had had to say it to Padma at night when Shanta was asleep. Shanta would not have allowed her to say it. Shanta would never have allowed Padma to consider it. She thought it was a sin, Shanta. Carrying her own second child, nurturing thoughts of adopting Padma's child. Always acting on her impulses, Shanta, never rational, never logical, never thinking of the long-term consequences. Rukmini found a doctor. Spent one day visiting private doctors, her gold bangles in her purse. Finally found one whose clinic looked clean and efficient. He said he did not want the money but the gold would do. Telling Padma about it and then saying, "No need to tell Shanta or Narayana. Then you come back home with me, and Appa and I will find a good boy for you—"

Padma had turned on her like a fury. "Appa does not want me." She had looked at her mother almost with horror, and said, "How can you talk about marriage, Amma, how can you?"

Calmly, her mother said, "No one knows, no one will know, and about Appa do not worry, I will see to that. Padma, my child, you are not the first woman to whom this has happened, you will not be the last. Think with your head, not your heart."

Padma had said, "I cannot come home." She said nothing about the abortion. Implicit in her silence was her consent.

They had set forth for the doctor the next day. In the taxi Rukmini had taken out a mangalsutra from her bag and given it to Padma. "I had it made for your marriage when Shanta got married," she said grimly. "Now wear it. I cannot give you mine." Padma had taken it and worn it silently.

Now she told the man sitting opposite her, "Padma and I went to a doctor for an abortion. At the doctor's office she told the taxi to go back."

Ah. He was waiting for every word of hers like a man dying of thirst who is being given water drop by drop. Was he capable of movement? Could he get up from that chair? She would see. She said, without turning, "The photograph behind me, it is lying face down on the mantelpiece. Look at it."

At first he did not get up. He kept looking at her the way a patient looks at a doctor who is giving him all the facts which will lead to the devastating but inevitable conclusion, like the patient who is fighting his realization, just in case. Then, very slowly, he got up. No, no. This was not the way. She would not be able to see his face when he was behind her. She got up, went to the mantelpiece, lifted the photo and walked across the room to where he still stood. She gave it to him. Still looking at her he took it, and without looking at it, sat. She went back to her chair.

He was looking at it, holding it with both hands. It had been taken by Shanta about eight months after Mallika's birth. It was one of the best photographs. Mallika had been a plump baby, chubby face and arms and legs, she was giving one of her rare smiles, her cheek against Padma's. A plump, happy, smiling child was a beautiful child. Padma was not smiling, her expression was grave, but she looked beautiful. Padma always photographed well. Shanta had had it enlarged and sent to her mother. She had almost wept when Shanta sent it to her, her stomach twisting with the urge to hold the child to her bosom, lay that soft, chubby cheek against her own, feel that tender body against her breasts. Such hunger she felt then, such hunger. But Mallika was twelve now. She had thought about it for years as she waited for this moment, wondering, which one will I show him, this one or the most recent one? It had come to her gradually that it had to be this one. This was how He should first see her. None of the others would evoke what this would. Let what this evoked not be tempered.

She did not recognize his voice when she heard it, "Do you have a recent photograph?" He did not lift his eyes from the one he held.

She hesitated. Then she walked to the cupboard, bent down and opened the door. From a brown envelope she sorted out the photos Shanta had sent her of Mallika every year, and took out one that had been taken a few months ago. Again Mallika and Padma—Mallika in her school uniform, two thick plaits, large eyes, grave expression as always; Padma, her arm around her, laughing, probably at something Shanta must have been saying as she clicked the camera, and looking, if possible, lovelier than ever, no sign of the bruised expression that Shanta said she still wore. She closed the cupboard. She gave him the photograph, then went back to her chair and sat.

It was like looking at a weeping statue. No movement of the body, no heaving shoulders, no sound. A face streaked with tears, that was all, his hands holding the second photo, the first on his lap. She marvelled. This was the way to cry, if one did. In such tears there was dignity. That was why she had never cried, not even when alone. She knew she could not do it this way, knew she would do it like Shanta—the sobs escaping, moans, shudders; reddening nose and eyes; thoughts, words, escaping unbidden. Everyone in the family knew she never cried—He, her children, his family, their friends. Even He, even He she had seen crying but He had never seen her do the same. She had seen him weep when his parents died. When Shanta's letter came, telling them about Padma, that night she had heard him weeping in the bathroom. It was a terrible sound because it was one He was trying to control but could not, he sounded like an animal in pain, she had not been able to stand it.

Now this man sitting before her would not say he did not know. Now he would know the futility of such a remark. He had done it to Padma. Like every man before him and every man after, he had not thought of the consequences of this act. The consequences were not his to bear. She, Rukmini, she could not even count the number of abortions and miscarriages she had had. After some time she had stopped telling Him, after some time He saw it as just another irritation she had to live with, like her periods. The bleeding was there, it seemed permanently. For Him her periods and miscarriages merged into one another; a "woman's problem," as they called it in those days, that's what it was for which she once in a while took to bed. On the rare occasions when she stayed in bed for more than one day, He expressed concern. If it truly caused Him concern then why did He not stop doing it to her? Why did He think what He did was divorced from what she suffered? No, no, she was asking the wrong question. The significance did not lie in the question: Why did He think. The significance lay in the answer: He did not.

Later, she could not remember how long they sat like that. It could have been five minutes, it could have been fifteen. Then he said, still looking at it, "She's twelve now." She nodded. "Yes." He looked up then, both hands still holding the photograph, a vast emptiness in those dark brown eyes.

Almost in full bloom the flower, in a giant, arid landscape.

After some time he said, "How did Padma—" He stopped, his face was twisted.

"Padma is a lecturer. Mallika is in a convent school." No more. Nothing about how she was managing. Let him imagine the worst.

He said, his voice sounding like another, "You help support her."

"Her father has not spoken to her or seen her since the day she left our house to go to Shanta's, when she found out she was going to have a baby. Her brother has not spoken to her since then. I have not seen her since then." It was as though he could not contain his thoughts, his words. She heard him say something. She said, "She manages. She takes tuitions."

She watched the horror on his face. "But on a lecturer's salary . . ."

"That is how it is."

"Madhav—"

She stopped him with a raised hand. "When Padma lost you she also lost her family. She lost her father, her brother and her mother." He said something. She answered, "Shanta is there for her. No one else."

Only she, Padma's mother, knew what these thirteen years had been for Him, her husband. It had eaten Him up, the loss of His youngest child. If she, Rukmini, had gone to Padma after that first time, then how would He have borne it? That was why she had not gone to Padma after that first time. Because if she had He would regard it as another betrayal. He would not have been able to bear it. It would have broken Him. That burden too He had put on her. All these years she had borne it. Borne the fact that she had betrayed Padma. Borne the fact that Padma did not forgive her. Borne the fact that Padma felt her mother's betrayal more deeply than she felt her father's. She understood her father's betrayal. She refused to understand her mother's. Shanta understood. None of this He knew. She had never forgiven Him for it.

The man sitting before her said, "My . . . daughter . . ."

She heard the singing in her ears. Once before she had felt it when she was very ill, just before she fainted. Now she felt the raging blood rush to her face and every sound outside faded; the singing in her ears filled the room. She waited for it to subside. After a long time, it did.

She said, "Padma told me you read a lot. That you used to write to her during the holidays."

"Yes."

He writes beautifully, Amma, Padma told her before they went to Lucknow. He has a very literary mind, Amma. What had Padma meant to convey by that? That they were kindred souls, he and Padma? Even then she had wanted to say, That is all very well at this stage, my child; later these things have no value. Later he will not appreciate you for your love of reading; it will interfere with other things. Silly child, she had wanted to say, you really think all this is important? Strange, how much Padma had talked to her before they went to Lucknow. She had expected her mother to . . . to what? Padma had not known what to expect—accusations, tears, condemnation. She had not expected her mother to hold her for so long, to say, finally, dry-eyed but compassionately, "What has happened has happened. Tell me about Him now." Slowly, Padma had.

"Now also, do you read a lot?"

"Yes." The thirst was consuming him. He was humouring her. He was saying to himself, Women are like that, they ask irrelevant questions. They cannot keep to the point. He was saying to himself, She will come to my question eventually. I can wait. Forever I can wait. I can wait till this thirst makes my body shrivel and curl.

"What have your books taught you then?" she asked. She examined the bewilderment on his face and shrugged slightly. "Nothing. Naturally. Padma, she fell in love with you. She thought, He is such a sensitive man, such an interesting man, look at what he reads, look at what he understands of his books. She thought, all that moves him about the people in his books, all that will be part of what he and I will share. She thought, so sensitive he is to the grief that he reads about, he will be as sensitive to my own. To everything that we share. That is how one thinks when one is young. One or two women I know still keep thinking that, keep waiting, never marry. Tragedy. What do you know of tragedy? For men like you tragedy, it is a luxury. Only from books you get it. It is a stimulus to the intellect. That is all. Allows you to build theories. Allows you to discuss them. That is your knowledge of tragedy. Vicariously, that is how you live it. Who is Lear? Who is Hamlet? Who is Othello? All names. Foreign names. I spit at them.

"You ask about *your daughter*? She is not your daughter. You think your seed, it makes you her father? These children, my grandchildren, whose photos you see on the mantelpiece, are they your children? If Mallika, she is your child, then they also are your children. As much right as you have to my other grandchildren, that much right you have to her. Every right you forsook when you forsook Padma. Even now, even now you think you are more sinned against than sinning, do you not? Now you think you can go to Padma and say, I had no choice, forgive me, let me get to know my daughter and provide for her. So simple. Listen to me. Hear me. You had a choice. Even if you chose what your heart did not want, it still remains what you chose. It does not mean you had no choice. Before you go back to your mother and your sisters, understand that. You did what you did because you did not have the strength to do otherwise. Padma, she used to say, Amma, he is a strong man, a principled man. You also thought that, did you not? You still think that. Because you thought that, Padma also thought that. Believed what you believed, said you never lied. She did not know that it was your belief which was a lie, any more than you knew it.

"What right have you to ask about them after thirteen years? You think I will tell you where they are? You think you will find out? I say that you will never find out because there will not be any will in you to find out. One more thing I have to tell you. After that let me see if you still want to find out."

She had not practiced this. She had never found the words for it even in her fantasies. But they had come, unpracticed, unbidden. They had come just when they should have, no sooner, no later, no more, no less. He had heard. The battered look was there again; he was ready for the final blow. The same expression of that man who after being hit again and again finally lay on the ground, and after the other two walked away, slowly got up and stood, his back against the wall of their apartment building. Then the other two turned. Slowly, as if they had all the time in the world, they began walking back towards him. When they reached him they began again till they finished what they had intended. After that he did not get up.

"But first let me answer the question that is written on your face. What is she like, my granddaughter? She is quiet. She is loving. She reads like a starving man eats. Just like her mother used to as a child. She stands first in her class. Now let me tell you the rest. Padma and Shanta told her her father had died in a car accident. As the years went by she used to ask them about him. What was he like? What did he like doing? How did her mother meet him? All that. Padma told her. Told her he was very bright, loved books, read a lot, was good and honest and handsome. Told her, He loved your mother very much. She wanted to know, What did he look like? Refused to believe that Padma did not have any photographs of you. You used to write to her, no, when she came home for the holidays? We never knew. She got so many letters, she wrote to her brother, her sister, her friend Sumi . . . Do you know, after what happened she has lost Sumi also? She kept saying, I have to begin afresh. Like a mantra she used to say it, I have to begin afresh. Terrified that people would find out about it. Not terrified for herself, but for Mallika. That is how she lives, even now. In fear. Mallika should never find out. Mallika should never meet anyone from her past in case they suspect.

"But Padma does not know the worst. We have kept it from her, Shanta and I. What will it achieve, telling her? Nothing, just give her one more thing to brood about, feel terrified of. Shanta found out. Then she told me. Mallika, she does not know that we know. She thinks it is her secret alone. Mallika has had this photograph for many years, kept it hidden in a secret place. Mallika must have found it in Padma's trunk. Must have been looking for it there."

For some time she could not speak. Why had Shanta told her? Why could Shanta not have kept it to herself? Had not her mother borne enough? What had telling her mother achieved? One more stone to carry. Problem was, Shanta could keep nothing from her, her mother. She told her everything—her arguments with Narayana, her mother-in-law's nastiness, her ups, her downs, Padma's ups, Padma's downs, everything. From the time she was a child she had done it, and she, her mother, had listened. No discrimination Shanta had, didn't know what should be said, what should not. It was not for a daughter to speak to her mother about her husband or about her in-laws. Other things, yes, but not this. Did Shanta not realize how difficult it was for her mother to listen? Which mother wanted to know about the unhappiness that seeped into a daughter's life after marriage? Which mother wanted to know its inevitability put into words? The problem was that even after all these years, even after she herself became a mother, Shanta like a child, thought her mother was invulnerable.

Once, when Shanta was ten, her mother had taken to bed. She lay quietly, her eyes closed, but at some point the cramps must have hurt more than usual, and she moaned softly. She sensed a movement next to her and opened her eyes. Shanta stood there, her eyes wide with terror.

"Child," she had exclaimed, holding on to the side of the bed and pulling herself up, "what has happened?"

"Amma," Shanta said, "are you going to die?"

She sank down into the bed again. "No," she said.

The terror had slowly receded from Shanta's eyes to be replaced by tears. She burst out accusingly, "Then why did you moan?"

Now Rukmini watched the lines grow deeper on his forehead. She said, "Mallika looks at the photograph every day. She talks to it. She knows every feature, every line. Shanta has heard her. In the afternoons when she thinks her mother and Shanta rest, then she takes out the photograph. When she argues with her mother—oh, yes, she argues—then she goes to the room and talks to her father. Shanta has heard her. At night when she sleeps, every night, she talks to her father. Shanta has heard her. Dada, she calls him. Dada."

"For years . . . she has had the photograph?"

Was it incomprehension that she saw on his face? Why that? What was so difficult to believe about what she was telling him? She said, "Yes, at least seven years. How does that matter. She has built another life around the photograph. She knows her father better than the lines on her hand. Everything Padma has told her about her father—and Shanta, poor thing, keeps adding to that from her own imagination. All that Mallika sees in the photograph. All that she uses when she talks to him. Around that she has built another father. This father is the arbiter of justice. The protector. The man who will keep her from harm. That is how she thinks." She paused.

His eyes were looking beyond her.

She said, "She thinks that he is alive. She thinks that one day he will come back to her. Shanta told me, every time the doorbell rings she looks up as though it might be him coming home to her."

It was as if the night had disappeared without a dawn, that swiftly his expression changed. This was how it had to be. Then she could bring back the night.

"It is her world of make-believe, a world where she is a child like any other with a mother and a father—and that, a father who is perfect. She has built on this fantasy for years and it has become real to her."

He said something. She leaned forward questioningly. He was asking about the photograph Mallika had. Which one, he was asking.

Strike.

"The photograph you took of Padma and Sumit. Her friend Sumi's brother."

At first he did not understand. He stared at her. Then she saw his lips moving soundlessly, *The photograph you took.* The photograph *I* took? He said, harshly, "That is not *my* photograph."

She nodded. "I did not say it was your photograph. I said it was the photograph of her father."

She watched the waves of shock on his face. "Sumit," he said, "Sumit was not—"

She looked at him dispassionately. "No, he was not Mallika's—not the man who fathered Mallika. He is the man who became Mallika's father. He is the man whom she thinks of as her father. That is the face that has become her father's. That is the man she has been talking to every afternoon and every night for all these years. Sumit. Sumi's brother."

Now she would not wait for him to ask. It would be like asking a man mortally wounded to get himself a glass of water. And she was not the one to give it. Enough to watch till the end.

She said, "If you go to them you will destroy Mallika."

This was how Padma had looked when Shanta had shown her another photograph that long-ago day in Lucknow. There was no expression worse than this, a face wiped clean of hope, hope sucked right out like marrow, the very bones hollow.

In full bloom the flower, blinding its beauty.

His fingers, long and strong, lay limply on the photographs. He would not look at them again. After some time she got up from her chair. She went across the room to him and put out her hand. He had his other hand across the lower part of his face, his eyes on the carpet. She waited. His eyes lifted, he looked up at her. Thus must dying men look, who knew it was happening. But were the eyes of dying men so clear, so full of knowledge? Did the eyes of dying men say without accusation, I understand. His fingers curled around the photographs. Very slightly, he shook his head. She continued standing before him, her outstretched hand began to tremble. He got up then, very slowly, the photographs in his hand, his long fingers covering the writing at the back of the first one, *Padma and Mallika, 1958.* Give, she wanted to say, give, but her throat would not move; even after he walked to the door and softly let himself out, her hand stayed outstretched, beseeching. This then, would be his last sight of her, this. With legs that no longer supported her she stumbled to the window, held on to the window bars with both hands, watched. He was having trouble opening the gate. Like a blind man, fumbling. Finally managing to open it, forgetting to close it, walking to the car. A black ambassador, his car, he wearing a pin-striped blue shirt and dark blue pants. She had seen it all before, the way he stood still, his back to her, his hand on the car handle, the other hand holding the photograph, his head resting on the car as though he needed its support, then slowly opening the door of the car, shutting it, sitting for several minutes, his head lowered, unmoving, then his hand on the ignition, the sound of the car starting, the burst of speed as it moved down the road; even the sound of the screeching brakes she had heard before, then the other horrible smashing, grinding sound, yes, even the silence that followed and then the scream of a woman, all that, exactly as Shanta, her daughter with the black tongue, had described thirteen years ago.

She and Shanta did not tell Padma all this. It was not the time for such a telling. Even later would not be the time for such a telling. Later they would tell her what she needed to be told, of how, like a treasure, he had cocooned his memories of her and lived off them for the rest of his life. That was what Padma needed to know to survive this.

But he did not know her. He only knew what it was to love her in the way of people in books, and in the end, who was to say if it was better or worse than the other way. At least he cherished what he believed her to be, what she had been all those years ago, none of which, of course, she was now. He had forsaken her, but he had cherished her. If he had not forsaken her he would not have cherished her. Either one or the other; one for the other.

That day as Padma sat beside her and Shanta, trembling, she only told her that He had come to her two weeks before her father died and why he had come. That he had had no choice about this marriage of his. That, some time after his marriage, he had come rushing to Bangalore to explain to her and that Appa had told him that Padma was married. That he knew, finally, about Mallika. That he took the photograph and left, and then, the accident. She had to tell Padma, she had to. Otherwise Padma would go back to Mallika and say to her, That man who came is not your father, he is not anyone of importance, it was a mistake, a mistake. Otherwise Padma would go back to Mallika and say, It is time for the truth now, I am tired of lies, they have destroyed everything; the truth is, your father is still alive but he does not know about you.

But of course, that too would not be the truth. So she had to tell Padma that he had died within minutes of leaving the house, that she and Shanta had meant to prepare her, tell her, gently, but now that was not possible.

"Blood, so much blood," the servant had told Rukmini, after she sent him to the site of the crash to find out. He was pale, shuddering. "All over. Finished," he had said. No need to tell Padma all that. Let her remember his face as it was when she first knew him.

Padma had not cried. She had just continued shivering as if she had malaria, her teeth chattering, her hands and feet ice cold, saying, Mallika, Mallika, Mallika. They had to make her lie down and put blankets over her, get her hot, sweet tea. That did not help, so then Shanta told Madhav and he opened His drink cabinet and poured out some brandy and Shanta got it and they forced Padma to drink it and that helped a little, at least, it helped the shivering to subside a little. Shanta also drank some brandy in small, quick gulps without coughing or spluttering. As though she had drunk it before, not once but several times—ah, so that secret Shanta had kept from her. And then it was time to go, Padma had to be strong for Mallika, she could not continue that way, she knew it, and so by the time she was ready and Madhav put her and Shanta in the back seat of the car, she was almost in control though her face and lips were white. Shanta was all right. At least, she looked all right—her hair intact, her lipstick intact, she had even put rouge on her cheeks, which she had never done before. When her mother pointed silently to Shanta's cheeks Shanta snapped at her, so then she knew that Shanta would be all right. Before they had left Shanta told her mother, "We will tell Mallika the truth when we go back. And later, depending on how she recovers, we will tell her everything."

Of course, *everything* was a relative term. No one told anyone everything. What needed to be told, that one told. Or rather, what one considered important. And sometimes there were things that one simply forgot. No one could tell anyone everything. Eventually, Shanta would tell Padma most of what their mother had written to her in her thirty-page letter. Eventually their mother would tell Padma again. The story would be told and retold, told and retold. Padma and Shanta and she would tell Mallika the child a condensed version of the story. Mallika the woman . . . who knew what they would tell Mallika the woman. Stories changed with time. Maybe there would be things that Padma would share with Mallika which she did with no one else. One could do that with a daughter in a way one could not with a mother or a sister, especially when the daughter became a woman. Maybe Shanta would share with Mallika what she shared with no one else. Oh yes, Shanta would, even if Padma did not. Maybe she, Rukmini, would tell Mallika what she had told no one else. Out of all this Mallika would create her own story. Perhaps the story Mallika the woman would carry would be a kinder story. Perhaps not. That depended on Mallika. Perhaps it would just be a different story. After all, would not Mallika the woman bring into it her own experiences and see it in that light? And she would see it one way at twenty, another way at thirty, another way at forty, fifty, sixty . . .

But now, for the present, they would tell her what had to be told. Nothing of curses, of the wife. No, none of that. Just why her father did not marry her mother and how he came seeking them, and how he died. It was important that she did not grow up hating her father. That was very, very important. Now she had to get to know him again, and then they would say, He is exactly as we described, only there is another face behind the story. God only knew. God only knew if then Mallika, instead of saying, I understand, would instead say, He forsook my mother and I will never forgive him. God only knew.

But it was inevitable that as the years passed Mallika would ask more and more, and other things would have to be told to her, about not only her father but her mother, her grandmother, her Shantamama, her uncle, her grandfather, the roles they all had played and why. Why, she would want to know, why. They would all have their versions of why. Which one would Mallika believe? Which one would she want to believe? Was belief a question of how much you loved someone? If it was, then Mallika would only believe Padma and Shanta. If it was, then Mallika would not only not believe her grandmother, but would never love her.

She would be prepared for that. Now that He was gone she knew that there was nothing you could be completely prepared for, but as far as it was possible, she would be prepared for it. Now that He had gone she knew that she had not been prepared to lose the one person for whom she was the sun and the moon and the stars. If she had died before Him He would have had no reason to live. That was what she had lost.

As for her, it was as if without Him she had burnt herself out. There was nothing left of herself, there was nothing she wanted. Not in this life. Talk to me, she would say at night, come to me, once at least. She knew women whose dead husbands came to them in their dreams, women who spoke to them in their sleep and sought their advice. But it had not happened to her. He never came. They did not know how she felt, her children. They were unaware that there was nothing left of the mother they had known, that she was like a star whose light continued to shine in the sky even though it no longer existed; her children still saw her as she had once been, when in fact, she was no longer there.

People saw what they wanted to see. It suited them to do that. Or perhaps, they could not help doing that. Her children wanted to see her as she was before. They would not be able to bear seeing anything else. Shanta especially. If Shanta knew her mother was a shell—no more—then Shanta would be lost, rudderless. She would close her eyes, her Shanta.

Padma too. After all, whom did Padma have but her mother and her sister and her daughter? Friends did not count. They counted for nothing. And Madhav, he did not see. He did not think of such things. He had never really known her. People saw what they wanted to see.

Rukmini knew now after all these years, that the knowledge people took away with them had to do less with what they observed than what they were. To every experience Mallika, Shanta and Padma brought something different, from every experience they would take away something different. Sumi had brought the rejection that she felt after her marriage broke up into her perception of others, rejection was what she had taken away from whatever she saw—Padma's rejection, Shanta's rejection, Rukmini's rejection. And He, the man who had loved Padma, what of him? What had He brought with him when he came to see her? What had he taken away? His clear look of comprehension—round and round in her mind it would go, round and round like an insect in her brain cells, night after night, when there was nothing to do but think, nothing to do but think.

If Mallika forgave her, then all this she would tell her one day. And more. She would tell her, each of us thinks so differently, each of us experiences so differently. Each making of it what she knew, what she could comprehend. Like these chappatis that you all make, all those acts of kneading, making into balls, rolling, putting on the fire—it seems the same, but each woman brings into it something different. Have you noticed, she would tell Mallika, how every little act of making it is so different for every woman—the sifting, the pouring of water, the way the knuckles knead, the thoughts that a woman thinks as she does it, which have nothing to do with what she is making? Have you realized, she would tell Mallika, that it is only in the act of cooking that we can think or talk to one another? Do you know, she would say to Mallika, how every woman thinks her mother makes the best food in the world and how every woman ends up cooking like her mother even if her mother has never taught her how to cook?

Many things she would tell Mallika if Mallika forgave her. Maybe to Mallika she would speak of all that had been in her mind as He sat before her, of the expressions His face had borne. Maybe to Mallika she would speak of the look of comprehension He had given her before He left the house. But she would have to wait till Mallika was older, till she could understand. Some things after a few years, other things after some more years. That is, if she, Mallika's grandmother, was alive after all that time. Many things Shanta and Padma would also tell Mallika. Many things Mallika's friends and their mothers would tell her. To her they would tell. In the telling Mallika would hear their stories too. Which way then would she see her own?

# MALLIKA AND PADMA, AFTER

 It came and then it went. Time passed. Then, like the earth disgorging its bowels, it was returned to her, all of it. She, Padma, head held down, hair held back, forced to look at the entrails. Unwind, unknot, straighten. Find the beginning. There the heart—she and Karan—there the tributaries branching out into other lives, the blood thick and heavy, running its inexorable course. There, look again, the beginning thirteen years old. No, not thirteen. Older. Sixteen years ago when they first met, or was it seventeen? Unwind, unknot, straighten. The end, then? Endless the tributaries, nowhere in sight the end.

All hope gone. Never. Understand that word. *Never.* Accept, said Shantacca. Accept. Must mourn, said Shantacca, must mourn. He would never come back to her. He would have. Now, never. Understand that word. *Never.* Time passes. You gave me my belief in you. One day at a time, that is the only way. One recovers. Really? Really, yes, really. You're laughing at me again. One can recover from anything. Really? Yes, really. Karan. Can't live without you. That simple. Padma. Whatever else I doubted I never doubted that. Or will. Try and enjoy the time we have together. We will have plenty of time later. I love your *mmm*s. I don't want to think about later. I want to enjoy what we have now. That's the only way to be happy. I destroyed your belief in me. I did it knowingly. Ma, like sunshine. Karan. Now I understand how much more I have destroyed. Like sunshine. Like sunshine in pink. One can recover from anything. Really? Ma, tell me. Karan. Tell me, Ma. Padma. I have no words for it or for what I feel now. Time passes.

. . .

Mallika's fever had been very high, Anu told them. She didn't tell them how she and Madhu had panicked, how Madhu had cried that night, saying, If something is happening to Mallika then what will Padma do, what she will do? The doctor attended to Mallika, and she and Madhu stayed up with her at night putting cold compresses on her head. Mallika had actually been quite delirious. She had asked for her mother and her Shanta-mama all the time. She had cried heartrendingly throughout. They hadn't wanted to scare Padma and Shanta by sending a telegram, but what else could they have done?

It was very difficult looking at Padma's face, and her sister's as she talked. Very difficult. Padma was pale as a ghost, her face suddenly thinner, her large black eyes stark against that whiteness. And a look almost of bewilderment on her face, as though she understood nothing—not her father's death, not her child's illness . . . nothing. Shanta looked collected and calm but her eyes were swollen. Shanta was the stronger of the two this time. Padma would break. The crack was widening. Padma would break.

It had happened in her house, Anu told them. The four girls were in Prabha's room, she and Madhu were in the kitchen, talking, when the doorbell rang. Anu opened it, and a man stood there, asking if Padma Rao lived next door, because he had rung the bell there and no one had answered it. She shook her head and said no, that Padma had gone to her parents' house since she had lost her father. He said he was sorry to hear that. Then he said that he knew Padma from her college days, and since he had come to Delhi on work, he thought he would drop by and see her. She invited him into the house. First he demurred, then her husband came to the door and said he must come and have something cold to drink, it was very hot outside, Padma's friends were their friends, come in. He came in, sat down, Anu's husband sat opposite him, they began to talk, she went into the kitchen to get some water and make some juice.

She didn't tell Padma and Shanta that she had had a premonition. But perhaps it had not been a premonition, perhaps it had to do with what had happened before. About a week before he came, the doorbell had rung and when she opened the door it was a woman who looked so familiar that she automatically smiled and invited her in, and in that instant realized who it was. Sita. Sita, her travelling companion. Sita had recognized her immediately, "Didi, you," Anu said. Her heart beginning to beat very fast, Anu invited her inside. Sita came in and said, "I will not stay, I just came to ask you where Padma Rao is—your neighbour."

Sita need not know she remembered everything she had told her. She need not let Sita know that she remembered the name on the horoscope. Her mind working very fast, she said, "She has gone to Bangalore. Her father died—" Sita nodded slowly. The questions on Anu's lips lay unasked. Why have you come? It has to do with your brother, does it not? Does he want to see her after all these years? Does he know about her child . . . his child? On what quest had Sita come . . . her own? Wanting to find out what story lay behind that long-ago incident? "Sita, come and sit, what will you have to drink?" But Sita refused, she had to go, she said.

And then, a week later, he had come. The minute he said he had known Padma during her college days, she knew. It was he. The man who had abandoned her Padma—Sita's brother. Panic seized her—Mallika, Mallika was there with Prabha and Gauri. What would happen now? What did he know? Why had he come? None of this could she tell Padma and Shanta.

When Anu went into the kitchen, Madhu continued, she told Anu that she had to go home and make lunch. She went out of the kitchen and saw him. She stopped in her tracks and rushed back into the kitchen.

She did not want to interfere, Madhu said to Shanta and Padma, but she did know and she would not tell anyone else, that she would swear on God, only she and Anu knew, on God's name they would not tell anyone, she was only trying to protect Mallika. The thing was, she knew this man was Mallika's father. It was all right, they did not have to explain anything to her, nothing at all, what were good friends for if they wanted explanations, everything good friends accepted, everything, that is what they were for, good friends. She had seen the photograph that Mallika had of her mother and father, Mahima had shown it to her. No harm her Mahima meant. She was so excited, her Mahima. She kept saying to her, See, Mumma, so handsome he is, so handsome he is. Very angry she was with Mahima for showing it to her, said to her, this was not a good thing to do, getting it from Mallika's house without asking her, and then her Mahima cried and cried and said she only wanted to show it to her to show her how handsome Mallika's father was. In her heart her Mahima was a pure, good girl, her intention was pure, that was the thing. Madhu had told Mahima, Now take it back and do not show it to anyone else, and that was what her

Mahima did. But see, she, Madhu, had seen the photograph, right in front of her the photograph was, so how could she not see it, yes, she saw it and the tears came to her eyes to think of him and Padma together and so beautiful they both looked, so innocent and so young. That was how she knew. Actually, the thing was, once by some mistake, she had bumped into this same man in the Cottage Industries Emporium, so when she saw the photograph she recognized him. Only Anu she had told this thing to, no one else. So then she knew that Mallika's father was alive and that actually they were divorced, and so what if they were divorced, these days it was happening, who was she to say anything about divorce, any man whom Padma divorced would be a man not worth living with, otherwise would their Padma ever do such a thing? This also she knew, that it happened before Mallika was born and that Padma did not want to tell him about Mallika because then he would take away her child from her. It was easy for men to do these things, they had better jobs and more money and influence, look at poor Mrs. Moitra not being able to ever see her son, of course Padma could not suffer the same fate. She, Madhu, was a mother too, she knew what lay in a mother's heart. So, she rushed into the kitchen and said, Anu, Anu, this man is the man in the photograph, this man is Mallika's father, Mallika is in the other room, Anu, I will take her away to my house, otherwise she will know it is her father and she thinks he is dead and then because of her he will get to know that he has a daughter and he will take her away, that is what she said. She went to the bedroom and said to the four girls, who were sitting on the bed and talking, Today we will have lunch in my house, hurry up, we are going now. Stupid thing to do, so stupid, how could they go out without entering the dining area and the sitting area, whether one went out from the front door or the kitchen back door, one had to first enter the dining room. So then she said, No, no, keep sitting, and she sat next to them, panting, wondering what to do. Then of course, it had to happen, stupid of her not to think of that, Mr. Prasad called Mallika, and she watched Mallika get up and go out of the bedroom and she could do nothing about it at all.

Anu continued. She was giving him his juice when her husband called Mallika and she said to him, Mallika isn't here, and Mallika came out that instant. She came to them and stopped, staring at him. He looked at her without recognition, smiled politely at her, Mr. Prasad began to say that this was Padma's child but he did not say it because Anu said, very loudly at that moment, Mallika, you are looking ill, go back to the room. Mallika didn't move. Her face was white as a sheet. He continued looking at her with a smile, one of those smiles that one gave to people one did not know very well. Mr. Prasad looked puzzled, he said again, This is—and he stopped as Mallika's hands slowly went up to her ears, covering them, closing her eyes, a horrible sound coming out of her stomach, as if she had been beaten very hard. Then Anu rushed to her, and Madhu, who had come out, rushed to her from the other end and they managed to catch hold of her before she fell.

Padma and Shanta did not have to worry, Madhu said. He did not know Mallika was Padma's daughter. Anu had called her husband into the room, and as they lay Mallika down on the bed, Madhu hissed to Anu, Tell your husband, tell your husband, but it was as if no words could come out of Anu's mouth, never had she seen such panic in Anu's face, as if she did not know what to say, what was there to say, it was so simple, so Madhu said to Anu's husband, this is Mallika's father and he is divorced from Padma and he does not know about Mallika because she is afraid he will take Mallika away from her so do not tell him anything. First Mr. Prasad he looked bewildered. He said, No, no, that is not possible, I was talking to him and— Then she, Madhu, said, Please do not say anything, I beg of you Prasad Sahib don't say anything. That man, whatever he told you, it is not the truth, I beg of you. So good he was, Mr. Prasad, so very good. No questions he asked, nothing, went back to the room to him, said goodbye to him in a few minutes, saw him to the door, went and got the doctor. Then Mallika got up and looked around her, and they said he had gone and not to worry about it anymore and that was when she became quite hysterical and her temperature began to rise till finally the next day they had to send the telegram to Padma.

Then Shanta spoke. She said there could be no friends as good as those her sister had, that no words could express what she felt for them. That she understood what they had done and that she would have done the same thing in their situation, they only had Padma's best interests at heart. But the truth was, the man they saw was not Mallika's father. The man they saw, the man in the photograph, was Padma's friend's brother. And Mallika had discovered the photograph and assumed it was her father. By the time she and Padma discovered this, it was too late to tell Mallika. They had thought, let it be, just let it be. Mallika's father was really and truly dead and he would never come back to her. They must tell this to Mr. Prasad too.

For the second time Anu and Madhu wept before Shanta. They wept harder than they had the first time, Anu especially. They didn't ask any questions, not even Madhu.

Most of those first two days after they returned, Mallika slept. Shanta gave Padma Amma's thirty-page letter, which told the whole story of his visit to her in all its terrible detail. Padma did not cry when she read the letter either. It terrified Shanta, seeing Padma's face—white and thin, with huge circles under the eyes and no colour at all in her lips. Like a ghost she looked. Like a ghost going mad. She sat by Mallika without saying a word, when Shanta produced food, she ate; when Shanta said, Sleep, she lay down obediently, her eyes open. When Mallika woke, she sat by her, fed her, took her to the bathroom. Then Mallika slept again and she would sit like a mad ghost again. She, Shanta, made up for her. She could not stop weeping. Someone had to cry—it might as well be her. It might as well be her who emerged from this sane. Cry, Shanta, cry. Cry for your father, cry for your daughter, cry for your sister. Cry, Shanta, cry. Otherwise, if something happened to Padma—and that seemed probable—then who would take care of Mallika?

The third day Mallika woke up with the question in her eyes. Padma spoke to her, her hand stroking her child's hair. Very plainly and simply she said, "Mallika, we could not tell you earlier. When we found the photograph in your room it was too late. The photo is one taken by your father. The man in the photo with me is my friend Sumi's brother. Sumi's brother was the man who came to Anu Aunty's house. Your father—"

The same cry Mallika gave that Anu and Madhu had described, as though she was being hit very hard, her hands in front of her to ward off any more words, "No," her hands going to her ears and her eyes closing, shouting, "I don't want to know *anything*—stop it, *stop it.*"

"Mallika, listen, your father—"

"*No.*"

Then she curled up like a foetus and lay still.

They didn't say anything to her after that.

Lying in bed, all three of them, Mallika between them. Mallika turning to Padma. Padma gathering her to her breast, murmuring. Mallika's body shaking, whimpering sounds emerging from her like an animal in pain. His fingers on Mallika's forehead, stroking it, his face ravaged with suffering. He could not rest. He had never rested. Not after he left her, not after he died. She had lived with him for almost eighteen years now. She had not let him go. He had not allowed her to let him go. Thirteen years without her, she living in his mind, he living with her in their house in Delhi, in their room, narrow bed, blue bedcover, desk with books. Ready after thirteen years to come back to her, dead in an instant, in that instant back in this house, back in this room, back to their child, palpable his pain or was it hers, no difference now, looking up, the fan whirring, a desk full of books, a small mirror on the cupboard, a calendar on the wall with dates marked in blue, crumpled blue bedcover, clothes on the floor, his face above her. Tea?

"*Padma!*"

Shantacca's face above her. Desperation in her voice. "Padma, let him go."

She looked at Mallika. She was fast asleep, breathing a little heavily.

"Padma." Shanta was talking to her above Mallika, her face frightened. "Padma, let him rest."

"Shantacca, he's always here, Shantacca, he's always here."

"I know, my darling, I know."

"Shantacca. Help me."

"Pray, pray."

"I can't."

The days going by, slowly, very slowly. Mallika lying in bed, resting, mute, Shantacca holding her, the whimpering beginning again. The very air in the house heavy, thick with grief. Eyes swollen, tongue thick, words unsaid, thoughts twisted. Unravel, unwind, untwist. Begin from the beginning—there the heart—she and Karan. Begin from the beginning.

Amma's letter. She had moved to Madhav's house. Their Bangalore house was rented out.

"Shantacca, I'll never go home again."

Shanta silent.

"Mallika will never know him."

Loud sobs racking Shantacca's body. Padma's arms around her. Mallika watching them quietly, her book in her hand. Later, Shantacca saying, "I feel anchorless, Padma, adrift."

. . .

Mallika had never seen them like that, her mother and her Shantamama. That was the most frightening part of all. Anchorless . . . adrift. Now she had another burden in addition to the one that she could not bear; now she had to protect her mother and her Shantamama from the sorrow that she bore for them; they must not know how much their suffering made her suffer. They must continue to think that it was only the other loss which had made her mute.

Too much knowledge had come upon her too suddenly. She did not know how to hold it. The knowledge of one loss, her father, and before she could comprehend it, the other knowledge—that neither Ma nor Shantamama were invulnerable. Terror seized her whenever she saw her mother's face. When she saw Shantamama's, she felt she could not contain her own grief, which grew so much out of theirs.

Only Prabha stood there like a sturdy rock. Only Prabha knew everything that she knew. Only Prabha could she talk to. Prabha knew without being told that she could have no father other than the one she had known for seven years, the one in the photograph, who was still alive, who had given her that polite smile. Prabha knew without being told that he had to be put to death and that he refused to be put to death. And the man who had fathered her whose face she did not know, whatever they wanted to tell her about him she did not want to hear—Prabha knew that too without being told.

Of course, Ma and Shantamama did not have to be told any of this either. But there was no strength to be got from them—what they suffered for her took it all away.

The story of the photograph they all knew—Madhu Aunty, Anu Aunty, Prasad Uncle. Of course, Madhu Aunty told Mahima. And Gauri probably knew too because Gauri always knew everything.

After a week she began spending the days in Prabha's house. She did not want to stay in her own. The griefs that it held smothered her every time she entered it. She did not want to look at her mother's face or her Shantamama's. They were both waiting for her to ask them sooner or later what they had to tell her about the man who had fathered her. The odour of this waiting was beginning to fill the house like unemptied rubbish in a plastic bucket. Only in Prabha's house was the air clear and fresh. She would spend the mornings with Prabha, and sometimes eat lunch there, or sometimes come home for lunch. Then she would sleep in the afternoon, which Ma and Shantacca insisted on because they felt she needed all the rest possible. Then after she got up she would have her milk and go again to Prabha's house, and come home a little before dinner.

The day the doorbell rang in the afternoon, she was lying in bed, unable to sleep. Ma was clearing up the dining room, and Shantamama had gone to Connaught Place with the boys to buy them shoes because both had outgrown theirs. The boys were as usual staying with their uncle in Old Delhi, and they were to meet Shantamama in Connaught Place after lunch. She heard Ma open the door, the murmur of voices, and after some time, absolute silence. She stepped out of bed silently and stood in the corridor that opened into the dining–living area and listened to a woman, who was not her mother or her Shantamama, beginning to laugh. What peculiar laughter. No, no, she was not laughing. Quite the opposite. It sounded the same, that was all.


How much grief in this little house, no space in the house for all it held, a strange woman coming in and crying . . . was this what the house did to people now . . . griefs leaning against its very walls. They would crack these walls, the house would crumble.

"I am Karan's sister. His youngest sister. Sita." She wiped her face.

*She's the baby of the family,* Padma remembered.

"Please . . . sit."

"My brother told me he had spoken of me . . . to you."

Chatter, chatter, chatter. She's different from all of us.

Padma got up, went to the fridge and poured out a glass of water. She took it to Sita. Sita drank it thirstily.

My mother calls her her ray of sunshine.

"Forgive him. Forgive all of us."

She tried to nod.

"For thirteen years, didi, he lived with you in his mind. Every day, every night."

Would it never end.

"You had to live all these years not knowing why he did what he did. But . . . you . . . cannot know what it was like for him. I . . . he could not come to you. He will . . . never . . . tell you about that."

Once again, she nodded.

"I have come to hear the truth and tell you the truth. You need not say it gently or kindly. Tell me, didi, what lies in your heart when you think of him."

"I . . . pain."

"Hate? Anger?"

"No. No." Never that, never.

Sita closed her eyes briefly. "Didi, he was coming to you."

She nodded.

"What he wanted to say to you, he could not—"

"I know what he wanted to say to me."

"Didi?"

"He . . . what he did to me . . . he must have been a damaged . . . man."

"Yes."

"He wanted to ask my forgiveness."

"Yes," Sita said. She was quiet for some time. "Perhaps it is a good thing that your sister and your mother cursed us. Otherwise the time might not have come when I would ask my brother."

"No . . . you—"

"If we had had normal lives, if I had had a normal life, I would have let it slip to the back of my mind. But there was nothing normal about our lives. My sisters—"

"I know. Everything."

"Didi, you do not know everything. Something happened to me that was worse than what happened to my sisters, and after that it was as if I had to find out, I began to believe as my mother and sisters did, that it all went back to that day when your mother and sister came to our house.

"One year after I got married I had a beautiful baby girl. Seven and a half pounds. Fair; thick black hair. Beautiful. So beautiful. Everyone said that—the nurses, the doctor, everyone."

Not this.

"Didi."

Padma opened her eyes.

"She was not alive. Strangled by the umbilical cord. After that my mother said, Do not have any more children, do not have any more children. Like a mad woman she used to keep saying it. Two years later when I told her I was expecting my second child, she screamed at me, What are you doing, do you have no sense? Then she put her hand to her mouth and began to cry loudly. "My second child was a boy. Seven pounds. Fair; black hair. Also dead. Also strangled by the umbilical cord. You cannot look at my face. The others also. No one could look at my face."

"Sita—"

"Didi, two babies. They were perfect. It seemed that at any moment their eyes would open. I did not believe them. I had to see. I had to touch. I tried to make them cry." She was silent for a minute, then she said, "I told my brother, All this what has happened to us, it is because two women cursed us. Bhaiya said that he had never come across such superstitious and foolish women.

"You are smiling a little. Yes, I also used to smile when he said things like this. But this time I did not. I told him we had been cursed. You should have seen his face. Such irritation on it, such impatience. He said to me, Why are you talking like an uneducated woman? Then he began asking me, Who were these women, when did they came, he began firing questions at me one after the other. Then I gave him your horoscope. I said, Her mother and sister had come to our house thirteen years ago, soon after you had got married. He stared at it. Then he said to me, *Her* mother and sister came to our house after my wedding? I said, Yes. It was as though someone had hit him very hard, that was how his expression was. He said, Why wasn't I told? I told him why, that Mataji and my sisters made me swear on the Gita not to tell anyone. He looked at me with disbelief. Then he strode out of the room. I followed him to the kitchen, where Mataji was cooking and he showed it to her and he said, Mataji, why was I not told of this? My mother looked at him and then at me, very calmly. She said, Beta, what was there to tell? They had an offer of marriage for you from this girl who was in your college. I told them that we could not accept it since you were already married. Then they got very angry, said all kinds of things. They even cursed us. That is why I did not tell you. We even made Sita swear on the Gita not to tell you, so terrible were the words these women flung at us.

"Yes, my mother is a clever woman. My brother had nothing to say. He just stood there, looking dazed. I had your letters in my hand. I held them up. I said to him without looking at my mother, I found these in Mataji's saree trunk. He took them from my hands and looked at the handwriting on them. His hands were shaking. I saw him looking at the postmarks, at the back and in the front. I waited for him to open them, but he did not.

It was as if the words were stuck in his throat. My mother said, What are these letters? I said to her, Do not pretend, Mataji, these are the letters Padma Rao wrote to Bhaiya thirteen years ago, which you read and hid from him. I found them in your saree trunk today. My mother did not look angry or anything. As if I was talking foolishly, she said, Sita what are you saying? Then she peered at the letters in my brother's hand and said, Beta, I do not know what the matter is with Sita. You think I would open your letters? I do not even know what this is that you are holding in your hands. I said to Mataji, If you do not know then why were they lying in your trunk? She said, So many things are lying in my trunk, so many old letters, you know I never throw away letters, if these were also lying there then I must have put them away with the others, if you say they are thirteen years old then in the confusion of the wedding and my illness I must have put them away with the rest and forgotten about them. I said, If that is so, Mataji, then why are they opened? She did not answer me. She looked at Bhaiya and said, Beta, I have nothing to say. Such accusations I will not even bother to answer, it is beneath me. If these letters have been opened, then ask the person who gave them to you why she opened them.

"I told Bhaiya, No Bhaiya, I did not read them. They were already opened. He did not reply. He went back to his room and sat on his bed, looking down at the carpet, the letters still in his hand. I sat down next to him and said, Bhaiya, they were already open. He did not answer. I don't think he was even aware that I was talking. I had seen that expression on his face before. I had never understood it. It was as though his mind was somewhere else, so far away that it was just his body that sat before me. Now, after all these years I did understand. He was with you. In the ten years that he was married, and the three years that followed, it was this expression which—"

"Three years after . . . ?"

"She went away to the ashram where her guru lives. None of us have seen her after that."

Sita continued as if there had been no interruption. "Bhaiya said to me, You should not have read them, Sita. I did not want to argue anymore. I said, Bhaiya, read them. Please read them now. He took a deep breath and shook his head, he put the letters next to him on the bed and said, No, this belongs to another time. I said, Bhaiya, what are you saying, don't you want to know what she says. He said, What she said, not what she says. I said, Bhaiya, it is the same thing. He shook his head again and said, She is living another life now. Thirteen years ago she wrote things to me that she wanted me to read. I did not read them then. She will not want me to read them now.

"After some time I said, Bhaiya, why did you not marry her? Then he told me what you already know. I understood what my mother had done.

"I said, Bhaiya, will you tell me about her.

"He said, I have nothing but contempt for myself.

"See, that was the thing. That was how he had lived for the last thirteen years. I had not known it till then. But you put it correctly—he was a damaged man. How hard he worked in his job. He got promotions faster than his colleagues. Everyone praised him, everyone spoke of his honesty, his integrity. He worked as though that was all that mattered."

"I said to him, Bhaiya, tell me about her.

"After some time he said, She was not like me.

"I said, How?

"He said, If it had happened to her she would not have got married." I came in. I sat next to him. I couldn't see his face at all. After some time he said, I'm going to Bangalore to her parents tomorrow. He got up and went out."

She should offer Sita tea, something cold, something . . . to eat. She couldn't get up. Her tongue was heavy, her eyes heavier.

"My brother will never speak to you of all this. That is why I am telling you."

Again, she tried to nod.

"Also, didi, I had to know how you feel towards . . . him. 'Specially . . . now."

Slowly her tongue was forming the words, "In this house I shared every day with him. Every moment with Mallika, I shared with him."

There was compassion in Sita's eyes. "Thirteen years. Like Bhaiya."

Waste.

"One thing I would have wished for. Only one," Padma said.

"What, didi?"

"That we had met, once, just once, before he . . . died."

"Didi?"

"So that I could have told him before he died what lay in my heart. I can never tell him now. He will never know."

"Didi, what are you saying."

"If he had met me once, and then gone, then I could let him go. He'll never know, now, Sita. He'll never know I hold nothing against him."

Was that horror on Sita's face or something else?

"Didi, the . . . accident—you know . . . that . . ."

"The accident was near my mother's house."

"She . . . what did your mother see?" Sita's voice was hoarse.

All that Sita had told her today, that too she now had to carry with her. "What . . . Sita?"

"Your mother saw the accident?"

She should offer Sita some lime-juice. Was there lime in the fridge? She nodded.

Sita tried to say something, failed. She got up and sat next to Padma, held her hand. She put her arm around her shoulder. Her arm was very strong, it held her in a vicelike grip. Sita said, "My brother is not dead."

Sita shook her. "Didi."

She hadn't offered her any juice. She said, "Sita, will you have lime-juice or would you prefer tea?"

Sita's grip was hurting. "Didi, I don't know why your mother thought he . . . he . . . had died. He was badly hurt. But he is recovering now. They shifted him to Delhi—he is still in Safdarjung Hospital. That is why he has not come to you."

Another one of those horrible dreams. Would they never end. Would this be the one that would now begin haunting her for the rest of her years? Was this one worse or better than the Mallika dream? She had borne that. Now she supposed she could bear this. One could bear anything.

She was a terrible hostess. Shantacca would have had a whole tray of snacks by now, beautifully served, and long lovely glasses of lime-juice. She said, "Sita, I'm so sorry for not giving you anything to drink. Tell me, tea or coffee or something cold?"

"Didi, my brother, Karan, is alive, he's alive, didi. Your child, Mallika's, father is alive."

When would this dream end. At what point. If she didn't talk at all, if she just watched Sita, said nothing . . . then what would happen? Would the room become dark and Sita merge into the darkness, and she be alone, waiting, Mallika asleep where she couldn't see or reach her . . . would that be the place where this new dream would take her? Because it would have to end with Mallika. As long as there was no white sheet in this new dream. Recently she had begun using old bedcovers as sheets for Mallika's bed. They weren't as smooth as proper sheets but Mallika didn't mind and Shantacca had insisted. I don't know why you didn't think of it before, Shantacca had said.

"Didi. Didi. Are you all right?" Sita's face was very frightened, her voice very high.

There. She had been right. There was Mallika coming towards them. It had to end with Mallika, like the other dream. Now what would happen? There was fear on her child's face. So now she would have to break her resolution not to talk in the dream and reassure her child. Even in dreams one could not ignore the fear on one's child's face. She spoke, and even her voice sounded different, so this was surely a new horrible dream, God help her. "Mallika, don't look frightened, my pet, come and sit here." Mallika wasn't coming and sitting next to her. Sita was looking at Mallika and her eyes were full of tears. Mallika was looking at her, Padma, the fear in her face growing. It always had to end with Mallika, her poor, poor child. All her fault. All Mallika's suffering was her mother's fault. She said, "Mallika, please make some lime-juice for our guest, and get some of Shantamama's cake too." She shook her head at Sita's expression. "No, Sita," she said firmly, "please don't be formal with me. You can't leave without having something to drink." But Mallika didn't go and Sita's expression didn't change, nor did her grip around Padma's shoulder. Padma sighed. Well then. She would have to wait and see what happened. Sita was fumbling with the purse on her lap. She managed to open it with one hand and took out a photograph. "Look at this, didi," she said, and there was a kind of desperation in her voice. "This is what he looks like now."

Sita should not have shown it to her. She should not have. It was a full-length close-up of him. He was standing, his hands in his pockets, looking unsmilingly at the camera. He had filled out, it was no longer the body she had known. Broader shoulders, stronger arms and legs. It was no longer the face she had known. Thinner. Wiped clean of any softness. The boy-man she remembered and of whom she had thought for thirteen years had gone. There was nothing left of him at all. His features were the same, the way he stood was the same, it was Karan. But not the Karan she had known. Gone. Gone. Now she could never dream of him without this new unknown face intruding. Now she could never dream of him again.

"Didi. Didi."

She was moaning loudly, the sounds racking her body, coming out of her stomach. She was back in the railway guest house, they had just come back with the news. She held her stomach and howled like an animal, Shantacca's arms around her or was it Sita's, which time was it now, where was she, the years moved in front of her, contracted, a desk full of books, crumpled blue bedcover, a calendar with marks on the wall, mirror high on the wall, clothes on the floor, Padma.

"Lie down. Lie down, didi. Here, put your head on the cushion. I'll get you water. Don't get up. Close your eyes. Mallika, beti, your neighbour, Mrs. Prasad—all right, go, beti, get her, hurry."

So this is where it ended? Three of them in the room with her, fear on their faces—imagine, fear, how peculiar. Anu, Sita, Mallika. No Shantacca this time, no Madhav, no Amma, no Appa. But Appa was dead wasn't he? Or was he not? Or was that too part of the dream? No Karan either. At least not one that she could see. In the other dream he was waiting outside the door. In this one he was waiting inside the photograph. Why was Mallika looking at the photograph in that manner? And anyway it wasn't him, it was an older man. At least thirteen years older. This is what dreams did, merging and mixing and going forwards and backwards. Who was making those dreadful sounds? It seemed to come from near her. Mallika, was Mallika all right? She put out her hand to her but Mallika was standing in the far corner just looking at her, her face full of terror. She could feel the room becoming dark as it had in the other dream. Mallika, she wanted to say, but the words would not come out. My baby, she wanted to say, but her tongue had curled up and died. So this, then, was the last part of the dream, the darkness like Rahu swallowing up her child and spitting out her child's terror, and that was all that she could see finally— Mallika's terror, like the Cheshire Cat—without Mallika's face.


They said it was a breakdown. Rest. That was what she needed, lots of rest. The nursing home wasn't far from the house, but it wasn't near either. Madhu Aunty would take them there and get them back twice a day. And she let them have their time with Ma, leaving them there and coming back after a decent interval to pick them up. After a few days they just visited once a day, since Ma spent all her time sleeping. Sita visited at separate times with lots of fruits, sometimes on their way in or out they would meet her. It would not have been easy for her—she lived very far away, in Old Delhi.

Shantamama had said to Mallika after the first day, "It is better this way than the other way. This way your ma will remain sane." Mallika tried to push That Day out of her mind. She would never forget the sounds Ma made for as long as she lived. She would never forget her face for as long as she lived.

A week later when Shantamama went to see Ma, she searched Shantamama's trunk and found it. Thirty pages, she counted them all. Over and over she had seen Ma reading it, over and over. All of it in Kannada.

Only Prabha could help her. She knew what she, Mallika, had heard between Ma and Sita. She knew about the man who had fathered her.

Shantamama didn't even notice that the letter had gone. She was too busy cooking and making soups for Ma, going with Madhu Aunty to the nursing home and back, cooking again, seeing to it that Mallika was having all her meals. Nothing ever ended for Shantamama, nothing.

Who, that was the question. Who would translate the letter for her? It couldn't be any grown-up they knew. No one in the colony. What to do? She and Prabha opened the letter and closed it, looked at the thirty sheets, stared at those round letters with curls that hid so many secrets. Who, who, who?

"Gauri."

Prabha struck upon it. Gauri knew Kannada. Her grandmother had taught her to read and write it. Gauri who was so terrible in studies had a flair for languages. She even read Kannada novels. And she would never betray its contents even if she had to die for it.

Gauri was overwhelmed. Just now she would do it, just now. She would not tell anyone, never never never—she promised on her mother's name, on her father's name, on her grandmother's name, on her sisters' names. She didn't have to make all those promises, they believed her, Prabha told her.

They sat in the veranda behind Gauri's house that hot summer afternoon when Gauri's mother and sisters slept. Prabha had an empty notebook with her into which she wrote what Gauri translated.

*My dearest child, Shanta. What I am going to write to you are for your eyes alone. It will have to be told to Padma sooner or later, but let it not be this un-*

*purged version. My child, things have come full circle. And once again, your words have fulfilled themselves.*

"Hai, Gauri, so nicely you translate," Prabha sighed.

He must have fallen asleep before she came to his room in the hospital. He did not know how long she had been sitting on that chair, watching him. Ten minutes? An hour? He had been sleeping on his side, facing her. He hadn't slept the previous night. He never slept at night. Sometimes he tried to fight off the sleep that overcame him in the mornings or afternoons so that it would come instead at night. It wouldn't work. Then the night would come and like a replay it would begin again.

He opened his eyes and she was there looking at him, sitting very close to his bed, crying, her hands clasped hard on her lap, her eyes and lips swollen. His lips mouthed her name. Mallika. She was trying not to make any sounds, but they escaped in spite of her effort. She wiped her nose against her sleeve, then her face against the other.

Slowly, he sat up in bed, waited for the dizziness to subside. Then he got up, walked to the cupboard and opened it. He took out a large, clean handkerchief and gave it to her. She took it from him and blew her nose. From a jug on the side table he poured out a glass of water and gave it to her. She drank it all. He poured out another. She drank most of that too. He took the glass back from her, washed it in the washbasin and put it back over the jug. He opened the cupboard again and took out a fresh towel. "You can wash your face in the washbasin," he said, giving it to her. Then he went back to bed and sat against the pillow, trying to fight the dizziness. He heard the tap running.

When he opened his eyes she was sitting down on the chair again. No, she didn't look like Padma. She was going to be a tall girl, unlike Padma. She was slim, but unlike Padma, not small built. The only thing she had inherited of Padma's was her skin, brown and smooth and glowing. No resemblance to him either. That familiar, grave expression. In that instant it hit him. It was his reserve that she had. It was his expression that she bore.

She too wouldn't take her eyes away from his face. Her own was getting contorted with the effort to hold back more tears. They began trickling out again.

"My child . . ."

*"I'm not your child."*

He flinched. He had heard that before too. Her body was heaving. She covered her face with his hanky. Through it he heard her muffled voice, "Tell your mother that the bastard does not carry your family's name. Tell your mother the bastard's name is Mallika *Rao.* Rao, Rao, Rao. Your mother called Ma—"

*"Mallika."*

"—a *randi.* Your mother called Ma a *randi.* You listen. You listen. I read the letter Ajji wrote to Shantamama after you went to her. I know everything. *Everything.*"

She was crying very hard again. She put the hanky on her lap and wiped her face with the towel. With dread he waited for the inevitable question.

"*How* could you have not known?"

He shook his head mutely.

"Why did you—"

He raised his hand as if warding off a blow. "Please. Don't ask me. I can't answer."

She stared at him. "You have to tell me."

"No," he said pleadingly. "Please. No."

"You didn't know?"

"No. No."

She stared at him, the tears still running down her cheeks. "But you—"

"I was coming to see you and your mother when I had the accident. If I had known earlier . . . you think I would have—" He couldn't speak.

Her face crumpled. "You should have gone to Ma," she sobbed. "Even if you thought she was married you should have gone to her. Even if you thought she was married."

He felt drained, bereft.

"You don't know *anything.* You don't know what you've *done* to her."

He didn't have the right to speak.

"You wanted to come to us for . . . ab . . . solution." She mouthed the word silently to see if she had got it right, nodded, said again, "For absolution."

How can either of you give me what I can't give myself.

There was no point denying anything. She had not come for answers.

"When will you be discharged?"

"Next week."

"Then you'll go to Ma. Then you'll ask for her forgiveness. Then she'll give it. Then you'll marry her."

His head was hammering so hard that he couldn't sit up. He lay down, facing her.

"Gauri, my friend, translated Ajji's letter from Kannada to English. She wouldn't tell us what *randi* meant in English."

And he had thought, just the night before, that the worst that he would have to face now was their rejection.

"I told Gauri, If you don't tell me, I'll ask Anu Aunty. So then she got scared and begged me, Mallika, please don't ask anyone. She couldn't say it. She tried to write it, but that also she couldn't do. So then she spelt it out in a whisper to Prabha and me: W - H - O - R - E." She spat it out in a sibilant whisper.

He had been prepared for rejection. But he had not imagined its odour.

"I told Gauri, You don't have to feel bad. I said, You're only translating it. Gauri kept crying, kept crying, kept saying, I'm sorry, I'm sorry. As though it were her fault."

She was quiet, thinking of something. The hammer in his head was beating a terrible beat.

"Our neighbour, Madhu Aunty, my friend Mahima's mother—her servant, an unmarried woman, had a baby. Madhu Aunty said, Oh those servants are like that. I thought she meant servants were different, like different . . . a different species. I thought she meant things could happen to people like them that could never happen to us."

She mulled over this for some time, opening and closing his hanky. "Our other neighbour, Anu Aunty, my friend Prabha's mother . . . once she told Prabha, Delhi girls are very fast—they go on motorcycles with boys."

There were three lines between her eyebrows. "They're Ma's only friends."

She thought he didn't understand. He said, "But they don't know do they?"

"No. Not yet."

"They need never know."

She shook her head.

What did she want him to say.

"They think Ma is good . . . and honest and . . ."

"She is all that."

"*You* don't have to tell *me* that. You don't have to tell me *anything* about Ma. I know her better than you *ever* knew her."

"I wasn't trying to tell you anything about your mother. I—"

"You never saw her suffer. How can you know someone whom you haven't seen suffering?"

It was no use. She found his silence unbearable. She found his words unbearable.

"You never knew Ma, never. You never went through any bad times with her. Then how can you know her? Shantamama says that true love is what is tested at bad times, through shared troubles. She says that if you stand by those you love in times of need, that is the true test. But at times of need only Shantamama and Madhu Aunty and Anu Aunty have stood by her. No one else. She's borne all her troubles without you."

"I know that."

"You *don't* know that. You don't even know *what* troubles she's had. You don't know *anything*."

Better to be silent.

"You think troubles mean things that have *happened* to her. They're not only that. They're also things you don't *talk* about."

I know.

"Ma hasn't talked about anything to me but I *know*. She hasn't talked about it to her friends but they also *know*."

Mallika. Mallika.

"You don't even understand what I'm saying. When I said her friends think she's good and honest, I meant what *they* think *good* and *honest* means. Not what *I* think it is."

I know.

"You want to marry her, don't you?"

He kept absolutely quiet, not taking his eyes away from her face.

"Then, after you marry her, you'll want to take her away from our house and our friends and from her job—to your house and there you'll make her look after your old mother and look after your sisters and their husbands when they come, and spend all her time in the kitchen. That's what you'll make her do. If Ma had married you then she would have had to become like that and forget books and music and her doctorate and everything. Ma would have become like Anu Aunty, my friend Prabha's mother, cooking, cleaning, looking after guests. That's what Shantamama says. Anu Aunty learnt singing for fourteen years. Now she's stopped singing. She doesn't even have five minutes for that. Her mother-in-law hates her. Your mother would also have hated Ma. She also would have said nasty things to my mother which you would never have heard. And Ma also would not have told you because you wouldn't have believed her just like Prasad Uncle doesn't believe Anu Aunty. Shantamama says men never believe anything bad about their mothers."

Her expression changed. Curiosity. "Do you believe that your mother did all those things?"

He could not answer.

"You have to tell me."

"It's all in the past. Try to . . . forget it."

*"Forget it!"* She sounded incredulous. "You're trying to excuse her."

"No."

"Of course you are."

"I believe it."

"No, you don't. I don't believe you. You don't believe it. You're just saying it because you know that is what I want you to say."

He was silent.

"*Nobody* has gone through what Ma has gone through. *Nobody.* And you're saying, Try and forget it." Her voice was shaking.

She put the back of her hand to her mouth and was quiet for some time. Then she said, "So what if you thought of her day and night for thirteen years. It doesn't count for anything. It's . . . easy to think of . . . someone day and night for years."

Familiar words again.

"Where did you and Ma go?"

He looked at her blankly.

"Did Ma come to your house when you were a lecturer—is that where?"

"Yes."

"She used to come to your house . . . often?"

"Yes."

"She . . . you . . . you asked her to come?"

"We . . . both wanted to be together."

"For two years?"

"Yes."

"Ma didn't think it was . . . wrong or . . . anything."

"No." He struggled for the words. "She . . . wouldn't do anything she felt was . . . wrong."

"Would you?"

Trapped.

"I'm not talking about how you ditched her. I mean . . . did you think she was . . . loose?"

"*No.* No. Never." Ditched her.

She was watching him very carefully.

"If I thought that way about your mother . . . do you think I—"

"You only wanted to come to us because you knew you had a . . . had given her a child. Otherwise you wouldn't have wanted to."

"No. Had I known she had never married I would have gone to her, whether or not she had had a . . . had you."

"But you were married."

"I would have got a separation."

"I don't understand. You married her because you couldn't say no to your mother. But you would have got a separation from her in spite of your mother?"

Mallika.

She said, "Tell me. I don't understand. I don't."

"It doesn't make any sense. But yes, that is what was . . . in my mind."

"You went to Ajji's house after your marriage and Ajja told you Ma was married. Suppose he hadn't told you that. Then?"

"Then I would have sought Padma out."

"Then?"

"Got a separation from my wife."

"I don't understand. All this going here and going there and getting separated and married again—why did you get married in the first place?"

"There didn't . . . seem to be a . . . choice. But of course . . . there was. There always is."

There always is. Going through the marriage ceremony in a daze, thinking, get it over with, get it over with, then go to Padma. All the while thinking, it will be over soon. Then I'll go to Padma. Nothing else in his mind, nothing. The wedding over, his mother ill, ready to die, saying she wanted him by her side during her last days, late for the training . . . no leave. There always is a choice.

"So if you knew Ma was unmarried, you would have got a separation from your wife and married Ma, and taken her to your house. Then your family would have welcomed her with open arms, especially your mother."

"I wasn't thinking of all that."

"That's what Shantamama says. She says men never think. She says men never know what their wives have to put up with from their families. Your wife also had to. I read all that in Ajji's letter. Shantamama says the worst thing about marrying a man you love is the disillusionment that follows. You made Ma suffer one way. If you had married her you would have made her suffer another way."

She was talking quite earnestly now. She had forgotten that he was the man who had fathered her. She was thinking about him and her mother as people in the distant past, disconnected from her. It would not last. She was still a child. Padma's child. She spoke well. She had a way with words. And yet, in the middle of all this, from time to time, the child in her would suddenly emerge.

"You're not listening to me."

Padma. Padma. He looked up at Mallika's face.

"I'm listening to every word."

"But you're not taking me seriously."

"I'm taking you very seriously." Padma.

She stared at him and her eyes grew still. He tried to speak but could not. He had to make that look on her face go away. What had she seen on his face to make her look that way.

She said, "Where do you live now?"

He was quiet for some time. Then he said, "I've been posted to . . . Delhi." She stared at him. He understood the look now. He watched her with compassion.

"Mallika," he said gently. "Don't try and ward me off. I'll keep away without it."

She said, without premeditation, "Ma won't let you keep away." She burst into loud tears.

He got out of bed, sat facing her. The dizziness had gone, he felt unnaturally calm. He heard her weep, "What will I do without Ma, what will I do without Ma."

He touched her arm. He shouldn't have. He could feel his insides shattering like so many splinters of glass. She moved her hand away.

"You won't ever have to do without your mother."

"Ma'll *die,* Ma'll *die.*"

"She won't die. She's had a breakdown. She needs rest. Then she'll get better."

She was crying even more now, "Suppose she goes mad . . ."

"She'll be all right."

Her sobs became louder. "No she won't, no she won't."

"Give her a little time. She will be back to normal."

"Now she'll never be back to normal. Never, never."

"She'll recover. Sita spoke to the doctor and he too said that."

Mallika wiped her face with the towel.

"I won't take your mother away from you."

She wiped her face again. The weeping was slowly subsiding. She looked up at him again and asked, "You can stay without her?"

He could feel the constriction in his chest becoming worse. He knew what she was asking of him. "Yes," he said. His voice was calm again. "I can stay without her and without you if I know both of you want it that way and as long as both of you are well and in good health."

"You want to meet her first . . . to . . . talk about . . . everything."

"Yes."

"You won't ask her to marry you."

"She won't want to."

"Why?"

"The burden of the past thirteen years."

"Even though she knows everything now?"

"Even though she knows everything now."

She was looking a little cheerful now. God help him.

"And you'll never want to see her after this?"

She saw his hesitation. Her eyes began to fill. He said, "Mallika, do you think I can sever all relations with you and your mother? Especially you?"

She looked down and said, "If you did it for thirteen years why can't you do it again?"

Padma had always said her hands got cold when she was overwrought. But Padma's hands and feet were always cold in the winter and cool in the summer. You're always overwrought, he would tease her, warming her feet and hands and the rest of her under the quilt. Now he could feel his own hands becoming very cold.

He said, "It also . . . depends . . . on how your mother feels, doesn't it?"

She looked up at him and said, "And what about how I feel?"

If this had been a film, bugles would have been blowing, drums beating. What a fool he had been. She had declared war right from the beginning. But he hadn't seen it for the tears. How did he fight her, his . . . no, not his daughter. Padma's daughter.

"Aren't I part of it too?" She was ready for war. No tears now. Far deadlier.

"Yes. What is it that you want me to do?"

"Why are you asking me? As though you're going to do what I want you to do. As though you're going to."

"I have to see your mother. I want to . . . keep . . . in touch with both of you."

"One minute you're saying one thing, another minute you're saying another thing."

"I won't do anything that you both don't want."

"And if Ma wants it?"

"She will not do what you don't want her to do."

"She always does what she wants to do."

"She does?" he asked, diverted.

"She thinks she doesn't. But she does."

"I see."

"If Ma does?"

"Pardon?"

"If Ma wants to keep contact?"

"We'll cross that bridge when we come to it."

"That means you will." She was looking distinctly unfriendly now. What to tell her.

"Ma's got a very good reputation in the colony. And in her college." Now what.

"Except Narayana Uncle when he comes home with Shantamama, no man ever comes to our house."

Ah. That was it.

"If you keep coming and seeing us then people will start gossiping about Ma."

She wasn't sure of her mother. For the first time in her life. She wanted him away. Out.

"If you keep coming home people may find out who . . . you . . . are. Ma won't tell you all this. *You* have to tell her."

Of course. Mallika would not, could not, tell Padma. She wanted him to ensure the severing. The look he had seen on her face had been one of terror.

"You don't have to look as though you're feeling sorry for me."

"I'm not feeling sorry for you."

"I'm going now." She made no move to get up.

There was a long silence.

"Does your mother know you're here?"

"Ma will get to know. Ma always gets to know."

"She does?" Gently. Gently.

"She knows how I think."

Don't say anything. Listen.

"But that I also know about her. You know?"

He nodded.

"No, you don't know. Shantamama says men don't understand these things. She says men only want logic. She told me, Mallika, you always know the texture of your mother's thoughts. I don't know what Ma's think-ing. But I always know what . . . feelings her thoughts give her."

Had he known?

"Did you know?"

"I . . . haven't thought about it."

"That means you didn't know. You don't have to think about these things. If it's there it's there, if it isn't there it isn't there."

"Perhaps."

"Not perhaps. Definitely. Ma must have known yours."

Mallika understood that.

"Ma is like that with everybody."

Oh.

"But most of all with me."

I understand what you're trying to tell me, child.

A stray tear trickled out of one eye. She wiped it.

He sat up on the bed and leaned against the back. "How did you come?"

"I took a bus."

"Does anyone know you're here?"

"Prabha. And Gauri."

"Your aunt, Shanta?"

"She's gone to her brother-in-law's house to spend a few days with her sons. In Old Delhi."

"Where are—"

"I'm staying in Prabha's house."

"Where does Prabha's mother think you are?"

"In Gauri's house."

"The three of you planned it all out."

She didn't answer.

He glanced at his watch. "You should go back. Wait. I'll give you the money for a scooter."

"I'm taking a bus."

"It's safer."

"It is *not*. Not in Delhi. If a bus isn't crowded it's safer than a scooter."

He took in a deep breath. "Do you have money for the ticket?"

She didn't look at him. She nodded.

"How is P— Your mother?"

"I don't know." She mumbled it into her lap.

"Please tell me."

"All this time, you didn't even ask. Not even once."

"Sita has been coming here regularly and telling me about her."

Already he could anticipate her response.

"Then why are you asking me."

"Because you know your mother better."

She played with the end of her plait. "I don't know. She sleeps most of the time. She hardly talks."

"I see."

She seemed to be about to say something else. With dread, he waited. She looked down at her lap. Then she looked up at him. No. No.

"Don't ask me anything else," he said.

She opened her mouth to ask the question.

He shook his head desperately, *"No."*

Accusation and betrayal in her eyes. As if unable to meet his, she looked down at her lap.

"Mallika."

She looked at him.

"Forgive me."

She looked down again. In misery and despair he watched her shoulders beginning to heave. She put up her arm and covered her eyes with it. The familiar sound of her weeping began again. Without taking her arm away from her eyes she put out her other arm to ward him off.

Thirteen years had worn it thin. Now, inside him, something was beginning to tear. He had to hold it together. He couldn't let it happen now.

The worst was, he knew why. If he hadn't, he might have been able to bear it better. Easier to wonder, to question. Easier to doubt. That gave one fortitude. It gave one grace. In his case he had the answer—it was all his doing. That simple. Living with his wife had been easier than living with this knowledge. He had managed to shut out his wife without much of an effort. She had allowed herself to be shut out. Hours would pass and he wouldn't even be aware that she was in the house. But from the other, there was no escape.

Once he had called Padma simple. But actually she had been wise. Wisdom, contrary to what he had once believed, was simple, not complicated. Mallika had put her finger on it when she said her mother knew how people thought. Its texture, as her sister, Shanta, had told Mallika. And all those other things that her aunt had told her, all so inappropriate for a child's ears. Mallika had assimilated and digested every bit of it. And quoted it to him faithfully, with conviction, and in a context, to boot.

Padma had known how he thought too. He had imagined it was this way because of what lay between them. But no, it was her. As she knew others, she had known him, known the shape of his thoughts and feelings long before she understood them. She had this same knowledge even now. She had told Sita that he must have been damaged by what he did to her. He could not have imagined that this was what she would be left with after thirteen years.

But before she knew of his going to her mother—what had she thought before that, for all those long years? What, what, what? Knowing him as she did, what *could* she have imagined? This was what he had lived with every day and night—her question. She wouldn't have believed it at first. Eventually she would have had to. She wouldn't have had a choice. Yet, Sita had said to him, he had lived with her day and night for thirteen years, as she had with him. Would this be what he would see when he went to her? Or would it be the unspoken splinters of those thirteen years? Or the other, which Mallika had come to tell him?

.   .   .

When he reached the nursing home he found that he couldn't enter. He stood at the door for a moment, then forced his hand upwards to open it. A slow paralysis was afflicting him. "Excuse me—you are going in?" He moved to let the man behind him enter, then followed him inside. "Padma Rao," he said at the reception. The nurse looked doubtful. "It is not visiting hours, sir." He looked at her mutely. "Are you her brother . . . husband?" He shook his head. "Then, sir, please come back between four and six in the evening. Only close relations they are allowed in the morning." She looked down at her register and began writing. "Which room is she in?" he asked. She looked up, abstractedly, "Twelve." She went back to her register. He walked down the corridor. On the left—one, three, five, seven, nine, eleven. On the right—two, four, six, eight, ten. Twelve.

He felt sick, nauseous. He stood outside the door blindly. It opened, a woman in her early thirties came out and almost walked into him. "Forgive me, forgive me," she said in Hindi, moving to the side as he moved backwards. "It's all right," he managed to say. She was about to move, then she looked up at him and he saw an almost frightened recognition in her eyes. She said, "You must be . . . Sita's brother." He nodded. "And you are Mrs. . . . Prasad?" She acknowledged it with a slight nod, folded her hands in a namaste. He folded his. She looked as though she would begin crying any minute. Apprehensively he pointed to the door. "Is . . . she all right?" Mrs. Prasad nodded, avoiding his eyes, her own very bright. "She is . . . very weak." He nodded. She said, "Not just her body, but otherwise also . . . you understand?" He nodded again. She wanted to say something more, he saw her throat move. She said, indistinctly, "Please, be . . . take care . . . do not . . . disturb her." Their eyes locked for a brief moment, then she folded her hands and was gone. He opened the door.

The bed was on the far side of the room, the window next to the bed had its curtain drawn against the sun. She was lying there, her back turned to him, covered with a white sheet. Her hair in its long plait was all he could see of her. It had grown. There was a chair on the side that she was facing. He closed the door softly and walked to her bed and around it.

She was asleep. He sat down.

. . .

An hour later she stirred. She opened her eyes. After some time, not taking her eyes away from him, she sat up, put the pillow behind her and sat back against the bed.

The look in her eyes hadn't been there before. You don't know what you've *done* to her. You don't know *anything*.

After a long time she said, "There's coffee in the flask." He picked up the flask and opened it, poured some into the cup of the flask and another into a mug that lay next to it. He handed her the mug. She drank, and he saw some colour return to her face. He felt the chill in his body slowly dissipating as he drank. He saw her eyes on his cup of coffee. No, not on that, on his hands. Were they still shaking? They finished their coffee in silence. Then he took her empty mug from her and went to the bathroom. He washed the two cups and the flask in the washbasin, then splashed water on his face. The bathroom smelt of her, as his once had. He wiped his face against his sleeves and went back to the room. She said, "There's a clean towel in the cupboard." He shook his head, put the flask and mug on the side table and sat down once again.

Face thinner. Longer hair, still slim, still that smooth, brown skin. The same large brown eyes, except that they had dark circles around them. Looked about eight years younger than her age. She hadn't taken her eyes off him. She was looking at him in the curious, questioning way that one looks at someone who seems very familiar but whom one can't place. Even if he had had any words they would have died at meeting that look.

"Where did you get hurt?"

He looked at her, dazed.

"Your accident."

"Concussion."

"You were unconscious?"

He nodded.

"Did you break any bones?"

"Ribs."

"You're all right now?"

He nodded.

"Was that a very deep cut on your temple?"

He nodded.

"The other vehicle?"

"A truck. He wasn't hurt."

"Your voice sounds the same."

And yours. I hear it every night.

Her eyes moved from his face to his arms, his hands. She lifted his hand. Hers were cool. They always had been. She rested his palm on the palm of her left hand, and with her right, felt his fingers, his knuckles, his nails. She turned his hand this way, then that. Then for a few seconds she held his hand between her own, her face very intent, her eyes looking beyond him, as though she was listening to something. Gently, she put it back on his lap. She shook her head slightly, almost to herself. She closed her eyes as if to shut him out, then opened them and continued looking at him with the same look.

He might have said something if she had not done this in the manner that she had. Was he looking at her the way Mallika had looked at him? Was the same terror there on his face?

He tried to speak.

She put out her hands, as though stopping something. "Please," she said gently, "don't say anything."

He tried to nod.

"I've told them too. Shantacca and Anu. And Madhu. Not to say anything."

She shifted her pillows, leaned back again.

"When . . . will they discharge you?" Don't look at me like that.

"In about a week."

This is not what I came to say to you.

"I'm not going home."

He repeated, "Not going . . ."

"Home."

Thoughts were congealing. "Where . . . then?"

"I have to go away."

Tread carefully.

She gave an infinitesimal smile. "It's all right. I just need to be alone. For some time."

"Mallika—"

"Shantacca'll be taking Mallika back with her next week. Mallika'll return to Delhi before her school opens."

"Don't you want to—"

"No, I don't want to take Mallika with me. We . . . need to be separate for some . . . time."

Nothing was making sense.

"I don't want . . . I can't give her . . . anything . . . at this point."

The chill was entering his body again.

"I don't want . . . anyone expecting . . . anything."

"Mallika—"

"Especially Mallika."

He tried to find his way. "They all come to . . . see you here."

She lay down on the bed and turned to her side facing him. "Then they go away."

"But—"

"At home no one goes away. Not even Karan."

The chill was entering his bones.

She covered herself up with the sheet all the way up to the neck. "Can't keep . . . it . . . up . . ." Her eyes began to droop. He thought she was asleep when she said, as though she hadn't stopped, "Even the marrow from my . . . bones sucked . . . dry."

Her face was calm, her brow unfurrowed.

She opened her eyes. "I'm not mad."

He shook his head—you're not.

"You were frightened too."

"Not because I thought you were mad."

"But for the same reason that the others get frightened?"

"Because it isn't . . . like you?"

She nodded.

He said, "Yes. For that reason."

Very reasonably she said, "But it is. Like me."

Padma.

"I felt like this so often. So often."

Padma.

"For years."

Padma.

"I just didn't let myself think about it. About anything."

It was coming. He could see it. He braced himself.

"Even about Karan. For thirteen years I didn't let myself think about what he had done to me."

Even so, he could feel the shock.

"The problem is," she said thoughtfully, "that I can't mourn him. Or my father. Or Madhav."

"Can I," he said, stopped, began again. "Can I talk to you?"

She gave him a doubtful look.

"There is . . . I want to say . . . talk to you."

She looked more doubtful.

"Whenever you're ready. Not now, if you don't want me to."

She looked relieved. "All right."

"Do . . . would you like some water?"

"No thank you."

He poured himself some and drank it.

"I should have mourned for all three, thirteen years ago. First for Karan. Then for my father. Then for Madhav."

Better if she shouted, raved, wept. Accused.

"It's very . . . tiring trying to look strong and Padma-like in front of them. Madhu comes here and starts weeping. Anu comes here and spends the whole hour trying not to weep. Shantacca comes here and cries about Mallika. Mallika comes here with one of them and then it's the worst."

"How is she?"

"She tries not to show it to me. But I can feel"—she put out her hand as though touching something—"it."

Did she know Mallika had come to him? No.

"She's suffering for me. She always has. Even when she didn't know . . . anything. Now it's worse. That's another reason we have to be apart for some time. We're . . . bad for each other . . . we don't . . . balance one . . . another."

Balance? "Your sister, she—"

"Mallika's coping because of her. Shantacca and she balance one another. They always have."

What was she saying?

"They enjoy each other more than Mallika and I enjoy one another. From the beginning they have."

He had no idea.

"It isn't healthy. From the time she was a baby Mallika used to know . . . the shape of my thoughts. Sometimes before even I knew them . . ."

She was plucking at the sheet, speaking aloud.

"I too. Every time I used to be awake a minute before she cried out in her sleep. Even now. A day before she falls sick I know she'll fall sick. I can feel it in my bones. When my father died and I went home after thirteen years, it was as if I was waiting for something to happen to Mallika. It did."

She turned her head to the side and looked at him. "Do you understand?"

He didn't answer.

"That's why we can't enjoy each other the way she and Shantacca can. We don't give each other much . . . laughter. We have no . . . protection from one another."

She was not talking to the man who had fathered her child. That was why she could talk.

"When Mallika was born, till we came to Delhi, Shantacca breastfed her as often as I did."

The baby. Plump, grave, big eyes. Soft skin. Soft hair.

Her eyes held a faraway look.

"She comes here at least twice a year. Stays for two, three months. She loves Mallika more than her own sons."

Her eyes focussed on him. "Mallika came to see you."

He was very still.

"She's very . . . secretive. We would never have known. But Shantacca felt uneasy and came back early from her brother-in-law's house. When Mrs. Prasad said Mallika was with Gauri, Shantacca went to Gauri's house. Then she waited at home till Mallika returned, and got it out of her."

"What . . . did she say?"

"Nothing. Just that she had gone to see you. Nothing else. Refused to talk. Just like Karan. He too wouldn't let a thing out if he didn't want to."

His stomach churned again.

"What do you think of her?" The same look of slight curiosity on her face.

He got up and walked to the window. He drew the curtain and looked out. The light blinded his eyes. He drew the curtain against it. He walked back to her bed and stood by it.

"Sit. Please."

He took a deep breath and sat.

"Tell me."

He shook his head slightly.

"It's difficult to see one's child clearly. Even if you know how the child feels, thinks . . . even then. That's why I'm asking you."

Padma. Padma.

"That's why I need to go away. I can't help her unless I do. I have to help her."

"Where?"

"Away from all of them. Where I don't have to be . . . Padma-like."

"Where will you go?"

"A colleague of mine—her parents, who live in Delhi, have a small house in Dehra Dun. They're not going there this summer. She said I could go and stay there as long as I liked."

"How long . . . ?"

"About three weeks. Perhaps four."

"Four weeks?"

"After that I'll have to come back and begin teaching."

"Isn't that a . . . long time?"

"No, no. It's a short time. I haven't been out of Delhi for thirteen years. Not even for a day. Nor has Mallika. Now she'll have a proper holiday. Shantacca's been longing to have her in her own house.

"Why not?"

"Why not?"

"Why haven't you taken Mallika anywhere?"

She looked at him for a minute, her head turned slightly to one side. Gently, she said, "Why do you think?"

He shook his head.

"Money."

He could have hit himself. He looked away from her. "I'm sorry."

"That's all right." If only she wouldn't be so polite, so considerate.

Fool to have asked. He should have known. Dear God, and this nursing home. Who was paying for this? Should he? Would Padma accept it? And for Mallika?

She was watching him curiously. After some time she said, "Thank God."

He looked at her.

"I almost thought you'd offer us money. Thank God you didn't."

"I was going to."

"Oh?" Again that curious look.

"I thought you would refuse. That's what I was thinking about."

"I see."

He waited. She didn't say anything.

"Can I—"

"No."

"Mallika—"

"No."

There was no animosity in her voice, no anger. He would have preferred that.

Where to go from here. Nowhere. There was nowhere to go.

He got up. "I'll come back . . . in a couple of days."

She shook her head. "No. Don't."

The feeling of nausea was returning.

Gently she said, "Please sit for a minute."

He sat.

"I need to be alone. I can't . . . listen. Or talk. Even . . . think."

"All right."

"I'm sorry."

"*You* don't have to say that." His voice was shaking. "I—"

She put up her hands again as though stopping something. "No. No. Don't say anything. Please." For a second he thought he saw fear. Hope surged. Her face was calm.

He got up. "Can I come and see you . . . both again?"

"Yes. Of course."

"I didn't think there was any *of course* about it."

For a minute she didn't reply, gazing up at him with the same curious, wondering expression. Then she said, "If Mallika doesn't want to see you?"

His legs wouldn't move. He sat down abruptly.

Softly, she said, "You can come and see me. I'll still be there."

"You're not." All around him cracks were widening, gaping. He could hardly hear himself.

Her voice came from a great distance. "What I meant was, I'll be ready to listen to you when I come back. You said, didn't you, that you wanted to talk to me?" He could no longer brace himself for what he knew was coming. "But you're right. I'm not."

The cracks were appearing all over. Once when he was a schoolboy there had been a small earthquake in Delhi and he still remembered the ominously low never-before-heard moan of the quake in his ears as the table on which he drank his milk began to move. Now the same sound was beginning. He did not want to hear it in this room. Spare Padma that. Sita, why did you give me hope.

He heard her pouring out a glass of water, felt it put into his hand. He took a couple of sips, put it down on the table. He heard her voice, close now, saying, "Listen to me."

He managed to raise his eyes from the heaving floor. Her face was blurred. "No one meant more to me than Karan. Do you think I can . . . turn my back on what . . . remains of him?"

Now it was he who put out his hand. Too late to stop her words, too late. "Not that. I don't want . . . that." He got up, trying to fight the sound that was filling his ears. He stood for a moment, then began the long walk out of her room.

The months went by. He buried himself in his work, keeping late hours in the office. The weekends were the worst. He made two trips to Lucknow for two days each, to see his mother. Sita and her husband came to see him. He went to see them. But the distance was too much; it could not be done often. After the first time, Sita did not ask him what had happened.

He could no longer read. He could no longer sleep. He began going for long walks after dinner, two or three miles. Even so, sleep did not come. July, August, September, October, November. The beginning of December. All that had congealed within him for so many years was now peeling off and floating about inside his mind like so much flotsam.

It would have been better if he had seen them anywhere else but where he did. But he did see them as soon as he entered the bookshop in Connaught Place, and it was too late to turn and walk away because Mallika, who was standing on a stool and looking at books, happened to turn and see him, and she froze. Padma's back was turned to him but it was like going back in time, her long, thick plait hanging down, that bright saree, except that she had no glass bangles and she wore a mangalsutra. There was nothing he could do, nothing, so he walked up to Mallika, who was still frozen, and said, softly, "Hullo." Then Padma turned and she froze too, tried to say something, failed. She looked up at Mallika and gave her her hand. Mallika took it and climbed down the stool, and stood next to her mother looking up at his face wordlessly. There was absolute silence.

Mallika's lips were beginning to tremble. He could not bear it. "I think

. . . I should go," he said to Padma. She didn't reply. Her face had become very pale. "Bye," he said to both of them and walked out of the shop. He wasn't sure which direction he was going. He kept walking.

"Listen."

He turned. It was Padma behind him. She must have been running. The colour had come back to her cheeks. No sound of glass bangles this time. Her arms were bare except for a thin gold bangle around her right wrist. Once he had told her to do her bangle-buying before she came to their bookshop, not after. She hadn't known how bereft he felt on the days when he saw her bare arms and heard no clinking sounds. That was why he had said it. The year when he had walked away from her, he had come once to their bookshop and heard the faint clink of her bangles above him. He had left the bookshop that instant.

This time her saree was purple and yellow, she had a large maroon bindi on her forehead, her skin was glowing, her lips were a deep pink. She hadn't worn lipstick those early days, hardly ever.

"Mallika wants to talk to you."

His mouth felt suddenly dry.

"Her exams finish at the end of this week. After that can you . . . ?"

"Yes."

She was opening her purse, taking out an envelope and a pen. "Here." She gave it to him. "I don't have your address and phone number." He wrote down his home and office addresses and phone numbers and gave it back to her. She put it in her bag and closed it. "I suppose you can only come on Sunday?"

"I can come any time."

She was thinking. "Next Monday . . ."

"Yes?"

"Can you come home . . . earlyish, around ten or so?"

He nodded.

"Do you have the address?"

He nodded.

"If Mallika wants to be alone with you, then I'll go out after you come, and come back for lunch. Ayaji will be there."

"All right."

She was tense. He could feel it. No curious, wondering expression this time. No expression at all. Very brisk, very matter-of-fact. But tense.

"I—"

"You—"

They both stopped. She said, "Mallika's waiting in the bookshop. I have to go."

"Padma."

*"Don't say that!"* Her face was ravaged. *"Don't say Padma."*

He found he was breathing very fast.

"I've heard the same voice saying it for thirteen years." Her voice was very low. "I don't want to hear it again."

*"Forgive me."*

Her hands flew to her ears, covering them, her eyes shut tightly. *"Don't."*

A man stopped to stare at them. Two women passing looked at them and then at each other. She stood there, her hands over her ears, her eyes shut, very still. He took her arm and entered the shop next to which they had been standing. It was a jewellery shop. A man came towards them, "Can I help you?" He shook his head and took her out of the shop. She had removed her hands from her ears. He said, "I have to talk to you."

Her eyes as they met his were dazed with pain. He looked away. He had seen the same expression once before. Then he had been able to withstand it. Or so he had thought.

After some time he said, "Are you teaching tomorrow?"

"College closed yesterday." Her voice was barely a murmur.

"Will Mallika be in school tomorrow?"

"Yes. But you can't keep coming home. I can't . . . explain you to my neighbours. I . . . have to . . . protect Mallika. And myself."

Ma's got a very good reputation in the colony.

"We can meet, somewhere . . . in a restaurant?"

"It's too public. I don't want to be seen with you."

"Come to my house."

"Your house?"

"If my neighbours are nosy I'll say you're my sister."

"That's the only way to do it, isn't it. Your sister. My brother."

He recoiled.

"I'll come to your house," she said. "What time?"

"I'll pick you up at ten?"

"Didn't you *hear* me? Don't you *understand*?" Her voice was low, the anger contained. "I can't have men coming to my house and picking me up and dropping me back. I've lived in the same neighbourhood, in the same house, for twelve years. They all know me. They all know Mallika."

"I'm sorry."

No man ever comes to our house.

"No gossip has ever *touched* us."

He said, "I thought, when I came to the nursing home—"

"When you came to the nursing home, I wasn't thinking."

"I see."

"This time when I had . . . the breakdown, every one of them came to see me at the nursing home with food and fruits. They all sent food home to Shantacca and Mallika because they knew Ayaji wasn't there. Every day for ten days."

The life he hadn't known was coming up in front of him in quick, sure strokes. It was not what he had imagined.

"They all think I'm a . . . sati savitri. And that . . . suits me."

But she could not ever know what he had imagined.

"I'll come tomorrow. I can't come after that."

She turned and he watched her walking back swiftly towards the bookshop. It was the same bookshop where he had first seen her eighteen years ago, spread over his books like a sunbeam.


He couldn't separate the child from the pain. He had felt its weight bear down on his chest when she came to him, and now, again, when he saw her. It was there now, all the time, corroding him the way Padma had for thirteen years. But Padma had had her roots not in pain but in its opposite. She had been his sunbeam. But the child, what of her beginnings in the man who had fathered her? Her beginnings lay in his ignorance. In his horror at reading Padma's letters. Her beginnings lay in his rejection—it was not possible, it could not be possible, let it not be possible. Her beginnings lay in his fear, and then, afterwards, in agony such as he had never known before. Such were his child's beginnings in him; not in the longing for confirmation, but in the hope of its opposite. And when the confirmation came, in the absolute absence of happiness.

Padma. What beginnings could the child have had in her? What thoughts did the child absorb in her womb? In her womb the same horror, shock, rejection, disbelief, grief. These were the child's beginnings in

Padma. When had that changed? Before she bore her? After? How long after?

He slept finally as dawn began to break. In the dream he heard the doorbell ring, and then, blessed silence. It rang again, twice, very distantly.

"Sahib."

He opened his eyes. His servant, Govind, stood uneasily next to his bed. "A . . . memsahib has come to see you, sahib."

Sita. Hadn't she said she would come this week. Damn. He would have to drop her back before Padma came. All the way to her house in Old Delhi. But today was Monday. Why would she come so early to his house. Something had happened. He sprang out of bed and went to the living room. It was Padma.

He was wide awake. "I'm sorry. I must have overslept. I—"

"No, I'm sorry, I'm very early . . . I didn't realize . . ." she was stammering. Govind was hovering in the background.

"Govind, two cups of tea." He turned to Padma. "Or coffee?"

"Anything."

He turned to Govind. "One tea, one coffee." Govind went inside. He sat opposite her.

"I'm sorry," Padma said. "I got up at five. I thought I might as well come early. Mallika went to school at seven." She was looking frightened.

"That's all right."

"I didn't mean to wake you up." Her eyes were slightly red.

"You didn't wake me," he said automatically. They were a little swollen too. "Have you had your breakfast?"

She nodded.

"Govind," he called.

Govind appeared.

"Breakfast also. For both of us."

"Ji, sahib."

When he turned to Padma she was trying to smile. "You do it well."

"Do I."

"Hmmm. Govind this, Govind that. You're . . . used to it."

"I suppose I am."

"He looks like a . . . nice man."

"Yes."

There was a sudden silence. He was conscious of his crumpled pyjama kurta, unshaven face, unbrushed teeth. "I'll just be back." He got up.

"It's all right. I've seen you in worse."

She hadn't intended to say it. The frightened expression was back.

He sat down again. "Do you still see only the . . . remains, then?"

He saw her hands clenched under her shawl. She didn't answer.

Govind came in with a tray of tea and coffee. He served Padma. She still took one and a half spoons of sugar. He took his tea, spooned in sugar. Govind went out.

In complete silence, not looking at him, she drank her coffee.

He finished his tea and got up. "I'll be out soon." She nodded.

After he was bathed and dressed he went to the kitchen. "Don't make lunch today, Govind. We will be out for lunch."

"Breakfast is on the table, sahib."

When he went to the sitting room she was looking at his books on the bookshelf. "Breakfast is ready," he said. They moved to the dining table and sat.

"I recognize most of those books," she said so softly that he could hardly hear her.

He passed her the plate of matar parathas and she took one. "There's chutney and dahi," he said, taking one. "Do you have all your books too?"

She helped herself to some chutney and dahi. "They're all Mallika's now. She keeps them in her room."

"She's reading them so early?"

"She's read most of them. Some, several times."

He had never written anything in the books he had given her. Except that one time. Mallika wouldn't know then.

"She even remembers which ones I bought and which ones—" She stopped looking at him as though cornered.

"Karan gave you."

She nodded, avoiding his eyes. After some time she said, "Tell me about your work."

He began to tell her, in spare, short sentences. She asked him questions and he found himself talking more. He could barely eat his paratha. By the time he managed to finish it, he realized that he had been talking for fifteen minutes. You never talk to me properly, she used to say to him once. She had hardly eaten.

"I haven't asked you about your job at all," he said, as Govind began clearing the table. They got up and she followed him to the washbasin in the enclosed veranda behind the living–dining area. She washed her hands and dried them on the towel. "Nothing to tell. It's quite routine now," she said. They went to the sitting room.

"Govind will leave in about half an hour," he said. "I've told him to come back in the evening. I thought . . . we could talk better without him hovering around."

She nodded.

"What subjects does Mallika plan to take in the ninth?"

"She isn't sure."

"Isn't she inclined towards the arts?"

"She is. But . . . it isn't very practical. Unless she wants to appear for the I.A.S. She'll have more options with a science background. She can become a doctor."

"Is that what she wants?"

"She doesn't know what she wants. I suppose it's what I want for her."

"Sita was telling me she comes first in class."

"She and Prabha—Mrs. Prasad's daughter, yes. One or the other."

"Wouldn't you like Mallika to teach, like you?"

"No."

"You don't enjoy it?"

"I love it."

She saw the surprise on his face and said, "I wouldn't have been able to support myself and a child on the salary. I've managed because my mother has helped support me, and I have the . . . the house. Mallika must be . . . self-supporting."

So. That.

"How does your sister feel?"

"Oh, she wants Mallika to get married as soon as she finishes college."

"And Mallika?"

"She can't think of anything beyond her books."

"Sahib."

It was Govind. "The work is finished, sahib."

"All right. Come back at tea time."

"Ji, sahib."

He went out of the room. The sound of the back veranda door shutting reached them softly.

Utter silence.

She broke the stillness, opening her handbag. She took out a packet of cigarettes and a box of matches. She took out one and lit it. Inhaling deeply, she looked around her. He picked up the ashtray on the table next to his chair, got up and placed it next to her. He went back to his chair.

"When did you start?"

"About . . . two years after Mallika was born."

"Just like that?"

"I was feeling . . . desperate one day. My colleague, Deepa, called me home for lunch—she lives near the college—and when she had one I said I'd have one too."

"No one knows."

"No."

"Padma."

She jerked. Frightened. Again.

"Why are we talking about cigarettes."

Her throat moved. She said nothing.

"You told Sita you knew what I wanted to say to you."

She was very still. "You're doing it again. After all these years you're doing it again." He could hardly hear her.

"Doing . . . what?"

"Yes, I did tell Sita that, when I thought you were dead. But you're not dead. Say what you want to say. After thirteen years don't make me say it for you. I'm not the Padma you knew thirteen years ago." Ice cold with fury, her voice, freezing every word of his that had slowly begun to surface.

"I wanted to ask your forgiveness. For what I did to you. For not knowing about Mallika all these years. For everything." All wrong. Everything wrong. The words, the tone, the meaning.

Was she waiting for him to go on? The expression on her face was completely unforthcoming. When he did not say any more she said, "All right. So now you've said it."

"You know what happened."

"I know what my mother told Shanta in her letter. And what Sita told me."

"I haven't been able to live with myself."

"I know that too." She had begun to shiver.

"Come and sit here," he said, pointing to the chair next to him by the window over which the sun streamed. "You'll be warmer." She got up and walked to the chair, sitting down and turning it away slightly so that the sun did not shine in her eyes.

"Do you want some more coffee?"

She shook her head, not looking at him.

Tell me what you thought I had done. Tell me how you coped. Tell me about the baby who could have been mine. About her, especially, tell me— month by month, year by year. When she walked and talked and what she said and when.

Her voice low, she said, "I don't want to talk about the past. If that's why you've called me here."

He had lost his bearings completely.

"You said what you had to say . . . a little while ago. Now . . . that's said. Don't say any . . . more."

Padma.

"And . . . please don't talk about . . . any future . . . or anything."

His mouth was very dry.

"I came because I thought . . . you'll want to know about Mallika. So . . . ask about . . . her. Don't ask me anything else." The last sentence came out in a rush.

In the silence he could hear her breathing fast. Minutes ticked by.

"How . . . is Mallika?"

"Very quiet. Withdrawn. Doesn't talk about what happened. Or ask any questions."

"She said she wanted to see me."

"She didn't mention you at all till . . . yesterday. I told her after I was discharged from the nursing home that you had come to see me. She never asked me what happened. I said you wanted to see both of us. She said, I don't want to see him."

He nodded.

"That day after you went out of the bookshop, Mallika began to cry. I told her to wait. Then I came running after you."

He got up and went to the window. Behind him he heard her say, "When I told you Mallika wanted to see you I was acting on instinct. She hadn't. Then, last night when I said goodnight to her, she said, Can I meet him?"

Her voice was very close. She was standing behind him. He turned to face her. She said, "Why don't you sit. I can't talk to you when you have your back turned to me."

He shook his head. They stood quietly together. After some time he said, "What did she say when you told her you were coming to see me?"

"Nothing."

"How did she . . . look?"

"Expressionless. Like you do sometimes."

What he said then came out before he could help it. "Did you want her after she was born?"

"Yes."

"You . . . she . . . was motherhood . . . did you feel . . ."

She was looking at him, not helping him with his question.

"What was it like . . . after you had her?"

"Debilitating."

Too late to hide his expression. She had seen it. "Debilitating?"

She didn't answer.

"Was she seriously ill?"

"No."

"Were you?" His worst nightmare.

"Was I what."

"Seriously ill . . . at any time?"

"No, I wasn't seriously ill at any time."

Thank God. Why was she looking like that? "With . . . everything . . . at least . . . thank God . . . at least you didn't have to . . ."

"I didn't have to?"

"Cope with any serious illness."

She continued looking at him with that expression.

"Was Mallika . . . she . . . as a baby . . . what was she like?"

"The way she is now."

He tried again, "I keep thinking . . . wondering . . . how you managed."

She didn't answer.

Desperately he went on. "I understand, it must have been difficult financially and . . ."

"You understand nothing."

The words stuck in his throat.

"You never did."

He looked at her incredulously.

"You only knew me as a lover."

"Is that all I meant to you?"

The whole atmosphere in the room changed.

"I didn't mean lover . . . in its limited sense."

"You were my truest friend."

"That too, was easy."

"I see."

"You don't."

"What . . . has this to do with . . . what I asked you?"

"Your shock. And incomprehension."

"*Debilitating* is a strong word."

"Not strong enough."

"What *happened*?"

"Nothing . . . *happened*."

No, she wouldn't. She wouldn't tell him anything.

After some time he said, "How has she taken all this?"

"The shock has been worse for her than for you or for me."

He waited for her to go on. She didn't.

They were looking at each other now. He couldn't say any more. As if unaware of what she was doing, her hand was going up, her palm resting against his cheek as it had done that very first time. He closed his eyes. Her hand did not move away and he felt his own rise and cover it, moving her palm to his lips, opening his eyes, kissing the scar, her old wound, murmuring, "Sixteen years . . . still there . . ." Padma's eyes so large, so close to his face, her hand suddenly limp in his. Then her fingers clenched and she withdrew her hand at the moment that he let it go, her breath indrawn in the same moan that he had heard sixteen years ago in the bookshop as the nail went into her.

She went and sat on the sofa, looking down, her arms hidden under the shawl. He continued standing where he was.

Five minutes passed. She was sitting in the same position, very still. He folded his arms across his chest and looked down. He heard the rustle of her saree. He looked up. She was closing her handbag, getting up.

He went across the room. "Don't go," he said.

She went to the front door, tried to unbolt it, fumbling, her head turned away from him. She couldn't do it. He put his hand up, unbolted the door, turned to her. She groped for the door, stumbled. He touched her arm, she shook it off, opened the door and went out.

Forty-five minutes later he stirred. His right leg had gone to sleep. He stood, picked up some change from a bowl on the mantelpiece and went out of the house towards the paan shop. He was walking back with the cigarettes when he saw her standing at the bus stop, her back turned to him. He quickened his steps, then began to run as he saw a bus coming to the stop and Padma moving towards it. It was full, people were hanging out from the door. A crowd of people rushed into the bus, Padma one of them, but she was the last to get in and the bus had begun to move as she hitched up her saree and, running, clambered in. She was hanging on at the door when he reached, unable to get in because of the crowd, holding on tight to the handle, her feet at the bottom step. He managed to leap on as the bus gathered speed, then felt himself losing balance and Padma's hand on his arm, pulling him in next to her. "Spare me the dramatics." It was her voice in his ear. "Get inside," he said, trying to help her move up. "I would if I could," she said through gritted teeth. Someone moved, she pushed her way inside, he moved close behind her, "I'll get the tickets." He felt for his wallet. It wasn't there. He had left it behind, taken only enough change for the cigarettes. She was standing a little ahead of him, hemmed in by two men behind her and a third next to her. He pushed his way through the crowd towards her, "I need money for the tickets." She opened her hand-bag and gave him a rupee. He pushed his way back to the conductor. "Bhai sahib, take some care," an irate old man said to him. The bus had stopped again, another wave of people was being pushed in through the door; he found himself being swept aside. He elbowed his way towards the conductor again and bought the tickets. "This is not the full change," he said to the conductor, counting the money. "There is no change—come back later," the conductor said, handing out more tickets. Karan began moving up towards Padma, who was now farther up the bus and hemmed in by four other people. He fought his way through and, pushing and shoving, managed to displace the two men behind her, placing himself where they had earlier been. She didn't turn. "Could we get down at the next stop, please?" he said into her ear. She didn't answer. He felt someone trying to squeeze past him and tried to move next to Padma but there was no space. She was looking out the window as though he didn't exist. "Let us move, bhai sahib," an irritated voice sounded behind him. He tried to move, the people behind him squeezed their way up ahead of him, he found himself being carried along with them and held on to the seat next to where Padma stood, then began pushing his way back to her again. "If you want to go in front then go in front, if you want to go at the back, then go at the back, why you are doing both?" an irritated woman said to him. He moved down towards Padma, but she wasn't there. He looked towards the front; she was standing farther up. He began pushing his way up towards her. "Again he has started," a thin man said to the irritated woman. By the time he reached the door the bus had stopped and Padma was getting down and the bus had started moving again. He shoved aside the man next to him and leapt down from the bus and would have fallen if a man standing at the bus stop hadn't put out his arm to hold him. "Take a little care," the man said. Padma was standing ahead of him, looking towards an approaching bus. The bus stopped and she got inside. He followed her into it. It wasn't crowded. She bought herself a ticket and moved ahead. He bought himself one with the change he had got in the first bus, then followed her and stood next to the seat where she was sitting. "Please listen," he said. Padma didn't look at him. The middle-aged woman sitting next to her glanced up at him. He said, "Padma." She flinched. "Beti," the middle-aged woman said to Padma, "what is the use of doing nakhra? All that works only before marriage." She gazed at Padma's face, then looked up at him accusingly, "What have you done to her, Bhaiya?" She bent down and whispered something to Padma. Padma nodded. The woman patted her hand and looked out of the window. After some time she got up from her seat. "You sit here," she said to him, "I have to get down." He stepped aside to let her move out. She said, "It is not a good thing, whatever you have done," and began moving towards the front of the bus.

He sat next to her. After some time she said, "Did you want to see how much I could withstand?"

His throat was full. Standing there, seeing her fall, hearing her moan as the nail went into her palm, she turning, seeing him there, not telling him, not knowing he knew, he waiting, watching.

"Your cruelty. That too, I never saw." She was saying it almost wonderingly.

She looked at him in the direct way he had never forgotten, her face so close that he could see himself reflected in her eyes. "I protected you. All those years."

Memories of other bus journeys crowded his mind.

"I didn't even know. I protected you from myself."

Sitting by her those days, in bus after bus, watching her clear eyes on his face, wanting to shake her out of her oblivion.

"You never knew what I carried. But you couldn't have. I didn't know myself."

Watching her talk, those days, so drenched in her, that sometimes he hardly heard what she was saying.

"I never spoke to you of what was on my mind."

Then she would look at him indignantly, and say, You're not listening to me.

"You're not listening to me."

It was another Padma looking at him now.

"I'm listening."

"You're not. You're thinking of something else."

"I heard what you said."

"When was the last time you were in a bus?"

"With you."

"Oh." She mused. "No wonder you're so incompetent."

"Could we please get off this bus and go back?"

She got up. They began to move towards the front of the bus. A couple of minutes later the bus stopped. He put out a hand for her but she ignored it and got down. "I'm not going back by bus," he said, hailing a scooter. She shrugged. The scooter stopped and they got into it.

When they reached his house they climbed upstairs and he went into his bedroom and took out money from his wallet for the scooter. "I'll be back in a minute," he said to her and went down.

When he came up she was standing next to his bookshelf, looking at the books. She moved to the chair and sat. He sat next to her.

"Are the buses you travel in usually as crowded?" he asked.

"Depends on the time. Often, yes."

"It must be . . . difficult."

He looked at her enquiringly.

"They rub themselves against you."

She was watching his expression. "You think I'm imagining it."

"I didn't say that."

"It's clear on your face. Your . . . disbelief."

"It couldn't be deliberate. In a crowded bus—"

"It happens in crowded buses. It happens in uncrowded buses."

"I've never heard of it."

"There's a lot you've never heard of."

He felt himself reeling at the viciousness in her voice.

"How can you even presume to tell me it doesn't exist? Because it'll never happen to you?"

"All right. Let's forget it."

"It happens everywhere, not just in buses. There. That look of disbelief on your face."

"I haven't said a word."

"It happens on the roads."

"You make it sound as if it's routine."

"It is. In Delhi."

"If it were I'd have seen it."

"Like you saw it when you and I were going for a walk sixteen years ago?"

"I don't know what you're talking about."

"But you should. You say you would have seen it if it happened." She was looking at him as though he were one of those men. "You always told me that I shouldn't be so uneasy about walking in the dark, because you were with me. In fact . . . you used to get . . . impatient when I did. You think it never happened to me those days?"

"You never told me."

"There's a lot I didn't tell you."

"And you blame me for that."

"Once it happened when you and I were walking together. A man came up to me and hit me on my breast and walked on. You were lighting a cigarette. We continued walking."

"When I was with you?"

"Yes. Didn't you say you'd see these things when they happened?" She opened her bag and took out a cigarette. "When did you stop smoking?" she asked lighting it.

"I haven't stopped. I have it once in a while."

"When?"

"When I feel I need it the most, that's when I don't."

"Really?"

"When I need it the most, then I . . . concentrate on something else."

"That sounds like your . . . affair."

He felt his chest tightening. He took out the packet of cigarettes from his pocket and lit one.

"The worst is over then," she said.

"The worst?"

"You're smoking. You said you didn't smoke when you needed it the most."

"I've just broken the resolution."

"I see."

He watched her warily.

"It's happened to Mallika too."

"What has?"

"All the things I just told you about."

"To *Mallika*?"

"And to her friends."

"Where?"

"In our neighbourhood."

"But—"

"She's very careful. She never goes out alone, never travels alone, doesn't talk to strangers. But one can't protect one's child all the time. I thought I could. But it happens to them anyway."

He was feeling slightly sick.

"I always thought a father could protect his daughters where such things were concerned. But even he can't." She closed her eyes and took in a deep breath. "I don't know," she whispered almost to herself. "I don't know how to . . . talk to you."

They were both quiet for some time. She said, "My students—they often come and tell me what happens to them. One girl, very brave, very spirited—hit the man who did it to her in a bus. The man punched her in the jaw and broke her two front teeth."

He looked at her incredulously.

"The people in the bus did nothing," she said, answering his unasked question. "They never do."

There was a short silence.

"Once when Madhu, Anu and I went to a mela, a crowd of men suddenly gathered around us and . . . assaulted us."

"A *crowd* of men?"

"Yes. After we went back home I thought of Karan. I thought he would have understood what I went through. I thought he could have taken it away."

"Why—they just assaulted you—just like that?"

She nodded. "This is the world Mallika is growing up in. The one I grew up in. Not you. I hadn't realized it before. I hadn't realized anything before."

It was coming. He could feel it gathering, moving towards him.

"Those days I used to think you would be my protector, like Appa was, like Madhav was. But my only protectors have been my sister, my friends, my mother. And Mallika."

She was waiting for him to say something. When he didn't, she said, almost tentatively, "Haven't you ever thought of what . . . it would have been like had we actually got married thirteen years ago?"

"We didn't get married."

"And so you didn't think about it."

"What's the point."

"The point . . ."

"I don't believe in ifs and coulds."

He could hear her thoughts gathering. He braced himself for the second onslaught.

"All these years, I felt imprisoned, trapped. I used to think it was because of my circumstances. But . . . my friends, my sister, the other women I've seen, my mother . . . they're as imprisoned."

"I'm not interested in the other women."

"I would have been one of them if I'd married you."

"Why are you talking of ifs and buts."

"I used to think," she said wonderingly, "that I was leading an unnatural life because of my circumstances. But now I realize it isn't only me. Women seem to lead lives opposed to their dreams and desires."

"Men do too."

"In a different way. Not in any . . . fundamental sense."

"Living opposed to one's dreams . . . that's life. It doesn't have anything to do with being men or women."

"Do you remember, once you said to me that your mother was a very strong woman because she always worked uncomplainingly?"

"No."

"You said it when I expressed my shock that she worked so hard for the wedding that she almost lost her baby."

"I told you about that?"

"You did. Don't you remember?" She was almost pleading.

"No."

"Those days . . . did it . . . occur to you that I wouldn't have been like . . . your mother? That I wouldn't have worked uncomplainingly? If we had married wouldn't you have thought . . . I was weak and undutiful?"

"So now you're holding me to something I was supposed to have said more than fifteen years ago?"

"You said that your mother did it uncomplainingly. You said that with such . . . admiration. Wouldn't you have . . . expected me to do it uncomplainingly too?"

"Do *what*?"

"All the things a woman has to do when she gets married. All the things that *you* didn't have to do when you got married. Give up all the things you love."

"*What* things?"

She was shaking her head, her eyes not moving from his face.

"Tell me."

Something like despair on her face.

"Do *what*? Give up *what*?"

"*Everything.* My . . . friend Anu, she learnt Indian classical music for years. She's never sung after her marriage. Madhu gave up her B.A. Shantacca topped the university throughout, she's a gold medalist, and all she does is cook and clean."

"Their husbands told them to give it all up?"

The same despairing expression on her face. "No. Their husbands never told them to give it all up."

"Then?"

She said nothing, still looking at him with that expression.

"If there was no one stopping them, whom are you blaming?"

Still no answer.

"If no one stopped them, they have only themselves to blame."

Her expression changed. She said, "Like your wife?"

In the silence he stared at her. "I don't want to discuss her."

"No, you don't." She stopped then said, "You don't want to face what you did to her."

Now he could read her expression.

"Shantacca has taken your celibacy as a confirmation of your loyalty to me. Imagine. Your *loyalty*!"

It was hatred.

"So *what* if you were celibate for thirteen years? So was I."

She was breathing very fast.

"Nobody thinks of your wife. Of what you did to her. Do you?"

She was waiting for him to speak.

"At least I wasn't alone like her."

Again she was waiting for him to speak.

"That day you said to me, referring to your mother—What has to be done has to be done. Wouldn't you have said the same thing to me if we had got married? If I hadn't, would your mother and sisters have accepted me? Would you? You think you'd have continuing indulging my love for books? Once that was what . . . mattered to you—that I did what I wished, spontaneously, that I never held back. You'd have ended up disliking those very things. It would have angered you if I didn't conform. My mother, whenever she used to get irritated with Shantacca or me, used to say, Get married and do what you want. What she actually meant, unknown to her, was, If you don't obey the rules in my house, then you better go to another house and obey the rules there."

She waited for him to speak. When he didn't speak, she shook her head. "The fact is, I've survived what happened. But would I have survived being married to you? Wouldn't it have been more debilitating being a wife and daughter-in-law? If we had got married, your family would never have accepted me. Now I know what that can mean in a marriage. I used to think marriage would be an extension of all that we shared those four years. Don't you *understand* that actually it would have grown to exclude all that?"

Mallika, my child. You know your mother better than I ever did or will.

"Don't you *see*? We loved in a vacuum. That was why it was so . . . wonderful. Do you know how old I was when I first met you?"

"Almost seventeen."

"Five years older than Mallika."

"Five . . ."

"Yes. Five. Two years after that I was in your bed."

"I see. You were too young to know what you were doing."

"You don't see," she said sadly. "I knew what I was doing. As Mallika would if she decided she wanted to do something."

"Why are you bringing Mallika into it?"

"Though . . . I don't think she would do what I did. She's like you . . . very circumspect, very reserved. In a woman that's more difficult to . . . break than in a man. Oh, why am I bringing Mallika into it. I don't know . . . perhaps because it struck me how long ago it was and how differently I saw things then."

She took out another cigarette. He watched her light it.

"So, we'll get married," she said, as though thinking aloud. "Then I'll shift to your house. Leave my friends, everybody, Mallika's friends. I'll keep house, manage the servants, be a good hostess, socialize with all your colleagues and their wives. Your mother will come and live with us and I'll look after her. Your sisters will come and stay with us and I'll look after them. Pretend that nothing happened. Then . . . Mallika . . . my child, whom your mother called a bastard . . . she will live with them too. My sister, Shantacca, will no longer come and visit me. Amma? She has never come to see me because of my father. Now Appa's gone, but Amma will still not come to me. And so we'll get married, and I lose my house, my friends, my sister, my mother. And my job, since yours is transferable. So we get married and I lose everything . . . for what?"

"I can't answer that question for you."

Unexpectedly, she laughed. "You haven't changed in that respect. Still no direct answers from you. So, tell me, what did Mallika say to you in the hospital?"

"She too sketched out what it would have been if we had got married. And what it would be like if we did marry. It . . . tallies with your picture."

He heard her take her breath in. She was staring at him, waiting for him to go on. When he didn't, she said, "You don't want to think about it."

"I'm . . . thinking about many . . . things."

"In my fantasies I used to imagine you coming back to me. I used to imagine it all pouring out of you, and I listening. It's working the other way. Tell me, what were your fantasies?" Her tone was light, mocking.

"That you would die or be very ill and that I wouldn't know."

She stared at him. "How would it have made a difference? I could have been either, at any point, all these years."

"You asked me what my . . . fantasies . . . were. I told you. It was no . . . more improbable than yours." He got up and went to the window. Don't get up, Padma. Don't come near me.

He heard the rustle of her saree as she came and stood next to him. "I can't talk to you when your back is turned to me."

He turned to her. "I don't see the point of this conversation. We didn't get married. I abandoned you. You had a child. You lost your family. You lived with that for thirteen years. I can't pretend to know what you went through or how. When you came here today that was what I thought you were going to speak of. Those were the . . . accusations I . . ."

"You wanted to hear."

"But you don't want to speak of that. You want to speak of other, completely irrelevant issues. I can't argue about that or defend myself because they're hypothetical. Yet you're putting me on the defensive about hypothetical situations. You're rejecting me on the basis of a past that didn't exist, and on the basis of a future that you've already concluded can't exist."

"Is that how you see it?"

"Why are you talking of what might have happened? It didn't happen. And don't speak for me. Speak for yourself."

"Did you at all *hear* what I said?"

"Loud and clear."

"You have to know how I *think*. *That's* the point."

"*I* don't think that way. That too, is the point."

"I know you don't think that way." Again that despair in her voice. "Nor do the husbands of the women I know. They all think their wives are happy."

"Don't equate me with them. Don't speak for all men and all women."

"I want you to know what lies in my mind. You never knew before either."

"I never knew *before*?"

"See. You weren't listening to what I was saying in the bus. That's what I was trying to tell you in the bus."

"You always spoke your mind."

"Whatever I told you those days was true, but easy to say because it was what lay on the surface. Now nothing that I say to you is easy to say. But it's truer." She was pleading with him again.

"You've talked about a hypothetical past. You've talked about an impossible future. You've spoken of the life you think I expect you to live and how you cannot live it. You've spoken of the life I would have expected you to live had we got married and how you could not have lived that either. Put all that aside for a moment."

"Put that aside?"

"Yes."

"How can I put it aside?"

"I said, 'for a moment.' "

"You *are* all that. You *are* all that might have been. You *are* all that could be."

"You're shivering."

"I'm overwrought."

"I am too. Should I get you some tea or coffee?"

"Coffee." Her shivering wasn't abating. She had her shawl wrapped tightly around her, her hands were crossed over her waist under it.

He went to his bedroom. He picked up the blanket from the chair and went back to the sitting room. "Put your feet up," he said. She removed her sandals and put her feet up. He opened the blanket and placed it around her. She closed her eyes.

Ten minutes later, when he returned with the coffee, she was asleep. He looked at his watch. He could feel a similar exhaustion sweeping him. His eyes were heavy with it. He picked up a cushion from the chair and placed it on the ground next to the sofa. He lay down, resting his head on it, turning slightly so that he was facing her. He could hear her breathing a little heavily. He reached up and touched her cheek. She didn't stir.

She had slept like this when he had known her too. If it was possible, she had loved her sleep as much as she loved making love. One dissolved easily and voluptuously into the other. Their lovemaking, like everything else about her, had taken him by surprise. It shouldn't have. How like her her lovemaking was. As she had sought and enjoyed him because she liked, and then, loved him, she now sought and enjoyed this. It made him laugh to see her unabashed curiosity, to hear her questions, astonished him how her longing for him had come with an equal measure of ignorance.

He had not expected the absolute joy. When she left his house she left its bubbling remnants behind. When she returned, the bubbling would resume. Once, fast asleep in the afternoon, he woke to her moving softly next to him. He opened his eyes and watched her lift her left hand up, feel the upper arm, then lift the right hand, feel the upper arm again. "What on earth are you doing?" he asked. She said, "Karan, do my arms—my upper arms—look any different?" He said, "Different?" She said, "From before?" He asked, "From before what?" She said, "From before I came to your house?" He said, "I hadn't seen them before." She said, "There's a girl in the hostel who says she can tell who is a virgin by looking at her arms." He had been rendered helpless with laughter.

The passion he had expected. That he had known before. Once he had told her in his confusion and anger that it wasn't the first time he was feeling this way. It had been too early to recognize the difference, and later he had been too close to see. She must have thought that he had come to her with knowledge and with experience. She could not have known, as he himself hadn't at the time, that neither mattered; that with or without knowledge and experience he would still have experienced joy as he had never known before—such was the radiance in which she enclosed him.

She, who had always been so enclosed in the love of her family, now seemed to envelope him in something similar, and it was as if even that was not enough for him. On the weekend as he worked at his desk at night, he wanted her in the same room, so she sat on the bed behind him, reading. He worked late into the night and she would fall asleep, a pillow over her head to shut out the light. Then when she was asleep, he would get into bed and lie down next to her, his lips against the back of her neck, his arm around her, and then, after some time, he would go back to work.

He opened his eyes. She was looking at him.

"You insisted I come for coffee. You prolonged it."

Her eyes dazed with pain, he waiting.

"That day, for the first time, you ordered rasmalais for yourself. You ate it slowly. Then you insisted I sit with you while you finished your cigarette."

He couldn't even look away.

"You asked me questions about what papers I was taking for my exams. You made me talk."

He lay very still.

"And then," she said, "You went to her."

Eight and a half months without Padma. That too he had withstood. Then, seeing her with Madhav twice. At the first concert he had managed not to go to her. Then again at the second concert, just before it began, her radiance undimmed, and even from that distance it had begun to enclose him again. She had been laughing at something that Madhav was saying. And after the concert he had found himself going towards them, and later, the same thing had pushed him up the stairs in the bookshop, raised his hand to enclose hers, apologize for what he had always known was his betrayal. He had not intended going towards her after the concert. He had not intended going up the stairs. Nothing he had ever done with her had been intended. Not the dosas, the coffees, the bookshops, the walks, the visits to her hostel, the talks. Not the lovemaking. He had not planned on any of it overtaking him the way it had. With Padma he had not known what he was heading towards. Unlike with "Her" (as Padma always called her). With her he had known, and unlike Padma, she had known too.

He should not have been *able* to go to Her with Padma inhabiting him as she was. But he had. Does She read, Padma had asked later. He had not told Padma how much. What did you talk about, Padma had asked. He had not told Padma, Most things. Did you spend the nights with her. He had known what Padma had actually been asking.

He had tried to tell her. That the last thing he had wanted was this, with either of them. What he hadn't told her was that he wanted his time to himself, without any distractions, to read, to write, to think, to reflect. Especially to write. He had done it before her. He hadn't been satisfied with what he wrote. His stories lacked something. None of the characters seemed real. He couldn't make them convincing. They spoke things that he put into their mouths, not out of any inner compulsion. He knew the faults in his writing but he did not seem to be able to do anything about them. He had planned to write those two years while he taught—expand his mind—as he had once told Madhav. But it appeared that his mind was contracting to exclude everybody and everything except Padma and he did not seem to have the will to fight it. Fight what? This thing so pristine and spontaneous, so innocent and unreserved? It had never been so simple from his side. Until that day when she walked into his house and poured the glass of water on his head.

"I should have an affair now. Exorcise Karan once and for all. Is that what you wanted to do to me sixteen years ago?"

"Forgive me, Padma."

Her whole body jerked, her hands flying up to her ears and covering them. "Don't," she whispered, "I've heard that too, for thirteen years. Don't."

After some time she sat up, put the blanket away at the foot, leaned back against the sofa.

"Padma—"

*"Don't say Padma."*

"All right. Calm down. I'm sorry."

She removed her hands from her ears.

"Perhaps," he said, his voice very low, "I was trying to see how much I could withstand."

"Don't talk such *drivel*. You sound like a Hindi film Hero." She stared at him, then said, "You're laughing."

He bit his lips. "I'm sorry." His laughter stopped as abruptly as it had begun. Her lipstick had gone, her kajal smudged, her hair almost undone.

She moved back slightly in the sofa.

"When you left my mother's house you were coming to us. What did you think would happen after that?"

"I wasn't thinking of any future. I was just thinking of you and the child and all I wanted was to come to you. That's all. To come to you."

She tried to speak, he saw her swallowing instead.

"If I had kicked the bucket when I had the accident, then you wouldn't have had all these . . . thoughts."

She nodded gravely. "That's true."

He found himself laughing again. "How like you to say that. I should have died, then. Literally, not figuratively."

She was looking at him as if . . . as if he were her old Karan. The laughter caught in his throat.

One more move of her head and her plait would be undone completely.

She wrapped the shawl tightly around herself, he watched her decide whether or not to put her feet down; she must have decided against it because her feet would then encounter him. She sat back, her hands around her knees.

Her plait was undone. Firmly, she put her hair behind her.

She looked at her watch. "Your Govind will be coming soon."

"He won't come for another two hours."

"Time enough for us to make violent love," she said bitterly. "Isn't that what you're thinking of just now?"

"Aren't you?"

"How typical your answer is."

"Yes, I'm thinking of that. But that isn't all I want."

"I've been thinking of it too. But that *is* all I want."

"You—what?"

"*That* isn't dead at any rate," she said even more bitterly.

"You can . . . do it and not want the rest?" he said incredulously.

Furiously she replied, "Couldn't *you*, with her?"

"So *that's* what I now mean to you."

In that instant he saw a flash of something on her face. Satisfaction? It was gone.

She looked away. "Could I have some coffee, please?"

"Did you really mean what you said just now?"

"What do you expect after thirteen years of abstinence?"

"I don't," he said softly, "believe that it's all that remains."

He could hear her breathing very fast. "You're confusing one with the other. I'm not. That's the difference."

"Don't," he said even more softly, "speak for me."

She put her feet down from the sofa, got up, looking around her as if she were trapped. He got up too, and in that instant his arms were around her, his mouth parting hers in a kiss of such violence that for a moment they swayed unsteadily. Her arms were so tight around him that her bangle hurt his neck. He was walking her backwards down an old, unforgotten path, the bed beneath them, their hands unbuttoning, unhooking, unknotting. Her cheek rubbing against his, nothing had happened, nothing, that had all been a terrible dream, he would not open his eyes yet, a terrible dream this, unfamiliar the taste of her tongue, the sounds in her throat, their limbs entwined, unfamiliar the sound of her breathing, his teeth at her neck, unfamiliar this new, brutal rhythm. Over, almost as soon as it had begun.

Don't open your eyes. His arms about her. His cheek resting against hers. Years and years of waking up and not finding her next to him, all the laughter gone, years and years of the nightmare that was her permanent absence. It was this nightmare from which he would now awaken, he would open his eyes and they would be in their old house which she had so loved, their old house which he hadn't known he loved. She, lying enclosed within him, her breathing still heavy, he opening his eyes, seeing that hers were still closed. Softly, "Padma." She not opening her eyes, not answering. He closing his eyes. No sleep this time, just to have her here, enough.

But he must have slept. When he awoke, the first shock gripped him. Not the room he had thought he would wake up in. He closed his eyes, then opened them again, prepared for the second shock—her absence. But she was there, enclosed in his arms as she used to be all those years ago. He had not trusted the physical sensation, having felt it so often before, since the time he walked away from her, having woken up for years and years with her warmth against his body, opening his eyes and knowing it was another illusion. Now he found that her eyes were still closed, her arms tightly wrapped around herself. She, like he, hadn't opened her eyes once from the moment they had moved together in this bed. She wasn't sleeping. He felt her move slightly against him. He would find her, this second time he would find her, his arms around her in a vicelike grip, barely any space to move his mouth from her eyes to her nose to her ears, simpler just to move back to her mouth, kiss it slowly this time, very slowly, the way he used to, why had he forgotten how, she had forgotten too, no gentle hands or mouths these strange, straining bodies, this woman no less savage than this man, no matter, no stopping, no thinking.

Finally, opening his eyes. Looking at her as she lay unmoving next to him, her eyes still closed.

"Padma." Kissing her eyes.

Her eyes still closed.

"Padma." Her cheek, her forehead.

Not moving.

Her ear, her hair.

"Padma." Gently, her mouth.

Her eyes opening. Seeing his unfamiliar room. Very still.

"I thought so too," he whispered.

So still.

"Padma."

She, unmoving.

"Is this all you want?" Could she hear him? "I don't believe this is all you want. Padma?"

A hideous sound emerged from her. She turned away from him towards herself, her whole body contracting, her arms going around her stomach, the sound not stopping. This was how she would sound if Mallika died. The thought came and went like one of those sudden illuminations on a dark night that for an instant reveal its hidden horrors. In terror he watched her as she lay curled in the foetal position, her arms wrapped tightly around her stomach, the sound emerging unrelentingly. Once, when he was a boy, a servant in their house had lost her child and he had heard similar sounds coming out of the servant's quarters, harsh and loud, with a rhythm that belonged only to itself. He had rushed out of his house to his friend who lived on another street, unable to contain the fear that grew out of hearing it. Now he felt the same terror, but tenfold, as he sat beside her, unable even to touch her. She wasn't aware of where she was. She wasn't aware he was next to her. She was in another time, in another place. In that instant, he knew where.

It went on and on without any sign of abating. There was no comfort to be given. It had gone far beyond that, long before this. I had expected accusations about what I did, he had told her. You had wanted accusations, she had interrupted. But you don't want to speak of that, he had said, You want to speak of other things that are completely irrelevant.

Now, unasked, she was giving him what he had said was relevant. She was giving it to him in its purest, most distilled form. She would never be able to give it to him in any other. It was there for him to see and hear— the same wordless thing which had been seeping into his own marrow all these years.

As he felt a similar rhythm beginning in him, begging to be sung, her sounds began to abate. When they finally stopped, she was still shuddering. He wiped her cheeks with his palm. "Wait," he said, getting up. He went to his cupboard and took out a fresh towel. He soaked part of it in the bucket in his bathroom, wrung it out. He opened his cupboard again and took out a handkerchief. Then he sat on the bed next to her and wiped her face with the towel. He gave her the hanky and she blew her nose into it. He wiped her face again, then mopped it dry with the other side of the towel. She submitted to his ministrations like a very sick child, unmoving. When he finished she continued lying where she was, her eyes and lips swollen, her whole body limp.

He was very cold. He picked up his clothes from the ground and began putting them on. After he had finished he picked up hers and put them on the chair next to the bed. She sat up on the bed, mute, pulling the quilt all the way up to her neck, her hair streaming behind her.

"Put on your clothes," he said after some time. "You'll catch a cold."

She wasn't looking at him. "Could you go out, please?"

When she came to the sitting room fifteen minutes later, she had repaired herself as best as she could, but her lips and eyes were badly swollen. She sat on the sofa and took out her cigarettes. She offered him one. He took it. She lit his, then hers. For a while they both smoked silently.

"If you get pregnant—"

"It's the wrong time."

"But—"

"It's all right. This had to happen."

"That's not what I meant."

"I know. It happened once. It could happen again. It's all right. I don't intend having another baby."

"You'd do that?"

"Yes."

She would. He could see it on her face.

"I shouldn't have—"

"I told you. It's all right. I wanted it as much as you did."

"Is that all it meant to you?"

He got up from his chair and walked across the room to where she sat. He sat next to her.

"You'd better make your bed before Govind comes."

He touched her cheek. She moved away from him slightly. "Please," she said without looking at him. He got up.

When he came back she was standing at the window. He joined her there. She turned to him and he felt it coming and he could not brace himself for it this time.

"All that's left is Mallika."

He looked out of the window.

"Mallika. That's all we have."

*"Don't speak for me. That might be all you have. It isn't all that I have."* He hadn't raised his voice, but he saw the surge of fright on her face. Stay calm. Stay calm.

"There was nothing irrevocable about what you felt for me." She too had lost her calm, her voice was shaking. "If I hadn't clung to you so relentlessly, you'd have let me go. You . . . allow . . . things to happen to you. You allowed me to . . . take over your life. You allowed your mother to marry you off. You allowed your marriage to go on and on, shutting out your wife for years and years and years. It never occurred to you what she might be going through. That thought also you shut out. When you were in college, you shut out your father. Then me, for almost a year. And now you've shut out your two sisters and mother."

There was a light tapping at the back door. He went to the back veranda. Govind.

"Coffee?" he said coming back. She was sitting on the sofa.

She shook her head.

"You don't want me to drop you back at your house."

"You can drop me at a scooter stand a mile from my house."

From the kitchen came the soft sounds of water running, dishes being washed.

"Was what happened only the result of thirteen years of abstinence?"

It was as though he had slapped her. Her head jerked back. For a minute they looked at each other. Then she said, "Neither of us is what we were thirteen years ago. Whatever you feel at this point belongs to another Padma. Not to me."

"I told you. Don't speak for me."

"All right. Whatever I feel now, belongs to the Karan I knew once. I don't know who you are."

"Is that why you made love to me like that?"

She was looking at him as though he were an enemy. "You don't understand anything. Anything. You think I gave you what I once did. I didn't. I can't. It's gone. I can't ever give that to you." Her voice was shaking.

"All right."

She became very still.

"I was coming to you prepared to accept the . . . inevitable," he said. Then, after the accident when Sita spoke to me . . . I had hope. Well, that's gone now. So, I accept . . . whatever you . . . feel."

He didn't want to look at her face anymore. He looked towards the window, where the curtains fluttered slightly. There was something else he wanted to ask her but he couldn't think properly. Something very important.

"Mallika's expecting you on Monday."

That was it. Suddenly everything became sharp again. "That's what I wanted to speak to you about."

She nodded.

"I don't know what will happen on Monday. But I was hoping that there was a small chance that Mallika might want to get to know me."

She nodded again.

"I want you to know," he said carefully, "that whether Mallika wishes to know me or not, I don't expect anything of you from now on, and that I won't do anything to . . . precipitate it either."

She nodded. She wasn't looking at him.

As they got up to leave she said, "When you come on Monday, please don't come in your car. Take a scooter."

Monday lay in wait.

He took a scooter. Ayaji opened the door for him. She gave him a strange look and asked him to come in and sit. "Bitiya," she called Mallika. Then she picked up a piece of paper from the table and gave it to him. "Memsahib said to give this to you."

The note was very brief. She didn't address him. She would be back for lunch. She hadn't signed the note.

Carefully, he put the note on the table, a wholly unknown sensation gripping him. It was the terrifying familiarity of the house. As though he had lived here before, in another life, as though he had seen it all before. Familiar the spare but comfortable furniture, familiar the mirrorwork cushions, the rug, the wall hanging, the two paintings on the wall, the small dining table, the fridge, the cabinet on the side. To the right, he knew, was Padma's bedroom; to the left, he knew, Mallika's bedroom. He was being sucked into a dark and endless tunnel.

Mallika entered. His hands were shaking. He got up, unable to speak.

"Will you have some tea?"

"Thank you." He sat, closed his eyes. Had he gone mad?

She went into the kitchen, then came back and sat in the chair next to him. He could hear the clatter of dishes in the kitchen. From outside came the voice of the vegetable woman making her rounds, Gobi, matar, aloooo.

He forced himself to speak. "How did your exams go?"

"All right."

"I suppose you'll come first again."

She didn't answer.

"So . . . your holidays have begun?"

She nodded without looking at him.

"Do you have plenty of books to read?"

She nodded again.

On the mantelpiece was the same photograph that Padma's mother had first shown him. He had known it would be there. He was going crazy.

"What did your mother and sisters say about what they did to Ma?"

No preliminaries, no prevarication.

"My mother said she didn't remember . . . it was too long ago."

"Your sisters?"

"They said they didn't know anything beyond what happened in that room."

"They made your youngest sister promise on the Gita not to tell any-one."

"They said that was because what had happened was . . . something they couldn't possibly tell me. They said they couldn't conceive of there being any truth in it."

"So they thought Ajji and Shantamama were there just for the fun of it."

"They thought I was not capable of . . . of . . ."

"Of promising to marry Ma, then making her pregnant, then marrying someone else."

"Yes."

"And you believe all of them."

"That's what they said."

"They're *lying*. After all they've done to Ma, you believe them."

"I didn't say that."

"You believe your mother's forgotten."

"There's a great deal that she's forgotten. After my youngest sister lost her two babies, my mother has . . . become a little . . ."

"Mad."

"Yes. She forgets that my father is dead. She forgets who my sisters are married to."

"But she lives by herself."

"Her youngest brother and wife live nearby. They look her up every day."

"Your mother hasn't forgotten."

"That's possible."

"Huh," she snorted in the way he had heard other schoolgirls do. "She's pretending."

Ayaji came in with the tea and held the tray to him. After he helped himself she gave him another strange look and went back to the kitchen.

"Then? What did you tell them."

"Nothing. It isn't going to change anything."

She threw him a mutinous look. "I *hate* them."

After a few minutes she said, "What do they know now?"

"The truth."

"Your mother also?"

"Yes."

"What did they say?"

"I don't think . . . my mother comprehended. My sisters didn't say anything."

"Didn't they say anything about what they'd *done?*"

"No."

"Why don't you talk *properly?* I wanted you to come here so that you would tell me *properly.*" There was a note of hysteria in her voice.

"When I told my mother she didn't respond at all. After I finished telling her she began to talk about something completely irrelevant. My sisters didn't say anything. They were together in the hospital when I told them. After that I haven't met them and we haven't written to each other. I have been to see my mother twice and she doesn't . . . appear to remember anything. She doesn't mention it at all."

"If I were you I wouldn't forgive them for the rest of my life. I wouldn't talk to them for the rest of my life. Never, never, *never.*"

Ayaji came out of the kitchen with the tea. "Bitiya. Are you all right?" She gave him the tea, looking at him as though he were a thief.

"I'm all right, Ayaji."

So that was why she had wanted him to come. Because she wanted to continue what she had been unable to finish in the hospital. Nothing more. No offer of friendship. Not a chance. Now Padma need have no apprehensions.

"What do you think of what your mother did to you and Ma?"

She would not let go. In her own words, never, never, *never.*

"It was I who did it."

Was there an ashtray anywhere. He looked around. She got up and picked up one from the mantelpiece. "Here." She placed it on the side table next to him.

"Thank you." He lit his cigarette.

She watched him for a minute. Then she burst out, "Because of *you* she also drowns her sorrows in *this.*"

He choked. After he finished coughing, she said, "You're shocked."

So. She hadn't given up her mission to steer him away from her mother. Of course not. That, then, was the second reason why she had wanted to meet him.

"You know already." Her tone was deadly.

He nodded.

"She did it when she came to see you." Deadlier.

What to say now.

"Why did you pretend to be shocked?"

"I didn't pretend. I was taken aback that you knew."

She looked at him in disbelief. "She's my *mother*."

He tried to nod placatingly.

"Just because she . . . did it in front of you and doesn't do it in front of me doesn't mean you know her better that I know her." The note of hysteria was back in her voice.

"She too feels that I don't know her," he said gently. "That's what she came to tell me."

"That's what she came to tell you?"

"She made it very clear that she wants to live the way she has always lived for all these years, and that I don't enter that picture."

"Oh."

"Yes."

"But if that's all she wanted to tell you, then why was she there with you the whole day?"

"Because to explain that, she had to talk about many other things. She felt I didn't understand what she was saying."

"For so many hours she was talking?"

"I was talking too." Was he red in the face? Thank God for his dark skin.

"And you still don't understand?"

"I . . . look at it differently. Anyway. That's not important. I told her I accept it and that I won't . . . expect anything of her."

"And of . . . me?" Her eyes were fixed on her lap.

"I had . . . hoped you would want to know me, as I want to know you. But if you don't, I understand."

Complete silence. She was looking at her hands.

"I'll accept that too," he said.

Silence.

He tore his eyes away from her. Where to look. He couldn't bear to look at the mantelpiece. He focussed his eyes on the centre table.

"*Everything* you accept. *Everything*." Her voice was trembling.

"Mallika?"

"You accept what your mother and sisters did. You accepted your marriage. You accepted that Ma was married. You didn't even try and tell her what had happened. You didn't even have the decency to write to her. I don't know what's *wrong* with you." She was breathing very hard.

"You should have *told* Ma. It was *cruel* of you never to tell her. One minute she says goodbye to you thinking you're going to get married. Next minute you get married to someone else and never even *tell* her. So what if your mother was sick. So what if you thought Ma had got married. You didn't even bother to *find* out where she was or how she was. For thirteen years . . . didn't you *want* to know how she was?"

Her face was flushed. She could barely control the pitch of her voice. "No *wonder* Ma doesn't want you. No *wonder*."

Nothing to say, nothing to say.

"Say *something*. You never *say* anything."

Nothing to say.

"You don't even *ask* any questions. You don't even want to *know* anything."

She was waiting.

"I don't want to ask gratuitous questions."

"For thirteen years you didn't bother. No wonder Ma hasn't forgiven you. No wonder she'll never forgive you."

"She told you that?"

"I know."

She knows the shape of my thoughts. Sometimes before even I know them.

A fairly long silence.

The expression that he recognized was coming to her face. With dread he waited.

"All these years—"

"Please."

"But—"

"No." Not this.

"I know about it. I know." She was looking at him as if she hated him. "Your . . . *affair*."

No. No. No. Padma. Padma.

"*You* don't tell me anything about Ma."

Padma. How could you.

"*She* told me about *you*."

"Please," he burst out. He saw the fleeting gleam of satisfaction on her face. This, then, was the third reason she had called him here. To find out what it was that he felt for her mother. Or perhaps, to find out what he had felt once. Not that her conclusion would make any difference to the outcome.

She was a child still. That was why she wanted him to wince, grimace, raise his voice. That was why she wanted him to "say something." What other way did she have of gauging?

Had he been her father then perhaps she would have known him too in the way she knew her mother. Him too she would have protected as fiercely. Strange. It had never occurred to him to think of receiving protection from one's child. Especially from one's daughter. Suddenly it hit him like a punch in the stomach. When he and Padma—

"When you and Ma went to Fatehpur Sikri, what did you wish for?"

He looked at her, stunned.

"Did Ma tell you what she wished for?"

"No."

"And you also didn't tell her."

He nodded.

"She won't tell me, even now."

It was coming.

"What did you wish for?"

He had not known what to ask for. He had watched Padma tying her red thread, closing her eyes, wishing. He had held his thread uncertainly. He couldn't think of a single thing he wanted. If he didn't have Padma he would have asked for her. He looked at Padma, who had finished, and was watching him. Of course. He had smiled at her, then turned his back to her and tied the thread.

"Your wish hasn't come true yet," Mallika said.

"It hasn't come true."

If there was any absolute truth, then that truth was that it had not come true. Mallika would say so too if she knew his wish. She would say, You wished for a daughter? I am not your daughter.

"Do you have the letters Ma wrote to you?"

"Yes."

"And photographs?"

He nodded.

"You read them and look at them often?"

He shook his head.

"Ma's burnt all your letters and photographs."

There had been enough shocks the last few months. He still hadn't recovered from the one Mallika had given him a few moments ago. He was still reeling with shock at the familiarity of the house. This shock was by no means worse than those. But his expression must have changed and she saw it. Now she was feeding upon it as she had upon the others.

So. Padma was being ruthless now. No other way to do it.

"She didn't do that now. She did it when she was expecting me." Was that compassion in her voice? He looked up at her, but he couldn't read her expression. "She didn't tell me till I asked her a few days ago."

He used to lie on the terrace at nights and talk to her. He would point out the different constellations to her, and tell her about his longing to travel to the Southern Hemisphere. Everything he saw began to be filtered through her eyes—his early morning walks, the changing colours of the sky, the bird sounds. These thoughts he would write to her. Then he would wait for her letters.

The doorbell rang. Ayaji came out of the kitchen and looked out the living room window. "Oho, open the door, Ayaji," he heard a woman's voice say.

"Madhu Aunty," Mallika said ominously.

Ayaji opened the door and a fat woman entered, carrying a large steel vessel. She stopped short when she saw him. He got up and folded his hands. She put the vessel down on the table and folded hers. "I have got dahivadas for you and your mummy, Mallika," she said, turning to Mallika.

"Thank you, Aunty."

"Where is Mummy?"

"She's gone out."

"Accha?" Astonishment in her voice. She looked suspiciously at him. "When she is coming back?"

"At lunchtime, aunty."

"She is . . . accha, at lunchtime. I am just coming." She went into the kitchen and he heard her conferring with Ayaji in the kitchen. Whatever Ayaji said to her must not have reassured her, because she came back and sat down opposite him and gave him a broad and very false smile.

So this was the other friend. Not someone who he would have imagined Padma would have anything in common with. For that matter, the other lady, Mrs. Prasad was also most unlike Padma.

"Oh!" she gave a little laugh. "I forgot to introduce myself. I am Mrs. Nanda, Padma's neighbour and old friend."

He nodded with a slight smile.

"And you are . . . ?"

Mallika threw him a frightened look. He introduced himself and said, "I knew Padma in college."

"*College?* Accha, accha. So long ago."

"Her brother and I were in the same college."

"Her brother . . . of course, of course. So, you are visiting Delhi?"

"I've recently been posted to Delhi."

"I see, I see. Where you are working?"

He told her.

"And where do you have accommodation?"

He told her.

"Very nice place. Very nice houses." She beamed at him.

She picked up a magazine from the table next to her and began thumbing through it. She looked up and beamed at him again. "I hope you don't mind. I am waiting for Padma. Ayaji said she is coming back soon."

"Mummy'll come back . . . for . . . lunch, aunty."

"Accha. So Padma she has called you for lunch?"

"Yes."

She looked at her watch.

It was eleven. What would she do now. He sat back in his chair. He could do with some comic relief.

She began thumbing through the magazine again. She looked up and gave him another smile. "I am just coming," she said getting up, and went into the kitchen again.

Mallika threw him an agonized look. "Now she's gone to find out if Ma has really called you for lunch," she said in a whisper.

"Is she always so curious?"

"She isn't curious—she's protective!" Mallika whispered indignantly. "She knows Ma never leaves me alone with strange men."

"Well, your Ayaji can reassure her on that score."

"Ayaji can't stand Madhu Aunty. She won't tell her a thing. Whenever Madhu Aunty asks her anything, Ayaji says, What do I know." She paused, then frowned. "I know what you're thinking, I know. You're thinking that Ma's friends are not like her."

She caught his expression before he could hide it and burst out, "I *knew* it, I *knew* it. That's so *snobbish* of you. They are the ones who have stood by Ma. Not you."

Mrs. Nanda came out of the kitchen, her face slightly flushed. She sat down again opposite him and tried to smile. Mallika said, "Aunty, if you want I'll call you as soon as Ma comes back."

"What is there in that. I will wait for your Ma." She picked up the magazine and began to read.

When he looked at Mallika she was looking at him, her expression unguarded and vulnerable. Then the mask descended again on her face.

"I think I have seen you before somewhere." Mrs. Nanda was scrutinizing his face.

He smiled. "I have a . . . common face."

"Vaise, I do not forget faces. You have come to Delhi before?"

"I've been here a few times. On work."

"Hmmm." She went back to her magazine.

For a few minutes there was silence. The doorbell rang. Mallika sprang up and opened the door. It was Mrs. Prasad holding a steel vessel in her hands. Mrs. Nanda almost embraced her in relief. "Anu, come in, Padma has gone and her brother's college friend he has come to see Padma, and I am also sitting and keeping him company till Padma comes. Come, come." She introduced them to each other. Mrs. Prasad put down the steel vessel on the table, avoiding his eyes.

"Sit, Anu, sit. Padma will just come now," Mrs. Nanda said, sitting on the sofa and patting the seat next to her.

Mallika came back and sat in her old chair.

Mrs. Prasad sat down very stiffly. There was complete silence.

"I know where I have seen you," Mrs. Nanda said triumphantly.

"Madhu," Mrs. Prasad said. "I need something from your house, can we go to your house now?"

"We will go, one minute. Now I remember. My memory is very sharp. Nothing I forget, 'specially faces I never forget. You also were so much younger. Don't you remember?"

"I'm afraid not."

"Ayaji and I were in the park with Mahima and Mallika and you also were in the park? Ten, eleven years ago?"

"I can't recall."

"It was you only. Try and remember. You told me something very sad, about your own child—afterwards I felt so bad."

Mallika and Mrs. Prasad were both staring at her.

"Yes, you remember. I am sorry, I did not mean to remind you about your child. Forgive me. Please forgive me." She looked away from him. "It was because you were holding Mallika with such love that I never forgot that day. For so long you were holding her and playing with her. One hour." Now she was sounding almost tearful. "You remember, no?"

"Madhu, I have to borrow something from you . . ." Mrs. Prasad's voice sounded a little breathless.

Mrs. Nanda got up. "Your wife . . . ?" she said delicately to him.

"My wife is no longer with me. She has joined an ashram."

Mrs. Nanda put her hand to her heart. "Yes. I understand. The loss of a child . . . nothing to live for . . . Anu, chalo. I will come again to check if you want anything—"

"No thank you, I—"

"Padma's friends are my friends, in five minutes I will come back. Chalo, Anu."

They went out.

Mallika said, "You—"

"Look who is here, look who is here," Mrs. Nanda's voice rang out joyfully. She opened the front door and put her head in, smiling from ear to ear. "Mallika, beti, look who is here, come come."

Mallika went to the door. From where he sat he could see two women stepping out of a taxi. "Shantamama," he heard Mallika scream joyfully. He saw her rush out and hug the tall woman who had just got out of the taxi. An older woman came out after her. Padma's mother. Mallika stood still. Padma's mother held out her arms. The next instant Mallika was in them. He saw Padma's mother weeping. The taxi driver opened the boot and Mallika's aunt began lifting a suitcase. Mallika broke away from her grandmother's embrace and went to help her aunt.

He got up and went swiftly to the taxi. Mrs. Prasad and Mrs. Nanda were both hugging Padma's mother. "Your telegram it did not come, Padma did not even know you were coming," he heard Mrs. Nanda say as she began leading Padma's mother to the house. They stopped as he came. He gave them both a faint smile and went to Mallika and her aunt. "Let me," he said, taking the suitcase from Shanta. Shanta's eyes widened. She looked at her mother and handed the suitcase to him wordlessly.

By the time he had carried the two trunks, two suitcases, two baskets and three handbags into the living room, the house swarmed with women.

Shanta was in the kitchen giving instructions to Ayaji. Her mother was sitting on the sofa, her arm around Mallika, the other hand caressing Mallika's cheek, saying something to her, her face suffused with tenderness and love. Mallika was looking up at her with a similar expression. Mrs. Nanda and Mrs. Prasad were standing in the dining room conferring animatedly.

He stood next to the luggage awkwardly. He bent down and began arranging the luggage next to the wall, picking up all the odds and ends and putting them on top of the trunks and suitcases. Now they were out of the way. When he stood up Padma's mother was standing next to him, grave and dignified. "You have been very kind," she said, "now please sit down. What would you like to drink?"

"Nothing, thank you." He sat down. Padma's mother sat down too. Mrs. Nanda came and sat next to her, held her hand, began to talk.

Even Padma's mother, who had never met Mallika in all her life, was now part of this house.

Mallika was looking at him and this time there was no mistaking the compassion on her face. She had caught him at an unguarded moment. He had caught her too. Too late to dissemble.

Shanta and the two friends seemed to know one other very well. There were loud, extended goodbyes. After closing the front door Shanta gave him a charming smile, said to Mallika, "Darling, come inside for a moment," and then to him, "I'll be back in a moment," and disappeared inside with Mallika.

Together once again with Padma's mother. Had he dreamt that day and all that had happened? She said to him, in English, as she would to any visitor sitting in the house, "So bad the telegraph service is. We sent a telegram about coming."

He nodded.

"She is a beautiful child." Her eyes were full of tears. This time, unlike the last, she spoke in English.

He nodded again.

"You have met Mallika before?"

"She came to the hospital to see me."

"These two ladies, Padma's friends—"

"They think I am Padma's brother's friend from college."

"Good. Good. Still. They will think it strange that you are here."

"Mallika wanted to see me. I won't be coming here again."

"Is that because of Padma? Or Mallika?" She was looking at him earnestly, her face concerned and soft. He marvelled.

"Both."

"Oho. So. Then?"

He shrugged.

"Of course, of course." She was actually managing to sound confused and apologetic. Incredible. "If you will excuse me. One minute." She got up and went inside.

Mallika came to the sitting room. "What was Madhu Aunty—"

Shanta entered the room, smiling. "I'm so sorry, rushing inside like that. Would you like some tea, coffee . . . ?"

"No thank you."

"Mallika, darling, please help Ayaji lay the table. And take out those other plates, the ones at the back. Tell Ayaji to rinse them first, though."

Mallika got up reluctantly and went to the cabinet.

"I'm so glad you're here." There was warmth in her voice and eyes.

His first welcome. He hadn't known how much he needed it till this moment.

"Just now in the bedroom I told Mallika, Tell me everything that has happened since your mother last wrote to me. But Mallika, she tells what she wants to tell. So now I have to ask you."

He nodded.

"Padma said you came to see her in the hospital. Nothing else. Mallika also never mentioned you. So then I wrote to Amma. So Amma came to me from Madhav's house and we came here." She was looking at him expectantly.

"Last week Padma and I talked. It's . . . over."

Shanta made a sound.

He tried to speak. "Mallika doesn't . . . I think she . . ."

"She doesn't think of you as her father. She thinks of you as . . . as . . ."

"Padma's lover," he said.

She looked over her shoulder to assure herself no one was there. Her face was slightly red. "Not just that," she said in a low voice. "Mallika hasn't . . . hasn't . . ."

"Forgiven me."

Shanta nodded apprehensively.

"I know."

"So," Shanta said, "what is going to happen?"

"Nothing."

"I can't bear this," she whispered. "Don't let it happen. I beg of you. Don't let it happen. You were allowed to live for a reason. Think of that. It is because of them that you were allowed to live. Otherwise what was the point of all this?"

He and Madhav had had innumerable arguments on the subject. No point, Madhav used to say. Everything was arbitrary. Chance was the ruler. Karan used to take the opposite point of view, not because he believed it but for the fun of it. On and on they would go, as Padma used to say to him later, on and on and on.

"You would have asked the same question if I had died."

"But you see, you didn't," she said triumphantly.

"I can't change the way they think or feel."

"They don't know how they think or feel." She almost sobbed this out. "Padma and her ideas. You can't live life from ideas."

"I don't think it's that."

"You don't know. She's become like my father. Full of theories and ideas. I keep telling her, those have no grounding in reality. But who can persuade her."

"Food is ready," Ayaji said from the kitchen. The doorbell rang. Shanta opened it. Three girls stood there, each holding a vessel of food. Prabha smiled at him sunnily, he smiled back. His second welcome. The one trying not to look at him must be Mahima. Very pretty, very petite. Gauri, dark, thin and graceful, standing at the kitchen door, looking at him when she thought he couldn't see. The three girls went into Mallika's room. A moment later Mallika came out of the other room and went into her own. He heard some giggling. A few minutes later they all came out and trooped into the dining room. Shanta beckoned to the girls. "They're Mallika's best friends," she said. They stood in front of him, smiling, radiant. Lovely, lovely children. Mallika's grandmother came with a plate full of sweets. "Here, have," she said tenderly to the girls, "I made them myself." They helped themselves. Mahima said, "Prabha, come on, we have to go home." Prabha sprang up and, with another wide smile, waved to him. The girls flew out like a flock of birds.

Lunch was a quiet meal. "Ma said she'd come back by lunchtime,"

Mallika said once. "The bus must be late," Shanta said reassuringly. "She should be back in an hour's time."

After lunch the mother went into the bedroom. Shanta glanced at Mallika, who was standing at the door, then said, "Mallika darling, come here and cut these guavas. I'll just make Amma's bed and come back." Mallika came slowly to the sofa, sat down, and began cutting the guavas, not looking at him.

The doorbell rang. Mallika's face lit up. She opened the door. It was Mrs. Nanda, carrying another steel vessel. "I have made some papri," she said coming in. "You can have it at tea time."

Mallika moaned. She had cut her hand. In horror he watched the blood oozing out. Before he could reach her side, Shanta had materialized from the other room and was taking her to the bathroom. Mrs. Nanda got up swiftly. "Padma keeps bandages and all in here," she murmured, going to the cabinet in the dining room and opening one of the drawers. From there she took out a bandage, some cotton, dettol, ointment and a pair of scissors, and without even looking at him, went into the bedroom. He stood next to the dining table for a minute, then slowly went back to the sitting room.

They all came out fifteen minutes later. Her finger was bandaged up. She went to the door again. Shanta came and sat next to him and began cutting the guava. "I'm sorry for leaving you like this," she said.

"You don't have to apologize to me for this," he said quietly.

Realization seemed to hit her. "I'm sorry," she said in a low voice.

"Is she—"

"No, no, just a small cut."

Mrs. Nanda looked at her, and then at Shanta. "I will go to the library and see," she said, making a move to get up.

"I can do that," he said.

Mrs. Nanda looked shocked. "Why you should do that? No, no, you are a guest."

Shanta said, "Don't panic. Wait for another half an hour. You know what these buses are like. And it's so far, anyway."

They all ate the guavas in silence. Mallika didn't move from where she stood. Then her grandmother came out of the bedroom, her face lined with worry. She saw them, said nothing, went to where Mallika stood and stood next to her. Shanta and Mrs. Nanda exchanged a worried look. No one looked at him.

He had relinquished all rights to his child that long-ago day when he said goodbye to Padma. The right to comfort her, tend to her, reassure her. It was not him she would ever seek for any of this. The tension that now clouded the room excluded him completely. No one looked at him for reassurance, no one exchanged worried glances with him. He was, as Mrs. Nanda said, the guest.

If Padma was dead, the others would mourn her but he would have relinquished that right too. He would have no right to offer support or comfort to his child. Offer? One did not offer these things. She would not seek it from him. It would not occur to her to do so. If Padma was dead Mallika would then belong to all these women. Even to her grandmother. Mallika would always be theirs. Never his.

"Amma, Mallika. Come and sit. It is of no use standing there like that." They turned and slowly came and sat. Then Shanta said to him, tentatively, "Are you in a hurry to—"

"No. I'm in no hurry." He got up and went out of the front door to the veranda. At the end of the street, coming towards him, was Padma, a cloth bag hung over her shoulder, full of what looked like books. He had waited in this veranda before, he knew it now, familiar the green and white chairs, familiar the sight of Padma walking towards him. She was absorbed in some thought and didn't see him at first. Then she looked towards the house and for a moment she slowed her pace and he saw the shock on her face.

He put his head in at the door and said, "She's back."

Mallika ran to the door, past him, down the veranda steps and into Padma's arms. He went inside. Shanta and her mother went out. Voices rose and fell—surprise, joy, complaint.

A few minutes later they all came in, smiling. Padma's mother had her arm around her daughter's waist. Padma's smile didn't include him. "I'm sorry," she said.

"The bus didn't come?" Shanta asked.

Padma nodded.

"You should have taken a scooter," he said unthinkingly.

Mallika said, "Scooters cost a lot of money."

He saw Mrs. Nanda finally getting up from her chair. "You gave us too much worry, Padma," she said reprovingly.

To his surprise, Padma looked stricken with guilt and said, "I'm terribly sorry, Madhu."

Mrs. Nanda gave her a hug, like a mother who was satisfied that her child had understood, then she folded her hands, including him in her goodbye, and went out.

The mother said, "Come, Padma, come and eat." Padma followed her mother to the dining table. Mallika joined them.

Padma's guilt-stricken, pleading face was still playing on his mind when Shanta sat next to him and said, "Thank God she's all right."

"I think I should go now."

"Amma and I will rest after this. You can be with Padma and Mallika. After tea, if you wish, you can leave."

He hesitated.

She said in a very low voice, "Please could I talk to you very frankly."

He nodded.

"You will mind. But I have to. For Mallika's sake."

He nodded again.

"You see, I don't know now what is going to happen."

"I told you. Nothing."

"Yes. Yes. You told me. So . . . what about Mallika?"

"Mallika?"

"Her future, her marriage, everything . . . Mallika's future."

He looked at her blankly. "Mallika's *marriage*?"

"Well, she will have to get married one day."

He continued looking at her blankly.

She shifted in her chair. "Padma has nothing saved for Mallika."

He understood.

"I'm sorry to sound so . . . sound like this. But she is my child too. And Padma, she is quite foolish about these things. All her theories are all very well, but one has to be practical about these things. She—"

"I don't know how to offer any financial support without Padma objecting."

She gave a sigh of relief. "Oh that. That is the least of the problem. Start an account in Mallika's name. When she gets married, the money will be there."

"They need money now."

"That they do. Padma's nursing home—my God—those bills."

"How did she pay?"

"I told Amma to send money. So she sent."

"I see."

"It wasn't easy. Amma's living with Madhav now. His wife is a witch. Wants to know everything. It is Amma's money. What business is it of Ratna how Amma spends it? But no, she had to find out where Ma was sending the money and why. And that too, when all the rent from the Bangalore house is going to Madhav."

"I see."

"Appa left the house to Madhav. Padma keeps saying, Appa should have left it to Amma, not to Madhav. Once, when I used to talk about these things Padma used to call me petty. Now she's the one who talks about it. Then it isn't petty? No, when she talks about it, she is talking about issues, about right and wrong and justice and injustice. Am I talking too much?"

He shook his head.

"What was I saying. Yes, my father. Whom to talk to, about him? Not Padma, not Amma, and Mallika's too young. The boys couldn't care less, and my husband . . . you can't talk to husbands about your parents. Then next time you have a fight they'll throw it back at you—whatever you told them. I want to tell her, Put your logic aside, Padma, put all your theories aside. But I listen. Who else will listen to her?"

"She hasn't talked to you about me?"

"No." She shook her head as she saw his face. "I don't understand her. She should do it for Mallika's sake at least."

"Do what?"

"Marry you."

"It's not something that can be done . . . for Mallika's sake."

"You too." Her tone was bitter.

"Padma says we're two different people now."

"Well, of course you are. So am I. So is my husband. Everyone changes. What a silly thing to say."

"And that she cannot give up everything that she has now. Her house, her friends, her independence."

"She said *that*?"

"She said married women are trapped more than she has ever been. She said they lead an unnatural life, opposed to their dreams and desires."

Shanta was looking down at her lap. "So," she said quietly. "Now I know how she sees all of us."

Too late to take back the words.

"You were talking about Mallika—her future."

She raised her eyes to him slowly. "Mallika?"

"I'll open a bank account in her name."

He heard her give a deep sigh of relief. "Don't even *mention* it to Padma. Just *do* it." He nodded.

"I didn't mean to complain about Padma. After she got her doctorate—"

"She's got her doctorate?"

"She never told you? Trust her. Yes. How she worked for it. She drove herself. Sometimes she used to stay up all night . . . the way she—"

Mallika came to them. Shanta rose. "Amma and I are going to rest for some time. We'll see you at tea time. Where's Ma, Mallika?"

"She's just coming."

Padma came out of the kitchen. She was pale. "Darling, you're tired, will you rest too?" Shanta said, looking worried. Padma shook her head. Shanta looked at her doubtfully, then went inside.


Mallika looked down at her toes. Padma looked at him. Padma, how could you. He couldn't bear to look at her face.

"What have you been hiding from me?" Padma's voice was shaking. Mallika's head jerked up. "What has been going on?"

He should have left earlier. He should not have let Shanta dissuade him. The old feeling of suffocation was coming back.

"I don't want your silences anymore." Padma's voice was shaking so much that he could hardly make out the words. "I bore with your silence for thirteen years. I won't bear with it for a minute more." Mallika's eyes were wide with fear. "Ayaji," Padma called.

She had been waiting. She made her entrance with aplomb and stood before them, not giving him one glance. "Now," Padma said, "say it in front of him."

She was doing it in front of Mallika. That was the worst of it. After she had stripped him, she would open him up and prise out that tender, stunted thing which he had nurtured for all these years when there had been nothing else to nurture. He had come prepared for the final closure. He would have gone knowing he still had this to hold on to. Not anymore. Now even this would have to become part of the rest.

Ayaji was in full form. "I know him," she said giving him a look. "Remember, memsahib, I used to take Baby to the park every day because you were too tired when you came back from college? He used to come to the park and play with Baby. Long time he used to stay in the park. Gentle he was, kind. I used to feel compassion for him. For someone so young he had a very sad face. He used to suddenly appear and disappear. He would come to the park for two days, then not come for months. That way he used to come and go for two, three years. When he came to this house today he recognized me, memsahib. Then why did he pretend not to recognize me? Now you ask him what has to be asked."

So saying she walked to the back door and let herself out.

He looked up. Mallika was shivering. Padma's face and lips were white. She had her arm around Mallika. Mallika was looking at him. Pleadingly. He said to Mallika, "No. I didn't know. I promise." His voice was clear, steady. Bewilderment on Mallika's face.

"Get her a blanket from her room." He got up and turning to the left, went to Mallika's room. He had seen this before too. The huge bookshelf full of books. He knew the books they held. The bed. The desk and chair. Familiar. He lifted the bedcover and picked up the blanket. He went back to the sitting room and put it around Mallika. He was going back to his chair when Mallika put out her arm and touched his sleeve. "Sit here," she said. The pleading look had not gone. There was no place on the sofa. He took off his shoes and sat down on the carpet next to the sofa.

Padma was taking the notebooks out of her cloth bag, one by one, till they lay in a pile next to her on the sofa. Eight in all.

"I found these in Mallika's room last night. When did you give them to her?"

Mallika looked at her mother, agonized.

"Ma, he—"

She didn't even look at Mallika. "*You* tell me. Everything."

No anger in her voice. Terror.

"I must have lost my mind." He tried to hold his voice but it cracked, "When . . . I . . . lost you."

Once, long ago, she had poured a glass of water over his head and he had made a declaration, the absolute nature of which he comprehended only years later. This time her terror, of him, had precipitated the other.

Now there was no mistaking the compassion on Mallika's face. He looked up at Mallika, spoke to Mallika.

"After your grandfather told me your mother had got married, I went back to Delhi to continue my training. Knowing she was married, I felt I couldn't write to her to explain, or, I thought, meet her. Only gradually did it come to me that I could end my marriage. She, hers. I didn't know where your mother was. Then I remembered that she had told me about her sister and brother-in-law—she had mentioned his designation in the railways. I was able to find out they were in Trichinopoli. I had no leave. We were not encouraged to take leave during the training period and I had taken more than I was entitled to because of my mother's health. The months passed. Then I managed some leave and went to Trichinopoli. They weren't at home. The servant told me they had gone away for a few days. He refused to tell me where. I asked him for a glass of water. When he went to get it, I opened the address book that was lying on the table and found your mother's name and her Delhi address.

"When I next managed to get leave, I came to Delhi. I found your house. I didn't know what to do. Knock and say to Padma's husband, I am an old friend of your wife's? Or if your mother opened the door, then . . . say what? Tell her I married someone else more than a year ago, and so did you, but now let us both leave them and be together? I realized how presumptuous I had been to think she would want me back. On the other hand, I felt that if I could meet her alone, without her husband, then I could try and explain. I thought, if she forgave me then it wasn't too late to make a life together again. It was evening. I thought I would come back the next morning, which was a Monday, at about eleven. Then her husband would have gone to work and she would probably be on her own. I drove away. On the way out I passed the market." He stopped.

She was there. Standing in front of the phalwalla, buying fruits. He got out of the car and began walking towards her. He saw the mangalsutra at the back of her neck. For a second it made him stop in his tracks. There was no one next to her except an ayah with a baby. He was perhaps fifteen feet from her when she turned to the ayah and took the baby from her. The ayah put the fruits in a basket and they both began walking away.

It was as though a hand was turning him around and pushing him back to the car. He opened the door and got inside. When he opened his eyes, she was walking away from him, holding the baby, the ayah walking beside her. She was walking very slowly. A hammer was hitting him on his head, beating a rhythm, saying, This should have been your baby, This should have been your baby. The hammer was beating a rhythm saying, Now you have lost her forever, Now you have lost her forever. The baby was chubby, with big eyes and black hair and a very solemn expression. The baby that should have been his.

So this too he had done to Padma—driven her to endure another man's body.

He went back to the car and drove to her house. He parked farther up the road. He saw her walking towards her house. She didn't even glance at the car. She was looking very tired. Pale and tired. Then he thought, it does not matter, it does not matter even if she has a child, if she is ready to take me back then we can start life together again with the child. He would bring up the child as his own and the child would never know otherwise. She went to her house and sat down in the veranda, the baby on her lap. The door opened. A man came out. Much older than her, at least thirty-five. A kind, gentle face. He sat next to her and put out his arms. She handed the baby to him. He held the child and they began to talk.

Reality hit him. Had he been mad? Here she was with a husband and a baby. More than a year had passed, she had a child, and he was actually contemplating going to her the next morning and asking her to leave her husband and come to him? After what he had done? She would never come. Even if she did she would lose the child to her husband. No court would give her custody of the child. They would say she was an unfit mother. He had been mad.

He drove away.

"You saw Ma in the market."

"Yes. With you. I drove to your house. She sat with you on her lap in the veranda. A man came out and sat with her and they began to talk."

"Narayana Uncle."

"I thought it was her husband. All my fantasies about being together again seemed . . . crazy."

It was the end. Now he had to lay Padma to rest.

Mallika's voice above his head, "But you came back."

"Yes."

"You saw me in the park with Ayaji and recognized us."

Unbearable. Unbearable the remembrance of her skin against his, the softness of her cheek, those large, grave eyes, the sudden, unexpected smiles. She would recognize him in her second year and put her arms up to him to be carried. She used to wear silver payals and silver bangles and sometimes there was a large black mark on her cheek to take away the nazar. Padma never came. Ayaji would watch him indulgently as he lay on the grass on his stomach, his nose nuzzling his child's. His child liked it when he blew into her face. She would close her eyes and smile as her hair blew back.

"You used to imagine that I was your child?"

He nodded.

"That's why you kept coming back."

Mallika knew the shape of his thoughts too.

"I remember you."

He could not look at her face.

"I remember you holding me up and saying something. I used to play with your watch."

"You couldn't remember." He could hardly hear himself speak.

"Didn't you make train noises for me?"

She had been fascinated. Over and over she would want him to do it. Her head turning to one side, then to the other, her eyes big with wonder.

Once, just once, he met Mrs. Nanda. She had seen his misery, asked questions. He had told her he had lost his child. It was true.

The child looked forward to his visits. She recognized him, would laugh with delight when he played with her. One day, as he held her, the pain in his chest unbearable, she saw his face and burst into tears.

He stopped going to the park.

"You stopped coming to the park when I was three."

He nodded.

He buried himself in his work.

"When did you come back?"

"A year later."

"You wanted to see Ma."

He nodded.

"You parked opposite our house, next to Mrs. Moitra's house."

"Yes."

Four years since he had seen Padma that time in the market. At four-thirty in the morning he saw the light go on in what must have been the bedroom. Then off in the bedroom, on in the living room. Twenty minutes later she drew the curtain that faced the street and he saw her framed against the window, holding a mug in her hand. Then she went to the dining table, which he could see too, and sat there, reading from a large pile of books. He drove away.

Sitting at his desk at work, thinking, Mallika's five now, if she were mine she would be listening to my stories. What would I tell her? He began to write. After a month of writing he tore it all up.

Back the following year. At four-thirty again the light came on. Twenty minutes later Padma framed against the window. Again back to the dining table to work.

The story that lay within him refused to be written. What he did write said so little of what he wished that he would give up every few weeks. Then he would go back to it again. It seemed that he had no words for this story that waited within him. At nights he would sit at his desk, trying to write. On the weekends he would do the same. He found himself thinking about it every waking moment, even as he went about his work. Then, one day, he discovered the girl Kiran, and the boy Abhimanyu. And the story began to, very slowly, grow roots. Even so, it was not easy. He found himself rewriting and revising endlessly. Suddenly, Kiran would do something in the magic land that changed everything he had planned for her. Or, without warning, Abhimanyu would respond in a completely unexpected way to a bird or an animal, and this would sweep the story to a wholly unpredictable climax. They would get themselves into situations not of his making and he would have no idea how to get them back out. What on earth would Kiran and Abhimanyu do now? He didn't know. And that was where the excitement of writing lay, in this unpredictability. It was a heady feeling, coming back from work every day and knowing the magic land was there, waiting for him, this land where things happened as if of their own volition. He wrote every night, every weekend. It was as if he were possessed. Now he knew joy again, and passion. Kiran and Abhimanyu refused to do what he planned for them. He learned to listen to them. The stories flowered. And he knew, those hours, what it was to be given life again.

The following year. No Padma. Perhaps she was working at nights and not in the morning? He returned at midnight and waited till almost five. No Padma.

"How often did you come?"

"Before I saw you again, three times."

"Once every year."

"Yes."

"You used to see Ma when she woke up to study?"

"Yes."

"Every time?"

"The year I met you and Prabha I didn't see her."

He came back in the evening the next day. Perhaps he would see her at the veranda as he drove past. He didn't. It hit him then. She could have left. He would never know where she was. She could be dead. He would never know that either. He turned into the street behind the line of houses where hers was, and then he saw two small girls getting the worst of a fight with two boys. Running out of the car, throwing the boys into the ditch, helping the girls up. Mallika. Big, brown, frightened eyes. It couldn't be. Then the other girl saying, "Mallika." Looking at her, gripped with joy. A joy that almost caved in when she spoke of her father who read. He had his briefcase in the car, the notebook in the briefcase where it always lay.

He looked up at Padma. "That year when I didn't see you at night, I came back the next evening. That's when I saw the two boys attacking Prabha and Mallika."

Padma wasn't looking at him. Her eyes were fixed on her lap.

"Then he threw them into the ditch, Ma, and checked that we were unhurt, then he gave us the first book, see, this one, and then he went away."

She didn't look at Mallika either. Even her hands were still.

The knowledge that it could never be put to rest.

Back in Delhi, a year later, driving through the colony at seven in the morning. Seeing Padma at the bus stop near the colony. Following the bus to the college where she taught. Seeing her laughing and talking to a student outside the college gates, then going inside.

She wasn't dead. She wasn't ill. She lived in the same house.

"You came then, the next year?"

"She was going to her college."

"You followed her there." No surprise in her voice.

"And the following year we saw you parked outside Mrs. Moitra's house."

He had borrowed Sita's husband's car after dinner and told them not to wait. On an impulse he put his briefcase with the two new stories in the car. Driving around aimlessly, for a few hours, then, driving to her house.

Waiting for it to be four-thirty. Someone prodding his back. Looking up, and there they were, Prabha and Mallika, in their pyjamas, their eyes wide with terror, the terror fading, delicious excitement filling their faces. After they flew back into the house, he waited for Padma to draw the curtain. She did. He drove back.

"Prabha and Mallika came out to where I was parked," he said to Padma. "They recognized me. We talked a little. I gave them the books."

"These two books, Ma. See. Did you see Ma after that?"

"Yes."

A year and a half later. Two nights in a row, waiting for Padma. No sign of her. She was dead. Going the next day to Mallika's school, meeting the Mother Superior, telling her that he wanted his daughter admitted to her school, asking if he could look around. She taking him around the school. Looking for Mallika as he passed classroom after classroom filled with children. Thanking the nun, saying goodbye, hearing the bell for the tiffin break. Turning back, walking around the corridors. And there she was.

"I came back a year and a half later, didn't see you. I went to Mallika's school, and I saw her there and talked to her. So I knew . . . you were all right. I gave her two more books."

"These two, Ma. You didn't see Ma that year?"

"No."

"You tried to?"

"Yes. She wasn't . . . I didn't . . . see her."

Seeing the tears in Mallika's eyes, touching her cheek and walking away, not letting himself think. Telling himself, Padma is all right, Padma is all right, now I don't have to see her. Driving away from the convent all the way to Padma's college. Waiting outside for two hours. No sign of her. Back to the colony, through the market and past her house. No sign. Out of the colony, back to her college, then back again to her colony. No Padma.

Then, after that, the last time. Two nights. No luck. He would never see her again. Circling the neighbourhood in the sizzling heat. Everything quiet, everyone inside their homes. In the compound, boys in white, playing cricket, exultant shouts. Parking the car there, watching them, filled with the urge to play. Going to the boys, joining their game. Prabha running towards him, jumping up and down, pointing to Mallika.

She should have been his child. And in the middle of all that, she spoke of her father, and his love for books. Of his buying books for Padma and for her. All joy squeezed out of him. Abruptly waving goodbye, driving away, past Padma's house, and there she was, walking into her neighbour's house, a flash of her green saree, a swing of her plait and she had gone inside.

"Then Ma, a year ago, when he was playing cricket in the maidan with the other boys, he saw me and we talked and he gave me two more. These two."

Silence. She hadn't moved at all.

"Did you see Ma that time?"

"I passed your house. She was going inside Mrs. Prasad's house."

A year later. Padma's five letters written thirteen years ago. His departure for Bangalore. Sometime during those nightmarish hours with Padma's mother he had actually thought Padma had died in the one year that he hadn't seen her. No, Padma's mother had said, Padma wasn't dead.

Finally, Padma was looking at him. In her face he was finally seeing what he had not known till this day—he had lost his mind.

"Ready for tea?"

It was Shanta. He looked up, dazed. Padma and Mallika were looking up at her too. He glanced at his watch. Had an hour already passed? Was that how long their silences had been?

Shanta's eyes went over them in a quick, appraising glance. "I take it that you are," she said, going to the back door.

When he came out of the bathroom, ten minutes later, they were all sitting at the dining table. He joined them, sitting at the place kept for him between Shanta and the mother. Shanta served the tea. Something had happened. She had lost her ebullience.

"Shanta, child, please serve the cake."

Her eyes focussed on him and he saw something he couldn't recognize on her face. Silently she passed him the plate. He shook his head. Padma was drinking her tea silently, not looking at anyone. Mallika was looking at Padma. The mother was looking at him.

Ah. That was how she must have looked as she cursed.

"Have dinner here," Mallika said. Shanta slowly turned towards her. "Ma?" Mallika said, looking at Padma, but Padma didn't seem to have heard.

"You must," Shanta said, as though it was being forced out of her.

He tried to speak.

"Come, let us go to the veranda," Shanta said to him. They went to the veranda and sat. He could see the Prasads on their lawn, the two children playing. On the other side was a man, probably Mr. Nanda, with Mahima. People were going for walks, sitting on their lawns and verandas. The mother came out and sat with them. A few minutes later, Mallika joined them. The mother turned to Mallika, took her hand in hers, her expression changing, her eyes suffused with love. He heard them murmuring.

A cozy picture for all to see.

Now he knew what lay under the coziness. Not acceptance. Far from it. What it was, was a public declaration, asserting his legitimacy. Not for his sake, but for Padma's. To protect her. The declaration said, He is with us, Padma's mother, Padma's sister, so don't you dare gossip or speculate. Mother, older daughter, he, all of them bound by the curse, by its echoes.

Dinner was a very quiet meal. Shanta had excelled herself. She served coffee after dinner. As a special concession Mallika was allowed a cup too.

He finished his coffee and got up. "Thank you," he said to Shanta. "It was a wonderful meal." She tried to smile. He folded his hands to the mother. She acknowledged it, folding her own with great dignity.

Padma. "Goodnight," he said to her. She was picking up her shawl from the sofa and wrapping it around herself. "Mallika and I'll walk with you to the scooter stand."

"It's not necessary."

"You might not get a scooter at this time. The taxi stand is on the other side."

"I'll find it." He turned to Mallika, who was watching her mother. "Goodnight."

"Spend the night here," Mallika said in a small voice.

Silence. No one looked at anyone else.

"Thank you. That's very . . . sweet of you. But I have to go back. Goodnight, Mallika." He raised his hand as Padma moved forward. "There's no need to come with me. Please."

He was out the door and into the cold night.

It was freezing. He walked fast towards the scooter stand. Not a single scooter. He stood on the road for ten minutes. No luck. The two he hailed refused to stop. Now what. Where the hell was the taxi stand. He asked a passerby, who pointed in the opposite direction. He began walking in that direction.

At first when he heard it he thought he was imagining it. The sound of someone panting behind him. It became louder. He turned. Mallika. Running towards him. Alone. He walked swiftly towards her and she stopped, unable to speak, taking deep breaths. "What are you doing here alone in the middle of the night," he said, unsteadily. She was too breathless to answer. He took her arm and walked to the side of the road. "Do they know you're out of the house?" She shook her head, still panting. "Come on then," he said, letting go of her arm. "Wait," she said, "Let . . . me catch . . . my . . . breath."

For a few minutes they stood there. "It's ten at night," he said, "and you come chasing me alone all the way here without telling anyone at home? Suppose something had happened to you?"

She was looking up at him.

"Come along."

They began walking towards the house.

"And don't ask me to stay the night."

"You can sleep in my room. I'll sleep with Ma in the sitting room."

"That isn't the reason I'm saying no."

"You're saying it because of Ma."

He glanced at her as she walked next to him. A shock ran through him. She was taller than Padma.

"All this time I thought you were having an affair with Mrs. Moitra."

He stopped in his tracks. "You thought *what*?"

"Your car was always parked outside her house. And everyone knows she has a . . . lover."

He looked at her speechlessly. She was looking up at him with Padma's clear eyes. "That's why I said I knew about your affair."

Forgive me, Padma. I should have known you wouldn't have. Forgive me.

Twice in the hospital, and once this morning, Mallika had begun to ask. Each time, she had allowed him his refusal to answer. Terrified that if she persisted, it would be confirmed.

They resumed walking.

"So they all know now."

"Mahima and Madhu Aunty don't."

"Mrs. Prasad?"

"Prabha told me that once when they were going by train to her grandmother's house—" She stopped abruptly.

"Yes?"

Padma was coming swiftly towards them, almost running. When she reached them she didn't even look at him, but caught hold of Mallika's arms with both her hands. "*Never . . . never . . . do . . . that . . . again,*" she said, shaking Mallika hard after each word. "Do . . . you . . . understand?"

Mallika's face crumpled. She burst into tears.

She stood at the side of the road weeping. Padma tried to wipe her cheeks with her saree palla but Mallika flung her hand away. "Here," he said, handing her a hanky. She took it and blew her nose violently into it. After five minutes she subsided as suddenly as she had begun, and without a word, began walking back. They followed two steps behind her. When they reached the house the mother and Shanta were standing in the veranda. Mallika stopped and looked up at him.

"All right," he said.


After all of them had gone to bed and the lights in the house were switched off, he gently closed Mallika's bedroom door and went to the bookshelf. It covered the entire wall of her room. She had arranged them in a particular order. On the topmost shelf were all her childhood books. On the next, the books she was probably reading now, or had read. On the third shelf, all the books he and Padma had collected at their bookshop. On the bottom one, comics and romances. He began looking at the third shelf. There it was. He took it out and opened it. *To Padma, my friend. Karan* he had written in the book. He turned the pages. The page had been torn out. Very neatly. He put the book back in its place.

Mallika's desk. Her textbooks, homework and classwork notebooks neatly covered with brown paper. Pens, pencils, ink. English classwork. Write an essay on the following subjects: the autobiography of a fountain pen; my most unforgettable character; the happiest day of my life.

He sat at the chair and began to read about the happiest day in her life. After some time he stopped. It was unbelievable. He continued reading till he came to the end. The poor child. The poor, poor child.

It had been written a year before and was a beautifully rendered description of her and her mother going back to Bangalore to visit her grandparents. Her first visit; they had not been able to go before because her grandfather had not forgiven her mother for marrying her father without permission. But finally they were going.

She described the train journey—this girl who had never been on a train till this year. And then, the scooter ride to the house—this girl who had never been to the house. She described the house and the garden and the servant and last of all, her grandparents. He had seen it. He knew how accurate her description was. He had seen the green gate and the profusion of flowers in the garden, he had seen the charming sitting room and the shelf full of books. All that she described. She enclosed her grandparents in this beautiful house, evoking the texture and warmth of each room. She described how her grandmother smelt, and the feel of her arms around her, how her grandfather greeted her and her mother, wordlessly. She wrote about the silence in her Delhi house, a silence punctuated only by the sound of Ayaji's grumbles in the kitchen and the sound of the pressure cooker, and sometimes, over the radio, the classical music that her mother so loved. But in the Bangalore house, she wrote, that first morning, the sun rose to the sounds of her grandparents and her Shantamama chanting their morning prayers. She described their table with the photographs and idols of the Gods, her Shantamama gathering the flowers from the garden in a brass plate and decorating the Gods with them, the smell of incense filling the house and, from outside, bird sounds wafting in. And later, the mutterings and murmurings, chimings and clinkings, cacklings and creakings, the radio blaring with Karnataka music, and in the kitchen her Ajji going clatter clatter, bang bang, her voice scolding the servants, rising and falling; in the brief lull the clinking of her Shantamama's bangles as she went about dusting the mantelpieces and all the corners that the servants had forgotten. From her bedroom window she could see the profusion of flowers in the garden. My grandfather had forgiven my mother long ago, she wrote, but could never tell her so.

The autobiography of a fountain pen. The pen was presented to a boy called Madhav by his mother for his tenth birthday. The essay went on to describe the boy's intelligence, his wit, his imagination. The pen transformed all this into words—in school, at home, in his letters to his favourite sister, Padma, in his diary. He wrote about his parents and his sisters and about a friend he had at college, called Kunal. The pen shared all Madhav's secrets, things that even his youngest sister did not know. It knew, for example, that there was no one he loved as much as he loved his sister, and when she went and got married to his friend Kunal without telling anyone, it broke his heart. Later, when Kunal died in an accident and his sister was expecting a baby, he told his sister that he would adopt the child. She would not part with the baby. In anger they said things to each other that neither ever forgot. All this Madhav recorded in his diary. But now he had his own wife and children and there was no time for writing. Now the fountain pen was no longer privy to the secrets that lay in his heart. All it knew now was what work he did in his office. Often the pen wondered what had happened to all these people who had mattered so much to Madhav.

*This is not the autobiography of a fountain pen,* the teacher had written below. *You have let your imagination run away with you. Next time read the title of the essay carefully before you begin writing.*

Bloody stupid woman.

He couldn't read anymore. He wasn't ready to discover her most unforgettable character. He hadn't been ready for what he had read.

He put the notebook back in its place and switched off the lamp at the desk. He got up and went to the bed, lay down, covering himself with the quilt. Shanta had given him a pyjama kurta of Narayana's that had been left behind in the house on his last trip. It was short for him, though fortunately, not tight. He had Mallika's bathroom to himself. There was another bathroom in Padma's room, Shanta had told him reassuringly. Padma had provided him with a toothbrush and a comb.

He got up from the bed, went to the desk, switched on the lamp again. He knew it before he opened the notebook. He must have known it even as he had switched off the lamp and got into bed. *My Most Unforgettable Character—my father, Kunal.* He closed the notebook, switched off the lamp and continued sitting at the desk.

Kunal. His name too she had not known. For thirteen years, another name, another face. He closed his eyes. Even if you can't sleep, his mother used to say, close your eyes. That itself will refresh you. During his boyhood he had never seen his mother sleeping. She went to sleep well past midnight every day, and got up before five. How else to look after them all and her ailing mother-in-law, and all the guests that they had? She had begun knitting a sweater for him when he was ten. She would try and find the time to knit at night, but invariably, would fall asleep while doing it. After four years, the sweater was ready. He wore it every day that winter till a cousin who came to stay with them decided to hide the sweater in the dustbin. That day, for the first and last time in his life, he had used his fists.

He looked at his watch. It was three. He walked to the door. For a minute he stood there, then he opened the door softly and went into the sitting room. Padma and Mallika were lying on a mattress on the ground, under a quilt, Padma stroking the child's head. He went up to them and sat down on the carpet next to Mallika. She was fast asleep. He watched Padma's hands on the child's forehead and hair, moving in a slow and steady rhythm. "Get your quilt," Padma said, her voice low. "Your blanket also," she added as he got up.

When he came back she got up and helped him spread the blanket next to Mallika. Then she went back to the other side, curling herself around Mallika again. He put his pillow over the blanket and got under the quilt, lying on his side, his head resting on his hand, looking at the child. How softly she was breathing. When he had held Mallika in his arms as a baby he had discovered this other physical longing, so different from the one he had known with Padma, and yet, in its fierceness, so akin. This was what they said mothers felt for their children. Surely fathers felt it too?

"What did I do to my child," Padma said. "What did I do to her."

"It's my fault. She hid it from you because I told her not to show the books to anyone."

"Not just that. I never knew her. Once she showed me what I had done to her. Even then I didn't see it."

No questions. Not now.

"I used to think I was a terrible mother for other reasons. I didn't even see this. What have I done to her."

He looked away from her face.

"This is what I have become. I never knew. Oh God, forgive me."

Much later, he turned his head towards her. She was lying on her side, her arm around the child. She said, without anger, "If Mallika hadn't been there we could have put each other aside once and for all. I couldn't forget you because I had your child. You couldn't forget me because you had your guilt."

"If after thirteen years I had found out that you were not married I would have come to you, child or no child."

Slowly, she shook her head.

"That day, just before you left my house, I said I accepted what you said you felt," he said. "It wasn't true."

"You mean it isn't true now."

"It wasn't true then either."

"The same old Karan," she said to herself, almost wonderingly.

He preferred the anger. A silent terror began gnawing at his stomach, and rising.

"Not the same. I think . . . I believe . . . differently."

"The way you think and what you believe in doesn't translate into your actions. You've never acted."

He closed his eyes, felt the darkness move.

"Once you used to think suffering in silence was ennobling."

He opened his eyes.

"That's how you used to perceive your mother."

Only sadness in her voice.

"And Mallika thinks suffering is . . . romantic. Your . . . futile visits to Delhi . . . she thinks it confirms your . . . fidelity to me. But . . . suffering's . . . not romantic. Or, ennobling. It's just . . . it's a waste."

She put her cheek against the child's. Almost to herself, she said, "When she found out who you were . . . what could she have imagined."

"She thought I was having an affair with some Mrs. Moitra."

He heard her intake of breath.

"She told me tonight. When she came running after me."

Something inside him must have snapped with awful finality thirteen years ago. How else could he, all these years, have done what he had done? Padma had broken down after he returned to her, after he had risen, literally, from the dead. But he had collapsed long before Padma, thirteen years ago, and this disintegration had, like a building crumbling from within, just gone on and on, while the outside edifice appeared strong and smooth with not even a hairline crack to hint at the ruins within.

"I used to think I couldn't live without Karan. But I did. Sustaining myself on those old memories. Like married women who find life more bearable reading romances. Easier that than having an affair, no? Except that Karan was my real life romance, not my fantasy romance. But it was a fantasy, nevertheless, wasn't it? As perverse as yours."

"I was a very sick man."

"And I, a very sick woman."

He watched her caress the child's head.

She said, "I hated myself too."

"You?"

"How else to understand what you did."

He had never asked her. It hit him now. The question that had haunted him for thirteen years—he had never asked her why she thought he had done it.

"You blamed *yourself* for what I did?"

"I thought that after you found out about how I broke the hostel rules, you realized that I was dishonest and deceitful and devious. And that . . . whatever you felt for me . . . died then."

So. This too.

"The way it happened with your father whom you . . . worshipped. You didn't tell him why, either."

Padma. Which one? The first time in the hospital. The dazed, far-removed Padma, looking at him the way one looks at a familiar face one can't quite recognize. Talking to him as though there had never been a past. Kind, considerate, removed. The second time in his house. Another Padma. Battering him with things he could barely comprehend. Such anger, such . . . hatred. Yet they had made . . . love? Then, here in her house, here in this very room, a third Padma, apologizing almost abjectly to that Mrs. Nanda. Full of diffidence, full of apprehension, wanting only to placate. Now, this Padma.

What bearing did this Padma have on the one he had once known most truly for her constancy? The constancy, in his mind, being not what she felt for him, but what she *was*. And in a fashion completely unthought and unconsidered, it had always been there, her belief in herself.

It wasn't there now.

Nor was his belief in her.

"Why the name Abhimanyu?" she asked.

"I intended him to be like Abhimanyu."

"But he turned out to be . . . partly . . . like you."

"When did you read them?"

"This morning. I took them with me. That's why I was late."

"Why . . . partly?"

"Your Abhimanyu acted."

"I . . . see."

Once she had given him his faith in her, given him his absolute belief in her integrity. Even as he had destroyed her faith in him, his own had remained intact. Intact those few years together, intact the long years after.

Not anymore. When Mallika had said to him, I know about your affair, he had thought that Padma had betrayed him, he who had once not known even the nature of such a thought.

Nothing familiar about her expression either. Once he had known every play of light and shadow on it. More light than shadow. Her radiance captivating and enclosing him. Continuing, in her absence, to enclose him for thirteen years.

It wasn't there anymore.

He felt his body jerk.

That light had been extinguished thirteen years ago. He had continued living within it for as long.

Mourn for Padma, Karan, mourn for Padma.

"Everything that we ever felt for each other has become . . . twisted and misshapen," she whispered.

"It can become whole again." He could hear the despair in his voice.

She shook her head as despairingly. "Whatever I was to you is now . . . contaminated with your guilt and . . . everything else that you've been . . . carrying inside you. I can't live with what I've become in your mind."

"And . . . what have I become in yours?"

Silence.

"The same thing. A sickness. Like cancer. You've consumed me. Nothing else has been possible."

Nothing else. For thirteen years, only Padma.

"You haven't asked me, Why the name Kiran," he said, his voice shaking.

She made a stifled sound.

He got up, went to the other side, where she lay, sat next to her. He leaned over her, covered Mallika with his quilt, then lay down next to Padma, covering himself with hers. He groped for her hands, found them, held them in both his as he had done many years ago. No words this time.

Mourn for Padma, Karan, mourn for Padma.

He could hardly hear her as she spoke. "I'm swamped. Swamped with those memories. Like the memories . . . of someone dead."

She was holding on to his hands as if she were drowning in a well.

He gripped her hands tighter as the well began pulling him in too.

In the darkness, enclosed within its waters, he could no longer see her, he had lost her completely, deeper, deeper, nothing left of her, only the water, its voice, Padma's voice. "All you had to do thirteen years ago was to come to me and tell me what had happened. That's all. Whether I was married or not. Whether I had a child by the marriage or not. Whether I would have gone back to you or not. Those considerations were less important, Karan, those considerations were not important." Had he heard it before, a dream, an echo, he had heard it before. Mallika. And then, the other echoes, of that magical and distant time, swamped, he was swamped, drowning, he could feel her hands pulling him out, see her face taking shape beside him, hear his shuddering sounds. Her hands disengaging themselves from his, her voice anguished, "This . . . this *compulsion*, it doesn't come out of the four years we knew each other, Karan—it comes out of the thirteen years we spent apart."

Such a long silence.

"It was worse for you." Her words came out like a sigh.

He shook his head.

"I've built up another life for myself. I have Mallika. Shantacca, Madhu, Anu. Amma."

"You have me." What was he saying? "Even if you don't want me," he said, the terror rising to his throat.

"But what do you have, Karan? Except the dream Padma?"

Even as she said it, she saw what lay in his face. She closed her eyes against it.

"The dream," he spoke as though he were being throttled, "is over."

He found that he was sitting upright. Without any conscious thought, he was getting up, going back to the other side, sitting down next to Mallika.

Time passed.

He looked at the child. He found his hand involuntarily rising, touching her hair. Her forehead. Her cheek.

Where do you come from, magic man?

From the land where stories grow, my magic girl.

The best books I have ever read in my whole life.

So she had said with shining eyes, this child whose flesh lay warm under his hand, this child who couldn't know how, in that useless, stunted time, his books had sustained him. So she had said breathlessly, this child who didn't know how death had stalked and preyed upon the secret years.

Padma's voice, shuddering, "Now I have to learn to live without Karan."

Without Padma.

"Padma." He could hardly see her as she turned towards him. "I only gave Mallika what you gave me once. I just returned it to her. It was all I had to give."

She was looking at him, as blinded as he.

The best books. All, now, that remained. All, now, that he could call his own.

From the window across the room, he could see the streetlight. The same window from where he had, thrice, seen her framed. Now, within that window, inside the house, enclosed in a dreamlike, echoing time. Now, outside, the silence. Silence cradling the echoing house, all, for a while, still.

# GLOSSARY

| | |
|---|---|
| Abhimanyu | a very young and brave warrior, son of Arjuna, in the epic *Mahabharata* |
| Acca | older sister |
| Accha | yes/O.K./indeed/I see (depending on the context) |
| Ahalya | a woman in the epic *Ramayana*, who was cursed by her husband and turned to stone for no fault of hers |
| Ajja | grandfather |
| Ajji | grandmother |
| Apsara | a celestial nymph |
| Ayaji | the woman servant who takes care of the house and children |
| Bahu | daughter-in-law |
| Bahurani | a term used to address one's daughter-in-law |
| Bechari | poor thing |
| Beti/Beta | child |
| Bewakoof | fool |
| Bhabi | elder brother's wife |
| Bhola-bhala | innocent, naive |
| Bindi | a red dot applied in the middle of the forehead—a sign of marriage. Traditionally not applied by widows. |
| Bua | father's sister |
| Chai | tea |

| | |
|---|---|
| Chalo | let us go |
| Charpai | a bed made out of jute coir |
| Chishti | the shrine of Khawaja Saleem Chishti built by Akbar at Fatehpur Sikri (Agra). People make wishes there by tying a red thread around the filagree work of the shrine. |
| Chupa rustam | a secretive person |
| Churail | a term of abuse used against women |
| Dadima | paternal grandmother |
| Dal | lentils |
| Dhobi | washerman |
| Didi | older sister |
| Diwali | the Hindu festival of lights ushering in the Hindu new year |
| Drishti | eye. The belief that when someone's eye falls on you, either with an excess of love or of dislike, you fall ill. |
| D.T.C. | Delhi Transport Corporation |
| Dusshera | Hindu festival in honour of Durga and Rama |
| Gajaras | a garland of flowers used to decorate one's hair |
| Ghungrus | a belt of bells tied around one's ankles for Indian dancing |
| Gita | song of the Lord in the epic *Mahabharata*, consisting of a philosophical conversation between Arjuna and his charioteer, Lord Krishna, where Krishna reveals to Arjuna the essential principles of life |
| Haraam zaadi | a term of abuse |
| Harishchandra | a king in Hindu mythology famous for total giving |
| Hawan | a religious ceremony |
| I.A.S. | Indian Administrative Service |
| Jamadarni/Jamardar | sweeperess/sweeper |
| Janampatri | horoscope |
| Jooda | hair styled in the form of a bun |
| Kabadiwalla | buyer of old bottles, newspapers, odds and ends |
| Kajal | kohl |

| | |
|---|---|
| Kannada | the language spoken in the southern state of Karnataka |
| Karnataka music | South Indian classical music |
| Katori | bowl |
| Kiran | a name for a girl, meaning "a ray of light" |
| Kum kum | the powder used to apply a bindi |
| Kuthi | bitch |
| Lakshmi | the Hindu goddess of wealth and good fortune |
| Lathis | long sticks used as weapons |
| Maang | the line parting one's hair |
| Madrasi | a condescending and misguided term for all South Indians, used by most North Indians |
| *Mahabharata* | a great Indian epic |
| Mali | gardener |
| Mangalsutra | a gold chain strung with black beads, only worn by married women |
| Manglik | a certain placement of Mars in one's horoscope makes one a Manglik. It is believed that one Manglik must marry only another Manglik, or else his/her spouse will die or be harmed. |
| Mataji | mother |
| Mela | a fair |
| Mithai | Indian sweets |
| Nada | a string used to tie one's underwear |
| Nahi | no |
| Nakhra | acting coy, hard to get |
| Namaste | a greeting with hands folded |
| Nazar | eye (the equivalent of Drishti) |
| Pandal | a small, beautifully decorated structure within which the wedding rites take place |
| Phalwalli/Phalwalla | fruit seller |
| Puja | prayer |
| Rahu | a star that eclipses the sun |
| *Ramayana* | the epic in Hindu mythology about Lord Rama |
| Ramleela | the ballet of the epic *Ramayana* through song and dance |
| Randi | whore |

| | |
|---|---|
| Sabji | vegetable |
| Sabjiwalla/Sabjiwalli | vegetable seller |
| Saj-dhaj | decking up |
| Sati Savitri | Savitri, the wife of Satyavan, who won her husband back from Yama, the god of death, by her devotion |
| Shamyana | a large, colourful tent, put up for weddings |
| Shastras | Hindu sacred texts |
| Shlokas | the chants in Sanskrit during prayer |
| Sidha-sadha | straightforward |
| Sindoor | vermillion applied to the parting of the hair, a sign of being married, and of the husband being alive |
| Suhagini | a woman whose husband is living |
| Tadka | a kind of seasoning |
| U.P. | the northern state of Uttar Pradesh |

# ACKNOWLEDGEMENTS

I give my deepest thanks to the following:

My parents, Parvathy Appachana and S. T. Appachana, from whom it all begins and grows. Padmini Mongia (Paddy), who knew the book from its inception to its end, who struggled with it as I did, who read its various versions with incredible patience, interest and belief, who nurtured it and helped it grow during the long years, and whose support and sustenance ultimately go far beyond the book. Victoria Gould Pryor (Tory), friend and agent, who painstakingly and patiently read and re-read my manuscript at its many stages, and whose steady belief sustained me throughout. Without Paddy and Tory, the book and I would have sunk. Kiran Grewal, Nandita Gupta, and Monisha Mukundan, for their feedback, for all that went before, all that happened during and all that has come after. The Mishara family, especially Veena, for their belief and sustenance. Judy Nichols, for her tremendous support. Anjali Potnis, Nandini Ramchandran and Sarita Srivastava, for being there for me in Pune in the most solid, steadfast way. Ian Jackman (Random House) for all his help. Mrs Usha Mongia for so readily giving me information about the Delhi University of yore.

And the writers' retreat at Hawthornden Castle, Scotland, where I was a Hawthornden Fellow in 1993. Writing uninterrupted for a month in that exquisite solitude is now one of my sweetest memories.

# ABOUT THE AUTHOR

ANJANA APPACHANA'S first book, *Incantations and Other Stories*, was published in England, India and the United States, and has also been translated into German. One of her short stories in the collection won an O. Henry Festival prize. Appachana is a recipient of the National Endowment for the Arts Creative Writing Fellowship for the year 1995–1996.

## ABOUT THE TYPE

This book was set in Garamond, a typeface originally designed by the Parisian type cutter Claude Garamond (1480–1561). This version of Garamond was modeled on a 1592 specimen sheet from the Egenolff-Berner foundry, which was produced from types assumed to have been brought to Frankfurt by the punch cutter Jacques Sabon (d. 1580).

Claude Garamond's distinguished romans and italics first appeared in *Opera Ciceronis* in 1543–44. The Garamond types are clear, open, and elegant.